Zen Omnibus

Michael Dibdin was born in 1947 and attended schools in Scotland and Ireland, and universities in England and Canada. He is the author of the internationally bestselling Aurelio Zen series, including *Blood Rain*, *And Then You Die* and, the last in the series, *End Games*. He died in 2007.

by the same author

THE LAST SHERLOCK HOLMES STORY
A RICH FULL DEATH
THE TRYST
DIRTY TRICKS
THE DYING OF THE LIGHT
DARK SPECTRE
THANKSGIVING

Aurelio Zen series

RATKING
VENDETTA
CABAL
DEAD LAGOON
COSI FAN TUTTI
A LONG FINISH
BLOOD RAIN
AND THEN YOU DIE
MEDUSA
BACK TO BOLOGNA
END GAMES

MICHAEL DIBDIN
The Aurelio Zen Omnibus

Ratking

Vendetta

Cabal

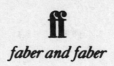

faber and faber

Ratking first published in 1988
Vendetta first published in 1990
Cabal first published in 1992
by Faber and Faber Limited
3 Queen Square London WC1N 3AU
This omnibus edition first published 2008

Printed and bound in Great Britain by
William Clowes Ltd, Beccles, Suffolk

A CIP record for this book
is available from the British Library

ISBN 978-0-571-24158-3

2 4 6 8 10 9 7 5 3 1

CONTENTS

Ratking

Agli amici di quel tempo

'Hello?'

'Hello? Who is it?'

'Who's calling?'

'I want to speak to Senator Rossi.'

'Speaking.'

'Ah, it's you, Senator? Forgive me! These phones make everyone sound like anyone, or rather no one. This is Antonio Crepi.'

'Commendatore! What a pleasure! Are you here in Rome?'

'In Rome? God forbid! No no. I'm in Perugia. At home, at the villa. You remember it?'

'But of course, of course. Of course.'

'When my eldest boy married.'

'Exactly. Precisely. An unforgettable occasion. A wonderful couple. How are they both?'

'I don't see that much of them. Corrado's moved to Milan and Annalisa's seeing some footballer, or so they tell me. Our paths don't cross very often.'

'Ah, what a shame.'

'These things happen nowadays! I don't really give a damn any more. At our age it's absurd to go on pretending. Let them do what they like. Just as long as I've got my vines and my olives, and one or two friends I can still talk to. People I understand and who understand me. You know what I'm talking about?'

'Of course, of course! Friendship is the most important thing in life, I always say. No question about that.'

'I'm glad to hear you say so. Because the fact is I'm phoning to ask for your help on behalf of a friend. A mutual friend. I'm talking about Ruggiero Miletti.'

'Ah. A tragic business.'

'Do you know how long it has been now?'

'Shocking.'

'Nearly four and a half months. A hundred and thirty-seven days and nights of agony for the Miletti family and for all their friends. To say nothing of Ruggiero himself.'

5

'Horrible.'

'A man as old as you or I, Senator, chained up in some shack in the mountains, in this bitter weather, at the mercy of a gang of callous bandits!'

'Dreadful. Scandalous. If only one could do something to help . . .'

'But you can help! You must help!'

'In any way I can, Commendatore! I am only too ready, believe me. But we must be realistic. Kidnapping is the scourge of society today, a plague and a peril in the face of which we are all equally vulnerable, equally powerless, equally . . .'

'Rubbish! Excuse me, but when something happens to one of you politicians the whole country is put into a state of siege! Nothing is too much trouble then, no expense is spared. But when it's an ordinary, decent, law-abiding citizen like our friend Ruggiero no one even takes any notice. Business as usual! "It's his own fault. Why didn't he take more precautions?"'

'Commendatore, do not let us fall into the trap of deluding ourselves that any responsible person might presume to deny the gravity of . . .'

'Keep that stuff for the press, Senator. This is Antonio Crepi you're talking to! Don't you try and tell me we are still equal. If you were kidnapped, God forbid, you would get the crack units, the top men. Well, that's what I want for Ruggiero.'

'Of course, of course! Naturally!'

'I'm not blaming the people here in Perugia. But let's face it, if they were the best they wouldn't be here, would they? They would be in Rome, looking after you politicians.'

'One should perhaps avoid exaggerating the effectiveness of the measures to which you refer, Commendatore.'

'Listen, if you get a pain in the chest you go to a specialist, right?'

'Our specialists couldn't save Aldo Moro.'

'Spare me the talk, Senator! God knows we've had enough talk. Now, I want action, and that's why I'm phoning. I want a top man sent up here to shake up the whole operation. A new face, a fresh approach. You can arrange that in a second, with your contacts.'

'Well . . .'

'Or is it too much to ask?'

'It's not . . .'

'Don't you think Ruggiero deserves the best?'

'Naturally.'

'Senator, I wouldn't have bothered to call you if I thought you were one of

those people with short memories. There are enough of them about, God knows! But no, I thought, Rossi's not like that. He hasn't forgotten what the Miletti family has meant to him. Senator, I beg you, think of them now! Think what they are going through. Think what it will mean to them to know that thanks to you one of the top policemen in Italy has been sent to Perugia to inspire the hunt for their beloved father! And then think that you can arrange all that with a single phone call, as easily as ordering a taxi.'

'You overestimate my power.'

'I hope not. I sincerely hope not. Because I have always thought of you as a friend and ally, and it would sadden me to feel that I could no longer count on your support. And you on mine, Senator, and on that of the Miletti family and their many friends.'

'For heaven's sake, Commendatore! What are you talking about? Do not please permit ourselves to be misled into imagining that . . .'

'Perfect! There is no more to say, then. When can I expect to hear?'

'Well, in a situation of this type one would perhaps be wise to avoid imposing rigid deadlines. Nevertheless, broadly speaking, I would by no means rule out the possibility of being in a position to . . .'

'I'd like to know by this afternoon.'

'Oh, you would, would you?'

'Or perhaps you have more important business to attend to?'

'Look here, Crepi, it's no good your expecting miracles, you know! Excuse me saying so.'

'I'm not asking for miracles, Senator. I'm asking for justice. Or does that take a miracle in this country?'

'Lapucci.'

'Did I wake you, Giorgio?'

'Who's this?'

'Gianpiero Rossi.'

'Ah, good morning, Senator! No, I was working in the other office. No one ever believes it, of course, but we do work here at Central Office.'

'Listen Giorgio, I have a little problem I think you may be able to help me with.'

'Consider it done.'

'You know about the Miletti kidnapping?'

'The tyre king from Modena?'

'*Modena! What do you mean, Modena? Would I give a damn if he was from Modena? Miletti, Miletti! Radios, televisions!*'

'Ah, of course. Excuse me. From Perugia.'

'*From Perugia, exactly. And that's my problem. Because some people there, friends of the family, feel that not enough is being done. You know how it is, everyone wants special attention. And these are people who are difficult to refuse. Do you follow?*'

'Perfectly.'

'*Like they say, the poor pray for miracles, the rich think they have a right to them. Now, I'm not trying to justify what cannot and should not be justified. I neither condone nor condemn. But the fact remains that I'm in a difficult situation. You see what I mean?*'

'Of course. But what exactly do they want, these people? If you don't mind my asking.'

'*They want a name.*'

'A name? Whose name?'

'*That is entirely up to you. It must be someone presentable, naturally. Don't make me look like an idiot. If he's well known so much the better.*'

'And what is this person to do?'

'*Why, go and sort things out.*'

'Go to Perugia?'

'*To Perugia, of course!*'

'A police official?'

'*Exactly. Can you help me?*'

'Well, I must say that this is a particularly difficult moment, Senator. Since the Cabinet reshuffle the party's relations with the Ministry have been . . .'

'*When you've been around as long as I have, Giorgio, you'll know that it's always a particularly difficult moment. That's why I rang you instead of some other people whose names came to mind. Now can you help me?*'

'Well, despite the changes I've just referred to, we do have various contacts, of course. There's one in particular I'm thinking of who may well be able . . .'

'*I'm not interested in the details, Giorgio. I just want to know if you can help me. Or should I ring someone else? Perhaps you could recommend someone?*'

'You must be joking, Senator. Anything that can be done, I'll do for you. By this time tomorrow you'll . . .'

'By this time tomorrow I'll be in Turin. Make it this afternoon. I'll be here till seven.'

'Very well.'

'Excellent. I knew I did right to call you. I've got a nose for these things. Giorgio's a man who can make things happen, I thought. A million thanks. I'll be expecting your call.'

'Yes?'

'Enrico?'

'Who's that?'

'Giorgio Lapucci.'

'Christ, I thought it was his royal highness. Excuse me while I change my trousers.'

'Why the panic?'

'He's at a conference in Strasbourg, and every so often he phones me and demands a complete update on the situation here. All part of this new managerial style you've been reading about. Keeps us on our toes, he says. Anyway, what can I do for you?'

'I suppose this line is safe?'

'Giorgio, this is the Ministry of the Interior you're talking to. Any phone tapping that goes on around here, we do it.'

'Of course.'

'So what's up?'

'Well, it's the old story, I'm afraid. Someone's leaning on someone who's leaning on me.'

'And you want to lean on me.'

'Isn't that what friends are for? But it shouldn't be too difficult. It's a question of getting a senior police official transferred temporarily to Perugia to take over a kidnapping case.'

'That's all?'

'That's all.'

'No problem. I can lose it in the routine postings and bang it through at departmental level. No one ever looks at that stuff. The only headache could be finding someone. When are we talking?'

'Now.'

'Shit. Look, I'll have to think a bit. Let me get back to you.'

'Today, though.'

'I'll do my best.'

'I appreciate it, Enrico. Give my best to Nicola.'

'*And mine to Emanuela. Listen, why don't we all get together some time?*'

'Yes, we should. We really should.'

'*Personnel.*'

'Mancini. I need someone we can send up to Perugia on a kidnapping. Who do you suggest?'

'*No one.*'

'What do you mean, no one?'

'*I mean there isn't anyone available.*'

'What about Fabri?'

'*In Genoa on that bank job.*'

'De Angelis?'

'*Sardinia. Where there were three kidnappings last week alone, in case you haven't seen the papers. This weekend we've got the visit of the President of France plus an English football team, God help us. Are you getting the picture? If not, I can go on.*'

'Calm down, Ciliani. I know things are difficult. But there's always somebody. Look harder.'

'*There's no one except Romizi, and he's going on leave.*'

'Well, tell him he'll have to put it off.'

'*Excuse me, dottore, but you tell him! He's booked a flight to America.*'

'What's he doing going to America?'

'*How should I know? Got relatives there or something.*'

'Well, what about people outside Criminalpol?'

'*You said this was operational.*'

'We could always stretch a point. Isn't there anyone who's had some experience? Couldn't stand the sight of blood and requested a desk job, that sort of thing. Use your head, Ciliani! I mean we're talking about a gesture here, not a new chief for the fucking Squadra Mobile.'

'*Doesn't help.*'

'What about what's-his-name, the one we've got doing Housekeeping?'

'*Zuccaroni?*'

'No, the other one.'

'*Zen?*'

'That's it.'

'But surely he's . . .'

'What?'

'Well, I thought there was, you know, some problem about using him.'

'Really? I haven't heard anything.'

'I don't mean anything official.'

'Well, as long as it's not official I can't see that there's any problem. A kidnapping, too! Wasn't he something of a specialist? Couldn't be better'

'If you say so, dottore.'

'It's perfect. Ideal from every point of view. The only thing that would ruin it is delay. And that's why I'm going to leave it in your lap, Ciliani. I want Zen and the relevant paperwork in my office within the hour. Got that?'

'Uh.'

'Caccamo?'

'Uh.'

'Ciliani. You seen Zen?'

'You tried his office?'

'No, I'm too stupid to think of that. Of course I've tried his fucking office.'

'Hang on, isn't he away somewhere? Treviso?'

'Trieste. He was due back this morning.'

'Did I ever tell you about this girl from Trieste I met the time I was doing beach duty down at Ostia? She was sunbathing totally nude behind a dune, and when I . . .'

'Fuck off, Caccamo. Christ, this is all I need. Where has that son of a bitch Zen got to?'

ONE

'No! I don't believe it! It isn't possible!'

'It isn't possible, but it happens. In short, it's a miracle!'

'Just a few hundred metres away from the station and they stop! This is going too far!'

'Not quite far enough, I'd say!'

'For the love of God, let us out of this damned train!'

'"And yet it does *not* move", as Galileo might have said. Ah well, let's be patient.'

'Patient! Patient! Excuse me, but in my humble opinion what this country needs is a few people who will no longer be patient! People who refuse to suffer patiently the bungling and incompetence with which we are surrounded! There! That's what I think!'

'It's better to travel hopefully than to arrive, they say. It should be the motto of the State Railways.'

'You choose to joke about it, signore, but in my humble opinion this is no joking matter. On the contrary, it is an issue of the very highest importance, symptomatic of all the gravest ills of our poor country. What does one expect of a train? That it goes reasonably fast and arrives within five or ten minutes of the time stated in the time-table. Is that too much? Does that require divine intervention to bring about? Not in any other country in the world! Nor used it to here.'

'You can always move to Switzerland, if that's how you feel.'

'But now what happens? The railway service, like everything else, is a disaster. And what is the government's response? To give their friends in the construction business billions and billions of lire to build a new railway line between Rome and Florence! And the result? The trains are slower than they were before the war! It's incredible! A national disgrace!'

The young man sitting near the door, Roman to his elegant finger-tips, smiled sarcastically.

'Ah yes, of course, everything was better before the war,' he murmured. 'We know all about that.'

'Excuse me, but you know nothing about it,' replied the vigorous, thick-set man with the shock of silver hair and the Veronese accent. 'Unless I am very much mistaken you weren't even born then!'

He turned to the third occupant of the compartment, sitting by the window, a distinguished-looking man of about fifty with a pale face whose most striking feature was a nose as sharply triangular as the jib of a sailing boat. There was a faintly exotic air about him, as though he were Greek or even Levantine. His expression was cynical, suave and aloof, and a distant smile flickered on his lips. But it was his eyes that compelled attention. They were grey with glints of blue, and a slightly sinister stillness which made the Veronese shiver. A cold fish, this one, he thought.

'What about you, signore?' he demanded. 'Don't you agree that it's a disgrace, a national disgrace?'

'The train was delayed at Mestre,' the stranger observed with a grave, deliberate courtesy that somehow seemed mocking. 'That has naturally upset the schedules. There were bound to be further delays.'

'I know the train was delayed at Mestre!' retorted the Veronese. 'You don't need to remind me that the train was delayed at Mestre. And why, may I ask, was the train delayed at Mestre? Because of an unofficial stoppage by the local section of one of the railway unions. Unofficial! As if we didn't have enough official strikes, we are also at the mercy of any local gang of workers with a grievance, who can throw the whole transport system of the nation into total chaos without, needless to say, the slightest fear of any reprisals whatsoever.'

The young Roman slapped the leg of his trousers with a rolled copy of a glossy news magazine.

'Certainly it's a nuisance,' he remarked. 'But don't let's exaggerate the inconvenience. Besides, there are worse things than chaos.'

'And what might they be?'

'Too much order.'

The Veronese made a contemptuously dismissive gesture.

'Too much order? Don't make me laugh! In this country too much order wouldn't even be enough. It's always the same. The trains are late? Build a new railway! The South is poor? Open a new factory! The young are illiterate delinquents? Hire more teachers! There are too many civil servants? Retire them earlier on big pensions! The crime rate is soaring? Pass new laws! But for the love of God don't expect us to make the railways or the factories we have run efficiently, or make the teachers or bureaucrats do an honest day's work, or make people respect the existing laws. Oh no! Because that would smack of dictatorship, and of tyranny, and we can't have that.'

'That's not the point!' The young Roman had finally given up his pose of ironic detachment. 'What you want, signore, this famous "order" of yours, is something un-Italian, un-Mediterranean. It's an idea of the North, and that's where it should stay. It's got no place here. Very well, so we have a few problems. There are problems everywhere in the world! Just look in the newspaper, watch the television. Do you think that this is the only country where life isn't perfect?'

'It's got nothing to do with perfection! And as for this beautiful Mediterranean myth of yours, signore, permit me to say that . . .'

The man at the window looked away at the blank wall of the Campo Verano cemetery on the other side of the tracks. Neither this further delay nor the argument to which it had given rise seemed able to touch the mood of serenity which had been with him since he awoke that morning. Perhaps it had been the dislocation of routine that had done it, the shock of finding himself not back in Rome but inexplicably stalled at Mestre, five hundred and sixty kilometres further north. For a moment it had seemed as though reality itself had broken down like a film projector and soon everyone would be demanding their money back. After a blind tussle with his clothes in the cramped darkness of the sleeping compartment he had stepped out into the misty early-morning air, laden with the salty stench of the lagoon and the acrid odours of petroleum and chemicals from the heavy industry he could hear murmuring all around, and wandered along the platform to the bar, where he pushed his way into a group of railwaymen, ordered an espresso laced with grappa and discovered that no trains would move out of Mestre until further notice due to a dispute regarding manning levels.

I could go, he had thought. I could have gone, he thought now, simply by boarding one of the orange buses which passed the station with illuminated signs bearing that magic combination of letters: VENEZIA. But he hadn't, and he'd been right. His mysterious mood of elation had been one to float on, gliding lightly as a shallow-bottomed skiff across the inlets and channels of the lagoon whose melancholy topography he had explored as a boy. At his age such gifts came rarely and should be handled with care, not asked to bear up under the tortuous coils of his relationship with his native city. His reward had been that the mood proved unexpectedly durable. Neither the delay at Mestre nor subsequent hold-ups at Bologna and Florence had been able to touch it, and despite the weather, grey and unseasonably cold for late March, even the return to the capital hadn't depressed him as much as usual. He would never learn to like Rome, never be at ease with the weight of centuries of power and corruption there in the dead centre of Italy, the symbol and source of its stagnation. How could he ever feel at home in the heaviest of all cities when he had been born and formed in its living antithesis, a city so light it seems to float? Nevertheless, if he were forced to take sides between the old Veronese and the young Roman there could be only one choice. He had no wish to live in some miserable Northern land where everything ran like clockwork. As if that was what life was about! No, it was about those two lads out there in the corridor, for instance, typical Roman working-class toughs in jeans and leather jackets staring into the first-class compartments as they strolled along the corridor with an easy natural insolence which no degree of poverty could touch, as if they owned the place! The country might have its problems, but as long as it could go on producing that burning energy, that irresistible drive and flair . . .

In a second, the door was closed again and the taller one inside, a plastic sports bag in one hand, an automatic pistol in the other. A brief smile flashed across his face.

'Don't worry, I'm not a terrorist!'

The bag landed on the floor at their feet.

'All the goodies in there! Wallets, watches, rings, lighters, lockets, trinkets, bangles, ear-rings, silk knickers, you name it. Foreign currency in major denominations only, all major credit cards accepted. Move it, move it!'

The snout of the automatic jabbed out towards each of the three passengers in turn.

'You piece of shit.'

It was hardly audible, a shiver of pent-up loathing finding its release. The pistol swung towards the silver-haired man.

'You said *what*, grandpa?'

The grey-eyed man by the window cleared his throat conspicuously.

'Don't shoot me, please,' he said. 'I'm just getting my wallet out.'

The pistol swung away from the Veronese. The other man's hand emerged holding a large brown leather wallet from which he extracted a plastic card.

'What's that?' the youth snapped.

'It's no use to you.'

'Let me see! And you two *move* it, for fuck's sake, or do you want to get kneecapped?'

Expensive leather and precious metals began to hit the bottom of the plastic bag. The youth glanced at the plastic card and laughed briefly.

'Commissioner of Police? Eh, sorry, dottore, I didn't know. That's OK, keep your stuff. Maybe one of these days you can do me a favour.'

'You're a police official?' demanded the Veronese as the carriage jerked violently and the train started to roll forward.

The door opened and the other youth beckoned urgently to his companion.

'Haven't you fucking finished yet? Let's go, for Christ sake!'

'Well, do something!' shrieked the silver-haired man as the pair scooped up the bag and vanished. 'If you're a policeman, do something! Stop them! Pursue them! Shoot them! Don't just sit there!'

The train was now moving slowly past the San Lorenzo goods yard. A carriage door slammed near by. The police official opened the window and looked out. There they were, haring away across the tracks towards the safety of the streets.

The Veronese was beside himself with rage.

'So you refuse to reply, do you? But that won't do! I *demand* an answer! You can't get out of it that easily, you know! God in heaven, do you feel no shame, Commissioner? You calmly allow innocent citizens to be robbed under your very nose while you hide behind the power of office and do precisely damn all about it! Mother of God! I mean, everybody knows that the police these days are a bad joke that makes us the laughing stock of every other country in Europe. That's taken for granted. But dear Christ, I never in my worst moments expected to witness such a blatant example of craven dereliction of duty as I have seen today! Eh? Very well. Excellent. We'll see about this. I'm not just some nobody you can push around, you know. Kindly give me your name and rank.'

The train was rounding the curve by the Porta Maggiore and the terminus was now visible up ahead.

'So, your name?' the silver-haired man insisted.

'Zen.'

'Zen? You're Venetian?'

'What of it?'

'But I am from Verona! And to think you disgrace us like this in front of these Southerners!'

'Who are you calling a Southerner?'

The young Roman was on his feet.

'Ah, ashamed of the name now, are you? A few minutes ago it was your proudest boast!'

'I'm ashamed of nothing, signore! But when a term is used as a deliberate insult by someone whose arrogance is matched only by his stupendous ignorance of the real meaning of Italian culture . . .'

'Culture! What do you know about culture? Don't make me laugh by using big words you don't understand.'

As the carriage jarred over several sets of points and began to run in alongside the platform Zen left the compartment and squeezed through the line of people waiting in the corridor.

'In a big hurry, eh?' remarked a sour-looking woman. 'Some people always have to be first, and just too bad for everyone else.'

The platform was packed with passengers who had been waiting for hours. As the train slowed to a halt they stormed it like assault troopers, intent on winning a seat for the long haul down to Naples and beyond. Zen struggled through them and out to the station con-course. The phones were all in use. At the nearest a tired-looking, poorly dressed woman was repeating 'I *know* . . . I *know* . . . I *know*' over and over again in a strident, unmodulated country voice. Zen waved his identity card at her.

'Police. This is an emergency. I need to use this phone.'

He took the receiver from the woman's unresisting hand and dialled 113.

'This is Commissioner Aurelio Zen. No, Zen. Z,E,N. No O. That's right. Attached to the Ministry of the Interior. I'm calling from the Stazione Termini. There's been a train job. They ran off towards Via Prenestina. Get a car off now and then I'll give you the descriptions. Ready? The first was about twenty. Height, one sixtyish. Short dark hair, military cut so possibly doing his service, dark-green leather jacket with twin zippered flaps, faded jeans, dark brown boots. The other slightly taller, longer lighter hair, moustache, big nose, brown leather jacket, new jeans, red, white and blue running shoes, carrying a green plastic sports bag with white lettering "Banca Popolare di Frosinone". He's got a small automatic, so be careful. Got that? Right, I'll leave a full report with the railway police.'

He hung up. The woman was gazing at him with an air of cautious fascination.

'Was it a local call?' he asked.

Fascination was replaced by fear.

'What?'

'Were you speaking to someone in Rome?'

'No, no! Salerno! I'm from Salerno.'

And she started rooting in her bag for the identity card which was her only poor talisman against the dark powers of the state.

Zen looked through his change until he found another telephone token, which he handed to her.

'Here. Now you can dial again.'

The woman stared at him suspiciously. He put the token down beside the phone and turned away.

'It's my sister,' she said suddenly, gripping his arm. 'She works for the Pope. At the Vatican! She's a cleaner. The pay's rotten, but it's still something to work for the Pope, isn't it? But her husband won't let me in the house because of what my brother found out about him, the dirty bastard. So I phone her whenever I come up to see my grandson. She hasn't got a phone, you see, so I phone from the station. They're stingy bastards, those priests. Still, it's better than packing anchovies, at least your fingers don't stink. But listen, can that criminal do that? Forbid me to see my own sister? Isn't there a law against that?'

Mumbling something about emergencies, Zen pulled away from the woman's grasp and crossed the concourse towards the distant neon sign reading POLIZIA FERROVIARIA.

'Welcome home,' he muttered under his breath. His earlier mood already seemed as remote and irrelevant as a childhood memory.

The heavy front door closed behind him with a definitive bang, shutting him in, shutting out the world. As he moved the switch the single bulb which lit the entrance hall ended its long, wan existence in an extravagant flash, leaving him in the dark, just back from school. Once he had kissed his mother he would run out to play football in the square outside. Astonishingly, he even seemed to hear the distant sound of lapping water. Then it faded and a didactic voice began pontificating about the ecology of the Po Delta. Those liquid ripples overlaying the constant rumble of traffic came not, of course, from the backwater canals of his childhood, but from the television.

He moved blindly along the passage, past pictures and furniture which had been part of his life for so long that he was no longer aware of their existence. As he approached the glass-panelled door the noise of the television grew louder. Once inside the living room it was deafening. In the dim mix of video glare and twilight seeping through the shutters he made out the frail figure of his mother staring with childlike intensity at the flickering screen.

'Aurelio! You're back!'

'Yes, mamma.'

He bent over her and they kissed.

'How was Fiume? Did you enjoy yourself?'

'Yes, mamma.'

He no longer bothered to correct her, even when her mistakes sent him astray not just in space but in time, to a city that had ceased to exist a third of a century earlier.

'And what about you, mamma? How have you been?'

'Fine, fine. You needn't worry, Maria Grazia is a treasure. All I've missed is seeing you. But I told you when you joined! You don't know what it's like in the services, I said. They send you here and then they send you there, and just when you're getting used to that they send you somewhere else, until you don't know which end to sit down on any more. And to think you could have had a nice job on the railways like your father, a nice supervising job, just as secure as the police and none of this roaming around. And we would never have had to move down here to the *South!*'

She broke off as Maria Grazia bustled in from the kitchen. But they had been speaking dialect, and the housekeeper had not understood.

'Welcome home, dottore!' she cried. 'They've been trying to get hold of you all day. I told them you hadn't got back yet, but . . .'

At that moment the phone started to ring in the inner hallway. It'll be that old fascist on the train, Zen thought. That type always has friends. But 'all day'? Maria Grazia must have exaggerated.

'Zen?'

'Speaking.'

'This is Enrico Mancini.'

Christ almighty! The Veronese had gone straight to the top. Zen gripped the receiver angrily.

'Listen, the little bastard had a gun and he was standing too far away for me to jump him. So what was I supposed to do, I'd like to know? Get myself shot so that the Commendatore could keep his lousy watch?'

There was a crackly pause.

'What are you talking about?'

'I'm talking about the train!'

'I don't know anything about any train. I'm calling to discuss your transfer to Perugia.'

'What? Foggia?'

The line was very poor, with heavy static and occasional cut-outs. For the hundredth time Zen wondered if it was still being tapped, and for the hundredth time he told himself that it wouldn't make any sense, not now. He wasn't important any more. Paranoia of that type was simply conceit turned inside out.

'Perugia! Perugia in Umbria! You leave tomorrow.'

What on earth was going on? Why should someone like Enrico Mancini concern himself with Zen's humdrum activities?

'For Perugia? But my next trip was supposed to be to Lecce, and that's not till . . .'

'Forget about that for now. You're being reassigned to investigative duties, Zen. Have you heard about the Miletti case? I'll get hold of all the documentation I can and send it round in the morning with the car. But basically it sounds quite straightforward. Anyway, as from tomorrow you're in charge.'

'In charge of what?'

'Of the Miletti investigation! Are you deaf?'

'In Perugia?'

'That's right. You're on temporary secondment.'

'Are you sure about this?'

'I beg your pardon?'

Mancini's voice was icy.

'I mean, I understood that, you know . . .'

'Well?'

'Well, I thought I'd been permanently suspended from investigative duty.'

'*First I've heard of it. In any case, such decisions are always open to review in the light of the prevailing circumstances. The Questore of Perugia has requested assistance and we have no one else available, it's as simple as that.*'

'So it's official.'

'*Of course it's official! Don't you worry about that, Zen. Just concentrate on the job in hand. It's important that we see results quickly, understand? We're counting on you.*'

Long after Mancini had hung up Zen stood there beside the phone, his head pressed against the wall. At length he lifted the receiver again and dialled. The number rang for a long time, but just as he was about to hang up she answered.

'Yes?'

'It's me.'

'*Aurelio! I wasn't expecting to hear from you till this evening. How did it go in wherever you were this time?*'

'Why did you take so long to answer?'

She was used to his moods by now.

'*I've got my lover here. No, actually I was in the bath. I wasn't going to bother, but then I thought it might be you.*'

He grunted, and there was a brief silence.

'Look, something's come up. I have to leave again tomorrow and I don't know when I'll be back. Can we meet?'

'*I'd love to. Shall we go out?*'

'All right. Ottavio's?'

'*Fine.*'

He hung up and looked round the hallway, confronting the furniture which having dominated his infancy had now returned to haunt his adult life. Everything in his apartment had been moved there from the family house in Venice when his mother had finally agreed, six years earlier, to leave. For many years she had resisted, long after it had become obvious that she could no longer manage on her own.

'Rome? Never!' she cried. 'I would be like a fish out of water.'

And her gasps and shudders had made the tired phrase vivid and painful. But in the end she had been forced to give in. Her only son could not come to her. Since the Moro affair his career was nailed down, stuffed and varnished, with years of dreary routine to go before they would let him retire. And there was simply no one else, except for a few distant relatives living in what was now Yugoslavia. So she had moved, avoiding the fate she had feared by the simple expedient of bringing all her belongings with her and trans-forming Zen's apartment into an aquarium from which she never emerged.

But if she was thus protected from suffocation, the effect on Zen was exactly the reverse. He had never particularly liked the apart-ment, in a drab, pompous street just north of the Vatican, but in Rome you had to take what you could get. The nearest he had come to a personal feeling for the place had been an appreciation of its anonymity: it had been like living in a hotel. But his mother's arrival had changed all that, swamping the sparse furnishings provided by the landlord with possessions laden with dull memories and obscure significance. At times Zen felt that he was choking, and then his thoughts would turn to the house in Venice, ideally empty now, the rooms full of nothing but pearly light, intimations of water, the cries of children and gulls. He had promised himself that one day he would retire there, and in the meantime he was often so intensely there in spirit that he wouldn't have been in the least surprised to learn that the place was believed to be haunted.

From the kitchen came a clatter of pans supplemented by Maria Grazia's voice alternately berating the ancient stove, encouraging a blunt knife, singing snatches of the spring's big hit and calling on the Madonna to witness the misery to which her life was reduced by the quality of the vegetables on offer at the local greengrocer's. He would have to eat something here before sneaking out to meet Ellen. His mother's birthday was in a week, he realized. He would almost cer-tainly still be away. At all events, he would have to tell her about the change of plans, which meant hearing once again how he should have got a nice job on the railways like his father. Did she really not realize that she told him this every single time he returned? Or was she, on the contrary, having a good laugh at his expense? That was the trouble with old people, you could never be sure. That was the trouble with living with someone you loved more than anyone else in the world, but had nothing in common with now but blood and bones.

'But I don't understand. Surely you're not a real policeman? I mean, you work for the Ministry, don't you? As a bureaucrat. That's what you told me, anyway.'

Ellen's implication was clear: she would never have had anything to do with him if she had thought he was a 'real' policeman.

'And it's the truth. Ever since I've known you that's what I've been doing. Going the rounds of provincial headquarters checking how many paperclips are being used, that sort of thing. Inspection duty, popularly known as Housekeeping, and just about as glamorous. The nearest I've got to real police work was smashing the great stolen toilet-roll racket at the Questura in Campobasso.'

She didn't smile.

'And before that?'

'Well, before it was different.'

'You were a real cop? A police officer?'

'Yes.'

There was so much shock in her look that he could not tell what else it might contain.

'Where was this?' she asked eventually.

'Oh, various places. Here, for example.'

'You worked in the Questura, here in Rome?'

'That's right.'

'Christ! Which department?'

She was looking hard at him.

'Not the Political Branch, if that's what you're worried about.'

It was, of course. Ellen's circle of expatriate acquaintances already regarded it as rather bizarre that she had got involved with an official from the Ministry of the Interior, just as Zen's few friends were clearly at a loss to know what to make of his liaison with this American divorcee, a classic *straniera* with her bright little apartment in Trastevere filled with artistic bric-à-brac and books in four languages and her Fiat 500 illegally parked in the street outside. The only answer in either case had been that whatever it was, it worked for both of them. It had seemed to be the only answer necessary. But now, without the slightest warning, Ellen found herself facing the possibility that her official had once been an active member of La Politica: one of those who beat up demonstrating students and striking workers and pushed suspects out of windows, while protecting the neo-fascists responsible for the indiscriminate bombings of public squares and cafeterias and trains.

'I asked you what you did do,' she insisted, 'not what you didn't.'

Her manner had become that of the tough brutal cop she perhaps assumed him to have been, bullying a statement out of a suspect.

'I was in the section concerned with kidnappings.'

At this, her features relaxed slightly. Kidnappings, eh? Well, that was all right, wasn't it? A nice uncontroversial area of police work. Which just left the question of why he had abandoned it for the inglorious role of Ministry snooper, spending half his time making exhausting trips to dreary provincial capitals where his presence was openly resented by everyone concerned, and the other half sitting in his windowless office at the Viminale typing up unreadable and no doubt unread reports. But before Ellen had a chance to ask him about this, Ottavio appeared in person at their table and the subject changed to that of food.

Ottavio outlined in pained tones his opinion that people were not eating enough these days. All they ever thought about was their figures, a selfish, short-sighted view contributing directly to the impoverishment of restaurateurs and the downfall of civilization as we know it. What the Goths, the Huns and the Turks had failed to do was now being achieved by a conspiracy of dietitians who were bringing the country to its knees with all this talk of cholesterols, calories and the evils of salt. Where were we getting to?

Such were his general grievances. His more particular wrath was reserved for Zen, who had told the waiter that he did not want anything to follow the huge bowl of *spaghetti alla carbonara* he had forced himself to eat on top of the vegetable soup Maria Grazia had prepared at home.

'What are you trying to do?' Ottavio demanded indignantly. 'Put me out of business? Listen, the lamb is fabulous today. And when I say fabulous I'm saying less than half the truth. Tender young sucklings, so sweet, so pretty it was a sin to kill them. But since they're dead already it would be a bigger sin not to eat them.'

Zen allowed himself to be persuaded, largely to get rid of Ottavio, who moved on to spread the good word to other tables.

'And how have you been?' Zen asked Ellen, when he had gone.

But she wasn't having that.

'Why haven't you told me this before?'

'I didn't think you'd be interested. Besides, it's all past history now.'

'When did all this happen, then?'

He sighed, frowned, rubbed his forehead and grimaced.

'Oh, I suppose it must be about . . . yes, about four years ago now. More or less.'

Surely he had overdone the uncertainty grotesquely? But she seemed satisfied.

'And now they're suddenly putting you back on that kind of work? This must be quite a surprise.'

'It certainly is.'

There was no need to conceal that, at any rate!

'So it was 1979 you quit?'

'The year before, actually.'

'And you got yourself transferred to a desk job?'

'More or less.'

He tensed himself for the follow-up, but it failed to materialize. Fair enough. If Ellen didn't appreciate how unlikely it was that anyone in that particular section of the Rome police would be allowed to transfer to a desk job in 1978 of all years, he certainly wasn't going to draw her attention to it.

'What made you do that?'

'Oh, I don't know. I suppose I was just fed up with the work.'

The food was brought to their table by Ottavio's youngest son, a speedy little whippet who, at fourteen, had already perfected his professional manner, contriving to suggest that he was engaged on some task of incalculable importance to humanity carried out against overwhelming odds under near-impossible conditions, and that while a monument in the piazza outside would be a barely adequate expression of the debt society owed him, he didn't even expect to get a decent tip.

They ate in silence for several minutes.

'So, what have you been up to?' Zen insisted. 'How's business?'

'Very quiet. There's a big sale on Tuesday, though.'

Ellen made a living acting as representative for a New York antique dealer, but it was a case of profiting from a lifelong hobby, and one that she had tried in vain to get him to share. Zen had had his fill of old furniture!

'How long will it be altogether?'

'Not long, I hope.'

'Do you know Perugia?'

Perugia, he thought. Chocolates, Etruscans, that fat painter, radios and gramophones, the University for Foreigners, sportswear. 'Umbria, the green heart of Italy', the tourist advertisements said. What did that make Latium, he had wondered, the bilious liver?

'I may have been there on a school trip, years ago.'

'But not for work?'

'Not a chance! There're two of us on Housekeeping. Zuccaroni is better regarded than me, so he gets the soft jobs, close to home.'

'Will it be difficult?'

He pushed his plate away and topped up their glasses with the flat, bland white wine.

'There's no way of knowing. A lot depends on the magistrate who's directing the investigation. Some of them want to take all the decisions themselves. Others just want to take the credit.'

She also finished eating and at last they could smoke. He took out his packet of Nazionali. Ellen as usual preferred her own cigarettes.

'Can I come and visit you?' she asked with a warm smile.

'It would be wonderful.'

She nodded

'No mother.'

He suddenly saw which way the conversation was heading.

'Don't you think it's ridiculous, at our age?' Ellen continued. 'She must know what's going on.'

'I expect she does. But as far as she's concerned I'm still married to Luisella and that's that. If I spend the night with you it's adultery. Since I'm a man that doesn't matter, but one doesn't mention it.'

'It matters to me.' Her tone had hardened. 'I don't like your mother thinking of me as your mistress.'

'Don't you? I quite enjoy it. It makes me feel young and irresponsible.'

The remark was deliberately provocative, but he had long ago decided that he was not going to be talked into matrimony a second time.

'Really?' she retorted. 'Well, it makes me feel old and insecure. And angry! Why should I have my life dominated by your mother? Why should you, for that matter? What's the matter with Italian men, letting their mammas terrorize them their whole life long? Why do you give them such power?'

'Perhaps we've found over the centuries that they're the only people who can be trusted with it.'

'Oh, I see. You can't trust me? Thanks very much!'

'I can't trust anyone in quite that way.'

It seemed perfectly obvious to him. Why was she getting so angry?

'Not because my mother's a saint,' he explained. 'It's just that mothers are like that. They can't help it, it's biological.'

'Oh, that's wonderful! Now you've insulted both of us.'

'On the contrary, I've complimented both of you. My mother for being what she is, and you for being everything else. And above all for being so understanding in what is a very difficult situation for both of us, but one that won't last for ever.'

She looked away, disarmed by this allusion, and Zen seized the opportunity to signal Ottavio for the bill.

The air outside was deliciously cool and fresh after the small, stuffy restaurant. They walked in silence towards the roar of traffic on Viale Trastevere. In Piazza Sonnino an office building was being refitted after a fire, and the hoarding put up by the builders had attracted the war-paint of rival political clans The Red Brigades' five-pointed star was the most conspicuous, but there were also contributions from Armed Struggle ('There's no escape – we shall strike everywhere!'), the Anarchists ('If voting changed anything they'd make it illegal'), and the neo-fascist New Order ('Honour to our fallen companions – they live on in our hearts!').

To Zen, the clash of slogans seemed eerily appropriate. Because if the events of 1978 had had a secret centre, and part of their horror was that he would never be sure, then in a sense it had been here, at the terminus of the 97C bus and the San Gallicano hospital opposite. If there had been an unspeakable secret, then one of the two men who had guessed it had died there. And since that moment, day and night, whatever else he might be doing or thinking, Zen had remained uneasily aware that he was the other.

TWO

'The entire resources of the Questura of Perugia are at your disposal. Eager to obey, my men await only your commanding word to spring into action. Your reputation of course precedes you, and the prospect of serving under your leadership has been an inspiration to us all. Who has not heard of your brilliant successes in the Fortuzzi and Castellano affairs, to name but two? And who can doubt that you will achieve a no less resounding triumph here on Umbrian soil, earning the heartfelt thanks of all by succeeding where others, less fortunate or deserving, have failed? The city of Perugia has a long and historic relationship with the capital, of which your posting here is a concrete symbol. My men will, I am sure, wish to join with me in bidding you welcome.'

There was a feeble flutter of applause from the group of senior officials assembled in the Questore's spacious top-floor office, all discreetly modern furniture, rows of law books, and potted plants. Aurelio Zen stood in their midst like a Siamese cat dropped into a cage full of stray dogs: tense and defiant, his eyes refusing to meet those fixed on him with expressions of more or less successfully concealed mockery. They knew what he was going through, poor bastard! And they knew that there was absolutely nothing he could do about it.

Salvatore Iovino, their chief, a corpulent, vivacious fifty-year-old from Catania, had given a masterly performance. Fulsome and vapid, laden with insincere warmth and hidden barbs, his speech had nevertheless left no legitimate grounds for complaint. He had spoken of Zen's 'reputation', without actually mentioning that his abrupt departure from the Rome Questura in 1978 had been the subject of the wildest rumours and speculations throughout the force. The two cases he had mentioned dated from the mid-seventies, underlining Zen's lack of recent operational experience. He had referred to the transfer as a 'posting', thus emphasizing that it had been imposed on him by the Ministry, and had called it a symbol of the historic relationship between Rome and Perugia, a relationship consisting of two thousand years of bitterly resented domination.

'Thank you,' Zen murmured, lowering his head in a proud and melancholy gesture of acknowledgement.

'And finally,' the Questore continued, 'let me introduce Vice-Questore Fabrizio Priorelli.'

Iovino's bland tone did nothing to prepare Zen for the glare of pure hostility with which he found himself transfixed by Priorelli. The Questore's next words followed an exquisitely judged pause during which the silence in the room assumed a palpable quality.

'Until today he was handling the Miletti case for us.'

Iovino laughed weightlessly.

'To be perfectly frank, that's one of the many problems your unexpected arrival has caused us. It's a matter of protocol, you see. Since Fabrizio outranks you I can't very well make him your second-in-command. Nevertheless, should you wish to consult him he has assured me that despite his numerous other duties he is in principle at your disposition at all times.'

Once again Zen murmured his thanks.

'Right, lads, lunch!' the Questore called briskly. 'I expect you're about ready for it, eh?'

As the officers filed out Iovino picked up the phone and yelled, 'Chiodini? Get up here!' Then he turned pointedly away and stood gazing out of the window until there was a knock at the door and a burly man with a bored brutal face appeared, at which point the Questore suddenly appeared to notice Zen's existence again.

'I'll leave you in Chiodini's safe hands, dottore. Remember, whatever you need, just say the word.'

'Thank you.'

As they walked downstairs Zen studied his escort: hair closely cropped on a head that looked muscle-bound, ears cauliflowered, no neck to speak of, shoulders and biceps that formed one inflexible block, the 'safe' hands swinging massively back and forth. Chiodini would be the one they sent for when old-fashioned interrogation methods were required.

At the third-floor landing the man jerked his thumb to the right.

'Along there, three five one,' he called without turning or breaking his stride.

Zen just managed to stop himself intoning another 'Thank you.'

Yes, it had all been consummately handled, no question about that. Iovino's speech had been a brilliant set piece, systematically exploiting all the weaknesses of Zen's position. Words are not everything, however, and the Questore had by no means neglected other possibilities of making his point, such as the contrast between the bombastic formality with which he had rolled out the red carpet and beaten the big drum and the perfunctory way he had then dismissed Zen into the 'safe hands' of the local third-degree specialist. The message was clear. Zen would be offered the moon and the stars, but if he wanted a coffee he'd have to go and fetch it himself.

He opened the door of the office and looked around warily. Everything seemed normal. On one wall hung the mandatory photograph of the President of the Republic, facing it on another the inevitable large calendar and a small crucifix. There was a grey metal filing cabinet in the corner, the top two drawers empty and the bottom one stuffed with plastic bags. In the centre of the office, dominating it, stood a desk of some sickly looking yellow wood which had seemingly been grown in imitation of one of the nastier synthetic materials. Like every other piece of furniture in the room this carried a tag inscribed 'Ministry of the Interior' and a stamped serial number. Screwed to the back of the door was a list itemizing every piece of furniture in the room, down to the metal rubbish bin, together with its serial number. It was not that the Ministry did not trust their employees. They were just tidy-minded and couldn't sleep at night unless they were sure that everything was in its place.

Zen walked over to the window and looked out. Down below was a small car park for police vehicles. Facing him was a windowless stone wall with a heavy gate guarded by two men, one in grey uniform with a cap, the other in battledress and a flak jacket. Both carried submachine guns, as did another guard patrolling the roof of the building. So that was it: they had given him an office with no view but the prison. He smiled sourly, acknowledging the hit. Sicilians were notoriously good at this kind of thing.

And the phone? He would never forget those first months at the Ministry, sitting in a windowless office in the basement, his only link to the outside world a telephone which was not connected. The repair men were always just about to come, but somehow they never did, and for over three months that telephone had squatted on his desk like a toad, symbol of a curse that would never be lifted. And when it finally was repaired Zen knew that this was not a token of victory but of total defeat. They could let him have a phone now. It didn't matter, because it never rang. Everyone knew about his 'reputation'. He had broken the rules of the tribe and been tabooed.

Here in Perugia his phone worked all right, but the same logic applied. Who was he going to call? What was he going to do? Should he fight back? Call Iovino's bluff and start throwing his weight around? The Ministry had sent him and they were bound to back him up, if only as a matter of form. With a bit of effort and energy he could soon bring the Questore and his men to heel. The problem was that he lacked the energy and was not going to make the effort. At heart he just didn't care enough about these provincial officials and their petty pride. He didn't even care about the case itself. Nine kidnappings out of ten were never solved anyway, and there was no reason to think that this one would be any different. In the end the family would pay up or the gang would back down. As a spectacle it was as uninspiring as an arm-wrestling contest between two strangers.

Outside the Questura he found the driver who had brought him there from Rome, a young Neapolitan named Luigi Palottino, still standing attentively beside the dark blue Alfetta. The sight of him just increased Zen's humiliation by reminding him of the scene at his apartment that morning when he'd returned, having spent the night with Ellen, to find Maria Grazia and his mother trying to organize his packing while the driver stood looking on with a bemused expression and everyone had to shout to be heard above the cheery chatter of the television, which had apparently turned itself on so as not to be left out of things.

'What are you doing here?' Zen snapped at him.

'Waiting for you, sir.'

'For me? I'm not in the mood for company, frankly.'

'I mean waiting for your orders, sir.'

'My orders? All right, you might as well take me to my hotel. Then you can go.'

The Neapolitan frowned.

'Sir?'

'You can go back to Rome.'

'No, sir.'

Zen looked at him with menacing attention.

'What do you mean, "no"?'

'My orders are to remain here in Perugia with you, sir. They've allocated me a bed in the barracks.'

They want to keep tabs on me, thought Zen. They don't trust me, of course. *Of course!* And who could say what other orders Luigi Palottino might have been given?

Half an hour later Zen was sitting in a café enjoying a late lunch, when he heard his name spoken by a complete stranger. The café was an old-world establishment quite unlike the usual chrome-and-glass filling stations for caffeine junkies, a long, narrow burrow of a place with a bar on one side and a few seats and small tables on the other. The walls were lined with tall wooden cabinets filled with German chocolates and English jam and shelves bending dangerously under the weight of undrinkably ancient bottles of wine. There were newspapers dangling from canes and waiters in scarlet jackets who seemed to have all the time in the world, and faded pastoral frescos presided amiably from the vaulted ceiling. Zen took the only free table, which was between the coat-stand and the telephone, so that he was continually being disturbed by people wanting to get at one or the other. But he paid no particular attention to the other clients until he heard his own name being laboriously spelt out.

'Z,E,N. Yes, that's right.'

The man was in his early sixties, short but powerfully built with an almost aggressively vigorous appearance that suggested a peasant background not many generations earlier. But this was no peasant. His clothes and grooming suggested wealth, and his manner was that of a man used to getting his own way.

'So I've been told. Perhaps he hasn't arrived yet? Ah, I see. Listen, Gianni, do me a favour, will you? When he comes back, tell him . . . No, nothing. Forget it. On second thoughts I'll call him myself later. Thanks.'

The receiver was replaced, and the man glanced down.

'Sorry for disturbing you, eh?'

He walked slowly away, greeting various acquaintances as he went.

The elderly cashier seemed to have no idea how much anything cost, and by the time the waiter who had served Zen had told her and she had manipulated the Chinese box of little drawers to extract the right change, the man had disappeared. But as soon as Zen got outside he almost bumped into him, standing just to the left of the doorway chatting to a younger bearded man. Zen walked past them and stopped some distance away in front of a glass case displaying the front page of the local edition of the *Nazione* newspaper with the headlines circled in red ink.

'TRAGEDY ON THE PERUGIA-TERNI: ATROCIOUS DEATH OF YOUNG COUPLE UNDER A TRUCK.' He could see the two men quite clearly, reflected on the glass surface in front of him, the younger protesting in a querulous whine, 'I still don't see why I should be expected to deal with it.' 'BUSES IN PERUGIA: EVERY-THING TO CHANGE – NEW ROUTES, NEW TIMETABLES.' 'It's agreed, then?' exclaimed the older man. 'But not Daniele, eh? God knows what he's capable of!' 'FOOTBALL: PERUGIA TO BUY ANOTHER FOREIGNER?' Zen scanned the newspaper for some reference to his arrival. Rivalries within the Questura usually ensured that an event which was bound to be damaging to someone's reputation would be reported in the local press. But of course there had been no time for that as yet.

When he next looked up he found that the two men had now separated and the older one was walking towards him.

'Excuse me!'

The man turned, suspicious and impatient.

'Yes?'

'I couldn't help overhearing your telephone call just now. I believe you wish to speak to me. I am Aurelio Zen.'

The man's impatience turned first to perplexity and then embarrassment.

'Ah, dottore, it was you, sitting there at the table? And there I was, talking about you like that! Whatever must you have thought?'

His voice drifted away. He seemed to be rapidly searching his memory, trying to recall what exactly he had said. Then with an apologetic gesture he went on, 'I am getting old, dottore! Old and indiscreet. Well, what's done is done. Forgive me, I haven't even introduced myself. Antonio Crepi. How do you do. Welcome to Perugia! Will you allow me to offer you a coffee?'

They returned to the café, where Crepi hailed the barman familiarly.

'Marco, this is Commissioner Zen, a friend of mine. Any time he comes in I want you to give him good service, you understand? No, nothing for me. You know, dottore, they say we must be careful not to drink too much coffee. I'm down to six cups a day, which is my limit. It's like a bridge, you know. You can reduce the number of supports up to a certain point, depending on the type of construction, nature of the soil and so on. After that the bridge collapses. For me the lower limit is six coffees. Fewer than that and I can't function. Anyway, how do you like Perugia? Beautiful, eh?'

'Well, I've only just . . .'

'It's a city on a human scale, not too big, not too small. Whenever I go to Rome, which nowadays is almost never, I feel like I am choking. It's like putting on a collar that's too tight, you know what I mean? Here one can breathe, at least. A friend of mine once told me, "Frankly, Antonio, the moment I set foot outside the city walls I just don't feel right." That's the way we are! Provincial and proud of it. But listen, dottore, I want to be able to talk to you properly, not standing in some bar. Can you come to dinner this evening?'

Zen avoided a reply by taking a sip of coffee. He still hadn't the faintest idea who he was talking to!

'I'm sure this is very different from the way you do things in Rome,' Antonio Crepi went on. 'Maybe you even think it's a bit strange, but I don't care! The only thing that interests me is getting Ruggiero released. The *only* thing! Do you understand? It is wonderful that you're here, your arrival gives us all new heart. Come to dinner! Valesio will be there too, the lawyer who's been handling the negotiations. Talk informally, off the record. Say what you like, ask any question you like. Be as indiscreet as I am, if you can! No one will mind, and when you start work tomorrow morning you'll know as much about the case as anyone in Perugia. What do you say?'

This time there was no way out.

'I'll be delighted.'

Crepi looked pleased.

'Thank you, dottore. Thank you. I'm glad you understand. We Umbrians are just simple, forthright country folk. Rome is another world. If at first you find us a bit rough, a bit blunt, that's just our way. After a while you'll get used to it. We lack polish, it's true, but the wood beneath is sound and solid. But you're not from Rome, surely? Excuse me asking.'

'I'm from the North.'

'I thought so. Milan?'

'Venice.'

'Ah. A beautiful city. But Perugia is beautiful too! I'll send some-one to collect you at about eight. No, I insist. It's easier than trying to give directions. You need to have been born here! Until this evening, then.'

As Zen walked back to his hotel he noticed several people staring at him curiously, but it was not until he caught sight of his reflection in a shop window that he realized that he was wearing one of those annoying little Mona Lisa smiles which makes everyone wonder why you're so pleased with yourself. It was just as well that no one knew him well enough to ask, for he had no idea what he would have replied.

Whatever the reason might have been, by eight o'clock the smile had definitely faded.

Zen had spent the afternoon and early evening reading the back-ground material he had been given on the Miletti case. Like most police drivers, Luigi Palottino clearly considered himself a Formula One contender *manqué*, and the relentless high speeds and a succes-sion of near misses had brought on a mild attack of the car sickness from which Zen often suffered, so that he just hadn't been able to face the pile of documents Enrico Mancini had sent round with the Alfetta. Not that he needed them, of course, to know who Ruggiero Miletti was. To any Italian of his generation the name was practically synonymous with the word gramophone. Ruggiero's father, Franco, had started the business, first repairing and later constructing the new-fangled machines in a spare room at the back of the family's furniture shop on Corso Vanucci, the main street of Perugia. That was in 1910. Ruggiero had been born the previous year. By the time he left school Miletti Phonographs had become a flourishing concern which had outgrown the original premises and moved to a site convenient to the railway line down in the valley.

Although by no means cheap, the Miletti instruments had enjoyed from the first the reputation of being well made, durable, and technically advanced, 'combining the ancient traditions of Umbrian craftsmanship with an irresistible surge towards the Future', as the advertisements put it. Franco had a flair for publicity, and before long such notables as D'Annunzio, Bartali the cycle ace and the composer Respighi had consented to be photographed with a Miletti machine. Franco's greatest coup came when he persuaded the Duce himself to issue a typically bombastic endorsement: 'I declare and pronounce that your phonographs are truly superior instruments and represent a triumph of Fascist civilization.' Meanwhile the radio age had arrived, and the Miletti company were soon producing the massive sets which formed the centrepiece of every wealthy family's sitting-room, around which friends and hangers-on would congregate on Sunday afternoons to listen to the programme called 'The Four Musketeers', which eventually became so popular that the football authorities had to delay matches until it was over.

The family's good fortune continued. Although Ruggiero's elder brother Marco was killed in Greece, the Milettis had a relatively easy war. Having sacrificed one son, it was easy for Franco to persuade influential friends that Ruggiero's brains were too valuable a commodity to be put at risk, and hostilities ended with them and the Miletti workshops intact. Both were quickly put to work. The postwar economic boom, artificially fuelled by the Americans to prevent Italy falling to the Communists, provided ideal conditions for rapid growth, while Ruggiero soon proved that he combined his father's technical genius with even greater ambition and vision. In the next decade the company steadily expanded and diversified, though often in the teeth of considerable opposition from Franco Miletti. When his father died in 1959, Ruggiero found himself at the head of one of the most successful business concerns in the country, producing hi-fi equipment, radios, televisions and tape recorders, exporting to every other country in Europe as well as to many in South America, and often cited as a glowing example of the nation's economic resurgence. In 1967 the firm became the Società Industriale Miletti di Perugia, or SIMP for short, but this fashionably ugly acronym changed nothing. The Miletti family, which in practice meant Ruggiero himself, remained in absolute and sole control.

The kidnap itself was described in a few pages of material copied over the teleprinter from Perugia. The contents proved to be highly predictable, but at least Zen discovered who Antonio Crepi was: the retired director of a construction company with whom Ruggiero Miletti was in the habit of spending Sunday evening playing cards. One week Crepi would motor over to the Miletti villa, the next Ruggiero would drive down to his friend's place, overlooking the Tiber valley. On the last Sunday in October, four and a half months earlier, it had been Ruggiero's turn to visit Crepi. He had left home as usual at eight o'clock and arrived at Crepi's twenty minutes later. The two had played cards and chatted until about a quarter past eleven, when Ruggiero left to drive home. He had never arrived.

The alarm had been given by Silvio, one of Ruggiero's three sons. It was rare for Ruggiero not to be back by midnight, and since there was a hard frost Silvio began to worry that his father might have had an accident. He therefore phoned Crepi, who had already gone to bed, and learned that Ruggiero had set out on his return journey an hour earlier. But, as so often, no one thought of a kidnapping. Daniele, the youngest son, arrived home while his brother was speaking to Crepi, and instead of alerting the police the two decided to search the road themselves. When they arrived at Crepi's villa without having found any trace of Ruggiero the police were finally informed. It was twelve thirty-seven.

Perugia is blessed with a crime rate among the lowest in Italy, and at that hour only a skeleton staff was on duty at the Questura. It took another quarter of an hour to call out the men on standby, and it was twenty past one before a complete set of roadblocks had been set up. Meanwhile the route Miletti had taken was thoroughly examined, revealing evidence of a struggle. Ruggiero's hat, tie and shoe were found lying on the verge, and not far away lay a muslin wad soaked in ether. But it wasn't until daybreak that the burnt-out shell of the car Ruggiero had been driving, one of a fleet of leased Fiat Argenta saloons used by both the family and the senior management of SIMP, was finally spotted by a helicopter in an abandoned quarry some eleven miles north of the city. The front bumper was dented and one of the headlamps cracked, indicating that the gang had front-tailed Ruggiero from the villa, then deliberately braked hard on a bend to cause a minor collision, immobilizing his car. They would have got out to examine the damage, all smiles and apologies. At the last moment their victim must have realized what was happening, for he had fought and kicked and struggled. But by then it was much too late. You could only defend yourself against kidnappers *before* they struck, by persuading them to strike somewhere else.

The remainder of the report on the Miletti kidnapping set out the investigators' provisional conclusions. The gang had had about two hours altogether in which to seize Miletti, dispose of his car, and make good their escape. Assuming the first two stages took about thirty minutes, that left an hour and a half before the road-blocks went up. It was more than enough. If they had continued north they could have been on any one of a dozen remote roads high up in the Apennines within an hour. It was quite possible that they had gone to ground there, in some isolated farm or mountain hut. On the other hand they might well have left the area altogether, taking the link road west to the motorway and spending the rest of the night driving south. By dawn they could have reached the Aspromonte mountains behind Reggio di Calabria, a territory fifty times the size of San Marino and considerably more independent of the Italian State.

In short, it had been a typical professional kidnapping, well planned and well executed. The victim had been carefully chosen to combine the maximum potential return with the minimum possible risk. Like many others, Ruggiero Miletti had regarded kidnapping as something that happened to other people in less fortunate areas of the country, and had scorned to take any precautions. Like many others, he had been wrong. For months, his movements had been logged and analysed, until the kidnappers knew more about his way of life than he did. They had taken him at the weekend. By Monday morning the snatch squad would be back at the garages or factories where they worked. Their companions would laugh as they yawned their way through the day and make crude jokes about their wives being too much for them. They wouldn't mind. They would be getting paid soon, their job over.

Meanwhile the central cell of the gang would be in touch with the family to get the negotiations moving. They wouldn't be too impatient at first, although they would sound it, phoning up with bloodcurdling threats about what would happen to their victim if they weren't paid by the day after tomorrow. But they had timed the operation for the autumn precisely to allow themselves the long winter months in which to break any resistance to their demands.

By now though, in late March, they would be starting to grow restless, wanting to see some return on their considerable investment. Summer was just around the corner, and they wouldn't want to risk missing their month at the seaside. Criminals have the same aspirations as everyone else. That's why they become criminals.

More recent details were skimpy in the extreme. The gang had apparently contacted the family soon after the kidnapping and it was understood that a ransom had been agreed. The sum remained unknown but was thought likely to have been in the region of ten thousand million lire. Payment was assumed to have taken place towards the end of November, but the hostage had not been released, and a local lawyer named Ubaldo Valesio was now believed to be negotiating on behalf of the family. This last snippet was dated mid-December, and unless someone had filleted the file before it was put on the teleprinter it was the most recent piece of information the police in Perugia had. The message was clear: '. . . was understood that a ransom had been paid . . . remained unknown but was thought to have been in the region of . . . was assumed to have taken place towards the end . . . believed to be negotiating . . .' Whoever had drafted the report wanted no one to be in the slightest doubt that the Miletti family had not been cooperating with the authorities.

There was nothing unusual in this, of course. The trouble with the authorities' line on kidnapping was that it sounded just too good to be true. Free the victim, punish the criminals *and* get your money back! Besides, most people were happier doing business with the kidnappers, whose motives they understood and who like them had a lot to lose, than with the impersonal and perfidious agencies of the State. If Zen was unpleasantly surprised to discover how little the Milettis had been cooperating, it was because it put paid to the theory he'd evolved to explain his sudden recall to active duty.

The explanation Enrico Mancini had given him was obviously false. In the first place, provincial detachments never requested intervention of this kind. A local Questura might ask for an expert from Criminalpol to advise them on some technical problem, but that was a very different thing to handing over control to someone from Rome. Such a procedure was always imposed by the Ministry, and was regarded as a humiliating reprimand for inefficiency or incompetence. But an even more serious objection to Mancini's story was simply that Mancini was telling it. Enrico Mancini was a very big fish indeed, whose natural habitat was the wider ocean of political life. At the moment he chose to swim in the local waters of the Interior Ministry, where indeed he had survived an abrupt change in the political temperature which had proved fatal to several of his species. But tomorrow he might well be sighted in one of the other branches of government, between which he moved as effortlessly as a porpoise moves from the Tyrrhenian to the Adriatic and back again. According to some observers, indeed, this rather too evident ease, together with Mancini's brashly confident manner, might prove to be his downfall in the long run.

At all events, the likes of Mancini did not concern themselves with such normal everyday matters as staff movements. The implication was clear. Despite appearances, this particular staff movement was neither normal nor everyday. When you got a personal phone call from an assistant under-secretary to the Minister and were told you were leaving the next morning, someone had been pulling strings. The obvious candidates had been the Miletti family, but if the Milettis were not cooperating with the authorities they would hardly run to the Ministry complaining that those authorities weren't doing enough. So what was going on?

Zen read and re-read the material, scribbling a few notes and a lot of convoluted designs in the margins. But it was no good. There were too many faceless names, or what was worse, names which had somehow acquired a totally misleading set of features and characteristics. Thus Pietro, Silvio, Cinzia and Daniele appeared as 'The Miletti Children', a quartet of child entertainers in matching outfits, and this despite Zen's knowledge that the youngest, Daniele, was twenty-six years old, while Pietro was already in his late thirties, married and living somewhere abroad. As for Cinzia, she could hardly be a winsome little pre-pubescent charmer since she already had two children of her own, the eldest twelve years old.

Meanwhile it was getting late, and the full implications of accepting Crepi's invitation were becoming clear to Zen. He'd acted without thinking, purely on reflex, paralysed by his ignorance of who Crepi was. But after what had happened at the Questura he could be in no doubt as to the weakness of his position in Perugia. To survive he must armour himself in authority, surround himself with as many of the signs and symbols of office as he could muster. Instead of which he had agreed to venture out on to dangerously ambiguous ground, half-social and half-official; a treacherous no man's land where all manner of elaborate games might be played at his expense, where any points he scored would count for nothing but the slightest slip might compromise his position for ever. Well, at least he would go in style. He had phoned the Questura and arranged for Palottino to meet him outside the hotel. They could follow Crepi's chauffeur back to the villa.

The call came at ten past eight.

'There's someone here to collect you. He says he's expected.'

'I'll be down at once.'

The lobby was empty except for a bearded man reading a newspaper and a French couple who were disputing some item on their bill with the receptionist. Zen had almost reached the revolving door when he was called.

'Excuse me!'

Suddenly Zen had an unpleasant sense that events were getting out of hand. It was the bearded man Crepi had been talking to outside the café earlier that afternoon.

'You are Commissioner Zen?'

'Yes?'

'I'm Silvio Miletti. How do you do?'

'I had no idea that you would be coming in person to fetch me,' Zen murmured in some confusion. 'You shouldn't have bothered.'

'It was no bother.'

The way this was said made it quite clear that exactly the opposite was the case. For a moment Zen was tempted to turn on his heel, refuse to go, invent some last-minute engagement. But they were outside now, and Silvio Miletti was pointing across the street.

'My car's over there.'

Palottino saved him. The Neapolitan had parked the Alfetta right in front of the hotel, practically blocking the entrance, and was now leaning in a nonchalantly heroic posture on the driving door, receiving the homage of the passers-by. As he caught sight of the superior from whom flowed his power to flaunt, dazzle and ignore the parking regulations, he snapped smartly to attention.

'And mine's right here,' Zen replied.

'No, no, dottore,' Silvio Miletti insisted fussily. 'You're travelling with me. That's why I've come, after all.'

'Signor Miletti, my driver gets so little work he's almost going crazy as it is. But if you would permit me to offer you . . .'

'No, no, I insist!'

'So do I.'

Zen softened the words with a pale smile, but there was nothing soft about his tone.

Silvio Miletti sighed massively.

'As you wish, dottore, as you wish. Perhaps you would have the goodness to wait just one moment, however, if it's not too much to ask.'

He walked across the street to a large blue Fiat saloon and spoke to someone inside. Zen stood watching, his brief triumph draining away. He had not only been rude, he had been uselessly rude. His petty insistence had demonstrated his weakness, not his strength. I've lost my touch, he thought bleakly. Then the blue saloon drove off and Zen saw that the driver was a woman. That made it perfect. He had succeeded in insulting not only Silvio Miletti but also his fiancée.

'I didn't realize you were with someone,' he remarked as the two men took their places in the back of the Alfetta.

Silvio Miletti shrugged.

'It's only my secretary. I don't drive.'

They followed the blue Fiat through a wedge-shaped piazza and down a steeply curving street. At the bottom it turned sharp right and disappeared through a narrow archway. Numerous scratches on the brickwork showed where drivers had misjudged the clearance, but Palottino revved up and took it like a lion going through a blazing hoop, almost crushing two pedestrians in the process.

Out of the corner of his eye Zen studied Silvio Miletti. Close to, Ruggiero's second son looked like an overweight ghost, at once insubstantial and corpulent. His features, which might have been strong and full of character, had sagged like paint applied too thickly. He was sturdily built, yet gave an impression not of vitality but of enormous lethargy, of a weary disgust with everything and everyone, like a man who has never reconciled himself to what he sees in the mirror every morning. His gestures were oddly prim and fussy for such a lumbering frame, and his voice was high and slightly querulous, with an underlying whine of self-pity.

As suddenly as in a medieval fresco, the city ended and the countryside began. One moment they were driving down a densely inhabited street, the next they were on a country road that dropped so steeply Zen felt his ears aching. A yellow sign flashed by: 'All vehicles using this road from 1 November to 31 March must carry snow-chains on board'. Palottino kept the Alfetta tucked tightly in behind the slowly moving Fiat, like a dog worrying a sheep.

'Tell me, when did the kidnappers last make contact?'

Zen dropped the question idly, just to test the water.

'The negotiations are being handled by Avvocato Valesio.'

Silvio Miletti's tone was so uncompromising that Zen asked himself why he had agreed to be present in the first place.

'Presumably he keeps you informed.'

'No doubt he tells us everything he feels we should know,' Miletti replied with a fastidious quiver, rearranging the folds of his coat 'On the other hand he fully understands how difficult this experience is for us, and I'm sure that he would avoid distressing us unnecessarily.'

He made it quite clear that the negotiator's tact and consideration could well serve as a model to other less thoughtful people.

As the road bottomed out in the valley Palottino swung out and booted the accelerator, leaving the Fiat for dead.

'For Christ's sake!' Zen exploded. 'We're supposed to be following that car!'

'Oh, fuck. Sorry, sir, I forgot.'

'I'll tell you when to turn,' Silvio Miletti told him with another sigh. These sighs were immensely expressive. The world, they seemed to suggest, had once again demonstrated its limitless capacity for stupidity, vulgarity and total insensitivity to his needs and desires. Not that this surprised him; on the contrary, he had long resigned himself to the unremitting awfulness of life. Nevertheless, each reminder was another pebble thoughtlessly tossed on to the already intolerable burden which he was expected to bear without complaint. It really was too bad!

'So when did the gang last make contact, to the best of your knowledge?' Zen continued remorselessly.

There was a rustle of clothing as Miletti changed position with a wriggle of his hips.

'I'm afraid I really can't discuss this. I'm sure you understand why.'

'No, as a matter of fact I don't understand at all. I'm aware that the Miletti family has not been cooperating with the police up to now, but since you have agreed to meet me tonight I assumed that you must have decided to change that attitude. I certainly can't imagine what we're going to talk about otherwise.'

The sigh emerged again in all its glory.

'As far as cooperation goes, I think the fact that I was prepared to come and pick you up from your hotel is sufficient proof of my personal goodwill. In my father's absence, however, decisions are being made jointly by the whole family, and the decision which had been made is that all dealings with the authorities are to be handled by our legal representative, Ubaldo Valesio. He will be present this evening and you will have ample opportunity to put your questions to him.'

The road ran along between two ridges, beside a small stream. The moon was almost full, and by its light the scenery looked flat and unconvincing, depthless shapes blocked out of black cardboard. Even the few clouds in the sky were as neat and motionless as a backdrop. To one side, up on the crest of the ridge, a row of cypresses and cedars led up to a ruin with a tall tower.

'In other words, Valesio will be acting as intermediary not just between you and the gang but also between you and me?'

Zen made no attempt to conceal his irony, and Silvio's reaction was to flare up.

'Yes, dottore, that's exactly what I mean! Despite what some people seem to think, I'm made of flesh and blood like everyone else and there's only so much I can stand. I just can't cope with anything more! I can't be expected to!'

He broke off abruptly to tell Palottino to turn left up a narrow dirt track.

'For over a month we have heard nothing,' he continued in the same self-pitying tone. 'Nothing!'

The headlights swept over rows of neatly pruned vines as the twists and turns of the steeply climbing track succeeded one another.

'Before, they used to make threats, to rant and rave and say God knows what. That seemed bad enough at the time, but now I almost miss their threats. They seem almost reassuring, compared with this terrible silence.'

The track became a driveway lined with cedars and cypresses and suddenly the house was there before them, a fantastic affair of mock-medieval turrets and towers with fishtail embattlements and coats of arms embedded in the walls which Zen realized with a slight shock was the ruin he had caught sight of from the road below. With a satisfying spray of gravel, Palottino brought the car to a halt beside a white Volvo parked in the forecourt.

Antonio Crepi must have been on the lookout, for when Zen got out he found his host at the door to welcome him.

'How do you like my little fortress? It's mostly fake, of course, but nowadays such things have a charm of their own. No craftsman alive could do those mouldings. There's even a romantic story behind it. Years ago, before the war with Austria, my grandfather met his future wife up here during a summer outing. There was nothing here then but the ruins of an old watchtower. Later he bought the land and had the ruins turned into this place as a present for their silver wedding anniversary. Look, this wall is original, over three metres thick! Pity you can't see the view. The Tiber's just down there, and on the other side the hills stretching away towards Gubbio. Better than any painting in the world in my opinion. Silvio, how are you?'

As they passed down a long hallway Zen had a confused impression of old furniture, elaborate paintwork in poor condition, of musty smells and cold, immobile air. Crepi opened one of the three sets of double doors opening off an anteroom at the end of the corridor and ushered his guests through into a large sitting room with a high frescoed ceiling. As they entered, a woman of about thirty moved quickly forward, her hand held out to Zen. She had a skiing tan and long honey-blonde hair and was wearing tawny leather slacks, a hazel-brown silk blouse and masses of gold everywhere.

'Cinzia Miletti, dottore, pleased to meet you, so glad you could come. Wonderful, really. We're counting on you, you know, please tell us there's hope. I'm sure there is, I don't know why but something tells me that father will be all right. Are you religious? I wish I was. And yet sometimes I feel I am. I don't go to church, of course, but that's not what religion is really about, is it? Sometimes I think I'm more religious than all the priests and nuns in Assisi. I have these tremendous feelings.'

Crepi broke in to introduce the other person in the room. Gianluigi Santucci, Cinzia's husband, was a wiry little man in his late thirties, with carefully sculpted, thick black hair, a neat moustache and something almost canine about his sharp, wary features. Zen sensed hostility in the brief glance and minimal nod with which he acknowledged his greeting without budging from where he stood in front of the log fire. Then Cinzia swept him away again.

'Where are you from? You're not Roman, are you? I can't stand Romans, arrogant, pushy people, think they still rule the world. Of course we have masses of friends in Rome. But your name, it reminds me of that book I keep meaning to read, a classic, by what's-his-name, about the man who's trying to give up smoking. Do you smoke? I really should stop, but I've been to the doctor and he told me to take pills which I simply refuse to do, it's worse than smoking. You read these horror stories in the magazines, years later your children are born deformed, though there's nothing wrong with my two, thank God. Have you got any children? But where are you from? No, let me guess. Sicily? Yes, you've got Norman blood, I can sense it. Am I right?'

'Not quite, my dear,' Crepi put in with heavy irony, and corrected her.

'Venice? Well, it's the same thing, an island.'

Just then a tall, plain woman came in from the hallway, closing the door quietly behind her. She was about forty years old, with medium-length mousy-brown hair tied up in a bun, and was dressed in a trouser-suit made from some synthetic material which reminded Zen of beach fashions at the Lido back in the fifties. It was meant to look stylish, but somehow succeeded in being both brash and drab at the same time. No one took the slightest notice of the newcomer. Gianluigi Santucci was saying something to Crepi in an intense whisper, while his wife wandered distractedly about asking everyone if they had seen her handbag and discussing how much easier life would be if handbags didn't exist but how could you survive without them although of course her friend Stefania had given up using hers completely, just thrown it away one day, and she still managed so perhaps it was possible, with time all things were possible.

'Are your brothers coming?' Zen asked Silvio, who shook his head briefly.

'Pietro's in London. And Daniele is not interested in this sort of thing.'

But Zen remembered hearing Crepi tell Silvio that afternoon, 'But not Daniele, eh? God knows what he's capable of!' So whatever sort of thing it was, the youngest Miletti was being deliberately kept out of it.

Gianluigi Santucci's raucous voice suddenly cut loose, as if someone had flicked the volume control on a badly tuned radio.

'Well, that's his tough shit, in my opinion! If people arrive late they can't expect everyone else to wait for them. It's not as if he's the head of the family or an honoured guest!'

Crepi explained to the others that they had been discussing whether or not to wait any longer for Ubaldo Valesio.

'What's the point in waiting?' Cinzia's husband demanded. 'These lawyers are always stuffing themselves, anyway. Lawyers and priests, they're the worst!'

'Yes, let's get on with it!' Silvio agreed. Judging by his tone, he meant 'Let's get it over with'.

Crepi turned to Zen.

'Dottore, you're the neutral party here,' he said with exaggerated heartiness. 'What do you say?'

Fortunately Cinzia saved him.

'Oh, I'm sure the Commissioner feels just the same as the rest of us!' she cried. 'Let's eat, for heaven's sake! I'm starving, and you know Lulu's digestion is always a problem. Standing around waiting just gets the juices going, you know, eating into the stomach lining. Horrible, disgusting. But he bears it like a lamb, don't you, Lulu?'

The dining room was cold and smelt damp. It was lit by a large number of naked bulbs stuck in a chandelier whose supporting chain ran up several metres to an anchorage planted with surreal effect in the midst of the elaborate frescos which covered the ceiling. Zen had plenty of time to study these buxom nymphs and shepherds disporting themselves in a variety of more or less suggestive poses as the meal proceeded at a funereal pace, presided over by an elderly retainer whose hands shook so alarmingly that it seemed just a matter of time before a load of food ended up in someone's lap.

The tagliatelle was home-made, the meat well grilled on a wood fire, Crepi's wine honest and his bottle-green oil magnificent, but the dinner was a disaster. Ubaldo Valesio did not arrive, and without him, by tacit consent, kidnapping of Ruggiero Miletti could not be mentioned. With this tremendous presence unacknowledged there was nothing to do but be relentlessly bright and superficial. Cinzia Miletti thus came into her own, dominating the table with a breathless display of frenetic verbiage which might almost have been mistaken for high spirits. Antonio Crepi punctuated her monologues with a succession of rather ponderous anecdotes about the history and traditions of Umbria in general and Perugia in particular, narrated in the emphatic declamatory style of university professors of the pre-1968 era.

Silvio sat eating his way steadily through his food with an expression midway between a squint and a scowl, as though he were looking at something repulsive through the wrong end of a telescope. Gianluigi Santucci contributed little beyond occasional explosive comments that were the verbal equivalent of the loud growls and rumbles emanating from his stomach. The woman in the grotesque trouser-suit, who was apparently Silvio's secretary, said not one word throughout, merely smiling ingratiatingly at everyone and no one, like a kindly nun watching children at play. As for Zen, he studied the ceiling and thanked God that time passed relatively quickly at his age. He could still remember half-hours from his childhood which seemed to have escaped the regulation of the clock altogether and to last for ever, until for no good reason they were over. Crepi's dinner party made the most of every one of its one hundred and thirteen minutes, but shortly after half past ten its time was up and they all filed back into the other room.

But despite the slightly more relaxed atmosphere, the situation remained blocked. There was continued speculation about what could have happened to Valesio, whose thoughtlessness in not ringing to apologize and explain was agreed to be typical. The origins of the problem were traced back to his mother, a Swede who had fallen in love first with Perugia and then with a Perugian, and who as a foreigner could not be expected to know how to bring up her son properly. But Zen was beginning to suspect that Crepi had been outmanoeuvred, that Valesio was staying away deliberately under orders from the Milettis in order to prevent any discussion of the kidnapping. So why didn't they all go, for God's sake? The farce had been played out to the bitter end and there was nothing to stop them making a graceful exit. The fact remained that no one appeared to have the slightest intention of doing anything of the kind.

At last the sound of a motor was heard outside, and everyone perked up.

'Ah, finally!' cried Cinzia. 'He's impossible, you know, really impossible, and yet such a nice person really. My mother always told me whatever I did never to marry a lawyer. He'll be late for his own funeral, she used to say, and I must say Gianluigi for all his faults is always on time.'

This paragon of punctuality exchanged a glance with Silvio.

'That's a motorcycle engine,' he remarked.

Crepi got up and walked over to the window.

'Well?' Cinzia demanded. 'Who is it?'

'There's nobody there.'

'Exactly, there's nobody here!' a new voice exclaimed.

Six heads turned in unison towards the other end of the room, where the door had opened a crack.

'Or rather I'm here,' the voice continued. 'It comes to the same thing, doesn't it?'

'Stop playing the fool, Daniele!' cried Cinzia sharply. 'You know what my nerves are like. What must you think of us, dottore? You must forgive him, he's a good boy really. It's my mother's fault, God rest her. A good woman, a wonderfully warm person, but she hadn't read Freud of course. I shudder to think how she must have toilet-trained us all.'

The door swung open, but Daniele remained standing on the threshold. He was tall and shared his sister's good looks, which were set off by about a million lire's worth of casually elegant clothing: Timberland shoes, tweed slacks, a lambswool sweater and a Montclair skiing jacket.

'What are you doing?' exclaimed Silvio in a tone of sullen irritation. 'Come in and close the door!'

A contrived look of surprise and puzzlement appeared on Daniele's handsome features.

'What do you think I am, some kind of gatecrasher? Someone who just barges into parties he hasn't been invited to? I wasn't brought up on a farm, you know.'

Antonio Crepi gestured impatiently.

'Oh, come along, Daniele! We haven't got time for this kind of thing. You know very well that I invited the whole family. If you couldn't be bothered to come that's your business, but don't waste our time with these childish scenes.'

'Oh, the whole family, eh? That's not what I was told.'

He came in and closed the door, staring pointedly at Silvio.

'If you're so fussy about your manners suddenly, then you might at least greet Antonio's guest,' chirped Cinzia. 'This is Commissioner Zen, who's come up specially from Rome to help save father. He's from Venice, lucky man. What a beautiful city! I'm just crazy about Venice.'

Daniele swung around and peered at Zen's feet with comically exaggerated interest. He frowned.

'That's odd. I've always been told that the policemen in Venice have one wet shoe. You know, because when they've finished their cigarettes they throw them in the canal and . . .'

He mimed someone stubbing out a cigarette with his foot and started to laugh loudly.

'But Commissioner Zen's feet are perfectly dry!' he resumed. 'So clearly he can't be from Venice. Either that or he's not a policeman.'

'Shut your face!'

The reprimand came not from Silvio or Crepi but from Gianluigi Santucci. Daniele continued to smile genially as though he had not heard him. He did not speak again, however. Neither did anyone else, and so silence fell.

In the end it was left to Silvio's secretary to save the situation.

'Well, I expect Commissioner Zen would like to get an early night,' she remarked, as she stood up.

It was the first thing Zen had heard her say all evening, and he realized with a shock that she was not Italian. Of course! With those clothes he should have guessed.

'That's very thoughtful of you, signora,' he said, rising to his feet to ensure that her gesture did not go for nothing.

'She's not a signora,' Cinzia corrected him. 'She's not married. Are you, Ivy?'

It was a horrible and quite deliberate insult. Any woman of a certain age is entitled to be addressed as signora whether or not she is married. Everyone tensed for the reaction, but it never came. The woman stood there like a statue, smiling as beatifically as she had all evening.

'That's quite true, Cinzia,' she replied evenly in her deep, chesty voice, enunciating every word with almost pedantic clarity. 'But the Commissioner hasn't been here long enough yet to know all these little details. However, I expect in a few days he'll know more about us than we do ourselves!'

It was a remarkable performance. The woman's foreignness made Zen think of Ellen, and so it was with genuine warmth that he replied, 'Good night, signora,' and received a beaming smile in return.

Everyone stood up, except for Daniele.

'I don't want to leave yet,' he complained. 'I only just got here.'

Gianluigi Santucci strolled over to the sofa where he was slumped and grabbed him by the ear.

'Ah, these young people today!' he cried with vicious playfulness. 'No energy, no initiative. It makes me sick!'

With a mocking laugh he hauled Daniele to his feet and pushed him over to join the others.

At the front door hands were shaken and formulas of farewell exchanged. At the last moment Crepi plucked at Zen's sleeve, holding him back.

'Not you, dottore.'

The Milettis exchanged a flicker of rapid glances.

'I thought he wanted to get an early night,' Silvio objected.

'Don't you worry about Commissioner Zen,' Crepi smiled, all cheerful consideration. 'Mind how you go yourselves, that driveway of mine is quite dangerous in places. I keep meaning to have it re-surfaced but what with one thing and another I never get around to it.'

'And if Valesio comes?'

Gianluigi Santucci's question, unlike that of his brother- in-law, had real meaning.

'If Valesio comes he'll get a dish of cold tagliatelle and a piece of my mind! But we won't discuss the kidnapping behind your backs, if that's what you're worried about.'

Santucci grimaced.

'Worried? Why should I be worried? It's for others to worry, not me!'

A few minutes later the disparate noises of the Fiat, the Santuccis' Volvo and Daniele's Enduro Trail bike had all faded to a distant intermittent drone that was finally indistinguishable from silence.

'Well, what did you think of them?' Crepi demanded as they returned to the living room. 'But first let me offer you something to drink. Do you like grappa? I'm told this one is good. It's from your part of the world. My youngest girl married a dentist from Udine and they send me a bottle made by one of the uncles every Christmas. Actually, my doctor has forbidden me to drink spirits, but I haven't the heart to tell them that.'

He handed him a glass of liquid as limpid as spring water.

'Now listen, dottore,' Crepi continued. 'You must be wondering why I should want to ruin your first evening in Perugia like this.'

Zen sniffed the grappa appreciatively.

'I'm even more curious to know why they agreed to come.'

'The Milettis? Oh, they came because each thought that the others were coming and no one wanted to be left out. This afternoon on the Corso, just before we spoke, I ran into Silvio. I mentioned the dinner and let him think that Cinzia and her husband were coming. Silvio didn't care for the idea of Cinzia and Gianluigi discussing matters with you behind his back, so he agreed to come. Then I phoned Cinzia and told her that Silvio was coming, with the same result. And no one wanted to be the first to leave. If it hadn't been for the foreigner I might have had to throw them out!'

He did not make this prospect sound too displeasing.

'And Daniele?'

'Daniele's less predictable. But you can usually get him to do something by convincing him that you don't want him to do it. I told Cinzia not to mention the dinner to him, which is like asking someone to carry water in a sieve. He assumed he was being excluded and barged in trying to be as rude as possible to everyone. Little did he suspect that that was precisely what I wanted! But there you are, you see. They think they're so clever, these children, but once you understand how they work you can do anything you like with them. It's just a shame that Valesio couldn't make it. If only we'd been able to discuss the kidnapping you'd really have seen what we're up against.'

Zen considered this for a moment.

'I thought we were up against a gang of kidnappers.'

'If only we were!' Crepi exclaimed. 'How simple that would be. But that's why I invited you here this evening. Because if you're to help, really help, the first thing you have to realize is that this is no ordinary kidnapping, for the simple reason that the Milettis are no ordinary family. Let's start with Silvio. Of the whole brood, he's the one who resembles his father most, physically I mean. In every other way they couldn't be more different. Silvio hasn't the slightest interest in the firm, or in anything else except his stamp collection, and one or two nastier hobbies. Ruggiero has never understood him. For example, when the time came for Silvio to do his military service everyone assumed that his father would make a few phone calls and get him exempted. Well, Ruggiero made the phone calls all right, but to make sure that Silvio not only did his full time but did it in some mosquito-ridden dump in Sardinia. He'd just begun to realize that his son was a bit of a pansy, you see, and he reckoned that was the way to make a man of him. I don't think Silvio's ever forgiven him for it. Not just the time in Sardinia, but above all the humiliation of having a father who thought so little of him he wouldn't even play a few cards in Rome to get him off the hook.'

Crepi stood up, opened a small ceramic jar on the mantelpiece and extracted a short cigar. He offered one to Zen, who shook his head and extracted one of the four Nazionali remaining. He realized with dismay that he had forgotten to bring a supply of those deliciously coarse cigarettes made from domestic tobacco, costing only a few hundred lire a pack but as difficult to find as wild mushrooms. In Rome he could count on getting them from a tobacconist to whose son he had once given a break, but in Perugia what would he do?

'I won't waste time on Cinzia,' Crepi continued. 'She's just a pretty child who's growing old without ever having grown up. There are only two important things about her. One is that husband of hers. I must admit to a sneaking admiration for Gianluigi, although he's undoubtedly one of the most appalling shits ever invented. He's not from round here, of course. You spotted those ugly Tuscan 'c's, like a cat being sick? Santucci's been on the make since the day he was conceived. Marrying Cinzia Miletti hasn't done his career any harm, of course, but he would have risen anyway, anywhere, under any circumstances.'

Zen smiled slyly.

'We have a saying in Venice. Whether the water is fresh or salt, turds rise to the top.'

He immediately regretted the comment. What was he doing talking to Crepi in this familiar fashion? But his host's laughter sounded genuine enough.

'Quite right, quite right! I've been at the top myself, so I should know! Oh yes, Gianluigi has done all right for himself. With Silvio taking no interest and Pietro abroad, he's wormed his way into the senior management level at SIMP. But of course Ruggiero still makes all the final decisions, and there's no love lost between those two, needless to say. It must be quite a relief for Gianluigi to have the old man out of the way. But we mustn't forget the other important thing about Cinzia, which also applies to her little brother. It's simply that when Ruggiero passes on, God forbid, they'll each inherit twenty-

five per cent of SIMP. A quarter of the company each! That's quite a
thought, isn't it? Particularly when you realize that our foxy little
Tuscan is married to one quarter and has the other very firmly under
his thumb. Daniele ignores me and treats Silvio like shit, but he obeys
his brother-in-law.'

Zen took another little sip of grappa, rolling it around his mouth.
The rough, stalky taste burned down his throat and up into his brain.
Why was Crepi telling him all this?

'What about Pietro?' he asked. 'Isn't it rather surprising that he's
not here in Perugia during his father's ordeal?'

Crepi nodded.

'He did come back at first, but when the negotiations began to drag
out he claimed that he had to go back to London to look after his
business interests. He takes after his father in that. Silvio inherited
Ruggiero's looks, Pietro got the brains. He's extremely sharp, but
much too intelligent to let it show. Ruggiero has a slow country manner which has deceived a lot of clever Milanese into not reading the
fine print. Pietro trades on his ten years in London. He originally
went there to organize the distribution of SIMP products that end,
then talked his father into letting him set up a semi-autonomous
subsidiary to import a range of products. But that's just a cover. His
real business is currency manipulation. He's organized a chain of
more-or-less fictitious companies and shifts funds around between
them, turning a tidy profit each time. Clever, eh? But Pietro *is* clever,
and fiercely ambitious, although you'd never guess it from his manner. He acts like the model of an English gentleman, all vague and
shy and diffident. But don't let it fool you. You could use his ego to
cut glass.'

Zen felt his head beginning to swim.

'I don't expect to have much to do with the family. They've made it
quite clear that they're not prepared to cooperate with the
authorities.'

'I know. What bothers me is that they're not prepared to cooperate
with the kidnappers either.'

'But haven't they already paid up?'

Crepi made an ambivalent gesture.

'They've paid once, back in November. We all thought that was
that. But instead of releasing Ruggiero those bastards came back for
more. That's when all the trouble started.'

'How much more did they want?'

'The same again. Ten thousand million lire.'

Zen made a face.

'God almighty, they've got it!' Crepi snorted impatiently. 'And if they haven't there are a hundred ways they could raise it. But they felt they'd agreed to the first demand too easily, and that this time they should strike a harder bargain, arguing over every last lira. Then there was the question of how to raise the money. More problems, more bickering. Exactly what should be sold? Should they borrow? Couldn't Piero help out? And what about Gianluigi's idea of doing a deal with a foreign firm interested in acquiring a stake in SIMP? Et cetera, et cetera. I won't bore you with all the details.'

'What about the police, the judiciary? Are they aware that Valesio is in regular contact with the gang?'

Crepi waggled his hands again.

'Yes and no. They know, of course. In Perugia everyone knows everything. But officially they've been kept out of it. You see, part of the problem all along has been that the investigating magistrate who's handling the case, Luciano Bartocci, is a Communist who's got it in for the Milettis on principle. Given half a chance Bartocci would like to use the kidnapping as an excuse to pry into the family's affairs for political reasons.'

'Couldn't he be replaced?'

After a moment Crepi gave another long, loud laugh.

'My answer to that, dottore, is the same as a certain politician gave his wife when they went to the Uffizi to see that Botticelli which was cleaned recently. The wife is in raptures. I can just see it over the fireplace at home, she says. Listen, her husband replies, I can't do *everything*, you know!'

Zen joined in his host's laughter.

'Anyway, this is really beside the point,' Crepi resumed. 'If the family were united, all the Bartoccis in the world couldn't touch them. As it is, they would starve to death for want of agreeing which sauce to have with their pasta if the cook didn't decide for them. And meanwhile Ruggiero's life is in the balance! He's over seventy years old, dottore, and his health is failing. Ever since the accident that killed his wife he has suffered from bouts of semi-paralysis down one side of his body. Two years ago it looked as though he would have to give up working altogether, but in the end he pulled through. Who knows how he's suffering at this very moment, while we sit here warm and well fed in front of the fire? He must be brought home! The family must pay whatever is being asked, immediately, with no further haggling! That's what you must tell them, dottore.'

To hide his look of dismay, Zen brought the glass to his lips and drained off the last drops of grappa.

'What makes you think they'll listen to me?'

'I don't mean the family.'

'Who, then?'

Crepi leaned forward.

'Your arrival here in Perugia will be widely reported. I'll see to that! You'll be interviewed. They'll ask you about your impressions of the case. Tell them! That's all. Just tell them.'

'Tell them what?'

'Tell them that you wonder how serious the Milettis really are about getting Ruggiero back! Tell them that the family gives no impression of having understood the extreme gravity and urgency of the situation. In a word, tell them that you're not convinced that the Milettis are in earnest! Naturally I'll give you my fullest backing. We'll shame them into paying! Do you see? Eh? What do you say?'

But at that moment the phone rang.

THREE

As the car leaned further and further into the curve he tensed for the inevitable smash. Cheated again! There was no getting used to it.

'If that's Valesio with his apologies I'll tell him what he can do with them!' Crepi had muttered as he went to answer the phone. 'Hello? Who? Oh. Yes? I don't understand. What? No! Oh, my God! Oh, Jesus!'

He bent over, taking deep breaths.

'What's happened?'

Crepi was panting as though about to faint. Zen took the receiver from him.

'Hello? Who's there?'

The line went dead.

'They've killed him,' Crepi murmured as he lurched towards the door, ignoring Zen's questions.

Zen dialled the Questura, but they didn't know anything. He told them to find out and call him back.

He walked over to the hearth, picked up a log and threw it on the embers. Some dried moss and a section of ivy still clinging to the bark flared up. Gradually the wood itself took hold, first smoking furiously and then bursting into flame.

A ladybird appeared from a crack and began exploring the surface of the log, now well alight. Zen took a splinter from the hearth and lowered the end of it into the path of the little creature, which promptly veered away. Again and again he tried to tempt the ladybird to safety, until his hand began to ache from the heat. Just as he had finally succeeded, the phone rang again. The insect fell and flamed up on the glowing embers at the front of the grate.

'The Carabinieri are handling it and they're not giving much away. The gist of it seems to be that someone's been killed out near Valfabbrica.'

He walked downstairs calling for Palottino, who emerged from the kitchen where he'd been watching television. It wasn't till they were getting into the car that Crepi appeared, looking for the first time like the old man he was.

'I'm coming too.'

It had been his contact in the Carabinieri who had called, he said. Ruggiero Miletti had been found murdered in the boot of a car.

The night was still mild and luminous, but a big gusty southerly breeze had sprung up and was pushing the clouds along, and when they cleared the moon the landscape was revealed, distinct and yet mysterious, in a way that made daylight seem as crudely functional as neon strip-lighting. Then the clouds closed in again and it was night, the headlights punching holes in the darkness. Black metal bicycle torches gripped tight as they ran shrieking barefoot through the sand dunes. At the Lido, it must have been, with Tommaso and that lot, more than forty years ago. To think that single memory had lain undisturbed in some crevice of his brain all these years, lovingly, uselessly preserved.

'There it is!'

Crepi's voice was uncomfortably close to Zen's ear. He just glimpsed the blue and white sign reading 'Valfabbrica'.

The main street was dark and tightly shuttered. Outside the Carabinieri station three men in uniform were chatting beside a dark blue Giulietta. A burly individual with a sergeant's stripes on his sleeve responded to Zen's request for directions by jerking his head at the open doorway behind him, but before Zen could get out Palottino leaned across him and started speaking in tongues. The sergeant said something in return and then got into the Giulietta.

'He's going to take us there,' the Neapolitan explained.

'Friend of yours?'

Palottino shook his head. The emergency was having a relaxing effect on his manners.

'He's from Naples, I recognized the accent. Says this is the first interesting thing that's happened here.'

'And what exactly *has* happened?'

Wonderful, thought Zen. I'm reduced to getting my information on the dialect grapevine.

'Somebody found shot in a car.'

Crepi groaned as though knifed.

About a kilometre outside town they turned left on to a dirt road winding through a desolate landscape created by the seasonal floods of the nearby river. After a while the Giulietta slowed, lights appeared ahead and the road was blocked by vehicles parked at all angles across it.

The scene was illuminated like a film set by a powerful searchlight mounted on a Carabinieri jeep. As they got out Zen made out a group of men standing talking near a large grey car. Then everything disappeared as the searchlight went out.

'Till tomorrow, then!'

'Excuse me!' Zen called.

'Who is it?'

'I'm from the police.'

The silence was broken only by the incomprehensible squawks and crackles of a short-wave radio.

'You're rather late.'

Someone laughed.

'As usual!'

'It's gone.'

'And we're off.'

'Is it true, then?'

It was Crepi's voice, just in front of Zen.

'Is what true?'

'He's dead?'

'Who are you?'

'I am Antonio Crepi. Who are *you*?'

Someone drew in their breath sharply.

'Forgive me, Commendatore, I had no idea! For God's sake, Volpi, tell your men to put that light back on. Ettore Di Leonardo, Deputy Public Prosecutor. My apologies, I thought you said you were from the police.'

'I'm from the police,' Zen began. 'Commissioner Aurelio . . .'

'Answer me!' Crepi repeated. 'Is he dead?'

The searchlight crackled back into life and they all covered their eyes.

'Unfortunately, Commendatore. Unfortunately.'

'The first murder victim I've ever seen,' said a younger man with a full black beard. 'And it wasn't a pretty sight, I can assure you.'

'Show a little respect, for Christ's sake!' Crepi protested angrily. 'He was my friend!'

The younger man shrugged.

'Mine too.'

'You, Bartocci?' Crepi's tone was bitterly sarcastic. 'A friend of Ruggiero Miletti? What the hell are you talking about?'

'Who said anything about Ruggiero Miletti?' asked the older of the two civilians.

'I was referring to the murdered man, Ubaldo Valesio,' explained his bearded colleague.

Crepi looked at the third man, a major of the Carabinieri.

'But I was told that it was Ruggiero who had been killed!' he exclaimed.

'There was initially some confusion as to the identity of the victim,' the officer replied smoothly.

The older civilian had turned his attention to Zen. He was short and stout, with a face as smooth and featureless as a balloon, and he glared at everyone, as though he knew very well how foolish he looked and had decided to brazen it out.

'You're from the police? Di Leonardo, Deputy Public Prosecutor. I'm by no means happy with the way this investigation has been handled. In my view the police have shown a lack of thoroughness bordering on the irresponsible, with the tragic results that we have seen tonight.'

Zen shook his head vaguely.

'Excuse me, I've only just arrived . . .'

'Quite, quite. This is in no sense intended as a personal reflection on you, Commissioner. Nevertheless I find it quite incredible that no attempt has been made to exploit the dead man's contacts with the gang, really quite incredible. If his movements had been monitored much might have been learned. As it is we now have a corpse on our hands without being any closer to tracing either the gang or Ruggiero Miletti's whereabouts. It is most unsatisfactory, really most unsatisfactory indeed.'

Zen gestured helplessly.

'As I say, I've only just arrived here, but I must point out that electronic surveillance of the kind you mention requires the co-operation of the subject. If no such attempt was made it's presumably because the police were respecting the wishes of the Miletti family.'

The Public Prosecutor waggled his finger to indicate that this wouldn't do.

'The constitution states quite clearly that the forces of the law

MICHAEL DIBDIN

operate autonomously under the direction of the judiciary. The wishes of members of the public have nothing whatever to do with it.'

'But the police can't be expected to contradict the wishes of the most powerful family in Perugia without specific instructions from the judiciary,' Zen protested.

Major Volpi intervened, holding out his hand as though he was directing traffic.

'I cannot of course speak for my colleagues in the police,' he remarked smugly, 'but I can assure you that in this case as in any other my men will at all times do whatever is necessary to ensure a successful outcome, regardless of who may be involved.'

A fierce rivalry had always existed between the civil police, responsible to the Ministry of the Interior, and the paramilitary Carabinieri controlled by the Defence Ministry. Indeed, it was deliberately cultivated on the grounds that competition helped to keep both sides efficient and honest.

'There you are, you see!' Di Leonardo told Zen. 'You can't expect us judges to do all your thinking for you, Commissioner. We expect to see some initiative on your part too.'

With that he turned away to speak to Antonio Crepi. The Carabinieri officer went off to supervise a tow-truck which had just arrived from the direction of the main road. Bartocci, the young investigating magistrate, was standing beside the car in which Valesio's body had been found, a grey BMW, almost new by the look of it. Zen walked over and looked down into the open boot. There was nothing to be seen except a small dark pool of blood held back by the edge of a plastic pouch containing an instruction booklet on the use of the jack.

'His wife's very close to my sister,' Bartocci remarked. 'She's only thirty-one. They've got three children.'

Zen had enough sense to keep quiet.

'The worst of it is that this wasn't his line at all! Ubaldo was a labour lawyer. Union disputes, contracts, that sort of thing. A good negotiator, of course.'

Luciano Bartocci provided the strongest possible contrast to his senior colleague from the Public Prosecutor's office. They had both been called out unexpectedly, but while Di Leonardo was turned out immaculately in a suit, pullover and tie complete with gold pin, the younger man was wearing a skiing jacket, open-necked shirt and jeans. He was about thirty-five years old, athletic and vigorous, with a frank and direct gaze. His beard almost hid his one weakness, a slight facial twitch, as if he were constantly restraining an impulse to smile.

'Why should they do such a thing?' he murmured.

'Perhaps it was a mistake.'

Zen was hardly conscious of having spoken until Bartocci rounded on him.

'You wouldn't say that if you'd seen him! They put the gun in his mouth, it blew the back of his head clean off. There was no mistake about it.'

'No, I meant . . .'

But before he could explain Bartocci was called away by Di Leonardo. All the vehicles were revving up their engines ready for departure. Without warning the searchlight went out again.

Zen hadn't been paying attention to his surroundings and at first he was afraid to move a step in case he walked into a ditch. But as his eyes adjusted he started to make his way towards the Alfetta, slowly at first, then with growing confidence. He was moving at almost his normal pace when he ran into someone.

'Sorry!'

'Sorry!'

He recognized Bartocci's voice.

'Is that the Police Commissioner from Rome?' the young magistrate asked.

'Yes.'

'Listen, I'd like to see you tomorrow morning. Can you come to my office?'

The voice was moving away.

'I'll have to break the news to his wife,' Bartocci continued, more and more distantly. 'I don't know how long that'll take. Shall we say nine o'clock? If I'm late perhaps you could wait.'

'Is there anything in particular you want?'

There was no reply. Zen walked cautiously forward, hands outstretched before him, but when the moon came out again he found that he was alone.

The Uncle of Italy, Sandro Pertini, looked down with his inimitable air of benevolent authority on Aurelio Zen, who stared blankly back.

This apparent lack of respect was due to the fact that he was not looking at the President of the Republic but at the glass covering the photograph, which reflected the doorway open to the adjoining room where his two assistants were sifting through the mound of documents that had been removed from Ubaldo Valesio's home and office that morning. Or rather, that is what they were supposed to be doing: the glazing of the presidential portrait revealed that in fact one of them was engaged in an intense whispered discussion with the other, punctuated by furtive glances in the direction of Zen's office.

Zen's face was even paler and more drawn than usual, and his eyes glittered from the combined effects of too little sleep and too much coffee. It had been after three o'clock before he'd finally got to bed. He awoke four hours later with the taste of blood in his mouth, the tip of his tongue aching fiercely where his teeth had nipped it. That was a bad sign, a sign of tension running deep, of nerves out of control. He got out of bed and opened the window for the first time. The noise of traffic from the broad boulevard directly below rushed in along with the icy pure air. In the middle distance two churches marked the route of a street running out of the city through a medieval suburb. The nearer was a broad structure of rough pink stone with a solid rectangular bell-tower, squatting amidst the cramped and jumbled houses with the massive poise of a peasant woman in the fields. The other, by contrast, was a complex conglomerate of buildings topped by a tall, slim spire. Far beyond them both, fifteen or twenty kilometres away, a mountain as round and smooth as a mound of dough rose from the plain. Zen had never seen it before, but he had the oddest sensation that he had known it all his life.

He had got up and searched through his luggage, still scattered untidily about the room, until he found the little transistor radio he took with him on his travels. The news had just begun, and he listened with one ear as he shaved. A minister had decided to respond with 'dignified silence' to calls for his resignation following claims that his name appeared on a list of those involved in a kickback scandal involving a chain of construction companies. The leader of one party had described as 'absolutely unacceptable' a statement made the day before by the secretary of another, whom he accused of 'typical arrogance and condescension'. A senior police officer in Palermo had been shot dead as he left a restaurant. The Pope had announced a forthcoming tour of ten countries. Flights were likely to be disrupted later that month by a planned strike by air traffic controllers. An accident on the Milan–Venice motorway had left three people dead and eleven more injured and had strengthened the calls for the building of an extra carriageway. The murder of a lawyer in Umbria had been squeezed in just before the weather forecast; the Carabinieri were said to be investigating, but there was no mention of Ruggiero Miletti.

Zen jerked his chair back, making it squeak loudly on the floor, and the two heads reflected in the rectangle of glass immediately bent over their respective piles of papers, covered with almost illegible notations in Ubaldo Valesio's minuscule handwriting. Zen shifted his gaze to the right, towards the small crucifix and the calendar showing cadets on parade at the training school at Nettuno. The calendar was still turned to February, although it was now March and his mother's birthday was in less than a week. He absolutely must not forget to get her a present.

On the desk in front of him lay the *Nazione* newspaper. The headline read 'BUTCHERED, THE MILETTIS' MOUTHPIECE: A MESSAGE TO THE "SUPERCOP" FROM ROME?' Below it appeared a photograph of a scene which had become as familiar a part of Italian life as a bowl of pasta. Lying in a stiff and unnatural foetal crouch with a rather fatuous lopsided grin on his face, Ubaldo Valesio made an extremely unconvincing corpse. But conviction was amply supplied by the pictures of the other side of the lawyer's head which Bartocci had shown him earlier, the pulpy mass of the brain hollowed out like a watermelon seeded with bits of shattered bone.

But he had not died in vain! Thanks to this development Zen had been able to enforce payment of the blank cheque which the Questore had so boldly dashed off the day before. He had requested and obtained the services of two inspectors and a detective-sergeant, together with an extra office and various communications and vehicle privileges which he had no reason to suppose he would need but had thrown in for good measure. But as the news had made clear, the Carabinieri had taken a stranglehold on the murder inquiry, and all that remained for the 'supercop from Rome' was to check Valesio's movements on the previous day and sift through the material which had been removed from his home and office. Lucaroni, one of the two inspectors, was handling the first chore, while the other, Geraci, was at work next door on the second. He was being assisted, if that was the word, by Chiodini, whose services Zen had specifically requested. The sight of the big brute straining to decipher Ubaldo Valesio's finicky jottings was some small compensation for the way he had treated Zen the day before.

Zen had arrived at Bartocci's office promptly at nine o'clock. The law courts were housed in a rambling Renaissance palace forming one side of the inevitable Piazza Matteotti. The portal was surmounted by a lunette containing a statue of Justice flanked by two creatures apparently consisting of a vulture's head and wings attached to the body of a hyena, a motif repeated extensively elsewhere in the building. Zen had plenty of time to admire the architectural features of the palace, since Luciano Bartocci did not put in an appearance until shortly after ten.

By day the young magistrate conformed rather more to the sartorial norm for members of his profession: a tweed jacket, lambswool pullover, check shirt, woollen tie and corduroy trousers. He, too, looked haggard, having been up until almost five o'clock that morning dealing with the victim's widow. Patrizia Valesio, it seemed, had at first reacted with eerie calm to the news of her husband's death.

'She was still up when we got there,' Bartocci explained, 'still waiting for her husband to come home. I'd taken my sister along to help out. I think Patrizia must have realized what had happened the moment she opened the door, but she invited us in as though nothing was the matter. We might have been paying a normal social call, except that it was the middle of the night. I told her that her husband had been involved in an accident. "He's dead, isn't he?" she replied. "They've killed him." I just nodded.'

They were outside the law courts, waiting for Palottino to bring the Alfetta over. Bartocci had explained that he wanted Zen to accompany him to Valesio's home and office, where he planned to remove any documents which might have a bearing on the lawyer's murder or his contacts with the kidnappers. The street was brilliantly sunny and busy, with people going into and out of the market building, whose entrance was through an arcade beneath the law courts.

'She stayed perfectly calm until I mentioned something about the car,' Bartocci went on. 'Then she went crazy. "No, it's not possible!" she shrieked. "It was brand-new, I gave it him for Christmas! Don't tell me it was damaged too!" Marisa and I just stood looking at each other. It sounded like the ultimate consumerist nightmare, a woman who accepts her husband's murder without blinking an eyelid and then breaks down because the car's been scratched. Then she started to get hysterical and incoherent, snatching up things from the shelves and throwing them across the room. Marisa tried to calm her while I rang for a doctor. It took him forty minutes to get there. I'll never forget that time as long as I live.'

A woman who looked like a barrel wearing a fur coat was waiting for the bus. Her son, perfectly dressed as a miniature man, stood staring unbelievingly up at the balloon whose string he had just lost hold of, now floating away high above the arriving Alfetta.

'The calmness was all a façade, of course,' Bartocci continued once they were settled in the car. 'Patrizia had been so terrified by what her husband was doing that she had convinced herself that nothing could happen to him. But she'd forgotten to extend this magic immunity to the BMW, which is why she went into hysterics as soon as I mentioned it.'

'Where is she now?'

'With relatives, under sedation.'

The Valesios' house was one of a number of modern apartments forming an exclusive development on the lower slopes of the city, all pink brick and double glazing and concrete balconies dripping with creeper. In the absence of Patrizia Valesio the family interests were represented by her mother, a formidable woman who followed Bartocci and Zen from room to room, personally checking every single item that was removed while bemoaning the fact that the authorities were permitted to make free with the private papers of a man above suspicion, a pillar of the community and a repository of every known human virtue. Ubaldo Valesio himself made a ghostly fourth presence, smiling at them from photographs, haunting a wardrobe full of clothes, proclaiming his taste in books and records, even trying to lay claim to a non-existent future by way of a scribbled note on his desk jotter reading 'Evasio Thursday re plumbing'.

It was not until they were driving back to the city centre that Bartocci produced the photographs.

'Just in case you still think it was a mistake,' he commented as Zen studied the images of horror.

'No, I meant that Valesio may have accidentally caught sight of one of the gang,' Zen explained. 'These would have been the top men, don't forget. No one else would be entrusted with the negotiations.

They might well have been worried that he would be able to identify them.'

Bartocci seemed to be about to say something, but in the end he just turned away and looked out of the window, leaving Zen to wonder once again why he had been invited along on this routine errand.

The studio which Ubaldo Valesio had shared with two other lawyers was in the centre of the city, just behind the cathedral, in a street so narrow there was barely room for Palottino to park. It consisted of one wing of the first floor of the building, two huge rooms divided into separate work areas by antique screens and potted shrubs. Valesio's partners were both present. They were very correct, very polite, and very unhelpful. Yes, they had known that Ubaldo was acting for the Milettis. No, they had never discussed it. They watched discreetly but attentively as the two representatives of the State looked through diaries, memo books, files and folders. Then they drew up an inventory of what had been taken, obtained a receipt, said goodbye, and went back to work.

'When may I expect your report on this material?' Bartocci asked Zen when they got back to the law courts.

'Tomorrow, I hope. But if anything important comes up I'll phone you.'

He turned back and started to get into the car, but Bartocci called him back.

'Listen, there are a few things I'd like to discuss with you. Off the record, as it were.'

Zen gazed at him, his face perfectly expressionless.

'In fact I thought we might have lunch. That little restaurant down the street there is where I usually eat, the one with the neon sign and the awning.'

'Today?'

'If that's convenient.'

Bartocci's tone was polite, almost deferential. It scared Zen stiff.

'I'd be delighted,' he replied with a ghost of a smile.

As Palottino drove him back to the Questura he saw that the restaurant Bartocci had indicated was called the Griffin and displayed a sign with a beast similar to those he had seen at the law courts.

Back in his office, Zen thought about griffins and Luciano Bartocci and Ubaldo Valesio. Griffins, he discovered from the dictionary kept in the desk drawer to help the less literate officials write their reports, were mythical creatures having the head and wings of an eagle and the legs and tail of a lion. He was still not quite sure why they had been carved above the entrance to the law courts. Were they symbols of Justice? Certainly Luciano Bartocci seemed to be something of a hybrid. Zen had never been invited to lunch by a member of the judiciary before, and he found the prospect as unattractive as the invitation to Crepi's the previous evening. Once again he felt that he was being drawn into an area where the stakes were high and the rules not clearly defined. 'A few things I'd like to discuss with you, off the record.' What was Bartocci up to?

Almost with relief, his thoughts turned back to Ubaldo Valesio. Although they had never met, Zen felt he knew the dead man well: a successful and ambitious lawyer in a city which despite its recent growth was still a small town at heart, a place where rumours spread as silently and effectively as a virus. His partners had been telling the truth, Zen felt sure, and the two men next door were almost certainly wasting their time. People like Valesio, who knew everything about someone and something about everyone, not only stopped talking to others about their affairs, they very soon stopped talking even to themselves. Above all they would never commit anything to paper unless it was absolutely necessary. Ubaldo Valesio would have kept the details of his dealings with Ruggiero Miletti's kidnappers in the only place he considered safe, his own head. With a shiver, Zen remembered the photographs Bartocci had shown him.

A clangour of bells suddenly rang out from churches near and far, calling the faithful to Mass and reminding the rest that their lunch was just an hour away. Zen fetched his coat and hat and walked through to the next room. Geraci looked up at him with an expression of intense anxiety. His face was heavy and fleshy, and the two deep furrows running from the corners of the nose to the edge of the mouth gave him a hangdog look. His chin had a weak and skimpy look, as though the material had run out before the job was quite finished, while his eyebrows were absurdly thick and bushy, with a life of their own.

'Anything?' Zen enquired.

Geraci shrugged. Chiodini pretended to be so intent on his labours that he did not even notice Zen's presence.

Outside, the sun illuminated every surface with uncompromising clarity. The air seemed full of disquieting hints of summer, but the illusion lasted no longer than it took to turn the corner into a narrow alley sunk deep in shadow, where the wind whetted the cold edge of the air like a knife. Bare walls faced with crumbling plaster rose up on both sides, pierced by the high, inaccessible windows of the prison, covered with heavy steel mesh. After going about a hundred metres Zen was beginning to feel he had made a mistake in turning off the broad avenue that led directly up to the centre, but he persisted, and was rewarded when the street widened out into a little square where the wind disappeared and a cherry tree was in sumptuous blossom in a garden high above. But at the next corner the wind was back, keener than ever. He turned left down a long flight of steps to get away from it.

In the grocery at the corner a sad, pale pig of a girl, a greasy sliver of cooked ham dangling from her mouth, jerked her thumb at a set of steps opposite in response to his request for directions to the centre. It was a staircase for mountain climbers, the steps seeming to get progressively higher as he climbed. The wall it ran up looked like the face of history itself. It was founded on massive blocks of rock whose dimensions were those of ancient days, presumably Etruscan. Above this layer came another, Roman work, where the blocks, though still large, had lost the epic scale. Then came a long stretch of small cubes of pinkish stone forming the wall of a medieval house, and finally an upper storey tacked on in brick and concrete.

He stopped to catch his breath, leaning against one of the giant blocks which had weathered to form intricate niches and cavities. In several of them tiny plants had somehow contrived to put down roots in a trace of dust, in another someone had wedged an empty Diet Coke can. On the other side a breathtaking view stretched away, line after line of hills rippling off into the hazy distance. He stepped carefully over a dead pigeon on the next step and clambered grimly to the top. The street in which he came out continued upwards without respite through an ancient gateway, and still up, darkly resonant and clangorous, past basement workshops where carpenters and furniture repairers and picture framers were at work. The air, fresh and cold and delicately flavoured with wood smoke, was a luxury in itself, an air for angels to breathe.

On the wall of a nearby building was a hoarding displaying two posters. The one on the right featured a garish picture of a woman in a bathing costume being pursued by a number of eager fish with teeth like daggers. 'For the first time in Italy,' the caption exclaimed, 'women and sharks in the same pool!!!' The name of a circus appeared beneath, with the dates of its next visit to Perugia. The other poster showed a famous footballer leering suggestively at a glass of milk, but what attracted Zen's attention was the top left-hand corner, where the mass of posters accumulated over several months was starting to curl back under its own weight, revealing a section of older strata far beneath. In the corner, in large red letters, he read 'LETTI'. The protruding curl was almost a centimetre thick, layered like plywood, and when Zen tugged at it the whole block peeled off and fell to the ground at his feet. Now he could see almost all the earlier poster, which was headed 'SIMP AND THE MILETTI FAMILY.' There were five short paragraphs of closely set writing:

The arrogance and intransigence of the Miletti family, amply demonstrated on innumerable occasions in the past, are once again in evidence. Not content with shutting down the Ponte San Giovanni subsidiary, or laying off more than 800 workers in Perugia – to say nothing of their continuing exploitation of female piece-work labour and well-known anti-union policies – they are now reported to be planning to sell off a controlling interest in the Società Industriale Miletti di Perugia to a Japanese electronics conglomerate.

Having crippled a once-prosperous enterprise by a combination of managerial incompetence and ill-advised speculation in the activities of such gentlemen as Calvi, Sindona and their like, the Milettis now intend to recoup their losses by auctioning off SIMP to the highest bidder.

The company named in the take-over bid already owns factories which are running well below their maximum potential production level due to the world economic recession and consequent shortage of demand. Their intention is to use SIMP as a means of eluding the EEC quotas by importing Japanese-produced goods to which nothing will be added in Umbria but a grille bearing one of the brand-names which generations of local workers have helped to make famous.

The Umbrian Communists totally condemn this example of cynical stock-market manipulation. SIMP is not to be sold off like a set of saucepans. The future of our jobs and those of our children must be decided here in Perugia after a process of consultation between representatives of the workforce, the owners, and the provincial and regional authorities.

Italian Communist Party
Umbrian Section

Zen turned away from the billboard and started to climb the ancient street paved with flagstones as smooth as the bed of a stream. An old woman lurched towards him, a bulging plastic bag in each hand, bellowing something incomprehensible at a man who stood looking up at the scaffolding hung with sacking that covered a house being renovated. A gang of boys on scooters swooped down the street, slabs of pizza in one hand, klaxons groaning like angry frogs, yelling insults at each other. They missed the old woman by inches, and a load of rubble gushing down a plastic chute into a hopper made a noise that sounded like a round of applause for their skill or her nonchalance.

'Anything else?'

The waiter perched like a sparrow beside their table, looking distractedly about him. Bartocci shook his head and glanced at Zen.

'Shall we go?'

At the cash desk the manager greeted Bartocci warmly. No bill was presented. Like the rest of the almost exclusively male clientele of the noisy little restaurant, the magistrate was clearly a regular who paid by the week or month.

'How about a little stroll before having coffee?' Bartocci suggested once they were outside. 'I must warn you, though, that it's uphill, like everything in Perugia!'

It was a measure of Zen's state of mind that he found himself wondering whether the words had more than one meaning. Lunch with Bartocci had indeed proved very much like dinner with the Milettis, except that the food was even better: macaroni in a sauce made with cream and spicy sausage meat, chunks of liver wrapped in a delicate net of membrane and charred over embers, thin dark green stalks of wild asparagus, strawberries soaked in lemon juice. But just as at Crepi's the evening before, the conversation had been dominated by what was *not* discussed. Bartocci had shown himself to be particularly interested in Zen's career and his views on various items of news: a scandal about kickbacks for building permits involving members of a Socialist city council, reports that a Christian Democrat ex-mayor had been a leading member of the Palermo Mafia, allegations that the wife of a Liberal senator in Turin was involved in the illegal export of currency. Zen knew what was happening, of course, and Bartocci knew that he knew. It was all part of the process. How would this police official from Rome react to being sounded out 'off the record' by a Communist investigating magistrate?

Zen tried to steer a middle course, neither clamming up nor trumpeting opinions, biding his time and hoping that Bartocci would get to the point. But unless he did so soon Zen was going to get very nervous indeed. He had even tried to precipitate matters by asking Bartocci about the Deputy Public Prosecutor's criticisms of the police. But Bartocci's response had been offhand: 'Let's enjoy our lunch, we'll talk later.'

The magistrate led the way up a broad flight of steps which at first appeared to lead to someone's front door. At the last moment they swerved to the left and continued into a tunnel burrowing underneath a conglomerate of interlocking houses, walls, gardens and yards deposited there over the centuries by generations of people neither more nor less dead than Ubaldo Valesio. It was dark and the wind whined emptily past them. On the wall a soccer fan had spray-gunned 'Rome are magic', while a dustbin opposite was inscribed 'Juventus Headquarters'.

After about fifty metres the subterranean arcade widened out slightly into a concrete yard where six Fiat 500s were packed in, so tightly that there was barely room to pass on foot. Bartocci led him on without a word, turning left and right without hesitation, always climbing, until they reached a small piazza in front of a church where the walls fell back to reveal a view similar to the one Zen had seen that morning from his bedroom window, centred by that strange mountain, full and rounded as a mound of risen dough.

Bartocci glanced around the square, which was empty except for a few parked cars.

'What were you saying about Di Leonardo?' he asked suddenly.

'Well, he implied last night that the police were at fault for not having exploited Valesio's contacts with the kidnappers. I wondered if you agreed.'

'No, I don't see things in quite the same way. In fact I should have preferred to pursue a much more active line in this case from the very start. I tried to have the family's assets frozen, to prevent any possibility of a ransom payment. I also sought to have Ubaldo's phone monitored. But there was considerable opposition to these initiatives, notably from Di Leonardo himself.'

'But you don't need higher authority to authorize those things,' Zen pointed out.

'I don't need higher authority to sign a warrant for the arrest of President Pertini, either. But it would be the last I ever signed. If I'd frozen the Miletti account and had the phone-tap put on, the net result would have been to destroy any chances I have of influencing the outcome of this case. Besides, people like the Milettis can always raise cash somewhere, and as for the phones, the gang must assume that they're all tapped anyway. We wouldn't have learned anything much without trying to follow Valesio, which would have been a very risky venture indeed. Di Leonardo tried to suggest that Ubaldo had been killed because of my negligence. I was his real target, not you. But just imagine how he would have responded had there been the slightest evidence that Valesio's death was the result of my interference! No, that's not the way to handle these things.'

Zen moved over to the parapet at the edge of the piazza, where stone benches were placed at intervals between trees giving shade on hot summer days. The wall dropped vertically away to the gardens of the houses far below. Beyond them rose a lengthy strip of high medieval city wall, then a valley cut steeply into hills dotted with modern villas, leading the eye away to the still more distant hills and the valley beyond, green and grey and brown beneath the azure sky, where the strange mountain rose. In the far distance, at the limit of vision, shimmered the snow-covered peaks of the Apennines.

Zen got out his packet of Nazionali. It contained only one cigarette, the last of the supply he had brought with him. As he lit up a flicker of movement down below caught his eye. A girl in jeans and a red sweater was standing at an open window in one of the houses, looking out at the garden with its rows of vegetables running up to a chicken coop at the foot of the high retaining wall. She was clearly unaware of being observed herself.

'Valesio's death has changed everything, of course,' Bartocci continued. 'Your arrival at the same moment is extremely convenient. The whole investigation will have to begin again from scratch. We must be prepared to re-examine all our assumptions, even the most fundamental, without allowing ourselves to be influenced by the thought that some people might find our conclusions difficult to swallow.'

Zen exhaled a long breath of the fragrant, earthy tobacco. The girl moved and the window was empty again.

'That's why I asked to speak to you today,' the magistrate went on in the same confidential tone. 'It's very refreshing for me to deal with an outsider, someone free of any preconceptions. You have no axe to grind here, no interests to protect. One can consider every possibility.'

The girl reappeared at the window. Her legs were now bare.

'About a month ago I received this,' Bartocci said, handing Zen a sheet of paper.

AREN'T THE MILETTIS CLEVER? THEY CAN TURN THEIR HAND TO ANYTHING – EVEN KIDNAPPING!!?? THEY'VE HAD PLENTY OF PRACTICE IN EXTORTION, ASK THEIR WORKERS! BUT IF YOU ARE NOT IN THEIR PAY TOO THEN KNOW THIS. OLD MILETTI GOT HIMSELF KIDNAPPED AT JUST THE RIGHT MOMENT. WITH HIM OUT OF THE WAY THE FAMILY CAN'T SIGN ANY TAKEOVER PAPERS WHICH MIGHT LET THE JAPS INTO THE GAME. AND WHAT IF THE RANSOM ENDED UP IN THE FAMILY'S POCKETS INTO THE BARGAIN? MAYBE THEN THEY COULD KEEP SCREWING US FOR ANOTHER FEW YEARS!

THINK ABOUT IT.

ONE WHO KNOWS

Zen gave the letter back to Bartocci, who replaced it carefully in his pocket.

'Of course, I get a lot of this sort of thing, and normally I would simply discount it as a hoax from someone with a grudge against the family. But in this case it seems to me that the writer knows what he's talking about.'

The girl had moved again, so that only her bare legs and feet were visible. Then she disappeared completely.

'What's this about a takeover?' Zen asked. 'I saw something about it on an old poster today, too.'

'SIMP has been in financial difficulties for some time now. The root cause is that Ruggiero has insisted all along on maintaining total personal control of every aspect of the business. But the company has diversified into areas he knows nothing about, the market has changed out of all recognition in the last ten or fifteen years, above all he is no longer the man he was. The result has been a gradual running-down of the whole operation. They've been forced to shut one of their factories and lay off about a quarter of the workforce at the other. But the real crunch came with the collapse of Calvi's financial empire. It seems that the Milettis had sunk quite a lot of money in it. Since then the company has been living from one loan to another, under increasing pressure to improve their performance and efficiency. Finally, just before Ruggiero was kidnapped, a Japanese company made an offer to put up the money SIMP needs in return for a licence to sell its products under the Miletti name. The old man wouldn't hear of it, of course.'

'That's not what the PCI poster suggested.'

'No, the Party quite correctly takes the line that unless prevented the family will do whatever makes sense from a financial point of view. Ruggiero's opposition is merely the sentimental stubbornness of an old man, and as such cannot be depended on to protect the interests of the workers.'

Again a flicker of movement below caught Zen's eye. The girl passed by the window, naked except for a yellow towel wrapped round her hair.

'I know this theory sounds fantastic,' Bartocci continued. 'But look at what else happens in this country. Look at Gelli, look at Calvi. Was that any more fantastic? When Michele Sindona got into difficulties with the law in New York he staged a fake kidnapping for himself so that he could go to Palermo and pressure people he thought might be helpful. What's to stop the Milettis doing the same thing? It's a scheme worthy of Calvi himself. Take Ruggiero out of circulation to prevent any takeover deals going through, and then use their own money, recycled through a faked payoff, to prop up the company's finances.'

Zen tried to keep his eye off the window below and his mind on what Bartocci was saying.

'But that would mean that they also murdered Valesio.'

Bartocci nodded.

'It's precisely Valesio's death which has made me take the theory seriously. You said that he may accidentally have caught sight of one of the members of the gang. But why should the kidnappers care if Valesio caught a glimpse of some Calabrian he'd never seen before and would never recognize again? But suppose that the person Valesio saw was *not* a stranger. Suppose it was someone he knew very well, someone anybody in Perugia would know well. Imagine his rage as he realizes the shameful game they have been playing on him and on everyone! And imagine the Milettis' horror as they face the certainty of a revelation which would smash the family's power for ever and send many of them to prison for years to come. What are they to do? Either kill Valesio or admit that all these months while we've been working tirelessly for Ruggiero Miletti's release he has in fact been comfortably holed up in some property of the family a few miles from here, perhaps even in his own house. Do you remember how long it took the family to get around to informing the police of his disappearance? They claimed it was because the idea of kidnapping never occurred to them, but it might equally be because they needed time to fake the accident and the evidence of the struggle, time to burn the car.'

Again a movement at the window below caught Zen's eye. But this time the figure was that of a man, who reached for the shutters and banged them shut.

'So you really believe that there's a conspiracy?' Zen asked Bartocci. He still wasn't sure whether the magistrate was completely serious.

'There's always a conspiracy. Everything that happens in society at a certain level is part of a conspiracy.'

Zen noted the evasive reply.

'If everything is, nothing is. If we're all conspirators then there's no conspiracy.'

'On the contrary, the condition of this conspiracy is that we're all part of it,' Bartocci retorted. 'It's a ratking.'

'A what?'

'A ratking. Do you know what that is?'

Zen shrugged.

'The king rat, I suppose. The dominant animal in the pack.'

'That's what everyone thinks. But it's not. A ratking is something that happens when too many rats live in too small a space under too much pressure. Their tails become entwined and the more they strain and stretch to free themselves the tighter grows the knot binding them, until at last it becomes a solid mass of embedded tissue. And the creature thus formed, as many as thirty rats tied together by the tail, is called a ratking. You wouldn't expect such a living contradiction to survive, would you? That's the most amazing thing of all. Most of the ratkings they find, in the plaster of old houses or beneath the floorboards of a barn, are healthy and flourishing. Evidently the creatures have evolved some way of coming to terms with their situation. That's not to say they like it, of course! In fact the reason they're discovered is because of their diabolical squealing. Not much fun, being chained to each other for life. How much sweeter it would be to run free! Nevertheless, they *do* survive, somehow. The wonders of nature, eh?'

He paused for a moment, to let Zen's exasperation mature.

'Now a lot of people believe that somewhere in the wainscotting of this country the king of all the rats is hiding,' he finally went on. 'The toughest brute of all, the most vicious and ruthless, the dominant animal in the pack, as you put it. Some thought it was Calvi, some thought it was Gelli. Others believe that it is someone else again, someone above and beyond either of them, a big name in the government perhaps, or on the contrary someone you've never even heard of. But the one thing they all agree is that he exists, this super-rat. It's a message of hope and of despair. Hope, because perhaps one fine day we'll finally trap him, run him down, finish him off and rid the house of rats for ever. Despair, because we know he's too shrewd and powerful and cunning ever to be trapped. But in fact that's all just a fairy story! What we're dealing with is not a creature but a condition, the condition of being crucified to your fellows, squealing madly, biting, spitting, lashing out, yet somehow surviving, somehow even vilely flourishing! That's what makes the conspiracy so formidable. There's no need for agendas or strategies, for lists of members or passwords or secret codes. The ratking is self-regulating. It responds automatically and effectively to any threat. Each rat defends the interests of the others. The strength of each is the strength of all.'

'I don't quite see what all this has to do with the present case,' Zen said.

Bartocci glanced at his watch.

'I'm sorry, I got rather carried away. But the fact remains that whether or not there is a conspiracy in progress in the Miletti case, I believe that the investigation has reached a point where I can no longer continue to ignore such a theory. However, it would be fatal for me to announce my intentions. If I were to conduct this investigation like any other the political repercussions would ensure that the truth never came to light.'

'Which is where I come in.'

The magistrate looked at him, the strange stalled smile straining away at the corner of his mouth.

'If you are prepared to help.'

Zen turned round, taking a deep breath. One of the first-floor windows of the houses giving on to the piazza was a painted dummy, but at the one next to it a portly, silver-haired man in a red dressing-gown stood staring down at them with undisguised curiosity.

'What do you want me to do?' Zen asked tonelessly.

'Just a few things that would be difficult for me to do without causing comment. First of all I'd like you to check what firearms are registered to members of the Miletti family. Don't forget to include the Santuccis. I also want you to make discreet inquiries as to the whereabouts of members of the family yesterday.'

'I can tell you where they were yesterday evening. They were having dinner with me at Antonio Crepi's.'

Bartocci gave him a look that modulated rapidly from astonishment through alarm and respect to suspicion. Then he laughed rather aggressively.

'Well, well! You do get around, don't you?'

'Apparently Crepi wanted me to meet the Milettis. To "see what we're up against" as he put it.'

At the other end of the piazza a young couple were hungrily necking, bent over a parked car. The fat man at the window was still looking on, his thumbs tucked under the belt of his dressing-gown.

'Did he say anything else?'

'Yes, quite a lot. In fact to some extent it seemed to tally with what you've been saying. Not that he suggested that the family had any complicity in the kidnapping . . .'

'Of course not! Anyway, he wouldn't know.'

'But he feels they're not doing enough to bring Ruggiero home. He asked me to make that plain to the press in an attempt to pressure the Milettis to pay up.'

The young magistrate smiled sourly.

'Typical. Anyway, one thing is certain. No additional pressure will be necessary now. Valesio's death will do more than any press conference to resolve this issue one way or the other. Within the next few days I expect the family to say that they've received a demand for the full amount of the ransom to be paid at once and that they are going to comply. That's why we need to move fast. Once that money is handed over and Ruggiero is back we'll never be able to prove anything. But we must be discreet, above all! This entire matter is politically sensitive in the very highest degree, and if any word of it leaks out I shall be forced to . . .'

He broke off suddenly, looking past Zen. The young man had produced a camera and was taking photographs of his girlfriend posed in various positions against the landscape.

'Anyway, I must go. No time for coffee, I'm afraid.'

As Bartocci hurried away the man with the camera came striding purposefully towards Zen, his girlfriend following more slowly behind.

'Pardon me! Would you be as good enough to mind making of us two both a photograph?'

Foreign, thought Zen with relief. The young magistrate's sudden haste had been unnecessary. One thing at least was certain: the bastards would never employ foreigners.

FOUR

That afternoon Aurelio Zen went boating.

After the shock of Valesio's murder and his almost sleepless night, lunch with Luciano Bartocci had really been the last straw. One thing he could have done without was an ambitious young investigating magistrate with a strong political bias, a prefabricated conspiracy theory and an itch to get his name in the news. At Zen's expense, needless to say, should anything go wrong.

Once upon a time magistrates had been dull, stolid figures, worthy but uninspiring, above all remote and anonymous. But the combination of television and terrorism had changed all that. A new breed of men had emerged from the vague grey ranks of the judiciary to stamp themselves on the nation's consciousness: the glamorous investigating magistrates and Public Prosecutors who were to be seen on the news every evening leading the fight against political violence and organized crime. Now all their colleagues craved stardom too, and almost overnight the once faceless bureaucrats had blossomed out in trendy clothes and bushy beards, and an anonymous letter was enough to get them as excited as any schoolboy.

Since Bartocci had been at pains to emphasize that his comments were 'off the record', Zen could of course simply ignore them. But that would be rash. There were an infinite number of ways in which the investigating magistrate could compromise or embarrass a police officer, whereas having the judiciary on your side was an invaluable asset. No, he had to try and keep Bartocci happy. On the other hand, the inquiries he had been asked to make, although apparently innocuous, were also fraught with risk. A great family such as the Milettis is like a sleeping bear: it may look massively apathetic and unimpressionable but each hair of its pelt is wired straight into the creature's brain, and if you twitch it the wrong way the thing will flex its tendons and turn on you, unzipping its claws. What was he to do? How was he to react? What was a safe course to take?

His immediate solution was to go boating. Not for long, of course.

With all these new developments pressing in on him the last thing he could afford was an afternoon off work. But neither was there any point in trying to take action with his head in this condition. So having made his way back to the hotel he closed the shutters, took off his shoes, jacket and tie, lay down on the bed and cast off. The image of the long shallow craft gliding forward through the reeds in regular surges, propelled by the oarsman's graceful double-handed sweeps, was a powerful agent of calm. Just ten or fifteen minutes of it now would see him right, a short trip out through the islets and mud-banks where you could let the boat drift, lean over the stern and watch the inner life of the dirty green water, the shreds of seaweed and small branches and other shapes that sometimes proved to be alive, or focus on the surface, a depthless sheet of scum on which the pearly light shimmered in continual shifting patterns, or even look up to see a huge modern building, several storeys high, going for a stroll along a neighbouring island, the superstructure of a freighter putting out to sea along the deep-water channel . . .

He got up and put the light on, shivering. Something was wrong. How could the room feel stuffy and cold at the same time? And it was totally silent, no distant murmur of traffic, no footsteps, no voices. Catching sight of the transistor radio, he clicked it on and fiddled with the tuning, encountering only heavy bands of static interspersed with the twittering gibberish of machines. He felt like the last person left alive.

'. . . very much and you get a fabulous Radio Subasio T-shirt so keep those calls coming out there this one is for Adriana in Gubbio it's Celentano's latest coming to you at fifteen before four this Thursday morning courtesy of your friend Tullio who says . . .'

Zen silenced the radio, walked to the window and opened the shutters. The deserted piazza glistened under the streetlights. He had slept right through the night.

Catching sight of his reflection in the window he felt a surge of self-pity and suddenly realized that he missed Ellen very badly, and that it was only at moments like this, when he surprised himself, that he could admit how much he needed her. Why couldn't he tell *her*? That was what she wanted, after all, and he knew that she was right to want it. For a moment he thought of phoning her, then and there, and telling her how he felt. But it would be ridiculous, of course. He imagined the phone ringing and ringing until it prodded her unwillingly out of sleep, and her uncomprehending response. 'For Christ's sake, Aurelio, couldn't this have waited? Do you know what time it is? I've got a sale to go to at nine, and you know how difficult it is for me to get back to sleep once I've been woken.' Instead he read a paper he'd bought in Trieste and forgotten to throw away, immersing himself in a debate over the council's delay in resurfacing the streets in an outlying zone of the city until it was time to go to work.

A crowd of people of various races, clutching passports and sheaves of official documents, were clustered around an office in the foyer of the Questura. A sheet of paper attached to the glass partition with sticky tape read 'Foreigners' in crude lettering. Behind the glass an official from the Political Branch scowled at a worried-looking black.

'And I suppose it's my fault you haven't got it?' he demanded.

As Zen approached his office, the inspector who had been trying to trace Ubaldo Valesio's movements poked his head around the door of the next room.

'Just a moment, chief!'

Lucaroni was short and rather sleazy-looking, with narrow-set eyes and a broad jaw blue with stubble. His movements were quick and furtive and he spoke in a speedy whisper, as though every word were classified information.

'You've got a visitor,' he muttered. 'The widow. Rolled in about five minutes ago demanding to see you. We weren't sure what to do with her.'

He looked doubtfully at Zen, who nodded.

'Turn up anything yesterday?'

Lucaroni shook his head.

'He phoned his office at nine to cancel all appointments. It was obviously unexpected. There were two clients waiting who had to be sent away.'

Zen looked into the inspectors' room. Chiodini was poring over a sports paper. Geraci was staring fixedly back at Zen, as though he was trying to remember whether he'd turned the gas off before leaving home.

'How about you two?' Zen asked.

Geraci's eyebrows wiggled briefly.

'Just a lot of stuff about his house and taxes and kids.'

'And those marks in the diary,' Chiodini put in without looking up from his paper.

'They're nothing,' Geraci commented dismissively.

'What marks?' asked Zen.

He was really just buying time before having to deal with Patrizia Valesio.

Chiodini took the diary from the pile of documents on his desk and showed him that the lawyer had marked several pages during the previous three months with a red asterisk, the last being two days earlier. Zen walked over to the door opening directly into his office, taking the diary with him.

'What do you want us to do now, chief?' Geraci asked. He sounded slightly panicky.

'Nothing, for now.'

He should never have asked for three assistants, he realized. Now he would always have them hanging about, making him feel guilty, getting in his way. Moreover one of them was bound to be reporting back to the Questore, and since there was no way of finding out which he would have to keep them all busy if he was to do what Bartocci had asked.

The spare chair in his office was occupied by a woman of about thirty dressed in an elegant black outfit. Her face was large and round and slightly concave, with a long sharp nose.

'You're the man they sent up from Rome?' she asked. 'I am Patrizia Valesio.'

'I'm very sorry . . .'

She waved dismissively.

'Please, don't let's waste time.'

Zen took out a notepad and pencil and laid them on the desk.

'Very well. What can I do for you?'

'I've come to make an accusation. You may find it bizarre, even unbelievable. I simply ask you to listen, and not to judge what I say until I have finished.'

She took a deep breath.

'My husband did not usually discuss the negotiations for Ruggiero Miletti's release with me, but on one occasion about a month ago, while we were having dinner . . .'

She paused. The strain of what she was saying showed on her face. Then she finished quickly.

'He suddenly blurted out, "Someone is going behind my back".'

The phone started to ring.

'Excuse me,' Zen said, and lifted the receiver.

'Good morning, Commissioner. This is Antonio Crepi. I'm just phoning to make it quite clear that our discussion the other night is no longer relevant. Pietro has flown in from London and he's assured me that as soon as the gang make contact the matter will be resolved without further delay. I don't need to tell you to keep what I said to yourself, of course.'

'Of course.'

'Incidentally, I hear you had lunch with young Bartocci yesterday.'

Zen watched Patrizia Valesio removing an invisible hair from her coat.

'I don't want to interfere, dottore, but remember what I told you about him. Luciano's a good lad at heart, but he's got a bee in his bonnet when it comes to the Milettis. You know how these lefties are, they read Marx and stop seeing reality. Now that's a dangerous attitude for an investigating magistrate, in my opinion. Still more so for a policeman. See what I mean? Just a friendly word of advice, from one who knows.'

Zen put the phone down. '. . . from one who knows.' Where had he heard that phrase before?

Patrizia Valesio was staring at him with the expression of one who is not to be put off by interruptions. Her face reminded Zen of an old-fashioned candlestick: a shallow dish with a spike in the middle.

'I'm sorry,' he murmured. 'You were saying that . . .'

'Ubaldo told me that someone was going behind his back,' she repeated. 'He said that every time he returned to the kidnappers to present an offer worked out after lengthy discussions with the family, claiming that this was the absolute maximum the Milettis could afford to pay, the gang accused him of lying. "Have you forgotten the villa at Punta Ala? And what about the olive grove at Spello? Why haven't you sold the shares in such and such a company?" And when Ubaldo asked the Milettis, lo and behold there *was* such a villa, such an olive grove, such shares! It was a negotiator's nightmare!'

Zen stared hard at the pad. He had been doodling obsessive box-like designs, a nest of interlocking right-angled lines locking out all possibility of error or surprise.

'What about Ruggiero himself?' he suggested. 'He knows more than anyone about the family assets, and he's totally in the gang's power. It wouldn't be difficult for them to make him talk.'

'That's what Ubaldo thought at first. But the gang knew about financial developments which had taken place *since* the kidnapping, things Ruggiero couldn't have known about. Eventually Ubaldo became convinced that someone in the family circle was supplying the gang with information on a day-to-day basis. Which means that my husband was the innocent victim of some hideous double-dealing within the Miletti family! That's why I have come. I want his murderers punished. Not just the ones who pulled the trigger but also the ones who stood behind them, in the shadows!'

She broke off, taking quick shallow breaths.

'This is all very interesting, signora . . .'

'I haven't finished!' she snapped. 'There's something else, a vital clue. The gang always used the same procedure when they wanted to make contact. The telephone would ring at one o'clock, just as we were sitting down to lunch. Only two words were spoken. The caller gave the name of a football team and Ubaldo had to reply with the name of the team they were playing the following Sunday. He kept the fixtures list by the phone. Then he hung up immediately, phoned his office and cancelled his afternoon appointments. That was the procedure, and it never varied. But on Tuesday . . .'

She broke off again, fighting for control.

'On Tuesday the call came not at lunchtime but early in the morning, about seven forty-five. I heard Ubaldo give the password and then say "Now?" in great surprise.'

She held Zen's eyes with hers.

'When did you arrive here in Perugia, Commissioner?'

'On Tuesday.'

'At what time?'

'About half past one.'

'And who knew you were coming?'

He frowned slightly.

'Various people in the Ministry and here at the Questura.'

'No one else?'

'Not as far as I know. Why?'

Was that a sound from the next room, from behind the closed door?

'Then how do you explain the fact that the kidnappers phoned urgently, demanding to see Ubaldo in person, at a time when you were still in Rome and no one supposedly knew you were coming except the authorities?'

Her voice was triumphant, as though this clinched the matter. Zen deliberately allowed his frown to deepen.

'I don't see there's anything to explain. What connection is there between the two events?'

She snorted indignantly.

'The connection? The connection is obvious to anyone who can put two and two together. Do you really believe that the first contact after weeks of silence just happened by sheer coincidence to fall on the same day as your arrival here? I'm sorry, but that would be just a little too convenient. But how could the kidnappers have known about your arrival in Perugia five hours before it happened? Obviously their contact in the family tipped them off!'

'But how did the Milettis know, for that matter?'

'Because it was they who had you sent here, of course! You don't, for heaven's sake, think that things like that happen without someone pulling strings, do you?'

Zen looked away. He had just remembered where he'd heard the phrase with which Crepi had rung off. It had been the signature of the anonymous letter Bartocci had received suggesting that the kidnapping of Ruggiero Miletti was a put-up job. He found himself writing CREPI??? in block capitals on the pad in front of him. He hastily crossed it out, then covered the whole area with tight scribbles until all trace of the name had been obliterated.

'I don't quite understand, signora,' he said. 'First you claim that the family is collaborating with the kidnappers, then you say they must have used their influence to have me sent here. Isn't there some contradiction in your ideas?'

With a convulsive movement Patrizia Valesio got to her feet.

'Don't you speak to me of contradictions! That whole family is a living contradiction, consuming anything and anyone that comes within its reach, one of them smiling in your face while another stabs you in the back. My poor husband, who wanted only to help, ended up as their victim. Be careful you don't share his fate!'

Zen also rose.

'Anyway, since this case is under investigation by the judiciary, the proper person to inform is the magistrate in charge, Luciano Bartocci.'

His visitor picked up her gloves and handbag.

'Oh, I *shall* inform him, don't worry! And I shall inform him that

I've informed you. And then I shall inform the Public Prosecutor's department that I've informed both of you. Do you know why I'm going to inform so many people, Commissioner? Because I am expecting there to be a conspiracy of silence on this matter and I intend to make it as difficult as possible for the Milettis and their friends. If there is to be a conspiracy, at least everyone will see that it exists and will know who is involved. That will be some poor consolation, at least.'

At the last moment Zen remembered the diary. He showed it to Patrizia Valesio and asked if she knew anything about the asterisks which Chiodini had pointed out. The sight of her husband's writing was clearly a great shock, but she held herself together.

'Those are the days on which Ubaldo had a meeting with the kidnappers,' she replied in a dull voice. 'He marked the diary as soon as they phoned. He thought it might be useful later.'

Well, perhaps it might, Zen thought when she had gone. But he couldn't see how.

He opened the door to the other room. Lucaroni was standing almost immediately inside, studying a notice concerning action to be taken in the event of fire breaking out in the building. Geraci was sitting at his desk, a paperback edition of the Penal Code open in front of him. Chiodini had slumped forward on his newspaper and seemed to be asleep.

'Well, I've got some work for you, lads,' Zen exclaimed breezily. 'From what Valesio's widow has told me, it's clear that her husband's contacts with the gang began with a telephone call that was simply a signal for him to go to some prearranged meeting-place. The chances are that it was a bar, somewhere not too far away. I want you to find it. Draw up a list and visit each in turn. Take a photograph of Valesio along. It shouldn't be too difficult. A smart young lawyer driving a BMW will have been noticed.'

When they had gone Zen went back to his office and dialled an internal number.

'Records.'

'I want a check run on any firearms licences issued to the following persons. Family name Miletti, first names Ruggiero, Pietro, Silvio and . . .'

Again that sound next door. Zen put the phone down, got up quietly and went over to the door into the corridor. He looked out.

The corridor was empty, but the door to the inspector's room was slightly ajar. Zen walked along the corridor and pushed it wide open. Geraci was standing by his desk. He whirled round as the door hit the rubbish bin with a loud clang.

'Forgot my notebook,' he explained.

Zen nodded.

'Listen, Geraci, I want you to keep an eye on the other two for me.'

The inspector stared uncertainly at Zen.

'Keep an eye on them?'

'That's it. Just in case.'

He winked and tapped the side of his nose.

'Better safe than sorry. Know what I mean?'

Geraci clearly didn't have the slightest idea what Zen was talking about.

'I should get going,' he muttered nervously.

'Good thinking. Don't want to make them suspicious.'

He watched Geraci walk all the way down the corridor before going back to his office, leaving the connecting door open so that if anyone came in he could see them reflected on Pertini's portrait. Then he picked up the receiver again.

'Hello?'

'*So far I've got Miletti Ruggiero, Pietro and Silvio.*'

'Right. Also Miletti Daniele, Santucci Gianluigi and Cinzia née Miletti.'

'*Who's speaking?*'

Zen seemed to see again that glare of hostility and hear the Questore murmur, 'Until today he was handling the Miletti case for us.'

'Fabrizio Priorelli.'

'*I'll call you straight back, dottore.*'

'Eh, no, my friend! Sorry, but you'll do it now, if you please. I'll hold.'

'*Of course, dottore! Right away.*'

There was a clunk as the receiver went down, followed by receding footsteps. While he waited Zen looked round his office. Something about it was slightly different today, but he couldn't decide what it was.

The footsteps returned.

'*There are three cards, dottore. A Luger 9mm pistol in the name of Miletti*'

Ruggiero, issued 27 04 53. Then Santucci Gianluigi registered a rifle on 19 10 75. Finally Miletti Cinzia, a Beretta pistol, 4.5mm, dated 11 01 81.'

Zen noted these details in the margin of his earlier doodles.

'Shall I send a written copy up to your office, dottore?'

'No! Definitely not. I've got what I wanted. Much obliged.' He hung up, studying the information. Ruggiero's Luger would be war loot, belatedly registered once the menace of an armed Communist insurrection had faded. That might possibly have done the damage to Valesio's head, at close range. So might Gianluigi's hunting rifle, for that matter. But he didn't really believe any of it, not for a moment.

He got an outside line, dialled the law courts and asked to speak to Luciano Bartocci. While he waited he looked round his office with a deepening frown, trying to track down the detail which had been altered. What *was* it? The filing cabinet, the coat-stand, the rubbish bin, that big ugly crucifix, the photograph of Pertini, the calendar. Of course, the calendar! Someone had thoughtfully turned the page to March and now the glossy colour photograph showed the Riot Squad drawn up in full battle gear in front of their armoured personnel carriers.

'Yes?'

'Dottor Bartocci? It's Zen, at the Questura.'

'Finally! I've been trying to get hold of you since yesterday afternoon! Where have you been?'

'Well, I was . . .'

'Listen, there've been developments. Come and see me at once.'

'Patrizia Valesio has been here. She claims that . . .'

'I've already seen her. This is something else. Be here in twenty minutes.'

Outside the weather was hazy and dull. In the car park between the Questura and the prison Palottino had taken a break from polishing the Alfetta to chat to a pair of patrolmen. He looked hopefully at Zen, who waggled his finger and walked off up the street.

It was market day, and the wide curving flight of steps leading up to the centre was lined with flimsy tables covered in kitchenware and watches and clothing and tools and toys. Music blared out from a stall selling bootleg cassette tapes. The traders called like barnyard cocks to the women moving from one pitch to the next, uncertain which to mate with.

'. . . at prices you simply won't believe . . .'

'. . . never before in Perugia . . .'
'. . . thanks to the miracle of American technology . . .'
'. . . ever wears out I will pay you twice the . . .'
'SOCKS!!! SOCKS!!! SOCKS!!!'
'. . . one for thirty thousand, two for fifty . . .'

A man sitting on a three-legged stool emptied a dustpan full of rubbish over his suit and then removed it with a battery-powered mini-vacuum cleaner. On the wall behind him the name UBALDO VALESIO appeared over and over again in large black capitals. It was a notice board devoted exclusively to funeral announcements, and the lawyer's death was well represented. There were posters signed by his partners, by the local lawyers' association, the Miletti family, various relatives, and of course his wife and children. The wording changed slightly, depending on the degree of intimacy involved, but certain formulas recurred like the tolling of a bell.

'. . . an innocent victim of barbarous cruelty . . .'
'. . . tragically plucked from the bosom of his loved ones by a callous hand . . .'
'. . . a virtuous and well-respected life extinguished by the criminal violence of evil men . . .'

The morning session at the law courts was in full swing, and the halls and corridors were crowded. Luciano Bartocci's office was tall and narrow, with shelves of books that seemed to lean inwards like the sides of a chimney as they rose towards the distant ceiling. Two lawyers were facing the magistrate across a desk that occupied most of the floor space. One was clearly asking some favour on behalf of a client: bail or a visitor's pass or access to official files. Meanwhile the other lawyer was growing impatient with Bartocci for allowing himself to be imposed upon in this way by his pushy and unscrupulous colleague instead of attending to *his* utterly reasonable request for bail or a visitor's pass or access to official files. In the end Bartocci solved the problem by shooing both of them out of the office and leading Zen downstairs.

'There's something I want you to hear.'

He took him to a long narrow room in the cellars of the law courts, where phone-taps were carried out. A bank of reel-to-reel tape recorders lined the wall. A man was monitoring one of them over a pair of headphones. He jumped slightly as Bartocci touched his shoulder.

'Morning, Aldo. Can you play us that recording I was listening to earlier?'

'Right away.'

He selected a tape from the rack and threaded it on to a spare machine.

'This was intercepted late yesterday afternoon on the Milettis' home phone,' the magistrate explained to Zen. 'That's why I've been trying to get hold of you.'

The technician handed Zen a pair of headphones and started the tape. There was a fragment of ringing tone and then a voice.

'Yes?'

'Signor Miletti?'

'Who is this?'

'*Go to the rubbish skip at the bottom of the hill, on the corner of the main road. Taped to the inside there is a letter for you. Get down there quickly, before the cops beat you to it.*'

The caller had a thick, raw Calabrian accent.

'*The time for games is over. You have three days to do what we say, otherwise we'll do to your father what we did to Valesio. Only more slowly.*'

Zen removed the headphones, looking for clues to Bartocci's reaction. The message had sounded genuine enough to him.

'What was in the letter?'

'That's what we're about to find out. Thank you, Aldo!'

As they walked back upstairs Bartocci went on, 'Pietro Miletti has agreed to see me. I'm expecting him shortly and I'd like you to be present. We've just time for a coffee.'

They went to a tiny bar in Piazza Matteotti. The only other person there was a woman eating a large cream-filled pastry as though her life depended on it.

'I had a phone call from Antonio Crepi,' Zen remarked casually.

'Really?'

Bartocci's voice, too, was carefully expressionless.

'He knows we had lunch.'

'I'm sure he does. In fifteen minutes he'll know we've had coffee, too.'

'What did you make of Patrizia Valesio's story?' Zen asked.

The magistrate shrugged.

'It doesn't get us anywhere. A hostile Public Prosecutor would make mincemeat of her. The distraught widow trying to assuage her grief for her husband's death by carrying out a vendetta against the Miletti family, that kind of thing. But this letter is another matter.'

It took Zen a moment to see what Bartocci was getting at.

'If they try and fake a letter from the kidnappers, you mean?' Bartocci nodded between sips of coffee.

'They can't fake it well enough to fool a forensic laboratory. I'm surprised they haven't realized that. So this meeting with Pietro Miletti may well prove to be decisive. That's why I want you to be there.'

The eldest of the Miletti children seemed about as unlike the others as was possible. Short and plump, with receding hair and a peeved expression, Pietro looked at first sight like an English tourist who had come to complain about his belongings being stolen from his hotel room, full of righteous indignation about Italy being a den of thieves and demanding to know when the authorities proposed to do something about it. From his tweed jacket to his patterned brogues he looked the part perfectly: not the usual designer mix from expensive shops in Milan or Rome, but the real thing, as plain and heavy as Zen imagined the English climate, character and cuisine to be.

Bartocci introduced Zen as 'one of the country's top experts on kidnapping, sent here specially by the Ministry to oversee the case'.

Pietro Miletti was politely dismayed.

'I understood this was to be a private meeting.'

'Nothing which is said in this room will go any further,' Bartocci assured him. 'We are simply here to discuss what measures to take in the light of recent developments. Please be seated.'

After a moment's hesitation Pietro leaned his rolled umbrella and leather briefcase against the desk and sat down. Bartocci took his place on the other side of the desk. There was no other chair, so Zen remained standing.

'Now then,' the magistrate continued smoothly, 'I understand that in the course of a telephone call yesterday afternoon the kidnappers informed you of the whereabouts of a letter from them, and that this letter was subsequently recovered. You've brought it with you, I take it.'

'Not the original, no.'

Pietro Miletti spoke as though the matter was of no consequence, but Bartocci glanced at Zen before replying.

'A copy of the letter is of very little use to our scientific experts.'

'I haven't brought a copy.'

Bartocci gestured impatiently.

'Excuse me, dottore. You haven't brought the original letter, you haven't brought a copy. Would you mind very much telling me what you *have* brought?'

Pietro Miletti opened his briefcase and took out a sheet of paper which he offered to the magistrate.

'I've brought a memorandum prepared from the original letter, itemizing every relevant piece of information it contained.'

Bartocci made no attempt to take the paper.

'Dottore, I strongly resent the assumption that anybody is in a position to dictate to me what is or is not relevant to a case I am investigating. If you are not prepared to let me see the original letter then this pretence of cooperation becomes a farce and I see no point in continuing it.'

Pietro Miletti gave a short laugh that sounded unpleasantly arrogant and mocking, although it might equally well have been nervous in origin.

'I'm afraid that's impossible.'

'Impossible? Allow me to remind you that you are head of the family in your father's absence. Nothing is impossible if you want it.'

'No, no, I mean it's literally impossible. The letter no longer exists.'

Bartocci shot Zen a triumphant glance. So the Milettis *had* realized the threat to their schemes which the fake letter would pose and had no intention of letting them see it!

Pietro balanced the sheet of paper on his knees.

'I should explain that although part of the letter was dictated by the kidnappers, most of it was written by my father. It was a personal letter addressed to his family, and like any personal letter it was not intended to be read by outsiders. It was, besides, a very long, rambling and really rather distressing document. Distressing, I mean, for the evidence it provided of my father's state of mind. The strain and anguish of his long ordeal has clearly had a terrible effect on him. Naturally no reasonable person would wish to hold him accountable for what he wrote, but certain passages nevertheless made very disturbing reading.'

Zen gazed up at the shelves loaded with rows of books as uniform as bricks.

'He accused you of having abandoned him,' he said. 'He recalled the innumerable sacrifices he has made on your behalf and reproached you for not being prepared to help him in his hour of need. He even compared your behaviour unfavourably with that of his kidnappers.'

Pietro Miletti looked round in amazement.

'How do you know that? It isn't possible! Unless . . .'

An idea flared up in his eyes for a moment and then went out.

'Such letters resemble one another,' Zen explained. 'Like love letters.'

'Ah, I see.'

Pietro had lost interest again.

Bartocci was staring angrily at Zen, who realized that he had made the mistake of speaking as though the letter really existed, as if the kidnapping was genuine. The magistrate rapped on his desk.

'What became of the letter?' he demanded.

'We burned it.'

'You did *what*?'

'My father specifically forbade us to communicate any of the information it contained to the authorities, or to cooperate with them in any way whatsoever. That position received the strongest support from various members of the family, and it was only by strenuous and prolonged efforts that I have been able to persuade them to let me bring you this memorandum, which contains, as I've said, all the relevant items in the letter.'

Zen suddenly understood that Bartocci had some move in mind, something which he was keeping up his sleeve for the moment.

'And what are these "relevant items" you mention?' the magistrate asked, deliberately postponing this initiative.

Pietro Miletti picked up the paper again and began to read in a calm, confident voice, a voice that was accustomed to being obeyed, that never needed to make a fuss. The full ten thousand million lire, in well-worn notes, not consecutively numbered, was to be made ready for delivery immediately. An untapped telephone number was to be communicated to the gang, who would use it to pass on further details, identifying themselves by the same method they had used with Valesio. The police were not to be informed of any of these arrangements or to be involved in the payoff in any way. Failure to comply with these instructions would result in the immediate death of the victim.

'And what do you intend to do?' Bartocci asked when Pietro had finished.

'We shall obey, of course. What else can we do?'

'What you've been doing for the past four months! Stalling for time, crying poor, haggling over every lira.'

Pietro Miletti replaced the sheet of paper carefully in his briefcase.

'That'll do, Bartocci. We already know what our enemies say about us.'

An effortless hardening had taken place in his tone. He got to his feet and looked at both of them in turn.

'Do you know why kidnapping flourishes here in Italy? Perhaps you think it's because we're saddled with a corrupt and inefficient police force directed by politically biased career judges lacking any practical training whatsoever. That is certainly a contributing factor, but similar conditions obtain in other countries where kidnapping is almost unknown. No, the real reason is that in our hearts we admire kidnappers. We don't like successful people. We like to see them brought low, made to suffer, made to pay. They used to call Russia an autocracy moderated by assassination. Well, Italy is a plutocracy moderated by kidnapping.'

'How do you propose to raise the money when for the past months you've been claiming that it just wasn't possible?'

But Pietro Miletti had no further interest in the exchange.

'That's our affair.'

'There's always SIMP, of course,' Bartocci insinuated.

'Yes, there's still SIMP left to bankrupt. No doubt some people would be very glad to see that happen. But if our company ever does go under, those are the very people who are going to moan loudest.'

'What about this untapped telephone number the gang have asked for? How are you going to communicate it to them?'

'If I told you that, I doubt whether the number would remain untapped for very long. We're paying an extremely high price to get my father back. We have no intention of putting the success of that operation at risk because of the usual bungling by the authorities.'

'I take it you've asked for guarantees,' Zen put in quietly.

Pietro Miletti turned at the door.

'What guarantees?'

'How do you know your father is still alive?'

'We just got a letter from him!'

'How do you know when he wrote it? You should make it a condition of payment that the gang supplies a Polaroid photograph of your father holding the morning's paper on the day the drop is made. That will incidentally also establish that the people you're dealing with have still got possession.'

'Possession of what?'

His tone was reasonable and polite, a senior manager seeking specialized information from a consultant.

'The negotiations for your father's release have been very long drawn out,' Zen explained. 'It may well be that the original kidnappers couldn't afford to wait so long. It would depend on their financial situation, how the other jobs they're involved in are going. If they need some quick cash they may have sold your father to another group as a long-term investment.'

Pietro Miletti repeated his short laugh.

'My God, are we talking about a business in second-hand victims?'

Luciano Bartocci had been shuffling papers about noisily on his desk in an attempt to disrupt this exchange from which he was excluded.

'There is just one other thing . . .' he began.

Pietro Miletti cut him off.

'But what does it matter, after all? We don't mind who we pay as long as we get my father back.'

'But you wouldn't want to pay one gang and then find that they'd sold your father to another, would you?'

'There is just one other thing,' the magistrate repeated. 'When the pay-off is made, one of the people present will be Commissioner Zen.'

Bartocci might previously have had some difficulty in making himself heard, but now he instantly had the total attention of both men. It was so still in the room that it seemed the three had suspended their dealings by mutual consent in order to catch the barely audible undulations of a distant ambulance siren.

'You must be crazy,' Pietro Miletti said at last.

The young magistrate did actually look slightly mad. His eyes were bright with determination, his face flushed with a sense of the risks he was taking, and the stillborn smile twitched away at the corner of his mouth as though he was trying to eat his beard.

'Should you refuse to cooperate,' he went on, 'I must warn you that as from this evening each member of your family and household staff will be under surveillance twenty-four hours a day by a team of Commissioner Zen's men from Rome.'

He gave Zen a long, level look, daring him to deny it.

'Naturally this flurry of police activity will get into the newspapers. The kidnappers will quite possibly call off the whole operation.'

'How dare you, Bartocci?'

Pietro Miletti's voice was quiet and curious. Despite its rhetorical form, the question seemed to have real meaning.

'How dare you make my father a pawn in your games?'

The investigating magistrate steepled his fingertips judiciously.

'Dottore, we are all here in our official capacities. You represent your family. Commissioner Zen and I represent the State. As such our duties are clearly laid down in the Criminal Code. They are to investigate crimes, prevent them from being carried out, discover the guilty parties and take any further steps necessary to uphold the law. In our official capacities that is *all* that we need do. But we are not simply judges or police officials, we are also human beings, and as human beings we sympathize deeply and sincerely with the terrible situation in which the Miletti family find themselves, and wish to do everything possible to bring it to a swift and satisfactory conclusion. At the same time, we cannot ignore our duty. And so, after long and careful deliberation, we have arrived at a compromise between our official responsibilities and our natural wish to avoid hindering your father's release in any way. It is this compromise which I have just outlined to you. I believe that you would be well advised to accept it.'

Pietro Miletti shook his head slowly.

'How can you even consider putting my father's safety at risk?'

'There is no risk,' Bartocci assured him. 'No risk whatsoever. Isn't that so, Commissioner?'

Zen's mouth opened and closed soundlessly. You bastard, he was thinking. You shifty little bastard.

But Pietro Miletti was not interested in Zen's opinion.

'The kidnappers have just given us quite explicit instructions not to involve the police in any way, yet you claim that we can send a senior officer along on the pay-off itself without there being any risk!'

Bartocci waved the objection aside.

'They won't know that he's a police official.'

Pietro Miletti stood staring intently at the magistrate.

'Why, Bartocci? You're going to alienate half the city, put my father's life at risk, all for what? What's in it for you? Why are you prepared to play such a desperate game, to put your whole future in jeopardy like this?'

'How dare you threaten me?' Bartocci shot back.

After a moment Pietro shrugged and turned away.

'I shall have to discuss the whole matter with the rest of the family.'

'Since when has the Miletti family been run as a cooperative?' Bartocci jeered.

'I shall contact you tomorrow morning.'

'You'll contact me by three o'clock this afternoon,' the magistrate insisted. 'Otherwise I shall have no alternative but to allow Commissioner Zen to put his men in position.'

Bartocci made Zen sound like a mad dog he was managing to restrain only with the greatest difficulty.

Pietro Miletti turned in the doorway.

'Needless to say, if we do agree, the responsibility for the consequences of that decision will be on your heads. You might like to think about that before committing yourselves to this course of action.'

'I tell you there isn't the slightest risk!'

'That's what they told Valesio.'

As the door closed, Zen let out a breath he realized he had been holding for a long time. And to think he'd been agonizing about what line to take on Bartocci's conspiracy theory! No need for that now. Henceforth, as far as the Milettis were concerned, Zen was Bartocci's accomplice, the henchman whose men were to be used to enforce their enemy's will.

'You're prepared to go, I suppose?' the magistrate asked him with a studied casualness Zen found rather insulting.

'It's my job. But I would have preferred to know you were going to do it.'

Bartocci laughed boyishly.

'I didn't know I was going to do it myself until it happened!'

He walked over to one of the shelves in the end wall and took down a large box-file. Zen thought he was going to be shown some decisive new piece of evidence, but Bartocci simply reached through the space left vacant on the shelf and with a grunt of effort manipulated a lever. There was a loud metallic click and the whole section of wall swung outwards.

'It was this business about the letter that decided me,' the magistrate continued, as a widening slice of the outside world appeared in the gap. 'Clearly the reason they claim to have burnt it is simply that they realize it would be too risky to let us examine it.'

The view expanded as he pushed the twin doors fully open. There was a small balcony just outside the hidden window, now inaccessible and covered in pigeon droppings.

'So according to the Milettis, what have we got?' Bartocci asked rhetorically, counting off the points on his outspread fingers. 'One telephone call which could easily have been faked from any phone box, a letter which no one outside the family has seen, and a pay-off which will supposedly take place once arrangements have been made over a telephone number they refuse to disclose. If I hadn't insisted on you going along on the drop we would have absolutely no proof that it had ever taken place! It's a conjuring trick! The money which has suddenly and mysteriously become available simply vanishes into thin air as Ruggiero Miletti magically reappears. And from that moment on there would be absolutely no way of ever proving that the whole thing had been faked. No, this pay-off is our last chance, and one that I wasn't prepared to let slip.'

They stood gazing out at the few early swallows looping around the hazy, fragrant air.

'It's all coming together!' Bartocci muttered excitedly, as though to himself. 'So many separate bits of evidence all pointing in the same direction. Yes, it's coming together!'

Despite his lingering feeling of resentment, Zen watched the young magistrate with an almost fatherly tenderness. He knew that he was feeling what Zen himself had felt often enough in the past, on one fateful occasion in particular: this time the bastards are not going to get away with it.

FIVE

Smiling! Everyone was smiling and applauding! The chubby, balding presenter was smiling, the blonde starlet was smiling, the famous politician was smiling, the best-selling journalist was smiling, while the clean, well-drilled young people dancing around them were smiling hardest of all. Even the balloons they released as they gambolled about seemed to have a sleek, benevolent look as they rose, passing a shower of confetti as dense and continuous as the applause on its way down.

'Make me a coffee, will you?'

The barman dragged himself away from the knot of men deep in conversation about the price fetched by a piece of land across the road.

'And not even big enough to have a decent crap on!' he hurled over his shoulder before turning to jab a finger at Zen.

'Coffee?' he demanded accusingly.

Zen popped two motion-sickness pills out of their plastic nests and put them in his mouth. One to two, the box said. Better safe than sorry.

On the way back to his conversation the barman punched a button on the television and suddenly they were in Texas, where folk lived and loved fit to bust and discussed it all in idiomatic but poorly synchronized Italian. When the call finally came, it took Zen several moments to realize that the phone wasn't ringing in Sue Ellen's en suite boudoir but in the dingy poolroom at the end of the bar, where a pack of the local rogue males were playing throwing-billiards. He just managed to beat one of them to the receiver.

'Avellino.'

He had the list of the First Division fixtures ready. Avellino were at home to the champions.

'Juventus.'

There was a loud clack behind him as one of the players hurled the white down the table, scattering the colours.

'Take the Cesena road. Stop at the sign "Sansepolcro one kilometre". At the base of the pole.'

The line went dead and a moment later he heard the characteristic click as the interception machinery disengaged.

Outside it was pitch-dark and spitting with rain. The large Fiat saloon parked in the piazza looked ridiculous with a yellow child's cot strapped to the roof, but this had seemingly been stipulated by the gang to make it easier for them to identify the car.

Zen climbed into the nearside front seat.

'Take the Cesena road.'

The faint light from the dashboard caught a gold filigree ear-ring spelling 'Ivy' in flowing script. The ear-ring was typical of its wearer's taste, he thought. It was presumably real gold, yet it somehow contrived to look brash and cheap, like junk jewellery trying to make up in flash what it lacked in value.

When the Fiat had emerged from the gateway of the Miletti villa at five o'clock that afternoon, Zen had been astonished to find that his driver for the ransom drop was to be Silvio's secretary, Ivy Cook. He had been waiting there since hearing from Bartocci, less than an hour earlier, that the kidnappers had been in touch and that the car would be leaving as soon as it got dark. Pietro had finally agreed to Zen's presence, on condition that there was no contact until the pay-off actually began, so during the intervening forty-eight hours he had had nothing to do with the case beyond having the ransom money photographed to record the serial numbers and finalizing the arrangements for collecting Ruggiero when he was released. The family's passive resistance continued right up to the last moment: Zen was not permitted to set foot on Miletti soil but had to wait for the Fiat in the street, beyond the imposing wrought-iron gates. He'd had plenty of time to speculate about who else would be in the car. He thought he had covered every possibility, but in the event the Milettis had amazed him.

But if the Milettis had scored a point with their choice of driver, Zen felt that he got one back when Ivy named their destination: the bar, identified by Lucaroni, where Ubaldo Valesio had gone to receive the phone calls from the gang, situated in a village about ten kilometres from Perugia. Calculating that the kidnappers might use the same initial rendezvous, Zen had informed Bartocci, who had authorized a phone-tap. The resulting tapes would be voice-printed and compared with existing samples.

The headlights of the Fiat swept from one side of the narrow winding road to the other, picking out an area of ploughed field, a thicket of scrub oaks with last year's brown leaves still clinging to the branches, an ancient wooden cart fitted with modern lorry tyres, an abandoned barn covered with posters for a dance band called 'The Lads of the Adriatic', a dirt track leading off into the hills. Ivy drove steadily but not too fast, and thanks to the pills he had taken Zen was not worried about the prospect of nausea. He even felt a rather pleasant sense of detachment from what was going on, almost as though everything around him were happening on television and the barman might switch to another channel at any moment. Perhaps it was just due to the way he'd been sleeping lately, a restless, shallow sleep full of dreams which never seemed to work themselves out properly, leaving him half-enmeshed in their elaborate complexities even after waking. In the morning his head felt as if the cast of a soap opera had moved in uninvited during the night, and the effort of following their interminable dreary intrigues left him mentally soiled and worn, less refreshed than when he'd gone to bed.

Or was it simply fear? For he was acutely aware that Ubaldo Valesio had waited in that bar, used that phone, and then walked out of that door, got into his car and never come back. Bartocci might be convinced of his conspiracy theory, but Zen just couldn't take it seriously, much as he would have liked to. He had never taken part in a ransom drop personally before, but he knew what an extremely delicate moment it was. In a way it mirrored the original kidnapping itself, and carried almost equal risks for everyone concerned. It was a time when nerves were tense and misunderstandings costly or even fatal, a time when anything and everything might go wrong.

He turned slightly so that he could see Ivy out of the corner of his eye. She didn't look frightened, but neither did she look as though she was faking anything. There was tension in the lines at the corners of her mouth, but also determination and a sense of great inner strength. Ivy Cook wouldn't crack easily, that was one thing.

'Is it far now?' he asked.

'About ten minutes.'

Her strange deep voice pronounced the words like a parody of someone from the Trento area, where the warm and cold currents of Italian and German meet and mingle.

'What are we supposed to do when we reach the Cesena road?' she went on.

It seemed to take him an age to remember.

'We have to find a sign beside the road reading "Sansepolcro one kilometre". I suppose they've left another message there.'

'It's like a treasure hunt.'

When he had met Ivy at Crepi's dinner party her appearance had struck him as so wilfully bizarre that he had written it off as a freak effect, as though all her luggage had been lost and she'd had to raid the oddments put aside for collection by the missionary brothers. But evidently her appearance that first evening had constituted a rule rather than an exception. Tonight's colour scheme was more sombre but just as tasteless: chocolate-brown slacks, a violet pullover and a green suede jacket.

'You're English, then?'

The association of thought was clear only to him, luckily!

'My family is. I was born in South Africa. And you're from Venice, I believe?'

'That's right. A district called Cannaregio, near the station.'

A fine rain blurred the view.

'Have you lived in Italy for long?'

Ivy turned on the wipers.

'Years!'

'How did that happen?'

'I was on a tour of Europe. People take a couple of years off, buy a camper and explore the world. Then they go back home, get steady jobs and never leave South Africa again. I just didn't go home.'

A patch of lights off to the right revealed the presence of a town which slowly orbited them and disappeared into the darkness. Slip-roads came and went, labelled with the names of famous cities: Arezzo, Gubbio, Urbino, Sansepolcro. Then the road stretched away before them again, bare and gleaming and straight and dark, like a tunnel . . .

'What?'

Ivy was looking at him with a peculiar expression. He realized that he had just murmured something under his breath.

'Nothing.'

Jesus, what was in those capsules? He hadn't even needed a prescription to buy them. Surely they were just like aspirin? The government should step in, warn people, ban the things.

He had said, 'Daddy?'

Then reality started to move so fast that by the time he caught up it was all over and they were parked on the hard shoulder. Replaying the sequence he realized that Ivy had braked hard, the car swerving slightly on the greasy surface, then backed up. Now she was looking at him expectantly.

'Yes?' he said.

She pointed out of the window.

'Isn't that it?'

He looked out and saw the sign.

Outside it was cold and blustery, speckled with droplets of water gusting against his face. The base of the circular grey pole was concealed in a clump of long brown grass. A large spider's web strung between the base of the sign and the pole bellied back and forth in the wind, the spider itself clinging fast to it.

Beneath the strands of dead grass his fingers touched something hard. He pulled out an empty pasta box sealed at one end with industrial adhesive tape. The damp cardboard showed a picture of a smiling mother serving a huge bowl of spaghetti to her smiling husband and two smiling children. 'Get this fabulous apron absolutely free!' exhorted a slash across the corner of the packet.

'Is everything all right?'

Ivy had the door open and was leaning out, looking impatient.

'I'm just coming.'

He tried to strip off the tape, but it was too tough and his fingers were numb and he couldn't find where it began. When he got back to the car Ivy took it away from him and opened the other end. Why hadn't that occurred to him?

She took out a cassette tape and pushed it into the car's tape-deck. After a short hissy silence there was the usual voice.

'Play this tape once only, then put it back where you found it. At the Sansepolcro turn-off take the road to Rimini. When you reach the crossroads beyond Novafeltria stop and wait.'

There was the sound of a car behind them and it suddenly became very light. Then a figure appeared on Ivy's side and rapped on the window. She opened it.

'See your papers?'

The Carabinieri patrolman had the raw look of a recruit freshly dug up from one of the no-hope regions of the deep South and put through the human equivalent of a potato-peeling machine. The uniform he was wearing seemed to have been assembled from outfits designed to fit several very different people: the sleeves were too long and the neck too wide, while the cap was so small it had left a pink welt around his forehead. He scrutinized the documents as if they were a puzzle picture in which he had to spot the deliberate mistakes. Then he looked suspiciously around the car.

'Having problems?'

'Just stopped for a look at the map,' Ivy told him.

'It's illegal to park on the hard shoulder except in case of emergency.'

'I'm sorry. We were just leaving.'

The patrolman grunted and walked back to his vehicle. Ivy started the engine.

'The tape,' Zen reminded her. 'We've got to put it back.'

They sat and waited. Fifteen seconds. Thirty seconds. The headlights behind showed no sign of moving.

Zen palmed the cassette and got out. He walked to the verge and made a show of urinating. After a few minutes the carabinieri vehicle revved up and screeched off down the road. Zen slipped the tape back in its nest of grass at the foot of the pole and hurried back.

It was only when they reached the turning to Sansepolcro that he felt something hard underneath his foot.

'Damn! I forgot to put the box back.'

'Does it matter?'

There was no telling, that was the problem. The responsibility for the consequences will be on your heads, Pietro Miletti had said. All along Zen had been haunted by the idea that he might make some blunder which would hang over him for the rest of his life, yet here he was behaving like a dope addict. He felt an overwhelming desire for a cigarette, but Ivy was a non-smoker and he had agreed not to smoke in the car.

The road to Rimini bypassed the town and in a few moments they were out in the wilds again, labouring up a steep, tortuous medieval track on which modern civilization had done no more than slap a layer of asphalt and a road number. The ascent was arduous and prolonged, twisting and turning upwards for more than twelve kilometres to the pass, almost a thousand metres high. The starkness of the landscape revealed by the headlights penetrated the car like a draught. Zen sat there unhappily taking it all in. He didn't much care for nature in the raw: it was messy and wasteful and there was too much of it. This was a fertile source of incomprehension between him and Ellen. The wilder and more extensive the view, the better she liked it. 'Look at that!' she would exclaim, indicating some appalling mass of barren rock. 'Isn't it magnificent?' Zen had long given up trying to understand. It all came of her being American, he supposed. Americans had more nature than anything else except money, and they got pretty excited about that too.

To take his mind off the scene outside he looked at his companion instead. Part of the oddness of her appearance, he realized, came from the fact that she didn't look like a woman so much as a rather inept female impersonator. Not that there was anything butch about her. On the contrary, it was precisely the excessive femininity, laid on with a trowel as it were, that created the effect of someone pretending to be a woman, someone in fact rather desperately hoping to be taken for one. But this desperation was perhaps understandable. Certainly her role in the Miletti household appeared to be anything but feminine. She was evidently their dogsbody, used for tasks which no one else was prepared to take on. Typically, it had been Ivy, he'd learned, who had been sent to collect the letter from Ruggiero which the gang had left in the rubbish skip.

'Are you married, Commissioner?' she asked suddenly.

It was the first remark she had volunteered all evening.

'Separated. And you?'

'What do you think?'

Zen had no idea what he was supposed to think. Eventually Ivy herself seemed to sense the need for an explanation.

'My association with Silvio rather precludes marriage.'

They rounded yet another bend, the headlights sweeping over a bald expanse of stricken scanty grass. It had started to rain more heavily, unless they were now actually up inside the clouds.

'If you really want a cigarette very badly I think on the whole I should prefer you to have one,' Ivy told him.

He gave an embarrassed laugh.

'Is it that obvious?'

'Well, you keep fiddling with the ashtray and pushing the cigarette lighter in and out. Just open the window a crack.'

'What about the rest of the Milettis?' Zen asked as he lit up. The wind burbled at his ear like frantic drumming.

'What about them?'

'How do you get on with them?'

She took a moment to think.

'They find me useful, on occasion.'

'I still remember how Cinzia Miletti treated you that evening at Crepi's.'

'Poor Cinzia!' murmured Ivy. 'She's terribly unhappy.'

'Isn't it a bit of a strain, though, living in the same house with them?'

'Oh, I don't. They would never stand for it. Ruggiero would have a fit!'

She laughed gaily, as though Ruggiero Miletti's attitude was frightfully amusing.

'No, I have a little flat of my own, although I have been spending more time than usual at the villa since the kidnapping. But I'll be very glad when it's all over and things return to normal.'

'But you and Ruggiero don't get on?'

That gave her pause.

'Well, he doesn't have a very high opinion of either foreigners or women,' she said at last. 'That places me at something of a disadvantage.'

Zen didn't reply at once. He was at the honeymoon stage with his cigarette, listening to the nicotine marching through his blood.

'And yet you're looking forward to his getting back? I don't understand.'

'It's a question of the lesser of two evils. At least we all know where we are when he's around. For the last few months everything has rather fallen apart. Ruggiero kept all the reins in his own hands, you see. So in a sense I'll be glad when he is back, despite his attitude to me.'

He decided to risk a shot in the dark.

'Is it your relationship with Silvio that Ruggiero objects to?'

'Why do you say that?' she snapped.

Clearly this was a sensitive topic. Then she laughed, as if to cover her outburst.

'Anyway, you're quite right. Silvio is a very complex and tormented personality, someone who has great difficulty in coming to terms with the demands of life. I help to ease that burden for him. Ruggiero doesn't accept that, perhaps because it would mean accepting responsibility for the way his son's turned out.'

'In what way is he responsible?'

The cigarette had suddenly turned bad on him.

'Oh, in all sorts of ways. He was responsible for Loredana's death, for one thing. Silvio has never really recovered from that.'

'What happened?'

'Ruggiero was driving her back from Rome late one night, and somehow the car left the road and ended up against a tree. Loredana was killed instantly. Ruggiero's legs and collar-bone were broken and he was trapped in the wreckage for almost seven hours, pinned beside her corpse. He was discovered the next morning by a boy on his way to school. People say he has never been the same since. Loredana moderated the violence of his personality, or at least sheltered the children from it. After her death they certainly took the full brunt, Silvio in particular. He was only thirteen and he'd been particularly close to his mother. Her death was a great blow to him, and I imagine Ruggiero handled it in exactly the wrong way, telling him to snap out of it, stop snivelling, that sort of thing. He's a man who has crushed all softness in himself, so why should his son be indulged, be allowed to cry and display his grief, be stroked and cuddled and consoled when he never was? Of course, Cinzia suffered terribly too. The others rather less, I think. Pietro was old enough to cope better, Daniele too young to understand.'

Zen wound down the window and let his half-smoked cigarette be sucked out into the airstream. The conversation no longer kept the landscape at bay but intensified it, showing its desolation to be a reality not merely natural but also human.

Eventually the car slowed to a halt. The rain was now pelting down, covering the windows with a coat of water as thick and opaque as glycerine. The headlights created a luminous swathe ahead of the car, but nothing was visible except a variety of shapes which obstinately refused to become more than that. Ivy turned the engine off. Nothing moved outside, and the only sound was the steady metallic drumming on the roof of the car.

'Why did you ask if I was married?' Zen asked.

She glanced at him briefly.

'I don't know. To break the silence, I suppose. Why does one ask anything?'

He leaned closer to the window, but saw even less as his breath fogged the glass.

'Well, in my case it's usually to get information out of people,' he said. 'Then after a while it becomes a habit, like those teachers who speak to everyone as though they're five years old.'

'I suppose I was trying to make you seem more human. I'm frightened of the police, you see, like most people. Almost as frightened as I am of this gang.'

The minutes slipped away, their passage recorded with unnecessary precision by the digital clock on the instrument panel.

'They don't ever attack people, do they?'

It sounded as though the reality of what they were doing had come home to her for the first time.

'Who, the police?' he joked.

Her expression showed that she no longer had any time for jokes.

'No, it's completely unheard of,' he assured her. 'All they want from us is the money that's in the boot. We won't even see them, probably.'

The rain ceased abruptly, as if it had been turned off.

'I think I'll just stretch my legs a bit,' Zen announced.

The whole night was in motion, its gusts glancing blows from currents active on the fringes of the turbulence centred somewhere in the clouds swirling about overhead. The visibility had improved slightly. What he had taken to be a gate turned out to be a wall, the hump on the ground near by a heap of gravel and the massive bulk on the other side of the road a barn whose gable end still bore the faded icon of a helmeted Mussolini and the slogan 'It is important to win, but still more important to fight.'

At first the sound might have been thunder, or an animal. Next a light appeared, and a moment later a shape swept out of the night, big as a centaur, its blinding eye striking him along with something solid. Then it was gone, leaving a weighted envelope lying on the wet black asphalt at his feet.

Back in the car he showed Ivy the black-and-white Polaroid photograph it contained.

'That's Ruggiero,' she confirmed.

The picture showed a stocky man with a shock of white hair and the typical Umbrian moon-face, wearing a chequered shirt open at the neck and holding up a newspaper. He looked resentful and slightly embarrassed, like an elderly relative who had grudgingly agreed to pose in order to keep the peace at a Christmas party. The photo might have been modelled on those sent by the Red Brigades during the Moro kidnapping, but where those middle-class intellectuals had used the centre-left *Repubblica* to mark the date, Ruggiero Miletti was holding the *Nazione*, just the kind of paper which a bunch of good Catholic boys like the kidnappers would choose.

Ivy took the envelope from him, widened the opening and extracted a small coil of blue plastic strip about a centimetre wide. A message had been punched out in capital letters with a labelling machine. 'PUT PHOTO AND MESSAGE BACK IN ENVELOPE LEAVE HERE FOLLOW BIKE.' Zen slipped the photo and tape back into the envelope, opened the door and let them drop out.

'Right, well, let's get on with it.'

For the next three hours the motorbike led them a nightmare chase over more than a hundred kilometres of mountain roads that were often little more than channels covered by scree and loose gravel, furrowed by rain-water and ridged by surfacing strata of rock. All they ever saw of their guide was a faint distant tail-light, and then only rarely, at irregular moments after long periods of doubt when it seemed that they had lost the scent, made the wrong decision at some unmarked junction up in the stormy darkness.

The driving demanded constant attention. Only a narrow range of speeds was viable. Below that the car risked bogging down in the mud or grounding on an obstacle, above it the tyres might lose adhesion on the continual twists and turns or cliff-like descents, or one of the vicious potholes or rock outcrops rupture the suspension or pierce the sump. They hardly exchanged a word. Ivy had her hands full with the driving, and although Zen soon gave up trying to follow their route on the maps he had brought with him, which proved to bear only a partial and rather disturbing resemblance to the landscape, like a mild hallucination, he kept up a show of poring over them to try and assuage his guilt at being a mere passenger, unable to share her burden. And still the faint red light up ahead came and went by fits and starts, leading them on across gale-swept open moorland, through massively still pine forests, up exposed dirt tracks and over passes whose names had vanished with the inhabitants of the farms where until a few decades earlier generation after generation of human beings had eked out lives of almost unimaginable deprivation.

It was after midnight when a set of headlights appeared behind them, flooding the interior of the car with light. Ivy squinted, trying to shut out the glare that made her task still more difficult.

'What's going on?' she asked edgily.

'They must be gating us in.'

Then everything happened at once. The motorbike slowed so that for the first time they could see the outlines of the rider, a derelict farmhouse appeared in its headlight beam and the car behind them started flashing its lights. Figures appeared in the road ahead, waving them into the yard of the farmhouse. Their faces were black and completely featureless except for two oval eye-slits, the head hooded, the body shrouded in shiny waterproof capes. There were piercing whistles, then a thump as they opened the boot, where the money was packed in cardboard boxes wrapped in plastic rubbish bags. With a series of dull thuds and strangely intimate bumps the unloading began, punctuated by more of the raucous, inhuman whistles which finally blew away the remaining shreds of doubt in Zen's mind about the reality of the kidnapping. That eerie keening, like the cry of a great predator, was used by shepherds to communicate across the vast wind-swept spaces in which they lived and worked. No outsider, no amateur, could ever fake that sound.

The rain, which had been coming and going, began to pour down again, spattering in big gobs all over the glass around them. In the still warmth of the car, bathed in the calm green glow of the instrument panel, it was impossible to imagine what conditions were like out there. Inside and outside seemed so absolutely separate that once again Zen, drifting off into pleasantly dopey inattention, had the sensation of being a mere spectator of screen images, some television documentary about hardy men who did dangerous work for big money.

'What's happening?' Ivy whispered fearfully.

The activity at the back of the car had ceased and it had fallen silent.

'They're probably checking the money.'

He could make out nothing in the darkness around the car. The headlights revealed only the worn flagstones of the farmyard, the archway into the byre on the ground floor of the house, the crumbling steps that had once given access to the living quarters above. The door was staved in and torn half off its hinges in what looked like an act of senseless violence. At one of the gaping window frames a bit of ragged cloth twitched and flapped spasmodically in the wind.

'Perhaps they've gone,' Ivy whispered.

He didn't answer.

'Can't we go?'

'Not yet.'

Even before he finished speaking a caped and hooded figure appeared at Ivy's shoulder, the door was wrenched open and a powerful torch shone into their faces.

'Out! Out! Out!'

The next instant the door behind him opened too, transforming the interior of the car into a wind tunnel. A huge hand grabbed Zen's shoulder and dragged him outside, shoving him up against the side of the car. Light hit his face as hard as the stinging raindrops. Then it abruptly disappeared, and all he could see were entrancing coloured patterns chasing each other about the glowing darkness like tropical fish.

The pain was so unexpected, so absolute, that he had no name for it and fell over without a sound, like a baby, too shocked to make any fuss.

'Fuckarse cocksucker of a cop!'

He could just make out the outline of the figure in front of him, sweeping its heavy cape to one side, then something smashed into the side of his head. They've shot me, he thought. They've shot me like they did Valesio. They're proving they exist, punishing us for not believing in them, like gods.

With a strange detachment he noted the final sequence of events: the roar of a car engine near by, the boot drawn back, the hiss of a tyre skidding past, the oddly painless blast which ended it.

Like Trotsky and the iceman, he thought. Of course! The solution was so obvious, so satisfying, that there was no need to try and understand it.

That explained the cold, too. Obviously if it weren't cold the ice would melt. In fact some of it already had. The hard, smooth surface pressed to his face was covered in water. As for the purposeful darkness tugging at his clothing, this must be the wind in the tunnel. The only question, in fact, was where his father had gone, why he had left him alone. No doubt there was an answer to that, too, but he couldn't think what it was.

Once again he called weakly, but as before there was no reply. He lay back, stretched out on the cold wet tracks, waiting for the express to Russia to come and chop off his head.

The telephone call could hardly have been vaguer.

'*One of your men is by the farm up above Santa Sofia there, above the river, up there on the way to the church.*'

The voice was male, adult, uneducated, with a strong Calabrian accent. It was one forty-three in the morning and the duty sergeant wasn't quite sure whether he was dealing with a wrong number, a hoax, or an emergency. But the next words made sense all right.

'*You'd better go get him before he dies.*'

The Carabinieri station was at Bagno di Romagna, a small town high up in the Apennines on the borders of Tuscany and Emilia-Romagna. The locals were a staid lot; the sergeant, who was Sicilian, privately thought them dull. They were not given to silly pranks at any time, let alone a quarter to two on Sunday morning. So what the hell was going on?

He phoned his provincial headquarters at Cesena, who called regional headquarters at Bologna, who checked with their opposite numbers in Florence before confirming that no member of the force had been reported missing on either side of the Apennines. Better get out there and have a look just the same, Cesena told him with a hint of malice. Even down there in the coastal flatlands it was a wild night. They could imagine what conditions must be like up in the mountains, having done their stint in the sticks at one time or another.

Out *where*, though? Apart from the undisputed fact that the farm in question was 'up', the sergeant knew only that it was near a village called Santa Sofia, above a river and on the way to a church. He pored over his 1:100000 maps and finally selected four possibilities. If none of them proved correct they would have to wait until dawn and call out a helicopter, by which time it would probably be too late. The wind howled about the building, driving rain against the shutters.

They had been at it for over two and a half hours before the searchlight finally picked out the slumped body in the yard of an abandoned farm at over a thousand metres on the slopes of Mount Guffone. The young private at the wheel let out a gasp of surprise.

'You see?' the sergeant exclaimed triumphantly.

His relief at not having been made a fool of was matched by his curiosity to find out who the devil he was, this man lying chest down on the wet flagstones, face turned to one side as though asleep. There were some quite nasty-looking cuts on his head, and the sergeant was a bit apprehensive about turning him over. He would never forget that time when a corporal had been machine-gunned in an ambush on a country road near Palermo. He'd been found lying face down too, and the only sign of what had happened was a slight discoloration on the back of his jacket, as though some of the red dye from the trimming had leached on to the body of the black fabric. But when they turned him over there was a sound like a fart and all his insides had sicked out, bits that weren't meant to be seen and which God accordingly hadn't bothered to finish off like the rest. Amazingly, nothing had seemed to take any notice! The sky was still blue, the sun still shone, somewhere near by a lark gibbered away. Only he had watched, fascinated, as the pool of blood collecting around the spilt innards suddenly burst its confines and set off down the road, finding its way slowly and with difficulty, its bright fresh surface soon matted with dust and drowning insects.

'What we going to do?' asked the young private, a little concerned at the way his superior was acting.

'Do? Well, we've got to find out who he is, haven't we?'

In the end it was all right. There were no serious injuries at all, in fact. The man even mumbled something, and his eyelids flickered for a moment without opening.

'No wonder no one knew about him!' the sergeant exclaimed as he studied the identity card he had found in the man's wallet. 'He's not one of ours at all. Stupid bastard didn't know the difference.'

Or more likely didn't care, he thought. The glorious traditions of the Service meant nothing to scum like that.

The man lying at their feet mumbled something again.

'Did you hear what he said?' the sergeant asked.

The private made a face.

'I'm not sure. It sounded like he said "Daddy".'

Yellowed light, stale warmth, a pervasive scent of chemicals: the contrast with his earlier dips into consciousness was total.

Zen was sitting on a stool under a bright light in a small white-curtained cubicle, thinking about Trotsky and the iceman. With his open-necked shirt, his air of dejected exhaustion and the newspaper spread open on his knee, he might almost have been a kidnap victim waiting to have his existence confirmed by means of a Polaroid photograph. But in fact he was waiting for a different kind of photograph, a different kind of confirmation.

Trotsky and the iceman had been his attempt to solve the problem of why he was still alive despite having been shot in the head. Leon Trotsky protested with his dying breath that he had been shot, not stabbed, even though Stalin's killer had been caught with the ice-pick still in his hand. Zen's mistake was less excusable, since all he'd suffered were a few hard kicks.

Then the wind and the darkness and the sense of utter abandonment had unlocked a memory which had already put in a passing appearance earlier that night. It was a memory he hadn't known he had, and even now he knew very little about it beyond the fact that it involved him and his father and a railway tunnel. He didn't know where or when it had happened. There they were, the two of them, walking into the tunnel. It must have been on a main line, because there were two sets of tracks, and the mouth of the tunnel had seemed to him – he might have been five, six? – bigger than anything he had ever seen, bigger than anything he had known could exist.

They had gone a very long way into the tunnel. He hadn't wanted to, but since his father was holding his hand it was all right. When he looked round he found that the tunnel mouth had changed polarity and become a little patch of brightness, quite faint and very far away. The silence echoed with large drips falling from the invisible curved mass above. The air smelt dank and trapped despite the wind that poured past them, forcing them deeper into the solid darkness ahead.

Meanwhile his father, his voice reverberating in a way that hinted at the extent of the invisible spaces about them, told him about the tunnel, when it was opened and how long it was and how deep below the surface. He pointed out the sloping white stripes on the walls, whose incline indicated the nearest of the niches providing protection for plate-layers who otherwise might end up under the wheels of one of the expresses which thundered over these rails, bound for famous foreign cities.

Then, without warning or explanation, the warm grip on his hand disappeared and the soothing voice fell silent.

It was only for a moment, no doubt, as adults measure time. It must have been a joke, a little trick of the kind fathers like to play on their children, toying idly with their power, whimsical tyrants. He knew that it had been a joke, because when it was over his father laughed so much that the laughter was still echoing around them as they started back towards the light. It had sounded almost as though the tunnel itself were enjoying some deeper, darker joke whose significance not even his father had fully understood.

An unshaven young man in a white coat slouched into the cubicle and handed Zen three dark rectangular sheets of plastic.

'No fractures.'

Zen held the X-rays up to the light. They looked as dubious as the photographs which are claimed to prove the existence of a spirit world: swirls and patches of white suspended in a grey mix.

'You're sure?'

It certainly hurt badly enough. But perhaps pain was no guide. Oddly enough the worst was his shoulder, where the man had seized it to pull him out of the car.

'It's only bruised,' the orderly insisted. 'But next time take it easy, eh? I might be in the other car.'

Zen had told them he'd been involved in a traffic accident, which had got a good laugh all round when it emerged that he was from Venice. For want of practice, Venetian drivers are proverbially supposed to be the worst in Italy.

He left the hospital and began to walk slowly along the boulevard leading back to the centre of Perugia. The morning was quiet and warm. The storm had blown itself out, leaving the sky pearly. There was a mild southerly breeze. A few people were about, returning from church or walking home with a newspaper or a neatly wrapped pastry. He was glad that he had dismissed Palottino, although the Neapolitan had made it clear that he strongly disapproved of this mania for walking. He had driven up to collect his superior from the Carabinieri post where he and his rescuers had returned as soon as Zen had recovered enough to assure the sergeant that he didn't need to call an ambulance. As soon as they reached Bagno di Romagna Zen had phoned Geraci, who he'd left holding the fort, and inquired about Ivy Cook. His greatest worry was that somehow his presence had compromised her, that he might have another corpse on his hands, another death on his conscience. But Geraci was able to reassure him: Ivy had arrived home three hours earlier, badly shocked but unharmed. The money had been taken but there had been no communication from the kidnappers.

While Zen waited for his driver to arrive, his hosts tried politely to find out who he was and what he'd been doing, but he remained deliberately vague. Even with Palottino he had been discreet, not mentioning what the kidnapper had said to him. And when the Neapolitan asked, 'You don't think they knew?' Zen had pretended not to understand.

'Knew what?'

'That you were from the police.'

'How could they?'

Palottino had no answer to that, any more than Zen himself, though the question had tormented him for the whole drive back to Perugia. How could they have known? But they had, that was certain. 'Fuckarse cocksucker of a cop,' the man had said. So they knew that their orders had been deliberately disobeyed. This gang had already killed one man for less. The thought of what they might even now be doing to Ruggiero Miletti took the sparkle and warmth out of the morning and made Zen realize how exhausted he was.

As he passed through a small piazza there was a shout and a boy appeared at a window holding a bulging plastic shopping bag which he let drop to a friend in the street who stood, arms raised to catch it. But it was immediately obvious that the bag was too heavy and was falling much too fast. At the last moment the boy below ran back. The bag struck the paving, bounced, and now the boy caught it and peeled away the bag to reveal a football which he struck in a high, curling shot which ricocheted off the wall slightly to the left of a priest who had emerged from the large church which closed off one end of the piazza. Through the open door Zen could just make out the huge ornate crucifix above the high altar.

'How could they?' he murmured to himself again.

SIX

Twenty-four hours later he was sitting out on the Corso. It was brilliantly sunny and the atmosphere was charged with vitality and optimism. One bar had even gone so far as to put a few tables outside, and on impulse Zen settled down to enjoy the sunlight and watch the show on the Corso. This broad, flat street was the city's living room, the one place where you didn't need a reason for being. Being there was reason enough, strolling back and forth, greeting your friends and acquaintances, window-shopping, showing off your new clothes or your new lover, occasionally dropping into one of the bars for a coffee or an ice-cream.

For about fifteen minutes he did nothing but sit there contentedly, sipping his coffee and watching the restless, flickering scene around him through half-open eyes: the tall, bearded man with a cigar and a fatuous grin who walked up and down at an unvarying even pace like a clockwork soldier, never looking at anybody; the plump ageing layabout in a Gestapo officer's leather coat and dark glasses holding court outside the door of the café, trading secrets and scandal with his men friends, assessing the passers-by as though they were for sale, calling after women and making hourglass gestures with his hairy, gold-ringed hands; a frail old man bent like an S, with a crazy harmless expression and a transistor radio pressed to his ear, walking with the exaggerated urgency of those who have nowhere to go; slim Africans with leatherwork belts and bangles laid out on a piece of cloth; a gypsy child sitting on the cold stone playing the same four notes over and over again on a cheap concertina; two foreigners with guitars and a small crowd around them; a beggar with his shirt pulled down over one shoulder to reveal the stump of an amputated arm; a pudgy, shapeless woman with an open suitcase full of cigarette lighters and bootleg cassettes; the two Nordic girls at the next table, basking half-naked in the weak March sun as though this might be the last time it appeared this year.

At length Zen lazily drew out of his pocket the three items of mail he had collected from the Questura. One was a letter stamped with the initials of the police trade union and addressed to Commissioner Italo Pompeo Baldoni. He replaced this in his pocket and picked up a heavy cream-coloured envelope with his own name printed on it, and a postcard showing the Forum at sunset in gaudy and unrealistic colour with a message reading 'Are you still alive? Give me a ring – if you have time. Ellen.'

Putting this aside, he tore open the cream-coloured envelope. It contained four sheets of paper closely covered in unfamiliar handwriting, and it was a measure of how relaxed he was that it took him the best part of a minute to realize that he was holding a photocopy of the letter written by Ruggiero Miletti to his family three days previously.

My children,
If I address you collectively, it is because I no longer know who to address individually. I no longer know who my friends are within the family. I no longer even know if I have any friends. Can you imagine how bitter it is for me to have to write that sentence?

I remember one day, long ago, when I was out hunting with my father. He showed me a farmhouse, a solid four-square Umbrian tenant farm, surrounded by a grove of trees to break the wind. Look, he said, that is what a family is. Have many children, he told me, for children are an old man's only defence against the blows of fate. I obeyed him. In those days children did obey their fathers. But what has it availed me? For you, my children, my only defence, my protection against the cruel winds of fate, what do you do? Instead of sheltering me, you turn to squabbling among yourselves, haggling over the cost of your own father's freedom as though I were an ox brought to market. It is not you but my kidnappers who care for me now, who feed me and clothe me and shelter me while you sit safe and secure at home trying to find new ways to avoid paying for my release!

No doubt this tone surprises you. It is incautious, ill-advised, is it not? I should not permit myself such liberties! After all, my life is in your hands. If you treat me like an ox to be bargained for, I should be the more careful not to annoy you. Swallow your pride and your anger, old man! Flatter, plead, ingratiate and abase yourself before your all-powerful children! Yes, that is what I should do, if I wished to match you in devious cunning. But I don't. You have refused to pay what has been asked for my return, but if you knew what I have become, a fearless old man with nothing left to lose, you would pay twice as much to have me kept away! Whatever happens now, my children, we can never be again as we were. Do you imagine that I could forgive and forget, knowing what I know now, or that any of you could meet my eye, knowing what you do? No! Though the ox escape the axe, it has smelt the blood and heard the bellows from the killing-floor, and it will never be fooled again. I know you now! And that knowledge is lodged in my heart like a splinter.

Nothing remains to me of the pleasures and possessions of my old life, which you now enjoy at my expense. I have been forced to give them up. But in recompense I have received a gift worth more than all the rest put together. It is called freedom. You laugh? Not for long, I assure you! For I shall prove to you how free I am. Not free to indulge myself, to be sure. Not free to come and go, to buy and sell, to control my destiny. You have taken those freedoms from me. Losing them was bitter, and my only reward is that now I can afford the one thing which with all my wealth and power I've never been able to permit myself until this moment. I can afford to tell the truth.

I have paid dearly for it, God knows! More than a hundred and forty days and nights of anguish to soul and body alike! My leg, which never mended properly after the accident, has not liked being cooped and cramped and bound, and like a mistreated animal it has turned against its master, making itself all pain. Yes, I have paid dearly. So let me show you what I mean by freedom. Let me tell you what I know, what I have learnt. Let me tell each of you the truth, one by one.

I shall start with you, Daniele, my youngest, the spoilt darling of the family. What a beautiful child you were! How everyone doted on you! Whatever happened to that little boy, all cuddles and kisses and cheeky sayings that set everyone in a roar? Back in the sixties, when the kids seemed to think of nothing but politics and sex, I used to pray God almighty that my Daniele would never turn out like that. It never occurred to me that he might turn out even worse, a vain, spineless, ignorant lout with no interest in anything but clothes and television and pop music, who would be rotting in gaol at this very minute if his family hadn't come to his rescue. But when his own father needs to be rescued little Daniele is too busy to lift a finger, like the rest of you.

Cinzia I pass over in silence. Women cannot betray me, for I have never made the mistake of trusting them. The worst she could do was to bring that Tuscan adventurer into the family, since when none of us has had a moment's peace. I can't claim to have had my eyes opened to your true character, Gianluigi, for they were wide open from the first. Ask my daughter what I said to her on the subject! However, she preferred to disobey me. You think you're so clever, Gianluigi, and that's your problem, for your cleverness gleams like a wolf's fangs. I at least was never fooled. Take this business of the Japanese offer, for example. Certainly the scheme you've worked out is very cunning. I really admire the way the structure of the holding company leaves you in effective control of SIMP through an apparently insignificant position in the marketing subsidiary. I suppose you thought that old Papa Miletti would be too stupid to spot that, wrapped up in a lot of technical detail about non-voting share blocks and nominal investment consortia? Of course the kidnapping has given you an extra edge. All you had to do was to hold up the negotiations until I got desperate and then bully me into authorizing the Japanese deal on the pretext of raising money to pay for my release! In fact the kidnapping was very well timed from your point of view, wasn't it? It wouldn't even surprise me to learn that you set it up! Beware of in-laws, my father used to say, and when he's Tuscan into the bargain I think we can expect just about anything.

But none of this really bothered me, it was all piss in the wind as long as my eldest boy was true. Silvio I had already written off, of course. I realized long ago that the only thing he has in common with other men is the prick between his legs. God knows why – I made him the same way I made the rest of you – but there it is. There's nothing manly to be expected from Silvio, unless that English witch knows something the rest of us don't. Let him spit in her mouth and breed toads. He'll never breed anything else, that's for sure.

But Pietro made up for all that and for everything else, or so I thought. The rest of you, choke on this last gobbet of my scorn! If he had been loyal I should never even have mentioned these playroom plots and tantrums of yours. But what I didn't realize, and what has proved the gravest shock to me, is that Pietro is the worst of you all. What a superb role he has invented for himself, the English gentleman who stands disdainfully aside from the vulgar squabbles of this Latin rabble to whom he has the misfortune to be related! I've got to hand it to you, son, you're the only one who really managed to deceive me, the only one who could break your father's heart And you have, you have. The others I could afford to lose, but you were too precious. I loved you, I needed you, and blinded by my love and need I never looked at you closely enough. But now I have, and I see what I should have seen a long time ago, the selfish, arrogant, unscrupulous fixer who has been quietly feathering his nest in London for the past ten years at our expense after turning his back on us as though we weren't good enough for him, who couldn't even be bothered to come home during this ordeal but just flew over on a weekend return when the mood took him, when he had nothing better to do, like the tourist he is!

Gianluigi likes to think he's clever, but you really are, Pietro. You've inherited my brains and Loredana's morals, God rest her. You don't instigate plots, because you know that plots get found out. Instead you manipulate the plots of the others to your own ends, playing one off against the others, letting them waste their energies in fruitless rivalries while you look on from a safe distance, waiting patiently for the moment to make your move, the day when I drop dead and you can come home and claim your own.

Well, there we are, I've had my say. How do you like yourselves, my children? When you lie down tonight in your soft warm beds, think over what I have said. Get up and look at yourselves in the mirror. Look hard and long, and then think of your father lying here tormented with cold and pain and fear and despair.

What follows has been dictated by my kidnappers. For some reason they seem to believe that you will obey them this time. First, then, the full ransom of ten milliard lire is to be paid immediately, in well-worn consecutively numbered notes . . .

There, at the foot of a page, the photocopy broke off. Zen inspected the envelope. It was of distinctive hand-laid paper with a griffin watermark and had been posted in Perugia the previous Thursday.

'A personal and private family letter,' Pietro Miletti had said. 'A rather distressing document, not intended to be read by outsiders. Certain passages made very disturbing reading.' Yes, it was easy to see why the family who, as Antonio Crepi had put it, couldn't agree which sauce to have with their pasta, had found no difficulty in agreeing to burn Ruggiero's letter on the spot. But this made it so obvious who had sent this copy that he was astonished that it had been sent at all. When Pietro Miletti thought Zen must have seen the letter, he'd burst out, 'But that's impossible!' Then an idea occurred to him, and he added, 'Unless . . .' Now Zen knew what he had been thinking. If the letter had been burnt in the presence of all the members of the family immediately after being read, then the copy could only have been sent to him before they received it, by the person who went to pick it up from the rubbish skip.

But that could wait. This was urgent news and he must inform Bartocci at once. Besides, he had not yet had a chance to speak to the investigating magistrate about the pay-off. He tucked a two-thousand lire note under one of the saucers on the tray and went inside the café to phone.

Luciano Bartocci wasted no time on small talk.

'*Jesus Christ almighty, Zen, what the hell do you think you've been up to?*'

He was too taken aback to reply.

'*The family are absolutely incensed, and quite naturally so. How could you do such a thing? I thought you were an experienced professional or I'd never have let you go in the first place! Don't you realize the position this puts me in?*'

'What are you talking about?'

'*I'm talking about what happened at the pay-off, when you were beaten up. The woman who drove you told us all about it. It's no use trying to cover up now.*'

'I'm not trying to . . .'

Another voice broke in.

'*Maurizio? Maurizio, is that you?*'

'*It's in use!*'

'*What? Who is this?*'

'*This line is in use, please put your phone down.*'

There was a grunt and a click.

'*Hello? Hello?*'

'I'm still here.'

'*The man who assaulted you called you a dirty cop, or words to that effect. So evidently they knew who you were. You must have given yourself away somehow. It's absolutely unforgivable.*'

'They didn't find out from me!'

'*Then how did they find out? Eh?*'

Zen decided to give him the only answer he had been able to come up with.

'Perhaps one of the family told them.'

'*That's nonsense! Why should they do that?*'

Zen put a hand out against the wall to steady himself.

'How should I know? The last I heard you thought they were behind the whole thing!'

'*Now, listen, that's enough! I don't want to hear any more talk of that kind. This is a very serious situation you've got us into. There's no telling what the gang may do now.*'

Zen lowered the receiver and stared at it, as though its expression might help him understand the words it was uttering.

'*Hello? Hello?*'

Bartocci's voice emerged in a comically diminished squawk, like a character in a cartoon film. The white-jacketed waiter scurried into the café carrying a tray on which a pyramid of empty cups and glasses was balanced. 'Four coffees two beers one mineral water!' he called to the barman. With a sigh Zen raised the receiver again.

'Look, dottore, they knew I was there before I got out of the car, before they'd even had a glimpse of me.'

'*I'd like to believe you, Zen. But it's just not credible. If the gang knew you were coming why did they allow the pay-off to continue? Why didn't they just cancel the whole thing?*'

'I don't know. All I know is that my presence was no surprise to them, but they decided to go ahead with the drop anyway. And afterwards they went to the trouble of calling out the Carabinieri to make sure I didn't die of exposure. So there's no reason to suppose that they're going to do anything stupid now.'

'*You and the kidnappers seem to have a perfect understanding, Zen. They know what you're doing, you know what they're thinking. I just hope you're right. For all our sakes.*'

The line went dead.

A young man with a bad case of acne approached and pointed at the phone.

'You finished?'

Yes, he had finished. There was no point now in telling Bartocci about the letter he had received. The young magistrate had embraced orthodoxy with the fervour of a recent convert. He was no longer interested in sensational revelations by anonymous informants.

As Zen turned away he glanced at the calendar hanging beside the phone, and suddenly realized what day it was. After all these years it had finally happened! Come hell or high water, he'd always managed to get his mother a present and to send her some flowers and a card. But this time he had forgotten, and tomorrow was her birthday.

Then he remembered Palottino. Since arriving in Perugia the Neapolitan's days had been spent slumped in the Alfetta in the car park beneath Zen's office window, reading comics and listening to the radio. Yet poor Luigi was not happy. He longed for action, yearned to be trusted with high responsibilities, to undertake prodigious feats requiring a cool head, a stout heart and nerves of steel. Delivering a gift to Zen's mother didn't quite come into that category, but it was better than nothing. Besides, he could pick up some Nazionali from Zen's tame tobacconist as well. So it only remained to find a suitable present.

Forty minutes later he was still empty-handed and beginning to panic. It was a feeling which often came over him in shops, a paralysis of the decision-making faculty. Nevertheless he had to get something, and quickly, before the shops closed for lunch. It was at this point that he found himself face to face with Cinzia Miletti.

'Show me where they hit you!' she cried. 'Oh, is that all? Surely it should be worse. But you must tell me all about it, I can't wait to hear. Come and have coffee, I'm just on my way home, you can help carry this. Gianluigi's away and if that woman thinks I'm going to wait one second longer . . .'

Zen murmured something about needing to find his mother a present, and Cinzia immediately took charge.

'Well now, let's see, it should be something traditional, characteristic, typical of the region. Embroidery, for example, or does she collect ceramics? I know, chocolates! We'll get her a nice presentation pack, that one over there, local pottery.'

Even once Cinzia had bullied one of the assistants into offering Zen a discount, the item she had selected came to about three times what he had reckoned to spend, but he paid up. A few minutes later the Deruta vase containing about half a kilo of assorted chocolates had been placed on the rear seat of the Volvo and he was sitting in the front watching Cinzia tear up the parking ticket which had been tucked under the windscreen wiper.

Cinzia Miletti drove as she talked, in a prolonged spasm character-ized by unpredictable leaps and frenetic darts and swerves, serenely unimpressed by the existence of other traffic. The drive to her house just outside Perugia was littered with miraculously unachieved colli-sions. Cinzia naturally also talked as she drove. If anything she seemed even more voluble than usual, which Zen put down to embarrassment. With her father's fate still undecided, he had caught her cruising the shops as though she hadn't a care in the world. She was therefore at some pains to explain that the only reason she had come into Perugia at all was because of an appointment with Ivy Cook, of all people, who had telephoned her earlier that morning.

'I must see you urgently, she tells me, shall I come out there or could you meet me in town? So out of the kindness of my heart I agreed to come in.'

The kindness of Cinzia Miletti's heart was a quality Zen had con-siderable difficulty in imagining where Ivy Cook was concerned, but he found it easy enough to believe that in her husband's absence Cinzia had been feeling bored and had welcomed any excuse for going into Perugia.

'Did she say what it was about?'

'She didn't want to discuss it on the phone, that's all I know. First of all I had the most awful trouble starting this thing. We should never have got rid of the little Fiat we used to have which started first time every time and if anything did go wrong you could fix it with an elastic band or a bit of string, Gianluigi used to say, although person-ally I'm hopeless with machinery. Anyway, when I got to the café where we were supposed to meet there's no sign of her! Well, you can't get near her flat, they've closed the street, they're turning the whole city centre into a museum, next thing they'll be charging admission and closing in the afternoon. I had to walk all the way round there in these shoes, they look good but believe me they're not meant for walking, and in the end she's not even home. Have you ever heard anything like it? I mean, it's really just the most infuriating thing conceivable, maddening, really.'

They were driving through the suburbs in the valley far below the ancient hill settlement forming the historic core of the city. In the midst of concrete towers and slabs, the office blocks and apartment buildings of the new Perugia, stood an old stone farmhouse, squat and sturdy, with its attendant chicken coops and vegetable garden, the walls dyed green by years of sulphur sprayed on the vines running up to form a pergola. Was this the one Franco Miletti had pointed out to his son Ruggiero as an image of the family? If so, the protective trees had gone, and the brutal buildings which had replaced them would channel the wind more fiercely, not screen it.

They crossed the strip of wasteland underneath the motorway link that came tunnelling and bridging its way through the hilly landscape, and entered a zone of fenced-off lots containing warehouses and sales-rooms, light industrial units and the offices of small businesses. The whole area was no more than ten or fifteen years old, straggling along either side of what had once been a country road and ending messily with the shell of an unfinished building of some indeterminate nature. Shortly afterwards Cinzia turned off along an unpaved minor road. High boundary fences marked the position of villas hiding coyly behind rows of evergreens. Guard dogs hurled themselves against the wire and then chased the car the length of the property, barking frantically, while Cinzia told Zen how she had persuaded Gianluigi to buy a place in the country although he couldn't see the point, but to her nature was not a luxury but something fundamental, a source of sanity and order, did he understand what she meant?

They drew up in front of a pair of steel gates topped with spikes. While Cinzia searched the glove compartment for the remote control unit, Zen noted the heavy-duty fencing with angled strands of barbed wire at the top and electronic sensors at the bottom, and the video camera mounted on a pole just inside the gates, all of it brand-new. The local security equipment retailers had clearly done well out of Ruggiero Miletti's kidnapping. Bartocci should have noticed details like that, thought Zen. People don't go out and spend millions turning their homes into prison camps unless there is real fear in the air.

They were barely inside the front door when the elderly housekeeper appeared and told Cinzia that Signorina Cook had been looking for her.

'What?' shrieked Cinzia. 'Here? But she must be mad!'

'She said you were supposed to meet her here. She waited about ten minutes and then left.'

'What nonsense! Would I have bothered to go all the way into town if we had arranged to meet here?'

The housekeeper held up her hands in a conciliatory gesture and started saying something about a mistake. But Cinzia was not to be mollified.

'Oh no, she did it deliberately! Well, I'll teach her to play tricks on me!'

She strode to the telephone and dialled. After a moment or two she passed the receiver to Zen with an exclamation of disgust.

'Just listen to this!'

'. . . *at the moment*,' Ivy's recorded voice said. '*If you wish to leave a message please speak after the tone.*'

'I'll leave her a message all right, when I see her,' Cinzia exclaimed, slamming the receiver down.

She turned to Zen, her anger apparently gone.

'I'm going to change. Look around, make yourself at home. Margherita, make us some coffee.'

Zen stood there in the elegant and spacious sitting room, listening to the insistent voices of the glass and steel coffee table supporting a spray of glossy magazines, the pouchy leather furniture over which a huge lamp on a curved stainless-steel pole craned like a vulture, the silver plates and the crystal bowls, the discreetly modern canvases, the shelves lined with works of literature, the expensive antiques, the handwoven rugs on the gleaming parquet floor, the baby grand piano with a Mozart sonata lying open on the stand, the fireplace piled high with logs. The view from the picture window showed a carefully landscaped garden, a swimming pool, a tennis court, and a field where a wiry old gardener in baggy peasant clothing and a felt hat was tending his master's vines and olives. Even nature was made to chatter.

'Ah, so you've found our little secret, with your policeman's flair!'

The room had as many entrances and exits as a stage set. Cinzia had appeared almost at his elbow. She picked up a small statuette which he hadn't been aware of before.

'But we didn't buy it from some grave-robber, you know. I mean, that's totally wrong, taking the national heritage for your own selfish private use. But you see, Gianluigi's cousin works in the museum and they've got so much stuff there they literally don't know what to do with it all, it just sits and rots in boxes in the cellar, no one ever sees it. At least here it's cared for, admired, which is what they would have wanted. Wonderful people, very sexual and full of life. I'm sure I have Etruscan blood in me.'

She was wearing a short skirt with a big broad belt, a soft woollen pullover with a deep V-neck and a double string of pearls. She had removed her shoes and stockings.

'This wood is magic,' she exclaimed. 'In winter it's warm and in summer it's cool, can you explain that? I can't, not that I want to. I hate explanations, they ruin everything. But you mustn't peek at my feet like that, poor horrible ugly deformed things.'

She moved restlessly about the room, lifting and rearranging things without any evident purpose.

'Kant,' she remarked, taking a book down from the shelf. 'Have you read Kant? I keep meaning to, but somehow I never get around to it.'

She curled up in the leather sofa that looked as comfortable as a bed and waved Zen into a matching armchair opposite.

'So your husband's away?' he queried.

'In Milan, lucky pig! Very urgent business which he'd been putting off. But there's no point in him being here anyway, as far as I can see. I mean there's nothing we can do, any of us. It's just a question of waiting.'

Despite her alleged impatience to hear about his experiences during the pay-off, she made no attempt to refer to it again, launching instead into a blow-by-blow account of a film she had seen the previous evening, going on to explain that she loved films, really loved them, that the only place to see them properly was the cinema, that her favourite was a wonderful old place in the centre of town called the Minerva, and what a shame it was that no one went to the cinema any more.

The housekeeper brought in the coffee in an ornate silver tray which she deposited on one level of the Scandinavian wall-system. I've been in the family for generations, said the tray, so you can see that they're not just a bunch of jumped-up farmers like so many around these days. Quite so, commented the wall-system, but despite their solid roots these are modern progressive people with a truly cosmopolitan outlook. Oh, shut up, Zen thought. Just shut up.

'Is your husband's trip to Milan connected with this Japanese deal I've been hearing about?' he asked.

Cinzia's air of boredom deepened significantly.

'He never discusses business with me.'

And you would do well to follow his example, her eyes added, because while I'm not very good at business there are other things that I am good at, very good indeed.

A lanky girl with a moody look walked in, strolled self-consciously over to the table and took a tangerine from a bowl.

'Fetch me my cigarettes, will you, Loredana darling?' Cinzia asked her.

'Fetch them yourself. You could use the exercise.'

Cinzia shot Zen a dazzling smile.

'Do forgive her manners. It's a difficult age, of course. She'll start menstruating soon.'

The girl threw the cigarettes at her mother.

'Much better talk openly about it!' Cinzia continued calmly. 'There's no need for us women to be ashamed of our bodies any more.'

'It's not your fucking body,' the girl shouted as she ran upstairs.

'She's a crazy mixed-up kid,' exclaimed Cinzia, as though this was one of her daughter's main virtues. 'At the moment she keeps threatening to become a nun, if you please. My other one's about somewhere too, little Sergio. He's a darling! Too much so, in fact. I'm reading him the Greek myths at bedtime and I just hope when we get to Oedipus the penny will drop. It's perfectly normal at that age, of course. At least I haven't taught him how to masturbate, like some mothers. Cigarette?'

As she leaned forward to offer them her pullover bellied out and he caught a glimpse of her breasts, almost adolescent in size, but with large and prominent nipples.

'I've always tried to be an understanding parent,' she continued. 'I treat my kids as friends and equals.'

'Is that how your parents treated you?'

'My mother's dead!' she replied vaguely.

'What about your father? Did he treat you as an equal?'

Cinzia laughed almost hysterically.

'Well, it depends what you mean. I suppose he does his best. But take the business of Daniele's arrest, for instance. That was typical.

For years father had been nagging away at him to take some interest and prove he had the Miletti flair, yet as soon as he tried to show a bit of initiative everyone got on their high horse about it, father especially, calling him a worthless junkie and I don't know what else besides. It was so unfair, I thought. I mean, I suppose what the others were doing was illegal, but it's not as if they were forcing anyone to take the stuff. If they hadn't sold it someone else would have. And as far as Daniele was concerned it was just a business arrangement, nothing else. He never actually took the stuff or got his hands dirty in any way.'

She rearranged herself in another pose, her legs curled under her like a cat. She was quite calm again now.

'As it was, the poor kid ended up losing everything. Not just the money he'd invested but his allowance from father as well. Lulu's been helping him out, but it's still been very hard on him. Now I don't call that being very understanding, do you? You'd think people would be more tolerant with their own family.'

Zen gulped down the rest of his coffee and announced that he had to be going.

'Already?' Cinzia queried with a pout. 'Why not stay to lunch? Margherita's a wonderful cook.'

Her disappointment appeared genuine, but he forced himself to phone Palottino. 'The family are absolutely incensed', Bartocci had told him. If Zen had survived more or less intact all this time it was thanks to the instinct that was telling him to leave now.

'You still haven't told me about your adventure,' Cinzia reminded him as they waited for Palottino to arrive. 'It must have been terrifying. I think you're very brave. To sit in a car with that Cook woman for however many hours it was, I simply couldn't do it! Did you talk a lot? Did she talk about me? She must have done. What did she say?'

'We didn't talk that much.'

'Oh come on, I don't believe that! I know the woman. What did she say? Whatever it was I've heard worse. Tell me. What did she say about me?'

He looked away, out of the window, then back at Cinzia.

'She said you were terribly unhappy,' he replied.

Her features abruptly slackened all over, making her look years older.

'Unhappy?'

It was a shriek.

'She's crazy! I've suspected it for a long time, but now it's absolutely clear! Absolutely and totally clear, plain and evident for everyone to see.'

She gripped Zen's arm tightly.

'I ask you, do I look unhappy? Do I seem unhappy? Have I got the slightest reason in the world to be unhappy? Look at this house! Look at my husband and my children, look at my whole life. Then look at her! What has she got? Unhappy? What a joke!'

She walked away a little distance, then came back to him.

'The truth is that she envies me,' she went on more calmly. 'She envies all of us, she's riddled with envy! That's the real problem. It's not me who's unhappy, it's her! She's projecting her problems on to me. I've read about it, it's a well-known thing that mad people do.'

She shook her head and tried to smile.

'I'm a little tense at the moment, with Gianluigi away and still no word about father.'

'I'm sure he'll be released very soon now,' Zen said as reassuringly as he knew how.

But an oddly vacant look had come over Cinzia's features. Deafened by thoughts he couldn't begin to guess at, she hadn't even heard him.

Back at the Questura Zen tried to put Cinzia Miletti out of his mind. He felt that a winning hand had been dealt him and that he had played it badly, perhaps even from a professional point of view. In any case, it was too late now.

He stuck his head round the door to the inspectors' room.

'Anyone know an officer called Baldoni?'

Geraci looked up.

'Baldoni? He's in Drugs.'

'Three five one,' Chiodini chimed in without raising his eyes from his newspaper.

'Don't be stupid,' Lucaroni told him. 'This is three five one.'

Chiodini stuck one fat finger thoughtfully up his right nostril.

'Used to be three five one,' he pronounced at last.

Lucaroni consulted the directory.

'He's in four two five,' he said. 'Do you want me to . . .?'

'That's all right,' Zen replied. 'I'll do it myself.'

Baldoni was a pudgy, balding man wearing a blue blazer with five silver buttons, a canary-yellow pullover and a red tie. He was picking his teeth with a match while someone on the phone talked his ear off. When he hung up Zen handed him the letter.

'Fucking union,' he frowned. 'All they ever do is ask for money. The reason I joined was I thought they were going to get more money for me, not take it away.'

'I'm on the Miletti kidnapping,' Zen began.

Baldoni looked at him more warily.

'Rather you than me.'

'I understand that Daniele Miletti got himself into some trouble with your section some time ago.'

Baldoni laughed briefly.

'Got himself into it and got himself out of it.'

He tried to sit casually on the edge of his desk, farted loudly and stood up again.

'You know about the University for Foreigners?' he demanded. His tone was suspicious and aggressive, as though the institution in question was missing and Zen was suspected of having stolen it.

'I've heard of it.'

'Forget what you've heard. I know what you've heard. You've heard about this symbol of the brotherhood of man set in welcoming Perugia with its ancient traditions of hospitality, where every year bright-eyed, bushy-tailed youngsters come from the four corners of the world to study Italian culture and promote peace and international understanding.'

He looked intently at Zen.

'You're not from round here, are you?'

Zen shook his head.

'In that case I can tell you that in my humble opinion this place is the meanest, tightest little arsehole in the entire fucking country. International understanding my bum! Christ, the people in this dump are so small-minded they treat the folk from the village down the hill as a bunch of aliens. So why do they put up with the real foreigners? For one very simple reason, my friend. It's spelt m,o,n,e,y.'

'And Daniele?' Zen prompted.

'Don't worry, I'm getting there. Now you also have to realize that the foreigners aren't like the ones you've heard about either. They used to come down from the North – German, Swiss, English, American. Girls, mostly. They came to read Dante, drink wine, sit in the sun and get laid. But those days are long gone. Now the Arabs have moved in, because you-know-who in Rome has done a deal for oil rights, including a fat kickback for you-know-who, naturally. Meanwhile you and I get paid worse than his housekeeper and the fucking union writes to ask *me* to send *them* money!

'So, anyway, all these Arabs start rolling up to learn engineering and dentistry and Christ knows what. Unfortunately the professors object to giving lessons in Arabic, so suddenly we've got hundreds of thousands of students who need to learn Italian. And where do they go? To the University for Foreigners, of course, right here in lovely medieval Perugia. Only these foreigners are a bit different from what we've been used to. Masculine like they don't make them any more, don't give a fuck about Dante, don't touch alcohol, find it cold here after their own country and are more interested in praying and politics than getting laid. Bright eyes and bushy tails are at a distinct premium among this bunch, and as for the brotherhood of man, their idea of that is that if someone disagrees with you, you kill him. Remember, Ali Agca, the man who shot the Pope? He was here. Remember the Palestinian commando that murdered half the Israeli athletes at the Munich games? They trained at a farmhouse in the hills just outside Perugia. The Jihad Islamica suicide squads, the pro-Khomeini mob, the anti-Khomeini mob, KGB spies, Bulgarian hit-men, you name it, it's been here. The Political Branch have installed a hot line direct to the Ministry's central computer in Rome and even so they can't keep up. At one time there were two and half thousand Iranians alone in town. Their consul in Rome came up on an official visit last year and there was nearly a diplomatic incident when he got thrown out of the new university canteen he'd come to inspect. Turned out the last time the staff had seen him he was a student here and he'd made such an arsehole of himself they'd sworn they'd never let him back in!

'All right, so that's the new Perugia, crossroads of international terrorism. A big headache for the Politicos upstairs but what's it got to do with yours truly, you're no doubt wondering, or with Daniele Miletti for that matter? Well, terrorists need cash. The official ones get it from the government back home, the rest have to earn it. And there's no quicker way to make money than drugs, particularly if you happen to come from a country where the stuff is sold like artichokes. So we start to take an interest, and among other things we're passed the names of a couple of Iranians who make frequent trips back home by train. That's one hell of a way to travel to Iran, unless of course you want to avoid the screening procedures at the airports. The next time through we have them picked up and lo and behold they've got a suitcase full of heroin. So we get to work on them and forty-eight hours later we have the whole ring, including one Gerhard Mayer, twenty-nine, from West Berlin, their linkman into the local drug community. Which is where everything starts to fuck up, because the moment we turn our attention to Herr Mayer he tells us that the money he used to pay the Iranians was put up by the son of a certain well-known local citizen.'

'Daniele Miletti.'

'You know the feeling? One minute I had a nice clean case bust wide open, stiff sentences all round and bonus promotion points for yours truly. The moment that fucking kraut mentioned Miletti I knew I could kiss that sweet dream goodbye. We went through the motions and pulled him in, of course, but by the time the magistrate spoke to him Mayer had changed his mind. He'd never met Daniele Miletti, never seen him, never heard of him. The kid was back home in time for lunch.'

'And Mayer's statement?' Zen queried.

'Extorted under duress. Duress my bum! Mayer couldn't fucking *wait* to shop his rich young pal.'

'What happened to Mayer?'

'He hopped on the first plane back to Germany.'

Zen gazed at him, frowning.

'They let him out? With a drug trafficking charge hanging over him?'

Baldoni nodded.

'Like I say, where the Milettis are concerned, rather you than me, my friend. Rather you than me.'

By the evening Zen was beginning to feel like a hostage himself. He had spent the entire afternoon in his office, pacing from the desk to the window, from the window to door and back to the desk again. It was now over forty hours since the money had been handed over, but there had been no word of Ruggiero Miletti's release. Despite the fact that he was powerless to influence events in any way, Zen felt bound to remain on watch, like the captain of a ship. But in the end he could stand it no longer and went out for a walk.

The evening was warm and calm, but the side-streets through which he wandered at random were almost deserted. Very occasionally his path crossed that of a couple walking home or a group of a young friends going up to the centre, and then the brief appraising glances they gave him left Zen feeling obscurely ill at ease, underlining as they did his lack of purpose or direction. Thoughts flitted to and fro in his brain like swallows: phrases from Ruggiero Miletti's letter, an insinuation of Antonio Crepi's, something Ivy had said in the car, what Valesio's widow had told him, Luciano Bartocci's brisk new manner, Italo Baldoni's story, Cinzia Miletti's breasts . . .

He felt simultaneously starved and stuffed, deafened and denied. It was the nature of the place, he thought, perched up there on its remote peak, its back turned to the world, all the more obsessed with its petty intrigues and scandals because it knew them to be of no interest whatever to anyone else. Nothing he had been told from the very first moment he had arrived in Perugia amounted to any more than salacious gossip, casual slanders, ill-informed rumours of no real value which elsewhere would never have reached his ears. But folk here were eager to let you into their neighbour's secrets, particularly if they thought it might distract your attention from their own. 'Mayer couldn't fucking *wait* to shop his rich young pal.' Yes, that was the style of the place. It was all a fuss about nothing, another example of the national genius for weaving intricate variations around the simplest event. Zen had always derived much amusement from Ellen's simple-minded approach to current affairs. Despite her intelligence, she could be quite amazingly naive and literal in her judgements. She seemed to believe that the truth was great and would prevail, so why waste time spinning a lot of fancy theories? Whereas Zen knew that the truth prevailed, if at all, only after so much time had passed that it had become meaningless, like a senile prisoner who can safely be released, his significance forgotten, his friends dead, a babbling idiot.

But in the present case it was time to take a stand, to declare once and for all that on this occasion at least the truth was as obvious and evident as it appeared to be. The crimes which had been committed were manifestly the work of hardened professionals who had no more to do with the incestuous dramas of this city than Zen himself. Any suggestion to the contrary was simply an excuse for the locals to feel self-important and settle a few scores with their neighbours.

Inevitably, his steps led him in the end to the Corso, where the evening promenade was in progress. People paraded up and down, displaying their furs and finery, hailing their friends, seeing and being seen, streaming back and forth continually like swimmers in a pool. The stars of either sex clustered in twos or threes, massing their power, or strode out alone, shining soloists, while the less attractive gathered for protection in groups outside the offices of some religious or political organization. Part of the street was thronged with teen-agers, and more were arriving every instant on their mopeds. The males dominated, bold gangling youths in brightly coloured designer anoraks and jeans turned up to reveal their American-style chunky leather boots. They threw their weight about with boisterous nonchalance while the girls, in frilly lace collars like doilies, tartan skirts and coloured tights, looked on admiringly. One of the most prominent of them was a tall youth with the extravagant gestures and loud voice of an actor who knows he's going down well. Only at the last moment, when he'd been recognized in turn, did Zen realize that it was Daniele Miletti.

It was almost predictable. The young trendies of the soft right, like their Fascist counterparts of half a century earlier, bragged about not giving a damn. Nothing would do more to boost Daniele's status than to be seen showing off on the Corso while his father's life still hung in the balance.

'A very good evening to you, dottore!' the boy called out in a bad parody of a Venetian accent. 'So sorry to hear about your accident. Do try and take more care in future!'

He turned to explain the joke to his companions, who all laughed loudly.

'Don't you dare beat me up, you nasty nasty man, I'm a police-man!' one of them shrieked in a mocking falsettto.

Zen pushed on, understanding how Italo Baldoni must have felt when the young Miletti slipped through his fingers. Increasingly it seemed to him that there were people who needed to spend a few hours locked in a room with the likes of Chiodini. The trouble with the system was that they were the ones who never did. But he would never admit to such a thought, and in fact felt guilty for even thinking it. Then he felt resentful for being made to feel guilty, so that by the time he got back to the Questura all the benefits of his walk had been cancelled out.

He'd had an irrational feeling that something must have happened in his absence, simply because he hadn't been there, but he was wrong. He was back where he'd started, staring at the wall with nothing to do but wait. As his eyes fell on the crucifix he realized that he'd always loathed it, and in a small gesture of defiance he lifted it off its hook and set it down on top of the filing cabinet. Then he remembered the copy of Ruggiero's letter, and realized that there was something he could do after all.

'*Seven double eight one eight.*'

'Good evening. This is Aurelio Zen. Am I disturbing you?'

'*No, no. Not at all. Well, not really . . .*'

Ivy sounded ill at ease. Had she already guessed why he was calling?

'I wanted to contact you this morning, but . . .'

'*I was out. I'd arranged to meet someone.*'

'Yes, I know. I met Cinzia Miletti in town. She'd been waiting for you.'

'*Well, I'd been waiting for her, too! We'd arranged to meet at her house.*'

'She told me that you phoned her and asked for a meeting in town.'

'*I really can't imagine why she should have said that, Commissioner. It's exactly the opposite of what happened. She phoned me and asked me to come straight over. She didn't say why, but obviously in my position . . .*'

It occurred to Zen that while they were talking any incoming call announcing Ruggiero's release would be blocked.

'Never mind about that,' he said briskly. 'There's something I want to discuss with you. It's about a letter I've received.'

'*A letter? What sort of letter?*'

'I'd rather not discuss it on the phone. Do you think you could drop into my office? It won't take long.'

'*Well, it's a bit difficult. It's a question of the family, you see. I'm not sure they'd approve, just at present.*'

They'd approve still less if they knew what it was about, thought Zen.

'Perhaps later on, once this is all over.'

'Very well. I'll contact you later then.'

He hung up, his hand hovering hopefully above the receiver. But the phone remained sullenly silent.

His suspicions were confirmed. The uncharacteristic fuss and fluster in Ivy's manner was surely a proof that she knew only too well which letter he was talking about and was in mortal dread of the family finding out.

He took out the letter and scanned the final lines again. That mistake was curious: '. . . well-worn consecutively numbered notes . . .' For a moment it had made him inclined to doubt the authenticity of the whole thing. But it was only a detail, and it didn't alter the fact that no one but Ivy could have done it. She must have taken the letter straight to a photocopy shop after collecting it from the skip and then posted the copy to Zen before returning to the house, calculating that if the copy came to light each of the Milettis would equally be under suspicion. But that calculation had gone up in smoke with the original letter, and since then she must have bitterly regretted her rashness. Why had she taken such a risk? Was it because she knew the Miletti family only too well, and was determined that this time at least everything should not be conveniently hushed up? Had sending Zen the letter been her humble way of serving the great principle upon which Luciano Bartocci had now apparently turned his back, of not letting the bastards get away with it? At all events, she had committed no crime, so there was no reason for him to pursue the matter any further.

He sat there until his eyelids began to droop, then phoned the switchboard and told them that he would be at his hotel. There was no point in continuing his lonely vigil.

But why couldn't he rid himself of the eerie sensation that it had *already happened*, that everyone knew except him, that he was being deliberately kept in the dark?

SEVEN

He was in bed, in the room in Venice where he had spent his child-hood, and he was still that child. A figure moved slowly through the uncertain light towards him, as faceless and monumental as Death in an old engraving. But he wasn't frightened, because he knew that it was all just a joke, a little comedy of the kind fathers like to play with their sons.

He'd always known his father would come back. Not that he'd ever admitted it before, even to himself. But nothing and no one could ever really convince him that a world where fathers just disap-peared one day and never returned could be anything other than a pitiful sham, a transparent hoax. He had never been taken in, not really, not inside, but he'd known moments of doubt, so his delight and relief were unbounded now he found that his instincts had been right all along! For here his father was, sitting down beside him, hugging and kissing him, taking his hand again and laughing at the silly terrors his little game had aroused in his son.

The phone beside his bed started to ring. It was the duty officer on the intercept desk at the law courts.

'We've just picked up a message on the Miletti family line, dottore. It was from the kidnappers. They've released Signor Miletti.'

Thank God, Zen thought with obscure fervour. Thank God.

'Have you informed Dottor Bartocci?'

'Yes. The pick-up arrangements are to be put into effect immediately.'

'Where has Signor Miletti been released?'

'If you've got a pen I'll read the directions as they gave them to the family.'

Zen scribbled the instructions on the back of an envelope. They were to take the road to Foligno, turn right towards Cannara just beyond Santa Maria degli Angeli and drive until they saw a tele-graph pole with a yellow mark. Here they were to turn left, then take the second right and go about a kilometre to a building site where Ruggiero Miletti was waiting, unable to move because of his bad leg. It had been this problem which had led to the complex arrangements for picking up Ruggiero on his release. Normally kidnap victims are simply turned loose in the middle of nowhere and left to find their own way to the nearest house or main road. But since Miletti was immobilized it had been agreed that he would be fetched by a group consisting of Pietro Miletti escorted by Zen and Palottino in the Alfetta, with an ambulance in attendance in case Ruggiero required immediate attention. After the events of Saturday night and Bartocci's angry phone call the previous day, Zen half expected to be rebuffed when he rang the Milettis. But Pietro, although cool, made no attempt to change the arrangements. Now the family's fears had been proved groundless, the bungled pay-off could be dismissed as just another example of clumsy incompetence on the part of the police, the latest in a long list of blunders.

Twenty minutes later the convoy set out. It was brilliantly sunny, as though summer had leapt forward a few months. People were moving more slowly and nonchalantly, without the pretext of a destination or purpose. They glanced curiously at the line of official vehicles which drove along the boulevard running along the lower ridges of the city, through a gateway and down in a series of long, lazy curves, dropping over two hundred metres to the valley floor. Shortly after passing the enormous domed basilica of Santa Maria degli Angeli Palottino swerved across a patch of loose gravel into a minor road. The land was dead flat, divided into large ploughed fields almost devoid of trees. Modern brick and concrete duplexes squatted here and there along the road, each with a few rows of vines trained along wires suspended from concrete posts behind them. This would all have been uninhabited malarial marshland until the post-war boom made it worth draining. The road ran straight ahead, the telegraph poles passing at regular intervals to the right.

The yellow splash of paint showed up hundreds of metres away in the bright sunshine. A farm track led off to the left opposite, flanked by deep drainage ditches. Speeds dropped now and the vehicles closed up. The fields appeared to have been abandoned, the broken stalks of the crop left to rot in a vast expanse of furrowed mud which the recent rains had reduced to a sticky mess. Could there really be a building site in the middle of this swamp rapidly reverting to nature after a brief and unsuccessful flirtation with civilization, Zen wondered? There had always been a possibility that the telephone call had been a hoax and this seemed to be getting more likely all the time.

The bleak landscape made Zen think back to his dream, to his *own* father's fate. When the Germans invaded the Soviet Union in 1941, Mussolini thought the war would be over in a matter of weeks, and so that he could claim a share of the spoils for Italy he offered to send troops to the Russian front. The Germans had no illusions about the military effectiveness of their principal ally, and at first they agreed to accept only a few divisions of the Alpini, the specialist mountain troops who could hold their own with any in Europe. But that was not enough to give Mussolini the bargaining leverage he wanted. He insisted on sending more, and so two hundred and thirty thousand Italians were packed into trains and sent off to Russia, Zen's father among them. But the war was not over in a matter of weeks, and the Italian conscripts had neither the training nor the equipment to fight a winter campaign in Russia. They suffered ninety thousand casualties. Sixty-six thousand more made the weary trek home again. As for the remaining seventy-five thousand, nothing more was ever heard of them. They simply disappeared without trace. The Soviet authorities had no reason to take any interest in the fate of a handful of foreign invaders when over twenty million of their own people had been killed, while as for the Italians, it had suddenly become clear that they had in fact been anti-Fascists to a man all along and could hardly be expected to sympathize with the relatives of those few fanatics who had been rash enough to fight for the despised Duce. In any case, the whole country was in ruins and there were more urgent matters to attend to.

'There it is!' Palottino burst out.

From a distance it resembled some piece of modern sculpture: disjointed planes, random angles, a lot of holes. It was only as they drew nearer that he began to make out that it was the concrete skeleton of an unfinished three-storey duplex, its half-built walls, pillars and floors rising out of a sea of mud. On each side a wide staircase led up in six zigzag sections, breaking off abruptly on an open landing about twenty metres above the ground.

They parked a short distance away. Zen got out, jumped over the ditch running alongside the track and began to work his way along the edge of the field towards the back of the concrete structure, his shoes rapidly clogging up with mud. The building site was surrounded by a token fence consisting of two slack strands of barbed wire. Pietro Miletti was slowly making his way after him.

On the south side of the structure the concrete was cleaner than to the north, where it was discoloured with moss. Here the stains were reddish-brown, from the twisted-off ends of the rusty reinforcing wire. It felt warm and sheltered. Plants had already seeded in crevices around the foundations, preparing to take over the instant man's will failed. A yellow butterfly loped by with its strange broken flight, like an early film.

Zen looked round at the floor of unfinished concrete littered with cement bags, lengths of wire, nails and lumps of wood, a lone glove. The upper storeys had not yet been floored and through the concrete joists and beams above the sky was visible. There was no sign that anyone had been there for months.

'Papa!'

Pietro Miletti appeared, his elegant shoes and trousers bespattered with mud.

Zen scraped some of the mud off his shoes on the bottom step of the staircase.

'I'm afraid it was a hoax.'

'But why should they do that? What have they got to gain?'

Pietro sounded indignant, as though the kidnappers had broken the rules of a game and ought to be penalized.

'Perhaps it wasn't really the gang who phoned you.'

'It was them, all right. Do you think I don't know his damned voice by now? Besides, who else would it be?'

'How should I know?' Zen snapped back, his tension finding an issue. 'Someone who hates your guts. There must be plenty of them around.'

He turned away towards the outside of the building, veering to the right to complete his circuit of the structure. In the distance someone sounded a horn several times. The view ahead was obscured by a section of partially completed walling at the east end, but when he reached the corner Zen found that the only unpredictable feature of the landscape was a river which cut across the track about a hundred metres further on. Once, no doubt, there would have been a bridge, since swept away by floods or war. Or perhaps it had never existed. It was hard to say whether the track continued on the other side or not.

It was only when he turned to the more immediate problem of finding a way through the waste of mud that Zen noticed the figure lying slumped against the wall. He just had time to turn, plant one hand on Pietro Miletti's chest and push him back, indignantly protesting.

The floor was made up of dark red hexagonal tiles touching at their points, separated by triangles of a deep chestnut colour. Another way of looking at it was that the basic form was a large lozenge consisting of a red hexagonal core surrounded by six brown triangular tips, or again, diagonal strips of red hexagons kept in place by pairs of triangular brown wedges. The strips ran in both directions, creating a number of crosses. It should have been possible, theoretically, to work out how many there were. But it would have taken more than just time and ingenuity. You would have needed something else, some understanding of the principles involved, access to formulae and equations, a head for figures. Something he hadn't got, at any rate. As it was, an irrelevant image kept popping up in the corner of his eye, dragging his attention away: the image of an old man lying slumped in the mud against a wall of concrete blocks, turned away, as though death were an act as shameful as intercourse or defecation, which he had sought to conceal as far as possible, even in the bleakly exposed place where it had come to him.

Zen forced his attention back to the floor. But now a new pattern emerged as the red and brown shapes blocked together to form overlapping triangles all pointing across the room at the double doors opposite. These doors were now firmly closed, but they had opened several times since Zen's arrival, admitting a succession of visitors who had forced their way through the mass of bodies and expectant faces in the corridor outside, sweltering under television lights and waving microphones in front of anyone who appeared.

It was six o'clock in the evening, four hours since the Deputy Public Prosecutor had summoned Zen to his office in the law courts. When he arrived he had been told to wait, and he had been waiting ever since. He was being put in his place, softened up for what was to come. And what was that? 'When they found a policeman at the pay-off they must have panicked,' Major Volpi had remarked to Di Leonardo when they arrived together at the scene in a Carabinieri helicopter. Yes, the death of Ruggiero Miletti was Zen's fault. He was completely innocent, but it was his fault. Even the tiles concurred, for now the arrows had all flipped over and were pointing at him, pointing out the guilty party, the incompetent official, the unworthy son. The pain that tugged at the muscles of his stomach and chest was so intimately hurtful that he knew it was nothing but useless unspent emotion. What he needed was to break down and howl like a child, and it was the effort not to do so that was tearing at him. It was all his fault, his fault, his fault. He had never known the man, but it was his fault. He was condemned by an image which had haunted him for over thirty years: a poor defenceless body lying curled up in a vast flat dismal landscape, a father abandoned to his lonely fate. He must be guilty. There could be no excuse for such a death.

It was almost a relief when the door opposite suddenly opened and Ettore Di Leonardo appeared, immaculate as ever in a dark suit and sober tie.

'This way!'

The Public Prosecutor called him like a dog as he strode towards the door behind which a continuous threatening murmur could be heard. Zen obediently rose and followed, wondering as a dog per- haps does at his stupidity in not understanding why they were going that way, where their enemies lay in wait.

The gentlemen of the press had had a fairly lean time of it so far. Di Leonardo's personal secretary had issued a statement shortly after midday, a masterpiece of prolixity that took about five minutes to say that Ruggiero Miletti had been found dead and that another state- ment would be issued in due course. Since then anyone who had been unwise enough to venture along the corridor had been pounced upon and picked clean. Magistrates, lawyers, various clerks, a court reporter, a telephone repair man, and even a number of ordinary human beings untouched by the grace of public office had been accosted, to no avail. So when the Deputy Public Prosecutor himself suddenly appeared in person the assembled newshounds reacted like a gaggle of novices witnessing an apparition of the Virgin Mary.

Appropriately enough Di Leonardo's first gesture, a hand raised to still the clamour, looked not unlike a blessing. When complete silence had fallen he then produced a sheet of paper from his pocket, folded it back on itself to remove the crease, smoothed it out a number of times and then read a statement to the effect that inquiries were proceeding, steps being taken, fruitful avenues opening up and con- crete results expected within a short space of time. Having done so he folded the sheet of paper again, replaced it in his pocket and made to leave.

The reporters protested vociferously and blocked his path. Di Leonardo looked flabbergasted, as though never before in his experience had the media failed to be satisfied by the reading of a prepared statement. But questions continued to be hurled at him from every side, and eventually, as an extraordinary mark of favour, he consented to answer one or two of them.

The first came from a man in the front row, a crumpled, resilient-looking individual with the look of someone who has been dropped on his head from a great height at some stage in his life.

'Is it true that the magistrate investigating the Miletti case is to be replaced?'

Di Leonardo glared back in frigid indignation.

'Certainly not! Dottor Bartocci is and will remain in charge of the investigation into the kidnapping of Ruggiero Miletti.'

'And into his murder?' called a younger reporter on the fringes of the group.

'That is another and quite separate development, whose importance and urgency I need hardly stress. In addition to the kidnapping case, Dottor Bartocci is already handling the murder of Avvocato Valesio. My wish, the wish of all of us, is simply that we may as quickly as possible get to the bottom of the shocking and cold-blooded crime which has stunned and appalled the entire country, and arrest and punish those responsible. In order to avoid placing an impossible burden on the shoulders of my young colleague, it has been decided that the investigation of the events whose tragic outcome was discovered this morning will be directed by Dottor Rosella Foria.'

'But the murder of Signor Miletti is evidently linked to the other two cases,' pointed out a well-known interviewer with a television news crew. 'Why is the same magistrate not investigating all three crimes?'

Di Leonardo smiled wearily and shook his head.

'You reporters may spin whatever theories you choose. Our task is to weigh the evidence objectively and impartially. At the present juncture there is no evidence to suggest that this crime is necessarily linked to those you have mentioned, or indeed to any others.'

There was a flurry of protest, which Di Leonardo once again stilled with a gesture of benediction.

'But it is too soon to pronounce on these matters with any certainty,' he went on smoothly. 'Should any such evidence come to light in the future we will of course be prepared to review the situation.'

'You mean Bartocci may lose the other two cases as well?' asked the crumpled man. There was a ripple of laughter.

A tall woman with the chic, efficient look that spells Milan held up her notebook, and Di Leonardo immediately nodded encouragingly at her. It's a fix, thought Zen, and he edged back against the wall. Mesmerized by the Public Prosecutor's performance, no one had yet noticed him, but he had a nasty feeling that this was about to change.

'The Miletti family have made a statement in which they lay the blame for the murder squarely on the shoulders of the police,' the woman began. 'They have named a Commissioner Zen, whom they claim demanded to be present when the ransom money was paid, threatening to wreck the pay-off by a show of force if they did not comply. They further assert that in the course of the pay-off Commissioner Zen's identity was revealed and that the gang were so incensed that they assaulted him. They conclude that the death of their father was a direct result of the kidnappers' instructions having been disobeyed, and demand that this official be subjected to the appropriate disciplinary procedures. Have you any comment to make?'

Di Leonardo smiled again. It was a beautiful smile, brimful of wisdom, understanding and compassion.

'I don't think I need remind anyone of the tragic blow which the Miletti family, and indeed the whole of Perugia, has suffered today. Far be it from me to criticize comments made in the heat of the moment, which should be understood for what they are, cries of unendurable suffering, a passionate outburst of all-too-comprehensible anguish. I am sure I speak for all of us here when I say that our thoughts are with the Miletti family in this ordeal.'

Di Leonardo paused for a moment, seemingly overcome by emotion. Then he looked up, brisk and businesslike again.

'Nevertheless the fact remains that disciplinary action against officials who may have exceeded their duties or wilfully abused the position of responsibility with which they have been entrusted is a purely internal matter which will be carried out, should the situation warrant it, by the appropriate authorities at the appropriate time. The views and wishes of private individuals, however comprehensible, cannot be permitted to influence whatever decision may eventually be arrived at.'

'Do you accept the family's account of the events surrounding the pay-off?' another reporter demanded.

'I have no further comment to make.'

'But this Zen is still in charge of the case?'

Di Leonardo shook his finger as though admonishing a backward pupil.

'As I have already explained, Dottor Foria is directing the investigation.'

The crumpled reporter who had started the questioning now sighed theatrically and rubbed his forehead.

'Let's see, have I got this right? As far as the police are concerned it's all one case and the same officer remains in charge, but when it comes to the judiciary it's a completely unrelated development and a new magistrate has been appointed.'

'If you study the answers I have given I think you will find that they are very clear,' Di Leonardo returned. 'Should you have any further questions, I suggest you put them to Commissioner Zen himself.'

The Public Prosecutor pointed Zen out with one finger, and as everyone turned to look he slipped through the suddenly passive ranks to the safety of his office, closing the door firmly behind him. Immediately all hell broke loose.

'What's your reaction, dottore?'

'How did it feel finding Miletti's body?'

'Do you accept responsibility for his death?'

'A spokesman for the family has described your handling of the case as a quote disgraceful and disastrous example of official interventionism unquote. Would you care to comment?'

'Isn't it true that during the Moro affair you were transferred from the active list of the Rome Questura to a desk job in the Ministry following a disciplinary inquiry? Would you describe today's events as a further setback to your career?'

As the lights glared, the cameras whirred and the microphones thrust and jabbed, Zen finally understood why he had been summoned to the law courts.

'If you study the answers the Deputy Public Prosecutor has given, I think you will find that they are very clear,' he told them. 'I have nothing further to add.'

The reporters didn't give up so easily, of course. But stolid stone-walling makes for poor copy and dull viewing, and eventually they let him go, although even then a few of the younger and hungrier among them followed him down the wide staircase and out into Piazza Matteotti, hoping for a belated indiscretion.

It was dusk, and the evening was as still and airless as the previous one when, impatient for news, Zen had gone out for a stroll. It was strange now, walking through the same streets, to know that by then it had already happened. But even on a cursory examination the doctor had been in no doubt.

'Rigor mortis is complete but there's no sign of it passing off. Body temperature almost down to the ambient level. He's been dead at least eighteen hours, more likely twenty-four.'

Zen had hardly heard him at the time, shocked by the sight of the man he had been summoned to Perugia to save lying naked on a plastic sheet with a thermometer sticking out of his anus. Ruggiero Miletti had been killed the day before, on Monday morning, and yet the gang had waited until this morning to alert the family with a cruel message of hope! In all his experience Zen could remember nothing like it. Kidnappers could be violent, but in the easy, unashamed manner of men to whom violence was natural and legit-imate. If they had killed their victim to teach the Milettis a lesson they would have said so, even bragged about it. But this crime, and above all the manner in which it was mockingly announced, had a twisted sophistication, a kink in the logic which Zen would have said was quite alien to a gang of Calabrian shepherds.

But he impatiently dismissed this line of thought. Little enough was left him now, but at least his dignity remained, though no one but himself could see it. If he were to start clutching at straws, hoping against hope for a way out, then even that would be lost.

Back in his office he reached for the phone and dialled his home number. As usual, Maria Grazia answered and then yelled to his mother to pick up the extension phone by her chair, in the deep underwater gloom of the living room. The connection was especially good, almost as if they were face to face, and Zen found himself resentful that he should be deprived of the usual screen of inter-ference on an occasion when he could find nothing to say.

'Happy birthday, mamma. Did you like the present?'

'Is this going to take long? Crissie's having her baby and I don't want to miss that. Wayne will be livid when he hears. And that half-brother of hers, do you know what he's done? Sold the property over their heads! That couldn't happen to us, could it?'

'No, mamma.'

'Why not?'

Was she having a sly laugh at his expense, talking nonsense and then cornering him with a sudden question?

'Is it because you're in the police?'

'Yes, that's it, mamma. They wouldn't dare do anything like that. You see, there are some advantages after all.'

'What?'

'To being in the police! You're always telling me that I should have got a job on the railways. Anyway, if you're still watching when the news comes on you might see me. I'm . . .'

'Oh, I haven't time to watch the news. There's the dolphins on Six right afterwards. They've kidnapped them, the bastards.'

'Who, the dolphins?'

'Anyway, if you were on the railways we'd get free tickets wherever we wanted to go.'

'I already get free travel, mamma.'

'I don't!'

'But you never even leave the apartment any more!'

'That's what I'm saying. If you had a nice job on the railways maybe I could get out and about a bit.'

There was a knock, the door opened and Luciano Bartocci appeared. 'May I?'

After a moment's hesitation Zen waved him forward.

'Look, I've got to go,' he said into the phone. 'Happy birthday. See you soon.'

He hung up.

'Sorry if I disturbed you,' Bartocci went on. 'I was just passing, and I thought I'd . . .'

He took off the heavy overcoat he was wearing and laid it across the top of the filing cabinet.

'I won't stay long.'

The smile trembling to be born at the corner of his mouth was even more active than usual.

'The thing is, you see, I realize that I've been rather stupid, and rather selfish, and I'd like to apologize.'

Zen stood staring at the younger man in considerable embarrassment. He had no idea how to deal with the situation. A judge apologizing to a policeman! What were we coming to?

'I asked you to collaborate unofficially,' Bartocci went on. 'That was irresponsible. You could have refused, of course, but it was a choice I shouldn't have forced you to make.'

Zen watched the younger man circling the office, inspecting the fixtures and fittings as though they were evidence at the scene of a crime. He's not apologizing to me, Zen realized. He's apologizing to himself, for letting himself down.

'My entire strategy was incorrect from the start,' the magistrate continued. 'It's mere bourgeois adventurism to think that the conspiracies of powerful vested interests can be defeated by individual efforts. I should have known better. The ratking is self-regulating, as I told you before. The strength of each rat is the strength of all. Any individual initiative against them is doomed from the start. The system can only be destroyed politically, by collective action, a stronger system.'

The distant smile was in place on Zen's lips. By a bigger and better ratking, he thought.

'Did you actually hear the recording of the message the Milettis received this morning?'

For a moment Bartocci appeared slightly confused.

'Hear it? Why?'

'Is anyone sure it was really the kidnappers who phoned?'

There was silence while Bartocci thought through the implications of this remark. Then he smiled and shook his head.

'I see what you're getting at,' he said. 'But I'm afraid it's not on. You've been away from active duty for a while, haven't you?'

Evidently the rumours about Zen's past were beginning to catch up with him.

'All interceptions are now subjected to voiceprint analysis as a matter of routine,' the magistrate explained. 'If the one this morning hadn't matched the pattern I'd have been informed. No, I'm afraid we must accept that Miletti was murdered by his kidnappers.'

'All right, perhaps they pulled the trigger. But there's still the question of how they knew I would be there at the pay-off. Ubaldo Valesio reckoned that someone in the family was passing on information. Isn't it possible that the informant deliberately told the kidnappers I would be there, knowing what the consequences were likely to be?'

'You mean that one of the family got the gang to do their murder for them? I doubt very much whether you'll be able to interest Rosella Foria in such a theory.'

'Why? Is she . . .?'

He paused, significantly. Bartocci shook his head.

'No, no, Rosella's straight enough. But she does everything strictly by the book. She has to. There still aren't many women in the judiciary, so everything they do tends to get scrutinized by their male colleagues, and not only those on the Right, I'm afraid to say. If a woman makes the slightest mistake it's pounced on as evidence of her general incompetence. The result is a natural tendency towards caution. And after what's happened to me Rosella's going to be treading very carefully indeed.'

For a moment Zen wondered whether he should tell Bartocci about the photocopy of Ruggiero's letter. Since the death of the writer the insults and threats he had dealt out to each member of his family took on a new significance. But in the end he decided against it. That letter was a card up his sleeve, the last one he had.

'What *has* happened to you?' he asked instead.

'I'll have to look for a new posting.'

'You're being transferred?'

'Nothing as simple as that. The judiciary only resort to disciplinary action in the most blatant cases, where the alternative would make us look even worse. All I've done is offend one or two of the wrong people, it's not the end of the world. No, nothing has changed. I'm quite free to stay in Perugia for the rest of my life, as an investigating magistrate. But if I want to move up the ladder I'll have to go elsewhere.'

'I still don't understand why the Milettis didn't try and stop you handling the investigation in the first place if they feel so strongly about you.'

'They did try! But they went about it the wrong way. It was Pietro's fault. He's been away too long, lost his touch, forgotten how things are done. When I was assigned to investigate Ruggiero's kidnapping, Pietro made a statement to the press drawing attention to my lack of experience and my political views and demanding that I be replaced immediately. After that I couldn't be touched, of course. This time they went about it correctly, which is to say incorrectly. A few discreet phone calls and suddenly I find myself shunted into a siding while the investigation into Ruggiero's murder passes me by.'

As Bartocci took his coat, the crucifix which Zen had laid on top of the filing cabinet the previous evening fell to the floor.

'Where you're concerned the Milettis got it wrong again,' the magistrate remarked to Zen as they stood at the door. 'The Ministry would have been only too happy to hand you over stuffed and pickled if they'd been asked in the proper way. But once Pietro started sounding off to the press they had to stand by you to avoid charges of bowing to pressure.'

'I expect it'll come to the same thing in the end,' Zen told him as they shook hands.

The crucifix had been broken by its fall. Zen wandered over to the window, trying to push it back together again.

One effect of the years of terrorism had been to abolish night in the vicinity of prisons, and the scene outside was bleakly bright. Every detail was picked out by the floodlights mounted high up on the walls behind protective grilles. Remote-control video cameras scanned back and forth, while up on the roof a nervous-looking teenager in grey overalls went his rounds, hugging a machine-gun for comfort.

That was another slight anomaly about Ruggiero Miletti's death, Zen reflected. Like Valesio, he had been shot through the mouth, but this time the only sign of damage was a single discreet exit wound in the back of the neck. The bullets fired into the victim's cranium were still lodged there. When the projectile that had escaped turned up in the mud all was explained: it was a 4.5mm, low-power ammunition for a small pistol. This choice of weapons seemed rather bizarre. The negotiating cell of the gang had brutally dismantled Ubaldo Valesio's skull with a submachine-gun while the hard men who had executed Ruggiero had done so with a small hand-gun, a bedside toy for nervous householders.

As Zen stood there fiddling with the crucifix, the end of the upright suddenly came away cleanly in his hand and he saw that it was hollow and that the lower part of the shaft contained a heavy rectangular pack about two centimetres long connected to a wire running back into the shaft and disappearing through a small hole into the figure of Christ. This figure was painted in the same syrupy pastel shades as the rest of the crucifix, but when Zen tapped it the head resounded not with the dull thud of plaster but with a light metallic ring.

He's been away too long, Bartocci had said of Pietro Miletti. He's lost his touch, forgotten how things are done. He wasn't the only one. Zen clearly remembered the occasion when he'd felt that some detail in his office had altered. He'd thought that it was just the calendar which had been turned to the correct month, but something else had been changed too. The original crucifix had been much smaller, too small in fact to contain whatever it was he was now cradling in his hand. And to think he hadn't noticed! At this rate he couldn't even count on keeping his Housekeeping job much longer. People would be auctioning off whole police stations under his nose.

The broken fragments of the crucifix looked like some bizarre act of desecration. He laid them out on the desk, got a plastic bag out of the bottom drawer of the filing cabinet and swept all the bits and pieces into it. Then he put on his overcoat and pushed the package deep into the pocket.

It was almost eight o'clock, and the streets were dead apart from a little through traffic. While he was still undecided as to what to do a bus appeared round the corner and slowed to a halt near by. The doors opened and the driver stared at him expectantly, and Zen got in. The bus wound its way through the ring of nineteenth-century villas on the upper slopes and the post-war apartments below them, down to the modern blocks and towers on the flat land around the station, where it pulled up. The engine died and everyone got out.

Zen went over to the row of luggage lockers, laid the plastic package in one, dropped in three-hundred-lire coins, locked the door and pocketed the key. On the wall opposite there was an illuminated display listing the tourist attractions of the city. The word 'cinemas' caught his eye, and one of the names seemed familiar. He gave it to the driver of the taxi he found outside, who whisked him back up the hill again, back through time to a medieval alley smelling of woodsmoke and urine. A more unlikely situation for a cinema was hard to imagine, but the driver pointed to a set of steps burrowing up between two houses and explained that it was as near as he could get in a car.

The small piazza into which Zen eventually emerged had an eerie, underwater look, due to a uniform coating of lurid green light from a neon sign mounted on a building otherwise no different from the others. 'CINEMA MINERVA', it read. Zen made no attempt to find out what was showing. He paid, walked down a dark corridor and pushed through a curtain into a deep pool of sound and flickering light. The auditorium was almost empty. He walked without hesitation to the very front row, sat down and lay back, gazing up at the screen. Enormous blurred masses swarmed into view and out again. An ear the size of a flying saucer appeared for a moment and then was whisked away and replaced by a no less monstrous nose and half an eye. Giant voices boomed at each other. He snuggled down in his seat with a blissful smile, battered by images, swamped by noise, letting the film wash over him.

It was the perfect mental massage, and when it was over he rose feeling slightly numb, but tingling and refreshed. In the foyer he paused to look at the posters, and learned that he had just seen a comedy called *Pull The Other One!* featuring a fat balding middle-aged clerk, the slim glamorous starlet madly in love with him, the clerk's wily roguish ne'er-do-well cousin and the cousin's battleaxe of a wife. As he stood there he felt a hand on his shoulder.

He would never have recognized Cinzia Miletti if she hadn't approached him, for she was virtually in disguise: a silk scarf entirely covering her hair, dark glasses and a long tweed coat buttoned right up to the chin. She lowered the glasses for an instant so that he could see her eyes, then raised them again.

'Did you enjoy it? We did, didn't we, Stefania?'

They were the classic female twosome, mouse and minx. Stefania played her role to perfection, managing to give the impression of existing only provisionally, to a limited extent, and being quite prepared at the drop of a hat either to become completely real or to vanish without trace, whichever was more convenient.

Zen was so astounded at finding Cinzia there on that particular evening that he could think of nothing whatever to say.

'I think he's just fantastic, don't you?' she went on unperturbed. 'I've seen all his films except *Do Me A Favour!* which funnily enough I've never managed to catch although it's on TV all the time. He's working in America this year, you know.'

By now the foyer was completely empty. On every side images of love and violence erupted from glass-fronted posters advertising coming attractions. In her booth the cashier sat knitting behind a tank in which a solitary goldfish swam in desultory circles.

Cinzia looked at her companion.

'I must go,' breathed Stefania, and was gone.

'Would you walk me home?' Cinzia asked Zen. 'I'm staying here in town, it's only five minutes' walk, not worth calling a taxi, but I don't like to go alone. There are so many Arabs about now. Of course I'm not racist, but let's face it, they've got a different culture, just like the South.'

Still he couldn't reply, his head too full of questions to which he didn't particularly want to know the answers. But he managed to nod agreement.

'Of course you think I'm shameless,' Cinzia remarked as they set off, the windless muffled night hardly disturbed by their footsteps. 'Do you believe in a life after death? I don't know what to think. But if there isn't one then nothing makes any difference, does it, and if there is I'm sure it'll all be far too spiritual for anyone to get in a huff over the way the rest of us carry on.'

The part of the city through which they were walking reminded Zen of Venice, but a Venice brutally fractured, as though each canal were a geological fault and the houses to either side had taken a plunge or been wrenched up all askew and left to tumble back on themselves, throwing out buttresses and retaining walls for support as best they could.

'I mean, do you really think the dead sit around counting who goes to the funeral and how many wreaths there are and how much they cost?' his companion carried on. 'I just hate cemeteries, anyway. They remind me of death.'

Her tone was even more strident than usual. Zen wondered if she wasn't slightly high on drink or drugs.

'Going home to stick it up her, eh? Filthy old bumfucker! Squeeze it tight and you might just manage to get a hard-on, you miserable little rat!'

The voice was just overhead, but when they looked up there was no one there.

'Good evening, Evelina,' Cinzia replied calmly.

'Don't you good evening me, you shameless cunt! You blow-job artist! I bet you beg for it on bended knees! I bet you let him shove it where he wants! Whore! Masturbator!'

They turned a corner and the malignant ravings became blurred and indistinct.

'Poor Evelina used to be one of the most fashionable women in Perugia,' Cinzia explained. 'Nobody seems to know what happened, but one day during a concert she suddenly stood up, took off her knickers and showed everyone her bottom. After that she was put away until they closed the asylums, since when she's lived in that place. It's one of her family's properties, they own half the city. Sometimes you hear her singing, in the summertime. But mostly she just sits up there like a spider, sticking her head out of the window to insult the passers-by. It's nothing personal, she says the same to everyone.'

For some time now Zen had been wondering where they were going. When Cinzia said she was staying 'in town', he'd assumed that she meant the Miletti villa. But although the structure of the city still defeated him in detail, he had got his bearings well enough to know that this could not be their destination. Eventually Cinzia turned up a set of steps rising steeply from the street and unlocked a door at the top.

'You'll come in for a moment, won't you?'

Without waiting for an answer she disappeared, leaving the door open.

Zen slowly mounted the steps, and then paused on the threshold. Ruggiero Miletti was dead and the family blamed him. What better revenge than to disgrace him by rigging a scandal involving the dead man's daughter, a married woman? But he told himself not to be crazy. How could they have known he was going to that cinema when he hadn't known himself until he saw the name at the station?

A narrow stairway of glossy marble led straight into a sitting room arranged around a huge open fireplace. There was no sign of Cinzia. The room had roughly plastered walls and a low ceiling supported on enormous joists trimmed out of whole trees. Everything was spick and span, more like a hotel than a home. Zen was instinctively drawn towards the one area of disorder, a desk piled with leaflets, envelopes, magazines, newspapers, letters and bills. He picked up one of the envelopes and held it up to the light: the watermark showed the heraldic hybrid with which he was becoming familiar, with the wings of an eagle and the body of a lion. Next to it lay a note from Cinzia to her husband about collecting their daughter from school.

'This is really Gianluigi's place,' Cinzia explained as she breezed in. She had changed into a striped shirt and a pair of faded jeans that were slightly too large for her. 'I only use it when he's away, there's no telling who I might find here otherwise. What do you want to drink?'

'Anything at all.'

Her bare feet padded across the polished terracotta tiles to the bottles lined along a shelf in the corner. Zen sat down on the large sofa which occupied most of one wall, thinking about that last card which he'd fondly thought he had up his sleeve. Thank God he hadn't tried to play it! The trap had been beautifully set, and he'd only avoided it because thanks to Bartocci's machinations he'd already fallen into another one.

Cinzia brought them both large measures of whisky and sat down astride the wicker chair in front of the writing desk, facing him over the ridged wooden back.

'I don't normally drink with strangers,' she remarked. 'It's quite a thrill. We do all our drinking in private, you see, in the family. Like everything else, for that matter!'

Cinzia was beginning to remind Zen more than a little of his wife. Luisella had also been the child of a successful businessman, owner of one of the most important chemist's shops in Treviso, and she too had had brothers who had dominated her childhood, driving her to defend herself in unorthodox ways. Life was a game like tennis, set up by men for men to win with powerful serves she would never be able to return. She countered by deliberately breaking the rules, exhausting her opponents and winning by default.

'That's a clue by the way,' she continued. 'You're never going to get anywhere if you don't understand the people involved.'

'I thought the people involved were Calabrian shepherds.'

'Oh, well, I don't know anything about them. You should have asked Stefania. Her brother's best friend is Calabrian, a medical student. But his family is extremely rich and I don't expect he knows any shepherds.'

She got up abruptly.

'Shall we have some music? Let's see, I can never remember how to work this thing.'

She pressed a button and one of the hit songs of the season emerged at full volume, the tough, shallow lyrics gloatingly declaimed by a star of the mid-sixties who had traded in her artless looks and girlish lispings for a streetwise manner and a voice laden with designer cynicism.

'I'd rather just talk,' Zen shouted.

With a flick of her finger she restored the silence.

'I thought you were bored. Well, what shall we talk about? How about sex? Let's see how you rate in that area. What do you think we go in for, here in Perugia? Wife-swapping? Open marriage? Group gropes? Singles bars?'

'None of those, I should have thought,' Zen replied with a slight smile.

'And quite right too. Bravo, you're improving. There's some of that around, of course, but it's not *traditional*. So what do you think is the speciality of the house? I'm talking about something typically Perugian, home-made from the very finest local ingredients only.'

She finished her drink in one gulp.

'No idea? I don't think you're a very good detective, I've given you loads of clues. It's incest, of course.'

She banged her empty glass down on the desk, as though she had expected to find the surface several centimetres lower than it actually was.

'Don't look so surprised, it makes perfect sense. From our point of view marriage has one big drawback, you see. It lets an outsider into the family. Much safer to stick to one's close relations. There's no trusting cousins and the like, of course. No, we're talking mother and son, father and daughter. See what I mean? If you don't know these things how can you hope to get anything right? For example, you disapprove of my going to the cinema this evening, but what do you think I should be doing? Cleaving to the bosom of my grieving family? What do you think they're doing? Daniele will be locked in his bedroom watching the latest batch of video nasties. Silvio? He'll be stripping for action with Helmut or whatever his name is this week. And Pietro will have gone to bed with a nice English murder story. Not much in the way of company, you see.'

'And your husband?'

Zen was still irrationally worried that Gianluigi might walk in at any moment, hunting rifle in hand. Or would he use the other gun, the little 4.5mm pistol registered in Cinzia's name? Where was that kept?

'He's still in Milan,' Cinzia replied carelessly. 'He couldn't get a flight back because of all the journalists wanting to get down here, or so he claims. Anyway, he has nothing to do with it, he's not family. Of course, he didn't realize that when he married me. But you don't break into the Miletti family as simply as that! So he's been reduced to other expedients.'

'And why did *you* marry *him*?'

Cinzia looked around vaguely, as if trying to remember.

'Well, he's very handsome. I know men don't think so, but he is. That might almost have been enough.'

'But it wasn't.'

'No. I married him to spite my father.'

Zen gave her a look of appraisal.

'You're not being very typically Perugian yourself, are you, telling me all this?'

Cinzia's eyes suddenly flashed and she smiled, displaying an excessive number of rather dirty teeth.

'It's strange, isn't it? I knew his death would be a release, but I thought it would be terrible, that I would suffer. I thought he would always make me suffer, whatever happened. But it's not like that at all. All this time, all these years, I've been lugging this weight around with me, for so long now that I've forgotten what it's like to be free of it. I'd even begun to mistake it for part of my own body, an incurable growth that I've got to learn to live with. But it's not, it's not! That disease, that horror, that swelling, it was all *his*! I'm whole and healthy and light, I find. Sorry for his death? I feel like dancing on his coffin!'

But there were tears in her eyes. For a moment it looked as though she was going to break down.

'There used to be this old-fashioned clothes shop on the Corso,' she went on more quietly. 'It's gone now, they've turned it into a bou-tique. It was full of wooden drawers and cupboards and enormous heavy mirrors on stands and boxes of buttons and threads and trim-ming. All the clothes were wrapped in tissue paper. I can still remember the sound it made, a lovely special sound, as light and thin as the clothes were thick and heavy. Everything smelt of mothballs and lavender and cedar. That shop was like a dream world to me, full of secrets and wonders. My mother took me there occasionally, and we used to pass the window every Sunday after mass. They always had beautiful things in the window. There was one I craved in particular, a pink nightdress with a lace hem and a frilly neck and a family of rabbits embroidered on the chest. I always stopped to look at it, although I knew it was much too expensive. But when my eighth birthday came I found it among my presents, with a little card from my father.'

He saw that she was weeping, not for her father but for herself, for the child she had been.

'Well, I expect you can guess the rest! That evening he came to my room, to see how I looked in my new nightdress. He told me to sit on his knee. That was normal, I didn't think twice about it. But what happened next wasn't normal. I knew it must be wrong, because afterwards he made me promise not to tell anyone about it, not even Mamma. What had happened was our secret, he said. That was the agreement we'd made. He'd kept his part by buying me the nightdress, now it was up to me to keep mine. I didn't remember making any agreement, but what could I do? Fathers know best, don't they? So although I didn't like him touching me the way he had, I decided not to tell anybody. I didn't realize that by keeping quiet I was walking into a trap.'

She sniffed loudly and picked up her cigarettes.

'After that he came to visit me almost every evening. After he had gone I found that my nightie was covered in a horrible sticky mess with a strange sour smell. I went to the bathroom and scrubbed myself until I was raw. But I still didn't tell anyone. In the end he stopped bothering to make any pretence of cuddles, it became fucking pure and simple. And his filth was no longer just on my skin, it was inside me.'

Zen tried to think of something to say, but it was useless. Faced with this ordinary everyday atrocity, he felt ashamed to be a man, ashamed to be human.

'Finally I threatened to tell Mamma. I was older now and more daring. It was then that he finally sprang his trap. If you do that, he told me, we shall go to prison, both of us. Because it's really all your fault. You encouraged me, you led me on. You must have enjoyed it, otherwise you would have told someone before now! You're as bad as me, my girl, or even worse.'

She lit her cigarette and smiled at Zen, inviting him to appreciate her father's cleverness.

'The worst thing about his lies was that they were partly true. Because although I hated it worse than anything, I *did* enjoy it too, once I got used to it. *Of course* it felt nice, what do you expect? And don't you think it was flattering, in a way, to be preferred to my mother? What a position to be in! On the one hand I could send us both to prison, shame my mother, beggar my brothers, scandalize the city and blacken the Miletti name for evermore. On the other hand, I could do, I *did*, exactly the opposite, keeping my father satisfied and happy and my mother ignorant, helping to shore up their marriage, holding the family together and preserving my unsuspecting brothers, who thought they were so superior to me, from disgrace. Half the time I felt like a vicious little whore and the other half like the heroine of a nineteenth-century novel. But mostly I just felt my power! My father used the carrot as well as the stick, of course, and that meant I got everything I wanted, clothes, jewellery, perfume. And when his friends and business associates came round, I would put on my finery and try out my power on them too. And it worked! Antonio Crepi, for example, used to give me looks that would have melted a candle. I was twelve at the time.'

'Did your mother never suspect what was going on?'

After a long time Cinzia looked up.

'That's a terrible question,' she said. 'At the time I was sure she didn't know. How could she have known, I thought, and not done anything about it? Now I'm not so sure. She would have had every reason to look the other way. Besides . . .'

She stopped.

'What?'

'Sometimes I think she deliberately ignored what was happening, in order to punish me. Perhaps it was her way of taking revenge. Perhaps she too thought that it was my fault, that I enjoyed it, that I was as bad as he was, or even worse.'

She straightened up, her voice bright and brisk again.

'Anyway, none of that matters now. There was a car crash, she died, he was in hospital for a long time and when he came out everything had changed. He may have seen her death as a judgement. I don't know, we never talked about it of course. But he never came near me again, and I was left high and dry with all that power lying idle inside me. It didn't lie idle long, needless to say.'

She gave him a wry smile.

163

'So now you know everything there is to know about me! Not even my husband knows what I've just told you. A rare privilege, and one you didn't deserve, to be perfectly honest. But I needed to tell someone, after all these years, and it had to be a stranger of course. You were just in the right place at the right time.'

Zen finished his whisky.

'There's still one thing I don't know.'

'What?'

'Why you sent me that copy of your father's letter.'

She barked out a little laugh.

'I thought at first it must have been Ivy Cook,' Zen went on. 'But that doesn't really make sense. Take the envelope, for example. Did she take it with her when she went to the rubbish skip or dash to a stationer's and buy it? And not just any old envelope, but a special luxury brand with a griffin watermark. Like the ones on your desk.'

She gave him a bored look.

'It's not my desk, it's Gianluigi's. I expect he sent you the letter. You've no idea how resourceful he is. He just about owns poor Daniele ever since that business with the drugs, not to mention those photographs he has of Silvio . . .'

'No, it wasn't your husband,' Zen interrupted. 'It was you. You rewrote the letter after the original had been burned, had your version photocopied and then sent me the copy. The handwriting is the same as that note on the desk asking your husband to collect Loredana from school.'

'Well, supposing I did? It's not a criminal offence, is it, sending information to the police? You should be grateful! I may have changed a word here or there, but apart from that it's all exact. I wrote it while the text was still fresh in my mind. It wasn't the kind of letter that is easy to forget! When Pietro told us that you were going on the pay-off I felt that you should know what you were getting yourself into.'

Zen smiled sceptically.

'I thought it might have something to do with the fact that when it emerged that I'd received the letter, Ivy Cook would become *persona non grata* in the Miletti family.'

Cinzia giggled.

'Well, why shouldn't I get something out of it too? That bitch has been a thorn in our flesh for too long. Help yourself to another drink, I'll be back in a moment.'

She lurched off across the room, reaching for the wall to steady herself, and disappeared upstairs. Some time later there was the sound of a lavatory flushing, but Cinzia did not reappear. Zen sat there, thinking over what she had told him. He felt heavy, saturated, crammed with more or less repulsive odds and ends he neither wanted nor needed to know. Someone had said that nowadays doctors had to double as priests, offering general consolation and advice to their patients. But there are things you would be ashamed to tell even your doctor, things so vile they can only be confessed to the lowest, most contemptible functionaries of all. There were days when Zen felt like the Bocca de Leone in the Doges' Palace: a stiff stone grimace clogged with vapid denunciations and false confessions, scribbles riddled with hatred or guilt, the anonymous rubbish of an entire city.

There was still no sign of Cinzia. Zen got up, walked to the foot of the stairs and called out. There was no reply. He put his foot on the first step and paused, listening.

'Signora?'

The high marble steps curved upwards, paralleling the flight leading up from the front door. Zen started to climb them. There were three doors in the passageway at the top. Feeling like a character in a fairy tale, he chose the one to the right and opened it carefully.

'Signora?'

The room inside was startlingly bare, reminding him of his mother's flat in Venice. Two empty cardboard boxes sat on the floor, one at each end of the room, ignoring each other. Between them a small window showed a blank stretch of wall on the other side of the alley.

The second door he tried was the bathroom. A quick search failed to reveal any suspiciously empty bottles of barbiturates, but of course she might have taken them with her. That left just one door, and he hesitated for a moment before opening it. But the scene which met his eyes was perfectly normal. A large high old-fashioned bed almost filled the room. Cinzia Miletti was lying across it on her back, bent slightly to one side, fully clothed, her eyes closed. Her breathing seemed steady.

Zen felt he should cover her up. Her body proved unexpectedly awkward and resistant. One arm kept getting entangled in the sheets, until he began to think that she was playing a trick on him. Paradoxically, it wasn't till her eyes opened that he knew he was wrong. Their unfocused glance passed over him without the slightest flicker of movement or response. Then they closed and she turned over and began to snore lightly. His last image before switching off the light was of Cinzia's head lying on the pillow in the centre of a mass of long blonde hair, her mouth placidly sucking her thumb.

Outside the night had turned clear and bitterly cold, and the stars were massed in all their intolerable profusion. The light cast by one of the infrequent street lamps glistened on a freshly pasted poster extolling the virtues of Commendatore Ruggiero Franco Miletti, whose funeral would be held the following afternoon.

EIGHT

By morning everything had changed: the sky was still clear, but the sun shone on a new landscape. The straggling hinder-parts of the town, the scree of recent building on the lower slopes, the patchy developments strung out beside road and railway in the valley, all this had vanished. Immediately beyond the two churches visible from Zen's window the world abruptly ended, to begin again fifteen or twenty kilometres away, where the upper slopes of the yeasty mountain survived as a small island rising from a frozen ocean. A few other islets were visible on the other side of the valley, but apart from these patches of high ground and the stranded city itself, a glistening white mass of fog covered everything.

The Questura was barely fifty metres down the hill, but it was below the surface, and as Zen walked there from his hotel he felt the invisible moisture beading his newly shaved skin. When he looked up the light was pearly and the sky a blue so tender he could hardly take his eyes off it, with the result that on several occasions he collided with people coming the other way. But everybody was in a good mood that morning, and his apologies were returned with a smile. He remembered a Chinese fable Ellen had once told him about a man who falls off a cliff, saves himself by clutching at a plant, and then notices that two mice are gnawing away the branch on which his life depends. There is a fruit growing on the branch, which the man plucks and eats. The fruit tastes wonderful.

'How did the mice come to be halfway down a cliff in the first place?' he had asked her. 'And why didn't they eat the fruit themselves?'

He couldn't see the point of the story at all, but Ellen refused to explain.

'You must experience it,' was all she would say. 'One day it'll suddenly hit you.'

He had been sceptical at the time, but she'd been quite right, for he had suddenly understood the story. 'It'll come to the same thing in the end,' he'd told Luciano Bartocci. His days in Perugia were clearly numbered, and he would spend them like the young magistrate, on a siding running parallel to the main line but going nowhere and ending abruptly. The process had begun the day before, at the scene of the crime. It was Major Volpi who had been given responsibility for putting up road-blocks and carrying out house-to-house searches. The police had made one mistake too many in this case and would be given no further opportunities to demonstrate their incompetence. As for Zen, any day now he would receive a telegram from the Ministry summoning him back to Rome, and that would be that.

But in the meantime, how sweet the fruit tasted! And although the bureaucratic mice were invisibly at work, he still went through the motions of shifting hands and improving his grip on the branch. Thus his first action on returning to the Questura the day before had been to send his inspectors out to question the people living in the houses along the road to Cannara and talk to the local farmers, just in case anyone had seen anything. When he arrived at work that morning the result of their labours was waiting for him in a blue folder.

Five minutes after entering his office Zen reappeared in the inspectors' room, where Geraci was watching Chiodini fill in a coupon for a competition promising the winner a lifetime supply of tomato concentrate.

'What *is* this?' he demanded.

Geraci looked warily at the folder Zen was holding up, his eyebrows working away like two caterpillars doing a mating dance.

'It's our report.'

'I've never seen a report like this. What's all this stuff down the side?'

'Those are computer codes.'

'Since when have we had a computer?'

'We haven't, it's at the law courts. All packed up in boxes, down in the basement. But we'll be getting terminals here, once it's working. You see, this report isn't meant to be read, it's meant to be put into the computer.'

Zen regarded him stonily.

'But there is no computer.'

'Not yet, no. But they want to be ready, you see. It's going to be wonderful! All the files from us, the Carabinieri, the Finance people, everything, is going to go straight into the computer. Anything you want to know, it'll be there at your fingertips. Say you've got a report about a small red car, and you want to compare it with all the other small red cars that have been reported in the area. With the old method it would take you hours looking through files, but with the computer you just push a button and it tells you right away. And the same for all the large red cars, or the red foreign cars of any size, or the small sports cars of any colour . . .'

Zen passed one hand across his forehead. There were clearly various possibilities which the Chinese hadn't thought of. For example, the mice stop gnawing, scamper down your arm, cock their legs and piss in your face.

'Listen, you don't mean to tell me that everyone around here gets their reports in this form. I simply don't believe it.'

'Of course they do! Isn't it the same in Rome?'

Zen looked away. Of course it was the same in Rome. It would be the same everywhere, that was how the system worked. What Geraci still didn't know was that Zen had no recent operational experience in Rome or anywhere else.

'Mind you, some of the older officers get us to do a back-up report in the old way,' Chiodini told him.

'But it's strictly unofficial,' Geraci added hurriedly. 'Can't be logged or filed.'

Zen was leafing through the folder. He seemed not to have heard.

'Did you speak to this witness?'

The inspector took the file and glanced at the entry pointed out by Zen's broad flat finger.

'No, that was Lucaroni.'

'But it's marked G.'

'That's right. G stands for Lucaroni.'

'Really? I suppose you're L?'

Geraci frowned.

'L? No, L is already in use by the system. For example here in the same entry it says L23, right? That means an unidentified foreign car.'

'Where is Lucaroni?'

Geraci seemed to hesitate for a moment.

'Upstairs,' said Chiodini.

That meant either the senior command structure or the Political Branch, whose rooms are situated on the top floor of every Questura. The fact that the same word is used for either reflects the general feeling that the distinction between them is fairly hazy.

'Tell him I want to see him as soon as he gets back.'

He closed the door behind him. So they were getting a computer, were they? Soon the intolerable mysteries of Mediterranean life would be swept away by the electronic wonders of real time and random access for all. And just to make sure that everything was fair and above-board, the computer, like the facilities for tapping phones, would be located at the law courts, safely out of the hands of the police. 'They're doing to small-time corruption what the multi-national corporations are doing to small-time business,' a cynical Sardinian friend had once remarked apropos of the latest initiative to clean up the police. 'It's not going to stop the abuse of power, it's just going to restrict it to the highest level. Anyone can afford to buy you or me, Aurelio, but only the big boys can manipulate judges.'

Zen glanced at the wall, where the calendar now looked oddly unbalanced. Yes, it might be time to phone Gilberto. He couldn't leave the crucifix in the luggage locker for ever.

Lucaroni appeared about ten minutes later, all apologies for the delay.

'I was just having a word with Personnel,' he explained. 'My sister's getting married next week and I wanted to know whether there'd be any chance of a spot of leave.'

Zen passed him a page of the report.

'Tell me about this woman who claims to have seen a large blue car near the scene of the crime.'

'Well, there's just what it says here,' the inspector replied, scanning the page. 'It was a large blue foreign saloon, she said, driven by someone with fair hair, going along the . . .'

'Tell me about the woman.'

'The driver? But we don't . . .'

'No, the woman you spoke to.'

Lucaroni made a conspicuous effort to remember.

'Well, she was oldish. Lives with her in-laws in one of those new houses along the road.'

'How did she see the car?'

'She was out gathering salad leaves for the evening meal. There's very little traffic on that road and she knows most of the people, so when she saw this strange car she noticed it.'

'She called it a "strange" car?'

'Yes.'

'So how did the idea that it was foreign come up?'

'I asked her about the make and she said she didn't know. I asked if it was foreign and she said that it was.'

Zen nodded. The old woman wouldn't have known a Rolls-Royce from a Renault. 'Foreign' just meant that the car was a large luxury saloon of a kind she'd never seen before.

'And there was only one person in it?'

'So she said. A woman with blonde hair.'

Zen took the report back again.

'It says "fair hair" here.'

'Well, you can't put blonde, can you?' Lucaroni pointed out. 'The computer won't accept it. Hair is either fair or yellow.'

Zen nodded.

'Oh, there's one other thing.'

He pointed to the wall.

'You remember the crucifix that used to be there? You don't happen to know where it came from, do you?'

Lucaroni's tongue emerged to dampen his lips. He shook his head.

'I had a visitor in here the other day, you see. There was an accident and the thing ended up in pieces. Most unfortunate.'

'In pieces?' Lucaroni whispered.

Zen nodded.

'Luckily my visitor was a Communist, so he's not superstitious about these things. I'd be happy to pay for a new one, but I have no idea where to go. Do you think you could get me one? I'd really appreciate it.'

There was a long silence.

'Well . . .' Lucaroni began.

Zen tapped his chest with one finger.

'But I want one that is the same. You understand? Exactly identical in every respect.'

Their glances met and held.

'Identical,' breathed the inspector.

'Absolutely. I was very fond of that crucifix. It had a certain something about it, know what I mean?'

Lucaroni's mouth was now completely out of control. His tongue shot out continually, dumping saliva on his lips, which barely had time to spread it around their shiny surfaces before the next load arrived. Zen hastened to dismiss him before he self-destructed.

A glance at the map revealed that there was a short cut down to the Miletti villa, so instead of summoning Palottino he decided to walk. What he was thinking of doing was risky enough as it was. The less official he could make it the better.

The short cut turned out to be a lane which started abruptly at the bottom of a flight of steps opposite the Questura and ran straight down the hillside like a ruled line. It must have been one of the old medieval roads into the city, now closed to traffic by the concrete retaining wall of the ring boulevard. To either side old farmhouses and new villas stood in uneasy proximity. Beyond them, a narrow fold in the hillside was being filled with rubbish to provide space for a car park. Down below, lost in the mist, he could just make out the holm-oaks and cypresses surrounding the Miletti property, a lugubrious baroque monstrosity built on a shoulder of land jutting out from the steep hillside.

Zen walked past it for another hundred and fifty metres to the separate entrance marked 'Società Industriale Miletti di Perugia'. At this depth the mist was still unwarmed by the sun, clinging glaucously to every surface. This was the site of Franco's original workshops, built just below the house. In those days captains of industry were not ashamed to live close to the source of their wealth. Since production had been moved out to Ponte San Giovanni the buildings had been gutted and transformed into the administrative headquarters of SIMP. He'd been expecting tight security at the entrance, but in the event the gates were open and unmanned, and a passing employee directed him along a concrete road leading to the garage where a man in blue overalls was washing one of the Fiat saloons. Behind him a dozen or so more of the cars were lined up, their paintwork gleaming.

Zen flashed his identification with contemptuous brevity and then allowed a little time for the mechanic's fear to be fruitful and multiply. Everyone has some reason to be afraid of the police, and fear, like money, can be spent on something quite unrelated to what has created it. When Zen judged that he had enough for his purposes he pointed to the Fiats.

'Are you responsible for these cars?'

The man nodded. Zen gave a satisfied smile, as though he had obtained a damning admission.

'Then what have you done with my cigarette lighter?'

'Cigarette lighter?' the mechanic stammered. 'What sort of cigarette lighter?'

Zen's smile vanished.

'Why, how many have you found?'

'None! I haven't found anything.'

'Then why did you ask what sort, eh? Think you can keep anything you find, eh? Supplement your lousy wages with a little private enterprise, is that it?'

The man flung his sponge down angrily.

'I've found nothing! I've just cleaned them all ready for this afternoon. There was no cigarette lighter in any of them.'

'They're going to use the company cars for the funeral?' Zen queried in a tone of deep disgust. 'Talk about cheap!'

'It's what Signor Ruggiero would have wanted.'

'Don't try and change the subject! You claim not to have found any lighter, is that it?'

'I don't claim anything! I didn't find any lighter and that's all there is to it. Have a look for yourself if you want, I've got nothing to hide!'

'Oh, I'm going to! Don't you worry about that, I'm going to.'

The mechanic watched him out of the corner of his eye as he went from car to car, making an elaborate pretence of examining the interiors.

The mud surrounding the building site where Ruggiero Miletti had been murdered had proved a rich source of impressions. A preliminary investigation, completed while Zen was still present, had yielded five different footprints and two distinct sets of tyre marks. One of the two sets consistently overlaid the other, and it was distinctive, in that one of the tyres did not match the other three. Zen had imagined that this would be a rarity, but in fact four of the cars in the garage had one odd tyre. Only one configuration, however, matched that found at the murder scene.

'What the fuck do you think you're doing, Zen?'

It was Gianluigi Santucci. The Tuscan turned on the mechanic.

'What has he been asking you, Massimo? If you've told him as much as the time, you're out!'

'Nothing!' protested the mechanic energetically. 'I've said nothing!'

'That's true,' Zen confirmed. 'He's been most unhelpful.'

'I haven't found any lighter, I don't know anything about any lighter,' Massimo went on. 'I told him so, but he wanted to look for himself. But he didn't touch anything, Signor Gianluigi. I kept my eye on him the whole time.'

Gianluigi Santucci glared at Zen.

'Cigarette lighter my bollocks! What are you up to? Come on!'

'I've lost my lighter and I thought I might have left it in the car the other day. I didn't want to disturb the family at a moment like this so I came to check in person. But I don't understand what you're getting so excited about. I mean, is this garage a secret research area or something?'

Too late, Gianluigi realized his error. In an attempt to compensate he forced a smile.

'You haven't understood, have you?' he sneered. 'You think you're still in the game, but you couldn't be more wrong. You're a foreigner here. No one wants you, no one likes you, no one needs you. If you haven't got your marching orders yet it just means no one can be bothered to tell you what's happening any more! Now kindly fuck off out of here and don't come back.'

When Zen reached the gate the security guard was back in his place, but he was so intent on the spluttering exclamations of his walkie-talkie, cradling it to his face and murmuring to it like a mother trying to calm a baby, that Zen's departure went as unremarked as his arrival.

He walked on down the hill until the lane joined the main road. At the corner stood a green plastic rubbish skip, presumably the one where Ruggiero's letter had been left. Opposite there was a bakery, an office furniture showroom, a driving school and a tobacconist displaying the familiar public telephone symbol of a blue receiver in a yellow circle. Zen went in, got two thousand lire's worth of tokens and dialled a number in Rome.

'Gilberto?'

'Who's this?'

'Aurelio.'

'Aurelio! How's it going?'

'Can you do me a favour?'

'Such as?'

'It means coming up here.'

'Where's here?'

'Perugia. I've got problems.'

'What kind of problems?'

'Can you come up this afternoon?'

'This afternoon! Jesus.'

Even at this depth the sunlight had finally started to filter down through the mist. There was a grove of olive trees opposite the shop, on the other side of the main road. Above the rush and scurry of the traffic they stood in monumental stillness, each leaf precisely outlined against the deep blue sky.

'What do you want done?'

'Can we talk on this line?'

'Listen, I'm in industrial espionage, you know. How long do you think I'd stay in business if I didn't keep my lines clean? You worry about your own end.'

Zen told his friend briefly about the murder and the large blue car that matched both the witness's description and the tyre marks found at the scene. Then he told him what he wanted him to do and Gilberto said he would, although it might mean losing a contract to proof a leading Rome estate agent against electronic surveillance. They arranged to meet at half past four at a village a kilometre or so beyond the cemetery.

That left lots of time to kill, so Zen rode a bus back up to the centre and wandered along the Corso. The steps of the cathedral were being used as a grandstand by some of the local young people and a few early tourists. A German youth whose exaggerated features looked as though they had been moulded from foam rubber explained loudly to his companion how he *needed* the sun, the sun for him was a physical necessity. The two Nordic girls he had seen two days before were now basking like seals outside another café. One of them had even contrived to get sunburned. Her friend was delicately pulling little wafers of flaking skin off her chest, watched hungrily by a group of young men in leather jackets, narrow ties and mirror sunglasses.

All at once Zen saw a vigorous bulky figure in a dark grey overcoat with a black arm-band walking towards him across the piazza. It was Antonio Crepi. He prepared a greeting, but the Perugian passed by without a word or gesture, leaving Zen with his hand still uncertainly raised in salutation.

It was the first time that someone had cut him dead, and it was a shock. He had always thought of it as a superficial and outmoded gesture found only in old novels. But what had just happened had nothing to do with etiquette: Antonio Crepi had made it clear that for him, and by extension for the whole of the Perugia that mattered, Zen had ceased to exist. That's why ghosts wail, he thought, condemned to haunt a world which has no further need of them. He walked away quickly, trying to shake off the unnerving effect of the encounter.

The air was carved into blocks by the buildings, soft and warm where the sun reached, chill and unyielding in the shadows. The continual passage from one to the other was initially as refreshing as a succession of hot and cold showers, and ultimately as enervating. Zen stopped in a small grocery and ordered a roll filled with anchovies sprinkled with vinegar and a little crushed chilli, which he ate with a glass of white wine. There was a newspaper open at the local pages on top of the freezer, and as he munched the roll Zen read an article describing the life and times of the late head of the Miletti family in such exorbitantly fulsome terms that Zen wondered in his dour Venetian way whether such a paragon would find Paradise quite good enough for him. He also wondered whether Ruggiero's daughter had seen the article, and if so what she thought of it. Cinzia had told him what kind of drinkers the Perugians were, and what kind of lovers. What he needed to know now was what kind of murderers they were.

By four o'clock the last of the mist had disappeared, even down in the valley below the cemetery. The warm air was scented with the heady reek of diesel oil from the bus which had brought him there and was now parked in the terminus circle near by. The driver was sitting on the step, smoking and reading a newspaper. Zen stood in the fading sunlight watching the courtship of two pigeons on the tiled roof of a shed below. The gurgling male, alternately bowing down and rearing up, chased the female from one row of tiles to the next. Eventually he appeared to lose interest, disheartened by her lack of appreciation, and turned away. Instantly the female stopped too, so that both birds came to a halt like toys whose batteries have run down. It seemed the end. Relationships were just too difficult, the sexes would never see eye to eye, it was all too much bother. Something essential had broken down and next year there wouldn't be any pigeons. Then, just as suddenly as he had stopped, the male was off again, perking up his feathers and hopping after his mate with a meaningful glint in his beady eyes. Zen had watched this cycle a dozen times or more when he felt a touch on his shoulder and turned to find Gilberto grinning up at him.

Gilberto Nieddu was so small that it wasn't clear how he had ever managed to get into the police force. There were the inevitable rumours of bribery and favouritism, but since Gilberto's father was only a small-time locksmith from Nuoro this seemed unlikely. Zen preferred to think that some alert recruiting officer somewhere, realizing the appalling threat a disgruntled Gilberto would pose *outside* the law, had bent the rules to let him in. For four years they had worked together in Rome. The Sardinian had resigned a week after Zen's transfer, and he was the only one of his former colleagues whom Zen still saw regularly.

'Any problems?' Zen asked him.

'Only getting back here after I dumped it. You had to choose a place in the middle of nowhere.'

'Close to the scene. Local colour.'

Gilberto was as compact as a squash ball, sallow, ugly and muscular, yet amazingly deft in his movements. For a bet, he had once broken into the flat where a certain Vice-Questore was entertaining a lady friend and removed the couple's clothes so stealthily that the Vice-Questore thought something supernatural must have occurred and came over all religious for a while. No, Gilberto wouldn't have had any problems stealing an unguarded car from outside a cemetery.

'Is this all really worth it?' the Sardinian asked Zen, who merely shrugged.

'How much do I owe you?'

Gilberto Nieddu spat thoughtfully at the pigeons on the roof below.

'Take me out to lunch when you get back. At the Pergola.'

'The Pergola! Wouldn't it work out cheaper just to pay your normal rates?'

'Now, don't try and wriggle out of it or I'll send Vittorio round to see you. He's my new enforcer. A great success. You may think you have problems now, but Vittorio can make them seem like fond memories.'

Zen handed him a key with a number stamped on the shaft.

'This opens a luggage locker at the station. There's something inside, wrapped up in a plastic bag. I'd like to know what it is.'

The Sardinian looked at him long and hard, shaking his head slowly.

'You know something, Aurelio? You aren't really cut out to be a cop.'

'Imagine living in a country where the cops are all people who're cut out for the job.'

'I'll phone you tomorrow morning.'

Zen shook his head.

'I'll phone *you*.'

The Sardinian spat once more.

'Christ, you have got problems.'

The bus driver started his engine again. Zen just had time to cross to the phone booth, dial the police emergency number and give the message he had prepared before boarding the bus as the doors were closing. A few moments later they passed Gilberto walking back up the hill to the place where he had left his own car, just below the massive wall of the columbarium in the cemetery where Ruggiero Miletti had been interred two hours previously.

The switchboard on the ground floor of the Questura was manned by a chubby youth who was holding a large roll, turning it from one side to the other and studying it closely like a wrestler looking for a hold. As Zen came through the door he suddenly saw an opening and lunged forward, so that for the next thirty seconds or so he was unable to reply to his visitor's question.

'He wouldn't give his name,' he said finally. 'Probably a hoax.'

'What exactly did he say?'

'Just said he wanted to report a blue Fiat abandoned on the road to Cannara, near the scene of the murder.'

He kept glancing warily at his roll out of the corner of his eye, as though it might attack him. Zen leant forward on the top of the switchboard.

'Listen, this could be very important. I want that car brought in, turned over to the laboratory and given the works.'

'They'll need confirmation in writing.'

'They'll get it.'

The telephonist nodded. He was too eager to get back to his roll to ask how Zen had found out about the anonymous phone call.

Upstairs on the third floor Zen stepped into the inspectors' room, but there was no one there. He was about to leave when he froze in an awkward position midway across the room. Then he heard it again, a slight but unmistakable sound from next door. Someone was in his office.

He moved as quietly as he could towards the connecting door, grasped the handle and with a single movement flung the door open.

'About time too! I was beginning to think I'd have to spend the night here.'

He leant back against the door, his body slowly untensing.

'Ellen.'

'Ah, so you remember my name!'

'It's wonderful to see you.'

'Really? I certainly wouldn't have guessed it from the way you've been behaving. Why haven't you telephoned me?'

'I did!' he lied automatically. 'You were never there!'

'I was!'

'Not when I phoned.'

'I've been home almost every evening. When did you phone?'

'Well, anyway, let's not quarrel. The important thing is that you're here. How long can you stay?'

'I'll have to see. It depends.'

He tried to kiss her, but she evaded him in a half-angry, half-flirtatious way, so they were in the middle of a clumsy clinch when Lucaroni walked in.

'Oh fuck!' he said, on his way out again.

Zen turned on him.

'Didn't anyone ever teach you to knock? You're not home on the farm now, you know!'

'Sorry, chief. Really sorry. I didn't think anybody was here. I was going to put it up for you.'

'Put what up?'

Lucaroni unwrapped the package he was carrying to reveal a brand-new crucifix, the wounds daubed with bright red paint.

'Just what you wanted, right?' the inspector prompted eagerly. 'Just like the other one.'

Zen glanced at Ellen, who was staring at him in horrified disbelief.

'I'll explain later,' he said wearily. 'Don't worry. I'll explain every-thing later.'

A small white plastic bag containing various packets of waxed paper marked 'For Foodstuffs' lay propped against the gear-lever of the little Fiat. The draught coming in through the ventilation ducts made it tremble continuously. They should never have come, thought Zen. What a crazy idea, picnicking up a mountain at this time of year. A crazy *foreign* idea.

It had all started the night before, when Ellen asked, 'Is that Assisi over there?' They were standing looking out of his hotel window. In the distance a mess of lights were spread out across the face of the night like a shovelful of glowing cinders, flickering and scintillating in the currents of air rising from the villages in the plain between. Let's go there tomorrow, she'd suggested, and then talked about her previous visits, enthusing about the place so much that he grew quite determined to dislike it. But it wasn't until Ellen came to pick him up that he discovered that she had already bought everything for a pic-nic lunch. One o'clock in Piazza dei Partigiani after a stressful morn-ing at work was very different from eleven o'clock the night before after making love, but Ellen was bubbling with such enthusiasm that he hadn't the heart to voice his reservations. But he still thought it was crazy, and he'd been right. Here they were, parked a thousand metres up the dough-shaped mountain, huddled in Ellen's Fiat 500 because despite the sun the wind outside was wicked. Even the view was all but invisible through a windscreen coated with Roman grime. Foreign craziness!

Ellen started to unwrap the food: a mound of ricotta, slices of cooked ham, olives in oil, half a loaf of bread. On a warm sunny day in the open air it might have been idyllic. Eaten off sheets of wrap-ping paper balanced precariously on their shivering knees the cheese looked a disgusting white excrescence, the ham pale and sickly and the olives slimy. Even the wine, a heavy red, was a failure. Cold and shaken from the journey, thick with sediment and drunk from a plas-tic beaker, it tasted like medicine. But like medicine it did him good, and the food tasted better than it looked, and after a while the silence grew less tense and they began to chat about the contrast between bloody-minded, earnest Perugia, just visible on its wind-swept ridge as a distant smudge of grey, and Assisi, symbol of everything nice and pretty and kind, whose pink stone made even its fortifications look as innocent as an illustration in a book of fairy tales. But as Zen pointed out, at least in Perugia you were spared the relentless commercialization of the pilgrim city, the three-dimensional postcards of a glamorous St Francis preaching to an audience of stuffed animals, the bottles of 'Monk's Delight' liqueur, the ceramic prayer texts suitable for mounting over the toilet, the little figurines of lovable monks with round bellies and mischievous smiles.

'Yes, but despite all that there really is something special about the place, isn't there?' Ellen insisted.

It was the sort of comment, at once vague and gushing, that always irritated him. Sometimes he wondered whether that was why she kept making them.

'To me it's just another pretty Umbrian hill town,' he retorted. 'It's a shame it's been ruined.'

He was going too far, pushing too hard, saying things he didn't really believe. It was quite deliberate. Something had gone wrong between them, and he intended to find out what it was. Normally he handed over responsibility for the routine maintenance of their relationship to Ellen, but she was letting him down, so he was going to try the only technique he knew: drop some explosive overboard and see what floated to the surface.

'How can you say that?' she demanded indignantly. 'What about all the churches? They wouldn't exist if it hadn't been for him. The basilica is one of the greatest buildings in the world. Or would you dispute that?'

'On the contrary, I think it's so great that it should be put to better use. I remember when I was at university in Padua we went to see the basilica there. It's magnificent, one of my friends said, after the revolution we'll turn it into a sports centre. The place here would make a good Turkish baths.'

'You're showing your age, Aurelio. That sort of knee-jerk anticlericalism has been out of date for years.'

'Or best of all, they could use it as an exhibition centre. They could start with a display about the concentration camp at Jasenovac.'

'Was that in Poland?' she repeated as she cleared away the food.

'Yugoslavia. No one's heard of it, it wasn't in the Auschwitz or Belsen class. They only killed forty thousand people there.'

'And what's that got to do with Assisi?'

'The commandant of Jasenovac concentration camp was a Franciscan monk.'

He opened the window a crack, but the wind made such a noise that he immediately closed it again.

'When the Germans turned Croatia into a puppet dictatorship the Catholics there immediately got to work settling old scores with the Serbs, packing them into their churches and burning them alive, that kind of thing. The Church knew what was going on and they could easily have stopped it. But the Pope kept quiet and the atrocities went on, many of them supervised by the followers of St Francis. At the end of the war Eva Peron, the wife of the Argentinian dictator, sent us a boat-load of brown cloth. Guess why.'

She shook her head.

'To dress the Croatian thugs up as Franciscan monks so that they could escape to Italy out of the clutches of Tito's partisans. They were fed and sheltered here in Assisi and in other monasteries and church buildings until they could get away to South America. They were good Catholic boys, after all.'

'I don't suppose Tito's men were angels either.'

'I don't suppose they were. But at least they didn't go around with beatific smiles mumbling about peace and goodwill.'

'Well, I'm relieved to see that you haven't changed after all,' Ellen remarked as they lit their cigarettes. 'I got a bit worried when I found you'd been sending your subordinates out to buy crucifixes.'

Zen smiled too, but privately he heard Gilberto Nieddu's voice again, the Sardinian accent strong and clear-cut even over the bad line from Rome.

'Oh yes, Aurelio, I've identified it. No problem. For me, that is. But you've got problems all right. Your crucifix contains a transistorized short-wave transmitter with a cadmium-cell feed. Korean job, cheap and easy to obtain, four to five months continuous operation, use once and throw away. The mike concealed in the head of the figure is only medium-quality, technically speaking, but it would pick up a flea farting in a smallish room. The transmitter would then beam that out about two hundred metres. Somewhere within that radius there'll be a receiver, probably rigged up to a voice-activated tape recorder. Once every so often someone comes along, swaps the cassette and takes away the highlights of your day at work.'

There was a long silence, during which the noise on the line seemed to become a third party in their conversation.

'What do you want me to do with it?'

'You'd better send it back.'

'Do you have any idea who it belongs to?'

The silence lasted even longer this time.

'Upstairs, maybe.'

Gilberto's next words had shaken Zen more than anything that had happened so far.

'Watch yourself, Aurelio. Remember Carella.'

Avoiding Ellen's eyes, Zen wrapped his coat more closely about him.

'Anyway, let's look on the bright side. The way things are going I should be back in Rome soon.'

'I still don't understand what all the fuss is about,' Ellen replied in a slightly peevish tone. 'Miletti's death was nothing to do with you, surely?'

'That remains to be proved.'

'Oh, I see. It's the old story. You're guilty until proven innocent.'

'Not necessarily. Sometimes you're guilty anyway.'

They sat there listening to the gush and scurry of the wind buffeting the car.

'You didn't tell me the whole truth that evening at Ottavio's, did you?' Ellen asked at last.

He didn't reply.

'I want to know, Aurelio. I need to know.'

He turned his pale, grave face towards her.

'When you were a child, did you have someone who used to tell you stories?'

She looked at him in surprise.

'My father used to read to me.'

'No, I don't mean that. If it comes out of a book you know it's not real. I mean someone who would just sit down and tell you things, as if they had just happened on the way home. I had an uncle who did that. For example once he went to Rome on business and when he got back he told me about a building which was like the sky at night, so big that even when you stood in front of it you couldn't believe you were actually seeing it. Yet it was completely useless, he said. It had no roof and no floor, just hundreds of brick arches piled one on top of another like a team of acrobats. He was describing the Colosseum.'

He opened the window and pushed his cigarette out.

'Once he was late arriving at our house. He told me that when the *vaporetto* arrived he had noticed something strange about it. The boat was lying far too low in the water, almost level with the surface, the decks awash. It made no sound, and even seemed to absorb the sounds around it, like a sponge soaking up water. The people who were waiting all boarded this strange boat, all except my uncle. I asked him why he hadn't got on with the other passengers. Because that was the ferry of death, he said. He explained that the people who had got on to that ferry would get off in another world, and would never be seen in this one again. There is another city all around us, he told me. We can't see it, but there are ways into it, although there is no way back. Anyone who boards a certain ferry or walks down a certain street or enters a certain building or goes through a certain door disappears for ever into that other city.'

Ellen was looking at him with an expression he had never seen before. For a moment he wondered if he was doing the right thing. But in some odd way the decision no longer seemed to be in his hands.

'My uncle's stories sounded unlikely, but they always turned out to be true. That parallel world really exists, and what happened to me in 1978 was that I unwittingly blundered into it.'

The wind surged around the little car, streaking past across the expanse of long brown grass still flattened from the snow that had lain on it over the winter.

'I was in the kidnapping section of the Criminal Investigation Branch at the time. I was considered to be doing well. Rome Central is one of the three top postings in the country, along with Milan and Naples, and I'd worked my way there through a succession of jobs in various provincial headquarters. Promotion to Vice-Questore seemed certain and the general feeling was that if I played my cards right I would make Questore in the end. When the Red Brigade kidnapped Moro we were all thrown into the investigation, under the direction of the Political Branch. The first thing we discovered was that there seemed to be almost no information to go on. Despite all the money the Politicals had been siphoning off for years, a very sore point with the rest of us, they claimed to have no material on the terrorists beyond a few isolated descriptions and photographs. It was almost unbelievable. Here was Aldo Moro, an ex-Prime Minister, the leader of the Christian Democrat Party and one of the most powerful and influential men in Italy, at the mercy of the best-known organization of political extremists, and the people responsible for combating political extremism told us there was nothing we could do except organize random house-to-house searches. So that's what we did, along with chasing after various red herrings which somebody provided to keep us busy. Then one day one of my inspectors, a man called Dario Carella, phoned in claiming to have seen one of the suspected terrorists. Carella had followed the man to a chemist's shop in Piazzale della Radio and then to a bus stop. But the suspect must have noticed him, because he suddenly waved down a passing taxi and drove off. Carella had taken the number of the taxi and we discovered that it had dropped the suspect outside the San Gallicano hospital in Trastevere. Meanwhile Carella went back to the chemist's to find out what the man had bought. The result was very interesting. The prescription had been forged, and the medicines listed were all among those regularly used by Aldo Moro. Besides suffering from Addison's disease, Moro was a bit of a hypochondriac and he used a lot of drugs. He had a supply with him when he was captured, but this would have run out by then. It looked as though one of his captors had been sent to get more. The Political Branch were informed and the hospital duly sealed off and searched, but there was no trace of the man. Next we did a door-to-door of the whole area. You probably remember that.'

'I certainly do. They almost wrecked my flat.'

'That wasn't any more successful. But Carella had an idea. The bus stop where the suspect had waited in Piazzale della Radio is served by three lines, the 97, 97C and 128. And just around the corner from the San Gallicano hospital, in Piazza Sonnino, is the terminus of the 97 and 97C. Suppose the suspect had taken the taxi to get rid of Carella, got out at the hospital to confuse matters further, walked around the corner to the terminus and then continued by bus to his original destination? In that case, this wouldn't be Trastevere but one of the districts to the south where those two lines go, Portuense or EUR. Carella explained his idea to me, and I thought it was worth following up. It wasn't as though we had a wealth of other leads. So I went upstairs and proposed that we should do a house-to-house on those two areas. There was nothing very original in this. It was just routine procedure, playing percentages, and I was very surprised when I heard that the proposal had been rejected. When I queried the decision I was told that it had been taken at the very highest level, as a result of information not available to me.'

He tried to remove a smudge from the windscreen with the tip of his finger, but it was on the other side of the glass.

'Well, all right, so I thought the decision was surprising, but I'd long since realized that if I allowed that sort of thing to keep me awake at night I was going to be a chronic insomniac. But Carella was not so phlegmatic. He was a Southerner and a devout Catholic, like Moro himself, and I think he felt guilty for not having made more of the best chance anyone had so far had to rescue his hero. In short, he got a bit obsessed with the whole thing and he couldn't accept the decision not to pursue it further. At least, that's what I assume. We didn't discuss it, and when he didn't appear at work the next day I thought he was just sulking. But that night one of my other inspectors phoned and told me that Carella was in hospital after being struck by a car in the Portuense district. It was the San Gallicano hospital, as it happened. By the time I got there he was dead.'

He looked up through the clear patch of windscreen at the clouds moving slowly and peacefully across the upper reaches of the sky. The wind up there must be a different quantity from the restless gusts at work where they were.

'This is where it gets difficult to explain. Because instead of just letting it go I allowed myself to get involved. I don't know why. I've been asking myself ever since. Dario Carella wasn't a relative or even a friend. I didn't actually like him very much. And yet I risked everything I had worked towards, all the hope of what I might do in a position of real power, for something that was obviously doomed to failure from the start. That bothers me, it really does. I've always thought of myself as a sensible person, yet I allowed myself to do that. I can't understand why.'

Ellen laughed, a short, mirthless noise.

'Oh Christ, Aurelio, I don't believe it!'

'You don't believe what?'

Her expression became opaque.

'Nothing. Go on.'

Apparently he'd got it wrong yet again.

'The next day I went to question the bus drivers. As I suspected, Carella had been there before me. One of the men I spoke to said that a colleague of his had indentified the terrorist suspect from a photograph Carella had shown him. I got the colleague's address and went to have a word with him. As I was walking up to his house two young bearded men in jeans and sweaters got out of a car and ran towards me. For a moment I thought they were terrorists, but I was wrong, they were Political Branch operatives. They drove me back to the ministry, where I was questioned by an officer I'd never seen before, a colonel. It was a small, stuffy room, and yet I distinctly felt a chill in the air, like a draught, and I knew that it must be coming from that other world my uncle had told me about, and that the threshold to it was somewhere very close at hand. The colonel wanted to know what I had been doing and who I had talked to. It wasn't an easy hand to play. On the one hand I needed to stress the bus driver's evidence in order to bolster my case, which was that Carella had somehow stumbled on a clue to Moro's whereabouts. On the other hand I was afraid that if I made the driver sound too important he might end up under the wheel of a bus instead of behind one. In the end I was told to go home and to stay there. The next day I received a telegram informing me that my request to be transferred to clerical duties at the Ministry of the Interior had been granted. I hadn't submitted any such request, of course.'

There was a long silence, broken only by the perpetual nudging of the wind, which seemed to be getting stronger all the time.

'Shall we go?' Ellen asked.

She started the engine without waiting for an answer and began to drive along the track winding down the mountain.

'The Red Brigade were holding Moro in Portuense, weren't they?' she commented suddenly.

'In a ground-floor flat in Via Montalcini. About four blocks from where Dario Carella was run over.'

It wasn't until they reached the walls of Assisi that she spoke again.

'It's no good, I don't understand. I'll never understand. Why should they let him be killed? It doesn't make any sense! After all, he was one of them.'

'Perhaps he was no longer really one of them. Perhaps they didn't know that until he was kidnapped. Perhaps once he'd gone they realized that they were better off without him. The ratking is self-regulating, it responds automatically and effectively to every situation.'

She took her eyes off the road for an instant to glance at him.

'What have rats got to do with it?'

'Oh, nothing. I was just trying to explain how Miletti came to be killed.'

'Miletti?'

'I mean Moro.'

'How much have you had to drink?'

'Enough to need a coffee.'

They stopped in a village strung out in ribbon development along the flat straight road from Assisi to Perugia. The air was still and it was pleasantly warm. The café was a brash new building full of old men playing cards.

'I'm going back this afternoon,' Ellen said as they stood at the bar, watched by every eye in the place.

Her visit had not been a success. The basic material of their relationship, the DNA itself, seemed to have gone wrong. As long as that condition lasted, the time they spent together, instead of adding to their store of shared experiences, depleted the existing one, leaving them more apart than when they were separated.

'I'll be back soon myself,' he told her, 'and then we'll forget all this and have a really good time again.'

When they reached Perugia she dropped him opposite the Questura. As he stooped to kiss her Zen noticed that her cheeks were wet.

'Why are you crying?'

She shook her head.

'I'm afraid.'

'Afraid of what?'

'Of everything.'

'There's no need to be afraid. It'll be all right.'

But he stood there watching until the little car had disappeared, as though Ellen were setting off on a long and dangerous journey from which she might never return.

NINE

One day towards the end of the war five ships had appeared in the lagoon off Venice. For a few weeks they lay moored together, like a new island between the city and the Lido, and then one day they were gone. Later Zen worked out that they must have been American warships of an obsolete type, waiting to be sold or scrapped, but at the time their slightly menacing presence seemed a pure challenge, and when his friend Tommaso dared him to try and get aboard one he naturally agreed.

Close up they were as big as churches: great solid slabs of crudely painted grey with black numbers too large to read. Only the end vessel was manned by a token guard, and it was merely terrifying to slip into one of the narrow channels between them, where the water slapped back and forth, tie their skiff to the anchor cable and then shin up it to the deck. The rest of that day they spent in an alien world of pipes and gauges and controls and levers and incomprehensible signs, like the first explorers of a ruined city.

With most of the staff going home at two o'clock, the end of the working day for employees of the state, the Questura had a faintly similar air of abandonment which Zen always found attractive. The rooms and corridors were empty except for a few elderly women cleaning up the male mess of scattered newspapers, stained coffee cups, overflowing ashtrays and the odd half-eaten sandwich. They had not yet reached Zen's office, but someone else had been there, for there was a telegram on his desk.

Although he had been expecting it, it was still a shock. He put it away in his pocket unopened, and mechanically leafed through the report on the forensic tests he had unofficially requested on the Fiat Argenta saloon which Gilberto Nieddu had stolen from outside the cemetery during Ruggiero Miletti's funeral and left abandoned near the scene of the murder. He had pinned all his hopes on this report providing him with some positive evidence to lay before the investigating magistrate, Rosella Foria, and when it had arrived that morning he'd been bitterly disappointed.

True, the three Pirellis and the odd Michelin on the car corresponded 'in their general type and configuration' to the marks found at the murder site, as he had confirmed when he checked the car at the SIMP garage. But in the absence of 'specific individuating features' a positive identification was not possible, while the soil samples found were merely 'consistent with types found throughout the area'. As for the interior, it was clear that the mechanic had done his work well. The only items found were inconclusive traces of paint and dust, some cigarette ash, a few yellow nylon threads and a fifty-lire coin which had fallen and lodged beside the seat support, whose metal base had protected it from the nozzle of Massimo's vacuum cleaner. In short, nothing that would persuade Rosella Foria that there was any case for pursuing this line of inquiry, when to do so would mean admitting that the Miletti family was under suspicion. To justify that you would need a lot more than the vague phrases of the report and the confused statements of a single witness. You would practically need a photograph of one of them pulling the trigger, and it had better be a bloody good photograph, and even then the smart thing to do would be to tear it up, burn the fragments and forget you'd ever seen it.

The door opened and a grizzled face bound in a green scarf appeared. At the same moment the phone began to ring.

'*May I speak to Commissioner Aurelio Zen, please.*'

A woman's voice, cool and distant.

'Speaking.'

'*This is Rosella Foria, investigating magistrate. I should like to see you in my office, please.*'

The cleaning woman was already hard at work, banging her mop into the corners of the room.

'Now?'

'*If that is convenient.*'

Her tone suggested that he'd better come even if it wasn't.

'It stinks!' the cleaning woman remarked as he hung up.

'What?'

'He can't control his pee.'

Her accent was so broad that Zen could barely understand.

'I rub and scrub from morning to night but it's no good, everything stinks.'

She waved at the crucifix Lucaroni had provided.

'He hangs up there doing sweet fuck all and they expect us to feel sorry for Him! I just wish we could change places, that's all! Half an hour of my life and He'd wish He was back on his nice cosy cross, believe you me.'

For once Zen accepted Palottino's offer of a lift up to the centre of town. On the way he amused himself by constructing a *prima facie* case against Cinzia Miletti. The gun used to kill Ruggiero was the same calibre as the pistol registered in her name, and the old salad-gatherer said that the driver of the Fiat had blonde hair. Cinzia claimed to have gone to Perugia to meet Ivy Cook, but Zen had discovered that she'd lied about the copy of Ruggiero's letter, and that lie too had been intended to throw suspicion on Ivy. Cinzia could have arranged the appointment in town, gone to avenge herself on the man who had abused her innocence, then driven into Perugia and made a point of accosting Zen in order to strengthen her alibi. She'd had the motive, the means and the opportunity, and if her second name hadn't been Miletti they would have run a ballistic check on that little pistol of hers, questioned her in detail about the time during which she claimed to have been waiting for Ivy and staged an identification parade to find out if the witness who had seen the blue Fiat and its blonde driver could pick her out. As it was, that was out of the question. Luciano Bartocci might have risked it, which was precisely why he had been replaced. Rosella Foria wouldn't make the same mistake. If only one of those nylon threads they'd found on the floor of the SIMP Fiat had been a blonde hair instead, Zen thought. But hair is either fair or yellow, Lucaroni had told him. It sounded like a line from a pop song, and he murmured it over and over to himself as the car burbled over the cobbles of Piazza Matteotti.

Rosella Foria turned out to be a rather primly dressed, fragile-looking woman in her early thirties. Although her manner was suitably authoritative, her face seemed to seek approval. Her office, although almost identical to Bartocci's, was impeccably neat and tidy.

'There are two matters which I wish to discuss with you, Commissioner,' she began. 'The first concerns a car belonging to the Miletti family which I understand has been impounded by the police.'

Zen had been expecting something of the kind.

'Two days ago I was informed that a blue Fiat Argenta saloon had been found abandoned near the scene of the murder,' he replied. 'Since such a car had been sighted by a witness near the scene and at the time of the murder I followed normal procedure and sent the vehicle for forensic analysis with a view to eliminating it from suspicion.'

'Yet you failed to notify the Public Prosecutor's office of this development. Why?'

Despite her uncompromising tone, she was still smiling. Zen was used to dealing with men, whose signals, ritualized over centuries of aggressive display, were clear and simple to follow. But Rosella Foria was unencumbered by such traditions.

'Because the correspondence with the car mentioned by the witness was only superficial, and I saw no reason to anticipate a positive identification.'

The magistrate drew her well-plucked brows together.

'I don't understand how you could fail to see the significance of your action for the investigation, given that the car belonged to the Miletti family.'

'I didn't know that it did.'

Rosella Foria's frown deepened.

'Do you mean to say that you failed to take the elementary step of tracing the registered owner of the vehicle?'

'On the contrary, that was the first thing I did. The car proved to be registered to a Fiat dealer. From what you have just told me I assume that it was one of those leased by the Miletti firm and used by the family.'

'It didn't occur to you to contact the dealer in question?'

'I certainly should have done so if the tests had produced any positive results. But in fact they were inconclusive.'

She looked at him long and hard, but he noticed her shoulders relax and knew that it would be all right. She might or might not believe him. The main thing was that he had given her a story she could pass on to Di Leonardo and the Milettis. She was off the hook.

'All the same, it's most unfortunate that this has happened. Needless to say, the family are extremely displeased.'

Zen did not need to ask how they had learned of it. Like every top family, they would have a contact in the force.

'The car was apparently stolen from outside the cemetery while they were attending their father's funeral,' the magistrate added, watching him carefully.

Zen's grey eyes remained impenetrably glazed.

'Probably some youngsters took it for a joy-ride and then dumped it.'

'Possibly. In any event, we may consider the incident closed. But in the present situation misunderstandings of this kind are to be avoided at all costs. I should like your assurance that you will take no further initiatives without consulting me.'

'Are you suggesting I have exceeded my powers?'

He knew very well that she wasn't, of course, just as he knew what she *was* doing: telling him to forget the legal niceties and please not lift so much as a finger without her consent, because the situation was so delicate, the moment so critical, the stakes so high.

'I don't feel it's the letter of the law that we ought to be concerned with here,' she went on in a conciliatory tone, fingering the single-strand pearl necklace which looped above the neck of her Benetton cardigan. 'It's more a question of not hurting people's feelings by hasty or ill-considered gestures, of not wounding a family which has just lost one of its members in deeply distressing circumstances. Above all it's a question of not doing this when it is demonstrably gratuitous and irrelevant to the purpose of apprehending those responsible for this crime.'

'But it's not demonstrably anything of the kind,' Zen protested. Although he lacked the hard evidence he'd hoped for, it was surely time to open this woman's eyes a little, to remind her of the possibilities that were being swept under the carpet. 'On the contrary, in my experience it's unheard of for criminals to phone a number they know is being monitored in order to give the location of the body of a man they have just killed. If they wanted to murder Miletti, why didn't they do it up in the mountains or wherever they were holding him? Why risk moving him to a spot close to Perugia only to shoot him dead?'

The investigating magistrate carefully rearranged the stack of papers on the desk in front of her so that the edges were perfectly aligned.

'If I chose, I could answer these objections with a much stronger one. You seem to forget that Dottor Miletti was murdered almost twenty-four hours *before* the call informing us that he had been released. During that period of time only the kidnappers knew where he was. So how could anyone else possibly have committed the crime? However, this is all beside the point. I said I had two things to tell you. The first concerned the Milettis' car. The second is that the Carabinieri in Florence have detained a number of men who are believed to be members of the gang which kidnapped and murdered Ruggiero Miletti. I'm going there tomorrow morning to conduct the formal interrogation, but I'm informed that they've already made a full confession.'

This was different, this was real. Zen felt like a child on the beach whose sandy battlements have melted beneath the first big wave. Appropriately, Rosella Foria's concluding words sounded almost maternal.

'Don't take it too hard, Commissioner. It's a pity that your efforts here have not been rewarded with success, but once you're back in Rome you will no doubt soon find other outlets for your energies.'

As soon as he got outside Zen took out the telegram which had been waiting for him at the Questura. As he had thought, it was from the Ministry, informing him that his temporary transfer to the Questura of Perugia would terminate at midnight on Friday and his normal duties at the Ministry resume with effect from 0800 Monday.

For at least a minute he stood motionless on the kerb, oblivious to the animated scene around him. Then he crumpled up the telegram and walked back to the Alfetta, where he made Palottino's day by telling him to drive to Florence as quickly as possible.

At Carabinieri headquarters in Florence Zen was received with just that air of polite suspicion that he had expected. When he announced that he had important information about the Miletti case he was taken upstairs and handed over to Captain Rivolta, a young officer with an aristocratic appearance and a languid manner who denied any personal involvement in what Zen referred to as 'this magnificent coup'.

'It was a tip-off, I suppose,' Zen suggested.

Captain Rivolta gave a minimal nod.

'From a Sardinian gang, I believe. The usual rivalry.'

'So they were based here in Florence?'

Rivolta repeated his fastidious gesture of assent.

'Two brothers. They ran a furniture showroom and recycled the ransom along with takings from the business. They handled the negotiations themselves. It was they who had the Miletti's representative killed. Apparently he caught sight of one of them during the negotiations.'

Zen nodded sagely. It was going quite well, he thought. The young captain was relaxing nicely.

'Anyway, I understand you have some information to pass on,' Rivolta murmured.

'No, that's just what I told them downstairs.'

Captain Rivolta appeared to wake up fully for the first time.

'I've come to see the prisoners,' Zen explained.

'Well, that's a bit difficult, I'm afraid. As you are no doubt aware, requests for interrogation rights must be presented through the appropriate channels.'

'That's all right, I don't want to interrogate them. I want to beat them up.'

The young officer's superior smile froze in place, as though he wasn't quite sure what to do with it.

'Beat them up,' he repeated mechanically.

'Well, just one of them actually. The one who called me a fuckarse and a cocksucker when they had me at their mercy during the pay-off, up there in the mountains. The one who kicked me in the balls and in the face and then left me there to die. If your men hadn't come out and found me, God bless them, I *would* have died! Phone them, if you don't believe me!'

The captain held up his hands placatingly. Zen gave an embarrassed smile.

'Anyway, perhaps you understand now why I came straight here as soon as I heard that you'd laid hands on the bastards. Just fifteen minutes, that's all I ask.'

'Well, I'm really not sure that I can agree to authorize you to, ah . . .'

'I won't leave a mark on him.'

'Possibly not, but . . .'

'I've done this sort of thing before.'

'Yes, I'm sure you have. Nevertheless, there is the question of . . .'

Zen shot out of his chair.

'There's the question of teaching these fucking bastards to respect authority, Captain, that's what the question is! Next time it might be you out there, remember. Now the politicians have taken away the death penalty what have these animals got to lose? We've got to stick together, Captain, make our own arrangements. Just fifteen minutes, that's all I ask.'

Rivolta stared up at Zen, seemingly mesmerized.

'You're sure there won't be any marks?' he murmured at last.

Zen smiled unpleasantly.

'Like I always say, it's the ones that don't show that hurt the most.'

The corridor was straight, evenly lit and apparently endless, with steel doors set at equal intervals on either side. Zen had unconsciously adopted the same pace as his escort, so their footsteps rapped out a single rhythm on the concrete floor. At length the sergeant stopped, produced a set of keys and unlocked one of the doors. Zen's nostrils flared at the smell which emerged, sheep and smoke and dirt and sweat all worked together, overpowering the antiseptic odour which he hadn't been aware of until it went under to this blast from another world.

There were two men in the cell, one lying on the bunk bed, the other leaning against the wall. They stared at the intruders. The Carabinieri sergeant produced a pair of handcuffs and snapped them with practised ease on to the wrists of the man on the bed.

'On your feet, shithead,' he remarked without animosity.

He grasped the man's left elbow between forefinger and thumb and pushed him towards the door. The man winced and said something in dialect to the other prisoner. Then the door slammed shut and they were walking again, three of them now rapping out the same rhythm along the corridor.

They passed through a set of doors like an air lock, separating the cells from the rest of the building. The prisoner didn't move fast enough for the sergeant's liking and again he made him wince, although the only contact between them was the two-fingered grip on the man's elbow. Then they turned left through a pair of swing doors into a small gymnasium.

'Jesus!' the Calabrian muttered.

The sergeant guided him over to a set of wall-bars.

'You'll fucking well speak when you're spoken to and not unless,' he remarked.

'But we talk already!'

'You don't understand,' the sergeant told him. 'That was work. This is pleasure.'

He spun the prisoner round, undid one end of the handcuffs, looped it through the wall-bars and locked it back on the man's wrist so that the handcuffs wrenched his arms up and back in the classic *strappado* position.

'OK?'

Zen nodded appreciatively.

'Very nice.'

The sergeant chopped the edge of his hand down on the elbow he had been gripping earlier. The prisoner groaned.

'Hurt his arm,' the sergeant commented conversationally. 'He's all yours, then. Fifteen minutes.'

The swing doors banged together behind him a few times and then all was quiet.

Zen lit a cigarette.

'You remember me,' he said, placing it between the prisoner's lips.

The man stared at him through the smoke which drifted up into his unblinking eyes.

'Was it you?'

The prisoner drew on the cigarette. His gaze was as absolute and incurious as a cat's. His head shook.

'They come looking for him but he is not there. They take the brother instead and later he is dead. From then he hates all police.'

For the Calabrian the Tuscan dialect called Italian was as foreign a language as Spanish, but Zen dimly perceived the general outlines of the story.

'We know this only after,' the prisoner went on. 'We phone them to get you. We don't want anyone killed.'

'Except Ruggiero Miletti.'

The man mouthed the cigarette to one side.

'We don't kill Miletti!'

'You've confessed to doing so.'

'We don't want to end like the brother. When the judge comes we deny everything.'

'I don't think she's going to be very impressed by that.'

The prisoner looked sharply at Zen.

'It's a woman?'

This seemed to disturb him more than anything else.

'What of it?'

'They're the worst.'

Zen sighed.

'Look, you had the means, the opportunity and a reasonable motive. Everyone is going to assume you did it, no matter what you say.'

The prisoner let the cigarette drop from his mouth and trod it out with the care of one from a land where fire is not completely domesticated.

'It's the same. At Milan innocent till guilty, at Rome guilty till innocent, in Calabria guilty till guilty.'

Zen glanced at his watch.

'I believe that you didn't kill Ruggiero Miletti.'

'Prison for kidnap, prison for murder. Same prison.'

He's always known this would happen one day, Zen thought, and now that it has he feels oddly reassured. And I'm cast in the role of a smart lawyer trying to make Oedipus believe that I've found a loophole in fate and given a sympathetic jury I can get him off with a suspended sentence.

'Look, I've read the letter Ruggiero sent to his family,' he told the prisoner. 'He made it clear that you treated him well. As far as the kidnapping goes you were small fry, manual workers. You'll go to prison, certainly, but with good behaviour and a bit of luck you'll get out one day. But if you're sent down for killing a defenceless old man in cold blood then that's the end. They won't bother locking your cell, they'll just weld up the door. And you'll know that whatever happens, however society changes, whichever party comes to power, you're going to die in prison and be buried in a pit of quicklime, because if any of your relatives still remember who you are they'll be too ashamed to come and claim your body.'

The prisoner stared stoically at the floor. Zen consulted his watch again.

'Tell me about the day you released Miletti.'

There was no reply.

'If I'm to help you I need to know!'

Eventually the deep voice ground unwillingly into action.

'We drive him there and leave him. That's all.'

'What time was this?'

'Before light.'

'On Monday? Four days ago?'

A grudging nod.

'And when did you phone the family?'

'Later.'

'Later the same morning? On Monday?'

Another nod.

'Which number did you phone?'

'The same as before.'

'When before?'

'When we go to get the money.'

He seemed bored, as if none of this concerned him and he simply wanted to get it over with as quickly as possible.

'And who did you speak to?'

'I don't speak.'

Of course. The gang would have picked someone more articulate as their spokesman.

'You don't know anything about who answered? A man? A woman? Young? Old?'

'A man, of course! Not of the family. Like you.'

'Like me?'

'From the North.'

Zen nodded, holding the man's eyes. Time must be getting desperately short, but he didn't dare break the concentration by glancing at his watch.

'The man who hates the police because of what they did to his brother, how did he know who I was?'

'He say he can smell them.'

Zen's foot hooked the man's ankles and pulled him off balance so that he fell forward with a short cry of pain.

'That was very brave of you,' Zen commented as the prisoner struggled back to his feet. 'But we don't have time for bravery. Who told you I was coming on the pay-off?'

The man stood motionless, eyes closed, breathing the pain away.

'Some people say Southerners are stupid,' Zen continued. 'I hope you're not going to prove them right. I can't help you unless I know who your contact was.'

He moved closer to the prisoner, inside the portable habitat of mountain odours that surrounded him like a sheath.

'Was it one of the family?'

No response.

'Or someone in the Questura?'

The man's eyelids flickered but did not open.

'Someone called Lucaroni?'

Zen's gaze swarmed over the prisoner's face. 'Chiodini?'

Behind him the doors banged open and boots rapped out across the parquet flooring.

'Geraci?'

Suddenly the eyes were on him again, pure and polished and utterly empty of expression.

'Everything go all right?' asked the sergeant, appearing at Zen's side. 'Didn't give you any trouble, did he?'

Zen turned slowly, rubbing his hands together.

'It went just fine, thank you.'

The sergeant unlocked the handcuffs and the prisoner straightened his arms with a long groan. Zen buttoned up his overcoat.

'I'll be going then.'

'Didn't know you were here,' the sergeant remarked.

The Alfetta was parked on the pavement outside, forcing pedestrians out into the street jammed with traffic. Palottino sat inside reading a comic featuring a naked woman with large breasts cowering in terror before an enormous spider brandishing a blood-stained chainsaw. It was drizzling lightly and the evening rush hour was at its peak, but thanks to a judicious use of the siren and a blatant disregard for the rules of the road the Neapolitan contrived to move the Alfetta through the traffic almost as though it did not exist. Meanwhile Zen sat gazing out at the narrow cobbled streets, teeming with quirky detail to an extent that seemed almost unreal, like the carefully contrived background to a film scene. But it was just the effect of the contrast with that other world, a world of carefully contrived monotony, designed for twenty thousand people but inhabited by more than twice that number, of whom several hundred killed themselves each year and another fifty or so were murdered, a world whose powerful disinfectant would seep into the blood and bones of the violent, gentle shepherds who had kidnapped Ruggiero Miletti, until it had driven them safely mad.

Zen lit a Nazionale and stretched luxuriously. What the Calabrian had told him made everything simple. All he had to do was get in touch with Rosella Foria before she left for Florence and pass on the information he had received and he could return to Rome exonerated and with a clear conscience. The key was that the kidnappers had telephoned on Monday, not on Tuesday, and that the number they had called was the one communicated to them by the family before the pay-off, as stipulated in Ruggiero's letter. Whoever had answered this telephone call was at the very least an accessory to Ruggiero's murder and could be arrested at once. The rest would follow.

As they hit the motorway, surging forward into the rain-filled darkness, Zen suddenly felt slightly light-headed, and he told Palottino to stop at a service area so that they could get something to eat. Ten minutes later they were sitting at a formica-topped table in a restaurant overlooking the motorway. Zen was chaffing his driver about a toy panda he had bought for his brother's little daughter, a great favourite of his. Palottino produced a number of photographs of the child, which they both admired. Encouraged by his superior's good humour, the Neapolitan asked how things were going, and Zen felt so relaxed and obliging that he told him what had happened in Florence. Palottino laughed admiringly at the clever ruse Zen had used to gain access to the kidnappers, and at his description of the languid young captain who had fallen for it. But when it came to the prisoner's revelations he unfortunately got the wrong end of the stick.

'Called another number on another day!' he jeered. 'Oh, yes, very clever! What do they take us for, idiots?'

'Sorry?'

'Well, I mean no one's going to believe that, are they? Not when there's a recording, logged and dated, of them actually making the call on Tuesday. I mean, it's a clear case of pull the other one, right?'

Zen stared at him. He seemed to be having difficulty focusing.

'No. No, you don't understand. They called *another* number, not the Miletti house. On Monday.'

Quickly reading the signals, Palottino did an abrupt U-turn.

'Oh, I see! You mean you *know* they did. Oh, well, that's different! Sorry, chief, I didn't realize that. I thought it was just their word against the official record. And like we say in Naples, never believe a Calabrian unless he tells you he's lying!'

Zen gazed down at the surface of the table gleaming dully under the flat neon light. He stood up abruptly.

'I've got to go to the toilet. I'll meet you in the car.'

As Zen washed his hands he gazed at his face in the mirror above the basin. How could he have failed to see what was obvious even to a knucklehead like Palottino? How could he have imagined for a second that the kidnappers' unsupported assertions would be taken seriously by anyone? On the contrary, they would be indignantly dismissed as a feeble and disgusting attempt by a gang of ruthless killers to add insult to injury by smearing the family of the man they had just savagely murdered.

It was Thursday evening now. His mandate in Perugia ran until midnight on Friday. That gave him just over twenty-four hours. He phoned the Night Duty Officer at the Questura in Perugia and then, since he had some tokens left, dialled Ellen's number in Rome. But as soon as it began to ring he pushed the rest down with his finger, breaking the connection.

He must have dozed off, for the next thing he was aware of was feeling chilled and anxious. Through the window he could see the upper limb of a huge planet which almost filled the night sky. The collision in which the earth would inevitably be destroyed was clearly only moments away, for despite its appalling size the planet's motion was perceptible. It was even close enough for him to make out the lights of the hundreds of cities dotted across its monstrous convex surface.

'Son of a *bitch*!'

The world swerved, veered, straightened up.

'Fucking lorry drivers, think they own the road,' Palottino commented.

When Zen looked again the rogue planet had become a ridge blanked in darkly on the clear moonlit sky and its alien cities the twinkling lights of Perugia.

It was only just gone ten o'clock, but the streets were deserted. Palottino pulled into the car park where it was never night and they got out, watched by the guard on the roof of the prison. In the blank wall of the Questura opposite a light showed in Zen's office on the third floor.

Geraci must have heard his footsteps, for he was standing by the window with a respectful and curious expression as Zen came in.

'Evening, chief. What's up, then?'

The Duty Officer had told him to report to the Questura and await further instructions. Motioning the inspector to a chair, Zen went round behind the desk and sat down, rubbing his eyes.

'I've just got back from Florence. The military have taken the whole gang. All of them. Well, not quite all.'

Geraci's expression shifted almost imperceptibly, like the face of someone who has just died. The silence re-formed. Zen felt himself starting to slip back into his interrupted sleep and he forced his eyes open, staring intently at Geraci until the inspector looked away.

'I would never have agreed if it hadn't been for the boy,' he said.

'How much did they offer you?'

'It wasn't the money,' Geraci replied scornfully. 'We're from the same place, from neighbouring villages. They simply asked me to help them out. I would gain nothing myself, just the goodwill of certain people, people who are respected.'

He shook his head at the impossibility of a Northerner understanding these things.

'Anyway, I said no. So they started to use threats, although they don't like doing that. To them it's a sign of weakness. But they had asked and I had refused. They can't allow that.'

He paused and sighed.

'Just before Christmas I heard from my sister. Her youngest boy, just three years old, a little darling, had been taken. A few days later a letter arrived for me. Inside there was a little scrap of skin and a tiny fingernail. They'd amputated his finger with a pair of wire-cutters. I never thought fingernails were beautiful until I saw this one, it was like a miniature work of art. That evening they phoned me again. The boy still had nine more fingers and ten toes, they said. I agreed to do what they asked.'

Zen pushed his chair back and stood up, trying to dominate the situation again, to rise above the pity that threatened to swamp him.

'And what was that?'

'Get myself transferred to the squad investigating the kidnapping and pass on any information which might be useful.'

'And they gave you the tape-recorder and the crucifix?'

'Not until you arrived. While Priorelli was in charge I didn't need it, he was very open about his plans. But no one ever knew what you were thinking or what you were going to do.'

Zen allowed himself a moment to savour the irony of this. He had been uncommunicative with his staff because he thought they were all hostile to him and reporting back to the Questore, if not the Ministry or the Security Services!

'Where was the receiver?'

'In the broom cupboard at the end of the corridor, hidden under a pile of old boxes and papers. I played back the tapes at home and noted down anything important.'

'And the contacts with the gang? Come on, Geraci! I want to get home, go to bed. Don't make me do all the work.'

'I put an advertisement in the newspaper offering a boat for sale. The day the advertisement appeared I took a certain train, got into the first carriage and left the envelope in the bin for used towels in the toilet.'

Zen shook his head slowly. His disgust was as much with himself as with Geraci, but the inspector suddenly flared up.

'I wasn't the biggest shit in all this! One of the Milettis was in on it too! Can you imagine that? Betraying your own father! At least I didn't sink that low.'

Zen waved his hand wearily.

'Don't waste time trying to do dirt on the family. I'm not interested.'

Geraci got to his feet.

'It's true, I tell you! I had to pick up his messages at a service area on the motorway and leave them on the train, same as my own. Once I got there early and saw him.'

'So who was it?'

'I don't know.'

Zen snorted his contempt.

'He was all wrapped up in a coat and a scarf and wearing dark glasses, and I was watching from a distance. I didn't want to risk being recognized either.'

'How did he get there?'

'In a blue Fiat Argenta saloon.'

'Was there anyone else in the car?'

'No.'

'Describe him.'

'Quite short. Medium build.'

'How do you know it wasn't a woman?'

'He phoned to let me know he was coming. It was a man, all right.'

Zen turned to the window, as though he feared that his thoughts might be visible in his face. Daniele and Silvio were out. Pietro, too. Ivy Cook's voice was deep enough to be mistaken for a man's, but she was too tall. Cinzia was the right size, but her voice was almost hysterically feminine. No, there was really only one person it could have been.

'How many times did this happen?'

'Four altogether. I can give you the dates.'

Geraci took out his diary and scribbled on a blank page which he then tore out and handed to Zen.

'Where did he leave the messages?'

'At the Valdichiana service area on the motorway. The envelope was inside the last magazine in the top right-hand row.'

Zen sighed.

'So let's sum up. You claim that an unknown person in male clothing driving a Fiat saloon left four envelopes in a motorway service station. You don't know who he was, why he was doing it or what was in the envelopes, and you can't prove any of it. Doesn't add up to much, does it?'

Geraci looked away in frustration.

'Ah, what's the use! It isn't doing wrong that counts, it's getting caught.'

The same was even more true of doing right, Zen reflected. The wrongdoer arouses sneaking admiration, but if you want to be merciful or generous without making people despise you then you have to be very careful indeed.

'Tomorrow is my last day here in Perugia,' he said wearily. 'My tour of duty hasn't exactly been a glittering success and the public disclosure that one of my inspectors was a spy for the gang I was supposed to be hunting would be the last straw. So you're going to get a break, Geraci. You don't deserve it, but I do.'

The inspector gazed at him with an immense caution, not daring to understand.

'My conversation with the kidnappers was private. As far as I'm concerned it can remain private. I'd much prefer to turn you in, but luckily for you I can't afford to.'

Geraci's eyes were glowing with emotion.

'Dottore, my mother will . . .'

'Stuff your mother, Geraci! It's me I'm thinking of, not your mother or anybody else. Now I'm sure someone like you must know a crooked doctor. I want you to take indefinite sick leave starting tomorrow. You can spend your free time writing an application for transfer to the Forestry Guards. You're not staying in the police, that's for damn sure! Now piss off out of here before I change my mind.'

Geraci backed up to the door.

'God bless you, sir.'

The door closed quietly behind him.

'God help us,' muttered Zen.

Nine o'clock was sounding as he walked out of his hotel the next morning, sniffing the delicious air enlivened by a frisky breeze. After this, he reflected, breathing the capital's miasmal vapours would be like drinking Tiber water after San Pellegrino. Halfway along the Corso workmen were setting up a platform, the ringing sounds of their hammers unsynchronized to the movements of the arms which produced them. As he walked towards them the problem gradually corrected itself, as though the projectionist had woken up and made the necessary adjustments. By the time he emerged from his favourite café, having consumed a good frothy cappuccino made with milk fresh from a churn, the foam stiff as whipped egg whites, the same process had taken place inside his head. But any impression that things were finally going his way did not last long.

'All that material has been transferred upstairs,' the technician on duty in the intercept room at the law courts told him.

'What about transcripts?'

The man shook his head.

'All upstairs with the judges. We've finished with that one. The line's been disconnected and everything.'

Zen hesitated for a moment.

'May I use your phone?'

'Help yourself.'

There was an internal directory pinned to the wall by the phone. He dialled Luciano Bartocci's number.

'Yes?'

'Well, it did come to the same thing in the end.'

'Who is this?'

'I'm going back to Rome tomorrow. But first I'd like to have a word with you. About ratkings.'

There was a silence.

'*I'm very busy.*'

'It'll only take a few moments.'

The technician was busy fitting a new leader to a reel of tape. His work probably left him little interest in listening to other people's conversations, but Zen kept his voice low.

'It's vitally important.'

Zen spoke slowly, stressing each word, giving Bartocci time to think.

'*In about half an hour. On the roof of the market building.*'

Zen pushed past the women selling doughnuts and flowers and through a group of African students giggling at the photos they had just had taken in the machine. The terrace on the roof of the market was deserted except for a flock of pigeons and the two Nordic girls, one of whom was sketching the view while the other basked in the sun, her head on her friend's lap. The puddle under a leaky tap near by had frozen overnight and not yet had time to thaw, so that the pigeons slipped and skidded as they came to drink.

When Luciano Bartocci appeared, tense and wary, Zen wasted no time.

'I need to consult a document.'

'Ask Foria.'

'She's not here. It's urgent.'

Bartocci shook his head.

'Out of the question.'

'I just need a copy of the transcript of the call the gang made to tell the Milettis that they had released Ruggiero.'

'Why?'

'The Carabinieri in Florence have arrested the kidnappers. I've been to see them. They didn't kill Ruggiero.'

'What's that got to do with you? Or with me, for that matter? Rosella Foria is investigating the Miletti murder. Let her investigate. That's her job. Or do you think you're cleverer than she is?'

'I think I understand the situation better, thanks to you.'

Bartocci smiled at this clumsy attempt at flattery.

'Remember what you told me about ratkings?' Zen reminded him. 'How each rat defends the interests of the others and so the strength of one is the strength of all? Well, I think there's one case where that doesn't apply, where the system goes into reverse and the rats all turn on each other.'

'And that is?'

'When they sense that one of their number is damaged.'

The magistrate shook his head.

'They would simply destroy the damaged rat.'

'But suppose they don't know which one it is?'

Bartocci considered this for a moment.

'It all sounds a bit theoretical.'

'I agree. What I want to do is to test the theory. And that's why I need to see that transcript.'

One or two pigeons were already scrabbling about at their feet, their beady eyes skinned for a hand-out. Bartocci would clearly have liked to tell Zen to go to hell, but he was trapped by the relationship which he himself had been at such pains to create, and which he wasn't quite cynical enough to disavow now that it served not him but the other person. It was less trouble in the end just to give in.

'You remember the bar we went to in Piazza Matteotti?' he asked. 'Be there later on this morning, about midday. If there's anything for you read it there and then, seal it up and hand it back. If there isn't then go away. And stay away.'

On the Corso the hammering had stopped and the platform was being decorated with flags and bunting and posters proclaiming a political address the following day. By then, Zen thought, I'll be back in Rome, whatever happens. He found this oddly comforting.

The civic library was staffed by the usual sullen crew, as though it were a branch of the prison service. Since Zen was not a registered member it took his police identity card even to get him past the door. He climbed up to the periodicals room on the second floor and announced to the female attendant that he wished to consult back numbers of the local newspaper.

'Fill in a request form,' she replied, without looking up from her knitting.

There were no forms to be seen, but one of the other inmates explained that they were kept in the corridor on the next floor up.

'And the accession number?' the woman demanded when Zen brought his form back. The tip of her steel knitting needle hovered over a space as blank as Zen's face.

'I don't know what the accession number is.'

'Look it up!'

'Can't you do it?'

'It's not my job to fill in the forms. You have to look in the card catalogue.'

The card catalogue was in the basement. It took Zen twenty minutes to locate the section dealing with the newspaper he wanted. Since each month's copies had a separate accession number he then had to make out six different forms, which meant going back to the third floor and copying out his name, address, profession, and reason for request twelve times.

By half past ten he was back. The woman's knitting was making good progress. She pushed his forms away.

'No more than three requests may be submitted at one time.'

He handed back the forms corresponding to the last three months. The woman scrutinized them in vain for further errors or omissions, laid down her knitting with a reluctant sigh and trotted off. As soon as she was out of sight Zen took out his pocket-knife and cut through a stitch in the middle of the work she had completed.

He needn't have hurried. A further ten minutes elapsed before she returned, pushing a trolley bearing three large folders fastened with black tape.

'Keep pages in order edges straight corners aligned do not crease crinkle or tear leave at your position after use,' she told him.

As he began his search through the classified advertisements columns, Zen realized why the kidnappers had chosen boats as their cover. Perugia is about as far from the sea as any Italian city can be, and particularly during the winter interest in buying and selling boats is low. As a result there was little chance of the gang overlooking one of the messages intended for them. The discovery of the advertisements which confirmed Geraci's story was gratifying, but what really excited Zen was an announcement which had appeared the previous Friday, the day after the Milettis received Ruggiero's letter giving the instructions for the final ransom payment. 'Two-way radio for sale,' it read. 'Phone 8818 after 7.'

It looked innocuous enough, and yet Zen felt like an astronomer sighting a planet whose existence he had predicted from his calculations. This was the clincher, the thing that made everything else make sense. It was like in a dream where, tired of beating your fists against a locked and bolted door, you step back and notice for the first time that there is no wall on either side. Of course! It was so simple, so obvious.

In the bar opposite the post office a street-sweeper was explaining how he would sort out the national football team.

'Too many solo artists, that's the problem. One of them gets the ball and sees a bit of open space, all he thinks about is going forward, the rest of the team might as well not exist. When it comes off it's magnificent, I grant you, but how often does that happen, eh? No, it's percentages that add up in the end, this is what they don't realize. What we need is more discipline, more organization, more team-work.'

'Well, this is it,' the barman said, turning to the new customer with an interrogatory lift of the chin.

Zen identified himself and was handed a white envelope which was tucked between two bottles of fruit syrup. He opened it and took out a photocopy of a typed page:

INTERCEPT: *Yes?*

CALLER: *Verona.*

INTERCEPT: *What? You've got the wrong number.*

CALLER: *OK, listen. We have released Dottor Miletti. Understand? But someone'll have to go and pick him up. It's his leg, he can't walk. Here's how to find him.*

INTERCEPT: *Wait a moment! Turn down that music, Daniele!*

CALLER: *. . . the road to Foligno. Just beyond Santa Maria degli Angeli turn right, the Cannara road. Go to the telegraph pole with the mark and turn left. Take the second right and go about a kilometre until you see a building site beside the road on the left. The Milettis' father is there.*

INTERCEPT: *Wait a minute! The second on the right or the left? Hello? Hello?*

Zen looked up, his breath coming short and fast. He sealed up the photocopy in the envelope enclosed and handed it back to the barman. Then he got a telephone token and dialled the police laboratory. Hair is either fair or yellow, Lucaroni had told him. But all that's yellow isn't hair, the laboratory confirmed. The yellow threads found in the Fiat they had examined were strands from a cheap synthetic wig.

He emerged into the bright sunlight, blinking like a mole. The last piece of the puzzle was in place. He knew who had done it and how it had been done, and with the exception of the murderer he was the only person who did know. For a few more hours the whole situation would remain fluid and he held the key cards in his hands. If he played them right then perhaps just this once the bastards wouldn't get away with it after all. He tried not to think about what might happen if he played them wrong.

TEN

Gianluigi Santucci sat at the head of the dining table watching his family feed. Although he had hardly noticed his wife take a mouthful, her plate was already empty. He wondered how she managed to do it, given that she had been talking almost uninterruptedly since the meal began. His daughter Loredana had originally taken only four pieces of ravioli, subsequently increased to five under sustained pressure from her mother. But since she had eaten only half of them this apparent victory revealed itself, like so many in the family circle, as illusory. Gianluigi didn't need to read Cinzia's trashy psychology magazines to know that Loredana worshipped the ground he trod on. One of the ways in which this manifested itself was by her mimicking of the meagre diet to which her father was reduced by his digestive problems. For though Gianluigi was proud of the good fare he provided for his family, that was about the only pleasure he could take in it since this vicious intruder had taken up residence in his gut.

How his mother would have triumphed! As a child Gianluigi had resembled not fastidious Loredana but little Sergio there, his face cheerily smeared with tomato sauce, putting away the sticky pouches with a single-mindedness he would soon devote to masturbation. Gianluigi too had been a stuffer, eating as though he had a secret mission to devour the world. His mother had never left him in peace on the subject. 'Don't eat so fast, it's bad for you. Don't eat bread before your pasta, it's bad for you. Don't put oil on your meat, it's bad for you.' But she had never understood the secret source of her son's appetite: a gnawing envy of an elder brother who seemed so much bigger and more successful. Pasquale could dominate a room just by walking into it, and even his absence usually appeared to be of more interest than Gianluigi's presence. 'If you don't eat you won't grow,' his mother told him. Gianluigi turned this logic on its head and determined to eat his way into a future where he would be bigger and better than anyone around. But the only result had been a stomach condition which left him unable to do more than nibble a few scraps while this pain roamed his innards like a rat.

His hunger hadn't disappeared, however. It had just taken a different form. His physical size he could do nothing about, but on every other score he had beaten his brother hollow! Pasquale was now a dentist responsible for curing half the tooth problems in Siena and causing the other half, as he himself liked to joke. But his three children were all girls, his wife was a whore – Gianluigi himself had had her three times last summer – and although his earnings were respectable enough, his rival could already match him lira for lira twice over. And that was only the beginning. The events of the past week had opened up perspectives which even Gianluigi found slightly dizzying.

Not that he was by any means unprepared for the pickings that Ruggiero's death promised to bring with it. On the contrary, he had been working towards that very goal from the moment he met Cinzia Miletti. For in the end Pasquale had proved to be a disappointment. Like many young achievers he had gone into an early decline, growing fat and complacent, no challenge for the pool of unused ambition that ached and burned like the excess gastric acids in Gianluigi's stomach. He needed roughage, and his solution had been to marry into a family full of brothers and take them all on. He had been counting on this using up his energies for many years to come, so his pleasure at the way things had worked out was mixed with a certain amount of regret that it was all over so quickly. The Japanese deal on which he had expended so much energy and cunning was irrelevant now. Ruggiero's will would hold no surprises. Each of the Miletti children would receive a twenty-five per cent holding in SIMP. Cinzia's share was already in his hands, of course, and he could count on Daniele's too. It was not just a question of the money he had been advancing the boy ever since he got himself into trouble over drugs, although by now that amounted to almost a hundred million lire. Daniele was hooked on something quite as addictive as hard drugs and almost as expensive: a fashion market whose sole function was to flaunt the spending power of its wearers, or rather their fathers. To admit that he could no longer compete because his father had turned his back on him would have been the ultimate humiliation for the boy, so he had been glad to accept his brother-in-law's help. But what made Gianluigi quite certain of Daniele's support was the fact that the boy admired him. Pietro had never understood that, never been prepared to admit that his younger brother's hero was the outsider in the family, the pushy, self-seeking Tuscan. He would have to pay for that. One of Gianluigi's axioms was that one always paid for any lack of clarity and realism. Meanwhile he accepted Daniele's homage as he did his daughter's, and with as little thought of consummating the relationship. The fact of the matter was that the boy hadn't a hope in hell of ever amounting to anything, being spoiled, weak, vain and without that bitter inner pain that drives a man on.

So there he was in effective control of fifty per cent of SIMP. But even if Pietro knew that, he would still be counting on Silvio to balance things out. Which was a mistake, because when the chips were down Silvio would support Gianluigi too. This was something that Pietro could have no inkling of, for the simple reason that Silvio didn't know himself and would have denied it strenuously if he'd been asked. Nevertheless when the time came he would vote with Gianluigi, because of the photographs. Gianluigi had paid a detective agency in Milan five million lire for them, but like Daniele's allowance it was money well spent. Those photographs would make him undisputed master of the Miletti empire. It had been a nerve-racking business, particularly the last few weeks. He wondered what his family would think if they knew the risks he had been running. But now it was all over and he had come out on top. The Milettis had made it clear from the beginning that they played winner-take-all. And he would, he would!

The doorbell sounded and Margherita set down the dish of fried fish she was serving to go and answer it.

'Who on earth can that be?' Cinzia wondered aloud. 'What an idea, not even lunchtime is sacred any more, no wonder there's so much tension and unhappiness in the world, finish your pasta, Loredana.'

The housekeeper reappeared in the doorway.

'It's the police, dottore.'

Gianluigi was accustomed to living with pains, but the one that shot across his chest now was a stranger.

'Tell them to come back later,' his wife told the housekeeper, as though it was as easy as that, as though there was nothing to worry about. 'It's really too bad, a total chaos and intrusion.'

'No, I'll sort them out.'

He got to his feet, gathering his strength, his courage, his wits.

Margherita's words had conjured up visions of armed men surrounding the house, and when Gianluigi reached the door he was relieved to find no one there but Aurelio Zen. But relief merely made him angry for having been given an unnecessary fright.

'What the hell do you want now, Zen? Don't you know it's lunchtime?'

'I'm sorry to disturb you, dottore, but it's a matter of the highest urgency.'

'It had better be.'

He was sure of himself again, in control of the situation. This sort of confrontation was the stuff of his life, for which he trained like an athlete. Once he had mastered that initial moment of panic it was a pleasure to exercise those considerable skills.

'According to our records,' Zen went on, 'your wife is the registered owner of a Beretta pistol. I would like to examine it with a view to eliminating it from our inquiries.'

'Let me see your search warrant.'

'I'm not conducting a search.'

Gianluigi allowed his eyebrows to rise.

'Oh? Then what the fuck are you doing, may I ask, disturbing me without the slightest warning in the middle of lunch?'

'I'm conducting a preliminary inquiry in the sense of article 225 of the Penal Code, the results of which will be communicated to the Public Prosecutor's office and a search warrant issued in due course, your refusal to cooperate having been noted. But what's the problem? You have got the gun, haven't you?'

'Of course.'

This automatic reply was his first error, conceding the man's right to question him. But the sudden change of tone had caught him by surprise.

'Then why not just show it to me?' Zen suggested. 'It'll save both of us a lot of unnecessary bother.'

There was a shuffle of bare feet as Cinzia appeared.

'What's going on, Lulu? Oh, Commissioner, I thought you were back in Rome. Surely you must be.'

She and Zen exchanged a lingering glance.

'Get on with your lunch,' Gianluigi told his wife. 'I'll handle this.'

Realizing that after this interruption his earlier position of rigid intransigence would seem stilted, Gianluigi told his visitor to wait, went through to the living room and opened the top drawer of the old desk where the pistol was always kept.

It was not there.

For thirty seconds he stood quite still, thinking. But though the disappearance of the pistol was both mysterious and annoying, there was nothing whatever to be worried about. He returned to the front door.

'Look, the thing appears to have been mislaid,' he told Zen, who was now leaning against the wall smoking a cigarette. 'Probably the cleaning lady has put it somewhere. We'll have a proper look this afternoon or tomorrow if you care to contact me later.'

He was starting to close the door as Zen replied.

'That's fine. I didn't really come about the gun at all.'

The door opened again.

'I beg your pardon?'

'There's been an unfortunate development, dottore. As the result of a tip-off the Carabinieri have arrested most of the gang that kidnapped your father-in-law. Among other things, they've been talking about their contact in the Miletti family, the one who left messages tucked in a magazine at that service area on the motorway. The last magazine in the top right-hand row, I think it was.'

The exotic pain returned to Gianluigi's chest.

'And what has this got to do with me?'

Articulating these words was one of the hardest tasks he could ever remember performing.

'Well, it depends how you look at it. On the face of it, all this amounts to is an unsupported allegation by a gang of known criminals. On the other hand, it's hard to see what they have to gain by lying. We've suspected for a long time that there was an informer passing on the strengths and weaknesses of the family's negotiating position to the gang, but we didn't know who it was. Pietro was in London for much of the time. If the pick-up point was on the motorway, that excludes Silvio, who can't drive. As for Daniele, the gang say that the person who left the messages was short and slightly built, so he won't do. In one sense it's just a question of who's left, really.'

He tossed the butt of his cigarette out on to the gravel of the drive, where it continued to smoulder.

'But there's more to it than that. Above all, the investigating magistrate is going to be looking for a motive. Now if he had just wanted to beggar the Milettis the informant could have revealed the true extent of the family's finances straight off, but instead he chose to pass on scraps of information so that the negotiations were drawn out as long as possible. The magistrate will therefore be looking for someone who stood to gain from a delay in Ruggiero's return coupled with the need for a massive injection of cash to prop up SIMP. Cash from a Japanese company, for instance.'

The silence that followed was as long and significant as the words that had preceded it. Whatever was said now would have extra-ordinary resonances, and that knowledge was as inhibiting as the acoustics of a great church.

'I think that you are full of shit,' Gianluigi finally murmured, slowly and distinctly. 'I'm going to find out. And if you are, I'll make sure you drown in it.'

He walked through to his study, his heart a madhouse filled with the shrieks of despairing wretches, his head a cool and airy library where shrewd men debated tactics. Norberto was the best route to take. As a member of the regional council he knew almost everything that was going on and could find out the rest quickly and discreetly.

'Norberto? Gianluigi Santucci. Yes, me too. I'm sorry, but it can't wait. Someone's just told me that there's been a break in the Miletti case, that arrests have been made. Have you heard anything?'

Sensing a movement, he looked round to find that Zen had fol-lowed him and was now standing in the doorway. For a moment Gianluigi was tempted to get rid of him, but he restrained himself. The news was good. Much better to show himself unconcerned, a man with nothing to hide.

'Nothing at all?' he confirmed. 'I thought as much!'

'Get him to check,' Zen warned. 'This happened in Florence and the military are keeping it quiet until the magistrate gets there.'

Gianluigi bit his lip.

'Would you mind just checking that?' he said into the phone. 'You'll call back? Very well.'

As he replaced the receiver Loredana's voice rang out from the dining room.

'Christ, not chocolate pudding again! What are you trying to do, poison me? You know I hate chocolate! It brings me out in spots.'

While he waited for Norberto to get through to his contact, Gian-luigi thought back to that other phone call, in the days shortly after Ruggiero was kidnapped. The gang had been given the Santuccis' number as a 'clean' telephone line on which to communicate. At first Gianluigi had played it absolutely straight, but when the gang's modest demands were swiftly met and it began to look as if Ruggiero would be released within days, it occurred to him how convenient it would be if the old man's return could be delayed. The whole question of the deal with the Japanese was hanging in the balance, and with it Gianluigi's future, for if it went through he was a made man. So when the gang next phoned he'd expressed slight surprise that they'd asked for so little, given the family's ability to pay. If they needed more information on this subject, he implied, this could be arranged. It had been a risk, of course, but very carefully calculated, like all the risks he took. The kidnappers could pose no threat unless they were caught, a possibility so remote that Gianluigi had discounted it.

The phone rang.

'Well, you seem to be better informed than I am, Santucci! The gang have indeed been arrested. A magistrate went to Florence this morning to question them. Hello? Hello, are you there?'

'Yes. Yes, I'm here. Thanks. I'll be in touch.'

I'll never see Loredana's children grow, he thought, never take Sergio hunting. But this uncharacteristic weakness lasted no more than a moment. Then he strode to the end of the room and opened the sliding door to the terrace, beckoning to Zen to follow him.

The terrace was covered by a pergola whose vines were just beginning to put out shoots. It was sunny, still and surprisingly hot.

'So you're accusing me of collaborating with my father-in- law's killers, is that it?' Gianluigi demanded point-blank.

Zen looked taken aback.

'Not at all, dottore! I just wanted to warn you of certain developments which could potentially cause problems unless steps are taken now. That's all.'

'What kind of steps did you have in mind?'

Zen held up his hand, shaking his head.

'That's your affair, dottore. I don't need to know anything about it. But whatever you decide, it'll take time, and time is precisely what we don't have at present. Rosella Foria is questioning the gang in Florence at this very moment. We must act right away.'

So that was the way of it, eh? Thank God for human nature, thought Gianluigi, rotten to the core!

'Excuse me, but what's in this for you?' he queried pointedly.

Zen made a small gesture of embarrassment.

'About four years ago I had a misunderstanding with my superiors in Rome. They transferred me from active service and stuck me away in the Ministry doing bureaucratic work. At this stage of my career I haven't got much to look forward to except retirement anyway, but my pension will be pegged to my rank. Before this thing happened I was in line for promotion to Vice-Questore, but now . . .'

Gianluigi nodded and smiled.

'And you'd still like that promotion.'

Zen shrugged, his eyes discreetly lowered.

'You spoke of taking action,' Gianluigi went on. 'What did you have in mind?'

'Well, there's another factor involved. The kidnappers admit shooting Valesio, but they deny the Miletti murder. Moreover, one of the SIMP Fiats was observed near the scene of the murder, driven by a woman with blonde hair. I identified the car that day you found me at the garage, and later I had it stolen and subjected to a forensic examination.'

Gianluigi was silent. A display of outrage seemed a bit beside the point under the circumstances, and anyway, he needed to save his energy.

'Several long threads were found,' Zen went on. 'Threads from a blonde wig. It almost looks as though someone was trying to frame your wife, particularly since Ruggiero was shot with a pistol similar to hers which you now tell me is missing. But the point is that all this presents us with both a risk and an opportunity.'

Gianluigi almost missed this last remark. A blonde wig, he was thinking. A blonde *wig*.

Feeling that the silence had gone on long enough, he murmured, 'A risk for my wife, you mean?'

To his surprise Zen laughed rather nastily.

'No, dottore! Look, Ruggiero was killed on Monday, twenty-four hours before the phone call saying he had been released. Only the kidnappers knew where he was then, so if they didn't kill him they must have told the person who did. And only one person was in touch with the gang.'

'I didn't kill him!'

Gianluigi's voice swooped from a scream to a whisper as he realized that he might be overheard.

Zen nodded earnestly.

'I know, dottore. I woudn't be here otherwise. I'm just pointing out that the investigating magistrate is bound to assume that the gang's informant and Ruggiero Miletti's murderer are one and the same person. That's a risk we shouldn't underestimate. But it also provides a way out of the original problem. Because if the informant and the murderer are assumed to be one and the same person, then providing we can persuade Rosella Foria that one of the others committed the murder, she'll naturally assume that person was also the informant.'

After a moment's silence Gianluigi burst out laughing, as if he had just been told a story about the bizarre customs of a foreign country.

'You know, Zen, I think I've been underestimating you,' he said.

'We have an unfair advantage in the police. Everyone assumes we're stupid.'

Gianluigi's smile abruptly disappeared.

'But it won't work! Do you think these magistrates are children? How can you hope to implicate one of the family in Ruggiero's murder? It's preposterous!'

'That doesn't matter. The point is just to create as much fuss and confusion as possible, to send the shit flying in every direction. And then while Rosella Foria is busy trying to clear it all up there'll be plenty of time to take whatever steps you feel are appropriate to bring about a satisfactory and lasting solution of the problem. But I don't need to know anything about that. What I *do* need are those photographs of Silvio.'

Once again Gianluigi lost his head.

'Who put you up to this, Zen? You're not big enough to be operating on your own. Who's behind you, eh? What's the game?'

A dark suspicion suddenly took form in his mind as he remembered the look Zen and his wife had exchanged. Yes, it had to be her. No one else knew about the photographs.

He stepped forward furiously.

'Look here, you fuck off! Just fuck off out of here right now!'

But Zen stood his ground, gazing at him with the stolid confidence of a dog or horse that knows its owner will see reason sooner or later. And Gianluigi immediately realized that he was right. He would deal with Cinzia later, in private. He mustn't make it a public shame, still less allow it to compromise the successful resolution of the appallingly dangerous situation he found himself in. To do that would be the folly of an impetuous amateur, not the astute and hardened professional that he was.

'What are you going to do with the photographs?'

His voice was as calm as marble, and as hard.

'Don't you think it might be better if I didn't tell you?' Zen replied. 'They're going to question you, you know. I think it would be best for you to know as little as possible. It's amazing what people give away without even realizing it. When I mentioned the blonde wig, for example, you reacted. A magistrate would notice that. As you said, they're not children. What was it about the wig, by the way?'

Gianluigi eyed him for a final long moment before deciding.

'I'll show you.'

He went back into his office, opened the wall-safe and took out a yellow envelope. There were nine prints in all. He selected two, snipped the corresponding negatives from the strip of film and attached them to the prints with a paperclip. The other prints and negatives, the pick of the set, he put back in the safe. They would still do their job when the time came. Indeed, this could be a useful try-out, to see how Silvio reacted to being blackmailed.

When he re-emerged Zen had his back to the house, gazing at the view Gianluigi greeted exultantly each morning on rising with the thought, 'I bought you!' He handed over the envelope and watched with undisguised amusement as Zen studied the first photograph. It showed Silvio, naked to the waist, dancing in a crowded disco-theque. His hairy chest and smooth shiny belly were bare and a leather dog-lead dangled from each of his pierced nipples. His head was covered in a startling profusion of long blonde locks.

'The wig,' murmured Zen.

Gianluigi nodded.

'Where was this taken?' Zen asked him.

'In Berlin.'

'Ah yes, of course. Home of Gerhard Mayer.'

Gianluigi decided that it was time to remind his new employee of the realities of their relationship.

'So you know about that too, do you? Very clever. But don't get so clever that you forget what's what, will you? Because if you do I promise that you'll regret it for the rest of your life. And I don't make empty threats, Zen.'

Zen looked at him with an expression brimming with earnest sincerity.

'Dottore, please! I'm one hundred per cent on your side!'

Gianluigi nodded.

'Then we'll say no more about it. Now let's see just how clever you are. What do you make of this, eh?'

The second picture apparently showed Silvio leaning back against a tiled wall. But what was that gleaming white mass of vaguely rump-like curves looming above his chest? And why did he have that expression of ecstatic martyrdom?

Gianluigi turned the print on its side, observing Zen's puzzlement with a knowing smirk. It really was very difficult if you hadn't seen some of the later and more explicit shots.

'Does that help?' he prompted.

Now Silvio was seen to be lying supine on a white tiled floor beneath the white structure. It might almost have been an altar of some sort. Certainly the scene had a ritual air about it, as though it formed part of a ceremony whose exact significance was revealed only to initiates.

'What's this?' Gianluigi asked teasingly, pointing out the white object.

Zen shook his head.

'Well, what does it look like?'

He was having his fun all right, getting his money's worth!

'To be perfectly honest, it looks like a toilet.'

Gianluigi applauded ironically.

'Bravo, my friend. It *is* a toilet. But a rather special toilet. It's not connected to a sewer, it's connected to Silvio. He's waiting for someone to come along and use it. One of the places our Silvio goes when he visits his boyfriend in Berlin is a club for people who like to be crapped on, and vice versa of course. Don't you wish you'd thought of it, eh? What a goldmine! They both pay for their fun, and you've got a flourishing little business in top-quality garden manure on the side.'

Zen laughed and replaced the photographs in the envelope. Gianluigi clapped him familiarly on the back, pushing him into the house. Now he must get rid of him quickly. He needed peace and quiet in which to think. It was no use alerting his usual contacts. For them to be effective they would have to know the truth, and if they knew the truth they would abandon him. There were limits to what you could get away with, and he was well aware that he'd overstepped them. It was a pity the judiciary were already involved. Magistrates were so bloody-minded that they would often pursue their investigations even when it had been made perfectly clear to them that it was against their own best interests. That sort of stubbornness was something that Gianluigi absolutely despised. As far as he was concerned it was an aberration like religious or political fanaticism, something quite out of place in a modern democratic society.

'I need to talk to Silvio as soon as possible,' Zen remarked as they reached the front door. 'Could you get someone to persuade him to go to Antonio Crepi's house this afternoon? Crepi himself needn't know anything about it.'

Gianluigi stared at him, his eyes narrowing.

'You're asking an awful lot and giving very little in return,' he observed sourly.

'I'm doing it all for you, dottore!' Zen exclaimed with a hurt expression.

After a moment Gianluigi broke into loud laughter.

'All for me, my arse! You're doing it for your pension, my friend, and don't think I don't know it.'

Zen shrugged awkwardly.

'Oh well, that too, of course.'

'What now?'

Silvio silently echoed his driver's exasperated murmur as he caught sight of the patrolman waving them down. What now, indeed? Another annoyance, another setback, another delay.

As the taxi slowed to a halt beside the unmarked police car parked at a bend in the road a massive sigh began its slow progress up from the bottom of Silvio's chest. For this was not the first vexation which the day had dropped on him, not by a long chalk! In fact it had been nothing but trials and tribulations from the moment his clock-radio had turned itself on at five o'clock that morning, shocking him into consciousness. It had been supposed to wake him from a nap the previous afternoon in time for an appointment with a young friend, but he must have set it wrong, for having messed up his evening by failing to go off, it had then ruined his sleep into the bargain. So there he was, wide awake at the crack of dawn, with no more chance of going back to sleep than of getting a turd back where it came from, as dear Gerhard used to say.

He really must get in touch with Gerhard soon. One of the most unpleasant features of the last few months had been having to suspend his trips to Berlin, but now everything was satisfactorily resolved he would be able to slip away again sometime soon. As Ivy pointed out, Ruggiero's death was not without its consolations.

'Rubbish!' she'd retorted when he claimed to be grief-stricken.

'But my father's dead!' he'd cried with a dramatic gesture. 'I've got a *right* to be upset. It's only natural!'

'But you're not upset. On the contrary, you're quite relieved.'

'Don't say that!'

But he had known that she was right. That was what was so amazing about Ivy, her ability to reach into his mind and show him things he had never dared admit to himself were there. It was terrible, sometimes, how right she could be.

The policeman, a rather attractive young fellow with an enormous moustache, was checking the driver's documents. Silvio thought he'd seen him somewhere before. And wasn't there something familiar about the spot where they had been stopped too? The sun was high and it was unpleasantly hot in the taxi. He felt grotesquely overdressed in his heavy underwear, thick suit and overcoat, perspiring all over. But the moisture remained trapped between flesh and fabric, unable to do its business properly. Silvio consulted his watch. The patrolman was now walking in a maddeningly leisurely fashion around the taxi, inspecting it closely, taking his time. If this went on much longer he was going to be really late.

After that rude awakening he'd tried in vain to get back to sleep, but in the end he'd given up all hope and gone downstairs, only to find that Daniele had scoffed all his special organic goat's yoghurt rich in the live bacilli which Silvio's homoeopathist was adamant he needed to maintain the precarious equilibrium of his health. The goaty taste was what attracted Silvio, though. Everything to do with goats came into that special category where pleasure and disgust struggled for supremacy like two naked wrestlers. Sweat was another, and farts and bad breath. Gianluigi's breath was quite overpowering sometimes, because of his indigestion problems no doubt, or those teeth of his which never saw a brush, packed with rich, undisturbed deposits of plaque, so that he wondered sometimes how Cinzia could stand it. But perhaps she too loved to loathe, longed to stretch herself languorously out and yield to the very thing that made her shudder with disgust.

After that his day had gone from bad to worse, the last straw being this lunchtime call from that creep Spinelli at the bank, insisting on meeting a representative of the family at Antonio Crepi's villa that very afternoon to discuss some urgent problem that was too sensitive to discuss on the phone. Silvio had been hoping to treat himself to an afternoon listening to Billie Holliday records and leafing through that auction catalogue of rare Haitian issues which Pietro had sent him from London, hoping to keep him sweet for the future now he represented twenty-five per cent of the company! Yes, there were certainly consolations to Ruggiero's death, just as Ivy had insisted. She should have been here to drive him, but by the time the call came she'd already left to keep an appointment. So he'd had to take a taxi, which of course had been late arriving and then got stuck in the traffic. And now this! It really was too bad.

An official in plain clothes had got out of the police car.

'How's it going?' Silvio heard him ask the young patrolman.

'Not too good. Fucking thing's in excellent shape.'

Suddenly Silvio realized why this spot had seemed familiar. It was at this very bend that his father's car had been forced off the road by the kidnappers.

'You planning to be much longer?' the taxi driver demanded.

'We're just noting the defects we've found on your vehicle,' the official told him.

'Defects? What defects?'

The patrolman consulted his notebook.

'Insufficient tread depth on nearside front tyre. Rear window partially obscured by sticker. Number-plate light defective.'

The driver laughed sarcastically.

'The cigarette lighter doesn't work, either.'

'Really?' queried the official. '*Two* faults in the electrical system, then. May I see your snow chains?'

'Snow chains?' the driver replied incredulously. 'What are you talking about?'

'All vehicles using this road between the beginning of October and the end of April are required to carry snow chains on board. Didn't you see the sign back there on the hill?'

'Can't you feel that sun? It's over twenty degrees!'

'That's the law.'

'Then the law's crazy!'

'I wouldn't say that if I were you. You could end up facing a charge for contempt.'

'For fuck's sake!' the driver murmured.

Silvio wound down his window.

'Excuse me!' he called testily. 'I'm already late for an appointment and . . .'

The official looked round.

'Why, Signor Miletti! Please forgive me, I had no idea it was you.'

Silvio squinted up into the sunlight.

'Oh, it's you, Zen. I thought you were back in Rome.'

'Not yet, dottore. Not yet.'

'They've put you on traffic duty, have they?'

As someone often accused of lacking a sense of humour, Silvio liked to draw attention to his jokes by laughing at them himself. Zen duly smiled, although this might have been at the sound of Silvio's squeaky laughter rather than the joke itself.

'Anyway, will you please fine the driver or whatever you intend doing, and let us proceed. As I say, I'm already late for an appointment.'

'Out of the question, I'm afraid. On a cursory examination alone this vehicle has been found to have five defects. As such it is clearly unfit to ply for hire as a public conveyance. However, I'd be delighted to offer you a lift.'

'I have no wish to travel with you, Zen.'

'Suit yourself. But it's a long walk.'

'Snow chains!' murmured the taxi driver disgustedly.

Silvio sat there stewing in the stuffy heat in the back of the car, thinking over what had just been said. A thrilling sense of peril had taken hold of him, and it was this that finally moved him to open the door and give himself up to whatever was about to happen.

'A long walk to where?' he murmured dreamily as the taxi screeched round in a tight turn and headed back to the city.

Zen opened the rear door of the Alfetta.

'To where you're going.'

'But you don't know where I'm going.'

'Oh, but I do, dottore, I do.'

'Where, then?'

It had been intended as a challenge, but Zen treated it as a real question.

'You'll see,' he replied complacently as they drove off down the hill.

Crepi's villa was visible in the distance, perched up on its ridge, but the countryside flashed by at such an insane rate that in no time at all they had passed the driveway.

'You've missed the turning!' Silvio told the driver. 'I'm going to Antonio Crepi's! He's expecting me.'

'Wrong on both counts,' Zen replied without turning round.

'You'll lose your jobs for this,' Silvio stammered, almost incoherent with excitement. 'This is kidnapping! You'll get twenty years, both of you!'

They had reached the flatlands near the Tiber, whose course was visible to the right, marked by a line of trees whose lower branches were festooned with scraps of plastic bags and other durable refuse.

'This one,' Zen told the driver, pointing to an abandoned track burrowing into a mass of wild brambles and scrub. The entrance was marked by a pair of imposing brick gateposts in a bad state of disrepair. A cloud of red dust rose up all around the car, almost blotting out the view.

They drew up and Zen got out. He removed his overcoat and threw it on the front seat. From the dashboard he removed a clipboard and a large yellow envelope. Then he opened the rear door of the car.

'Get out, dottore.'

Silvio got out.

As the dust settled he could see the massive piles of bricks all around the clearing where they were parked. They still preserved the vague outlines of the barracks, ovens and chimneys they had once been, but fallen out of rank and order like an army of deserters. It reminded him of the old factory below the house which had been his private playground for many years, despite his mother's dire warnings about venturing into it. He had been a solitary child, and those deserted alleys, yards and warehouses provided the perfect environment for his fantasies to flourish. They were fantasies of war, for the most part, or rather of suffering. His victims were Swedish wooden matchsticks, which he arranged behind bits of wall or in trenches scooped from the dirt and then bombarded mercilessly with bricks, from a distance at first but gradually closing in until you could see the sharp edges of the missile gouging into the ground. But the best bit was afterwards, picking through the bent and broken splinters, picturing the appalling injuries, the grotesque mutilations, the agony, the screams, the pathetic pleas to be finished off. He played all the parts himself, his voice mimicking shells and explosions, sirens and screams. In that secret playworld he was blissfully transparent, secure in the knowledge that the gates of the abandoned factory were locked and guarded, the walls too high to climb and topped with shards of broken glass.

Then one day he looked up and found a pair of eyes on him.

The man was lean and hard and dirty, his clothes greasy and torn. Silvio had never seen a Communist before, but he knew instinctively that this was one. His father had told him how the Communists were going to take over the factories and kill the owners and their families. Silvio fled, and for weeks he stayed away. Then, gradually at first, he found that the danger was no longer a reason for avoiding the factory but rather an irresistible temptation to return. He had no further interest in his innocent games. They were lost to him for ever, he knew, part of something he now thought of for the first time as his childhood. If he was to go back it would be in exploration of a new dimension he felt opening up within himself. It was not a comfortable sensation. He felt wrenched apart internally, split and fractured like one of his matchstick heroes. But there was no denying that urge. He already knew he would be its willing slave for the rest of his life.

The second time he saw the man it was Silvio who had the advantage of surprise. He had rounded a length of wall, moving stealthily, and there in a corner he saw the figure, turned away, head bent, intent on some furtive task. He knew he should run for his life, but instead he found himself moving towards the man, who remained quite still, apparently unaware of his presence. Then, when Silvio was almost close enough to touch him, he suddenly whirled around and sent a high spray of urine flying through the air, splashing Silvio's clothes and face, his lips, his mouth.

Afterwards he drenched himself with the garden hose and told his parents that the rough boys near the station had thrown him in the fountain. His clothes came back unspotted from the laundry, but the obscene warmth and acrid taste of the bright yellow liquid had marked his flesh as indelibly as a tattoo. He never returned to the factory, which shortly afterwards was spruced up into offices and parking space for the management of what would soon become SIMP. But those barren desolate landscapes were now a part of him, like that stain which no water could wash off. Whenever he touched himself in bed at night he was there again, at risk from merciless mocking strangers, drenched in their stink and slime, both cringing and exultant.

'You see, dottore?' Zen remarked ironically. 'I told you I knew where you were going.'

It was suffocatingly hot. The great mounds of bricks were high enough to prevent the slightest breeze from entering but not to give any shade from the sun. Silvio could feel little rivulets of sweat running down the creases and furrows in his body, trickling through the hairy parts and soaking into his underclothes.

'Naturally I didn't just happen to be waiting at that bend in the road by pure coincidence,' Zen went on.

'It's a plot!' Silvio muttered.

'Yes, it's a plot. But you're only the means, not the end. All I need from you is your signature on these papers.'

Zen handed him the clipboard. The sun made a dazzling blank of the page, and Silvio had to turn so that the clipboard was in his shadow before he was able to make out anything except the crest printed at the top. Even then it took him a long time to see what it was about, because of the florid formulas and the stilted tone of the text. When understanding suddenly came he almost cried out with a pain as different from the gaudy agonies of his fantasies as a gallon of make-up blood is from a drop of the real thing.

He had never forgotten his mother's strict orders not to venture into the site where he had first experienced those horrid thrills, and when she was taken from him a few years later he knew that he was being punished for his disobedience. Not that this stopped him indulging; on the contrary, guilt made his forbidden pleasures taste still sourer and stronger. But the gentle hurt of her absence was something else. Nothing could assuage that, until Ivy came. And now . . .

'You must be out of your mind!'

Unfortunately, as so often happened when he got angry, his voice let him down, and the words emerged as an imperious squeak.

'It's nothing to do with me, dottore,' Zen assured him. 'I'm only following orders.'

'Whose orders?'

'Can't you work it out for yourself?'

Silvio struggled to summon up the small residue of cunning which he had inherited from his father. This man had known that he would be passing that spot on the road. Therefore he must have known that he was going to Crepi's, although he claimed that Crepi himself hadn't known. In other words, the summons from Spinelli had been nothing but a ruse designed to draw him into an ambush. So the banker must be part of the plot. But he was only a minor figure, like this man Zen. Who controlled them both? The obvious answer was Gianluigi Santucci, the banker's patron. But Gianluigi wouldn't waste his energy on petty vendettas of this type. No, it could only be . . .

'Cinzia,' he murmured.

Silvio threw the clipboard to the ground at Zen's feet.

'You can go fuck yourself.'

'We don't expect you to do it for nothing, of course,' Zen said mildly, dusting down the papers.

'You're trying to *bribe* me?'

Although eminently unworldly in his way, Silvio was enough of a Miletti to resent the idea that anyone would presume to patronize him financially.

'No, it's a question of a few souvenirs, that's all. Souvenirs of Berlin.'

Zen took two photographs from the large yellow envelope and held them up.

Instantly Silvio's real pain and righteous anger were overwhelmed by stronger sensations. To think that all the time this beast had *known*, had *seen!*

'No, I won't do it!'

He knew very well that this petulant refusal wasn't worth the paper it was wiped with, as dear Gerhard would put it. But Zen seemed to have been taken in.

'In that case I'm afraid that prints of these photographs will begin to circulate among friends and enemies of the Miletti family in

Perugia and elsewhere. Just imagine the scene, dottore! There they are, early in the morning, still dewy-eyed over that first cup of coffee, when bang! Hello! What's this? Good God! It looks like Silvio Miletti waiting for someone to come and take a dump on him! What do you think their reaction is going to be, dottore? Oh, well, it takes all sorts, different strokes for different folks, don't knock it till you've tried it?'

Silvio was literally speechless. The idea of those images being seen by people who inhabited a quite separate zone of his life, whom he met at receptions and conferences, at dinners and concerts, who greeted him on the Corso every day! Yes, he would have to sign, no question about that. The revelation of his secret pleasures to the whole of Perugia would be a humiliation so monumental, so absolute, so *perfect*, that he knew he would never survive the excitement it would generate.

But at the thought of what he was about to do, these thrills faded and the real pain returned.

'But it's all lies! Filthy obscene lies and nothing else!'

To his amazement, Zen winked conspiratorially.

'Of course it is! That's why it doesn't matter. In fact the kidnappers are already under arrest in Florence. They've confessed to the whole thing. Believe me, dottore, if I thought for a single moment that these allegations would be taken seriously, I'd never have agreed to be a party to this! But it's just a question of stirring up a bit of scandal, a bit of dirt. Quite harmless really.'

The man's whinging hypocrisy made Silvio feel sick, but what he said made sense. If the gang had confessed then the papers he was being asked to sign were totally worthless except precisely to someone like Cinzia, someone who would stoop to any trick to sully the honour of the woman he loved and whose love sustained him. But they would deal with Cinzia later. Meanwhile he must get this over with and warn Ivy immediately. It was awful to think how she might suffer if she was suddenly confronted with his apparent treachery.

'Just put your name on the dotted line at the bottom, dottore,' Zen prompted. 'Where it says that you made the statement freely and voluntarily.'

Silvio took out his pen and signed. When the yellow envelope was safe in his hands he turned to Zen.

'I may be dirty in superficial ways,' he remarked, 'but you're dirty through and through! You're a filthy putrid rancid cesspit, a walking shit-heap.'

The final proof of the official's total degeneracy was that he didn't even try to defend himself, merely getting into the waiting car, his despicable job done. Silvio followed, but more slowly. Despite the varied splendours and miseries of his existence, the pleasure of moral superiority was one that very rarely came his way. As a connoisseur of exotic sensations he was determined to savour it to the utmost.

ELEVEN

She almost changed her mind at the last moment. It was the place itself that did it, the smell of cheap power, making her realize just how far she had come since those early days, the days of secretarial work and English lessons. The world Ivy lived in now was drenched in power too, of course, but quite different from the low-grade kind that pervaded places where you came to post a parcel or cash a cheque or renew your residence permit. How she'd always hated the bitter, envious midgets who patrol these internal boundaries of the state, malicious goblins wringing the most out of their single dingy magic spell. Her Italian friends claimed to feel the same way, but Ivy had never been convinced. The opium of these people was not religion but power, or rather power *was* their religion. Everyone believed, everyone was hooked. And everyone was rewarded with at least a tiny scrap of the stuff, enough to make them feel needed. What people hated in the system was being subjected to others' power, but they would all resist any change which threatened to modify or limit their own. The situation was thus both stable and rewarding, especially for those who were rich in power and could bypass it with a few phone calls, a hint dropped here, a threat there. At length Ivy had come to appreciate its advantages, and to realize that she could make just as good use of them as the natives, if not rather better in fact. In the end she'd come to admire the Italians as the great realists who saw life as it really was, free of the crippling hypocrisy of the Anglo-Saxon world in which she had been brought up.

She'd learned her lesson well. Gone were the days when she had to hang around under that sign with its contemptuous scrawl 'Foreigners', waiting for the Political Branch officials who would swan in and out as it suited them, or not turn up at all, or send you away for not having enough sheets of the special franked paper which could only be bought at a tobacconist's shop which meant another half-hour's delay and then starting from scratch again having lost your place in the queue. Nowadays she went over their heads and dealt directly with the people with real power. The snag, of course, is that they won't speak to you unless you have real power too, or know some-one who does. Only since her association with Silvio Miletti had she been able to make full use of the lessons she had learned, to put her newly acquired skills to the test. Yes, she had come a long way.

'You looking for something?'

Hovering there at the foot of the stairs, hesitating, reflecting, she'd attracted the attention of the guard, who was fixing her with a supercilious stare.

'I have an appointment with Commissioner Zen,' she replied coldly.

'Never heard of him.'

'It's all right, I know the room number.'

She tried to move forward to the stairs, but the man barred her with one arm and yelled to a colleague, 'We got a Zen?'

The man consulted a list taped to the wall.

'Three five one!' he yelled back.

'Three five one,' the guard repeated slowly. 'Third floor. Think you can make it on your own?'

'Just about, I should think, thank you very much.'

Her attempt at irony did not make the slightest impression on the man's fatuous complacency. You couldn't beat them at their own game, of course; the mistake had been agreeing to come in the first place. Normally she would not have done so. In the circles in which she now moved one did not call on policemen unless they were on the payroll, in which case the meeting would be on neutral ground, in a café or on the street. But when Zen had phoned, just before lunch, Ivy had agreed with hardly a moment's thought. He was going back to Rome that evening, he said, and he'd like to clear up that matter they had discussed on the phone at the beginning of the week, did she remember? She remembered all right! Not the subject of the phone call, which had been rather vague in any case, some-thing about a letter he had received. But she wasn't likely to forget the way he'd quizzed her about her appointment with Cinzia that morning. At all events, today he'd suggested that she stop by his office in the afternoon, and to her surprise she had agreed. The prob-lem, she was forced to admit, was that her reflexes had not yet adjusted to her new position. Silvio would have got it right instinc-tively, but you had to have been born powerful for that. In her heart of hearts Ivy still feared and respected the police as her parents had taught her to do. She might have come a long way, she recognized, but there was still a long way to go.

Her sensible rubber heels made hardly a sound as she walked along the third-floor corridor. With some surprise she noticed that her palms were slightly damp. The place was having its effect. That shiny travertine cladding they used everywhere, cold and slippery, seemed to exude unease. Get a grip on yourself, she thought, as she knocked at the door.

The occupant of the office was a rough, common-looking individual of the brawn and no brain variety. She thought she must have made a mistake, but he called her in.

'The chief'll be back directly. He says you're to wait.'

Ivy glanced at her watch. She was by no means certain that it had been a good idea to come and this provided the perfect excuse for leaving.

'I'm sorry, I've got another appointment.'

But the man had taken up a position with his back to the door.

'Take it easy, relax!' he told her in an insultingly familiar tone. 'You want to read the paper?'

He picked a pink sports paper from the dustbin and held it out to her. There was a long smear of some viscous matter down the front page.

The man's body was bulging with muscle. His nose had been broken and his ears were grotesquely swollen. He had an air of ingrained damage about him, as though his life had been spent running into things and coming off second-best. The effect was both comical and threatening.

Ivy consulted her watch again.

'I shall wait for fifteen minutes.'

Why hadn't she insisted on leaving immediately? It had something to do with the man's physical presence. There was no denying it, he intimidated her. He was staring at her with an expression which to her alarm she found that she recognized. She had discovered its meaning back in the days when she was working at the hospital, where she'd been secretary to one of the directors, an unmarried man in his mid-forties. He was distinguished, witty and charming, and seemed intrigued by his 'English' secretary, amused by her, concerned about her welfare. He gave her flowers and chocolates occasionally, helped her find a flat at a rent she could afford, and once even took her out to eat at a restaurant outside Perugia. He had never made the ghost of a pass at her.

One weekend there was a conference in Bologna which he was due to attend, and at the last moment he proposed that Ivy accompany him. When she hesitated he showed her the receipt for the hotel booking he had already made, for two single rooms. She could assist him in various small ways in return for a little paid holiday, he explained. He made it sound as though she would be doing him a favour. He appealed to her as an attractive, vivacious woman, a fellow-conspirator against life's drabness, the ideal companion for such a jaunt as this. Nothing quite like it had ever happened to her before. The experience seemed to sum up everything she loved about this country where people knew what life was worth and understood how to get the best out of it.

They put up at a luxury hotel and dined out that evening at one of the city's famous restaurants. Ivy's pleasure was dimmed only by a slight anxiety as to what would happen when they got back to the hotel, or rather as to how she would deal with it. Ivy was not attracted to her employer physically, but she had long ago been forced to face the fact that the men she found attractive did not feel the same way about her. They were younger than her, for one thing, handsome, reckless types who didn't give a damn about anything. Unfortunately they didn't give a damn about her, even as a one-night stand, so she had learned to compromise. And when someone had been as attentive and thoughtful as her employer, taking such pains to ensure that the weekend was a success, not to mention the various practical possibilities for the future this opened up, well, why not, she thought.

Only it didn't happen. It didn't happen that night, when he simply kissed her hand and wished her a good night's sleep, nor the next, when they went out with a group of his colleagues to a restaurant in the country outside Bologna. The men all talked loudly and continuously and so fast that Ivy wasn't always able to follow the conversation. There were even moments when she doubted whether they meant her to. After the meal a bottle of whisky was brought to the table. As it circulated through the fog of endless cigarettes, Ivy watched meaning coming and going like a landscape glimpsed through cloud from a plane. She felt lost, discarded. Her employer had moved into the world which men inhabit with other men and where women are not at home. From time to time he glanced at her, made some comment or smiled, but he was no longer there, not really. She was alone in spirit, and later quite literally, for in the confusion of leaving the restaurant she ended up in a car with four men she hadn't even been introduced to, and had to spend the whole forty minutes of the drive back to Bologna fielding crassly insensitive questions about her private life, her family, why she was living in Italy and whether she liked spaghetti. Back at her hotel her employer was nowhere to be found. She made her way alone to her room, cursing herself for a stupid sentimental bitch.

The next morning a waiter awakened her with a bouquet of roses and a hand-written card covered in fulsome apologies and inviting her to take coffee on the terrace. There the apologies were repeated in person. He had drunk too much and become confused, the group he was with had wanted to go on to a nightclub despite his objections, and so on and so forth. Later he drove her back to Perugia. Nothing seemed to have changed.

But something *had*. She noticed it immediately in the eyes of the other men at the hospital and in the way they treated her. But she had no idea what it meant until about a week later, when she overheard two administrative assistants chatting on the stairs.

'. . . for the weekend with that English bit.'

'But he's a pansy!'

'That's what everyone thought! Looks like we've been underestimating him.'

'Or maybe he gets it coming and going, eh? Crafty old bugger!'

It was so cruel, so nasty! Above all, it was so unfair! 'But we didn't do anything!' she felt like screaming. 'He *is* a pansy! He didn't lay a finger on me!' But of course no one would have believed her. 'Where I come from,' an Italian girl had once told her, 'if a man and a woman are alone together in a room for fifteen minutes, it's assumed that they've made love.' Her employer had managed to salvage his reputation with the other men at the hospital – and how much depends on that reputation! – at no cost to himself. How very clever. Even in the intensity of her hatred and hurt at the way she had been used, Ivy remained coolly appreciative of how cleverly it had been done. Having realized at an early age that stupidity makes a poor sauce to plain looks, she had always sought to give cleverness its due.

But now, incredibly, this brutal policeman was looking at her in the same way as those men at the hospital, the way a man looks at a woman he knows to be sexually available. But that didn't make sense! The situation was utterly different in every respect. What was going on?

Ivy felt immensely reassured when Zen finally arrived. He didn't look at her in that vulgar impertinent way. His expression was detached, calculating and morose, as if to say that he would do his job to the best of his ability even though he had no illusions as to its value.

'All right, Chiodini, that'll do,' he said, summarily dismissing the man who had been keeping the door like some mastiff. As he settled in his chair Ivy noticed that his shoes and trousers were coated with a fine red dust.

'Is this going to take long?' she asked a little tetchily. 'You said two o'clock and I'm in rather a hurry.'

Zen took a sheet of paper from his pocket and passed it to her without a word. It was covered in the same fine red dust as his clothing. Was this the letter which he'd referred to? But she could see from the printed heading *Polizia dello Stato* that it was official. The typed text began with one of those formulas which the judicial system employs to eliminate the ambiguities of normal human utterance.

I, the undersigned, depose as follows.

On the morning of Monday 22 March at 0920 approximately I observed Cook, Ivy Elaine, outside the garage below our family residence at Via del Capanno 5, Perugia. She was carrying a small green plastic bag. She got into one of the Fiat saloons and drove away. Since Cook is entitled to the use of these cars I thought no more of it at the time.

Later the same morning, at 1145 approximately, I saw Cook walking upstairs to the room she occupied in our house during this period. She was carrying the same plastic bag as before. I wished her to type some letters for me and called to attract her attention. When she did not respond I followed her upstairs. Her room was empty and I could hear the sound of the shower from the bathroom next door. The plastic bag she had been carrying lay on the table. To my surprise, I found that it contained a blonde wig which I had bought the previous year to attend a Carnival party, and a small automatic pistol which I recognized as belonging to my sister Cinzia.

Ivy surveyed the effect this text was having on her body: the thudding of her heart, the swelling pressure of her blood, the dryness of her mouth, the moisture erupting all over her skin, the weight on her chest against which she had to struggle to draw breath, the numbness and trembling, the urge to break out in short sharp howls like a hyena.

When Cook returned to the room I asked her about the wig and the pistol. She appeared confused, and then said that she had just been playing a joke on Cinzia. I was appalled that she could contemplate such a thing at a moment when we were all anxiously awaiting news of my father's release. I demanded further details, but Cook's replies were incoherent and when I pressed her she became hysterical.

I assumed at first that this episode was due to the tremendous strain under which we were all living at the time. But when my father was subsequently found dead, and it emerged that he had been shot during the period that Cook had been absent from the house and with a pistol similar to the one I had observed in her possession, I began to suspect the horrifying truth.

As it got worse, it got better. This is a pack of lies, she thought.

Appalled by the idea that I had been responsible for introducing a viper into the bosom of the family, I threw caution to the winds and decided to confront Cook. To my astonishment she claimed that I had imagined the sequence of events described above. She admitted going out at the time in question, but asserted that my sister had telephoned and asked Cook to meet her at the Santucci house, outside Perugia. On arriving there, she said, she had found Cinzia absent, and after waiting for some time had returned to the city. As for the wig and the pistol, she denied all knowledge of them.

When I questioned my sister about this I discovered that the truth was that Cook had phoned Cinzia and asked for a meeting in Perugia, at which she had failed to appear. Clearly her motive in decoying my sister away from home had been to obtain entrance to the Santucci property, where she was admitted by the housekeeper and left unobserved for some time, in order to take the pistol which I had subsequently observed in her possession.

Upon searching the house I discovered that my wig had been replaced in the chest of drawers where it is kept. Of the pistol I could find no trace. Faced with Cook's angry denials and the assurance of the authorities that the murder had been committed by the kidnappers, I decided to keep my doubts to myself. But I now feel that this decision was mistaken, and have decided to come forward.

The above statement has been made freely and of my own volition and my legal rights were fully respected throughout.

(signed) Silvio Agostino Miletti

Perhaps in an attempt to counter its reputation for gross inefficiency in everything that matters, the State is a stickler for precision when it comes to trivia. The legal system which takes so long to bring people to trial that they are often released after being found guilty, having already been imprisoned for longer than the period of their sentence, insists that statements to the authorities record not only the date on which they were made but also the time. Thus it was that Ivy learned that Silvio's statement to the police had supposedly been made at twelve forty-two that day. Which was very interesting, because she remembered quite clearly that Silvio had spent the half-hour before lunch whining about the selfish and thoughtless behaviour of his brother Daniele and in particular his habit of eating the Bulgarian yoghurt which he, Silvio, went to considerable time and trouble to obtain from a stockist in Rome. That meant that the statement was not just a pack of lies but a transparent forgery. But this didn't reassure Ivy, quite the contrary. Because that big loopy signature at the bottom was genuine all right, so that Silvio had to be a party to whatever monstrous conspiracy was afoot.

She looked up at Zen, conscious that nothing of all this showed in her face.

'I don't know what to say. I feel like asking if this is some kind of joke. But it quite obviously isn't.'

The grey eyes regarded her cryptically.

'So what *is* it?' she demanded with a nervous laugh.

'It's a statement made to me by Silvio Miletti.'

'It's a pack of lies!' she cried. 'It's rubbish, sheer invention, as you must know very well! And not even very clever invention! Do you really think that if I'd committed a murder I would bring the gun back to the house in a plastic bag and leave it lying in my room in full view while I went to have a shower?'

'The witness describes you as hysterical. Hysterical people do irrational things.'

'I was *not* hysterical!' She sounded it now, though. 'I wasn't even there! After I got back from Cinzia's I went home to my flat, for heaven's sake.'

'What time was that?'

'I don't know, late morning. I remember I had to do some shopping, to get something for lunch. Yes, that's right, and then I ran into a friend on the Corso. We had an aperitif together. There, that proves it. He'll verify my story!'

'What about earlier, before the appointment with Cinzia? Where were you then?'

She was about to reply, but checked herself.

'If you're going to question me then I'm entitled to the presence of a lawyer.'

Zen acknowledged the point with a fractional inflexion of his lips, not so much a smile as the memory of a smile.

'But this isn't an interrogation,' he said.

His words were such an unexpected relief that Ivy felt quite faint. The riot in her body had been put down, but at too great a cost.

'I really must go,' she murmured.

Zen stared at her in silence. His expression was even more alarming than Chiodini's, although quite different. He was looking at her as though she was dead.

'I'm afraid that's not possible.'

'What do you mean?'

'Signora, an eminent citizen has come forward and made a statement implicating you in the murder of his father. Now I don't know exactly what conception you have of the duties of the police, but I can assure you that I wouldn't be performing mine if I simply ignored this allegation on the grounds that the person accused claims that it's all a pack of lies.'

'Are you saying I'm under arrest?'

'Not exactly. You're being held on suspicion of having committed a crime punishable by life imprisonment. This will be communicated to the Public Prosecutor's office, who will in turn inform the investigating magistrate. She will want to question you, I imagine. But that won't be for a day or two. She's in Florence at the moment. The kidnappers are under arrest there.'

So far Ivy had been proud of her control, but now a little manic giggle escaped her. Dear Christ, how much more could she take?

'Obviously she's got her hands full with that at the moment,' Zen continued. 'The Public Prosecutor is supposed to be informed within forty-eight hours, and the magistrate is bound to interrogate you within a further forty-eight. In practice that tends to get run together to suit everyone's convenience, but at the worst it shouldn't be later than Tuesday.'

'Tuesday.'

The word seemed meaningless.

'And until then?' she asked.

'Until then you'll be held here. Chiodini!'

The bruiser came back in.

'Take Signora Cook down to the cells.'

The word was like an electric shock, and Ivy sprang to her feet.

'Just a moment! I'm entitled to make a phone call first. It's my legal right!'

Zen ignored her.

'Now listen to me, Chiodini,' he said. 'I won't be here to supervise this, so I'm depending on you. Until Rosella Foria gets back from Florence Signora Cook is out of bounds, in quarantine. Understand? She speaks to no one and no one speaks to her. And I mean no one!'

'Right, chief. Come on, you!'

Chiodini made a grab at Ivy's arm, but she evaded him and stalked out, deliberately repressing all thought. There'll be time for that when I'm alone, she told herself.

As it was, she had to fight even for the small privilege of solitude. The cells were in the basement of the Questura, which clearly predated the rest of the building by several centuries. The doors had an air of total impenetrability which Ivy found oddly reassuring. Her privacy was very important to her, and she saw the doors not as shutting her in but as keeping others out. What had always terrified her most about prisons was the overcrowding, four or five people shut up together in a cell intended to be barely tolerable for two. Italians seemed to be able to stand such enforced intimacy, but Ivy knew that it would drive her mad. She simply couldn't function adequately without a space she could call her own, and she was acutely aware that in the hours ahead she was going to need to function not just adequately but quite extraordinarily well.

So it was a nasty shock when the cell door swung open to reveal a strange-looking woman with a smell on her and a wild look in her black eyes.

'I'm not going in there,' Ivy said firmly.

'Oh, you're not, eh?' Chiodini replied.

He stared at her in some confusion, unsure how to proceed. If it had been a man he would have hit him. But with women things were different; you could only hit them if they were married to you.

'There are lots of other cells,' she pointed out.

'They're being painted.'

'For God's sake, man, she's a *gypsy*! How would you like it?'

Chiodini could see her point. His mother had told him about gypsies. With a bad grace he locked the cell up again and installed Ivy in the one next door.

She slumped down on the bed. To think that on her way to the Questura, just an hour ago, she'd been worrying about whether or not to splash out on that slinky but hideously expensive Lurex trouser-suit she'd had her eye on for some time. The contrast between that reality and this cell, this mean pallet bed, that door as massive as the slab over a tomb, was so disturbing that she felt black waves of panic lapping up at her. But she refused to give in. To do so would be sheer self-indulgence. She had managed before, after all. When she discovered the reason why she had been invited for that weekend in Bologna she had calmly set about reviewing the options open to her. They fell into two categories, revenge and reward. There was no question that revenge was a very attractive option, but in the end Ivy had rejected it in favour of reward. Damaging your enemies is satisfying, but doing yourself a favour is more important in the long run. Only in exceptional circumstances is it possible to combine the two.

Like everyone else, Ivy had envied those who had a secure job, guaranteed by the State, which could not be taken away no matter how lazy or incompetent you were and whose admittedly meagre salary could be supplemented by tax-free moonlighting in the afternoon. Her position at the hospital was, as they said, 'precarious'. To keep it she had to please, which meant everything from picking up one man's suit from the cleaners and buying fresh pasta for another to queuing for over an hour in the pouring rain to get theatre tickets for one of the patients, quite apart from being expected to do the work of an entire typing pool single-handed. But she didn't dare complain. 'Don't give yourself airs!' the old fascist who served as porter remarked when she'd made the mistake of letting herself be provoked by his rudeness. 'The day the director decides he doesn't like the colour of your knickers you'll be out on the street.' He had no need to add, 'On the other hand I'm here for ever, whether he likes it or not.' That was implicit in everything he did, or more usually failed to do.

Ivy didn't necessarily want to work at the hospital for ever, but she did want to be the one who would decide if she would or not, and that meant getting a secure position. The director had the granting of such posts, but he knew what they were worth and wasn't going to hand them out to some foreigner when the telephone was ringing off the hook with locals offering him this that and the other if he would see to it that Tizio or Cosetta was fixed up. So Ivy bided her time and kept her eyes and ears open, waiting for events to take her where she wanted to go.

Then one day her employer came storming into the poky annexe where she worked and grilled her for over half an hour about some documents which he said had disappeared. From a man who habitually paraded his velvet gloves this display of iron fist was disconcerting, the more so in that Ivy knew nothing of the existence of the documents, never mind their disappearance. But now she did, and she knew that he half-suspected her of having taken them. All of which added up to the opportunity she had been waiting for, because despite this, the porter's prophecy was not fulfilled. Her job hung on a whim, but it was not indulged. The conclusion was obvious, and brought with it the reflection that her employer was not as clever as she had previously thought.

That afternoon she returned to the hospital after lunch, supposedly to catch up on her work. The other porter who, just to balance things out, was a Stalinist, responded to her request for the key to the supply cupboard as she had known he would, by tossing her a huge bunch opening every door on the top floor of the building. Identifying and labelling the keys was a task which the porters considered too onerous to undertake, and since their jobs were not precarious no one could make them do so. So if anyone wanted the spare key to a particular room they were given the bunch for the entire floor in question and had to find the key themselves.

It took Ivy twelve minutes to do so, but that was the hardest part of the whole business. Men did not hide things very well, she knew. Their minds ran in predictable ways. Once inside the director's office she quickly found the spare key to the filing cabinet, taped to the back of it, and a few seconds later the missing documents were in her hand. They had been where she had known they must be, lying on the floor of the metal drawer. They had been carelessly replaced between two files and had then worked their way down as the drawer was opened and closed. It was obvious, it happened all the time, and yet her employer had not thought of it. Part of the reason was that predictability of the male mind she had already noted, but it was also due to a structural defect of the system under which they all lived. The great weakness of paranoia is that it cannot take account of chance. Because the documents were sensitive and might be damaging to him if they fell into the wrong hands, the director had assumed that their disappearance must have been due to a deliberate act on someone's part. To think otherwise would have been to run the risk of being exposed as gullible and unrealistic, the very things that a man in his position could least afford to be.

Back home in her little flat Ivy examined the documents at her leisure. They looked innocuous enough, mere lists of figures and dates and initials, but the next morning before work she dropped into her bank, opened a safety deposit box and placed the documents in it. She did well, for when she got home she found that her flat had been ransacked.

That evening she phoned her employer, rambling on incoherently about how she couldn't go on living in an atmosphere of insecurity and lack of trust, of groundless accusations and the perpetual fear of losing her job. If she had a secure position perhaps she would feel differently, but as it was, well, she didn't know what she might do. Really, she felt capable of almost anything.

A month later her post was made permanent.

She'd done it once, and if she could do it once then couldn't she do it again? But it wasn't as simple as that. The situation was quite different this time. She didn't know whether to laugh or cry when she remembered Zen's panicky orders about keeping her 'in quarantine'. As though anyone was going to lift a finger to save her! Didn't he understand that she had no support whatever apart from Silvio? Her relationship had always been exclusively with him. That was the way he had wanted it. Evidently there was something about her that attracted homosexuals, perhaps the same thing that repelled the young men she would have preferred to attract. But you had to make the best of things, and Silvio Miletti was a pretty good catch, all things considered.

Ironically enough, it had been Ivy's boss at the hospital who had introduced her to Silvio. That was before the two men fell out over their mutual infatuation with a young German called Gerhard Mayer. Never one to do things by halves, Silvio had deprived his rival not only of Mayer's services but of Ivy's as well. For three years now they had been a couple in all respects but one. Ivy's only stipulation had been to insist on keeping her job at the hospital, although the work was actually done by a succession of temporary secretaries paid through a Miletti subsidiary. It was partly a form of insurance to hold on to the salaried position and the promise of a pension that went with it, but it was mostly spite. The director had not been very happy about the arrangement, to say the least, but what with the Miletti's leaning on him from one side and the fear that the missing documents might one day surface gnawing at him from the other, he had ended by agreeing.

Silvio and Ivy had proved to be a very effective couple, complementing each other perfectly. She had the vision, the will, the patience; he had the power, the contacts, and the influence. So far their exploits had been relatively modest. The anonymous letter she'd sent to the investigating magistrate Bartocci, alleging that the kidnapping was a put-up job, was a typical example. Ivy's method was to seize the opportunity when it arose, and meanwhile to stir things up so that opportunities were more likely to arise. The letter to Bartocci had in fact succeeded beyond her wildest dreams, for it had indirectly created the circumstances leading to Ruggiero Miletti's death, which had in turn removed the one remaining impediment to the brilliant future which beckoned to her and Silvio.

Or rather had seemed to beckon, until just a few hours ago. For now the unthinkable had occurred, the one eventuality which Ivy had left out of her calculations. Cautiously at first, but with increasing confidence as she recognized Silvio's dependence on her, she had sacrificed all her minor allegiances to this one relationship, which offered far more than all the others put together. It was often a considerable effort to remember that despite his fecklessness and petulance, his timidity and sloth, Silvio was a man of considerable power. And that power was now at her disposal, to use as though it were her own. It was a dizzying sensation, like finding yourself at the controls of a jet after a lifetime of flying gliders. Only now did she appreciate the more sinister implications of this image. Gliders rode the buoyant winds, versatile and questing, finding alternative currents if one failed, but when jets went wrong disaster was swift and inevitable. But it had never seemed possible that anything *could* go wrong. Silvio needed her as he needed food and drink, not to mention more esoteric satisfactions. He could no more deny her than he could deny himself.

At least, so she'd always supposed. But apparently she'd been mistaken, and with catastrophic results. The police could relax. No one would be pulling strings on her behalf, for she had deliberately cut them all except for those which bound her to Silvio. And he – even now she could hardly bring herself to believe it! – had not merely abandoned her but turned viciously against her, perjuring himself in the vilest way so that she could be thrown into a common lock-up like some gypsy beggar. No, Zen had nothing to worry about on that score!

Then an even more terrifying thought occurred to her. The discrepancy in the time of the statement proved that Zen and Silvio were hand in glove. He must *know* that the Milettis were not going to intervene to save her. Was he perhaps worried that their intervention might take a quite different form? A cup of coffee, for example, laced with something that would have her flopping about the cell like a landed fish, gasping out the classic words, 'They've poisoned me!'

That deposit box at the bank now contained much more than her employer's precious documents, as Silvio well knew. There were photocopies of letters, account books and papers of all kinds, and above all the tapes, boxes of them. The answering machine had been a stroke of genius. For some reason they were always regarded as slightly comical annoyances. No one liked having to deal with them, so callers were always relieved when you answered in person, too relieved to remember that the machine was still there, still connected and possibly recording every word they said. For some reason that never seemed to occur to anyone. But it was a meagre consolation just the same, not nearly enough to keep the rising tide of panic away. She might take a couple of the bastards with her, or at least scratch up their pretty rich faces a bit, but that would not save her. Nothing could save her now.

When the door of the cell opened she hoped it might be a familiar face, even a visitor to see her, but it was only the hard man who had brought her down there.

'Come on!' he said, beckoning impatiently.

Ivy felt as reluctant to leave her cell as a condemned prisoner being led away to execution.

'Where are we going?'

The man just stared at her in his insolent way, like those bastards at the hospital when they thought they had her where they wanted her.

'So you're called Chiodini, are you?' Ivy asked him.

'What about it?' the man demanded, suddenly on his guard.

'Nothing.'

But if I ever get out of here, she thought, I'm going to call a certain number I know and pay whatever it takes to have one of those arrogant eyes of yours sliced in two like a bull's testicle, my friend.

Chiodini led her away along a narrow passage constantly switching direction, like a sewer following the turnings of the street above. The walls here were a world away from the shiny, polished façades of the Questura – rough, grainy slabs of stone beaded with moisture like a sweaty brow, infilled with chunks of saturated brick and rubble. Here and there diminishing islands of plasterwork still clung on, but most of it had gone to make a gritty porridge that scratched and slithered underfoot. It felt like part of the complex system of tunnels and passages underlying the ancient city, into which it was said that children occasionally strayed and were never seen again.

At length they turned a corner to find a man who seemed to have been waiting for them. He was short and fleshy, with a melancholy face and heavy eyebrows, dressed in a heavy-duty suit of the kind farmers wear on Sundays. To Ivy, he was the image of an executioner.

'What are you doing here, Geraci?' Ivy's escort demanded. 'They said you were off ill.'

'I'm all right. I'll take over now, you run along.'

'But the chief said . . .'

'Never you mind about that! I'll look after her.'

Chiodini looked at Ivy, then at the other man.

'Go on, beat it!' Geraci insisted.

When Chiodini had gone, he led Ivy along the passage to a metal door. So lost was she in evil dreams that she expected to see a white-washed stall inside, with a dangling noose, the wooden shutters of the trap and the lever that springs them back to reveal the pit beneath. But in fact the room was large and high-ceilinged, bare of any features whatever except for a crucifix on one wall and a small barred window high up on the other. Through the window Ivy could just make out a section of exterior wall, bright with sunlight. The fact of their being outside, in the real world where life was going on in its reassuring humdrum way, imbued those stones with infinite fascination for Ivy. She wished she could see them more clearly, admire the tiny plants sprouting in the crevices, watch the insects coming and going, study the shifting subtleties of colour and shade. She longed to lavish a passionate attention on that poor patch of wall, to astonish it with her unwearying love.

Then she heard a sound behind her. Someone had spoken her name. On the other side of the great naked space a figure stood gazing at her with imploring eyes. Silvio, it's Silvio, she thought.

'I'll give you as long as I can, dottore,' Geraci murmured.

Silvio nodded impatiently.

'Yes, yes. Thank you.'

The man bowed slightly as he backed towards the door.

'Thank *you*, dottore. Thank *you*.'

Despite his impatience, once they were alone Silvio seemed unable to speak.

'What are you doing here?' Ivy demanded coldly.

'That man telephoned me and told me what had happened. I've been trying to get hold of you all afternoon! I had no idea they would move so quickly!'

At his words something Ivy thought had died for ever flickered into life again.

'But how did he get you in?' she asked guardedly. 'They said I was to see no one.'

'He's one of them. Apparently he's in some trouble, wants me to put in a word for him. But let me explain what happened, you have no idea . . .'

'Excuse me, I know exactly what happened! I've seen the whole thing, read every one of the lies you put your name to.'

Silvio rubbed his hands together in anguish.

'You don't think I signed that thing willingly, do you? Ivy, you must understand!'

'I don't care how you signed it! It's quite sufficient that you did. Do you know how I've spent the last few hours? Sitting all alone in a stinking cell, totally humiliated and despairing! And you have the gall to try and interest me in your state of mind when you signed the libellous rubbish that made that possible? You expect me to *understand*? No, no, those days are over, Silvio. I don't feel very understanding any more. I don't have time to worry about your problems. I've got problems of my own.'

'But you haven't! It's all meaningless!'

He blundered blindly towards her.

'Ivy, you must understand! It's all just a trivial vendetta by Cinzia. It doesn't amount to anything. You'll be out of here by this evening, I promise. I'll retract the whole statement, deny everything. They'll have to let you go.'

She turned towards him, a new light in her eyes.

'Cinzia?'

'That's right. She got hold of some photographs taken in Berlin and gave them to that bastard Zen. They threatened to make them public unless I signed. What could I do? I was taken completely by surprise. I thought I'd have time to warn you, at least. But it doesn't amount to anything, that's the important thing. She just wanted to stir up a bit of scandal, to give you a bad time for a day or two. But we'll soon sort her out, won't we? We'll make her sorry!'

Ivy was silent. The nightmare was beginning to fade, but something still remained, some real cry of distress which the dream had taken up and used for its own purposes. What had it been?

Meanwhile Silvio told her the whole story, starting with the call from the banker which had set him up to be waylaid by Zen. It was all Cinzia's fault, he repeated. But Ivy knew better. She had long recognized Gianluigi Santucci as her most formidable opponent. Like her, he was an outsider; like her, he had a personal hold over one member of the family; like her, he was ambitious and unscrupulous.

In different circumstances they might have been natural allies. As it was they were rivals. Ivy had always known that sooner or later she would have to deal with Gianluigi. Evidently he'd had the same idea, and had struck first. It should have occurred to her that he would have had Silvio followed to that club and his indiscretions photographed. After all, she would have done exactly the same thing in his position.

But there was still that other fact nagging at the back of her mind, that real nightmare. It was something Zen had told her almost casually and which she had immediately forgotten, not because it didn't matter but because it mattered far too much, because coming on top of Silvio's apparent stab in the back it was just too hideous to contemplate. But now that she wanted and needed to deal with it Ivy found that repression had done its job too efficiently. Try as she would, she simply couldn't recall what it had been.

'By the way, do you know that they've arrested the kidnappers?' Silvio asked her eagerly.

They had often remarked on the fact that one of them would mention something that had been on the tip of the other's tongue, as though they were able to read each other's minds. Now it had happened again. And now Ivy understood why she had deliberately forgotten. This was the worst news in the world.

There was only one way. She dreaded it as one might dread a painful and risky operation, even knowing that there was no alternative. It would have to be very quick, before she could change her mind.

'Silvio, the kidnappers didn't kill Ruggiero.'

He tossed his head impatiently.

'But they've confessed!'

'They didn't do it.'

'How do *you* know?'

It was his scornful, cocksure tone of voice that tipped the balance in the end, that made it possible for her to tell him.

'Because I did.'

It took him a moment to react.

'That's silly.'

He frowned.

'Don't say things like that. It's horrible. It frightens me.'

'It frightens me too. But if we face it together it won't be so frightening. You know that nothing can frighten us as long as we're together.'

She moved towards him.

'And now we'll never have to be apart again.'

His mouth opened a crack.

'But . . . you . . .'

'When they phoned to say he'd been released I suddenly realized what that would mean. We've been happy these past months, haven't we? Happy as never before. And that happiness is precious, because people like us know so little of it. The others are rich in happiness, yet they want to take away what little we've got. You remember the letter he sent. You remember what he said about us. Why should people be allowed to say things like that? You know it's unfair, you know it's wrong. And it was all about to start again. We would have been separated again, kept apart from one another. You would have been trapped at home, having to listen to his cruel, obscene gibes. You couldn't stand that. Why should you be expected to stand it?'

Although she was very close to him now, she still did not touch him. He turned away, and for a moment she thought that she'd lost him, that he was about to rush to the door, scream for the guards, denounce her.

'Perhaps I've done the wrong thing,' she went on, almost whispering. 'Perhaps I've made a terrible mistake. Even mummies aren't perfect, they make mistakes sometimes. But babies have to forgive them, don't they?'

After an interminable moment he looked back at her, and she knew she was safe. That dash to the door would never happen, for it would be like running off a cliff.

'What are we going to do?' he moaned.

'We must plan and act, Silvio. That statement will be used against me.'

'But since it's all lies . . .'

'It's all lies, yes. But it's not all untrue.'

Just as she had once paid tribute to her employer's cleverness, she now gave Gianluigi Santucci his due. It was very cunning, the way he had woven details like the wig and the pistol and the fake appointment with Cinzia into a tissue of lies. Yes, there was enough truth there to give the investigators plenty of material to get their teeth into.

'Besides, if they've arrested the kidnappers then sooner or later they'll find out that it was my number they called on Monday morning to announce Ruggiero's release.'

'But that's not true! They called us at the house on Tuesday! I remember that perfectly well. Pietro took the call.'

Ivy shook her head wearily.

'No, that was a recording I made when they phoned me the day before. The gang was given my number before the ransom drop, because it wasn't being tapped by the police. Don't you remember?'

Silvio gestured impatiently.

'Who cares what they say? It's just their word against yours. I'll get you the finest lawyers in the country . . .'

'That's not enough. The judicial investigation is secret, don't forget. However good a lawyer you get, there's nothing he can do initially. Besides, the Santuccis will be working against us, and there's no telling what line Daniele and Pietro will take. No, it's going to be a struggle, I'm afraid. We must prepare to fight on a much wider front, and that means we're going to need friends, all the friends we can get. Russo, for example, and Fratini. Possibly Carletti. I'll send you a list later. We must think flexibly. We might make it seem all a grotesque plot which Gianluigi is orchestrating in order to compromise the Miletti family. The new investigating magistrate will remember what happened to Bartocci. Hopefully she'll think twice about venturing too far on flimsy evidence in the teeth of sustained opposition. And if she does, we'll put it about that her zeal is not wholly inspired by a fervour for the truth, tie her in to Gianluigi's interests in some way.'

She had been thinking aloud, her eyes gleaming with enthusiasm as she began to see her way clear. But Silvio just moved his big head from side to side as though trying to dodge a blow.

'I can't do all that!' he wailed.

This brought her down to earth with a bump. She gripped his arms tightly, pouring her strength and determination into him.

'Nonsense! Remember what happened with Gerhard, after they arrested Daniele. You managed then.'

'But you were there too!'

'And I'll be here this time, to help you and tell you what to do. But you must do it, because I can't. Don't you see that? You must! No one but you can.'

But his look remained vague and distracted. She took his head in both her hands, forcing him to look her in the eyes.

'You know what happened to your real mummy, don't you?'

He bridled like a horse, but her grip was firm, holding him steady.

'She died, Silvio. She died because you didn't love her enough. Because you were too tiny, too weak. Do you want that to happen to me, too?'

He twisted away, a look of unspeakable horror on his face. After a moment he sighed massively and turned back towards her.

'I'll do whatever you want. Whatever has to be done.'

Satisfied, Ivy drew him down, tucking his nose into the hollow in her shoulder-blade where it loved to nestle.

As they embraced she gazed up at the crucifix on the wall. The figure on the cross was oddly distorted, suggesting not the consolations of the Christian faith but the realities of an atrocious torture. It looked as though the crucifix had been broken and then crudely glued together again, she thought idly.

'There, there,' she murmured. 'Everything's going to be all right.'

'By the way, do you know that they've arrested the kidnappers?'

'Silvio, the kidnappers didn't kill Ruggiero.'

'But they've confessed!'

'They didn't do it.'

'How do you know?'

'Because I did.'

'That's silly. Don't say things like that. It's horrible. It frightens me.'

'It frightens me too. But if we face it together it won't be so frightening. You know that nothing can frighten us as long as we're together.'

'Right, that'll do.'

Geraci pressed a button on the tape recorder and Chiodini clapped his enormous hands together.

'We got the bastards, didn't we? We really got them!'

Zen looked at them both.

'You can never be sure, can you? But on balance, yes, I would say that this time we've got them.'

TWELVE

It was raining in Rome. People said Venice was wet, but it seemed to Zen that it rained even more in the city of his exile. It had something to do with the way the two places coped with this basic fact of life. Venice welcomed water in any form, perfectly at home with drizzle or downpour. The city was rich in cosy bars where the inhabitants could go to shelter and dry out over a glass or two, secretly glad of this assurance that their great ark would never run aground. But Rome was a fair-weather city, a playground for the young and the beautiful and the rich, and it dealt with bad weather as it dealt with ageing, ugliness and poverty, by turning its back. The inhabitants huddled miserably in their draughty cafés, gazing out at this dapper passer-by with his large green umbrella and his bouquet of flowers, taking the rain in his stride.

Two weeks had passed since Zen's return from Perugia. His working days had been dominated by the readjustment to the humdrum world of Housekeeping and his personal life by the apparent impossibility of getting together with Ellen. Whenever he tried to arrange to see her it seemed to be the wrong day or the wrong time. In the end he'd begun to suspect that she was putting him off deliberately, but then this morning she had phoned out of the blue and invited him round to her flat for dinner.

'I'll get us something to eat. It won't be much, but . . .'

He knew what she meant by throwaway phrases like that! She had probably been planning the meal for days.

Ellen's attitude to food had initially been one of the sharpest indicators of her very different background. Brought up to assume that women cooked the regional dishes they had learned from their mothers, Zen had at first been both amazed and appalled by Ellen's eclecticism. He would no more have expected Maria Grazia to make a Venetian dish, let alone a French or Austrian one, than she would have expected to be asked. But at Ellen's you had to expect anything and everything. A typical meal might begin with a starter from the Middle East followed by a main course from Mexico and a German pudding. Presumably this was an example of the famous American melting-pot, only far from melting, the contents seemed to have retained all their rugged individuality and to jostle each other in a way Zen had found as disquieting as the discovery that the source of these riches was not family or cultural tradition but a shelf of cookery books which Ellen read like novels. Nevertheless, with time he had come to appreciate the experience. If the menu was bizarre, the food itself was very good, and it all made him feel pleasantly sophisticated and cosmopolitan. What new discoveries would he make tonight?

Ellen was given to dressing casually, but the outfit in which she came to the door seemed fairly extreme even by her standards: a sloppy, shapeless sweater and a pair of jeans with paint stains whose colour dated them back more than two years, when she'd redecorated the bathroom. The flowers he presented her with seemed to make her slightly ill at ease.

'Oh, how lovely. I'll put them in water.'

'There's no hurry, I expect they're wet enough.'

She led him into the kitchen.

'I really meant it about the food being simple, you know.'

She held up a colourful shiny packet. *Findus 100% Beef American-style Hamburgers*, he read incredulously. Was this one of her strange foreign jokes, the kind you had to be a child or an idiot to find funny?

'I imagine you ate well in Perugia, didn't you?' she continued with restless energy. 'Tell me all about it. What I don't understand is how the Cook woman ever thought she could get away with it. Surely it was an insane risk to take.'

He sat down at the kitchen table.

'It only seems like that because the kidnappers were arrested. Of course once I knew what had happened then I started to notice other things. For example, in the phone call to the Milettis which we recorded on the Tuesday, the gang's spokesman gave the name of a football team, Verona, as a codeword. Pietro should have responded with the name of the team Verona were playing the following Sunday, but he didn't understand and simply assumed it was a wrong number. Yet the kidnapper, instead of insisting or hanging up, says that's fine and goes ahead as if the correct response had been given. Which it had, of course, in the original conversation with Ivy. Also the spokesman refers to "the Milettis' father", because he knows that

the person he's speaking to is not a member of the family. If he'd
been phoning the Milettis direct he'd have said "your father".'

Ellen ignited the gas under the grill.

'Go on!' she told him as she peeled away the rectangles of plastic
which kept the hamburgers separate. She seemed more concerned
that he might fall silent than interested in what he had to say.

'Well, you know most of the rest. The kidnapper I spoke to in
Florence told me that they'd phoned the same number as was used to
arrange details of the kidnapping. The family had never revealed
what this was, and I obviously couldn't approach them directly. But I
knew that the gang had used advertisements in a local newspaper as
a way for people to get in touch with them. I went to the library and
looked through the paper until I found an advertisement that was
supposedly for a two-way radio. Phone 8818 after 7, it said. There are
no four-digit telephone numbers in a big city like Perugia. But if you
read the instructions literally you get a five-digit one, 78818. That was
Ivy Cook's number.'

There was a crinkling sound as Ellen tore off a sheet of aluminium
foil to line the grill-pan.

'What confused the issue slightly was that the kidnapper told me
that the person who answered was a man with an accent like mine.
For a moment I thought it might have been Daniele. But Ivy's voice is
deep enough to be mistaken for a man's, and to a shepherd from
Calabria her foreign accent sounded like someone from the North.
She recorded the kidnappers' call on the answering machine attached
to her phone, edited the tape to cut out her own voice, then
telephoned the Milettis the next morning and played it back to
Pietro.'

Ellen laid the patties on the foil and slid the pan under the grill.

'I'm surprised she and Silvio weren't more cautious,' she
remarked. 'Talking freely like that in a police station.'

'They weren't in a police station, just an anonymous room in an
annexe of the prison. But what really put them at their ease was that
it all seemed to have been rigged in their favour. I arranged for one of
my inspectors to call Silvio and offer to get him in to see Ivy in return
for various unspecified favours. It's the sort of thing that happens all
the time to people in Silvio's position, so he found it completely
natural. When he arrived, the inspector got rid of Ivy's guard and
made a big point of the fact that he was leaving the two of them alone

together. They both assumed that the Miletti family power was working for them as usual. After that it never occurred to them to watch what they were saying. They felt they were on their home ground, as though they owned the place.'

The patties were sizzling away loudly. Ellen kept busy slicing up buns and laying them on top of the grill to warm.

'Can I do anything?' he asked.

'No, you just take it easy.'

Normally she would have asked him to lay the table, but this evening he was being treated as an honoured guest, except that she'd hardly bothered to cook at all. Zen had once seen a film in which people were taken over by aliens from outer space. They looked the same and sounded the same, but somehow they weren't the same. What had Ellen been taken over by? No sooner had he posed the question than the answer, the only possible answer, presented itself, and everything made sense. But the sense it made was too painful, and he pushed it aside.

'All the same, so much scheming just to bring one guilty person to justice!' she exclaimed. 'Do you always go to this much trouble?'

'Not usually, no. But I was practically being accused of responsibility for Miletti's death myself. Besides . . .'

'What?'

Zen had been going to say that he had personal reasons for wishing fathers' deaths to be avenged, but he realized that it might sound as if he was fishing for sympathy.

'It's not that I'm criticizing you, Aurelio,' Ellen went on. 'I'm just staggered, as always, at the way this country works.'

'Oh, not that again!'

It was intended as a joke, but it misfired.

'I'm sorry,' she said in a tone that was half contrite and half defiant. 'I won't say another word.'

She served the hamburgers wrapped in sheets of kitchen paper and brought a litre bottle of Peroni from the fridge. The hamburgers were an unhappy hybrid of American and European elements. The meat, processed cheese and ketchup tried to be as cheerfully undemanding as a good hamburger should, but were shouted down by the Dijon mustard, the pungent onions and the chewy rolls.

Zen began dismantling his hamburger, eating the more appetizing bits with the fork and discarding the rest. Ellen wolfed hers down as though her life depended on it. After a few minutes she lit another cigarette without asking. He took the opportunity to push his plate away.

'Don't you like it?'

She sounded almost pleased.

'It's delicious. But I had to eat something with my mother. You know how it is.'

Ellen laughed quietly.

'I surely do.'

The conversation stalled, as if they were two strangers who had exhausted the few topics they had in common.

'Anyway, what have you been up to?' he asked her.

She refilled her glass with beer.

'Well . . .'

She broke off to puff at her cigarette. But he already knew what she was going to say. She had met someone else, these things happened, she'd been meaning to tell him for some time, she hoped they would remain friends. This was what he had glimpsed earlier, the answer to the question of what was making her act in this odd way, of what it was that had taken her over. The only possible answer was another man.

'The thing is, I'm going home, Aurelio.'

But you *are* at home, he thought. Then he realized what she meant.

'For a holiday?'

She shook her head.

'You're joking,' he said.

She walked over to the glass jars where she kept rice and pulses, pulled out an envelope tucked under one and handed it to him. 'Whether you travel for business or pleasure, MONDITURIST!' it read. 'Our business is to make travelling a pleasure!' Inside there was an airline ticket to New York in her name.

'I decided one night last week. For some reason I had woken up and then I couldn't get back to sleep. I just lay there and thought about this and that. And it suddenly struck me how foreign I feel here, and what that was doing to me.'

She paused, biting one fingernail.

'People who have been exiles too long seem to end up as either zombies or vampires. I don't want that to happen to me.'

There was a roar from the street outside as a metal shutter was hauled down, then a gentler rumble as it was eased into position and the lock attached. The greengrocer opposite was closing up and going home to his family.

'I think we should get married,' Zen said, to his total astonishment.

Ellen gave a yelp of laughter.

'Married?'

One of the other tenants had put on some rock music whose bass notes penetrated to where they sat as a series of dull thumps. Somewhere else, seemingly quite unrelated to them, a tinny melody line faintly wailed.

'You don't know how many times I've imagined that you might say this, Aurelio,' Ellen sighed. 'I always thought that it was the one thing needed to make everything right.'

'It is. It will.'

But his voice lacked conviction, even to himself.

He looked around slowly, conscious that all this was about to join his huge gallery of memories. The latest addition to our collection. A significant acquisition. 'They're turning the whole city into a museum,' Cinzia Miletti had complained. But it wasn't only cities that suffered that fate.

'I'd better go.'

She made no attempt to stop him.

'I'm sorry, Aurelio. I really am.'

The rain had almost stopped. Zen stood waiting at the tram stop, his mind completely blank. The shock of what had just happened was so severe that he found it literally impossible to think about. The last thing he could clearly remember was eating the hamburger and telling Ellen about the Miletti case. He had not mentioned the most recent development, which had occurred just the day before.

The arrest of Ivy Cook had had the unusual effect of uniting both sides of the political spectrum. On the one hand there was talk of a carefully orchestrated attempt by the forces of the Left to undermine the Milettis, on the other of a typically cynical solution by the Right to the embarrassing problem of the family's involvement in Ruggiero's death. In short, whatever your political leanings, Ivy Cook appeared as a humble employee who was being made to carry the can for others, a foreigner without influence or power, the perfect scapegoat. Di Leonardo, the Deputy Public Prosecutor, contributed to the debate with some widely quoted off-the-record criticisms of 'serious irregularities in the procedures adopted by the police', Senator Gianpiero Rossi publicly expressed the opinion that the tape recording was inadmissible evidence since it had neither been authorized by the judiciary nor made on official equipment, while Pietro Miletti flew back from London to demand an end to 'the continual harassment of the Miletti family and their dependants'. The net result was that Rosella Foria had finally granted an application for Ivy Cook's release on bail pending a full investigation. The case still hung in the balance, but Ivy was free.

The tram arrived and Zen was rumbled and jolted across the Tiber, over the Aventine hill and past the Colosseum to Porta Maggiore. He then walked three blocks to the street where Gilberto Nieddu lived with a dark-haired beauty who treated him with bantering humour, as though Gilberto's clumsy attempts to woo her aroused nothing but her amusement. In fact they had been married eight years and had four children, who sat open-mouthed and wide-eyed as Uncle Aurelio described the dramatic end of his relationship with 'l'americana'.

Rosella Nieddu diagnosed a lack of proper food and made Zen eat a bowl of ravioli, while Gilberto opened a bottle of the smooth and lethal rosé made by a relative of his. Then the children were packed off to bed and the adults spent the evening playing cards.

'Unlucky at love, lucky at cards,' Gilberto joked to his friend, but as usual Rosella Nieddu easily beat both of them, even with one eye on the television. Then the phone rang, and while the Sardinian went to answer it Rosella changed channels for the late movie, catching the end of the late-night newscast. There were stories about the seizure of a shipment of heroin by the Customs in Naples, a conference on the economic problems of the Third World due to open in Rome the following afternoon and a trade fair promoting Italian agricultural machinery which had just opened in Genoa.

'And finally the main news again. In a dramatic development in the Miletti murder case, Signora Ivy Cook, the foreign woman formerly being held in connection with this crime today failed to report to the police in Perugia as laid down in the conditions of her release. According to as yet unconfirmed reports she may already have left the country. Investigators are attempting to trace the person who chartered a light aircraft from Perugia to an airfield in Austria late this afternoon. And now for a round-up of the weekend sports action here's . . .'

'I have to go,' Zen said as soon as Gilberto came back. 'Mamma will get anxious.'

It had stopped raining. He started to walk home through the almost deserted streets. The chartered plane to Austria would no doubt have been followed by an international flight to South Africa, from which she could not be extradited. Ivy's plans would have been laid for days, carefully worked out in the course of her meetings with Silvio. Her passport had been impounded, so he must have obtained false papers for her as well as putting up bail and arranging the flight. Money would have been no problem. All sorts of people would have been happy to contribute financially to ensure that the contents of the famous safety-deposit box vanished with Ivy.

So she was in the clear. For Silvio the consequences were likely to be more serious, at least in the short run. The fickle public mood was about to turn very ugly indeed. Important people had been made to look foolish. The Miletti name would no longer be enough to protect Silvio. Her hands freed, Rosella Foria would have him arrested and charged with conspiring to pervert the course of justice. The case would drag on and on, getting bogged down in tedious details until everyone had lost interest, and then in a year or so, when the whole thing had been forgotten, Silvio would be quietly released for lack of evidence.

Suddenly Zen felt something give way inside his chest. It's my heart, he thought, I'm dying. Unable to go on walking, or even stand upright, he bent over a parked car, fighting for breath. Only very gradually did he realize what was happening. He was weeping. It was the first time for years, a brutal and convulsive release, as painful as retching on an empty stomach.

'Waiting for a bum-fuck, grandpa?'

Hands gripped his shoulders, pulling him round.

'Rim-job you're after, is it? Up from the provinces for a bit of fun, or are you local? I can fix you up, no problem. Not personally, you understand, but for the right money up front I can lay on a kid who went down on Pasolini. Meanwhile, let's check your financial standing. Wallet, fuckface! Wallet!'

A torch flashed in his face. Then he heard a gentle chuckle.

'Well, well, dottore, what a coincidence! Don't you remember me? That time on the train a few weeks back, with the old fart who tried to act tough.'

He looked more closely at Zen.

'But what's the matter?'

'Nothing.'

'What have the bastards done to you?'

'I'm all right.'

Unconvinced, the youth tugged his arm.

'Come and have something warm to drink, dottore. There's a place open just round the corner.'

'No, I'm all right, really.'

But his whole body was trembling uncontrollably, and he allowed himself to be led away.

'You shouldn't hang around here at this time of night, you know,' his companion remarked casually. 'This is a very tough neighbourhood.'

The only other customer in the all-night bar was an old prostitute sitting in the corner, talking to herself and obsessively shaking out her hair with both hands. The youth greeted the barman familiarly and ordered two cappuccinos. He produced a packet of Nazionali from his jacket.

'Smoke, dottore?'

'Thanks.'

'Fucking bastards. Don't ever let them get you down, though. You let them do that, it's the end.'

As their coffees arrived there was a screech of tyres outside. The door slammed open and two patrolmen walked in.

'Evening, Alfredo.'

'Evening lads. What can I get you?'

'For me a *cappucio*, really hot, lots of froth on it.'

'And a hot chocolate.'

'Right away. Cold out there?'

'It's not warm. See the game last night?'

'That Tardelli.'

'Beautiful.'

The patrolmen stood looking round the bar, rubbing their hands together and stroking their moustaches, staring with insolent directness at the other customers. The muffled squawks of their car's short-wave radio could be heard outside.

The youth looked down the room to the door at the end, beyond the video machine and the pinball table. Then he glanced at the barman, who shook his head almost imperceptibly.

'Had any trouble lately, Alfredo?' asked one of the patrolmen.

'No, no. We never have any trouble here,' the barman assured him, a shade too hastily.

'Glad to hear it.'

Time passed, marked by the slow coiling of smoke from their cigarettes.

'Was that us?' one of the patrolmen finally remarked.

His colleague ambled to the door and held it open, listening to the radio. He turned and nodded.

'Domestic altercation, Via Tasso.'

'Someone giving the wife a bit of stick,' the patrolman guffawed to Alfredo. 'What do we owe you?'

'You joking?'

'Thanks. See you, then. Don't work too hard.'

'No fear.'

The patrolmen went out, leaving the door wide open. A moment later their car roared away.

The barman started towards the door.

'I'll get it,' the youth told him, gulping down the rest of his coffee.

He gave Zen a little nod.

'Take care now, dottore.'

He sauntered to the door and disappeared.

'How much do I owe you?' Zen muttered to the barman.

'It's already taken care of.'

'How much?'

The barman looked at him more carefully.

'Cappuccino's eight hundred lire.'

As he took out his wallet, Zen came across the internal memorandum he had received that morning and put away unopened. It was bound to be bad news, probably disciplinary action of some kind resulting from his irregular handling of the Miletti case. But now he had nothing left to lose. Let's know the worst and have done with it, he thought, as he tore the envelope open.

> To: Chief Commissioner Zen Aurelio
> From: Enrico Mancini, Assistant Under-Secretary.
> You are hereby informed of your promotion to the rank of Vice-Questore with effect from the 1st of May and consequent on this your

transfer from inspection duties to the active rosta of the Polizia Criminale.

It took him a moment to realize what had happened. His deal with Gianluigi Santucci had only been intended to disguise his real purpose, which was to arrest Ruggiero's murderer. But the Tuscan's double-dealing had evidently gone undetected, and here was Zen's reward.

I'm back in the pack, he thought. A functioning member of the ratking once again.

Outside the sky was clear and littered with stars. Zen began to walk home through a silence broken only by the thin, insistent ringing of a distant telephone.

Vendetta

To Moselle

ROME

Wednesday, 01.50–02.45

Aurelio Zen lounged on the sofa like a listless god, bringing the dead back to life. With a flick of his finger he made them rise again. One by one the shapeless, blood-drenched bundles stirred, shook themselves, crawled about a bit, then floated upwards until they were on their feet again. This extremely literal resurrection had taken them by surprise, to judge by their expressions, or perhaps it was the sight of each others' bodies that was so shocking, the hideous injuries and disfigurements, the pools and spatters of blood everywhere. But as Zen continued to apply his miraculous intervention, all this was set to rights too: the gaping rents in flesh and fabric healed themselves, the blood mopped itself up, and in no time at all the scene looked almost like the ordinary dinner party it had been until the impossible occurred. None of the four seemed to notice the one remarkable feature of this spurious afterlife, namely that everything happened backwards.

'He did it.'

Zen's mother was standing in the doorway, her nightdress clutched around her skimpy form.

'What's wrong, mamma?'

She pointed at the television, which now showed a beach of brilliant white sand framed by smoothly curved rocks. A man was swimming backwards through the wavelets. He casually dived up out of the water, landed neatly on one of the rocks and strolled backwards to the shaded lounging chairs where the others sat sucking smoke out of the air and blowing it into cigarettes.

'The one in the swimming costume. He did it. He was in love with his wife so he killed him. He was in another one too, last week, on Channel Five. They thought he was a spy but it was his twin brother. He was both of them. They do it with mirrors.'

Mother and son gazed at each other across the room lit by the electronically preserved sunlight of a summer now more than three months in the past. It was almost two o'clock in the morning, and even the streets of Rome were hushed.

273

Zen pressed the pause button of the remote control unit, stilling the video.

'Why are you up, mamma?' he asked, trying to keep his irritation out of his voice. This was breaking the rules. Once she had retired to her room, his mother never reappeared. It was respect for these unwritten laws that made their life together just about tolerable from his point of view.

'I thought I heard something.'

Their eyes still held. The woman who had given Zen life might have been the child he had never had, awakened by a nightmare and seeking comfort. He got up and walked over to her.

'I'm sorry, mamma. I turned the sound right down . . .'

'I don't mean the TV.'

He interrogated those bleary, evasive eyes more closely.

'What, then?'

She shrugged pettishly.

'A sort of scraping.'

'Scraping? What do you mean?'

'Like old Umberto's boat.'

Zen was often brought up short by his mother's references to a past which for her was infinitely more real than the present would ever be. He had quite forgotten Umberto, the portly, dignified proprietor of a general grocery near the San Geremia bridge. He used the boat to transport fruit and vegetables from the Rialto market, as well as boxes, cases, bottles and jars to and from the cellars of his house, which the ten-year-old Zen had visualized as an Aladdin's cave crammed with exotic delights. When not in use, the boat was moored to a post in the little canal opposite the Zens' house. The post had a tin collar to protect the wood, and a few moments after each *vaporetto* passed down the Cannaregio the wash would reach Umberto's boat and set it rubbing its gunwale against the collar, producing a series of metallic rasps.

'It was probably me moving around in here that you heard,' Zen told her. 'Now go back to bed, before you catch cold.'

'It didn't come from in here. It came from the other side. Across the canal. Just like that damned boat.'

Zen took her by the arm, which felt alarmingly fragile. Widowed by the war, his mother had confronted the world alone on his behalf, wresting concessions from tradesmen and bureaucrats, labouring at menial jobs to eke out her pension, cooking, cleaning, sewing, mending and making do, tirelessly and ingeniously hollowing out and shoring up a space for her son to grow up in. Small wonder, he thought, that the effort had reduced her to this pittance of a person, scared of noises and the dark, with no interest in anything but the television serials she watched, whose plots and characters were gradually becoming confused in her mind. Such motherhood as she had known was like those industrial jobs that leave workers crippled and broken, the only difference being that there was no one mothers could sue for damages.

Zen led her back into the musty bedroom she occupied at the back of the apartment, filled with the furniture she had brought with her from their home in Venice. The pieces were all elaborately carved from some wood as hard, dark and heavy as iron. They covered every inch of wall space, blocking up the fire escape as well as most of the window, which anyway she always kept tightly shuttered.

'Are you going to stay up and watch the rest of that film?' she asked as he tucked her in.

'Yes, mamma, don't worry, I'll be just in there. If you hear anything, it's only me.'

'It didn't come from in there! Anyway, I told you who did it. The skinny one in the swimming costume.'

'I know, mamma,' he murmured wearily. 'That's what everyone thinks.'

He wandered back to the living room just as two o'clock began to strike from the churches in the Vatican. Zen stood surveying the familiar faces locked up on the flickering screen. They were familiar not just to him, but to everyone who had watched television or looked at the papers that autumn. For months the news had been dominated by the dramatic events and still more sensational implications of the 'Burolo affair'.

In a way it was quite understandable that Zen's mother had confused the characters involved with the cast of a film she had seen. Indeed, it *was* a film that Zen was watching, but a film of a special kind, not intended for commercial release and only available to him, as an officer of the Criminalpol section of the Ministry of the Interior, in connection with the report he had been asked to prepare, summarizing the case to date. He wasn't really supposed to take it home, but the Ministry didn't run to video machines for its employees, even those of Vice-Questorial rank. So what was he supposed to do – Zen had demanded, in his ignorance of the nature of video tape – hold it up to the window, frame by frame?

He sat down on the sofa again, groped for the remote control unit and pressed the play button, releasing the blurred figures to laugh, chat and generally ham it up for the camera. They knew it was there, of course. Oscar Burolo made no secret of his mania for recording the highpoints of his life. On the contrary, every visitor to the entrepreneur's Sardinian hideaway had been impressed by the underground vault containing hundreds of video tapes, as well as computer discs all carefully shelved and indexed. Like all good libraries, Oscar's collection was constantly expanding. Indeed, shortly before his death a complete new section of shelving had been installed to accommodate the latest additions.

'But do you actually ever watch any of them?' the guest might ask.

'I don't need to watch them,' Oscar would reply, smiling in a peculiar way. 'It's enough to know that they're there.'

If the six people relaxing at the water's edge were in any way uneasy about the prospect of having their antics preserved for posterity, they certainly didn't show it. An invitation to the Villa Burolo was so sought-after that no one was going to quibble about the conditions. Quite apart from the experience itself it was something to brag about at dinner parties for months to come. 'You mean to say you've actually *been* there?' people would ask, their envy showing like an ill-adjusted slip. 'Tell me, is it true that he has lions and tigers freely roaming the grounds and that the only way in is by helicopter?' Secure in the knowledge that no one was likely to contradict him, Oscar Burolo's ex-guest could freely choose whether to distort the facts . . . . ('and I solemnly assure you, I who have been there and seen it with my own eyes, that Burolo has a staff of over thirty servants – or rather *slaves*! – whom he bought, cash down, from the president of a certain African country. . .') or, in more sophisticated company, to suggest that the truth was actually stranger than the various lurid and vulgar fictions which had been circulating.

On the face of it, this degree of interest was itself almost the oddest feature of the business. Nothing could be more banal than for a rich Italian to buy himself a villa in Sardinia. By 'Sardinia', of course, one meant the Costa Smeralda on the northern coast of the island, which the Aga Khan had bought for a pittance from the local peasant farmers and turned into a holiday paradise for the super-wealthy, a mini-state which sprang into being every summer for two months. Its citizens hailed from all parts of the world and from all walks of life: film stars, industrialists, sheikhs, politicians, criminals, pop singers, bankers. Their cosmopolitan enclave was protected by an extremely efficient private police force, but its internal regime was admirably democratic and egalitarian. Religious, political or racial discrimination were unknown. The only requirement was money, and lots of it.

As founder and owner of a construction company whose rapid success was almost uncanny, there was no question that Oscar Burolo satisfied that requirement. But instead of meekly buying his way into the Costa like everyone else, he did something unheard-of, something so bizarre and outlandish that some people claimed afterwards that they had always thought it was ill-omened from the start. For *his* Sardinian retreat, Oscar chose an abandoned farmhouse half-way down the island's almost uninhabited eastern coast, and not even on the sea, for God's sake, but several kilometres inland!

Italians have no great respect for eccentricity, and this kind of idio-syncrasy might very easily have aroused nothing but ridicule and contempt. It was a measure of the panache with which Oscar carried off his whims that exactly the opposite was the case. The full resources of Burolo Construction were brought to bear on the humble farmhouse, which was swiftly altered out of all recognition. One by one, the arguments against Oscar's choice were made to look small-minded and unconvincing.

The security aspect, so important in an area notorious for kidnap-pings, was taken care of by hiring the top firm in the country to make the villa intruder-proof, no expense spared. Used to having to cut corners to make security cost-effective, the consultant was delighted for once to have an opportunity to design a system without com-promises. 'If anyone ever manages to break into this place, I'll believe in ghosts,' he assured his client when the work was completed. Hav-ing purchased peace of mind with hard cash, Oscar then added a characteristic touch by buying a pair of rather moth-eaten lions from a bankrupt safari park outside Cagliari and turning them loose in the grounds, calculating that the resulting publicity would do as much as any amount of high technology to deter intruders.

But even Oscar couldn't change the fact that the villa was situated almost 200 kilometres from the nearest airport and the glamorous nightspots of the Costa Smeralda, 200 kilometres of tortuous and poorly maintained road where no electronic fences could protect him from kidnappers. Wasn't that a drawback? Well it might be, Oscar retorted, for someone who still thought of personal transport in terms of cars. But Olbia and the Costa were only half that distance as the crow flies, and when the crow in question was capable of 220 kph ... To clinch the argument, Oscar would bundle his guests into the 'crow' – an Agusta helicopter – and pilot them personally to Palau or Porto Cervo for aperitifs.

As for swimming, since Oscar would not go to the coast like everyone else, the coast was made to come to him. A wide irregular hollow the size of a small lake was scooped out of the parched red soil behind the farm. This was lined with concrete, filled with water and decorated with a sandy beach and wave-smoothed rocks dynamited and bulldozed out of the foreshore, barnacles and all. And the barnacles throve, because one of the biggest surprises awaiting Burolo's guests as they padded off for their first dip was that the water was *salt*. 'Fresh from the Mediterranean,' Oscar would explain proudly, 'pumped up here through 5,437 metres of sixty-centimetre duct, filtered for impurities, agitated by six asynchronous wave simulators and continuously monitored to maintain a constant level of salinity.' Oscar liked using words like 'asynchronous' and 'salinity' and quoting squads of figures: it clinched the effect which the villa was already beginning to have on his listener. But he knew when to stop, and at this point would usually slap his guest on the back – or, if it was a woman, place his hand familiarly at the base of her spine, just above the buttocks – and say, 'So what's missing, except for a lot of fish and crabs and lobsters? Mind you, we have those too, but they know their place here – on a plate!'

Zen paused the video again as footsteps sounded in the street outside. A car door slammed shut. But instead of the expected sound of the car starting up and driving away, the footsteps returned the way they had come, ceasing somewhere close by.

He walked over to the window and opened the shutters. The wooden jalousies beyond the glass were closed, but segments of the scene outside were visible by looking down through the angled slats. Both sides of the street were packed with cars, parked on the road, on either side of the trees lining it and all over the pavement. Some distance from the house a red saloon was parked beyond all these, all by itself, facing towards the house. It appeared to be empty.

The scene was abruptly plunged into darkness as the street-lamp attached to the wall just below went out. Something had gone wrong with its automatic switch, so that the lamp was continually fooled into thinking that its own light was that of the dawn and therefore turned itself off. Then, after some time, it would start to glow faintly again, gradually growing brighter and brighter until the whole cycle repeated itself.

Zen closed the shutters and walked back to the sofa. Catching sight of his reflection in the large mirror above the fireplace, he paused, as though the person he saw there might hold the key to what was puzzling him. The prominent bones and slight tautness of the skin especially around the eyes, gave his face a slightly exotic air, probably due to Slav or even Semitic blood somewhere in the family's Venetian past. It was a face that gave nothing away, yet seemed always to tremble on the brink of some expression that never quite appeared. His face had made Zen's reputation as an interrogator, for it was a perfect screen on to which others could project their own suspicions, fears and apprehensions. Where other policemen confronted criminals, using the carrot or the stick, according to the situation, Zen's subjects found themselves shut up with a man who barely seemed to exist, yet who mirrored back to them the innermost secrets of their hearts. They read their every fleeting emotion accurately imaged on those scrupulously blank features, and knew that they were lost.

Like all the other furniture in the apartment, the mirror was old without being valuable, and the silvering was wearing off in places. One particularly large worn patch covered much of Zen's chest, reminding him of the last terrible scenes of the video he was watching, of Oscar Burolo reeling away from the shotgun blasts which had come from nowhere, passing through the elaborate electronic defences of his property as though they did not exist.

With a shiver, Zen deliberately stepped to one side, moving the stain of darkness away. There was something about the Burolo case which was different from any other he had ever been involved in. He had known cases which obsessed him professionally, taking over his life until he was unable to sleep properly or to think about anything else, but this was even more disturbing. It was as though the aura of mystery and horror surrounding the killings had extended itself even to him, as though he too was somehow in danger from the faceless power which had ravaged the Villa Burolo. This was absurd, of course. The case was closed, an arrest had been made, and Zen's involvement with it was temporary, second-hand and superficial. But despite that the sensation of menace remained, and the sound of footsteps was enough to make him rush to the window, a car parked half-way down the street seemed to pose some threat.

The fact was that it was time to go to bed, long past it in fact. He walked back to the sofa and picked up his crumpled pack of Nazionali cigarettes, considered briefly whether to have one more before turning in, decided against it, then lit up anyway. He yawned and glanced at his watch. A quarter past two. No wonder he was feeling so strange. Seen through the mists of sleeplessness, everything had the insubstantial, fluid quality of a dream. He picked up the remote control, pressed the play button and tried to concentrate on the screen again.

You had to hand it to Oscar! No doubt the camera angle had been carefully chosen, but it was really very difficult to believe that this beach, these rocks, those plashing wavelets were not part of a natural coastline, but a swimming pool five kilometres inland. As for the members of the group sitting around the table in the shadow of a huge green and blue parasol, toying with iced drinks, packs of cards and magazines full of games and puzzles, they were fairly typical of anyone who might have been found at the villa on any given day during July and August that summer. Besides Oscar and his wife there were only four guests: Burolo assiduously preserved the mystique of the villa by restricting the number of visitors, thus increasing their sense of being privileged intimates. His excuse was that the household was not able to cope with huge parties. Despite the tall tales of resident slave communities, Oscar's staff was in fact limited to an elderly caretaker and wife, together with a young man who had come with the lions and also helped to look after the garden. Oscar made much of being a self-made man with no wish for ostentatious display. 'I am what I am,' he declared, 'a simple builder and nothing more.' The truth was that he had realized that it was easier to dominate and manipulate small groups than large ones. The video made this very clear. In every scene, inside or out, it was the host himself who was invariably the focus of attention. Lounging on his personalized beach in silver shorts and a clashing pink and blue silk shirt, his head exaggerated in size as though by a caricaturist's pen, Oscar looked like the love child of the Michelin man and an overweight gorilla. One of his unsuccessful rivals had remarked that anyone who still doubted the theory of evolution obviously hadn't met Oscar Burolo. But it was a waste of time trying to be witty at Oscar's expense. He promptly took up the story, telling it himself with great relish, and concluding, 'Which is why I've survived and Roberto's gone to the wall, like the dinosaur he is!' Oscar the ebullient, the irrepressible Oscar! Nothing could touch him, or so it seemed.

Such was the spell cast by Burolo that it was only by an effort of attention that one became aware of the others present. The slightly saturnine man with thinning grey hair and a wedge-shaped face sitting to Oscar's left was a Sicilian architect named Vianello who had collaborated with Burolo Construction on the plans for a new electricity generating station at Rieti. Unfortunately their tender had been rejected on technical grounds – a previously unheard-of eventuality – and the contract had gone to another firm. Dottor Vianello was wearing an immaculate pale cream cotton suit and a slightly strained smile, possibly due to the fact that he was having to listen to Oscar's wife's account of an abortive shopping trip to Olbia. Rita Burolo had once been an exceptionally attractive woman, and the sense of power which this had given her had remained, even now that her charms were visibly wilting. Her inane comments had commanded total attention for so long that Rita had at last come to believe that she had more to offer the world than her legs and breasts, which was a consolation now that the latter were no longer quite first-division material. Opposite her sat the Sicilian architect's wife, a diminutive pixie of a woman with frightened eyes and a faint moustache. Maria Pia Vianello gazed at the spectacle of her hostess in full career with a kind of awestruck amazement, like a schoolgirl with a crush on her teacher. Clearly, *she* would never dream of trying to dominate a gathering in this way.

Despite these superficial dissimilarities, however, the Vianellos and the Burolos basically had much in common. No longer young, but rich enough to keep age at bay for a few years yet, the men ponderous with professional gravitas, like those toy figurines which cannot be knocked over because they are loaded with lead, the women exuding the sullen peevishness of those who have been pampered with every luxury except freedom and responsibility. The remaining couple were different.

Zen reversed the tape again briefly, hauling the swimmer up out of the water once more, and then froze the picture, studying the man who had dominated the news for the previous three months. Renato Favelloni's sharp, ferrety features and weak chest and limbs, coupled with greasy hair and an over-ready smile, gave him the air of a small-town playboy, by turns truculent and toadying, convinced of being God's gift to the world in general and women in particular, but quite prepared to lower himself to any dirty work in the interests of getting ahead. At first Zen had found it almost incomprehensible that such a man could have been the linchpin of the deals that were rumoured to have taken place between Oscar Burolo and the senior political figure who was referred to in the press as *'l'onorevole'*, the formula reputedly used by Burolo in his secret memoranda of their relationship. Only gradually had he come to understand that it was precisely Favelloni's blatant sleaziness which made him acceptable as a go-between. There are degrees even in the most cynical corruption and manipulation. By embodying the most despicable possible grade, Renato Favelloni made his clients feel relatively decent by comparison.

His wife, like Renato himself, was a good ten years younger than the other four people present, and exactly the kind of stunning bimbo that Rita Burolo must have been at the same age. This cannot have recommended Nadia Favelloni to Oscar's wife any more than the younger woman's habit of wandering around the place half-naked. Having reached the age at which women begin to employ clothing for purposes of concealment rather than display, Signora Burolo discreetly retained a flowing wrap of some material that was a good deal less transparent than it first appeared.

A sense of revulsion suddenly overcame Zen at the thought of what was shortly to happen to that pampered, veiled flesh. Vanity, lust, jealousy, boredom, bitchiness, beauty, wit – what did any of it matter? As the doomed faces glanced flirtatiously at the camera, wondering how they were coming across, Zen felt like screaming at them, 'Go away! Get out of that house now!'

The Favellonis had done precisely that, of course, which was one reason why everyone in Italy from the magistrate investigating the case to the know-all in your local bar agreed with Zen's mother that

Renato Favelloni was 'the one who did it'. With the seedy fixer and his disturbingly bare-breasted wife out of the way, the two maturer couples had settled down to a quiet dinner in the villa's dining room, with its rough tiled floor and huge trestle table which had originally graced the refectory of a Franciscan monastery. The meal had been eaten and coffee and liqueurs served when Oscar once again switched on the camera to record the after-dinner talk, dominated as always by his booming, emphatic voice, punctuated by blows of his hairy fist on the table-top.

Apart from a distant metallic crash whose source and relevance were in dispute, the first sign of what was about to happen appeared in Signora Vianello's nervous eyes. The architect's wife was sitting next to their host, who was in the middle of a bawdy tale concerning a well-known TV presenter and a stripper turned member of parliament who had appeared on his talk show, and what they had reputedly got up to during the commercial break. Maria Pia Vianello had been listening with a vague, blurry smile, as though she wasn't quite sure whether it was proper for her to appear to understand. Then her eyes were attracted by something on the other side of the room, something which made such considerations irrelevant. The vague smile abruptly vanished, leaving her features completely blank.

No one else had noticed anything. The only sound in the room was Oscar's voice. Whatever Signora Vianello had seen was on the move, and her eyes tracked it across the room until Oscar saw it too. He broke off in mid-sentence, threw his napkin on the table and stood up.

'What do you want?'

There was no answer, no sound whatever. Oscar's wife and Dottor Vianello, who were sitting with their backs to the camera, looked round. Rita Burolo emitted a scream of terror. Vianello's expression did not change, except to harden slightly.

'What do you want?' Burolo repeated, his brows knitted in puzzlement and annoyance. Abruptly, he pushed his chair aside and strode towards the intruder, staring masterfully downwards as though to cow an unruly child. You could say what you liked, thought Zen, but the man had guts. Or was he just foolhardy, trying to show off to his guests, to preserve an image of bravado to the last? At all events, it was only in the final moment that any fear entered

Oscar's eyes, as he flung up his hands in an instinctive attempt to protect his face.

A brutal eruption of noise swamped the soundtrack. Literally disintegrated by the blast, Oscar's hands disappeared, while bright red blotches appeared all over his face and neck like an instant infection. He reeled away, holding up the stumps of his wrists. Somehow he managed to recover his balance and turn back, only to receive the second discharge, which carried away half his chest and flung him against the corner of the dining table, where he collapsed in a bloody heap at his wife's feet.

Rita Burolo scrambled desperately away from the corpse as Vianello dived under the table, a pistol appearing in his hand. The ratchet sound of a shotgun being reloaded by pump action mingled with two sharp light cracks from the architect's pistol. Then the soundtrack was bludgeoned twice more in quick succession. The first barrel scoured the space below the table, gouging splinters out of the wood, shattering plates and glasses, wounding Signora Vianello terribly in the legs and reducing her husband to a nightmare figure crawling about on the floor like a tormented animal. The second caught Rita Burolo trying desperately to climb out of the window that lay open on to the terrace. As she was further away than the others, the wounds she sustained were more dispersed, covering her in a spray as fine and evenly distributed as drizzle on a windscreen. With a despairing cry she fell through the window to the paving stones of the terrace, where she slowly bled to death.

Despite her lacerated legs, Maria Pia Vianello somehow struggled to her feet. For all her diminutive stature, she too gave the impression of looking down at the intruder.

'Just a moment, please,' she muttered over the dry, clinical sound of the gun being reloaded. 'I'm afraid I'm not quite ready yet. I'm sorry.'

The shot took her at close range, flaying her so fearfully that loops of intestine protruded through the wall of her abdomen in places. Then the second barrel spun her round. She clutched the wall briefly, then collapsed into a dishevelled heap, leaving a complex pattern of dark streaks on the whitewashed plaster.

It had taken less than twenty seconds to turn the room into an abattoir. Fifteen seconds later, the caretaker would appear, having run from the two-room service flat where he and his wife had been watching a variety show on television. Until then, apart from wine dripping from a broken bottle at the edge of the table and a swishing caused by the convulsive twitches of the dying Vianello's arm, there was no sound whatsoever. 'If anyone ever manages to break into this place, I'll believe in ghosts,' the security analyst had assured Oscar Burolo. Nevertheless, someone or something *had* got in, butchered the inhabitants and then vanished without trace, all in less than a minute and in perfect silence. Even in broad daylight and the company of others it was difficult to ignore this almost supernatural dimension of the killings. In the eerie doldrums of the night, all alone, it seemed impossible to believe that there could be a rational explanation for them.

The silence of the running tape was broken by a distant scraping sound. Zen felt his skin crawl and the hairs on his head stir. He reached for the remote control unit and stilled the video. The noise continued, a low persistent scraping. 'Like old Umberto's boat,' his mother had said.

Zen walked quietly across to the inner hallway of the apartment, opened the door to his mother's bedroom and looked inside.

'Can you hear it?' a voice murmured in the darkness.

'Yes, mamma.'

'Oh good. I thought it might be me, imagining it. I'm not quite right in the head sometimes, you know.'

He gazed towards the invisible bed. It was the first time that she had ever made such an admission. They were both silent for some time, but the noise did not recur.

'Where is it coming from?' he asked.

'The wardrobe.'

'Which wardrobe?'

There were three of them in the room, filled with clothes that no one would ever wear again, carefully preserved from moths by liberal doses of napthalene, which gave the room its basic funereal odour.

'The big one,' his mother replied.

The biggest wardrobe occupied the central third of the wall giving on to the internal courtyard of the building. Its positioning had occasioned Zen some anxiety at the time, since it obstructed access to the fire escape, but the wardrobe was too big to fit anywhere else.

Zen walked over to the bed and straightened the counterpane and sheets. Then he patted the hand which emerged from the covers, all the obsolete paraphernalia of muscles and arteries disturbingly revealed by the parchment-like skin.

'It was just a rat, mamma.'

The best way of dispelling her formless, childish fears was by giving her a specific unpleasantness to focus on.

'But it sounded like metal.'

'The skirting's lined with zinc,' he improvised. 'To stop them gnawing through. I'll speak to Giuseppe in the morning and we'll get the exterminators in. You try and get some sleep now.'

Back in the living room, he turned off the television and rewound the video tape, trying to dispel his vague sense of unease by thinking about the report which he had to write the next day. It was the late-ness of the hour that made everything seem strange and threatening now, the time when – according to what his uncle had once told him – a house belongs not to the people who happen to live there now, but to all those who have preceded them over the centuries. Tomorrow morning everything would have snapped back into proportion and the uncanny aspects of the Burolo case would seem mere freakish curiosities. The only real question was whether to mention them at all. It wasn't that he wanted or needed to conceal anything. For that matter he wouldn't have known where to begin, since he had no idea who the report was destined for. The problem was that there were certain aspects of the Burolo case which were very difficult to men-tion without laying yourself open to the charge of being a credulous nincompoop. For example, the statement made by the seven-year-old daughter of Oscar Burolo's lawyer, who had visited the villa in late July. As a special treat she had been allowed to stay up for dinner with the adults, and in the excitement of the moment had sneaked some of her father's coffee, with the result that she couldn't sleep. It was a luminous summer night, and eventually the child left her room and set out to explore the house. According to her statement, in one of the rooms in the older part of the villa she saw a figure moving about. 'At first I was pleased,' she said. 'I thought it was a child, and I was lonely for someone to play with. But then I remembered that there were no children at the villa. I got scared and ran back to my room.'

Including things like that could easily make him the laughing-stock of the department, while if he left them out he laid himself open to the charge of suppressing evidence. Fortunately, it was no part of Zen's brief to draw conclusions or offer opinions. All that was needed was a concise report describing the various lines of investigation which had been conducted by the police and the Carabinieri and outlining the evidence against the various suspects. A clerical chore, in short, to which he was bringing nothing but an ability to read between the lines of official documents, picking out the grain of what was not being said from the overwhelming chaff of what was. Watching the video had been the last stage in this procedure. There was nothing left to do except sit down and write the thing, and this he would do the next morning, while it was all fresh in his mind. By the afternoon, the Burolo affair would have no more significance for him than for any other member of the public.

Once again, footsteps sounded in the street below. A few minutes later the silence was abruptly shattered as a car started up and accelerated away with a squeal of tyres. By the time Zen reached the window it had already passed far beyond the area of street visible through the closed jalousies. The sound of its engine gradually faded away, echoing and reverberating ever more distantly through the intersecting channels of streets. The streetlight was in its waxing phase, and as the light gradually intensified Zen saw that the red car which had been parked further along the street was no longer there. He closed the shutters, wondering why its presence or absence should be of any concern to him. Finding no answer, he decided it was time to go to bed.

Nearly over now. Everything's going, the doubts, the fears, the cares, the confusion, even the pain. All draining away of its own accord. There's nothing I need do, nothing more to be done.

When I saw him standing there, the gun in his hand, it was like seeing myself in a mirror. He had taken my part, emerging from nowhere, implacable, confident, unsurprised. He sounded impatient, taunting me with a strange name, threatening me. 'There's no point in trying to hide,' he said. 'Let's get it over with.' As usual, I did what I was told.

He cried out, in rage and disbelief. Whatever he had been expecting, it wasn't that. Then something overwhelmed me, knocking me over, opening me up. I couldn't have resisted even if I'd wanted to. It wasn't like the first time, the man under the table wounding me with his pistol. All he gave me was pain. This was different. I knew at once that I was carrying a death.

It won't be long now. Already I feel light and insubstantial, as though I were dissolving. The darkness is on the move, billowing out to enshroud me, winding me in its endless folds. Everything is in flux. Solid rock gives way at my touch, the ground flows beneath me as though the river had returned to its courses, unexplored caverns burst open like fireworks as I advance. I am lost, I who know this place better than I know my own body!

Wednesday, 07.20–12.30

As Zen closed the front door behind him its hinges emitted their characteristic squeal, which was promptly echoed from the floor above. One of the tenants there kept a caged bird which was apparently under the illusion that Zen's front door was a fellow inmate and responded to its mournful cry with encouraging chirps.

Zen clattered down the stairs two at a time, ignoring the ancient lift in its wrought-iron cage. Thank God for work, he thought, which gave him an unquestionable excuse to escape from his dark, cluttered apartment and the elderly woman who had taken it over to such an extent that he felt like a child again, with no rights or independent existence. What would happen when he no longer had this ready-made way of filling his days? The government had recently been making noises about the need to reduce the size of the bloated public sector. Early retirement for senior staff was one obvious option. Fortunately it was unlikely that anything more than talk would come of it. A government consisting of a coalition of five parties, each with an axe to grind and clients to keep happy, found it almost impossible to pass legislation that was likely to prove mildly unpopular with anyone, never mind tackle the bureaucratic hydra which kept almost a third of the working population in guaranteed employment. Nevertheless, he would have to retire one day. The thought of it continued to haunt him like the prospect of some chronic illness. How would he get through the day? What would he do? His life had turned into a dead end.

Giuseppe, the janitor, was keeping a watchful eye on the comings and goings from the window of his mezzanine flat. Zen didn't stop to mention the scraping noises he had seemed to hear the night before. In broad daylight the whole thing seemed as unreal as a dream.

The streets were steeped in mild November sunlight and ringing with sounds. Gangs of noisy schoolchildren passed by, flaunting the personalities that would be buried alive for the next five hours. The metallic roars of shutters announced that the shops in the area were opening for business. A staccato hammering and the swishing of a paint sprayer issued from the open windows of the basement work-shops where craftsmen performed mysterious operations on lengths of moulded wood. But the traffic dominated: the uniform hum of new cars, the idiosyncratic racket of the old, the throaty gurgle of diesels, the angry buzzing of scooters and three-wheeled vans, the buses' hollow roar, the chainsaw of an unsilenced trail bike, the squeal of brakes, the strident discord of horns in conflict.

At the corner of the block the newsagent was adding the final touches to the display of newspapers and magazines which were draped around his stall in a complex overlapping pattern. As usual, Zen stopped to buy a paper, but he did not even glance at the head-lines. He felt good, serene and carefree, released from whatever black magic had gripped his soul the night before. There would be time enough later to read about disasters and scandals which had nothing whatever to do with him.

Across the street from the newsstand at the corner of the next block was the café which Zen frequented, largely because it had resisted the spreading blight of skimmed milk, which reduced the rich foam of a proper *cappuccino* to an insipid froth. The barman, who sported a luxuriant moustache to compensate for his glossily bald skull, greeted Zen with respectful warmth and turned away unbidden to prepare his coffee.

'Barbarians!' exclaimed a thickset man in a tweed suit, looking up from the newspaper spread out before him on the bar. 'Maniacs! What's the sense of it all? What can they hope to achieve?'

Zen helped himself to a flaky brioche before broaching the chocolate-speckled foam on the *cappuccino* which Ernesto placed before him. It was only after they had been meeting in the bar each morning for several years that Zen had finally discovered, thanks to an inflamed molar requiring urgent attention, that the indignant newspaper-reader was the dentist whose name appeared on one of the two brass plates which Giuseppe burnished religiously every morning. He congratulated himself on having resisted the tempta-tion to look at the paper. No doubt there had been some dramatic new revelation about the Burolo affair. Hardly a day went by without one. But while for the dentist such things were a form of entertain-ment, a pretext for a display of moral temperament, for Zen it was work, and he didn't start work for another half hour. Idly, he won-dered what the other men in the bar would say if they knew that he was carrying a video tape showing the Burolo killings in every last horrific detail.

At the thought, he put down his coffee cup and patted his coat pocket, reassuring himself that the video cassette was still there. That was one mistake he certainly couldn't allow himself. There had already been one leak, when stills from the tape Burolo had made showing love scenes between his wife and the young lion-keeper had been published in a trashy scandal magazine. Such a magazine, or even one of the less scrupulous private TV stations, would be willing to pay a small fortune for a video of the killings themselves. The missing tape would immediately be traced to Zen, who had signed it out from Archives. Everyone would assume that Zen himself had sold the tape, and the denials of the magazine or TV station – if they bothered to deny it – would be discounted as part of the deal. Vincenzo Fabri had been waiting for months for just such an opportunity to present itself. He wouldn't let it go to waste!

Zen now knew that he had badly bungled his unexpected promotion from his previous menial duties to the ranks of the Ministry's prestigious Criminalpol division. This had been due to a widespread but mistaken idea of the work which this group did. The press, intoxicated by the allure of élite units, portrayed it as a team of high-powered 'supercops' who sped about the peninsula cracking the cases which proved too difficult for the local officials. Zen, as he had ruefully reflected many times since, should have known better. He of all people should have realized that police work never took any account of individual abilities. It was a question of carrying out certain procedures, that was all. Occasionally these procedures resulted in crimes being solved, but that was incidental to their real purpose, which was to maintain or adjust the balance of power within the organization itself. The result was a continual shuffling and fidgeting, a ceaseless and frenetic activity which it was easy to mistake for purposeful action.

Nevertheless, it was a mistake which Zen should never have made, and which had cost him dearly. When dispatched to Bari or Bergamo or wherever it might be, he had thrown himself wholeheartedly into the cases he had been assigned, asking probing questions, dishing out criticism, reorganizing the investigation and generally stirring things up as much as possible. This was the quickest way to get results, he fondly imagined, not having realized that the results desired by the Ministry flowed automatically from his having been sent. He didn't have to lift a finger, in fact it was important that he didn't. Far from being the '007 from the Ministry' which the press liked to portray, Criminalpol personnel were comparable to inspectors of schools or airports. Their visits provided a chance for the Ministry to get a reasonably reliable picture of what was happening, a reminder to the local authorities that all power ultimately lay with Rome, and a signal to concerned pressure groups that something was being done. No one wanted Zen to solve the case he had been sent to look into. Not the local police, who would then be asked why they had failed to achieve similar results unaided, nor the Ministry, to whom any solution would merely pose a fresh set of problems. All he needed to do in order to keep everyone happy was just go through the motions.

Unfortunately, by the time he finally realized this, Zen had already alienated most of his new colleagues. Admittedly he had started with a serious handicap, owing to the manner of his appointment, which had been engineered by one of the suspects in the Miletti kidnapping case he had investigated in Perugia. Zen's subsequent promotion had naturally been regarded by many people as a form of pay-off, which was bound to cause resentment. But this might eventually have been forgiven, if it hadn't been for the newcomer's tactless display of energy, together with the bad luck of his having made an enemy of one of the most articulate and popular men on the staff. Vincenzo Fabri had tried unsuccessfully on a number of occasions to use political influence to have himself promoted, and he couldn't forgive Zen for succeeding where he had failed. Fabri provided a focus for the feelings of antipathy which Zen had aroused, and which he kept alive with a succession of witty, malicious anecdotes that only came to Zen's ears when the damage had been done. And because Fabri's grudge was completely irrational, Zen knew that it was all the more likely to last.

He crumpled his paper napkin into a ball, tossed it into the rubbish bin and went to pay the cashier sitting at a desk in the angle between the two doors of the café. The newspaper the dentist had been reading lay open on the bar, and Zen couldn't ignore the thunderous headline: 'THE RED BRIGADES RETURN'. Scanning the article beneath, he learned that a judge had been gunned down at his home in Milan the night before.

So that was what the dentist's rhetorical questions had referred to. What indeed was the sense of it all? There had been a time when such mindless acts of terrorism, however shocking, had at least seemed epic gestures of undeniable significance. But that time had long passed, and re-runs were not only as morally disgusting as the originals, but also dated and second-hand.

As he walked to the bus stop, Zen read in his own paper about the shooting. The murdered judge, one Bertolini, had been gunned down when returning home from work. His chauffeur, who had also been killed, had fired at the attackers and was thought to have wounded one of them. Bertolini was not a particularly important figure, nor did he appear to have had any connection with the trials of Red Brigades' activists. The impression was that he had been chosen because he represented a soft target, itself a humiliating comment on the decline in the power of the terrorists from the days when they had seemed able to strike at will.

Zen's eyes drifted off to the smaller headlines further down the page. 'BURNED ALIVE FOR ADULTERY', read one. The story described how a husband in Genova had caught his wife with another man, poured petrol over them both and set them alight. He abruptly folded the paper up and tucked it under his arm. Not that he had anything to worry about on that score, of course. He should be so lucky!

As a bus approached the stop, the various figures who had been loitering in the vicinity marched out into the street to try their chances at the lottery of guessing where the rear doors would be when the bus stopped. Zen did reasonably well this morning, with the result that he was ruthlessly jostled from every side as the less fortunate tried to improve on their luck. Someone at his back used his elbow so enterprisingly that Zen turned round to protest, almost losing his place as a result. But in the end justice prevailed, and Zen managed to squeeze aboard just as the doors closed.

The events reported in the newspaper had already had their effect at the Viminale. The approaches leading up to the Ministry building were guarded by armoured personnel carriers with machine-gun turrets on the roof. The barriers were lowered and all vehicles were being carefully searched. Pedestrian access, up a flight of steps from the piazza, was through a screen of heavy metal railings whose gate was normally left open, but today each person was stopped in the cage and had to present his or her identification, watched carefully by two guards wearing bulletproof vests and carrying submachine-guns.

Having penetrated these security checks, Zen walked up to the third floor, where Criminalpol occupied a suite of rooms at the front of the building. The contrast with the windowless cell to which Zen had previously been confined could hardly have been more striking. Tasteful renovation, supplemented by a scattering of potted plants and antique engravings, had created a pleasant working ambience without the oppressive scale traditionally associated with govern-ment premises.

'Quite like the old days!' was Giorgio De Angelis's comment as Zen passed by. 'The lads upstairs are loving it, of course. A few more like this and they'll be able to claw back all the special powers they've been stripped of since things quietened down.'

De Angelis was a big, burly man with a hairline which had receded dramatically to reveal a large, shiny forehead of the type popularly associated with noble and unworldly intellects. What spoiled this impression was his bulbous nose, with nostrils of almost negroid proportions from which hairs sprouted like plants that have found themselves a niche in crumbling masonry. He was from the town of Crotone, east of the Sila mountains in central Calabria. One of the odd facts still lodged in Zen's brain from school was that Crotone had been the home of Pythagoras. This perhaps explained why De Angelis reminded him of a cross between a Greek philosopher and a Barbary pirate, thus neatly summing up Zen's uncertainty about his character and motives.

'Frankly, I shouldn't be a bit surprised if they set up the whole thing,' the Calabrian went on breezily. 'Apparently the Red Brigades have denied responsibility. Anyway, this Bertolini had nothing to do with terrorism. Why pick on him?'

Zen took off his overcoat and went to hang it up. He would have liked to be able to like De Angelis, the only one of his new colleagues who had made any effort to be friendly. But this very fact, coupled with the politically provocative comments which De Angelis was given to making, aroused a suspicion in Zen's mind that the Calab-rian had been deliberately assigned to sound him out and try and trap him into damaging confidences. Even given the mutual hostility between the criminal investigation personnel and their political colleagues 'upstairs', De Angelis's last remark had been totally out of line.

'Have you seen the papers?' De Angelis demanded. ' "The terrorists return". "Fear stalks the corridors of power". Load of crap if you ask me. The fucking Red Brigades don't go round spraying people with shotgun pellets. Nothing but the best hardware for our yuppie terrorists. M42s, Armalites, Kalashnikovs, state-of-the-art stuff. Shotguns are either old-style crime or DIY.'

He looked at Zen, who was patting his overcoat with a frown.

'You lost something?'

Zen looked round distractedly.

'What? Yes, I suppose so. But in that case it can hardly have been the Politicals either.'

'How do you mean?'

Zen's hands searched each of the pockets of the overcoat at some length, returning empty.

'Well, they'd have used the right gun, presumably.'

De Angelis looked puzzled. Then he understood, and whistled meaningfully.

'Oh, you mean . . . Listen Aurelio, I'd keep my voice down if you're going to say things like that.'

Too late, Zen realized that he had walked into a trap.

'I didn't mean that they'd killed him,' De Angelis explained, 'only that they'd orchestrated the media response to his death. I mean, you surely don't believe . . .'

'No, of course not.'

He turned away with a sickly smile. He had just given himself away in the worst possible fashion, voicing what everyone no doubt suspected but no Ministry employee who wanted to succeed could afford to say out loud. But that didn't matter, not now. All that mattered was that the video cassette of the Burolo killings was missing from his pocket.

Zen walked through the gap in the hessian-clad screens which divided off the space allotted to each official, slumped down behind his desk and lit a cigarette. He recalled with horrible clarity what had happened as he boarded the bus. It was a classic pickpocket's technique, using heavy blows in a 'safe' area like the back and shoulders to cover the light disturbance as a wallet or pocket-book was removed. The thief must have spotted the bulge in Zen's coat pocket and thought it looked promising.

Looking on the bright side, there was a good chance – well, a chance, anyway – that when the thief saw that he'd made a mistake he would simply throw the tape away. Even if he was curious enough to watch it, the first scenes were not particularly interesting. Unless you happened to recognize Burolo and the others, it looked much like any other home video, a souvenir of someone's summer holiday. Everything depended on whether the thief realized that his 'mistake' had netted him something worth more than all the wallets he could steal in a lifetime. He might, or he might not. The only sure thing was that Zen could do absolutely nothing to influence the outcome one way or the other.

He had expected writing the report to be a chore, but after what had just happened it was a positive relief to pull the typewriter over, insert a sheet of paper and immerse himself in work. The first section, summarizing the scene-of-crime findings, went very fast. Owing to the evidence of the video recording and the caretaker's prompt arrival, there was no dispute about the method or timing of the killings. The murder weapon had not been recovered, but was assumed to have been the Remington shotgun that was missing from the collection Oscar kept in a rack next door to the dining room. The spent cartridges found at the scene were of the same make, type and batch as those stored in the drawers beneath this rack. Unidentified fingerprints had been found on the rack and elsewhere in the house. The nature of the victims' wounds indicated that the shots had been angled upwards, suggesting that the weapon had apparently been fired from the hip. At that range it was unnecessary to take precise aim, as the video all too vividly demonstrated.

The two pistol bullets fired by Vianello had been recovered, and one of them revealed traces of blood of a group matching stains found at a point consistent with the assassin's estimated position. A series of stains of the same blood group – which was also that of Oscar Burolo, Maria Pia Vianello and Renato Favelloni – were found leading to the vault beneath the house where Oscar's collection of video tapes and computer discs was housed. When the villa was searched, this room was found to be in a state of complete disorder: the new section of shelving Oscar had recently installed had been thrown over, and video cassettes and floppy discs lay scattered everywhere. The fingerprints found on the gun-rack were also present in profusion here.

Zen stopped typing to stub out his cigarette. From behind the hessian screen he could hear male voices raised in dispute about the merits and demerits of the new Fiat hatchback. He recognized the voices of Vincenzo Fabri and another official, Bernardo Travaglini. Then a flicker of movement nearby caught his eye and he looked round to find Tania Biacis standing by his desk.

'Sorry?' he muttered.

'I didn't say anything.'

'Oh.'

He gazed at her helplessly, paralysed by his desire to reach out and touch her. These exchanges, full of *non sequiturs* and dead ends, were typical of their conversation. Presumably Tania just assumed that Zen was a bit scatterbrained and thought no more about it. He hoped so, anyway.

'This is for you.'

She handed him an envelope from the batch of internal mail she was delivering.

'So what was it last night?' Zen asked. 'The opera, the new Fellini?'

'The Opera's on strike,' she said after a momentary hesitation. 'As for Federico, we gave up on him after that last one. Granted the man used to be a genius, but enough's enough. No, we went out to eat at this little place out in the country near Tivoli. Have you been there? It's all the rage at the moment. Enrico Montesano was there, with the most peculiar woman I've ever seen in my life, if she *was* a woman. But you'd better hurry, if you want to go. The food's going downhill already. In another week it'll be ruined.'

Zen sat looking at her, hardly heeding what she said. Tall, large-boned and small-breasted, with brows that arched high above her deep brown eyes, prominent cheekbones, a strong neck and a light down on her protruding upper lip, which was usually curved as if in suppressed amusement, Tania Biacis resembled a Byzantine Madonna come down from her mosaic in some chilly apse, a Madonna not of sorrow but of joy, of secret glee, who knew that the universe was actually the most tremendous joke and could hardly believe that everyone else was taking it seriously. Like himself, Tania was a northerner, from a village in the Friuli region east of Udine. This had created an immediate bond between them, and as the days went by Zen had learned of her interest in films, music, sailing, skiing, cookery, travel and foreign languages. He also discovered that she was fourteen years younger than him, and married.

'I don't care what your dealer told you,' Vincenzo Fabri proclaimed loudly. 'Until a gearbox has done 100,000 kilometres – under on-road conditions, not on some test track in Turin – not even Agnelli himself knows how it's going to hold up.'

'What do I care?' retorted Travaglini. 'With the discount I'm getting I can drive it until the warranty runs out and still break even on the trade-in. That's a year's free motoring.'

'Would you do me a favour?' Tania whispered hurriedly.

'Of course.'

'You don't know what it is yet.'

'It doesn't matter.'

Zen saw nothing wild or extravagant in this claim, which represented the simple truth. But as she turned away with a disconcerted look he realized that it had sounded all wrong, either too gushing or too casual.

'Forget it,' she told him, disappearing through a gap in the screens like an actor leaving the stage.

Zen sat there taking in her absence with a sharp pain he'd forgotten about, the kind that comes with love you don't ask for or even necessarily want, but which finds you out. It was normal to suffer like this in one's youth, of course, but what had he done to deserve such a fate at his age?

He tore open the memorandum she had brought him.

From: Dogliotti, Assistant Registrar, Archives.
To: Zeno, Vice-Questore, Polizia Criminale.
Subject: 46429 BUR 433/K/95 (Video cassette, one).
You are requested to return the above item at your
earliest convenience since it is ....

In the blank space, someone had scrawled an illegible phrase.

Zen stuffed the memorandum into his pocket with a weary sigh. He had been so concerned about the large-scale repercussions if the tape fell into the wrong hands that he had completely forgotten the immediate problems involved. The Ministry's copy of the Burolo video was of course just that, a copy, the original being retained by the magistrates in Nuoro. Technically speaking its loss was no more than an inconvenience, but that didn't mean that Zen could just drop down to Archives and tell them what had happened. In theory, official files could only be taken out of the Ministry with a written exeat permit signed by the relevant departmental head. In practice no one took the slightest notice of this, but the moment anything went wrong the letter of the law would be strictly applied.

Once again, Zen turned to the task in hand as an escape from these problems. The next section of the report was considerably less straightforward than the one he had just written. While the facts of the Burolo case were simple enough, the interpretations which could be placed on them were political dynamite. Zen's completed report would be stored in the Ministry's central database, accessible by anyone with the appropriate terminal and codeword, his views and conclusions electronically enshrined for ever. At least he didn't have to deal with the dreaded glowing screens himself! The use of computers was spreading inexorably through the various law enforcement agencies, although the dream of a unified electronic data pool had faded with the discovery that the systems chosen by the Carabinieri and the police were incompatible, both with each other and with the quite different system used by the judiciary. It was a sign of their élite status that those Criminalpol officials who wished to do so had been allowed to retain their battered manual Olivettis with the curvy fifties' styling that was now fashionable once more.

Zen lit another of the coarse-flavoured domestic cigarettes, looked up at the rectangular tiles of the suspended ceiling for inspiration, then began to pound the keys again.

'Because of the exceptional difficulty of unauthorized access to the villa, the number of suspects was extremely limited. Nevertheless, five possibilities have at various times been considered worthy of investigation. The first, chronologically, concerns Alfonso and Giuseppina Bini. Bini acted as caretaker and general handyman at the villa, while his wife cooked and cleaned. Both had worked for Burolo for over ten years. At the time of the murders, the couple claim to have been watching television in their quarters in the north wing of the property. This is separated from the dining room by the width of the whole building, including the massive exterior walls of the original farm house. As Giuseppina Bini is slightly deaf, the volume of the television was turned quite high. Subsequent tests confirmed the couple's story that the gunshots were at first almost inaudible. It was only when they were repeated that Alfonso went to investigate.

'The evidence against the Binis never amounted to more than the fact of their presence at the villa at the relevant time, but since the only other people present were all dead, and it was apparently impossible for any intruder to have entered the property, it is understandable that the couple came under suspicion. However, the case against them, which already lacked any viable motive, was further weakened by the discovery of the video tape recording Alfonso Bini's evidently genuine shock on discovering the bodies, and by the fact that a meticulous search failed to uncover any trace of the murder weapon at the villa, where the couple had remained throughout.'

Zen paused to give his numbed fingers a chance to recover. Next on his list was the vendetta theory, which involved filling in the background about the attempted kidnapping of Oscar Burolo. This had surprised no one, except for the fact that the intended victim had got away with nothing but a scratch on his shoulder. God damn it, people had murmured in tones of exasperated admiration, how does he do it? Kidnapping was notoriously a way of life in Sardinia, and what had Burolo done but choose a property on the very edge of the Barbagia massif itself, the heartland of the kidnapping gangs and the location of the underground lairs where they hid their victims? He was asking for it!

And he duly got it. Fortunately for Oscar, the Lincoln Continental he had been driving at the time was a rather special model, built for the African president who figured in the fictitious 'slave' story. Oscar did a lot of work in Africa, which he liked to describe as 'a land of opportunity', rolling his eyes comically to suggest what kind of opportunities he had in mind. The president in question was unfortunately toppled from power just after taking delivery of the vehicle and just before Oscar could collect on the contract the president had signed for the construction of a new airport in the country's second-largest city, a job which had promised to be even more lucrative than most of those which Oscar was involved in.

Where other companies might reckon on a profit margin of 20 or 30 per cent, regarding anything above that as an extraordinary windfall, the projects which Burolo Construction undertook seemed able to generate profits that were often in excess of the total original budget.

Oscar had earned the sobriquet 'King Midas' for his ability to turn the hardest rock, the most arid soil and the foulest marshland into pure gold. In the case of the African airport, his bill had already soared to a sum amounting to almost 4 per cent of the country's gross national product, but on this occasion Oscar was constrained to realism. Even if the new regime had been disposed to honour the commitments of the former president, it would have had considerable difficulty in doing so, since the latter had prudently diverted another considerable slice of the country's GNP to the Swiss bank account that was now financing his premature retirement. All this was very regrettable, but Oscar was a realist. He knew that while governments come and go, business goes on for ever. So rather than stymie his chances of profitable intervention in the country's future by pointless litigation, he reluctantly agreed to accept a settlement which barely covered his expenses. To sweeten the pill, he asked for and was given the Lincoln Continental as well.

At the time Oscar had seen the car as just another of the fancy gadgets with which he loved to surround himself, but it undoubtedly saved his life when the kidnappers tried to take him. He was driving back from the local village church when it happened. Much to most people's surprise, Oscar never missed Sunday Mass. Experience had taught him the importance of keeping on the right side of those in power, and compared with the kind of kickbacks, favours and general dancing of attendance which some of his patrons expected, God seemed positively modest in His demands. It was true that you could never be absolutely certain that He was there, and if so whether He was prepared to come up with the goods, but much the same could be said about most of the people in Rome too. As long as all that was needed to stay in with Him was taking communion every Sunday, Oscar thought it was well worth the effort. Unfortunately the local village church lacked a suitable landing place for the Agusta, so he had to drive.

As he rounded one of the many sharp bends that Sunday, Oscar found the road blocked by what appeared to be a minor accident. A car was lying on its side in the ditch, while the lorry which had apparently forced it off the road was slewed around broadside on to the approaching limousine. Three men were kneeling beside a fourth who was lying face-down in the road.

As Oscar got out to help, the men turned towards him.

'Instantly, I *knew*!' he told countless listeners later. 'Don't ask me how. I just knew!'

He leapt back into the car as the 'accident victim' rolled to one side, revealing the rifles and shotguns on which he'd been lying. Several shots were fired, one of which wounded Oscar slightly in the shoulder. He didn't even notice. He threw the Lincoln into reverse and accelerated back up the road.

The kidnappers gave chase on foot, firing as they ran. But the African president, even more of a realist than Burolo himself, had specified armour-plating and bullet-proof windows, and the kidnappers' shots rattled harmlessly away. When he reached the corner, Oscar reversed on to the shoulder to turn the car round. As he did so, the youngest of the four men sprinted forward, leaped on to the bonnet, pressed the muzzle of his rifle against the windscreen and fired. In the event, the shot barely chipped the toughened glass, but for a second Oscar had stared death in the face. His reaction was to slam on the brakes, sending the man reeling into the road, and then accelerate right over him.

By the time the police arrived at the scene there was nothing to see except a few tyre marks and a little blood mixed in with the loose gravel in the centre of the road. A few days later the funeral of a young shepherd named Antonio Melega took place in a mountain village some forty kilometres to the north-west. According to his grim-faced, taciturn relatives, he had been struck by a hit-and-run driver while walking home from his pastures.

The abortive kidnap made Oscar Burolo an instant hero among the island's villa-owning fraternity, eminently kidnappable every one. One enterprising shopkeeper did a brisk trade in T-shirts reading 'Italians 1, Sardinians 0' until the local mayor protested. But although Burolo was quite happy to be lionized, in private he was a frightened man, haunted by the memory of that dull bump beneath the car and the man's muffled cry as the tons of armour- plating crushed the life out of him. He knew that by killing one of the kidnappers he had opened an account that would only be closed with his own death. Burolo had been born in the north, but his father had been from a little village in the province of Matera, and he had told his son about blood feuds and the terrible obligation of vendetta which could be placed on a man against his will, destroying him and everyone close to him because of something he had nothing to do with and of which he perhaps even disapproved. Young Oscar had been deeply impressed by these stories. To his childish ear they had the ring of absolute truth, matching as they did the violent and arbitrary rituals of the world he shared with other boys his age. Just as he had known the kidnappers the moment their eyes met, so now he knew they would not rest until they had avenged the death of their colleague.

Faced with this knowledge, a lesser man might have called it quits, sold off the villa – if he could find a purchaser! – and taken his holidays elsewhere in future. But Oscar's realism had its limits, and it ended where his vanity began. Had it been a business deal, with no one but himself and the other party any the wiser, he might have cut and run. But he had invested all his self-esteem in the villa, to say nothing of several billion lira, and it would take more than some bunch of small-time sheep-shaggers, as he jeeringly referred to them, to see him off.

Nevertheless, someone *had* seen him off, and the friends and relatives of the late Antonio Melega naturally came under suspicion. Apart from the sheer ferocity of the killings, some of the physical evidence seemed to support this hypothesis. Sardinians, particularly those from the poorer mountain areas, are the shortest of all Mediterranean peoples. The fingerprints found on the ejected shotgun cartridges were exceptionally small – 'like a child's', the Carabinieri's expert had remarked, an unfortunate phrase which had provoked much mirth in the rival force. But an adult gunman of small stature was another matter, and would also explain the low angle of fire which had previously been attributed to the gun being held at hip level. Moreover, sheep rustlers would necessarily be skilled in moving and acting soundlessly, hence the eerie silence which had so impressed everyone who had seen the video tape.

'Unfortunately,' Zen typed, 'there was an insurmountable problem about this attractive hypothesis, namely the question of access. The defences of the Villa Burolo had been specifically designed to prevent an incursion of precisely this kind. It is true that the control room itself was not manned at the time of the murders, but the system was designed to set off alarms all over the villa in the event of any intrusion. In order to test the effectiveness of these alarms, a specialist alpine unit of the Carabinieri attempted to break into the villa by a variety of means, including the use of parachutes and hang-gliders. In every case, the alarms were activated. Any direct assault of the premises, whether by local kidnappers or any other group, thus had to be ruled out.'

Placing an asterisk after 'group', Zen added at the foot of the page: 'Subsequent to an assessment of the situation undertaken by this department in late September, Dottor Vincenzo Fabri suggested that the intended victim of the killings might not have been Oscar Burolo, who was unarmed and whose demeanour throughout the video recording showed him to be unafraid of the intruder, but his guest Edoardo Vianello. Fabri pointed out that the fact that the architect was carrying a pistol showed that he feared for his safety, and raised the possibility that an investigation into Vianello's professional affairs might reveal an involvement with the organized crime for which his native Sicily is notorious. To overcome the problem of access, Fabri suggested that Giuseppina Bini was secretly working for the Mafia, drawing attention to the fact that in 1861 her maternal grandfather had been born in Agrigento. For some reason, however, this ingenious theory failed to attract the serious attention it no doubt merited.'

Zen smiled sourly. It was rare for him to get an opportunity to put one over on Vincenzo Fabri. What the hell had the man been up to, he wondered, floating this kind of wild and unsubstantiated rumour?

The next candidate on Zen's list came into the category of light relief.

'Furio Pizzoni was detained on his return to the villa about two hours after the killings had taken place. When questioned as to his earlier whereabouts, he claimed to have spent the evening in a bar in the local village. This alibi was subsequently confirmed by the owner of the bar and several customers. Pizzoni undoubtedly had access to the remote control device mentioned below (see Favelloni, Renato), but given his alibi and the absence of any evident motive, interest in him soon faded, although it was briefly revived by the discovery of video tapes showing amorous encounters between him and Rita Burolo.'

Zen drew the last fragrant wisps of smoke from his cigarette and crushed it out. After a moment's thought, he decided against going into any more details. Even the magazine which had paid so dearly for the photographs made from one of those video tapes had drawn a discreet veil of verbiage over the exact nature of this little love triangle. It was difficult to offer a tasteful account of the fact that the murdered woman had been in the habit of meeting Pizzoni by moon-light in the hut which the lions used during the day and rolling nude on the straw bedaubed with their sweat and excrement while the young man pleasured her in a variety of ways undreamt of in the animal kingdom. For some people it was still more difficult to accept that Oscar Burolo had known about these orgies and had done nothing whatever about them apart from rigging up a small video camera in the rafters of the hut to record the scene for his future delectation.

Suddenly Zen caught the sound of Tania's voice behind the screens.

'You promise?'

She sounded anxious.

'But of course!'

The heavy, monotonous voice was that of an official called Romizi.

'Otherwise it'll mean a lot of trouble for me,' Tania stressed.

'Don't worry! I'll take care of it.'

Zen slumped forward until his forehead touched the cool metal casing of the typewriter. So she had found someone else to ask her favour of, after he had scared her away with his tactless impetuosity. He took a deep breath, expelled it as a long sigh, and began to pound the Olivetti's stubborn keys again.

'Given the killer's need of specialized knowledge to overcome the villa's security defences, it was inevitable that the only surviving member of Oscar Burolo's immediate family, his son Enzo, should come under suspicion. Relations between Enzo and his father had reportedly been strained for some time, largely owing to the young man's refusal to agree to give up his attempt to become a professional violinist in favour of a career in law or medicine. That August, Enzo Burolo was attending a music school in America, and inquiries by the FBI confirmed that he had been in the Boston area during the period immediately preceding and following the murders. This line of investigation was therefore also dropped.'

Zen flexed his fingers, making the joints creak like old wood. He had now disposed of the suspects the judiciary had rejected. It only remained to discuss their eventual choice, currently awaiting trial in Nuoro prison. And here he had to tread very carefully indeed.

'The remaining possibility centred on Renato Favelloni,' he wrote. 'Favelloni had visited the Burolo property on many previous occasions, and had been staying there during the period immediately prior to the murders. Early that evening he and his wife were flown by Oscar Burolo to Olbia airport to catch Alisarda flight IG113 to Rome. According to Nadia Favelloni, shortly before the flight was called her husband told her that he had forgotten a very important document at the villa and had to return to get it. She was to go on to Rome while he would take a later flight. Nadia Favelloni duly left on IG113, but an examination of passenger lists revealed that Favelloni had made no booking for a later flight. Under questioning, Favelloni first claimed that he had flown to Milan instead. When it was pointed out to him that his name did not appear on the passenger list of the Milan flight either, he stated that the purpose of his trip had been to visit his mistress. This was why he had told his wife the false story about leaving a document at the Villa Burolo, and why he had booked under a false name. His wife was jealous, and had once hired a private detective to check on his movements. However, none of the staff or passengers on the Milan flight was able to identify Favelloni, and since his mistress's testimony is suspect, there is no proof that he ever left Sardinia on the night of the murders.

'The key to the Burolo case throughout has been the question of access. Oscar Burolo had paid an enormous sum of money to turn his property into a fortress, yet the murderer was able to enter and leave the property without setting off any of the alarms, all within a few minutes. How was this possible?

'The most likely explanation requires some consideration of the provision made to enable the inhabitants of the villa themselves to come and go. Since Burolo refused to employ security guards to man the gates or the control room, this had to be done automatically, by means of a remote control or 'proximity' device similar to those used for opening garage doors. But while most commercially available models are of little value in security terms, since their codes can easily be duplicated, the system at the Villa Burolo was virtually unbreakable, because the code changed every time it was used. Along with the existing code, causing the gates to open, the remote control unit transmitted a new randomly-generated cluster, replacing the previous code, which would serve to operate the mechanism at the next occasion. Since each signal was unique, it was impossible for a would-be intruder to duplicate it. But anyone who had been admitted to the villa could easily remove the device and use it to re-enter the property without triggering the alarms.'

So far, so good, thought Zen. Technical jargon about remote control devices was no problem. Where the Favelloni angle got sticky was when it came to dealing not with means and opportunity but with motive. It was widely assumed that the reason Renato Favelloni had paid so many visits to the Villa Burolo that summer was that he was involved in negotiations between Oscar Burolo and the politician referred to as *l'onorevole*, whose influence had allegedly been instrumental in getting Burolo Construction its lucrative public-sector contracts. According to the rumours circulating in the press and elsewhere, the two men had recently fallen out, and Oscar had threatened to make public the records he kept detailing their mutually rewarding transactions over the years. Before he could carry out this threat, however, he and his guests had been gunned down, his documentary collection of video tapes and floppy discs ransacked, and *l'onorevole* spared any possible future embarrassment.

This was the aspect of the case which was presumably occupying the attention of the investigating magistrate, but Aurelio Zen, unprotected by the might and majesty of the judiciary, wanted to give the subject the widest possible berth. Fortunately, he had a convenient excuse for doing so. Although these theories had been widely touted, because of the secrecy in which the prosecution case was prepared they remained mere theories, lacking any substantive backing whatsoever. Once Renato Favelloni was brought to trial – in a few weeks, perhaps – all this would very rapidly change, but until then no one could know the extent or gravity of the evidence against him. Thus all Zen needed to do was to plead ignorance.

'As already stressed, the details for the case remain *sub judice*,' Zen concluded, 'but the fact that the charge is one of conspiracy to murder indicates that another person or persons are thought to be implicated. This might indeed have been inferred from the fact that Dottor Vianello's pistol shot apparently wounded the assassin, probably in the leg, while a medical examination of the accused revealed no recent lesions. In this hypothesis, Renato Favelloni would have removed the remote-control device from the villa and passed it on to an accomplice, probably a professional gunman, who used it to enter Villa Burolo and leave again, having carried out the murders. One would of course expect a professional killer to use his own weapon, probably with a silencer. It can be argued that this anomaly merely strengthens the case against Favelloni, indicating that an attempt was made to disguise the fact that the crime was a premeditated conspiracy against the life of Oscar Burolo.'

Zen knocked the pages into order and read through what he had written, making a few corrections here and there. Then he put the report into a cardboard folder and carried it through the gap in the screens separating his work area from that of Carlo Romizi.

'How's it going?' he remarked.

Romizi looked up from the railway timetable he had been studying.

'Did you know that there's a train listed in here that doesn't exist?'

In every organization there is at least one person of whom all his colleagues think, 'How on earth did he get the job?' In Criminalpol, that person was Carlo Romizi, an Umbrian with a face like the man in the moon. Even after some gruelling tour of duty, Romizi always looked as fresh as a new-laid egg, and his expression of childlike astonishment never varied.

'No, I didn't know that,' Zen replied.

'De Angelis just told me.'

'Which one is it?'

'That's the whole point! They don't say. Every year they invent a train which just goes from one bit of the timetable to another. Each individual bit looks all right, but if you put it all together you discover that the train just goes round and round in circles, never getting anywhere. Apparently it started one year when they made a mistake. Now they do it on purpose, as a sort of joke. I haven't found it yet, but it must be here. De Angelis told me about it.'

Zen nodded non-committally.

'What did la Biacis want?' he asked casually.

The effort of memory made Romizi frown.

'Oh, she was nagging me about some expense claim I put in. Apparently Moscati thinks it was excessive. I mean excessively excessive. I said I'd send in a revised claim, only I forgot.'

Youth is only a lightness of the heart, Zen thought as he walked away, as happy as a bird and all because Tania had not treated Romizi to her confidences after all.

In stark contrast to the Criminalpol suite, the administrative offices on the ground floor were designed in the old style, with massive desks drawn up in rows like tanks on parade. Tania was nowhere to be seen. One of her colleagues directed Zen to the accounts department, where he spent some time trying to attract the attention of a clerk who sat gazing into the middle distance, a telephone receiver hunched under each ear, repeating 'But of course!' and 'But of course not!' Without looking up, he handed Zen a form marked *'Do not fold, spindle or mutilate'*, on which he had scribbled 'Personnel?'

In the personnel department on the fourth floor, Franco Ciliani revealed that the Biacis woman had just left after breaking his balls so comprehensively that he doubted whether they would ever recover.

'You know what her problem is?' Ciliani demanded rhetorically. 'She's not getting enough. The thing with women is, if you don't fuck them silly every few days they lose all sense of proportion. We should drop her husband a line, remind him of his duties.'

Apart from these words of wisdom, Ciliani was unable to help, but as Zen was walking disconsolately downstairs again, Tania suddenly materialized beside him.

'I've been looking for you everywhere,' he said.

'Except the women's toilet, presumably.'

'Ah.'

He handed her the folder as they continued downstairs together.

'This is the report Moscati asked for. Can you get a couple of copies up there before lunch?'

'Of course!' Tania replied rather tartly. 'That's what I'm here for.'

'What's the matter? Did Ciliani say something to you?'

She shrugged. 'No, he just gets on my nerves, that's all. It's not his fault. He reminds me of my husband.'

This remark was so bizarre that Zen ignored it. Everything Tania had said so far had suggested that she and her husband were blissfully happy together, a perfect couple.

As they reached the third-floor landing, Zen reached over and took her arm.

'What was it you wanted me to do for you?'

She looked at him, then looked away. 'Nothing. It doesn't matter.'

She didn't move, however, and he didn't let go of her arm. With his free hand he gestured towards the stairs. Whoever had designed the Ministry of the Interior had been a firm believer in the idea that an institution's prestige is directly proportional to the dimensions of its main staircase, which was built on a scale that seemed to demand heroic gestures and sumptuous costumes.

'Perhaps it would work better if we sang,' Zen suggested with a slightly hysterical smile.

'Sang?' Tania repeated blankly.

He knew he should never have opened his mouth, but he was feeling light-headed because of her presence there beside him.

'This place reminds me of an opera. I mean, talking doesn't seem quite enough. You know what I mean?'

He released her, stretched out one arm, laid his other hand on his chest and intoned, 'What was it you wanted me to do for you?'

Tania's face softened into a smile.

'And what would I say?'

'You'd have an aria where you told me. About twenty times over.'

They looked at each other for a moment. Then Tania scribbled something on a piece of paper.

'Ring this number at seven o'clock this evening. Say you're phoning from here and that because of the murder of that judge there's an emergency on and I'm needed till midnight.'

Zen took the paper from her.

'That's all?'

'That's all.'

He nodded slowly, as though he understood, and turned away.

Blood everywhere, my blood. I'm collapsing like a sack of grain the rats have gnawed a hole in. No one will ever find me. No one but me knows about this place. I will have disappeared.

I made things disappear. People too, but that came later, and caused less stir. People drop dead all the time anyway. Things are more durable. A bowl or chair, a spade, a knife, can hang around a house so long that no one remembers where it came from. It seems that it's always been there. When it suddenly disappeared, everyone tried to hush up the scandal. 'It must be somewhere! Don't worry, it'll turn up, just wait and see.' A crack had appeared in their world. And through it, for a moment, they felt the chill and caught a glimpse of the darkness that awaited them, too.

I've got together quite a collection, one way and another. What will become of it now, I wonder? Cups, pens, string, ribbon, playing cards, wallets, nails, clothing, tools, all piled up in the darkness like offerings to the god whose absence I sense at night, in the space between the stars, featureless and vast.

Things don't just disappear for no reason. 'There's a reason for everything,' as old Tommaso likes to say, nodding that misshapen head of his that looks like a lump of rock left standing in a field for farmers to curse and plough around, or else blow up. I'd like to blow it up, his wise old head. 'What's the reason for this, then?' I'd ask as I pulled the trigger. Too late for that now.

Perhaps he would have understood, at the last. Perhaps the others did, too. Perhaps the look on their faces was not just pain and terror, but understanding. At all events, the crack was there, the possibility of grace, thanks to me. Things are not what they seem. There's more to this place than meets the eye. I was living proof of that.

And they proved it too, dying.

Wednesday, 20.25–22.05

'Is this going to take much longer?' the taxi driver asked plaintively, twisting around to the back seat.

His passenger regarded him without enthusiasm.

'What do you care? You're getting paid, aren't you?'

The driver banged his palm on the steering-wheel, making it ring dully.

'Eh, I hope so! But there's more to life than getting paid, you know. It's almost an hour we've been sitting here. I usually have a bite to eat around now. I mean, if you wanted me for the evening, you should have said so.'

The street in which they were parked stretched straight ahead between the evenly spaced blocks of flats built on reinforced concrete stilts, the ground-floor level consisting of a car park. In the nearest block, half of this space had been filled in to provide a few shops, all closed. Between two of them was a lit plate-glass frontage, above which a blue neon sign read 'BAR'.

'Well?' the driver demanded.

'All right. But don't take all night about it.'

The driver clambered awkwardly out of the car, wheezing heavily. Years of high tension and low exercise seemed to have converted all his bone and muscle to flab.

'I'm talking about a snack, that's all!' he complained. 'Even the fucking car won't go unless you fill it up.'

Hitching up his ample trousers, he waddled off past three metal rubbish skips overflowing with plastic bags and sacks. Zen watched him pick his way across the hummocks and gullies that looked like piles of frozen snow in the cheerless light of the ultra-modern streetlamps.

Nothing else moved. No one was about. Apart from the bar, there was nothing in the vicinity to tempt the inhabitants out of doors after dark. The whole area had a provisional, half-finished look, as though the developer had lost interest half-way through the job. The reason was no doubt to be found in one of those get-out clauses which

Burolo Construction's contracts had invariably included, allowing them to suck the lucrative marrow out of a project without having to tackle the boring bits.

Like the others, the block near which they were parked was brand-new and looked as if it had been put together in about five minutes from prefabricated sections, like a child's toy. Access to the four floors of flats was by rectangular stairwells which descended like lift shafts to the car park at ground level. The flat roof bristled with television aerials resembling the reeds which had flourished in this marshy land before the developers moved in.

Some of the windows were unshuttered, and from time to time figures appeared in these lighted panels, providing Zen with his only glimpse so far of the inhabitants of the zone. There was no way of knowing whether their shadowy gestures had any relevance to his concerns or not. He had checked the list of residents posted outside each stairwell. The name Bevilacqua appeared opposite flat 14, but the door to the stairs was locked and Zen hadn't gone as far as trying to gain entry to the block. It seemed to him that he'd gone quite far enough as it was.

Most of his afternoon had been spent trying to find a solution to the problem of the stolen video tape. A visit to an electronics shop had revealed the existence of complexities he had never guessed at, involving choices of type, brand and length. In the end he'd selected one which had the practical advantage of being sold separately rather than in packs of three. It didn't really matter, he told himself. Either they would check or they wouldn't. If they did, they weren't going to feel any better disposed towards Zen because he had replaced the missing video with exactly the right kind of blank tape, or even given them a Bugs Bunny cartoon in exchange.

Back at the Ministry, he walked down two flights of drably functional concrete stairs to the sub-basement where the archives department was housed. As he had foreseen, only one clerk was on duty at that time of day, so Zen's request to inspect the files relating to one of his old cases, selected at random, resulted in the desk being left unmanned for over five minutes. This was quite long enough for Zen to browse through the rubber-stamp collection, find the one reading 'Property of the Ministry of the Interior – Index No. . . .', apply this to the labels on the face and spine of the video cassette and then copy the index number from the memorandum he had been sent.

When the clerk returned with the file he had asked for, Zen spent a few minutes leafing through it for appearances' sake. The case was one that dated back almost twenty years, to the time when Zen had been attached to the Questura in Milan. He scanned the pages with affection and nostalgia, savouring the contrast between the old-fashioned report forms and the keen flourish of his youthful hand-writing. But as the details of the case began to emerge, these innocent pleasures were overshadowed by darker memories. Why had he asked for this, of all files?

The question was also the answer, for the Spadola case was not just another of the many investigations Zen had been involved with in the course of his career. It had been at once his first great triumph and his first great disillusionment.

After the war, when the fighting in Italy came to an end, many left-wing partisans were ready and willing to carry the armed struggle one stage further, to overthrow the government and set up a workers' state. Some had ideological motives, others were just intoxicated by the thrills and glamour of making history and couldn't stomach the prospect of returning to a life of mundane, poorly paid work, even supposing there was work to be had. To such men, and Vasco Spadola was one, the decision of the Communist leader Togliatti to follow a path of reform rather than revolution represented a betrayal. Once it became clear that a national uprising of the Italian working class was not going to happen, Spadola and his comrades put their weapons and training to use in a sporadic campaign of bank raids and hold-ups which they tried to justify as 'acts of class warfare'.

The success of these ventures soon caused considerable strains and stresses within the group. On one side were those led by Ugo and Carlo Trocchio, who still adhered to a doctrinaire political line, and on the other Spadola's followers, who were beginning to appreciate the possibilities of this kind of private enterprise. These problems were eventually resolved when the Trocchio brothers were shot dead in a café in the Milan suburb of Rho.

With their departure, the gang abandoned all pretence of waging a political struggle and concentrated instead on consolidating its grip on every aspect of the city's criminal life. High-risk bank raids were replaced by unspectacular percentage operations such as gambling, prostitution, drugs and extortion. Spadola's involvement in these areas was well known to the police, but one aspect of his partisan training which he had not forgotten was how to structure an organization in such a way that it could survive the penetration or capture of individual units. No matter how many of his operations were foiled or his associates arrested, Spadola himself was never implicated until the Tondelli affair.

Bruno Tondelli himself was not one of Milan's most savoury characters, but when he was done to death with a butcher's knife it was still murder. The Tondellis had been engaged in a long-running territorial dispute with Spadola's men, which no doubt explained why Spadola found it expedient to disappear from sight immediately after the murder. Nevertheless, no one in the police would have wagered a piece of used chewing-gum on their chances of pinning it on him.

Then one day Zen, who had been given the thankless task of investigating Tondelli's stabbing, received a message from an informer asking for a meeting. In order to protect them, informers' real names and addresses were kept in a locked file to which only a very few high-ranking officials had access; everyone else referred to them by their code name. The man who telephoned Zen, known as 'the nightingale', was one of the police's most trusted and reliable sources of information.

The meeting duly took place in a second-class compartment of one of the *Ferrovia Nord* trains trundling up the line to Seveso. It was a foggy night in February. At one of the intermediate stations a man joined Zen in the prearranged compartment. Pale, balding, slight and diffident, he might have been a filing clerk or a university professor. Vasco Spadola, he said, was hiding out in a farmhouse to the east of the city.

'I was there the night Tondelli got killed,' the informer went on. 'Spadola stabbed him with his own hand. "This'll teach the whole litter of them a lesson," he said.'

'A lot of use that is to us if you won't testify,' Zen retorted irritably.

The man gave him an arch look.

'Who said I wouldn't testify?'

And testify he duly did. Not only that, but when the police raided the farm house near the village of Melzo, they found not only Vasco Spadola but also a knife which proved to have traces of blood of the same group that had once flowed in Bruno Tondelli's veins.

Spadola was sentenced to life imprisonment and Aurelio Zen

spent three days basking in glory. Then he learned from an envious colleague that the knife had been smeared with a sample of Tondelli's blood and planted at the scene by the police themselves, and that the reason why 'the nightingale' had been prepared to come into court and testify that he had seen Spadola commit murder was that the Tondellis had paid him handsomely to do so.

Zen closed the file and handed it back to the clerk with the blank video cassette.

'Oh by the way, if it isn't too much trouble, do you think you could manage to get my name right next time?' he asked sarcastically, flourishing the memorandum.

'What's wrong with it?' the clerk demanded, taking the substitute video without a second glance.

'My name happens to be Zen, not Zeno.'

'Zen's not Italian.'

'Quite right, it's Venetian. But since it's only three letters long, I'd have thought that even you lot would be capable of spelling it correctly. And while we're at it, what the hell does this say?'

He indicated the phrase scribbled in the blank space.

' "... since it is needed by another official",' the clerk read aloud. 'Maybe you need glasses.'

Zen frowned, ignoring the comment.

'Who asked for it?'

The clerk sighed mightily, pulled open a filing cabinet and flicked through the cards.

'Fabri, Vincenzo.'

Even now, sitting in the taxi, looking out at the deserted streets of the dormitory suburb, Zen could feel the sense of panic these words had induced. Why should Vincenzo Fabri, of all people, have put in a request for the Burolo video? He had nothing to do with the case, no legitimate reason for wishing to view the tape. If nothing more, it was monstrously unfortunate. Not only would Zen's substitution of the blank tape come to light, but it would do so through the offices of his sworn enemy. Nervously Zen lit a cigarette, ignoring the sign on the taxi's dashboard thanking him for not doing so, and reflected uneasily that Vincenzo Fabri couldn't have contrived a better opportunity to disgrace his rival if he'd planned it himself.

The earlier part of Zen's evening had not improved his mood. Dinner was always the most difficult part of his day. In the morning he could escape to work, and when he got home in the afternoon Maria Grazia, the housekeeper, was there to dilute the situation with her bustling, loquacious presence. Later in the evening things got easier once again, as his mother switched the lights off and settled down in front of the television, flipping from channel to channel as the whim took her, dipping into the various serials like someone dropping in on the neighbours for a few minutes' inconsequential chat. But first there was dinner to be got through.

Today, to make matters worse, his mother was having one of her 'deaf' phases, when she was – or pretended to be – unable to hear anything that was said to her until it had been repeated three or four times at an ever higher volume. Since their conversation had long been reduced to the lowest of common denominators, Zen found himself having to shout at the top of his voice remarks that were so meaningless it would have been an effort even to mumble them.

To Zen's intense relief, the television news made no reference to the discovery of exclusive video footage showing every gory detail of the Burolo murders. Indeed, for once the case was not even mentioned. The news was dominated by the shooting of Judge Giulio Bertolini and featured an emotional interview with the victim's widow, in the course of which she denounced the lack of protection given to her husband.

'Even when Giulio received threats, nothing whatever was done! We begged, we pleaded, we . . .'

'Your husband was warned that he would be killed?' the reporter interrupted eagerly.

Signora Bertolini made a gesture of qualification.

'Not in so many words, no. But there were tokens, signs, strange disturbing things. For example an envelope pushed through our letter-box with nothing inside but a lot of tiny little metal balls, like caviare, only hard. And then Giulio's wallet was stolen, and later we found it in the living room, the papers and money all scattered about the floor. But when we informed the public prosecutor he said there were no grounds for giving my husband an armed guard. And just a few days later he was gunned down, a helpless victim, betrayed by the very people who should . . .'

Zen glanced at his mother. So far neither of them had referred to the mysterious metallic scraping which had disturbed her the previous night, and which he had explained away as a rat in the skirting.

He hoped Signora Bertolini's words did not make her think of another possible explanation which had occurred to him: that someone had been trying to break into the flat.

'Don't you like your soup?' he remarked to his mother, who was moodily pushing the vegetables and pasta around in her plate.

'What?'

'YOUR SOUP! AREN'T YOU GOING TO EAT IT?'

'It's got turnip in.'

'What's wrong with that?'

'Turnips are for cattle, not people,' his mother declared, her deafness miraculously improved.

'You ate them last time.'

'What?'

Zen took a deep breath.

'PUT THEM TO ONE SIDE AND EAT THE REST!' he yelled, repeating word for word the formula she had once used with him.

'I'm not hungry,' his mother retorted sulkily.

'That won't stop you eating half a box of chocolates while you watch TV.'

'What?'

'NOTHING.'

Zen pushed his plate away and lit a cigarette. From the television set, Signora Bertolini continued her confused and vapid accusations. Although he naturally sympathized with her, Zen also felt a sense of revulsion. It was becoming too convenient to blame the authorities for everything that happened. Soon the relatives of motorists killed on the motorway would appear on television claiming that their deaths were due not to the fact that they had been doing 200 kilometres an hour on the hard shoulder in the middle of a contraflow system, but to the criminal negligence of the authorities in not providing for the needs of people who were exercising their constitutional right to drive like maniacs.

At one minute to seven exactly Zen walked through to the inner hallway where the phone was and dialled the number Tania had given him. A woman answered.

'Yes?'

'Good evening. I have a message for Signora Biacis.'

'Who's this?'

318

The woman's voice was frugal and clipped, as though she had to pay for each word and resented the expense.

'The Ministry of the Interior.'

Muffled squawks penetrated to the mouthpiece which the woman had covered with her hand while she talked to someone else.

'Who's this?' a man abruptly demanded.

'I'm calling from the Ministry,' Zen recited. 'I have a message for Signora Biacis.'

'I'm her husband. What have you got to say?'

'You've no doubt heard about the recent terrorist outrage, Signor Biacis . . .'

'Bevilacqua, Mauro Bevilacqua,' the man cut in.

Zen noted the name on the scratch pad by the phone. Evidently Tania Biacis, like many Italian married women, had retained her maiden name.

'As a result, ministerial staff have been placed on an emergency alert. Your wife is liable for a half-shift this evening.'

The man snorted angrily.

'This has never happened before!'

'On the contrary, it has happened all too often.'

'I mean she's never been called in at this time before!'

'Then she's been very lucky,' Zen declared with finality, and hung up.

That was all he'd needed to do, Zen thought as he sat in the taxi, waiting for the driver to return. It was all he'd been asked to do, it was all he had any right to do. But instead of returning to the living room and his mother's company, he'd lifted the phone again and called a taxi.

The address listed in the telephone directory after 'Bevilacqua Mauro' did not exist on Zen's map of Rome. The taxi driver hadn't known where it was either, but after consultations with the dispatcher it had finally been located in one of the new suburbs on the eastern fringes of the city, beyond the Grande Raccordo Anulare.

Whether it was that the dispatcher's instructions had been unclear or that the driver had forgotten them, they had only found the street after a lengthy excursion through unsurfaced streets that briefly became country roads pocked with potholes and ridged into steps, where concrete-covered drainage pipes ran across the eroded surface. Until recently this had all been unfenced grazing land, open *campagna* where sheep roamed amid the striding aqueducts and squat round towers that now gave their names to the new suburbs which had sprung up as the capital began its pathological post-war growth. Laid out piecemeal as the area grew, the streets rambled aimlessly about, often ending abruptly in culs-de-sac that forced the driver to make long and disorientating detours. Here was a zone of abusive development from the early sixties, a shanty town of troglodytic hutches run up by immigrants from the south, each surrounded by a patch of enclosed ground where chickens and donkeys roamed amid old lavatories and piles of abandoned pallets. Next came an older section of villas for the well-to-do, thick with pines and guard dogs, giving way abruptly to a huge cleared expanse of asphalt illuminated by gigantic searchlights trained down from steel masts, where a band of gypsies had set up home in caravans linked by canopies of plastic sheeting. After that there was a field with sheep grazing, and then the tower blocks began, fourteen storeys high, spaced evenly across the landscape like the pieces in a board-game for giants, on tracts of land that had been brutally assaulted and left to die. Finally, they had found the development of walk-up apartments where Mauro Bevilacqua and Tania Biacis had made their home.

Zen sank back in the seat, wondering why on earth he had come. As soon as the driver returned from his snack he would go home. Tania must have left long ago, while the taxi was lost in this bewildering urban hinterland. Not that he had really intended to follow her, anyway. Putting together her comment about her husband that morning and then her request that Zen phone up with a fictitious reason for her to leave the house, it seemed pretty clear what she was up to. The last thing he wanted was proof of that. He had accepted the fact that Tania was happily and irrevocably married. He didn't now want to have to accept that, on the contrary, she was having an illicit affair, but not with him.

A silhouetted figure appeared at one of the windows of the nearby block. Zen imagined the scene viewed from that window: the deserted street, the parked car. It made him think of the night before, and suddenly he understood what he had found disturbing about the red car. Like the taxi, it had been about fifty metres from his house and on the opposite side of the street, the classic surveillance position. But he had no time to follow up the implications of this thought, because at that moment a woman emerged from one of the staircases of the apartment block.

She started to walk towards the taxi, then suddenly stopped, turned, and hurried back the way she had come. At the same moment, as if on cue, the taxi driver reappeared from the bar and a swarthy man in shirtsleeves ran out into the car park underneath the apartment block, looking round wildly. The woman veered sharply to her left, making for the bar, but the man easily cut her off. They started to struggle, the man gripping her by the arms and trying to pull her back towards the door of the block.

Zen got out of the taxi and walked over to them, unfolding his identity card.

'Police!'

Locked in their clumsy tussle, the couple took no notice. Zen shook the man roughly by the shoulder.

'Let her go!'

The man swung round and aimed a wild punch at Zen, who dodged the blow with ease, seized the man by the collar and pulled him off balance, then shoved him backwards, sending him reeling headlong to the ground.

'Right, what would you like to be arrested for?' he asked. 'Assaulting a police officer . . .'

'You assaulted *me!*' the man interrupted indignantly as he got to his feet.

'. . . or interfering with this lady,' Zen concluded.

The man laughed coarsely. He was short and slightly-built, with a compensatory air of bluster and braggadocio which seemed to emanate from his neatly clipped moustache.

'Lady? What do you mean, lady? She's my wife! Understand? This is a family affair!'

Zen turned to Tania Biacis, who was looking at him in utter amazement.

'What happened, signora?'

'She was running away from her home and her duties!' her husband exclaimed. His arms were outstretched to an invisible audience.

'I . . . that taxi . . . I thought it was free,' Tania said. She was evidently completely thrown by Zen's presence. 'I was going to take it. Then I saw there was someone in it, so I was going to the bar to phone for one.'

Mauro Bevilacqua glared at Zen.

'What the hell are you doing lurking about here, anyway? It's as bad as Russia, policemen on every street corner!'

'There happens to be a terrorist alert on,' Zen told him coldly.

Tania turned triumphantly on her husband.

'You see! I told you!'

Having recovered her presence of mind, she appealed to Zen.

'I work at the Ministry of the Interior. I was called in for emergency duties this evening, but my husband wouldn't believe me. He wouldn't let me use the car. He said it was all a lie, a plot to get out of the house!'

Zen shook his head in disgust.

'So it's come to this! Here's your wife, signore, a key member of a dedicated team who are giving their all, night and day, to defend this country of ours from a gang of ruthless anarchists, and all you can do is to hurl puerile and scandalous accusations at her! You ought to be ashamed of yourself.'

'It's none of your business!' Bevilacqua snapped.

'On the contrary,' Zen warned him. 'If I choose to make it my business, you could be facing a prison sentence for assault.'

He paused to let that sink in.

'Luckily for you, however, I have more important things to do. Just as your wife does. But to set your fears at rest, I'll accompany her personally to the Ministry. Will that satisfy you? Or perhaps you'd like me to summon an armed escort to make sure that she reaches her place of work safely?'

Mauro Bevilacqua flapped his arms up and down like a flightless bird trying vainly to take off.

'What I'd like! What I'd like! What I'd like is for her to start behaving like a wife should instead of gadding about on her own at this time of night!'

He swung round to face her.

'You should never have gone to work in the first place! I never wanted you to go.'

'If you brought home a decent income from that stinking bank I wouldn't have to!'

Mauro Bevilacqua looked at her with hatred in his eyes. 'We'll settle this when you get home!' he spat out, turning on his heel.

Zen ushered Tania into the back of the taxi. He got into the front seat, beside the driver.

'What *were* you doing there?' Tania asked after they had driven in silence for some time.

He did not reply. Now that their little farce had been played to its conclusion, all his confidence had left him. He felt ill at ease and constrained by the situation.

'You weren't really on a stake-out, were you?' she prompted.

Zen usually had no difficulty in thinking up plausible stories to conceal his real motives, but on this occasion he found himself at a loss. He couldn't tell Tania the truth and he wouldn't lie to her.

'Not an official one.'

He glanced round at her. As they passed each streetlamp, its light moved across her in a steady stroking movement, revealing the contours of her face and body.

'You sounded very convincing,' she said.

He shrugged. 'If you're going to tell someone a pack of lies, there's no point in doing it half-heartedly.'

With the help of Tania's directions, they quickly regained Via Casilina, and soon the city had closed in around them again. Zen felt as though he had returned to earth from outer space.

'How can you stand living in that place?' he demanded.

As soon as he had spoken, he realized how rude the question sounded. But Tania seemed unoffended.

'That's what I ask myself every morning when I leave and every evening when I get back. The answer is simple. Money.'

You could always economize on your social life, thought Zen sourly, cut out the fancy dinners and the season ticket to the opera and the weekends ski-ing and skin-diving. He was rapidly going off Tania Biacis, he found. But he didn't say anything. Mauro Bevilacqua had been quite right. It was none of his business.

'So where's it to?' the driver asked as they neared Porta Maggiore.

Zen said nothing. He wanted Tania to decide, and he wanted her to have all the time she needed to do so. Although Zen had aided and abetted her deception of her husband, he actually felt every bit as resentful of her behaviour as Mauro Bevilacqua, though of course *he* couldn't let it show. He was also aware that Tania would have to invent a different cover story for his consumption, since the one she had used with her husband clearly wouldn't do. He wanted it to be a good one, something convincing, something that would spare his feelings. He'd done the dirty work she'd requested. Now let her cover her tracks with him, too.

'Eh, oh, signori!' the driver exclaimed. 'A bit of information, that's all I need. This car isn't a mule, you know. It won't go by itself. You have to turn the wheel. So, which way?'

Tania gave an embarrassed laugh.

'To tell you the truth, I just wanted to go to the cinema.'

Well, it was better than saying outright that she was going to meet her lover, Zen supposed. But not much better. Not when she had been regaling him for months with her views of the latest films as they came out, flaunting the fact that she and her husband went to the cinema the way other people turned on the television.

To lie so crudely, so transparently, was tantamount to an insult. No wonder she sounded embarrassed She couldn't have expected to be believed, not for a moment. She must have done it deliberately, as a way of getting the truth across to her faithful, stupid, besotted admirer. Well, it had worked! He'd understood, finally!

'Did you have any particular film in mind?' he inquired sarcastically.

'Anything at all.'

She sounded dismissive, no doubt impatient with him, thinking that he'd missed the point. He'd soon put her right about that.

'Via Nazionale,' he told the driver. Turning to Tania, he added, 'I'm sure you'll be able to find what you want there. Whatever it happens to be.'

As their eyes met, he had the uneasy feeling that he'd somehow misunderstood. But how could he? What other explanation was there?

'Please stop,' Tania said to the driver.

'We're not there yet.'

'It doesn't matter! Just stop.'

The taxi cut across two lanes of traffic, unleashing a chorus of horns from behind. Tania handed the driver a ten thousand lire note.

'Deduct that from whatever he owes you.'

She got out, slammed the door and walked away.

'Where now?' queried the driver.

'Same place you picked me up,' Zen told him.

They drove down Via Nazionale and through Piazza Venezia. The driver jerked his thumb towards the white mass of the monument to Vittorio Emanuele.

'You know what I heard the other day? I had this city councillor in the back of the cab, we were going past here. You know the Unknown Soldier they have buried up there? This councillor, he told me they were doing maintenance work a couple of years ago and they had to dig up the body. You know what they found? The poor bastard had been shot in the back! Must have been a deserter, they reckoned. Ran away during the battle and got shot by the military police. Isn't that the end? Fucking monument to military valour, with the two sentries on guard all the time, and it turns out the poor fucker buried there was a deserter! Makes you think, eh?'

Zen agreed that such things did indeed make you think, but in fact his thoughts were elsewhere. The history of his relationships with women was passing in review before his eyes like the life of a drowning man. And indeed Zen felt that he was drowning, in a pool of black indifference and icy inertia. His failed marriage could be written off to experience: he and Luisella had married too early and for all the wrong reasons. That was a common enough story. It was what had happened since then that was so disturbing, or rather what had *not* happened. For Zen was acutely aware that in the fifteen years since his marriage broke up, he had failed to create a single lasting bond to take its place.

The final blow had been the departure of Ellen, the American divorcee he had been seeing on and off for over three years. The manner of her going had hurt as much as the fact. Ellen had made it clear that Zen had failed her in just about every conceivable way, and once he had got over his anger at being rejected he found this hard to deny. The opportunity had been there for the taking, but he had hesitated and dithered and messed about, using his mother as an excuse, until things had come to a crisis. Then it had been a case of too much, too late, as he had blurted out an unconsidered offer of marriage which must have seemed like the final insult. It wasn't marriage for its own sake that Ellen had wanted but a sense of Zen's commitment to her. And he just hadn't been able to feel such a commitment.

It was no surprise, of course, at his age. With every year that passed the number of things he really cared about decreased, and Zen soon convinced himself that his failure with Ellen had been an indication that love was fast coming to seem more trouble than it was worth. Why else should he have let the opportunity slip? And why did he never get round to answering the postcards and letters Ellen sent him from New York? The whole affair had been nothing but the self-delusion of an ageing man who couldn't accept that love, too, was something he must learn to give up gracefully.

Zen had just got all this nicely sorted out when Tania Biacis walked into his life. It was the first day of his new duties at the Ministry. Tania introduced herself as one of the administrative assistants and proceeded to explain the bureaucratic ins and outs of the department. Zen nodded, smiled, grunted and even managed to ask one or two relevant questions, but in fact he was on autopilot throughout, all his second-hand wisdom swept away by the living, breathing presence of this woman whom, to his delight and despair, he found that he desired in the old, familiar, raw, painful, hopeless way.

Unlike the Genoese couple who had featured in the paper that morning, however, he and Tania ran no risk of being barbecued by an irate husband, for the simple reason that Mauro Bevilacqua had nothing whatever to feel jealous about, at least as far as Zen was concerned. True, he and Tania had become very friendly, but nothing precludes the possibility of passion as surely as friendliness. Those long casual chats which had once seemed so promising to Zen now depressed him more than anything else. It was almost as if Tania was treating him as a surrogate female friend, as though for her he was so utterly unsexed that she could talk to him for ever without any risk of compromising herself.

Sometimes her tone became more personal, particularly when she talked about her father. He had been the village schoolteacher, an utterly impractical idealist who escaped into the mountains at every opportunity. Tania's name was not a diminutive of Stefania, as Zen had assumed, but of Tatania, her father having named her after Gramsci's sister-in-law, who stood by the communist thinker throughout the eleven years of his imprisonment by the Fascists. But despite this degree of intimacy, Tania had never given Zen the slightest hint that she had any personal interest in him, while he had of course been careful not to reveal his own feelings. He quailed at the thought of Tania's reaction if she guessed the truth. It was clear from what she said that she and her husband lived a rich, full, exciting life.

What on earth could Zen offer her that she could possibly want or need?

It was therefore a sickening blow to discover that Tania apparently *did* want or need things that her marriage didn't provide. Not only hadn't she thought of turning to him to provide them, but she had treated him as someone she could use and then lie to.

This was so painful that it triggered a mechanism which had been created back in the mists of Zen's childhood, when his father had disappeared into an anonymous grave somewhere in Russia. That loss still ached like an old fracture on a damp day, but at the time the pain had been too fierce to bear. To survive, Zen had withdrawn totally into the present, denying the past all reality, taking refuge in the here and now. That was his response to Tania's betrayal, and it was so successful that when they arrived and the taxi driver told him how much he owed, Zen thought the man was trying to cheat him.

'129,000 lire for a short ride across the city!'

'What the hell are you talking about?' the driver retorted. 'Two and a quarter hours you've had! I could have picked up three times the money doing short trips instead of freezing to death in some shitty suburb!'

Zen gradually counted out the notes. Well, that was the last amateur stake-out he'd be doing, he vowed, as the taxi roared away past a red saloon parked about fifty metres along the street, on the other side.

The only people about were an elderly couple making their way at a snail's pace along the opposite pavement. Zen crossed over to the car, an Alfa Romeo with Rome registration plates. There were several deep scratches and dents in the bodywork and one of the hub-caps was missing, although the vehicle was quite new. Zen looked in through the dirty window. A packet of Marlboro cigarettes lay on one of the leather seats, which looked almost unused. The floor was covered in cigarette butts and scorched with burn marks. The empty box of an Adriano Celentano tape lay in the tray behind the gear-lever, the cassette itself protruding from the player.

He straightened up as footsteps approached, but it was only the elderly couple. They trudged past, the man several paces ahead of his wife. Neither of them looked at the other, although they kept up a desultory patter the whole time.

'Then we can . . .'

'Right.'

'Or not. Who knows?'

'Well, anyway . . .'

Zen noted down the registration number of the car and walked back to the house. Giuseppe was off duty, so the front door was closed and locked. The lift was on one of the upper floors. Zen pressed the light switch and set off up the stairs, taking the shallow marble steps two at a time. A rumble overhead was followed by a whining sound as the lift started down. A few moments later the lighted cubicle passed by, its single occupant revealed in fuzzy silhouette on the frosted glass.

By the time he reached the fourth floor, Zen was breathless. He paused briefly to recover before unlocking his front door. There was a clanking far below as the lift shuddered to a halt. Then the landing was abruptly plunged into darkness as the time switch expired. Zen groped his way to the door, opened it and turned on the hall light. As he closed the door again, he noticed an envelope lying on the sideboard. He picked it up and walked along the passage, past the lugubrious cupboards, carved chests and occasional tables for which no suitable occasion had ever presented itself. As he neared the living room, he heard the sound of voices raised in argument.

'. . . never in a hundred years, never in a thousand, will I permit you to marry this man!'

'But Papa, I love Alfonso more than life itself!'

'Do not dare breathe his accursed name again! Tomorrow you leave for the convent, there to take vows more sacred and more binding than those with which you seek to dishonour our house.'

'The convent! No, do not condemn me to a living death, dear Father . . .'

Zen pushed open the glass-panelled door. By the flickering light of the television he saw his mother asleep in her armchair. He crossed the darkened room and turned down the volume, silencing the voices but leaving the costumed figures to go through their melodramatic motions. Then he went to the window, opened the shutters and peered out through the slats in the outer jalousies. The red car was no longer there.

He held the envelope so that it caught the light from the television. It seemed to be empty, although it was surprisingly heavy. His name was printed in block capitals, but there was no stamp or address. He wondered how it had come to be left on the sideboard. Normally post was put in the box in the hallway downstairs, or left with Giuseppe. If a message was delivered to the door, Maria Grazia would take it into the living room.

He ripped the envelope open. It still seemed empty, but something inside made a scratching sound, and when he pulled the paper walls apart he saw, clustered together at the very bottom, a quantity of tiny silvery balls. He let them roll out into his palm. In the flickering glimmer of the television they could have been almost anything: medicine, seeds, even cake decorations. But Zen knew they were none of these.

They were shotgun pellets.

*The nights brought relief. At night I moved freely, I felt my strength return-
ing. The others never venture out once darkness has fallen. Dissolved by
darkness, the world is no longer theirs. They stay at home, lock their doors
and watch moving pictures made with light.*

They are afraid of the dark. They are right to be afraid.

*Beyond their locked doors and shuttered windows I came into my own,
flitting effortlessly from place to place, appearing and disappearing at will,
yielding to the darkness as though to the embraces of a secret lover. Until the
lights came on, the inmates stirred, and the prison awoke to another day.*

*It was easy to find my way back here. I'd always come and gone as I liked.
They never understood that. They never tried to understand. No one asked
me anything. They told me things. They told me my imprisonment, as they
called it, had been an accident, a mistake. 'What you must have suffered!'
they said. I'd lost my home and family, but they weren't satisfied with that.
They wanted me to lose myself as well. What am I, but what the darkness
made me? If that was a mistake, an accident, then so am I.*

*Sometimes the priest came. He had things to tell me too, about a loving
father, a tortured son, a virgin mother. Not like my family, I thought, the
father who came home drunk and fucked his wife until she screamed, and
screamed again when the son was born, a pampered brat, arrogant and
selfish, strutting about as though he owned the place, and all because of that
thing dangling between his legs, barely the size of my little finger! But I kept
my mouth shut. I didn't think the priest would want to know about them.*

*And who was I, when the family was together? The holy ghost, I suppose.
The unholy ghost.*

Thursday, 07.55–13.20

All the talk at the café the next morning was of the overnight swoop by the police and Carabinieri on leftist sympathizers in Milan, Turin and Genoa. 'About time too,' was the dentist's comment, but one of the craftsmen from the basement workshops disagreed.

'The real terrorists don't have anything to do with those *sinistrini*. It's just the cops trying to make a good impression. A week from now they'll all have been turned loose again and we'll be back where we started!'

The barman Ernesto and the dentist looked at Zen, who maintained a stony silence. The reason for this was neither professional reserve nor disapproval of the craftsman's cynical tone. Zen simply wasn't paying any attention to the conversation. He had problems of his own that were too pressing to allow him the luxury of discussing other people's, problems which were quite literally closer to home.

Once again he had stayed up until the small hours of the morning, trying without success to find the missing link that would explain the events of the previous days. Not only had he not succeeded, he wasn't even sure that success was possible. The temptation to fit everything into a neat pattern, he knew, should be resisted. It might well be that two or more quite unrelated patterns were at work.

One thing was sure. During the three hours he had been absent from home the night before, someone had entered his flat and left an envelope filled with shotgun pellets on the sideboard in the hallway. Zen had locked the front door on leaving and it had still been locked on his return. Questioning his mother obliquely, to avoid frightening her, he had confirmed that she had not let anyone in. The only other person with a key was Maria Grazia. Before leaving for work Zen had interrogated her without result. The key was kept in her handbag, which hadn't been lost or stolen. Her family were all strict Catholics of the type who would have guilt pangs about picking up a hundred-lire coin they found in the street. It was out of the question that any of them might have been bribed to pass on the key to a third party. Zen also questioned Giuseppe, who had duplicate keys to all the apartments. He was equally categorical in his denials, and given the fanatical vigilance with which he carried out his duties it seemed unlikely that the intruder could have gained access in this way.

Which left only the metallic scraping Zen's mother had reported hearing the night before. It had come from the other side of the room, she said, where the large wardrobe stood. It now seemed clear that the noise had been made by someone picking the lock of the door leading to the fire escape, only to find that it was blocked by the wardrobe which had been placed in front of it. Since this attempt had failed, the intruder had returned during Zen's absence the evening before and tried the riskier option of picking the lock of the front door.

Almost the most disturbing thing about the incident was what had *not* happened. Nothing had been stolen, nothing had been disarranged. Apart from the envelope, the intruder had left no sign whatever of his presence. He had come to leave a message, and perhaps the most important element of that message was that he had done nothing else. As a demonstration of power, of arrogant self-confidence, it made Zen think of the Villa Burolo killer. 'I can come and go whenever I wish,' was the message. 'This time I have chosen simply to deliver an envelope. Next time . . . who knows?'

Determined that there should not be a next time, Zen had made Maria Grazia swear by Santa Rita of Cascia, whose image she wore as a lucky charm, that she would bolt the front door after his departure and not leave the apartment until he returned.

'But what about the shopping?' she protested.

'I'll get something from the *tavola calda*,' Zen snapped impatiently. 'It's not important!'

Cowed by her employer's unaccustomed brusqueness, Maria Grazia timidly reminded him that she would have to leave by six o'clock at the latest in order to deal with her own family's needs.

'I'll be back by then,' he replied. 'Just don't leave the apartment unattended, not even for a moment. Understand? Keep the door bolted and don't open it except for me.'

As soon as he got to work, Zen called the vehicle registration department and requested details of the red Alfa Romeo he had seen in the street the night before. It was a long shot, but there was something about the car that made him suspicious, although he wasn't quite clear what it was.

The information he received was not encouraging. The owner of the vehicle turned out to be one Rino Attilio Lusetti, with an address in the fashionable Parioli area north of the Villa Borghese. A phone call to the Questura elicited the information that Lusetti had no criminal record. By now Zen knew that this was a wild-goose chase, but having nothing better to do he looked up Lusetti in the telephone directory and rang the number. An uneducated female voice informed him that Dottor Lusetti was at the university. After a series of abortive phone calls to various departments of this institution, Zen eventually discovered that the car which had been parked near his house for the two previous nights was owned by the professor of Philology in the Faculty of Humanities at the University of Rome.

Giorgio De Angelis wandered into Zen's cubicle while he was making the last of these calls.

'Problems?' he asked as Zen hung up.

Zen shrugged. 'Just a private matter. Someone keeps parking his car in front of my door.'

'Give his windscreen a good coat of varnish,' De Angelis advised. 'Polyurethane's the best. Weatherproof, durable, opaque. An absolute bastard to get off.'

Zen nodded. 'What's this you've been telling Romizi about a train that goes round in circles?'

De Angelis laughed raucously, throwing his head back and showing his teeth. Then he glanced round the screens to check that the official in question wasn't within earshot.

'That fucking Romizi! He'd believe anything. You know he loves anchovy paste? But he's a tight bastard, so he's always moaning about how much it costs. So I said to him, "Listen, do you want to know how to make it yourself? You get a cat, right? You feed the cat on anchovies and olive oil, nothing else. What comes out the other end is anchovy paste."'

'He didn't believe you, did he?'

'I don't know. I wouldn't be surprised if he gives it a try. I just wish I could be there. What I'd give to see him spreading cat shit on a cracker!'

As De Angelis burst out laughing again, a movement nearby attracted Zen's attention. He turned to find Vincenzo Fabri looking at them through a gap in the screens. He was wearing a canary yellow pullover and a pale blue tie, with a maroon sports jacket and slacks, and chunky hand-stitched shoes. Expensive leisurewear was Fabri's hallmark, matching his gestures, slow and calm, and his deep, melodious voice. 'I'm so relaxed, so laid back,' the look said, 'just a lazy old softy who wants an easy time.'

Zen, who still wore a suit to work, felt by comparison like an old-fashioned ministerial *apparatchik*, a dull, dedicated workaholic. The irony was that Vincenzo Fabri was the most fiercely ambitious person Zen had come across in the whole of his career. His conversation was larded with references to country clubs, horses, tennis, sailing and holidays in Brazil. Fabri wanted all that and more. He wanted villas and cars and yachts and clothes and women. Compared to the Oscar Burolos of the world, Fabri was a third-rater, of course. He wasn't interested in the real thing: power, influence, prestige. All he wanted were the trinkets and trappings, the toys and the bangles. But he wanted them so *badly*. Zen, who no longer wanted anything very much except Tania Biacis, didn't know whether to envy or despise Fabri for the childlike voracity of his desires.

'Giorgio!' Fabri called softly, beckoning to De Angelis. His expression was one of amused complicity, as though he wanted to share a secret with the only man in the world who could really appreciate it.

At the same moment, the phone on Zen's desk began to warble.

'Yes?'

'Is this, ah . . . that's to say, am I speaking to, ah, Dottor Aurelio Zen?'

Fabri, who had ignored Zen's presence until now, was staring at him insistently whilst he murmured something in De Angelis's ear.

'Speaking.'

'Ah, this is, ah . . . that's to say I'm calling from, ah, Palazzo Sisti.'

The voice paused significantly. Zen grunted neutrally. He knew that he had heard of Palazzo Sisti, but he had no idea in what context.

'There's been some, ah . . . interest in the possibility of seeing whether it might be feasible to arrange . . .'

The rest of the sentence was lost on Zen as Tania Biacis suddenly appeared beside him, saying something which was garbled by the obscure formulations of his caller. Zen covered the mouthpiece of the phone with one hand.

'Sorry?'

'Immediately,' Tania said emphatically, as though she had already said it once too often. She looked tired and drawn and there were dark rings under her eyes.

'Are you all right?' Zen asked her.

'Me? What have I got to do with it?'

The phrase was delivered like a slap in the face. From the uncovered earpiece of the phone, the caller's voice squawked on like a radio programme no one is listening to.

'So you'll see to that, will you?' Tania insisted.

'See to what?'

'The video tape! They were extremely unpleasant about it. I said you'd call them back within the hour. I don't see why I should have to deal with it. It's got nothing whatever to do with me!'

She turned angrily away, pushing past De Angelis, who was on his way back to his desk. He looked glum and preoccupied, his former high spirits quite doused. Fabri had disappeared again.

Zen uncovered the phone. 'I'm sorry. I was interrupted.'

'So that's agreed, is it?' the voice said. It was a question in form only.

'Well . . .'

'I'll expect you in about twenty minutes.'

The line went dead.

Zen thought briefly about calling Archives, but what was the point? It was obvious what had happened. Fabri had told them that the tape of the Burolo killings was blank and they were urgently trying to contact Zen to find out what had happened to the original. This was no doubt the news that he had been gleefully passing on to De Angelis.

But how had Fabri found out so quickly that Zen had been the previous borrower? Presumably Archives must have told him. Unless, of course . . .

Unless it had been the video tape, and not a wallet or pocket-book, that had been the thief's target all along. It would have been a simple matter for Fabri to find some pickpocket who would have been only too glad to do a favour for such an influential man. Once the tape was in his hands, Fabri had put in an urgent request for the tape at Archives, ensuring that Zen was officially compromised. Now he would no doubt sell the original to the highest bidder, thus making himself a small fortune and at the same time creating a scandal which might well lead to criminal charges being brought against his enemy.

It was a masterpiece of unscrupulousness against which Zen was absolutely defenceless.

As he emerged from the portals of the Ministry and made his way down the steps and through the steel barrier under the eye of the armed sentries, Zen wondered if he was letting his imagination run away with him. In the warm hazy sunlight the whole thing suddenly seemed a bit far-fetched. He lit a cigarette as he waited for the taxi he had ordered. He had decided against using an official car, since the caller had left him in some doubt as to whether or not this was an official visit. In fact, he had left him in doubt about almost everything, including his name. The only thing Zen knew for certain was that the call had come from Palazzo Sisti. The significance of this was still obscure to Zen, but the name was evidently familiar enough to the taxi driver, who switched on his meter without requesting further directions.

They drove down the shallow valley between the Viminale and Quirinale hills, leaving behind the broad utilitarian boulevards of the nineteenth-century suburbs, across Piazza Venezia and into the cramped, crooked intestines of the ancient centre. Zen stared blankly out of the window, lost in troubled thoughts. Whatever the truth about the video tape, there was still the other threat hanging over him. The form of the message he had received the night before had been disturbing enough, but its content was even more so. According to Signora Bertolini, her husband had 'received threats' before his death. 'There were tokens, signs,' she had said. 'For example an envelope pushed through our letter-box with nothing inside but a lot of tiny little metal balls, like caviare, only hard.'

It was no doubt symptomatic of their respective lifestyles that the contents of the envelope had made Zen think of cake decorations and Signora Bertolini of caviare, but there was little doubt that they had been the same. And a few days after receiving his 'message', Judge Giulio Bertolini had been killed by just such little metal balls, fired at high velocity from a shotgun.

Zen had no intention of letting his imagination run away with him to the extent of supposing that there was any direct connection between the two events. What he did suspect was that someone, probably Vincenzo Fabri, was trying to put the wind up him, to knock him off balance so that he would be too agitated to think clearly and perceive the real nature of the threat to him. No doubt

Fabri's thief had first attempted to enter Zen's flat to steal the video, and, having been foiled by the blocked emergency exit, had picked Zen's pocket in the bus queue the following morning. Then Fabri had seen the newscast in which the judge's widow spoke about the envelope, and with typical opportunism had seen a way to further ensure the success of his scheme, by keeping Zen preoccupied with false alarms on another front.

The taxi wound slowly through the back streets just north of the Tiber, finally drawing up in a small piazza. By the standards of its period, Palazzo Sisti was modest in scale, but it made up for this by a wealth of architectural detail. The Sisti clan had clearly known their place in the complex hierarchy of sixteenth-century Roman society, but had wished to demonstrate that despite this their taste and distinction was no whit inferior to that of the Farnese or Barberini families. But neither their taste nor their modesty had availed them anything in the long run, and today their creation could well have been just another white elephant that had been divided up into flats and offices, if it had not been for the two armed Carabinieri sitting in their jeep on the other side of the piazza and the large white banner stretched across the façade of the building, bearing the slogan 'A FAIRER ALTERNATIVE' and the initials of one of the smaller political parties which made up the government's majority in parliament.

Zen nodded slowly. Of course, that was where he had heard the name before. 'Palazzo Sisti' was used by newscasters to refer to the party leadership, just as 'Piazza del Gesú' indicated the Christian Democrats. This particular party had been much in the news recently, the reason being that prominent among its leaders was a certain ex-Minister of Public Works who was rumoured to have enjoyed a close and mutually profitable relationship with Oscar Burolo, prior to the latter's untimely demise.

The entrance was as dark as a tunnel, wide and high enough to accommodate a carriage and team, lit only by a single dim lantern suspended from the curved ceiling. At the other end it opened into a small courtyard tightly packed with limousines, whose drivers, dressed in neat cheap suits like funeral attendants, were standing around swapping gossip and polishing the chrome.

A glass door to the left suddenly opened, and an elderly man no bigger than a large dwarf scuttled out.

'Yes?' he called brusquely to Zen.

337

A young woman carrying a large pile of files followed him out of the lodge.

'Well?' she demanded.

'I don't know!' the porter cried exasperatedly. 'Understand? I don't know!'

'It's your job to know.'

'Don't tell me what my job is!'

'Very well, you tell me!'

Zen walked over to them.

'Excuse me.'

They both turned to glare at him.

'Aurelio Zen, from the Ministry of the Interior.'

The porter shrugged.

'What about it?'

'I'm expected.'

'Who by?'

'If I knew that, I wouldn't need to waste my time talking to a prick like you, would I?'

The woman burst into hoots of laughter. A phone started to ring shrilly in the lodge. Throwing them both a look of deep disgust, the porter went to answer it.

'Yes? Yes, dottore. Yes, dottore. No, he just got here. Very good, dottore. Right away.'

Emerging from his lodge, the porter jerked his thumb at a flight of stairs opposite.

'First floor. They're expecting you.'

'And the Youth Section?' the young woman asked.

'How many times do I have to tell you, I don't know!'

The staircase was a genteel cascade of indolently curving marble which made the one at the Ministry look vulgar and cheap. As Zen reached the first-floor landing, a figure he had taken to be a statue detached itself from the niche where it had been standing and walked towards him. The man had an air of having been assembled, like Frankenstein's monster, from a set of parts, each of which might have looked quite all right in another context, but didn't get along at all well together. He stopped some distance away, his gaze running over Zen's clothing.

'I'm not carrying one,' Zen told him. 'Never do, in fact.' The man looked at him as though he had spoken in a foreign language.

'You see, it's no use carrying a gun unless you're prepared to use it,' Zen went on, discursively. 'If you're not, it just makes matters worse. It gives you a false sense of security and makes everyone else nervous. So you're better off without it really.'

The man stared at Zen expressionlessly for a moment, then turned his back.

'This way.'

He led Zen along a corridor which at first sight appeared to extend further than the length of the building. This illusion was explained when it became clear that the two men walking towards them were in fact their own reflections in the huge mirror that covered the end wall. The corridor was lit at intervals by tall windows giving on to the courtyard. Opposite each window a double door of polished walnut gleamed sweetly in the mellow light.

Zen's escort knocked at one of the doors and stood listening intently, holding the wrought silver handle.

'Come!' a distant voice instructed.

The room was long and relatively narrow. One wall was covered by an enormous tapestry, so faded that it was impossible to make out anything except the general impression of a hunting scene. Facing this stood a glass-fronted bookcase, where an array of more or less massive tomes lay slumbering in a manner that suggested they had not been disturbed for a considerable time.

At the far end of the room, a young man was sitting at an antique desk in front of a window that reached all the way up to the distant ceiling. As Zen came in, he put down the sheaf of typed pages he had been perusing and walked round the desk, his hand held out in greeting.

'Good morning, dottore. So glad that you felt able to see your way clear to, ah . . .'

He was in his early thirties, slim and refined, with thin straight lips, delicate features, and eyes that goggled slightly, as though they were perpetually astonished by what they saw. His fastidious gestures and diffident manner gave him the air of a *fin de siècle* aesthete, rather than a political animal.

He waved Zen towards a chair made of thin struts of some precious wood, with a woven cane seat. It looked extremely valuable and horribly fragile. Zen lowered himself on to it apprehensively. The young man returned to the other side of the desk, where he remained standing for a moment with hands outspread, like a priest at the altar.

'First of all, dottore, let me express, on behalf of . . . the interest and, ah . . . that's to say, the really quite extraordinary excitement aroused by your, ah . . .'

He picked up the pages he had been reading and let them fall back to the desk again, as a knock resounded in the cavernous space behind.

'Come!' the young man enunciated.

A waiter appeared carrying a tray with two coffee cups.

'Ah, yes. I took the liberty of, ah . . .'

He waggled his forefinger at the two cups.

'And which one is . . .?'

'With the red rim,' the waiter told him.

The young man sighed expressively as the door closed again.

'Unfortunately caffeine, for certain people . . .'

Zen took his cup of undecaffeinated espresso and unwrapped the two lumps of sugar supplied by the bar, studying the 'Interesting Facts about the World of Nature' printed on the wrapper, while he waited for his host to proceed.

'As you are no doubt aware, dottore, this has been a sad and difficult time for us. Naturally, we already knew what your report makes abundantly clear, namely that the evidence against Renato Favelloni is both flimsy and entirely circumstantial. There is not the slightest question that his innocence would eventually be established by due process of law.'

Zen noted the conditional as the coffee seared its way down his throat.

'But by then, alas, the damage will have been done!' the young man continued. His seemingly compulsive hesitations and rephrasings had now been set aside like a disguise that has served its purpose. 'If mud is thrown as viciously as it has been and will be, some of it is bound to stick. Not just to Favelloni himself, but to all those who were in any way associated with him, or who had occasion to, ah, call on his services at some time. This is the problem we face, dottore. I trust you will not judge me indiscreet if I add that it is one we were beginning to despair of solving. Imagine, then, the emotions elicited by your report! So much hope! So many interesting new perspectives! "Light at the end of the tunnel", as l'onorevole saw fit to put it.'

Zen set his empty cup back in its saucer on the leather surface of the desk.

'My report was merely a resumé of the investigations carried out by others.'

'Exactly! That was precisely its strength. If you had been one of our, ah, contacts at the Ministry, your findings would have excited considerably less interest. To be perfectly frank, we have been let down before by people who promised us this, that and the other, and then couldn't deliver. Why, only a few days ago we asked our man there to obtain a copy of the video tape showing the tragic events at the Villa Burolo. A simple enough request, you would think, but even that proved beyond the powers of the individual in question. Nor was this the first time that he had disappointed us. So we felt it was time to bring in someone fresh, with the proper qualifications. Someone with a track record in this sort of work. And I must say that, so far, we have had no reason to regret our decision. Of course, the real test is still to come, but already we have been very favourably impressed by the way in which your report both exposed the inherent weaknesses of the case against Favelloni, and revealed the existence of various equally possible scenarios which, for purely political reasons, have never been properly investigated.'

The young man stood quite still for a moment, his slender fingers steepled as though in prayer.

'The task we now face is to ensure that we do not suffer as much damage from this innocent man being brought to trial and acquitted as we would do if he were really guilty. In a word, this show trial of Renato Favelloni, and by implication of *l'onorevole* himself, engineered by our enemies, must be blocked before it starts. Your report makes it perfectly clear that the evidence against Favelloni has been cobbled together from a mass of disjointed and unrelated fragments. Those same fragments, with a little initiative and enterprise, could be used to make an even more convincing case against one of the other suspects you mention.'

Perched precariously on the low, fragile chair, Zen felt like a spectator in the front row of the stalls trying to make out what was happening on stage. The young man's expression seemed to suggest that the next move was up to Zen, but he was unwilling to make it until he had a clearer idea of what was involved.

'Do you mind if I smoke?' he asked finally.

The young man impatiently waved assent.

'Which of the other suspects did you have in mind?' Zen murmured casually as he lit up.

'Well, it seems to us that there are a number of avenues which might be explored with profit.'

'For example?'

'Well, Burolo's son, for example.'

'But he was in Boston at the time.'

'He could have hired someone.'

'He wouldn't have known how. Anyway, sons don't go around putting out contracts on their fathers because they want them to study law instead of music.'

The young man acknowledged the point with a prolonged blink.

'I agree that such a hypothesis would have needed a good deal of work before it became credible, but the possibility remains open. In fact, however, Enzo Burolo has close links with one of our allies in the government, so it would in any case have been inopportune to pursue the matter. I cited it merely as one example among many. Another, which appears to us considerably more fruitful, is the fellow Burolo employed to look after those absurd lions he bought.'

Zen breathed out a cloud of smoke.

'Pizzoni? He had an alibi too.'

'Yes, he had an alibi. And what does that mean? That half-a-dozen of the local peasantry have been bribed or bullied to lie about seeing him in the bar that evening.'

'Why should anyone want to protect Pizzoni? He was a nobody, an outsider.'

The young man leaned forward across the desk.

'Supposing that wasn't the case? Supposing I were to tell you that the man's real name was not Pizzoni but Padedda, and that he was not from the Abruzzi, as his papers claim, but from Sardinia, from a village in the Gennargentu mountains not far from Nuoro. What would you say to that?'

Zen flicked ash into a pewter bowl that might or might not have been intended for this purpose.

'Well, in the first instance I'd want to know why you haven't informed the authorities investigating the case.'

The young man turned away to face the window. The tall panes of glass were covered with a thick patina of grime which reflected his features clearly. Zen saw him smile, as though at the fatuity of this comment.

'When one's opponent is cheating, only a fool continues to play by the rules,' he recited quietly, as though quoting. 'This piece of information came to light as a result of research carried out privately on our behalf. We know only too well what would happen if we communicated it to the judiciary. The magistrates have decided to charge Favelloni for reasons which had nothing to do with the facts of the case. They aren't going to review that decision unless some dramatic new development forces them to do so. Isolated, inconvenient facts, which do not directly bear on the case they are preparing, would simply be swept under the carpet.'

He swung round to confront Zen.

'Rather than squander our advantage in this way, we propose to launch our own initiative, reopening the investigation that was so hastily slammed shut for ill-judged political reasons. And who better to conduct this operation than the man whose incisive and comprehensive review of the case has given us all fresh hope?'

Zen crushed out his cigarette carelessly, burning his fingertip on the hot ash.

'In my official capacity?'

'Absolutely, dottore! That's the whole point. Everything must be open and above board.'

'In that case, I would need a directive from my department.'

'You'll get one, don't worry about that! Your orders will be communicated to you in the usual way, through the usual channels. The purpose of this briefing is simply and purely to ensure that you understand the situation. From the moment you leave here today you will have no further contact with us. You'll be posted to Sardinia as a matter of absolute routine. You will visit the scene of the crime, interview witnesses, interrogate suspects. As always, you will naturally have at your disposal the full facilities of the local force. In the course of your investigations you will discover concrete evidence demolishing Pizzoni's alibi, and linking him to the murder of Oscar Burolo. All this will take no more than a few days at the most. You will then submit your findings to the judiciary in the normal way, while we for our part ensure that their implications are not lost on anyone concerned.'

Zen stared across the room at a detail in the corner of the tapestry, showing a nymph taking refuge from the hunters in a grotto.

'Why me?'

The young man's finely manicured hands spread open in a gesture of benediction.

'As I said, dottore, you have a good track record. Once your accomplishments in the Miletti case had been brought to our attention, well, quite frankly, the facts spoke for themselves.'

Zen gaped at him. 'The Miletti case?'

'I'm sure you will recall that your methods attracted, ah, a certain amount of criticism at the time,' the young man remarked with a touch of indulgent jocularity. 'I believe that in certain quarters they were even condemned as irregular and improper. What no one could deny was that you got results! The conspiracy against the Miletti family was smashed at a single stroke by your arrest of that foreign woman. Their enemies were completely disconcerted, and by the time they re-formed to cope with this unexpected development, the critical moment had passed and it was too late.'

He came round the desk, towering above Zen.

'The parallel with the present case is obvious. Here, too, timing is of the essence. As I say, the truth would in any case emerge in due course, but not before *l'onorevole's* reputation had been foully smeared. We have no intention of allowing that to happen, which is why we are entrusting you with this delicate and critical mission. In short, we're counting on you to apply in Sardinia the same methods which proved so effective in Perugia.'

Zen said nothing. After a few moments a slight crease appeared on the young man's brow.

'I need hardly add that a successful outcome to this affair is also in your own best interests. I'm sure you're only too well aware of how swiftly one's position in an organization such as the Ministry can change, often without one even being aware of it. Your triumph in the Miletti case might easily be undermined by those who take, ah, a narrow-minded view of things. The size of the Criminalpol squad is constantly under review, and given the attrition rate amongst senior police officials in places such as Palermo, the possibility of transfers cannot be ruled out. On the other hand, success in the Burolo case would consolidate your position beyond question.'

He reached behind him and depressed a lever on the intercom.

'Lino? Dottor Zen is just leaving.'

Once again, Zen felt the pale, cool touch of the young man's hand.

'It really was most good of you to come, dottore. I trust that your work has not been . . . that's to say, that no serious disruption will make itself felt in . . .'

The appearance of the stocky Lino rescued them both from these incoherent politenesses. Like a man in a dream, Zen walked back through the dim vastness of the room to the walnut door, which Lino closed behind them as softly as the lid of an expensive coffin.

'This way.'

'That's very good,' Zen remarked as they set off along the corridor. 'Have they trained you to say anything else?'

Lino turned round looking tough.

'You want your teeth kicked in?'

'That depends on whether you want to be turned into low-grade dog food. Because that's what's liable to happen to anyone round here who fails to treat me with the proper respect.'

'Bullshit!'

'On the contrary, chum. All I have to do is mention that I don't like your face and by tomorrow you won't *have* a face.'

Lino sneered.

'You're crazy,' he said, without total conviction.

'That's not what *l'onorevole* thinks. Now beat it. I'll find my own way out.'

For a moment Lino tried bravely to stare Zen out, but doubt had leaked into his eyes and he had to give up the attempt.

'Crazy!' he repeated, turning away with a contemptuous sniff.

Zen left the portal of Palazzo Sisti with a confident, unfaltering stride, a man with places to go to and people to see. The moment he was out of sight around the nearest corner, his manner changed beyond all recognition. He might now have been taken for a member of one of the geriatric tourist groups that descend on Rome once the high season is over. Far from having an urgent goal in mind, he turned right and left at random, obeying impulses of which he wasn't even aware and which in any case were of no importance. All that mattered was to let the tension seep slowly out of his body, draining out through the soles of his feet as they traversed the grimy undulating cobbles, scattering pigeons and sending the feral cats scuttling for cover under parked cars.

In due course he emerged into an open space which he recognized with pleasure as the Piazza Campo dei Fiori, almost Venetian in its intimacy and hence one of Zen's favourite spots in Rome. The morning vegetable market created a gentle bustle of activity that was supremely restful. He made his way across the cobbles strewn with discarded leaves and stalks, past zinc bathtubs and buckets full of ashes from the wooden boxes burned earlier against the morning chill. Now the sun was high enough to flood most of the piazza with its light. The stall-holders were still hard at work, washing and trimming salad greens under the communal tap. Elderly women in heavy dark overcoats with fur collars walked from stall to stall, looking doubtfully at the produce.

Zen walked over to a wine shop he knew, where he ordered a glass of *vino novello*. He leaned against the doorpost, smoking a cigarette and sipping the frothy young wine, which had still been in the grapes when Oscar Burolo and his guests were murdered. A gang of labourers working on a house nearby were shouting from one level of scaffolding to another in a dialect so dense that Zen could understand nothing except that God and the Virgin Mary were coming in for the usual steady stream of abuse. A neat, compact group of Japanese tourists passed by, accompanied by two burly Italian bodyguards. The female guide, clutching a furled pink umbrella, was giving a running commentary in which Zen was surprised to make out the name 'Giordano Bruno', like a fish sighted under water. She pointed with her umbrella to the centre of the square, where the statue of the philosopher stood on a plinth, its base covered with the usual incomprehensible graffiti.

Nearby an old woman bent double like a wooden doll hinged at the hips was feeding last night's spaghetti to a gang of mangy cats. Zen thought nostalgically of the cats of his native city, carved or living, monumental or obscure, the countless avatars of the Lion of the Republic itself. In Venice, cats were the familiars of the city, as much a part of it as the stones and the water, but the cats of Rome were just vermin to be periodically exterminated. It somehow seemed typical of the gulf which separated the two cities. For while Zen liked Campo dei Fiori, he could never forget that the statue at its centre commemorated a philosopher who was burnt alive on that spot at about the same time that the gracious and exquisite Palazzo Sisti was taking shape a few hundred metres away.

As he took his empty glass back inside, Zen found himself drawn to the scene at the bar. One of the labourers, wearing dusty blue overalls and a hat made from newspaper like an inverted toy boat, was knocking back a glass of the local white wine. Further along, two businessmen stood talking in low voices. On the bar before them were their empty glasses, a saucer filled with nuts and cocktail biscuits, two folded newspapers and a removable in-car cassette player.

Zen turned away. That was what had attracted his attention. But why? Nothing was more normal. No one left a cassette deck in their car any more, unless they wanted to have the windows smashed in and the unit stolen.

It wasn't until Zen stepped into the band of shadow cast by the houses on the other side of the piazza that the point of the incident suddenly became clear to him. He *had* seen a cassette player in a parked car recently, in a brand-new luxury car parked in a secluded street late at night. Such negligence, coupled with the scratches and dents in the bodywork and the use of the floor as an ashtray, suggested a possibility that really should have occurred to him long before. Still, better late than never, he thought.

Or were there cases where that reassuring formula didn't hold, where late was just too late, and there were no second chances?

Back at the Ministry, Zen phoned the Questura and asked whether Professor Lusetti's red Alfa Romeo appeared on their list of stolen vehicles. Thanks to the recent computerization of this department, he had his answer within seconds. The car in question had been reported stolen ten days earlier.

He put the receiver down, then lifted it again and dialled another number. After some time the ringing tone was replaced by a robotic voice. 'Thank you for calling Paragon Security Consultants. The office is closed for lunch until three o'clock. If you wish to leave a message, please speak now.'

'It's Aurelio, Gilberto. I was hoping to . . .'

'Aurelio! How are things?'

Zen stared at the receiver as though it had stung him. 'But . . . I thought that was a recorded message.'

'That's what I wanted you to think. At least, not you, but any of the five thousand people I don't want to speak to at this moment.'

'Why don't you get a real answering machine?'

'I have, but I can't use it just at the moment. One of my competitors has found a way to fake the electronic tone I can send down the line to have it play back the recorded messages to a distant phone. The result is that he downloaded a hundred million lire's worth of business, as well as making me look an idiot. Anyway, what can I do for you?'

'Well, I was hoping we could have a talk. I don't suppose you're free for lunch?'

'Today? Actually that's a bit . . . well, I don't know. Come to think of it, that might work quite well. Yes! Listen, I'll see you at Licio's. Do you know where it is?'

'I'll find it.'

Zen pressed the rest down to get a dialling tone, then rang his home and asked Maria Grazia if everything was all right.

'Everything's fine now,' she assured him. 'But this morning! Madonna, I was terrified!'

Zen tightened his grip on the receiver. 'What happened?'

'It was frightful, awful! The Signora didn't notice anything, thanks be to God, but I was looking straight at the window when it happened!'

'When *what* happened?'

'Why, this man suddenly appeared!'

'Where?'

'At the window.'

Zen took a deep breath. 'All right, now listen. I want you to describe him to me as carefully as you can. All right? What did he look like?'

Maria Grazia made a reflective noise. 'Well, let's see. He was young. Dark, quite tall. Handsome! Twenty years ago, maybe, I'd have . . .'

'What did he do?'

'Do? Nothing! He just disappeared. I went over and had a look. Sure enough, there he was, in one of those cages. He was trying to mend it but he couldn't. In the end they had to take it off the wall and put up a new one.'

'A new *what*, for the love of Christ?'

Stunned by this blasphemy, the housekeeper murmured, 'Why, the streetlamp! The one that was forever turning itself on and off. But when I saw him floating there in mid-air I got such a shock! I didn't know what to think! It looked like an apparition, only I don't know if you can have apparitions of men. It always seems to be women, doesn't it? One of my cousins claimed she saw Santa Rita once, but it turned out she made it all up. She'd got the idea from an article in *Gente* about these little girls who . . .'

Zen repeated his earlier instructions about keeping the front door bolted and not leaving his mother alone, and hung up.

On his way downstairs, he met Giorgio De Angelis coming up. The Calabrian looked morose.

'Anything the matter?' Zen asked him.

De Angelis glanced quickly up and down the stairs, then gripped Zen's arm impulsively. 'If you're into anything you shouldn't be, get out fast!'

He let go of Zen's arm and continued on his way.

'What do you mean?' Zen called after him.

De Angelis just kept on walking. Zen hurried up the steps after him.

'Why did you say that?' he demanded breathlessly.

The Calabrian paused, allowing him to catch him up.

'What's going on?' Zen demanded.

De Angelis shook his head slowly. 'I don't know, Aurelio. I don't want to know. But whatever it is, stop doing it, or don't start.'

'What are you talking about?'

De Angelis looked again up and down the stairs.

'Fabri came to see me this morning. He advised me to keep away from you. When I asked why, he said that you were being measured for the drop.'

The two men looked at one another in silence.

'Thank you,' Zen murmured almost inaudibly.

De Angelis nodded fractionally. Then he continued up the steps while Zen turned to begin the long walk down.

I never used to dream. Like saying, I never used to go mad. The others do it every night, jerking and tossing, sweating like pigs, groaning and crying out. 'I had a terrible dream last night! I dreamt I'd killed someone and they were coming to arrest me, they'd guessed where I was hiding! It was horrible, so real!' You'd think that might teach them something about this world of theirs that also seems 'so real'!

Then one night it happened to me. In the dream I was like the others, living in the light, fearing the dark. I had done something wrong, I never knew what, killed someone perhaps. As a punishment, they locked me up in the darkness. Not my darkness, gentle and consoling, but a cold dank airless pit, a narrow tube of stone like a dry well. The executioner was my father. He rammed me down, arms bound to my sides, and capped the tomb with huge blocks of masonry. I lay tightly wedged, the stones pressing in on me from every side. In front of my eyes was a chink through which I could just see the outside world where people passed by about their business, unaware of my terrible plight. Air seeped in through the hole, but not enough, not enough air! I was slowly suffocating, smothered beneath that intolerable dead weight of rock. I screamed and screamed, but no sound penetrated to the people outside. They passed by, smiling and nodding and chatting to each other, just as though nothing was happening!

It was only a dream, of course.

'So what's the problem, Aurelio? A little trip to Sardinia, all expenses paid. I should be so lucky! But once you're in business for yourself you learn that the boss works harder than . . .'

'I've already explained the problem, Gilberto! Christ, what's the matter with you today?'

It was the question that Zen had been asking himself ever since arriving at the restaurant. Finding his friend free for lunch at such short notice had seemed a stroke of luck which might help Zen gain control of the avalanche of events which had overrun his life.

Gilberto Nieddu, an ex-colleague who now ran an industrial counter-espionage firm, was the person Zen was closest to. Serious, determined and utterly reliable, there was an air of strength and density about him, as though all his volatility had been distilled away. Whatever he did, he did in earnest. Zen hadn't of course expected Gilberto to produce instant solutions, but he had counted on him to listen attentively and then bring a calm, objective view to bear on the problems. As a Sardinian himself, his advice and knowledge might make all the difference.

But Gilberto was not his usual self today. Distracted and preoccupied, continually glancing over his shoulder, he paid little attention to Zen's account of his visit to Palazzo Sisti and its implications.

'Relax, Aurelio! Enjoy yourself. I'll bet you haven't been here that often, eh?'

This was true enough. In fact Zen had never been to Licio's, a legendary name among Roman luxury restaurants. The entrance was in a small street near the Pantheon. You could easily pass by without noticing it. Apart from a discreet brass plate beside the door, there was no indication of the nature of the business carried on there. No menu was displayed, no exaggerated claims made for the quality of the cooking or the cellar.

Inside you were met by Licio himself, a eunuch-like figure whose expression of transcendental serenity never varied. It was only once you were seated that the unique attraction of Licio's became clear, for thanks to the position of the tables, in widely-separated niches concealed from each other by painted screens and potted plants, you had the illusion of being the only people there. The prices at Licio's were roughly double the going rate for the class of cuisine on offer, but this was only logical since there were only half as many tables. In any case, the clientèle came almost exclusively from the business and political worlds, and was happy to pay whatever Licio wished to ask in return for the privilege of being able to discuss sensitive matters in a normal tone of voice with no risk of being either overheard or deafened by the neighbours. Hence the place's unique cachet: you went to other restaurants to see and be seen; at Licio's you paid more to pass unnoticed.

On the rare occasions when Zen spent this kind of money on a meal he went to places where the food, rather than the ambience, was the attraction, so Gilberto Nieddu's remark had been accurate enough. That didn't make Zen feel any happier about the slightly patronizing tone in which it had been made. Matters were not improved when Gilberto patted his arm familiarly and whispered, 'Don't worry! This one's on me.'

Zen made a final attempt to get his friend to appreciate the gravity of the situation.

'Look, I'll spell it out for you. They're asking me to frame someone. Do you understand? I'm to go to Sardinia and fake some bit of evidence, come up with a surprise witness, anything. They don't care what I do or how I do it as long as it gets the charges against Favelloni withdrawn, or at least puts the trial dates back several months.'

Gilberto nodded vaguely. He was still glancing compulsively around the restaurant.

'This could be your big chance, Aurelio,' he murmured, checking his watch yet again.

Zen stared at him with a fixed intensity that was a reproach.

'Gilberto, we are talking here about sending an innocent person to prison for twenty years, to say nothing of allowing a man who has gunned down four people in cold blood to walk free. Quite apart from the moral aspect, that is seriously *illegal*.'

The Sardinian shrugged. 'So don't do it. Phone in sick or something.'

'For fuck's sake, this is not just another job! I've been *recommended* to these people! They've been told that I'm an unscrupulous self-seeker, that I cooked the books in the Miletti case and wouldn't think twice about doing so again. They've briefed me, they've cut me in. I know what they're planning to do and how they're planning to do it. If I try and get out of it now, they're not just going to say, "Fine, suit yourself, we'll find someone else." They've already hinted that if I don't play along I could expect to become another statistic in somewhere like Palermo. Down there you can get a contract hit done for a few million lire. There are even people who'll do it for free, just to make a name for themselves! And no one's going to notice if another cop goes missing. Are you listening to any of this?'

'Ah, finally!' Gilberto cried aloud. 'A big client, Aurelio, very big,' he hissed in an undertone to Zen. 'If we swing this one, I can take a year off to listen to your problems. Just play along, follow my lead.'

He sprang to his feet to greet a stocky, balding man with an air of immense self-satisfaction who was being guided to their table by the unctuous Licio.

'Commendatore! Good morning, welcome, how are you? Permit me to present Vice-Questore Aurelio Zen. Aurelio, Dottor Dario Ochetto of SIFAS Enterprises.' Lowering his voice suggestively, Nieddu added, 'Dottor Zen works directly for the Ministry of the Interior.'

Zen felt like walking out, but he knew he couldn't do it. His friendship with Gilberto was too important for him to risk losing it by a show of pique. The fact that Gilberto had probably counted on this reaction didn't make Zen feel any happier about listening to the totally fictitious account of Paragon Security's dealings with the Ministry of the Interior which Nieddu used as a warm-up before presenting his sales pitch. Meanwhile, Zen ate his way through the food that was placed before them and drank rather more wine than he would normally have done. Occasionally Gilberto turned in his direction and said, 'Right, Aurelio?' Fortunately neither he nor Ochetto seemed to expect a reply.

Zen found it impossible to tell whether Ochetto was impressed, favourably or otherwise, by this farce, but as soon as he had departed, amid scenes of compulsive handshaking, Gilberto exploded in jubilation and summoned the waiter to bring over a bottle of their best malt whisky.

'It's in the bag, Aurelio!' he exclaimed triumphantly. 'An exclusive contract to install and maintain anti-bugging equipment at all their offices throughout the country, and at five times the going rate because what isn't in the contract is the work they want done on the competition.'

Zen sipped the whisky, which reminded him of a tar-based patent medicine with which his mother had used to dose him liberally on the slightest pretext.

'What kind of work?'

Nieddu gave him a sly look. 'Well, what do you think?'

'I don't think anything,' Zen retorted aggressively. 'Why don't you answer the question?'

Nieddu threw up his hands in mock surrender. 'Oh! What is this, an interrogation?'

'You've gone into the bugging business?' Zen demanded.

'Have you got any objection?'

'I certainly have! I object to being tricked into appearing to sanction illegal activities when I haven't even been told what they are, much less asked whether I mind being dragged in! Jesus Christ almighty, Gilberto, I don't fucking well need this! Not any time, and especially not now.'

Gilberto Nieddu gestured for calm, moving his hands smoothly through the air as though stroking silk.

'This lunch has been arranged for weeks, Aurelio. I didn't ask you to come along. On the contrary, *you* phoned *me* at the last moment. I would normally have said I was busy, but because you sounded so desperate I went out of my way to see you. But I had to explain your presence to Ochetto, otherwise he would have been suspicious. This way, he'll just think I was trying to impress him with my contacts at the Ministry. It worked beautifully. You were very convincing. And don't worry about repercussions. He's already forgotten you exist.'

Zen smiled wanly as he dug a Nazionale out of his rapidly collapsing pack. 'You were very convincing.' Tania had said the same thing the night before, and it had apparently been Zen's 'convincing' performance in the Miletti case which had recommended him to Palazzo Sisti. Everyone who used him for their own purposes seemed very satisfied with the results.

'So you're in the shit again, eh?' continued Nieddu, lighting a cigar and settling back in his chair. 'What's it all about this time?'

Zen pushed his glass about on the tablecloth stained with traces of the various courses they had consumed. He no longer had any desire to share his troubles with the Sardinian.

'Oh, nothing. I'm probably just imagining it.'

Nieddu eyed his friend through a screen of richly fragrant smoke.

'It's time you got out of the police, Aurelio. What's the point of slogging away like this at your age, putting your life on the line? Leave that to the young ambitious pricks who still think they're immortal. Let's face it, it's a mug's game. There's nothing in it unless you're bent, and even then it's just small change really.'

He clicked his fingers to summon the bill.

'You know, I never had any idea what was going on in the world until I went into business. I simply never realized what life was about. I mean, they don't teach you this stuff at school. What you have to grasp is, *it's all there for the taking*. Somebody's going to get it. If it isn't you, it'll be someone else.'

He sipped his whisky and drew at his cigar.

'All these cases you get so excited about, the Burolos and all the rest of it, do you know what that amounts to? Traffic accidents, that's all. If you have roads and cars, a certain number of people are going to get killed and injured. Those people attract a lot of attention, but they're really just a tiny percentage of the number who arrive safely without any fuss or bother. It's the same in business, Aurelio. The system's there, people are going to use it. The only question is whether you want to spend your time cleaning up after other people's pile-ups or driving off where you want to go. Fancy a cognac or something?'

It was after three o'clock when the two men emerged, blinking, into the afternoon sunlight. They shook hands and parted amicably enough, but as Zen walked away it felt as though a door had slammed shut behind him.

People changed, that was the inconvenient thing one always forgot. It was years now since Gilberto had left the police in disgust at the way Zen had been treated over the Moro affair, but Zen still saw him as a loyal colleague, formed in the same professional mould, sharing the same perceptions and prejudices. But Gilberto Nieddu was no longer an ex-policeman, but a prosperous and successful businessman, and his views and attitudes had changed accordingly.

On a day-to-day level this had been no more apparent than the movement of a clock's hands. It had taken this crisis to reveal the distance that now separated the two men. The Sardinian still wished Zen well, of course, and would help him if he could. But he found it increasingly difficult to take Aurelio's problems very seriously. To him they seemed trivial, irrelevant and self-inflicted. What was the point of getting into trouble and taking risks with no prospect of profit at the end of it all?

Gilberto's attitude made it impossible for Zen to ask him for help, yet help was what he desperately needed for the project that was beginning to form in his mind. If he couldn't get it through official channels or friendly contacts then there was only one other possibility.

The first sighting was just north of Piazza Venezia. After the calm of the narrow streets from which most traffic was banned, the renewed contact with the brutal realities of Roman life was even more traumatic than usual. I'm getting too old, Zen thought as he hovered indecisively at the kerb. My reactions are slowing down. I'm losing my nerve, my confidence. So he was reassured to see that a tough-looking young man in a leather jacket and jeans was apparently just as reluctant to take the plunge. In the end, indeed, it was Zen who was the first to step out boldly into the traffic, trusting that the drivers would choose not to exercise their power to kill or maim him.

It was marginally less reassuring to catch sight of the same young man just a few minutes later in Piazza del Campidoglio. Zen had taken this route because it avoided the maelstrom of Piazza Venezia, although it meant climbing the long steep flights of steps up the Capitoline hill. Nevertheless, when he paused for breath by the plinth where a statue of his namesake had stood until recently succumbing to air pollution, there was the young man in the leather jacket, about twenty metres behind, bending down to adjust his shoelaces.

Zen swung left and walked down past the Mamertine prison to Via dei Fori Imperiali. He paused to light a cigarette. Twenty metres back, Leather Jacket was lounging against a railing, admiring the view. As Zen replaced his cigarettes, a piece of paper fluttered from his pocket to the ground. He continued on his way, counting his strides. When he reached twenty he looked round again. The young man in the leather jacket was bending to pick up the paper he had dropped.

The only thing he would learn from it was that Zen had spent 1200 lire in a wine shop in Piazza Campo dei Fiori that morning. Zen, on the other hand, had learnt two things: the man was following him, and he wasn't very good at it. Without breaking his pace, he continued along the broad boulevard towards the Colisseum. This, or rather the underground station of the same name, had been his destination from the start, but he would have to lose the tail first. The men he was planning to visit had a code of etiquette as complex and inflexible as any member of Rome's vestigial aristocracy, and would take a particularly poor view of anyone arriving with an unidentified guest in tow.

Without knowing who Leather Jacket was working for, it was difficult to choose the best way of disposing of him. If he was an independent operator, the easiest thing would be to have him arrested on some pretext. This would also be quick – a phone call would bring a patrol car in minutes – and Zen was already concerned about getting back to the house before six o'clock, when Maria Grazia went home. But if Leather Jacket was part of an organization, then this solution would sacrifice Zen's long-term advantage by showing the tail that he had been burned. He would simply be replaced by someone unknown to Zen, and quite possibly someone more experienced and harder to spot. Zen therefore reluctantly decided to go for the most difficult option, that of losing the young man without allowing him to realize what had happened. It was not until the last moment, as he was passing the entrance, that it dawned on him that the perfect territory for this purpose was conveniently to hand.

In the ticket office, three men in shirtsleeves were engaged in a heated argument about Craxi's line on combatting inflation. Zen flashed his police identity card at them and then at the woman perched on a stool at the entrance, a two-way radio in one hand and a paperback novel in the other. Without looking round to see if Leather Jacket was following, he walked through the gateway and into the Forum.

To his untutored eye, the scene before him resembled nothing so much as a building site. All that was missing were the tall green cranes clustered together in groups like extraterrestrial invaders. It seemed as if this project had only just passed the foundation level, and only then in a fragmentary and irregular way. Some areas were still pitted and troughed, awaiting the installation of drainage and wiring, while in others a few pillars and columns provided a tantalizing hint of the building to come. Elsewhere, whole sections of the massive brick structures – factories? warehouses? – which had formerly occupied the area had still not been demolished completely. For the moment, work seemed to have ground to a halt. No dump-trucks or concrete-pourers moved along the rough track running the length of the site. Perhaps some snag had arisen over the financing, Zen thought whimsically. Perhaps the government had been reshuffled yet again, and the new minister was reluctant to authorize further expenditure on a project which had already over-run its estimated cost by several hundred per cent – or was at least holding out for some financial incentive on a scale similar to that which had induced his predecessor to sign the contract in the first place.

A Carabinieri helicopter was thrashing about overhead like a shark circling for the kill. Zen tossed away his cigarette and strolled along a path in the patchy grass between the ruins. A fine dust covered everything, beaten into the air by passing feet from the bone-dry soil. The sun crouched low in a cloudless sky, its weak rays absorbed and reflected by the marble and brick on every side. Overhead the helicopter swept past periodically, watchful, alien, remote. Halfway up the path, which veered off to the right and started to climb the Palatine hill, Zen paused to survey the scene. At that time of year there were only a few tourists about. Among them was a young man in a leather jacket and jeans. Oddly enough, he was once again having problems with his laces.

Zen resumed his walk with a fastidious smile. If Leather Jacket thought that bending down to tie up your shoes made you invisible then he shouldn't prove too difficult to unload. In fact he felt slightly piqued that such a third-rate operator had been considered adequate for the task of shadowing him. Evidently he couldn't even inspire respect in his enemies.

The path ran up a shallow valley, between masses of ancient brickwork emerging from the grass like weathered rocky outcroppings. The signs and fences installed by the authorities had imposed some superficial order on the hill's chaotic topography, but this simply made its endless anomalies all the more incomprehensible. Nothing here was what it appeared to be, having been recycled and cannibalized so many times that its original name and function was often unclear even to experts. Although no archaeologist, Zen was intimately familiar with the many-layered complexities of the Palatine, thanks to the Angela Barilli affair.

The daughter of a leading Rome jeweller, eighteeen-year-old Angela had been kidnapped in 1975. After months of negotiations and a bungled pay-off the kidnappers had broken off contact. In desperation, the Barilli family had turned to the supernatural, engaging a clairvoyant from Turin who claimed to have led the police to three other kidnap victims. The medium duly informed Angela's mother that her daughter was being held in an underground cell somewhere in the vast network of rooms and passages on the lower floors of the Imperial palace at the heart of the Palatine.

Unlikely as this seemed, the political clout wielded by the family was enough to ensure that Zen, who was directing the investigation, had to waste three days organizing a painstaking search of the area. The Barilli girl's corpse was in fact discovered the following year in a shallow concrete pit beneath a garage in the Primavalle suburb where she had been held during her ordeal, but Zen had never forgotten the three days he had spent exploring the honeycomb of caverns, tunnels, cisterns and cellars that lay beneath the surface of the Palatine. It was an area so rich in possibilities that Zen could simply disappear into the mathematics, leaving his follower to solve an equation with too many variables.

When he reached the plateau at the top of the hill, Zen turned left behind the high stone wall which closed off a large rectangle of ground surrounding a church, and waited for Leather Jacket to catch up. There was no one about, and the only sound was the distant buzzing of the helicopter. It had now moved further to the east, circling over the group of hospitals near San Giovanni in Laterano. No doubt an important criminal was being transferred from Regina Coeli prison for treatment, with the helicopter acting as an eye in the sky against any attempt to snatch him.

Footsteps approached quickly, almost at a run. At the last moment, Zen stepped out from behind the wall.

'Sorry!'

'Excuse me!'

The collision had only been slight, but the young man in the leather jacket looked deeply startled, as Zen had intended he should be. Close to, his sheen of toughness fell apart like an actress's glamour on the wrong side of the footlights. Despite a virile stubble, due no doubt to shaving last thing at night, his skin looked babyish, and his eyes were weak and evasive.

'It always happens!' Zen remarked.

The man stared at him, mystified.

'When there's no one about, I mean,' Zen explained. 'Have you noticed? You can walk right through the Stazione Termini at rush hour and never touch anyone, but go for a stroll up here and you end up walking straight into the only other person about!'

The man muttered something inconclusive and turned away. Zen set off in the opposite direction. Not only would the encounter have shaken Leather Jacket, but it would now be impossible for him to pass off any future contacts as mere coincidence. That constraint would force him to hang back in order to keep well out of sight, thus giving Zen the margin he needed.

He made his way through a maze of gravelled paths winding among sections of ruined brick wall several metres thick. Lumps of marble lay scattered about like discarded playthings. Isolated stone-pines rose from the ruins, their rough straight trunks cantilevering out at the top to support the broad green canopy. Here and there, excavations had scraped away the soil to expose a fraction of the hidden landscape beneath the surface. Fenced off and covered with sloping roofs of corrugated plastic sheeting, they looked like the primitive shelters of some future tribe, bringing the long history of this ancient hill full circle in the eternal darkness of a nuclear winter.

A line of pines divided this area from a formal garden with alleys flanked by close-clipped hedges. Screened by the dense thickets of evergreen trees and shrubs, Zen was able to move quickly along the paved path leading to a parterre with gravel walks, a dilapidated pavilion and terrace overlooking the Forum. A fountain dripped, bright dabs of orange fruit peeped through the greenery, paths led away in every direction. In the centre, a flight of steps led down into a subterranean corridor running back the way he had come. Dimly lit by lunettes let into the wall just below the arched ceiling, the passage seemed to extend itself as Zen hurried along it. The walls, rough, pitted plaster, were hung with cobwebs as large and thick as handkerchiefs, which fluttered in the cool draught.

At length the passage ended in another flight of steps leading up into the middle of the maze of brickwork and gravel paths which Zen had passed through earlier. Keeping under cover of the fragments of wall, he worked his way towards the massive ruins of the Imperial palace itself. The gate was just where he remembered it, giving access to a yard used for storing odds and ends of unidentified marble. It was supposed to be locked, but one of the things that Zen had learned in the course of his abortive search for Angela Barilli was that it was left open during the day because the staff used it as a short cut. Ignoring the sign reading 'No Admission To Unauthorized Persons', Zen walked through the yard to a passage at the back. To the left, a modern doorway led into a museum. Zen turned the other way, down an ancient metal staircase descending into the bowels of the hill.

At first, the staircase burrowed through a channel cut into the solid brickwork of the palace. As Zen walked down, the light diminished above, and simultaneously the darkness beneath began to glow. Then, without warning, he emerged into a vast underground space in which the staircase was suspended vertiginously, bolted to the brickwork. The other walls were immeasurably distant, mere banks of shadow, presences hinted at by the light seeping in far below, obscuring the ground like thick mist. Zen clutched the handrail, overwhelmed by vertigo. Everything had been turned on its head: the ground above, the light below.

Step by step, he made his way down the zigzag staircase through layers of cavernous gloom. The floor was a bare expanse of beaten earth illuminated by light streaming in through large rectangular openings giving on to the sunken courtyard at the heart of the palace. Zen walked across it, glancing up at the metal railings high above, where a trio of tourists stood reading aloud from a guidebook. A rectangular opening in the brickwork opposite led into a dark passage which passed through a number of sombre gutted spaces and then a huge enclosed arena consisting of rows of truncated columns flanking a large grassy area.

He sat down on one of the broken columns, out of sight of the path above, and lit a cigarette. At the base of the column lay a large pine cone, its scales splayed back like the pads of a great cat's paw. The air was still, the light pale and mild, as though it too was antique. The matchstick figures displayed on Zen's digital watch continued their elaborate ballet, but the resulting patterns seemed to have lost all meaning. The only real measure of time was the slow disappearance of the cigarette smouldering between Zen's fingers and the equally deliberate progress of his thoughts.

Who could Leather Jacket be working for? Until this moment Zen had assumed that he must be connected with the break-in at his flat and the envelope full of shotgun pellets which had been left there, but now, after some consideration, he rejected this idea. Leather Jacket simply didn't look nasty enough to have a hand in the attempt to scare Zen by copying the warnings sent to Judge Giulio Bertolini before his death. He didn't *care* enough. It wasn't a personal vendetta he was involved in, Zen was sure of that. He was in it for the money, a cut-rate employee hired by the hour to keep track of Zen's movements. But who had hired him? The longer Zen thought about it, the more significant it seemed that Leather Jacket had put in his first appearance shortly after Zen's interview at Palazzo Sisti.

The only surprising feature of this solution was that they should have chosen such a low-grade operative to do the job, but this was no doubt explained by the fact that Lino was in charge of that department. They might even prefer Zen to know that they were keeping tabs on him. He was their man now, after all. Why shouldn't they keep him under surveillance? What reason had they to trust him?

It was only when he had posed this question to himself that Zen realized that it wasn't rhetorical. 'Once your accomplishments in the Miletti case had been brought to our attention,' the young man had told him, 'the facts spoke for themselves.' But who had brought those 'accomplishments' to their attention in the first place? Presumably one of the 'contacts at the Ministry' the young man had mentioned earlier. 'We have been let down before by people who promised us this, that and the other, and then couldn't deliver. Why, only a few days ago we asked our man there to obtain a copy of the video tape showing the tragic events at the Villa Burolo. A simple enough request, you would think, but even that proved beyond the powers of the individual in question. Nor was this the first time that he had disappointed us.'

Zen looked up with a start. The sheer stone walls of the arena appeared to have crept closer, hemming him in. Only the day before he had asked himself why Vincenzo Fabri had gone out on a limb with his hare-brained notion about Burolo not being the murderer's intended victim, that the killings had actually been a Mafia hit on the architect Vianello. The answer, of course, was that this had been a bungled attempt to divert suspicion from Renato Favelloni. Fabri's mission to Sardinia had only nominally been undertaken on behalf of

Criminalpol. His real client had been *l'onorevole*. And he'd blown it! That was why Fabri had not been offered the chance to exploit the new evidence about Furio Pizzoni's real identity. It was too good a chance for Palazzo Sisti to risk wasting on someone in whom they no longer had any faith. Instead, they had plumped for Zen, whose record 'spoke for itself'. Only it hadn't, of course. Someone had spoken for it first. Someone had brought Zen's 'accomplishments in the Miletti case' to the attention of Palazzo Sisti, and suggested that this unscrupulous manipulator of evidence and witnesses might be just the right man to bring the Burolo imbroglio to a satisfactory conclusion. And that someone, it was now clear, could only be the Party's 'man at the Ministry', Vincenzo Fabri himself.

Zen lit another cigarette from the butt of the first, a habit he normally despised. But normality was rapidly losing its grip on his life. Vincenzo Fabri had recommended Zen to his masters as the white knight who could save Renato Favelloni from prison and *l'onorevole* from disgrace. By doing so, he had not only given his most bitter enemy a chance to succeed, but to do so on the very ground where he himself had recently suffered a humiliating failure. Why would he do a thing like that?

The only possible answer was that Fabri knew damn well that Zen was not going to succeed. So far from doing his enemy a good turn, Fabri had placed him in a trap with only two exits, each potentially fatal. If Zen failed to satisfy Palazzo Sisti, they would have him transferred to a city where his life could be terminated without attracting attention. If, on the other hand, he did what was necessary to get the Favelloni trial postponed, Fabri would tip off the judiciary and have Zen arrested for conspiracy to pervert the course of justice. Whatever happened, Zen was bound to lose. If his new friends didn't get him, his old enemy would.

By now the sun had disappeared behind the grove of pines whose foliage was just visible above the far end of the sunken stadium. All at once the air revealed its inner coldness, the chill at its heart. It was time to go. Leather Jacket would most likely have given up the search by now and be waiting near the entrance on Via dei Fori Imperiali.

Zen got to his feet and started to pick his way through the jumble of ruins opposite. A brick staircase and a circuitous path scuffed through the grass brought him out on a track flanked by pines leading down to the exit on Via di San Gregorio. The odours of summer, pine sap and dried shit, lingered faintly in the undergrowth. There was no sign of Leather Jacket, but in any case Zen no longer greatly cared about him. Being tailed was the least of his worries now, as for that matter was the missing video tape. To think that just that morning he had worked out an elaborate theory to explain the fact that Fabri had put in a request for it. The reason for this was now clear: he had been told to get hold of a copy by Palazzo Sisto. As for the theft, it must indeed have been the work of a pickpocket, as Zen had originally supposed. Vincenzo Fabri had bigger and better schemes in mind than pilfered videos. Had he not warned De Angelis that very morning to keep away from Zen because he was being 'measured for the drop'? The exact nature of that drop now seemed terrifyingly clear.

I was always biddable, a born follower. Like those ducklings we had, a fox killed the mother and they would follow whoever was wearing the green rubber boots that were the first thing they saw on opening their eyes. If the boots had been able to walk by themselves, they would have followed the boots, or a bit of rubbish blown past by the wind, whatever happened to be there when the darkness cracked open. Even the fox that killed their mother.

I can see him now, standing there, the light at his back, and all the forces of the light. Come with me, he said. I can't, I told him, I mustn't. It seemed that all this had happened before. Where do they come from, these memories and dreams? They must belong to someone else. There was nothing before the darkness. How could there be? We come from darkness and to darkness we return. There is nothing else.

It's all right, he said, I'm a policeman. Come with me. I did what he told me. He would have taken me anyway, by force.

The light burned so much I had to close my eyes. When I opened them there were men everywhere, rushing about, shouting at each other, crowding in, their eyes swishing to and fro like scythes. They took it in turns to pour their lies into me, filling me with unease. Everything that had happened had been a mistake. I'd done nothing wrong, it was all a mistake, a scandal, a tragic and shocking crime. When I tried to say something my voice astonished me, a raven's croak passing through my body, nothing to do with me. After that I kept silent. There was no point in trying to resist. They were too strong, their desires too urgent. Sooner or later, I knew, they would have their way with me.

In the end they tired and let me go. You're free, they said. Like the follower I was, I believed them. I thought I could go back as though nothing had happened, as though it had all been a dream!

Thursday, 17.20–19.10

By the time the grubby blue and grey Metropolitana train emerged above ground at the Piramide stop, it was getting dark. Zen walked up the broad dim steps beneath a Fascist mural depicting the army, the family and the workers, and out into the street.

The city's starlings were in the grip of the madness that seizes them at the changing of the light, turning the trees into loudspeakers broadcasting their gibberish, then swarming up out of the foliage to circle about in the dusky air like scraps of windborne rubbish. In the piazza below gleaming tramlines crisscrossed in intricate patterns leading off in every direction, only to finish abruptly a few metres further on under a coat of tarmac or running headlong into a traffic divider.

Instead of making a detour to the traffic lights on Via Ostiense, Zen walked straight out into the vehicles converging on the piazza from every direction. Maybe that was where the starlings got the idea, he thought. Maybe their frenzied swarming was just an attempt to imitate the behaviour patterns of the dominant life-form. But tonight the traffic didn't bother him. He was as invulnerable to accidents as a prisoner under sentence of death. Respecting his doomed self-assurance, the traffic flowed around him, casting him ashore on the far side of the piazza, at the foot of the marble pyramid.

The most direct route to where he was going lay through Porta San Paolo and along Via Marmorata. But now that he was nearly there Zen's fears about being followed revived, so instead of the busy main road he took the smaller and quieter street flanked by the city walls on one side and dull apartment blocks on the other. Apart from a few prostitutes setting up their pitches in the strip of grass and shrubs between the street and the wall, there was no one about. He turned right through the arches opened in the wall, then left, circling the bulky mound which gave its name to the Testaccio district. At the base of the hill stood a line of squat, formless, jerry-built huts, guarded by savage dogs. Here metal was worked and spray-painted, engines mended, bodywork repaired, serial numbers altered. During

Zen's time at the Questura this had been one of the most important areas in the city for recycling stolen vehicles.

The other main business of the district had been killing, but that had ceased with the closure of the slaughterhouse complex that lay between the Testaccio hill and the river. Any killing that went on now was related to the part-time activities of some of the inhabitants, of which the trade in second-hand cars was only the most notable example. As for the abattoir, it was now a mecca for aspirant yuppies like Vincerzo Fabri, who thronged to the former killing floors in their Mercedes and BMWs to acquire the art of sitting on a horse. Opposite, a few exclusive night-clubs had sprung up to attract those of the city's gilded youth who liked to go slumming in safety.

Skirting the ox-blood-red walls of the slaughterhouse, Zen walked on into the grid of streets beyond. Although no more lovely than the suburb where Tania and her husband lived, Testaccio was quite different. It had a history, for one thing: two thousand years of it, dating back to the time when the area was the port of Rome and the hill in its midst had gradually been built up from fragments of amphorae broken in transit or handling. The four-square, turn-of-the-century tenements which now lined the streets were merely the latest expression of its essentially gritty, no-nonsense character. The merest change in the economic climate would be enough to sweep away the outer suburbs as though they had never existed, but the Testaccio quarter would be there for ever, lodged in Rome's throat like a bone.

Night had fallen. The street was sparsely lit by lamps suspended on cables strung across from one apartment-block to another. Rows of jalousies painted a dull institutional green punctuated the expanses of bare walling. In an area where cars were a medium of exchange rather than a symbol of disposable income, it was still possible to park in an orderly fashion at an angle to the kerb, leaving the pavements free for pedestrians. Zen walked steadily along, neither hurrying nor loitering, showing no particular interest in his surroundings. This was enemy territory, and he had particular reasons for not wanting to draw attention to himself. After crossing two streets running at right angles, he caught sight of his destination, a block of shops and businesses comprising a butcher's, a barber's, a grocery and a paint wholesaler's. Between the barber's and the butcher's lay the Rally Bar.

It was years since Zen had set foot there, but as soon as he walked in he saw that nothing had changed. The walls and the high ceiling were painted in the same terminal shade of brown and decorated with large photographs of motor-racing scenes and the Juventus football team, and posters illustrating the various ice-creams available from the freezer at the end of the bar. Two bare neon strips suspended by chains from the ceiling dispensed a frigid, even glare reflected back by the indestructible slabs of highly polished aggregate on the floor. Above the bar hung a tear-off calendar distributed by an automobile spare-parts company, featuring a colour photograph of a peacock, along with framed permits from the city council, a price list, a notice declaring the establishment's legal closing day as Wednesday, advertisements for various brands of *amaro* and beer, and a drawing of a tramp inscribed 'He always gave discounts and credit to everyone'.

The three men talking in low voices at the bar fell silent as Zen entered. He walked up to them, pushing against their silent stares as though into a strong wind.

'A glass of beer.'

The barman, gaunt and lantern-jawed, plucked a bottle of beer from the fridge, levered the cap off the bottle and dumped half the beer into a glass still dripping from the draining-board. The glass was thick and scored with scratches. At the bottom, a few centimetres of beer lay inaccessible beneath a layer of bubbles as thick and white as shaving-foam.

The barman picked up a copy of the *Gazzetta dello Sport*. The other customers gazed up over their empty coffee cups at the bottles of half-drunk spirits and cordials stacked on the glass shelving. Above the bar, in pride of place, stood a clock whose dial consisted of a china plate painted with a list showing the amount of time the proprietor was allegedly prepared to spend on tax collectors, rich aged relatives, door-to-door salesmen, sexy housewives and the like. Plain-clothes policemen on unofficial business were not mentioned.

Zen carefully poured the rest of the beer into the glass, dousing the bubbles. He drank half of it and then lit a cigarette.

'Fausto been in tonight?'

The second hand described an almost complete revolution of the china plate before the barman swivelled smoothly to face Zen, as though his feet were on castors.

'What?'

Zen looked him in the eye. He said nothing. Eventually the barman turned away again and picked up his newspaper. The second hand on the clock moved from 'mothers-in-law' through 'the blonde next door' and back to its starting place.

'This beer tastes like piss,' Zen said.

The pink newspaper slowly descended.

'And what do you expect me to do about it?' the barman demanded menacingly.

'Give me another one.'

The barman rocked backwards and forwards on his feet for a moment. Then he snapped open the heavy wooden door of the fridge, fished out another bottle, decapitated it and banged it down on the zinc counter. Zen took the bottle and his glass and sat down at one of the three small round metal tables covered in blue and red plastic wickerwork.

As if they had been waiting for this, the other two customers suddenly came to life. One of them fed some coins into the video-game machine, which responded with a deafening burst of electronic screams and shots. The other man strode over to Zen's table. He had slicked-back dark hair and ears that stood out from his skull like a pair of gesturing hands. There was a large soggy bruise on his forehead, his nose was broken, and his cheek had recently been slit from top to bottom. Wary of the fearful things that had happened to the rest of his face, the man's eyes cowered in deep, heavy-lidded sockets.

'All right if I sit down?' he asked, doing so.

On the video screen, a gaunt grim detective in a trench-coat stalked a nocturnal city street. Menacing figures wielding guns appeared at windows or popped out from behind walls. If the detective shot them accurately they collapsed in a pool of blood and a number of points was added to the score, but if he missed then there was a female scream and a glimpse of the busty half-naked victim.

'I couldn't help overhearing what you said,' Zen's new companion remarked.

Zen stubbed out his cigarette in a smoked-glass ashtray printed with the name, address and telephone number of a wholesale meat supplier. *All home-killed produce*, read the slogan. *Bulk orders our speciality.*

'I'm a friend of Fausto's,' the man went on. 'Unfortunately he's out of town at the moment. Perhaps I could help.'

Zen moved the ashtray about on the table as if it were a counter in a game and he hadn't quite decided on his move.

'That would depend on what I wanted,' he said.

'And on who you are.'

So that the attractions of the video game should not be lost on those unable to see the screen, the manufacturers had thoughtfully provided it with a range of sound-effects which were repeated at regular intervals. One in particular, a mocking little motif like an electronic sneer, invariably caused the player to blaspheme and slap the side of the machine with his palm. At length he turned away in disgust, crossed over to the bar and slapped down a banknote.

'Gimme five,' he said.

The barman laid down his pink sports paper, massively unmoved by the shattering events referred to in the headline: 'JUVE WHAT A LETDOWN!!! ROMA WHAT A LETOFF!!!' He tossed the coins on the stainless-steel surface. A moment later the other man was lost to the world again, his buttocks twisting and swivelling as though copulating with the machine.

'I'm also a friend of Fausto's,' said Zen.

The man raised his eyebrows. 'Strange we haven't met before.'

'Fausto has a lot of friends. A lot of enemies, too. Maybe that's why he's out of town.'

'He didn't tell me.'

'That's no way to treat a friend,' Zen remarked.

The barman tossed his newspaper aside and stepped down from the raised wooden stage from which he lorded it over the customers. An oddly insignificant figure now, he moved restlessly about, straightening chairs and tables and polishing ashtrays.

'Anyway, if I run into Fausto, I'll let him know you were asking for him,' the man said. 'What did you say your name was?'

Zen wrote his telephone number on a piece of paper and handed it to the man.

'Tell him to ring me this evening.'

'Why would he want to do that?'

'For the same reason he's out of town. For his health, for his future, for his peace of mind.'

He got up and started to walk to the door.

'Hey, what about the beers?' the barman called.

Zen jerked his thumb at the table.

'My friend's buying,' he said.

He walked down the street without looking back. Once he had rounded the corner, he stopped in a patch of shadow cast by a large delivery van, keeping an eye on the door of the Rally Bar. A cloying odour emanated from the van, the odour of blood, of death. It had its own smell, quite distinct from all others. Zen recalled a visit he had made to another abattoir in the course of an investigation into an extortion racket, maybe even the Spadola case. He had watched the animals being prodded and kicked to their deaths, squealing piteously, showing the whites of their eyes. Men in blue overalls and red rubber aprons went about the killing in an atmosphere of rough, good-natured camaraderie, and at lunchtime went home to their wives and children and ate fried back muscles and veins and intestine and stomach lining.

A figure emerged from the bar and started to walk straight towards him. Zen backed into the shadows, keeping in the lee of the van, then ran quickly into the courtyard of a nearby apartment-block. Palms and small evergreen shrubs surrounded a dripping communal tap. The courtyard was separated from the street by a wall topped with high iron railings. Zen took shelter immediately inside, behind the wall, ready to follow the man once he had passed by.

But he didn't pass by. The footsteps came closer and closer, and then he was there, no more than a metre away. He crossed the courtyard and disappeared into one of the doorways. Zen followed.

Inside the door a narrow marble staircase with a heavy wooden banister on wrought-iron supports ran up to a landing. The man was already out of sight. Zen stopped still, listening to his footsteps in the stairwell above. One, two, three, four, five, six, seven, eight, then a brief pause as he reached the landing. This pattern was repeated twice. Then there was a faint knocking, repeated after some time. The murmur of voices was cut off by the sound of a door closing.

Zen ran up the stairs to the second floor. As on the other landings, there were two flats, one to the left and the other facing the stairs. There were numbers on the doors, but no names. Zen continued halfway up the next flight of steps, where he stopped, waiting for the man to emerge again.

The voice of a television newscaster was blaring away in one of the apartments nearby: '. . . investigation appears to have ground to halt. The authorities have denied that a fresh wave of arrests is imminent.

The secretary of the Radical Party today called for alternatives to the terrorist hypothesis to be considered, pointing out that Judge Bertolini never presided in political . . .'

A door opened on the floor above and women's voices drowned out the rest of the sentence.

'Bye, then!'

'Bye! I'll make the pasta, but don't forget the artichokes, eh?'

'Don't worry. Some thrushes too, if Gabriele has any luck.'

'A bit of good wine wouldn't come amiss, either.'

'That goes without saying.'

'And remind Stefania to bring a pudding, you know what she's like!'

The door closed. An elderly woman appeared on the stairs. She was wearing a long coat of some heavy, dark, dowdy-looking material, trimmed with cheap fur at the collar, and wore a woollen scarf over her shoulders. She paused to take in Zen, leaning against the wall.

'No more puff, eh?' she cackled.

Zen nodded ruefully. 'It's my heart. I have to be careful.'

'Quite right! You can't be too careful. Not that it makes any difference in the end. My sister's brother-in-law, that's by her second marriage, to someone from Ancona, although now they live here in Rome because he got a job with the radio, her husband I mean, he does the sound for the football matches.'

'The brother-in-law?'

'Eh, no, the husband! The brother-in-law doesn't do anything, that's what I'm telling you, he just dropped dead one day. And do you know the funny thing?'

There was the sound of a door opening on the second floor. Zen glanced round the angle of staircase. In the doorway facing the steps the man from the Rally Bar stood nodding and muttering something to someone inside the flat.

'The funny thing is,' the woman went on, 'that very evening he had to go to Turin to see his cousin's twin girls who'd been born the weekend before, and the train, the one he'd been going to take, you know what happened? It came off the rails, just outside Bologna! And there was another train coming the other way that would have run straight into the wreckage, except that it was late so they had time to stop it. Otherwise it would have been a terrible disaster with hundreds and hundreds of people killed, including poor Carlo, who was dead already, as I said. It all goes to show that when your time comes, there's nothing you can do about it.'

The door below had closed and the man's footsteps could be faintly heard descending the steps and echoing in the courtyard outside. The old woman cackled again and hobbled downstairs past Zen. As soon as she had gone, he walked down to the landing and knocked on the door in an authoritative way.

There was a scurry of steps inside. 'Who is it?' piped a childish voice.

'Gas Board. We've got a suspected leak to the building, got to check all the apartments.'

The door opened a crack, secured by a chain. There seemed to be no one there.

'Let me see your identification.'

Looking much lower down the opening, Zen finally spotted a small face and two eyes fixed unblinkingly on him. He got his police identity card out and dropped it through the centimetre-wide crack.

'Show this to your father.'

The eyes regarded him doubtfully. The girl couldn't have been more than about seven or eight years old. She tried to shut the door, but Zen had planted his foot in it.

The child turned away, the card held like something dangerous or disgusting between her index finger and thumb. After some time an even younger girl appeared, keeping well away from the door but watching Zen with an air of fascination.

Zen smiled at her.

'Hello, there.'

'Have you come to kill my daddy?' she asked brightly.

Before Zen could reply, the child was shooed away by a man's voice.

'Good evening, Fausto,' called Zen. 'It's been a long time.'

A figure scarcely larger than the children's appeared round the rim of the door.

'Dottore!' breathed a hushed voice. 'What an honour. What a pleasure. You're alone?'

'Alone.'

'You'll have to move your foot. I can't get the chain undone.'

'I just want to ask you a small favour, Fausto. Maybe I can do you one in return.'

'Just move your fucking foot!'

Zen did so. There was a metallic rattle and in a single movement the door opened, a hand pulled Zen inside and the door closed again.

'Please forgive my language, dottore. I'm a bit nervous at the moment.'

Fausto was a small, wiry man with the extreme skinniness that betrays an undernourished childhood. His face was marked by a scar which split his upper lip. He claimed that he'd got it in a knife fight, but Zen thought it was more likely the result of a bungled operation for a cleft palate.

In compensation for the rigours of his childhood, Fausto had survived the passing years with remarkably little sign of ageing. That he had survived at all was a minor miracle, given the number of men he had betrayed. The recruitment of Fausto Arcuti had led directly to one of the great successes of Zen's years at the Questura in Rome, the smashing of the kidnap and extortion ring organized by a playboy named Francesco Fortuzzi. Arcuti had worked from inside the gang, continuing to supply information right up until the last minute. Then, when the police swooped, he had been allowed a slip through the net along with various other minor figures who never realized that they owed their escape to the fact that Zen was covering Fausto's tracks. The long-term prospects for informers were bleak. Once a man had sold his soul to the authorities, they could always threaten to expose him if he refused to collaborate again, and the risks of such collaboration grew with every successful prosecution. Sooner or later the criminal milieu worked out where the leaks were coming from. Against all the odds, however, Arcuti had survived.

'Come in!' he said, leading Zen inside. 'What a pleasure! And so unexpected! Maria, bring us something to drink. You other kids, get the fuck out of here.'

The apartment consisted of two small, smelly rooms crudely lit by exposed high-wattage bulbs. Forlorn pieces of ill-assorted furniture stood scattered about like refugees in transit. The walls were bedecked with images of the Virgin, the Bleeding Heart of Jesus and various saints. Over the television hung a large three-dimensional picture of the crucifixion. As you moved your head, Christ's eyes opened and closed and blood seeped from his wounds.

'Sit down, dottore, sit down!' Arcuti exclaimed, clearing the sofa of toys and clothes. 'Sorry about the mess. The wife's out at work all day, so we never seem to get things sorted out.'

The eldest girl carried in a bottle of *amaro* and two glasses.

'I'd prefer to take you out to the bar,' Arcuti said, pouring them each a drink, 'but the way things are . . .'

'I've just come from there,' Zen told him.

'I suppose you followed Mario?'

'If that's his name. The one with the Mickey Mouse ears.'

Arcuti nodded wearily.

'Half-smart, that's Mario. It's OK when they're clever and it's OK when they're stupid. It's the ones in between that kill you.'

'So what's the problem?' Zen murmured, sipping his drink.

Arcuti sighed.

'It's this Parrucci business. It's got us all spooked.'

'Parrucci?' Zen frowned. The name meant nothing to him.

'You probably haven't heard about it. There's no reason why you should have, he wasn't working for you. In fact he wasn't working for anyone, that's what makes it worse. He'd given it all up years ago. Of course in this business you never really retire, but Parrucci had been out of it for so long he must have thought he was safe. No one even knew he'd been in the game until it happened.'

The informer drained his glass in a single gulp and poured himself another.

'We found out because of the way they did it. So we asked around, and it turned out that Parrucci had been one of the top informers up north, years ago. But he'd put all that behind him. Wanted to settle down and bring up his kids normally. That's why they picked him, I reckon.'

'How do you mean?'

'Well, if they knock off someone who's still active, it looks like a personal vendetta. People who are not involved don't take much notice. But something like this is a warning to everyone. Once you inform, you're marked for life. We'll come for you, even if it takes years. That's what they're saying.'

Zen lit a cigarette. He knew he was smoking too much, but this was not the time to worry about it.

'What did they do to him?' he asked.

Arcuti shook his head. 'I don't even want to think about it.'

He sat staring at the carpet for some time, balanced on the forward edge of the threadbare armchair. Then he grabbed a cigarette from the packet lying open beside him and lit up, glaring defiantly at Zen.

'You really want to know? All right, I'll tell you. In dialect, if a man is full of energy and drive, they say he has fire in his belly. That's a good thing, unless you have too much, unless you break the rules and start playing the game on your own account. What they used to do with traitors, down south, was to get a big iron cooking-pot and build a charcoal fire inside. Then they stretched the poor bastard out on his back, tied him up, set the pot on his stomach and then used the bellows until the metal got red-hot. Eventually the pot burnt its way down into the man's stomach under its own weight. It could take hours, depending on how much they used the bellows.'

'That's what they did to Parrucci?'

'Not exactly. That's the traditional method, but you know how it is these days, people can't be bothered. Parrucci they kidnapped from his house and took him out to the country, out near Viterbo somewhere. They broke into a weekend cottage, stripped him naked, laid him out across the electric cooker with his wrists and ankles roped together, and then turned on the hot plates.'

'Jesus.'

Arcuti knocked back the second glass of *amaro* amid frantic puffs at his cigarette.

'Now do you see why I'm nervous, dottore? Because I could be the next name on the list!'

'How do you know there'll be any more?'

'Because no one's claimed responsibility. Usually when something like this happens, you find out who did it and why. They make damn sure you know! That's the whole point. But this time no one's saying anything. The only reason for that is that the job isn't finished yet.'

Zen glanced at his watch. To his dismay, he found that it was almost ten to six. At six o'clock Maria Grazia would leave to go home, and from then on Zen's mother would be alone in the apartment.

Fausto Arcuti had noticed his visitor's gesture.

'Anyway, that's enough of my problems. What can I do for you, dottore?'

'It's a question of borrowing a car for a few days, Fausto.'

'Any particular sort of car?'

'Something fairly classy, if you can. But the main thing is, it needs to be registered in Switzerland.'

'Actually registered?'

Zen corrected himself.

'It needs to have Swiss number plates.'

Arcuti drew the final puff of smoke from his cigarette and let it drown in the dregs of *amaro*.

'This car, how long do you want it for?'

'Let's say the inside of a week.'

'And afterwards, will it be, er, compromised in any way?'

Zen gave him a pained look.

'Fausto, if I wanted to do anything illegal, I'd use a police car.'

Arcuti conceded a thin smile.

'And how soon do you need it?'

'Tomorrow, ideally, but I don't suppose there's any chance of that.'

The informer shrugged.

'Why ever not, dottore? You're doing business with the Italy that works! I may be shut up in this lousy, rotten, stinking hole, but I still have my contacts.'

He produced the piece of paper Zen had given the man called Mario.

'I can contact you at this number?'

'In the evening. During the day I'm at the Ministry.'

'Which department?'

'Criminalpol.'

Arcuti whistled.

'Congratulations! Well, if I have any luck I'll phone you in the morning. I won't give any name. I'll just say that I wanted to confirm our lunch date. There'll be a message for you at the bar here.'

'Thanks, Fausto. In return, I'll see what I can do to shed some light on this Parrucci business.'

'I'd appreciate it, dottore. It's not just for me, though that's not exactly the way I'd choose to go. But the girls, it's wrong for them to have to grow up like this.'

Zen walked away past the shuttered and gated market towards the bustle of activity on Via Marmorata. He was well satisfied with the way things had gone. Fausto Arcuti's lifestyle might appear unimpressive, but as a broker for favours and information he was second to none. Moreover, Zen knew that he would want to make up for the poor figure he had cut, cowering in fear of his life in a squalid flat.

Zen's main preoccupation now was to get home with as little delay as possible. He was in luck, for no sooner had he turned on to the main traffic artery than a taxi stopped just in front of him. The family which emerged from it seemed numerous enough to fill a bus, never mind a taxi, and still the matriarch in charge kept pulling them out, like a conjuror producing rabbits from a hat. At last the supply was exhausted, however, and after an acrimonious squabble about extras, discounts and tips, they all trooped away. In solitary splendour Zen climbed into the cab, which was as hot and smelly as a football team's changing-room, and had himself driven home.

To his relief, the red Alfa Romeo was nowhere to be seen. The lift was ready and waiting, for once, and Zen rode it up to the fourth floor. The experiences of the day had left him utterly drained.

He saw it immediately he opened the front door, a narrow black strip as thin as a razor blade and seemingly endless. It continued all the way along the hallway, gleaming where the light from the living room reflected off its surface. He bent down and picked it up. It felt cold, smooth and slippery.

He walked slowly down the hallway, gathering in the shiny strip as he went. As he passed the glass-panelled door to the living room, music welled up from the television, as though to signify his relief at finding his mother alive and well, her eyes glued to the play of light and shadow on the screen. Then he looked past her, uncomprehending, disbelieving. The gleaming strip ran riot over the entire room, heaped in coils on the sofa and chairs, running around the legs of the chairs, draped over the table. In its midst lay a small rectangular box with tape sprouting from slits in either end. Zen picked it up. *'Ministry of the Interior,'* he read, *'Index No.46429 BUR 433/K/95'.*

'What's the matter with you tonight?' his mother snapped. 'I asked you to bring me my camomile tea ages ago and you didn't even bother to answer.'

Zen slowly straightened up, staring at her.

'But mamma, I've only just got home.'

'Don't be ridiculous! Do you think I didn't see you? I may be old but I'm not so old I don't recognize my own son! Besides, who else would be here once Maria Grazia's gone home, eh?'

A cold shiver ran through Zen's body.

'I'm sorry, mamma.'

'You didn't even have the common decency to reply when I spoke to you! You always bring me my camomile tea before *Dynasty* starts, you know that. But tonight you were too busy cluttering the place up with that ribbon or string or whatever it is.'

'I'll fetch it straight away,' Zen mumbled.

But he didn't do so, for at that moment he heard a sound from the hallway, and remembered that he had left the front door standing wide open.

Among the furniture stored in the hall was a wardrobe inset with long rectangular mirrors which reflected an image of the front door on to the glass panel of the living-room door. Thus it was that even before he set foot in the hallway, Zen could see that the entrance to the apartment was now blocked by a figure thrown into silhouette by the landing light. The next moment this switched itself off, plunging everything into obscurity.

'Aurelio?' said a voice from the darkness.

Zen's breathing started again. He groped for the switch and turned on the light.

'Gilberto,' he croaked. 'Come in. Close the door.'

What is the worst, the most obscene and loathsome thing that one person can do to another? Go on, rack your brains! Let your invention run riot! (I often used to talk to myself like this as I scuttled about.)

Well? Is that all? I can think of far worse things than that! I've done far worse things than that. But let's not restrict ourselves to your hand-me-down imaginations. Because whatever you or I or anyone else can think up, no matter how hideous or improbable, one thing is sure. It has happened. Not just once but time and time again.

This prison is also a torture house. No one cares what goes on here.

You know Vasco, the blacksmith? Everyone still calls him the blacksmith, though he repairs cars now. What do you think of him? A steady sort, a bit obstinate, gives himself airs? As I was passing his workshop one morning I saw him pick up his three-year-old daughter by the hair, hold her dangling there a while, then let her fall to the floor. A moment later he was back to work, moulding some metal tubing while the child wept in a heap on the ground, her little world in pieces all around her. I wanted to comfort her, to tell her how lucky she had been. All her daddy had done was pull her hair. He could have done other things. He could have used the blowtorch on her. He could have buried her alive in the pit beneath the cars. He could have done anything.

He could have done anything.

Friday, 11.15–14.20

While the archives section presented a slightly more animated appearance during office hours than on Zen's previous visit, it could by no means have been described as a hive of activity. True, there were now about a dozen clerks on duty, but this manning level had evidently been dictated by some notional bureaucratic quota rather than the actual demands of the job, which was being carried on almost entirely by one man. He had a neurotically intense expression, compulsive, jerky movements, and the guilty air of someone concealing a shameful secret.

Unlike the others, he couldn't just sit back and read the paper or chat all morning. If there was work to be done, he just couldn't help doing it. It was this that made him a figure of fun in his colleagues' eyes. They watched him scurry about, collecting and dispatching the files which had been ordered, sorting and reshelving those which had been returned, cataloguing and indexing new material, typing replies to demands and queries. Their looks were derisory, openly contemptuous. They despised him for his weakness, as he did himself for that matter. Poor fellow! What could you do with people like that? Still, he had his uses.

As on his previous visit, Zen asked to consult the file on the Vasco Spadola case. While it was being fetched, he called to the clerk who had been on duty the last time he had been there.

The man looked up from the crossword puzzle he was completing.

'You want to speak to me?' he demanded, with the incredulous tone of a surgeon interrupted while performing an open-heart operation.

Zen shook his head. '*You* want to speak to *me*. At least, so I've been told. Something about a video tape.'

An anticipatory smile dawned on the clerk's lips.

'Ah, so it was you, was it? Yes, I remember now!'

The other clerks had all fallen silent and were watching with curiosity. Their colleague strode languidly over to the counter where Zen was standing.

'Yes, I'm afraid there's been a slight problem with that tape, dottore.'

'Really?'

'Yes, really.'

'And what might it be?'

'Well it *might* be almost anything,' the clerk returned wittily. 'But what it *is*, quite simply, is that the tape you gave us back is not the same tape that you took out.'

'What do you mean, not the same?'

'I mean it's not the same. It's blank. There's nothing on it.'

'But . . . but . . .' Zen stammered.

'Also, the tapes we use here are specially made up for us and are not available commercially, whereas what you handed in is an ordinary BASF ferrous oxide cassette obtainable at any dealer.'

'But that's absurd! You must have muddled them up somehow.'

At that moment, the other clerk interrupted to hand Zen the file he had requested. But his colleague had no intention of letting Zen get away with his clumsy attempt to shift the blame for what had happened.

'No, dottore! That's not the problem. The problem is that the tape you brought back is a blank. Raw plastic.'

Zen fiddled nervously with the Spadola file.

'What exactly are you accusing me of?' he blustered.

The clerk gestured loftily.

'I'm not accusing anyone of anything, dottore. Naturally, everyone knows how easy it is to push the wrong button on one of those machines and wipe out the previous recording . . .'

'I'm sure I didn't do that.'

'I *know* you didn't,' the clerk replied with a steely smile that revealed the trap Zen had almost fallen into. 'Our tapes are all copy-protected, so that's impossible. Besides, as I said, the brand was different. So a substitution must have taken place. The question is, where is the original?'

There was a crash as the Spadola file fell to the floor, spilling documents everywhere. As Zen bent down to pick them up, the assembled clerks signalled their colleague's triumph with a round of laughter.

Zen straightened up, holding a video cassette.

'46429 BUR 433/K/95,' he read from the label. 'Isn't that the one you've been making so much fuss about?'

'Where did that come from?' the clerk demanded.

'It was inside the file.'

Without another word, he went back to picking up the scattered documents. The clerk snatched the tape and bustled off, muttering angrily about checking its authenticity.

Zen wasn't worried about that, having played it through the night before, after he and Gilberto spent the best part of an hour rewinding the damn thing into the cassette by hand. His mother had gone to bed by then, still blissfully ignorant that a stranger had entered the apartment while she had been watching television.

Zen himself was still in shock from what had happened, and it was left to Gilberto to bring up the question of what was to become of his mother during his absence in Sardinia, now that their home was demonstrably under threat. In the end, Gilberto insisted that she stay with him and his wife until Zen returned.

'Quite impossible!' Zen had replied. His mother hadn't left the apartment for years. She would be lost without the familiar surroundings that replicated the family home in Venice. Anyway, she was practically senile much of the time. It was very difficult even for him to communicate with her or understand what she wanted, and it didn't help that she often forgot that her Venetian dialect was incomprehensible to other people. She could be demanding, irrational, bad-tempered and devious. Rosella Nieddu already had her hands full looking after her own family. It would be an intolerable imposition for her to have to take on a moody old woman, contemptuous and distrustful of strangers, someone who in her heart of hearts believed that the civilized world ended at Mestre.

But Gilberto had brushed these objections aside.

'So what *are* you going to do with her, Aurelio? Because she can't stay here.'

Zen had no answer to that.

And so it came about that early that morning an ambulance rolled up to the front door of Zen's house. The attendants brought a mobile bed up to the apartment, placed Zen's mother on it and took her downstairs in the lift before sweeping off, siren whooping and lights flashing, to the General Hospital. Thirty seconds later, siren stilled and flasher turned off, the ambulance quietly emerged on the other side of the hospital complex and drove to the modern apartment block where the Nieddus lived.

Throughout her ordeal the old lady had hardly spoken a word, though her eyes and the way she clutched her son's hand showed clearly how shocked she was. Zen had explained that there was something wrong with their apartment, something connected with the noises she had heard, and that it was necessary for them both to move out for a few days while it was put right. It made no difference what he said. His mother sat rigidly as the ambulancemen wheeled her into the neat and tidy bedroom which Rosella Nieddu had prepared for her, having shooed out the two youngest children to join their elder siblings next door. Zen thanked Rosella with a warmth that elicited a hug and a kiss he found oddly disturbing. Gilberto's wife was a very attractive woman, and the contact had made Zen realize that he had neglected that side of his life for too long.

The archives clerks had gone back to their desks, now that the fun was over. Zen gathered up the papers relating to the Spadola case and started to put them into some sort of order while he awaited confirmation that the video tape he had produced from his pocket after dropping the file was indeed the genuine article.

Suddenly his hands ceased their mechanical activity. Zen scanned the smudgy carbon-copied document he was holding, looking for the name which had leapt off the page at him.

. . . informed that Spadola was in hiding at a farmhouse near the village of Melzo. At 04.00 hours on 16 July personnel of the Squadra Mobile under the direction of Ispettor Aurelio Zen entered the house and arrested Spadola. An extensive search of the premises revealed various items of material evidence (see Appendix A), in particular a knife which proved to be marked with traces of blood consistent with that of the victim. Spadola continued to deny all involvement in the affair, even after the damning nature of the evidence had been explained to him. At the judicial confrontation with Parrucci, the accused uttered violent threats against the witness . . .

Once again, Zen felt the superstitious chill that had come over him that night after viewing the Burolo video. Parrucci! The informer whose gruesome death had thrown Fausto Arcuti into a state of mortal terror! It seemed quite uncanny that the same man should figure again in the file which Zen had asked to see two days before as part of his stratagem for substituting the blank video tape.

But he had no more time to consider the matter, for at that moment the clerk reappeared, video cassette in hand.

'It's the right one,' he confirmed grudgingly. 'So where did the other come from, I'd like to know?'

Zen shrugged.

'I'd say that's pretty obvious. When I brought the tape back the other day, you got it muddled up with the file I asked to consult at the same time. When you couldn't find it you started to panic, because you knew that it had been handed back and that you would be responsible. So you substituted a blank tape, hoping that no one would notice. Unfortunately, one of my colleagues had asked to see the tape, and he immediately discovered that . . .'

'That's a lie!' the man shouted.

Snatching the Spadola file from Zen, he abruptly went on to the attack.

'Look at this mess you've made! It would be no wonder if things sometimes *did* get confused around here with people like you wandering in and upsetting everything. Leave it, leave it! You're just making a worse muddle. These documents must be filed in chronological order. Look, this judicial review shouldn't be here. It must come at the end.'

'Let me see that!'

The form was stiff and heavy, imitation parchment. The text, set in antique type and printed in the blackest of inks, was as dense and lapidary as Latin, clogged with odd abbreviations and foreshortenings, totally impenetrable. But there was no need to read it to understand the import of the document. It was enough to scan the brief phrases inserted by hand in the spaces left blank by the printer. '29 April 1964 . . . Milan . . . Spadola, Vasco Ernesto . . . culpable homicide . . . life imprisonment . . . investigating magistrate Giulio Bertolini . . .'

It was enough to scan the spaces, read the messages, make the connections. That was enough, thought Zen. But he had failed to do it, and now it might be too late.

Back at his desk in the Criminalpol offices, which were deserted that morning, Zen phoned the Ministry of Justice and inquired about the penal status of Vasco Ernesto Spadola, who had been sentenced to life imprisonment in Milan on 29 April 1964. A remote and disembodied voice announced that he would be rung back with the information in due course.

Zen lit a cigarette and wandered over to the window, looking down at the forecourt of the Ministry with its pines and shrubbery which flanked the sweep of steps leading down to the huge shallow bath of the fountain in Piazza del Viminale. Although the implications of the facts he had just stumbled on were anything but cheering, he felt relieved to find that there was at least a rational explanation for the things that had been going on. It was not just an uncanny coincidence that Zen had happened to ask for the Spadola file the day that he had read about the killing of Judge Bertolini. At some level beneath his conscious thoughts he must have recalled the one occasion on which his and the murdered judge's paths had crossed. As for Parrucci, the reason why the name had meant nothing to Zen was that he knew the informer only by his codename, 'the nightingale'. When Parrucci agreed to testify against Spadola, his name had been revealed, but by that time Zen's involvement with the case was at an end.

A thin Roman haze softened the November sunlight, giving it an almost summery languor. At a window on the other side of the piazza a woman was hanging out bedding to air on the balcony. A three-wheeled Ape van was unloading cases of mineral water outside the bar below, while on the steps of the Ministry itself three chauffeurs were having an animated discussion involving sharp decisive stabs of the index finger, exaggerated shrugs and waves of dismissal, cupped palms pleading for sanity and attention-claiming grabs at each other's sleeves. Zen only gradually became aware of an interference with these sharply etched scenes, a movement seemingly on the other side of the glass, where the ghostly figure of Tania Biacis was shimmering towards him in mid-air.

'I've been looking for you all morning.'

He turned to face the original of the reflection. She was looking at him with a slightly playful air, as though she knew that he would be wondering what she meant. But Zen had no heart for such tricks.

'I was down in Archives, sorting out that video tape business. Where is everyone, anyway?'

A distant phone began to ring.

'Don't go!' Zen called as he hurried back to his desk.

He snatched up the phone.

'Yes?'

'Good morning, dottore,' a voice whispered confidentially. It sounded like some tiny creature curled up in the receiver itself. 'Just calling to remind you of our lunch appointment. I hope you can still make it.'

'Lunch? Who is this?'

There was long silence.

'We talked last night,' the voice remarked pointedly.

Zen finally remembered his arrangement with Fausto Arcuti.

'Oh, right! Good. Fine. Thanks. I'll be there.'

He put the receiver down and turned. Tania Biacis was standing close behind him and his movement brought them into contact for a moment. Zen's arm skimmed her breast, their hands jangled briefly together like bells.

'Oh, there you are,' he cried. 'Where's everyone gone to?'

It was as though he regretted being alone with her!

'They're at a briefing. The chief wants to see you.'

'Immediately?'

'When else?'

He frowned. The Ministry of Justice might phone back at any minute, and as it was Friday the staff would go off duty for the weekend in half-an-hour. He *had* to have that information.

'Would you do me a favour?' he asked.

The words were exactly the ones she had used to him two days earlier. It was clear from her expression that she remembered.

'Of course,' she replied, with a faint smile that grew wider, as he responded, 'You don't know what it is yet.'

'You decided before I told you what I wanted,' she pointed out.

'But I had reasons which you may not have.'

Tania sighed.

'I don't know what you must think of me,' she said despondently.

'Don't you? Don't you really?'

They looked at each other in silence for some time.

'So what is it you want?' she asked eventually.

Zen looked at her in some embarrassment. Now that his request had become the subject of so much flirtatious persiflage, it would be ridiculous to admit that he had only wanted her to field a phone call for him.

'I can't tell you here,' he said. 'It's a bit complicated, and . . . well, there're various reasons. Look, I don't suppose you could have lunch with me?'

It was a delaying tactic. He was counting on her to refuse.

'But you've already got a lunch engagement,' she objected.

It took him a little while to understand.

'Oh, the phone call! No, that's . . . that's for another day.'

Tania inspected her fingernails for a moment. Then she reached out and lightly, deliberately, scratched the back of his hand. The skin turned white and then red, as though burned.

'I'd have to be home by three,' she told him. She sounded like an adolescent arranging a date.

Zen was about to reply when the phone rang again.

'Ministry of Justice, Records Section, calling with reference to your inquiry *in re* Spadola, Vasco Ernesto.'

'Yes?'

'The subject was released from Asinara prison on 7 October of this year.'

Zen's response was a silence so profound that even the disembodied voice unbent sufficiently to add, 'Hello? Anyone there?'

'Thank you. That's all.'

He hung up and turned back to Tania Biacis.

'Shall we meet downstairs then?' he suggested casually, as though they'd been lunching together for years.

She nodded. 'Fine. Now please go and see what Moscati wants before he takes it out on me.'

Lorenzo Moscati, head of Criminalpol, was a short stout man with smooth, rounded features which looked as though they were being flattened out by an invisible stocking-mask.

'Eh, finally!' he exclaimed when Zen appeared. 'I've been able to round up everyone except you. Where did you get to? Never mind, no point in you attending the briefing anyway. All about security for the Camorra trial in Naples next week. But that won't concern you, because you're off to Sardinia, you lucky dog! That report you did on the Burolo case was well received, very well received indeed. Now we want you to go and put flesh on the bones, as it were. You leave on Monday. See Ciliani for details of flights and so on.'

Zen nodded.

'While I'm here, there's something else I'd like to discuss,' he said.

Moscati consulted his watch. 'Is it urgent?'

'You could say that. I think someone's trying to kill me.'

Moscati glanced at his subordinate to check that he'd heard right, then again to see if Zen was joking.

'What makes you think that?'

Zen paused, wondering where to begin.

'Strange things have been happening to me recently. Someone's picked the lock to my apartment and broken in while I'm not there. But instead of taking anything, they leave things instead.'

'What sort of things?'

'First an envelope full of shotgun pellets. Then something which had been stolen from me at the bus-stop a couple of days earlier.'

'What?'

Zen hesitated. He obviously couldn't tell Moscati about the theft of the Ministry's video.

'A book I was carrying in my pocket. I assumed some thief thought it was my wallet. But last night I got home to find my apartment covered in paper. The book had been torn apart page by page and scattered all over the floor.'

'Sounds like some prankster with a twisted sense of humour,' Moscati remarked dismissively. 'I wouldn't . . .'

'That's what I thought, at first.' He didn't mention that his principal suspect had been Vincenzo Fabri. 'Then I remembered that the widow of the judge who was shot said that exactly the same things had happened to her husband just before he was murdered. Meanwhile someone has been watching my apartment from a stolen Alfa Romeo recently, and yesterday I was followed half-way across the city. Nevertheless, it didn't seem to add up to anything until I heard that an informer named Parrucci had been found roasted to death near Viterbo. Parrucci was the key witness in a murder investigation case I handled twenty years ago, when I was working in Milan. The investigating magistrate in that case was Giulio Bertolini.'

All trace of impatience had vanished from Moscati's manner. He was following Zen's words avidly.

'A gangster named Vasco Spadola was convicted of the murder and sentenced to life imprisonment. He was released from prison about a month ago. Since then both the judge who prepared the case and the man who gave evidence against Spadola have been killed. It doesn't seem too far-fetched to conclude that the police officer who conducted the investigation is next on his list.'

A strange light burned in Lorenzo Moscati's eyes.

'So it's *not* political, after all!'

'The killing of Bertolini? No, it was straight revenge, a personal vendetta. You see, the evidence against Spadola was faked and Parrucci's testimony paid for by the victim's family. Presumably Bertolini didn't know that, but . . .'

'Do you realize what this means?' Moscati enthused. 'The Politicals have been holding up this Bertolini affair as proof that terrorism isn't finished after all and so they still need big budgets and lots of manpower. If we can show that it's not political at all they'll never live it down! That bastard Cataneo won't dare show his face in public for a month!'

Zen nodded wearily as he understood the reasons for his superior's sudden interest in the affair.

'Meanwhile my life is in danger,' he reminded him. 'Two men have been killed and I'm number three. I want protection.'

Moscati grasped Zen's right arm just above the elbow, as though giving him a transfusion of courage and confidence.

'Don't worry, you'll get it! The very best. A crack squad has been set up to handle just this sort of situation. All hand-picked men, weapons experts, highly skilled, using the very finest and most modern equipment. With them looking after you, you'll be as safe as the President of the Republic himself.'

Zen raised his eyebrows. This sounded too good to be true.

'When will this become effective?'

Moscati held up his hands in a plea for patience and understanding.

'Naturally there are a lot of calls on their time at the moment. In the wake of the Bertolini killing, everyone's a bit anxious. It'll be a question of reviewing the situation on an on-going basis, assessing the threat as it develops and then allocating the available resources accordingly.'

Zen nodded. It *had* been too good to be true.

'But in the meantime you'll put a man outside my house?'

Moscati gestured regretfully. 'It's out of my hands, Zen. Now this new squad exists, all applications for protection have to be routed through them. It's so they can draw up a map of potential threats at any given time, then put it on the computer and see if any overall patterns emerge. Or so they claim. If you ask me, they're just protecting their territory. Either way, my hands are tied, unfortunately. If I start allocating men to protection duties they'll cry foul and we'll never hear the end of it.'

Zen nodded and turned to leave. From a bureaucratic point of view, the logic of Moscati's position was flawless. He knew only too well that it would be a sheer waste of time to point out any discrepancy between that logic and common sense.

As the working day for state employees came to an end, doors could be heard opening all over the Ministry. The corridors began to hum with voices which, amplified by the resonant acoustic, rapidly became a babble, a tumult which prefigured the crowds surging invisibly towards the entrance hall where Zen stood waiting. Within a minute they were everywhere. The enormous staircase was barely able to contain the human throng eager to get home, have lunch and relax, or else hasten to their clandestine afternoon jobs in the booming black economy, 'the Italy that works', as Fausto Arcuti had joked.

Ever since Tania Biacis had accepted his invitation to lunch, Zen had been racking his brains over the choice of restaurant. Given her wide and sophisticated experience of eating out in Rome, this was not something to be taken lightly. The only places he knew personally these days were those close to the Ministry and therefore regularly patronized by its staff, and it would clearly be unwise to go there. Quite apart from the risk of compromising Tania, Zen didn't want to have to deal with winks, nudges or loaded questions from his colleagues. Again, it was important to get the class of establishment right. Nothing cheap or seedy, of course, but neither anything so grand or pretentious that it might make her feel that he was trying the crude old 'I'm spending a lot of money on you so you'll have to come across' approach. Finally, there were the practicalities to consider. If Tania had to be home by three, it had to be somewhere in the centre, where by this time most of the better restaurants might well be full. Every possibility that occurred to Zen failed one of these tests. He was still at a loss when Tania appeared.

'So, where are we going?' she demanded.

She sounded tense and snappy, as though she was already regretting having agreed to come. Zen panicked. He should never have confused his fantasies with reality like this. The situation was all wrong. It would end in disaster and humiliation.

'There's a place in Piazza Navona,' he found himself saying as he led the way out into the pale sunlight. 'It's crowded with tourists in summer, but at this time of year . . .'

He didn't add that the last time he was there had been with Ellen.

Outside the Ministry Zen hailed a taxi. The brief journey did nothing to alleviate his fears that a major fiasco was in the offing. He and Tania sat as far apart as possible, exchanging brief banalities like a married couple after a row.

The taxi dropped them by the small fountain at the south end of the piazza. As they walked out into its superb amplitude, two kids sped past on a moped, one standing on the pillion grasping the driver's shoulders. The noise scattered a flock of pigeons which rose like a single being and went winging around the obelisk rising above the central fountain, while a second flock of shadows mimicked its progress across the grey stones below. The breeze caught the water spurting out of cleavages in the fountain, winnowing it out in an aerosol of fine drops where a fragmentary rainbow briefly shimmered. Just for a moment Zen thought that everything was going to be all right after all. Then he caught sight of the restaurant, shuttered and bolted, the chairs and tables piled high, and knew that he'd been right the first time. '*Chiuso per turno*' read a sign in the window.

Tania Biacis looked at her watch. 'It's getting late.'

Zen nodded. 'Perhaps we'd better leave it till another time.'

He knew that there would be no other time.

Tania stared intently at the façade of the palazzo opposite, as though trying to decipher a message written in the whorls and curlicues of stone.

'Your place isn't very far away, is it? We could pick up something from a *rosticceria* and take it back there, if you don't mind that is. The food's not that important. What we really want to do is talk, isn't it?'

She made it sound so natural and sensible that Zen was almost unsurprised.

'Well, if that's . . . all right.'

'All right?'

'I mean, it's all right with me.'

'With me, too. Otherwise I wouldn't have suggested it.'

'Then it's all right.'

'It looks like it,' she said with a slightly ironic smile.

'How do you know where I live?' Zen asked, as they walked up the piazza.

'I looked you up in the phone book. I thought you'd be the only Zen, but there are about a dozen of you in Rome. Are the others relatives?'

Zen shook his head absently. He was wondering whether Vasco Spadola had employed the same simple method to track him down.

In a *rosticceria* just north of the piazza they bought a double portion of the only main dish left, a rabbit stew, and two of the egg-shaped rice croquettes called 'telephone wires', because when you pull them apart the ball of melted mozzarella in the middle separates into long curving strands. Then they walked on, out of the clutches of the old city and across the river. Zen paused to draw Tania's attention to the view downstream towards the island, the serried plane trees lining the stone-faced embankment, the river below as smooth and still as a darker vein in polished marble. While she was looking, he looked over his shoulder again. This time there was no doubt.

They moved on, towards the wildly exuberant façade which might have been a grand opera house or the palace of a mad king, but was in fact the law courts. Here they paused until the traffic lights brought the cars to a reluctant, grudging halt, then crossed the Lungotevere and turned right down the side of the law courts.

'Wait a minute,' Zen told Tania as they passed the corner.

A few moments later a young man in a denim suit trimmed with a sheepskin collar appeared, striding quickly along. Zen stepped in front of him, flourishing his identity card.

'Police! Your papers!'

The man gawked at him open-mouthed.

'I haven't done anything!'

'I didn't say you had.'

The man took out his wallet and produced a battered identity card in the name of Roberto Augusto Dentice. In the photograph he looked younger, timid and studious. Zen plucked the wallet out of his hand.

'You've got no right to do that!' the man protested.

Ignoring him, Zen riffled through the compartments of the wallet, inspecting papers and photographs. Among them was a permit issued by the Rome Questura, authorizing Roberto Augusto Dentice to practise as a private detective within the limits of the Province of Rome.

'All right, what's going on?' Zen demanded.

'What do you mean?'

'Someone's hired you to follow me. Who and why?'

'I don't know what you're talking about. I was just going for a walk.'

'And I suppose you were just going for a walk yesterday, when you followed me all the way from that restaurant to the Palatine? You really like walking, don't you? You should join the *Club Alpino*.'

On the main road behind them, a chorus of horns sounded out like the siren of a great ocean liner.

'What are you talking about?' the man said. 'I was at home all day yesterday.'

Zen's instinct was to arrest Dentice on some pretext and shut him up in a room with one of the heavier-handed officials, but he no longer worked at the Questura where such facilities were available, and besides, Tania was waiting.

'All right,' he said in a voice laden with quiet menace. 'Let me explain what I'm talking about. This job you're doing, whatever it may be, ends here. If I so much as catch sight of you again, even casually, on a bus or in a bar, anywhere at all, then this permit of yours will be withdrawn and I'll make damn sure that you never get another. Do we understand each other?'

These tactics proved unexpectedly successful. Faced with violence and menaces the man might have remained defiant, but at the threat of unemployment his resistance suddenly collapsed.

'No one told me you were a cop!' he complained.

'What *did* they tell you?'

'Just to follow you after work.'

'How did you report?'

'He phoned me in the evening. And he paid cash. I don't know who he is, honest to God!'

Zen handed back the man's wallet and papers and turned away without another word.

'What was all that about?' Tania asked as they resumed their walk.

'My mistake. I thought he looked like someone wanted for questioning in the Bertolini killing.'

That was the second time that afternoon that he had broken his rule about not lying to Tania, Zen reflected. No doubt it had been an unrealistic ideal in the first place.

It felt odd to be walking home with the woman who had occupied so much of his thoughts recently, to pass the café at the corner in her company, to walk into the entrance hall together under Giuseppe's eagle eye, travel up in the lift to the fourth floor, unlock the front door, admit her to his home, his other life.

He was acutely aware that, for the first time in years, his mother was not there. Freed from the grid of rules and regulations her presence imposed, the apartment seemed larger and less cluttered than usual, full of possibilities. Zen felt a momentary stab of guilt, as though he had manoeuvred her transfer to the Nieddus just so that he could bring Tania back to the flat. It was strangely exciting, and he caught himself speculating on what might happen after lunch. Rather to his surprise, Zen found that he could quite easily imagine going to bed with Tania. Without any voyeuristic thrill, he visualized the two of them lying in the big brass bed he had occupied alone for so long. Naked, Tania looked thinner and taller than ever, but that didn't matter. She looked like she belonged there.

Zen put these thoughts out of his mind, not from a sense of shame but out of pure superstition. Life rarely turns out the way you imagine it is going to, he reasoned, so the more likely it seemed that he and Tania would end up in bed together, the less likely it was to happen.

Maria Grazia had been told to stay away for the time being, and since Zen had no idea where she kept the everyday cutlery and crockery, he and Tania foraged around in the kitchen and the sideboard in the dining room, assembling china, silverware and crystal that Zen had last seen about twelve years previously, at a dinner to celebrate his wedding anniversary. Unintimidated by these formal splendours, they ate the rice croquettes with their fingers, mopped up the stew with yesterday's bread and drank a lukewarm bottle of Pinot Spumante which had been standing on a shelf in the living room since the Christmas before last. Tania ate hungrily and without the slightest self-consciousness. When they finally set aside their little piles of rabbit bones, she announced, 'That's the best meal I've had for ages.'

Zen pushed the fruit bowl in her direction.

'I find that hard to believe.'

She gave him a surprised glance.

'Given the life you lead,' he explained.

'Oh, that!'

She skinned a tangerine and started dividing it into segments.

'Look, there's something we'd better clear up,' she said. 'You see, I didn't quite tell you the truth.'

He thought of them sitting together in the speeding taxi, the bands of light outlining the swell of her breasts, the line of her thigh.

'I know,' he said.

It was her turn to look surprised.

'Was it that obvious?'

'Oh come on!' he exclaimed. 'Did you honestly think I'd believe that you went to all that trouble, getting me to fake a phone call from work and all the rest of it, just so that you could go out to the cinema? I mean you don't have to explain. I don't care what you were doing. And even supposing I did, it's none of my business.'

Tania was gazing at him with dawning comprehension.

'But that *was* what I was doing! Just that! It was all the other times that were lies, when I told you about the films I'd seen, and going to the opera and the theatre and all the rest of it.'

She looked away as tears swelled in her eyes.

'That's why I got so embarrassed in the taxi, when you asked where I was going. It wasn't that I had a guilty secret, at least not the kind you thought! It was just that my pathetic little deception had been found out and I felt so ashamed of myself!

'It all started when you mentioned some film I'd read about in the paper. That's all I ever *did* do, read about it. So I thought it would be fun to pretend that I'd seen it. Then I started doing it with other things, building a whole fantasy life that I shared with you every morning at work. It was never real, Aurelio, none of it! On the contrary! We never go anywhere, never do anything. All Mauro wants to do is sit at home with his mother and his sister and any cousins or aunts or uncles who happen to be around.

'The irony of it is that that's one thing that attracted me to Mauro in the first place, the fact that he came with a ready-made family. My own parents are dead, as you know, and my only brother emigrated to Australia years ago. Well, I've got myself a family now, all right, and *what* a family! Do you know what his mother calls me? "The tall cunt." I've heard them discussing me behind my back. "Why did you want to marry that tall cunt?" she asks him. They think I can't understand their miserable dialect. "It's your own fault," she says. "You should never have married a foreigner. 'Wife and herd from your own backyard.'" This is the way they talk! This is the way they think!'

She fell silent. A car door slammed in the street outside. Footsteps approached the house. Zen got to his feet, listening intently.

'What is it, Aurelio?'

He went to the window and looked out. Then he walked quickly through to the inner hallway, closing the door behind him. He lifted the phone and dialled 113, the police emergency number. Keeping his voice low so that Tania would not hear, Zen gave his name, address and rank.

'There's a stolen vehicle in the street outside my house. A red Alfa Romeo, registration number Roma 84693 P. Get a car here immediately, arrest the occupant and charge him with theft. Approach with caution, however. He may be armed.'

'Very good, dottore.'

As Zen replaced the phone, he heard a sound from the living room. No, it was more distant, beyond the living room. From the hall.

His heart began to beat very fast and his breath came in gulps. Slowly, deliberately, he walked through the doorway and past the television, brushing his fingertips along the back of his mother's chair. How could he have been so stupid, so thoughtless and selfish? To imagine that no harm could come to him in the daylight but only after dark, like a child! To put a person he loved at risk by bringing her to a place he knew to be under deadly threat. They'd been watching the house. They'd seen him and Tania enter, and they'd had plenty of time to prepare their move. Now they had come for him.

As he approached the glass-panelled door that lay open into the hall there was a loud click, followed by the characteristic squeal as the front door opened. On the floor above, the canary chirped plaintively in response.

The scene reflected on the glass door was almost a replica of the one the night before. But this time Zen knew that he had not left the door open, and the dark figure walking towards him along the hallway did not call his name in a familiar voice, and it was carrying a shotgun.

'What's going on, Aurelio?'

Tania was standing on the threshold of the inner hallway, looking anxiously at him. Zen waved her away, but she took no notice. Outside in the streets a siren rose and fell, gradually emerging from the urban backdrop as it rapidly neared the house. The gunman, now half-way along the hall, paused. The siren wound down to a low growl, directly outside the house.

Zen jumped as something touched his shoulder. He whirled round, staring wildly at Tania's hand. She was close behind him, gazing at him with an expression of affectionate concern. He looked at the reflection of the hallway on the surface of the glass door. The gunman had vanished. Zen grabbed Tania suddenly, holding her tightly, gasping for breath, trembling all over.

Then abruptly he thrust her away again.

'I'm sorry! I'm sorry!' he exclaimed repeatedly. 'I didn't mean to! I couldn't help it!'

After a moment she came back to him of her own accord and took him in her arms.

'It's all right,' she told him. 'It's all right.'

I didn't mean to do it. I was just paying a visit, like before. They shouldn't have tried to shut me out, though, or else done it properly. As it was, I just pushed and twisted until the whole thing came crashing down. But it made me angry. They shouldn't have done that.

l thought the noise might bring them running, but they were as deaf and blind as usual. To get my own back, I decided to make the gun disappear. I'm no stranger to guns. My father was famous for his marksmanship. After Sunday lunch, when the animals had been corralled and lassooed, wrestled to the ground like baby giants and dosed with medicine or branded, the men would hurl beer bottles up into the air to fire at. Drunk as he was, the sweet grease of the piglet they had roasted before the fire still glistening on his lips and chin, my father could always hit the target and make the valley ring with the sound of breaking glass. 'There's nothing to it!' he used to joke. 'You just pull the trigger and the gun does the rest.'

As I lifted it from the rack, I heard someone laugh in the next room. It was sleek and fat and arrogant, his laugh, like one of the young men lounging in the street, fingering their cocks like a pocketful of money. That was when I decided to show myself. That would stop the laughter. That would give them something to think about.

After that things happened without consulting me. A man came at me. A woman ran. I worked the trigger again and again.

Father was quite right. The gun did the rest.

SARDINIA

Saturday, 05.05–12.50

A chill, tangy wind, laden with salt and darkness, whined and blus-tered about the ship, testing for weaknesses. By contrast, the sea was calm. Its shiny black surface merged imperceptibly into the darkness all around, ridged into folds, tucks and creases, heaving and tilting in the moonlight. The short choppy waves slapping the metal plates below seemed to have no perceptible effect on the ship itself, which lay as still as if it were already roped to the quay.

A man stood grasping the metal rail pudgy with innumerable coats of paint, staring out into the night as keenly as an officer of the watch. The unbuttoned overcoat flapping about him like a cloak gave him an illusory air of corpulence, but when the wind failed for a moment he was revealed as quite slender for his height. Beneath the overcoat he was wearing a rumpled suit. A tie of some nondescript hue was plastered to his shirt by the wind in a lazy curve, like a question mark. His face was lean and smooth, with an aquiline nose, and slate-blue eyes, their gaze as disconcertingly direct as a child's. His hair, its basic undistinguished brown now flecked with silvery-grey high-lights at the temples, was naturally curly, and the wind tossed it back and forth like frantic wavelets in a storm scene on a Greek vase.

A few hundred metres astern of the ship, the full moon was reflected in the sea's unstable surface. The shuddering patch of brightness had an eerie illusion of depth, as if created by a gigantic searchlight aimed upwards from the ocean bed. It *was* deep here, off the eastern coast of the island, where the mountains plunged down to meet the sea and then kept going. Zen stood breathing in the wild air and scanning the horizon for some hint of their landfall. But there was nothing to betray the presence of the coast, unless it was the fact that the darkness ahead seemed even more unyielding, solid and impenetrable. The steward had knocked on the cabin door to wake him twenty minutes earlier, claiming that their arrival was imminent. Emerging on deck, Zen had expected lights, bustling activity, a first view of his destination. But there was nothing. The ship might have been becalmed in mid-ocean.

He didn't care. He felt weightless, anonymous, stripped of all superfluous baggage. Rome was already inconceivably distant. Sardinia lay somewhere ahead, unknown, a blank. As for the reasons why he was there, standing on the deck of a Tirrenia Line ferry at five o'clock in the morning, they seemed utterly unreal and irrelevant.

When he looked again, it was over. The wall of darkness ahead had divided in two: a high mountain range below, dappled with a suggestion of contours, and the sky above, hollow with the coming dawn. Harbour lights emerged from behind the spit of land which had concealed them earlier, now differentiated from the open sea and the small bay beyond. Reading them like constellations, Zen mapped out quays and jetties, cranes and roads in the half-light. Things were beginning to put on shape and form, to wake up, get dressed and make themselves presentable. The moment had passed. Soon it would be just another day.

Down below in the bar, the process was already well advanced. A predominantly male crowd, more or less dishevelled and bad-tempered, clustered around a sleepy cashier to buy a printed receipt which they then took to the bar and traded in for a plastic thimble filled with strong black coffee. On the bench seats all around young people were awakening from a rough night, rubbing their eyes, scratching their backs, exchanging little jokes and caresses. Zen had just succeeded in ordering his coffee when a robotic voice from the tannoy directed all drivers to make their way to the car deck to disembark. He downed the coffee hurriedly, scalding his mouth and throat, before heading down into the bowels of the ship.

The vehicles bound for this small port of call on the way to Cagliari, the ship's destination, were almost exclusively commercial and military. Neither category took the slightest notice of the signs asking drivers not to switch on their engines until the bow doors had been opened. Zen made his way through clouds of diesel fumes to his car, sandwiched between a large lorry and a coach filled with military conscripts looking considerably less lively than they had the night before, when they had made the harbour at Civitavecchia ring with the forced gaiety of desperate men. He unlocked the door and climbed in. Fausto Arcuto had done him well, there was no question about that. Returning to the Rally Bar the previous afternoon, Zen had collected an envelope containing a set of keys and a piece of paper reading 'Outside Via Florio, 63'. He turned the paper over and wrote, 'Many thanks for prompt delivery. The Parrucci affair has nothing, repeat nothing, to do with you. Regards.' He handed this to the barman and walked round the corner to Via Florio.

There was no need to check the house number. The car, a white Mercedes saloon with cream leather upholstery, stood out a mile among the battered utility compacts of the Testaccio residents. It had been fitted with Zurich number plates, fairly recently to judge by the bright scratches on the rusty nuts. No registration or insurance documents were displayed on the windscreen, but this would have been a bit much to expect at such short notice. Zen took out his wallet and inspected the Swiss identity card in the name of Reto Gurtner which he had retained following an undercover job six years earlier. It was a fake, but extremely high quality, a product of the secret services' operation at Prato where, it was rumoured, a large number of the top forgers in the country offered their skills to SISMI in lieu of a prison sentence. The primitive lighting and Zen's constrained pose made the photograph look like a police mug-shot, not surprisingly, since it had been taken on the same equipment. Herr Gurtner of Zurich looked capable of just about anything, thought Zen, even framing an innocent man to order.

As he sat there, muffled by the Mercedes' luxurious coachwork from the farting lorries and buses all around, Zen reflected that whatever happened in Sardinia, he had at least been able to clear up his outstanding problems in Rome before leaving. The Volante patrol summoned by his 113 call from the flat had arrested a man attempting to escape in the red Alfa Romeo. He turned out to be one Giuliano Acciari, a local hoodlum with a lengthy criminal record for housebreaking and minor thuggery. Zen recognized him as the man who had picked his pocket in the bus queue, although he did not mention this to the police. Acciari was unarmed, and a search failed to turn up the shotgun which he was assumed to have dumped upon hearing the sirens. But the police were holding Acciari for the theft of the Alfa Romeo, and had assured Zen that they would spare no effort to extract any information he might have as to the whereabouts of Vasco Spadola.

A series of shudders and a change in the pitch of the turbines announced that the ship had docked, but another ten minutes passed before a crack of daylight finally penetrated the murky reaches of the car deck. The coaches and lorries to either side of Zen rumbled into motion, and then, too soon, it was his turn.

Zen had learnt to drive back in the late fifties, but he had never really developed a taste for it. As the roads filled up, speeds increased and drivers' tempers shortened, he had seen no reason to change his views, although he was careful to keep them to himself, well aware that they would be considered dissident if not heretical. But in the present case there had been no alternative: he couldn't drag anyone else along to act as his chauffeur, and it would not be credible for Herr Reto Gurtner, the wealthy burgher of Zurich, to travel through the wilds of Sardinia by public transport.

Zen's style behind the wheel was similar to that of an elderly peasant farmer phut-phutting along at 20 kph in a clapped-out Fiat truck with bald tyres and no acceleration, blithely oblivious to the hooting, light-flashing hysteria building up in his wake. The drive from Rome to the port at Civitavecchia had been a two-and-a-half-hour ordeal, but getting off the ferry presented even greater problems of clutch control and touch-steering than had the innumerable traffic lights of the Via Aurelia, at each of which the Mercedes had seemed to take fright like a horse at a fence. Having stalled three times and then nearly rammed the side of the ship by over-revving, Zen finally managed to negotiate the metal ramp leading to Sardinian soil, or rather the stone jetty to which the ferry was moored. Rather to his surprise, there were no formalities, no passports, no customs. But bureaucratically, of course, he was still in Italy.

It was Zen's first visit to the island. In Italy all police officials have to do a stint in one of the three 'problem areas' of the country, but Zen had chosen the Alto Adige rather than Sicily or Sardinia, because from there he could easily get back to Venice to see his mother.

The port amounted to no more than a couple of wharves where the ferries to and from the mainland touched once a week and Russian freighters periodically unloaded cargoes of timber pulp for the local papermill. At the end of the quay a narrow, badly-surfaced road curved away between outcrops of jagged pink rock. Zen drove through a straggling collection of makeshift houses that never quite became a village and along the spit of land projecting out to the harbour from the main coastline. The sun was still hidden behind the mountains, but the sky overhead was clear, a delicate, pale wintry blue. Seagulls swept back and forth foraging for food, their cries pealing out in the crisp air.

As he drove through the small town where the road inland crossed the main coastal highway, Zen's instinct was to stop the car, drop into a café and start picking up the clues, sniffing the air, getting his bearings. But he couldn't, for in Sardinia he was not Aurelio Zen but Reto Gurtner, and although he had as yet only a vague idea of Gurtner's character, he was sure that pausing to soak up the atmosphere formed no part of it. Or rather, he was sure that that was what the locals would assume, and it was their view of things that mattered. A rich Swiss stopping his Mercedes outside some rural dive for an early-morning *cappuccino* would instantly become a suspect Swiss, and that of all things was the one Zen could least afford. He must not let the clear sky, pure air and early-morning sense of elation go to his head, he knew. In those mountains blocking off the sun, turning their back on the sea, lived men who had survived thousands of years of foreign domination by using their wits and their intimate knowledge of the land. Generations of policemen, occasionally supplemented by the army, had been drafted there in a succession of attempts to break the complex, archaic, unwritten rules of the *Codice Barbaricine* and impose the laws passed in Rome. They had failed. Even Mussolini's strong-arm tactics, successful against the largely urban Mafia, had been ineffectual with these shepherds, who could simply vanish into the mountains. The mass arrests of their relatives in raids on whole villages merely served to strengthen the hands of the outlaws by making them into local folk heroes. Any collaboration with the authorities was considered treachery of the most vile kind and punished accordingly. To Sardinians, mainland Italians were either policemen, soldiers, teachers, tax gatherers, bureaucrats or, more recently, tourists. They stayed for a while, took what they wanted, and then left, as ignorant as when they had arrived of the local inhabitants, the harsh brand of Latin they spoke and the complex and often violent code for resolving conflicts among shepherds whose flocks roamed freely across the open mountains. This was why Zen had decided to go about this unofficial undercover operation in the guise of a foreigner. All outsiders were suspect in Sardinia, but a foreigner was much less likely to attract suspicion than a lone Italian, who would automatically be assumed to be a government spy of some type. Besides, Herr Reto Gurtner had a good reason for visiting this out-of-the-way corner of the island at this unseasonable time of the year. He was looking for a property.

The Mercedes hummed purposefully along the road that wound and twisted its way up from the coast through a parched, scorched landscape. To either side, jagged crags of limestone rose like molars out of acres of sterile red soil. Giant cactuses with enormous prickly ears grew there, and small groves of eucalyptus and olive and the odd patch of wild-looking stunted vines. There was a gratifying absence of traffic on the road, and Zen was just getting into his stride when he was brought to a halt at a level-crossing consisting of a chain with a metal plate dangling from it. He had been vaguely aware of a set of narrow-gauge railway tracks running alongside the road, but they looked so poorly maintained that he had assumed the line was disused.

On the other side of the chain, an elderly woman was chatting to a schoolboy wearing a satchel with the inscription 'Iron Maiden' in fluorescent orange and green. They both turned to stare at the Mercedes. Zen gave them a bland, blank look he imagined to be typically Swiss. They continued to stare. Zen took the opportunity of consulting the map. That too was surely a typically Swiss thing to do.

A train consisting of an ancient diesel locomotive and two decrepit carriages staggered to a stop at the crossing. The Iron Maiden fan climbed in to join a mob of other schoolchildren, the locomotive belched a cloud of fumes and a moment later the road was clear again. Zen put the car in gear, stalled, let off the handbrake, started to roll backwards, engaged the clutch, restarted the motor, stalled, engaged the handbrake, released the clutch, restarted the motor, released the handbrake, engaged the clutch and drove away. None of this, he felt, was typically Swiss. The look the crossing-keeper gave him suggested that she felt the same.

Fortified by the information from the map and the occasional faded and rusted road sign, Zen continued inland for a dozen kilometres before turning left on to a steep road twisting up the mountainside in a series of switchback loops. At each corner he caught a glimpse of the village above. The nearer he got, the less attractive it looked. From a distance, it resembled some natural disaster, a landslip perhaps. Close up, it looked like a gigantic rubbish tip. There was nothing distinctively Sardinian about it. It could have been any one of thousands of communities in the south kept alive by injections of cash from migrant workers, the houses piled together higgledy-piggledy, many of them unfinished, awaiting the next cheque from abroad. The dominant colours were white and ochre, the basic shape the rectangle. Strewn across the steep slope, the place had a freakish, temporary air, as though by the next day it might all have been dismantled and moved elsewhere. And yet it might well have been there when Rome itself was but a village.

The final curves of the road had already been colonized by the zone of new buildings. Some were mere skeletons of reinforced concrete, others had a shell of outer walling but remained uninhabited. A few were being built storey by storey, the lower floor already in use while the first floor formed a temporary flat roof from which the rusted reinforcement wires for the next stage protruded like the stalks of some super-hardy local plant that had learned to flourish in cement. The road gradually narrowed and became the main street of the village proper. Zen painfully squeezed the Mercedes past parked vans and lorries, cravenly giving way to any oncoming traffic, until he reached a small piazza that was really no more than a broadening of the main street. The line of buildings was broken here by a terrace planted with stocky trees overlooking a stunning panorama that stretched all the way down to the distant coastline and the sea beyond. Somewhere down there, Zen knew, indistinguishable to the naked eye, lay the Villa Burolo.

He parked on the other side of the piazza, in front of a squat, fairly new building with a sign reading 'Bar – Restaurant – Hotel'. It was still early and the few people about were all intent on business of one kind or another, but Zen was conscious that their eyes were on him as he got out of the car and removed his suitcase from the boot. 'Stranger in town,' they were thinking. 'Foreign car. Tourist? At this time of year?' Zen was acutely aware of their puzzlement, their suspicion. He wanted to cultivate it briefly, to let the questions form and the implications be raised before he supplied an answer which, he hoped, would come as a satisfying relief.

He pushed through the plate-glass doors into a bar which might have looked glamorously stylish when it had been built, some time in the mid sixties, but which had aged gracelessly. The stippled plaster was laden with dust, the tinted metal façades were dented and scratched, the pine trim had been bleached by sunlight and stained by liquids and was warping off the wall in places. All these details were mercilessly reflected from every angle by a series of mirrors designed to increase the apparent size of the room, but which in fact reduced it to a nightmarish maze of illusory perspectives and visual culs-de-sac.

'With or without?' the proprietor demanded when Zen asked if he had a room available.

Zen had given some thought to the question of how Reto Gurtner should speak, eventually deciding against funny accents or deliberate mistakes. It would be typically Swiss, he decided, to speak pedantically correct Italian, but slowly and heavily, as though all the words were equal citizens and it was invidious and undemocratic to emphasize some at the expense of others.

'I beg your pardon?'

'A shower.'

'Yes, please. With a shower.'

The proprietor plucked a key from a row of hooks and slapped it down on the counter. He was plump, with a bushy black beard and receding hair. His manner was deliberately ungracious, as though the shameful calling of taking in guests for money had been forced on him by stern necessity, and he loathed it as a form of prostitution. He took Zen's faked papers without a second glance and started copying the relevant details on to a police registration form.

'Would it be possible to have a *cappuccino*?' Zen inquired politely.

'At the bar.'

Zen duly took the four paces needed to reach this installation. The proprietor completed the form, held it up to the light as though to admire the watermark, folded it in two with exaggerated precision, and placed it with the papers in a small safe let into the wall. He then walked over to the bar, where he set about washing up some glasses.

An elderly man came into the bar. He was wearing a brown corduroy suit with leather patches on the seat and behind the knees, and a flat cap. His face was as hard and smooth and irregular as a piece of granite exposed to centuries of harsh weather.

'Oh, Tommaso!' the proprietor called, setting a glass of wine on the counter. The man knocked the wine back in one gulp and started rolling a cigarette. Meanwhile he and the proprietor conversed animatedly in a language that might have been Arabic as far as Zen was concerned.

'May I have my *cappuccino*, please?' he asked plaintively.

The proprietor glanced at him as though he had never seen him before, and was both puzzled and annoyed to find him there.

'*Cappuccino*?' he demanded in a tone which suggested that this drink was some exotic foreign speciality.

Zen's instinct was to match rudeness with rudeness, but Reto Gurtner, he felt sure, would remain palely polite under any provocation.

'If you please. Perhaps you would also be good enough to direct me to the offices of Dottor Confalone,' he added.

The elderly man looked up from licking the gummed edge of his cigarette paper. He spat out a shred of tobacco which had found its way on to his tongue.

'Opposite the post office,' he said.

'Is it far?'

There was a brief roar as the proprietor frothed the milk with steam. 'Five minutes,' he said quickly, as though to forestall the old man from making any further unwise disclosures.

Zen stirred sugar into his coffee. He himself never took sugar, but he felt that Reto Gurtner would have a sweet tooth. Similarly, the cigarettes he produced were not his usual Nazionali but cosmopolitan Marlboros.

'I have an appointment, you see,' he explained laboriously, to no one in particular. 'In half an hour. I don't know how it is here in Italy, but in Switzerland it is very important to be punctual. Especially when it's business.'

Neither the proprietor nor the old man showed the slightest interest in this observation, but from the studious way they avoided glancing at each other Zen knew that the point had been taken. The disturbing mystery of Herr Gurtner's descent on the village had been reduced to a specific, localized puzzle.

It was just after nine o'clock when Zen, spruce and clean-shaven, emerged from the hotel. The main street of the village was a deep canyon of shadow, but the alleys and steps running off to either side were slashed with sunshine, revealing panels of brilliant white wall inset with dark rectangular openings. Behind and above them rose a rugged chaos of rock and tough green shrubs, the ancient mountain backbone of the island, last vestige of the submerged Tyrrhenian continent.

Zen walked purposefully along, smiling in a pleasant, meaningless way at everyone he passed, like a benevolent but rather simple-minded giant. The Sards were the shortest of all Mediterranean races, while Zen was above average height for an Italian, thanks perhaps in part to his father's quirky theories about food. A self-educated social-ist, he had been an enthusiast for many useless things, of which Mussolini's vapid patriotism had, briefly, been the last. Another had been a primitive vegetarianism, in particular the notion that beans and milk were the foundation of a healthy diet. From the moment Aurelio was weaned, he had eaten a large dish of these two ingre-dients mashed together every lunchtime. His father's belief in the virtues of this wonder-food had been based on a hotchpotch of half-baked ideas culled from his wide and eclectic reading, but by the purest chance he had happened to hit on two cheap and easily obtainable sources of complementary protein, with the result that Zen had grown up unaffected by the shortages of meat and fish which stunted the development of other children in wartime Venice.

The reactions to Herr Gurtner's bland Swiss smile varied interest-ingly. The young men hanging about in the piazza, as though work were not so much unavailable as beneath their dignity, surveyed the tall stranger like an exotic animal on display in a travelling circus: odd and slightly absurd, but also potentially dangerous. To their elders, clustered on the stone benches between the trees, he was just another piece in the hopeless puzzle which life had become, over which they shook their heads loosely and muttered incoherent comments.

The men, old and young, massed in groups, using the public spaces as an extension of their living rooms, but the women Zen saw were always alone and on the move. They had right of passage only, and scurried along as though liable to be challenged at any moment, clutching their wicker shopping baskets like official permits. The married ones ignored Zen totally, the nubile shot him glances as keen and challenging as a thrown knife. Only the old women, having nothing more to fear or hope from the enemy, gave him cool but not unfriendly looks of appraisal. Dressed all in black, they looked like pyramids of different-sized tyres, their bodies narrowing from massive hips through bulbous waists to tiny scarf-wrapped heads.

The exception which proved this rule of female purpose and activ-ity was a half-witted woman who approached Zen just as he reached his destination, asking for money. Even by Sardinian standards, she was exceptionally small, almost dwarf-like. She was wearing a dark brown pullover and a long full skirt of some heavy navy-blue material. Her head and feet were bare and dirty, and she limped so aggressively that Zen assumed that she was faking or at least exaggerating her disability for professional reasons. He offered her 500 lire before realizing that Herr Reto Gurtner, coming from a nation which prided itself on providing for all its citizens, would disapprove of begging on principle. Fortunately the woman was clearly too crazy to pick up on any such subtleties. Zen forced the money into her hand while she stared fixedly at him like someone who has mistaken a stranger for an old acquaintance. He turned away into the doorway flanked by a large plastic sign reading 'Dott. Angelo Confalone – Solicitor – Notary Public – Estate Agent – Chartered Accountant – Insurance Broker – Tax and Investment Specialist'. Also teeth pulled and horoscopes cast, thought Zen as he climbed the steps to the second floor.

Angelo Confalone was a plush young man who received Herr Gurtner with an expansive warmth, in marked contrast to the cold stares and hostile glances which had been his lot thus far. It was a pleasure, he intimated, to have dealings with someone so distinguished and sophisticated, so different from the usual run of his clients. He wasn't Sardinian himself, it soon emerged, from Genoa in fact, but his sister had married someone from the area who had pointed out that there was an opening in the village, it was a long story and one he would not bore Herr Gurtner with, but the long and short of it was that one had to start somewhere.

Zen nodded his agreement.

'We have a saying in my country. No matter how high the mountain, you have to start climbing at the bottom.'

The lawyer laughed with vivacious insincerity and complimented Herr Gurtner on his Italian.

'And now to business, if you please,' Zen told him. 'You have, I believe, something for me to look at.'

'Indeed.'

Indeed! When Reto Gurtner had phoned him the day before with regard to finding a suitable holiday property for a client in Switzerland, Angelo Confalone could hardly believe his luck. Ever since Oscar Burolo's son had instructed him to put his father's ill-fated Sardinian retreat on the market, Confalone had been asking himself who on earth in his right mind would ever want to buy the Villa Burolo after the lurid publicity given to the horrors that had occurred there. Mindful of this, Enzo Burolo had offered to double the usual commission in order to get the place off their hands quickly, but Confalone still couldn't see any way that he would be able to take advantage of this desirable sweetener. Unless some rich foreigner happens along, he had concluded, then I'm just wasting my time.

And lo and behold, just a few weeks later, Reto Gurtner had telephoned. He had inspected several properties in the north of the island, he said, but his client had specifically asked him to look on the east coast, where he had vacationed several years earlier and of whose spectacular and rugged beauty he retained fond memories. If Dottor Confalone by any chance knew of any suitable properties on the market . . .

A man wearing even one of the many hats mentioned on Angelo Confalone's business plate should perhaps have been shrewd enough to frown momentarily at this happy coincidence, but the young lawyer was too busy calculating his percentage from the sale of the property, which was now of course in a very different price bracket from the subsistence-level farm whose original purchase by Oscar Burolo he had also negotiated.

Confalone regarded his visitor complacently.

'As you are no doubt aware, Herr Gurtner, properties of a standard high enough to satisfy your client's requirements are few and far between in this area. As for one coming on the market, you would normally have to wait years. It so happens, however, that I am in a position to offer you a villa which has only just become available, and which I can truly and honestly describe, without risk of hyperbole, as the finest example of its type to be found anywhere in the island, the Costa Smeralda included.'

He went on in this vein for some time, expatiating on the imaginative way in which the original farmhouse had been modernized and extended without sacrificing the unique authenticity of its humble origins.

'The original owner was a man of vision and daring who brought his unlimited resources and great expertise in the construction business to bear on the . . .'

'He was realizing a dream?' Zen suggested.

Confalone nodded vigorously.

'Exactly. Precisely. I couldn't have put it better myself. He was realizing a dream.'

'And why is he now selling it, his dream?'

The lawyer's vivacity vanished.

'For family reasons,' he murmured. 'There was . . . a death. In the family.'

He awaited Herr Gurtner's response with some trepidation. For the kind of money the Burolos were offering, Confalone was quite prepared to try and conceal the truth. But money wasn't everything. He had his career to consider, and that meant that he couldn't afford to lie.

But Reto Gurtner appeared satisfied.

'I should like to see this most interesting property at once,' he declared, rising to his feet.

Confalone's relief was apparent in his voice.

'Certainly, certainly! I shall be privileged to accompany you personally and . . .'

'Thank you, that will not be necessary. There is a caretaker at the house? If you will be good enough to ring and let them know that I am coming, I prefer to look around on my own. We Swiss, you know, are very methodical. I do not wish to try your patience!'

After some polite insistence, Angelo Confalone gave way gracefully. Double commission and no time wasted doing the honours! He could hardly believe his luck.

Zen emerged from the lawyer's offices to a chorus of horns, the street having been blocked by a lorry delivering cartons of dairy produce to a nearby grocery. He slipped through the narrow space between the lorry and the wall and made his way along the cracked concrete slabs with which the street was paved, well pleased with the way things were going. Back in Rome, the idea of forestalling his official mission with a bit of private enterprise had appeared at best a forlorn attempt to leave no stone unturned, at worst a foolhardy scheme which might well end in disaster and humiliation. But from his present perspective, Rome itself seemed an irrelevance, a city as distant and as foreign as Marseilles or Madrid. It was here, and only here, that Zen could hope to find the solution to his problems.

Not that he expected to 'crack' the Burolo case, of course. There was nothing to crack, anyway. The evidence against Renato Favelloni was overwhelming. The only question was whether he had done the job personally or hired it out to a professional. The key to the whole affair had been the video tapes and computer diskettes stored in the underground vault at Oscar Burolo's villa. Here Burolo had kept in electronic form all the information recording in meticulous detail the history of his construction company's irresistible rise. After the murders, this material had been impounded by the authorities, but when the investigating magistrate's staff came to examine them, they found that the computer data had been irretrievably corrupted, probably by exposure to a powerful magnetic field.

Insistent rumours began to circulate to the effect that the discs had been in perfect condition when they were seized by the Carabinieri, and these were strengthened about a month later when a leading news magazine published what purported to be a transcription of part of Burolo's records. The material concerned a contract agreed in 1979 for the construction of a new prison near Latina, a creation of the Fascist era on the Lazio coast, popularly known as 'Latrina'. Burolo Construction had undercut the estimated minimum tender for the project by almost 60 per cent. Their bid was duly accepted, despite the fact that the plan which accompanied it was vague in some places and full of inaccuracies in others.

No sooner had work begun than the site proved to be marshy and totally unsuitable for the type of construction envisaged. Burolo Construction promptly applied to the Ministry of Public Works for the first of a series of revised budgets which eventually pushed the cost of the prison from the 4,000 million lire specified in the original contract to over 36,000 million. This much was public knowledge. What the news magazine's article showed was how it had been done.

Although the article did not name the politician referred to in Burolo's electronic notes as 'l'onorevole', it left little doubt in the reader's mind that he was a leading figure in one of the smaller parties making up the governing coalition, who had been Minister of Public Works at the time the prison contract was agreed. According to his notes, Oscar Burolo had paid Renato Favelloni 350 million lire to ensure that Burolo Construction would get the contract. A comment which some claimed to find typical of Oscar's sardonic style noted that this handout exceeded the normal rate, which apparently varied between 6 and 8 per cent of the contract fee. The records also listed the dates and places on which Oscar had contacted Favelloni, and one on which he had met l'onorevole himself.

No sooner has this article appeared than the journalists responsible were summoned to the law courts in Nuoro and directed to disclose where they had obtained the information. On refusing, they were promptly jailed for culpable reticence. But that wasn't the end of the affair, for the following issue of the magazine contained an interview with Oscar's son. Enzo Burolo not only substantiated the claims made in the original article, but advanced new and even more damaging allegations. In particular, he claimed that six months prior to the killings his father had paid 70 million lire to obtain the contract for a new generating station for ENEL, the electricity board. Despite this exorbitant backhander, Burolo Construction did not get the contract.

According to Enzo, Oscar Burolo was so infuriated that he vowed to stop paying kickbacks altogether. From that point on, his company's fortunes went into a nosedive. In a desperate attempt to break the system, Oscar had leagued together with other construction firms to form a ring that tendered for contracts at realistic prices, but in each case the bidding was declared invalid on some technicality and the contract subsequently awarded to a company outside the ring.

Burolo Construction soon found itself on the verge of bankruptcy, but when Oscar applied to the banks for a line of credit he discovered that he was no longer a favoured client. His letters were mislaid, his calls not returned, the people he had plied with gifts and favours were permanently unavailable. Furious and desperate, Oscar had played his last card, contacting Renato Favelloni to demand the protection of *l'onorevole* himself. If this was not forthcoming, he warned Favelloni, he would reveal the full extent of their collaboration, including detailed accounts of the payoffs over the Latina prison job and a video tape showing Favelloni himself in an unguarded moment discussing his relationship with various men of power, *l'onorevole* included. Discussions and negotiations had continued throughout the summer, but according to Enzo this had been a mere delaying tactic which his father's enemies used to gain time in which to prepare their definitive response, which duly came on that fateful day in August, just hours after Renato Favelloni had left the Villa Burolo.

From that moment on, the case against Favelloni developed an irresistible momentum. True, there were still those who raised doubts. For example, if the destruction of Burolo's records had been as vital to the success of the conspiracy as the murder of Oscar himself, how was it that the magazine had been able to obtain an uncorrupted copy of one of the most incriminating of the discs? Even more to the point, why did the killer use a weapon as noisy as a shotgun if he needed time to destroy the records and make good his escape? But these questions were soon answered. The magazine's information, it was suggested, came not from the original disc but from a copy which the wily Burolo had deposited elsewhere, to be made public in the event of his death. As for the noise factor, there was nothing to show that the discs and videos had not been erased before the killings. Indeed, the metallic crash reproduced on the video recording seemed to strengthen this hypothesis. As for the weapon, this had presumably been chosen with a view to making the crime appear a savage act of casual violence. In short, such details appeared niggling attempts to undermine the case against Renato Favelloni and his masters at Palazzo Sisti, a case which now appeared overwhelming.

Luckily for Zen, the case itself was only peripherally his concern. There was no way he could realistically hope to get Favelloni off the hook. His aim was simply to avoid making powerful and dangerous enemies at Palazzo Sisti, and the best way to do this seemed to be to take a leaf out of Vincenzo Fabri's book. In other words, he had to make it look as if he had done his crooked best to frame Padedda, but that his best just hadn't been good enough. This wasn't as easy as it sounded. The thing had to be handled very carefully indeed if he was to avoid sending an innocent man to prison and yet convince Palazzo Sisti that he was not a disloyal employee to be ruthlessly disposed of but, like Fabri, a well-meaning sympathizer who was unfortunately not up to the demands of the job. In Rome his prospects of achieving this had appeared extremely dubious, but he was now beginning to feel that he could bring it off. The tide had turned with the arrest of Giuliano Acciari and – yes, why not admit it? – with that lunch with Tania and the embrace with which it had concluded. A fatalist at heart, Zen had learnt from bitter experience that when things weren't going his way there was no point in trying to force them to do so. Now that they were, it would be equally foolish not to take advantage of the situation.

He strolled along the street, glancing into shop windows and along the dark alleys that opened off to either side, scanning the features and gestures of the people he met. He felt that he was beginning to get the feel of the place, to sense the possibilities it offered.

Then he saw – or seemed to see – something that brought all his confident reasoning crashing down around him. In an alleyway to the left of the main street, a cul-de-sac filled with plastic rubbish sacks, a few empty oil drums and some building debris, stood a figure holding what looked like a gun.

A moment later it was gone, and a moment after that Zen found himself questioning whether it had ever existed. Don't be absurd, he told himself as he stepped into the alley, determined to dispel this mirage created by his own overheated imagination. The man who had broken into his house in Rome was safely under arrest, and even if Spadola had taken up his vendetta in person, how could he have tracked his quarry down so quickly? Zen had had every reason to take the greatest care when collecting the Mercedes and driving it to Civitaveccia. He wasn't thinking of Spadola so much as Vincenzo Fabri and the people at Palazzo Sisti. But he hadn't been followed, he was sure of that.

The alley narrowed to a crevice between the buildings on each side, barely wide enough for one person to pass. As his eyes adjusted to the gloom, Zen saw that it continued for some distance, dipping steeply, and then turned sharply left, presumably leading to a street below. There was no sign that anyone had been there recently.

When he heard the footsteps behind him, closing off his escape, he whirled around. For a moment everything seemed to be repeating itself in mirror-image: once again he was faced with a figure holding a gun. But this time the weapon was a stubby submachine-gun, the man was wearing battledress, and there was no doubt about the reality of the experience At the end of the alley, in the street, stood a blue jeep marked 'Carabinieri'.

'Papers!' the man barked.

Zen reached automatically for his wallet. Then his hand dropped again.

'They took them at the hotel,' he explained, accentuating his northern intonation slightly.

The Carabiniere looked him up and down. 'This isn't the way to the hotel.'

'I know. I was just curious. I'm from Switzerland, you see. By us the towns are more rational built, without these so interesting and picturesque aspects.'

You're overdoing it, he told himself. But the Carabiniere appeared to relax slightly.

'Tourist?' he nodded.

Zen ran through his well-rehearsed spiel, taking care to mention Angelo Confalone several times. The Carabiniere's expression gradually shifted from suspicion to a slightly patronizing complacency. Finally he ushered Zen back to the street.

'All the same,' he said as they reached the jeep, 'it's maybe better not to go exploring too much. There was a case last spring, a couple of German tourists in a camper found shot through the head. They must have stumbled on something they weren't supposed to see. It can happen to anyone, round here. All you need is to be in the wrong place at the wrong time.'

The jeep roared away.

I thought their deaths would change everything, but nothing changed. Night after night I returned, as though next time the sentence might be revoked, the dream broken. In vain. Even here, where the darkness is entire, I knew I was only on parole. Nothing would ever change that. I was banished, exiled for life into this world of light which divides and pierces, driving its aching distances into us.

Perhaps I had not done enough, I thought. Perhaps a further offering was required, another death. But whose? I lost myself in futile speculations. There is a power that punishes us, that much seemed clear. Its influence extends everywhere, pervasive and mysterious, but can it also be influenced? Since we are punished, we must have offended. Can that offence be redeemed? And so on, endlessly, round and round, dizzying myself in the search for some flaw in the walls that shut me in, that shut me out.

A good butcher doesn't stain the meat, my father used to say, though everything else was stained, clothes and skin and face, as he wrestled the animal to the ground and stuck the long knife into its throat, panting, drenched in blood from head to toe, the pig still twitching. Yet when he strung it up and peeled away the skin, the meat was unblemished. That's all I need be, I thought. A good butcher, calm, patient and indifferent. All I lacked was the chosen victim.

Then the policeman came.

Saturday, 20.10–22.25

By eight o'clock that evening, Herr Reto Gurtner was in a philosophical mood. Aurelio Zen, on the other hand, was drunk and lonely.

The night was heavy and close, with occasional rumbles of thunder. The bar was crowded with men of all ages, talking, smoking, drinking, playing cards. Apart from the occasional oblique glance, they ignored the stranger sitting at a table near the back of the room. But his presence disturbed them, no question about that. They would much rather he had not been there. In an earlier, rougher era they would have seen him off the premises and out of the village. That was no longer possible, and so, reflected the philosophical Gurtner, they were willing him into non-existence, freezing him out, closing the circle against him.

Despite evident differences in age, education and income, all the men were dressed in very similar clothes: sturdy, drab and functional. In Rome it was the clothes you noticed first these days, not the mass-produced figures whose purpose seemed to be to display them to advantage. But here in this dingy backward Sardinian bar it was still the people that mattered. We've thrown out the baby with the bathwater, reflected the philosophical Gurtner. Eradicating poverty and prejudice, we've eradicated something else too, something as rare as any of the threatened species the ecologists make so much fuss about, and just as impossible to replace once it has become extinct.

Bullshit, Aurelio Zen exclaimed angrily, pouring himself another glass of *vernaccia* from the carafe he had ordered. The storm-laden atmosphere, the distasteful nature of his business, his sense of total isolation, the fact that he was missing Tania badly, all these had combined to put him in a sour and irrational mood. This priggish, patronizing Zuricher was the last straw. Who did he think he was, coming over here and going on as though poverty was something romantic and valuable? Only a nation as crassly and smugly materialistic as the Swiss could afford to indulge in that sort of sentimentality.

He gulped the tawny wine that clung to the sides of the glass like spirits. It was tasting better all the time. Once again he thought of phoning Tania, and once again he rejected the idea. The more he lovingly recalled, detail by detail, what had happened that lunchtime, the more unlikely it appeared. He must surely have imagined the light in her eyes, the lift in her voice. The facts were not in dispute, it was a question of how you interpreted them. It was the same with the Burolo case. It was the same with *everything*.

Zen peered intently at the tabletop, which swam in and out of focus in a fascinating way. For a moment he seemed to have caught a glimpse of a great truth, a unified field theory of human existence, a simple basic formula that explained everything.

This wine is very strong, Reto Gurtner explained in his slightly pedantic accent. You have drunk a lot of it on an empty stomach. It has gone to your head. The thing to do now is to get something to eat.

Well, it was easy to say that! Hadn't he been waiting all this time for some sign of life in the restaurant area? It was now nearly a quarter past eight, and the lights were still dimmed and the curtain drawn. What time did they eat here, for God's sake?

Once again the thunder growled distantly, reminding Zen of the jet fighter which had startled him at the villa. There had been no hint of a storm then. On the contrary, the sky was free from any suspicion of cloud, a perfect dome of pale bleached blue from which the winter sun shone brilliantly yet without ferocity, a tyrant mellowed by age. The route to the villa lay along the same road by which he had arrived, but in this direction it looked quite different. Instead of a forbidding wall of mountains closing off the view, the land swept down and away, rippling over hillocks and outcrops, reaching down to the sea, a shimmering inconclusive extension of the panorama like the row of dots after an incomplete sentence. The predominant colours were reddish ochre and olive green, mingled together like the ingredients of a sauce, retaining their individuality yet also creating something new. In all that vast landscape there was no sign of man's presence, except for a distant plume of smoke from the papermill near the harbour where he had disembarked that morning. The only eyesore was a large patch of greenery off to the left, on the flanks of the mountain range. Its almost fluorescent shade reminded Zen of the unsuccessful colour postcards of his youth. Presumably it was a forest, but how did any forest rooted in that grudging soil come to glow in that hysterical way?

The road looped down to the main road leading up over the mountains towards Nuoro, the provincial capital where Renato Favelloni now languished in judicial custody. According to the map, the unsurfaced track opposite petered out after a short distance at an isolated station on the metre-gauge railway. Zen turned right, then after a few kilometres forked left on to a road badly in need of repair which ran across the lower slopes of the valley, crossing the railway line, before climbing the other side to join the main coastal highway.

Some distance before the junction, a high wire-mesh fence came down from the ridge to Zen's left to run alongside the road. At regular intervals, large signs warned 'Private Property – Keep Out – Electrified Fencing – Beware of the Lions'. The landscape was bare and windswept, a desolate chaos of rock, scrub and stunted trees. After some time a surfaced driveway opened off the road to the left, leading to a gate of solid steel set in the wire-mesh fence.

Even before the Mercedes had come to a complete halt, the gate started to swing open. Zen pressed his foot down on the accelerator and the car, still in third gear, promptly stalled. Managing to restart it at the third attempt, he drove through the barrier, only to find his way blocked by a second gate, identical to the first, which had meanwhile closed behind him, trapping the car between the wire-mesh fencing and a parallel inner perimeter of razor-barbed wire. Remote-control cameras mounted on the inner gateposts scanned the Mercedes with impersonal curiosity. After about thirty seconds the inner gate swung silently open, admitting Zen to the late Oscar Burolo's private domain.

The narrow strip of tarmac wound lazily up the hillside. After about fifty metres, Zen spotted the line of stumpy metal posts planted at irregular intervals, depending on the contours of the land, which marked the villa's third and most sophisticated defence of all: a phase-seeking microwave fence, invisible, intangible, impossible to cross undetected. Within the triply-defended perimeter, the whole property was protected by heat-seeking infra-red detectors, a move-alarm TV system and microwave radar. All the experts were agreed that security at the Villa Burolo was, if anything, excessive. It just hadn't been sufficient.

Oscar's private road continued to climb steadily upwards,

smashing its way through ancient stretches of dry-stone walling that were almost indistinguishable from outbreaks of the rock that was never far from the surface, loose boulders of all sizes lying scattered about like some kind of crop, but in fact nothing grew there except a low scrub of juniper, privet, laurel, heather, rosemary and gorse, a prickly stubble as tough and enduring as the rocks themselves.

Finally the land levelled out briefly, then fell away more steeply to a hollow where the house appeared, sheltered from the bitter northerly winds. From this angle, the Villa Burolo seemed a completely modern creation. The south and east sides of the original farmhouse were concealed by new wings containing the guest suites, kitchen, scullery, laundry room, garage and service accommodation. To the right, in a quarry-like area scooped out of the hillside, was the helicopter landing pad and a steel mast housing the radio beacon for night landings and aerials for Oscar's extensive communications equipment.

Zen parked the Mercedes and walked over to the main entrance, surmounted by a pointed arch of vaguely Moorish appearance. There was no bell or knocker in sight, when the door opened at his approach and the caretaker appeared, Zen realized that it had been absurd to expect one. No one dropped in unexpectedly at the Villa Burolo, not when their every movement from the entrance gate to the front door was being monitored by four independent electronic surveillance systems.

As soon as he set eyes on Alfonso Bini, Zen knew why the caretaker had been ruled out as a suspect virtually from the start. Bini was one of those men so neutered by a lifetime of service that it was difficult to imagine them being able to tie their own shoe-laces unless instructed to do so. He greeted the distinguished foreign visitor with pallid correctness. Yes, Dottor Confalone had explained the situation. Yes, he would be glad to show Signor Gurtner around.

No doubt on Confalone's instructions, the tour started with the new wing, in order to dispel any idea that the property was in any way primitive or rustic. Zen patiently endured an interminable exhibition of modern conveniences, ranging from *en suite* jacuzzis and a fully equipped gymnasium to a kitchen that would have done credit to a three-star hotel. In the laundry room, a frightened-looking woman was folding towels. Zen guessed that this was the caretaker's wife, although Bini ignored her as though she was just another of the appliances stacked in neatly forbidding ranks along the wall. The only aspect of all this which was of any interest to Zen was a small room packed with video monitors and banks of switches.

'Security?' he queried.

Bini nodded and pointed to a row of red switches near the door, labelled with the names of the various alarm systems. The only ones switched on were the field sensors on the inner perimeter fence and the microwave radar.

'So someone has to be here all the time?' Zen asked.

Bini made a negative tutting sound.

'Only if you want to check the screens. If any of the systems picks up anything irregular, an alarm goes off.'

He threw a switch marked 'Test'. A chorus of electronic shrieks rose from every part of the building.

'Very impressive,' murmured Zen. 'My client certainly need have no worries about anyone breaking in.'

The caretaker said nothing. His face was set so hard it looked as though it might crack.

Once the villa's luxury credentials had been established, Zen was taken into the older part of the house to appreciate its aesthetic qualities. A short passageway cut through the thick outer walls of the original farm brought them into a large lounge furnished with leather armchairs, inlaid hardwood tables, Afghan carpets and bookcases full of antique bindings. The head of a disgruntled-looking wild boar emerged from the stonework above an enormous open fireplace as though the animal had charged through the wall and got stuck.

Zen walked over to a carved rosewood gun-rack near the door and inspected the shotguns on display, including an early Beretta and a fine Purdy.

'Do they go with the property?' he asked.

The caretaker shrugged.

'There seems to be one missing,' Zen pursued, indicating the empty slot.

Bini turned pointedly away towards the sliding doors opening on to the terrace.

'What's this?' Zen called after him, pointing to a wooden hatch in the flooring.

'The cellar,' replied the caretaker tonelessly.

'And next door?'

Bini pretended not to hear. Ignoring him, Zen walked through the doorway into the dining room of the villa. In the lounge, the stones of the original walls had been left uncovered as a design feature, but here they had been plastered and painted white. Zen looked around the room that was horribly familiar to him from the video. It was a shock, somehow, to find the walls not splashed and flecked and streaked with blood, but pristine and spotless. A shuffling in the doorway behind him announced the caretaker's presence.

'Fresh paint?' Zen queried, sniffing the air.

Just for a moment, something stirred into life in the old man's passive gaze. Angelo Confalone would have briefed him carefully, of course. 'Say nothing about what happened! Don't mention Burolo's name! Just keep your mouth shut and with any luck you might keep your job.'

Bini had done his best to obey these instructions so far, but now the strain was beginning to show.

'Nice and clean,' Zen commented approvingly.

The caretaker's mouth cracked open in a ghastly grin. 'My wife, she cleans everything, every day . . .'

Zen nodded. He had read the investigators' reports on the couple. Giuseppina Bini was one of those elderly women who, having grown up when doctors were expensive and often ineffective, strove obsessively to keep the powers of sickness and death at bay by banishing their agents, dirt and dust, from every corner of the house. This had made it virtually certain that the dried spots of blood found on the dining-room floor and on the steps leading to the cellar must have been deposited by the lightly-wounded killer. In which case, thought Zen, he must have destroyed the discs and tapes *after* the murders, despite the horrendous risks involved in staying at the scene once the alarm had been raised and the police were on their way. It didn't make any sense, he told himself for the fiftieth time. If the object was to destroy both Burolo and his records, surely the killer would either have used a silenced weapon or eliminated Bini and his wife as well, thus giving himself ample time to erase Burolo's records before making good his escape. And if the discs and tapes had been erased after they were seized by the Carabinieri – the long arm of Palazzo Sisti would no doubt have been capable of this – then why did the killer make his way down to the cellar and ransack the shelves at all?

It made no sense, no sense at all, although Zen had a tantalizing feeling that the solution was in fact right under his nose, simple and obvious. But that was no concern of his in any case. His reason for visiting the villa had nothing to do with viewing the scene of the crime. Nevertheless, for the sake of appearances he asked Bini to show him the cellar before they went outside. The caretaker duly levered up a brass ring and lifted the hatch to reveal a set of worn stone steps leading down.

'It's not locked?' Zen asked.

Bini clicked a switch on the wall and a neon light flickered into life below.

'There are no locks here,' he said. 'If you keep your jewels in a safe, you don't need to lock the jewel case.'

The cellar was large, stretching the entire width of the original farm. Zen sniffed the air.

'Nice and fresh down here.'

The caretaker indicated a narrow fissure at floor level.

'The air comes in there. They used to cure cheeses and hams here in the old days. Even in the summer it stays cool.'

Zen nodded. This constant temperature was no doubt why Oscar had used the place as a storage vault. But now the twin neon bars illuminated an empty expanse of whitewashed walls and bare stone floor. There was nothing to show that this had once been the nerve-centre of an operation which had apparently succeeded in fulfilling the alchemist's dream of turning dross into gold.

Once they got above ground again, the caretaker led Zen out on to the terrace.

'The swimming-pool,' he announced.

Wild follies and outrageous whims die with the outsized ego that created them, and their corpses make depressing viewing. Even drained and boarded over, a swimming-pool is still a swimming-pool, but Oscar's designer beach was an all-or-nothing affair. Once the plug had been pulled and the machinery turned off, it stood revealed for what it was: a tacky, pretentious monstrosity. The transplanted sand was dirty and threadbare, the rocks showed their cement joints, and the mystery of those azure depths stood revealed as a coat of blue paint applied to the vast concrete pit where the body of some small animal lay drowned in a shrinking puddle of water.

'We can get everything going again,' Bini assured his visitor. 'It's all set up.'

But he sounded unconvinced. Even if some crazy foreigner did buy the place, nothing would ever be the same again. Villa Burolo was not a house, it was a performance. Now the star was dead it would always be a flop.

'Well, it certainly seems to be a very pleasant and impressive property,' Zen remarked with a suitably Swiss lack of enthusiasm. 'I'll just have a look around the grounds, on my own.'

Bini turned back into the house, clearly relieved that his ordeal was over.

When he had gone, Zen strolled slowly along the terrace, rounding the corner of the original farmhouse. Despite the encircling wire, there was no sense of being in a guarded enclosure, for the boundaries of the property had been cleverly situated so as to be invisible from the villa. The view was extensive, ranging from the sea, across the wide valley he had crossed in the Mercedes, to the mountain slopes where the village was just visible as an intrusive smudge.

When he reached the dining-room window, Zen looked round to ensure that he was unobserved, then crouched down to examine the slight discolouration of the flagstones marking the spot where Rita Burolo had bled to death. Another thing that made no sense, he thought. None of the investigators had commented on the remarkable fact that the murderer had made no attempt to find out whether Signora Burolo was dead or not. As it happened, she had gone into an irreversible coma by the time she was found, but how was the killer to know that? A few minutes either way, a stronger constitution or a lesser loss of blood, and the Burolo case would have been solved before it began.

Nor was this the only instance in which the killer had displayed a most unprofessional carelessness. For although Oscar Burolo had concealed video equipment about the villa to tape the compromising material he stored in the vault, he camouflaged these clandestine operations behind a very public obsession with recording poolside frolics and informal dinner parties. Thus no attempt had been made to disguise the large video camera mounted on its tripod in the corner of the dining room. In the event, no glimpse of the murderer had been recorded on the tape, but how could he have been absolutely sure of that? And if there was even the slightest possibility that some damning clue had been captured by the camera, why had he made no attempt to remove or destroy the tape?

Once again, Zen felt his reason swamped by the sense of something grossly abnormal about the Burolo case. What did this almost supernatural indifference indicate, if not the killer's knowledge that he was *invulnerable*? There was no need for him to take precautions. The efforts of the police and judiciary were as vain as Oscar Burolo's expensive security measures. The murderer could not be caught any more than he could be stopped.

He walked back along the terrace to the west face of the villa. Beyond the sad ruins of the pool, the land sloped steeply upwards towards the lurid forest he had noticed earlier. The trees were conifers of some kind, packed together in a tight, orderly mass that looked like a re-afforestation project. Beyond them lay the main mountain range, a mass of shattered granite briefly interrupted by a smooth grey wall, presumably a dam. Zen continued along the terrace to the wall which concealed the service block and helicopter pad, a half-hearted imitation of the traditional pasture enclosures, higher and with the stones cemented together. On the other side was a neat kitchen garden with a system of channels to carry water to the growing vegetables from the hosepipe connected to an outside tap. Zen took a path leading uphill towards a group of low concrete huts about fifty metres away from the house and partially concealed by a row of cherry trees.

As he passed the line of trees, a low growl made the air vibrate with a melancholy resonance that brought Zen out in goose-flesh. There were three huts, a small one and two large structures which backed on to an enclosure of heavy-duty mesh fencing. Both of these had metal doors mounted on runners. One of them was slightly open, and it was from here that the noise had come.

The inside of the hut was in complete darkness. A hot, smothering, acrid odour filled the air. Something rustled restlessly in the further reaches of the dark. As Zen's eyes gradually adjusted, he made out a figure bending over a heap of some sort on the ground. The resonant vibration thrilled the air again, like a giant breathing stertorously in a drunken slumber. The bending figure suddenly whirled round, as though caught in some guilty act.

'Who are you?'

Zen advanced a step or two into the hut.

'Stay there!'

The man walked towards him with swift, light strides. He was short and stocky, with wiry black hair and the face of a pugnacious gnome.

'What are you doing?'

'Looking over the house.'

'This is not the house.'

Zen switched on his fatuous Swiss smile. 'Looking over the property, I should have said.'

The man was staring at him with an air of deep suspicion.

'Who are you?' he repeated.

Zen held out his hand, which was ignored.

'Reto Gurtner.'

'You're Italian?'

'Swiss.'

The low growl sounded out again. Inside the hut, its weight of emotion seemed even greater, an expression of grief and loss that was almost unbearable.

'What was that noise?' Zen asked.

The man continued to eye him with open hostility, as though trying to stare him out.

'A lion,' he said at last.

'Ah, a lion.'

Zen's tone remained politely conversational, as though lions were an amenity without which no home was complete.

'Where in Switzerland?' the man demanded.

He was wearing jeans and a blue tee-shirt. A large hunting knife in a leather sheath was attached to his belt. His bare arms were hairy and muscular. A long white scar ran in a straight line from just below his right elbow to the wrist.

'From Zurich,' Zen replied.

'You want to buy the house?'

'Not personally. I am here on behalf of a client.'

The words of the young man at Palazzo Sisti echoed in his mind. *'You will visit the scene of the crime, interview witnesses, interrogate suspects. In the course of your investigations you will discover concrete evidence demolishing Furio Padedda's alibi and linking him to the murder of Oscar Burolo. All this will take no more than a few days at the most.'*

Something inconceivably huge and fast passed overhead, blocking out the light for an instant like a rapid eclipse of the sun. An instant later there was an earth-shattering noise, as if a tall stone column had collapsed on top of the hut. Even after the moment had passed, the rumbles and echoes continued to reverberate in the walls and ground for several seconds.

The lion-keeper was on his knees at the far end of the hut, bent over the heap on the ground. Zen started towards him, his shoes rustling on the straw underfoot.

'Stay there!' the man shouted.

Zen stopped. He looked around the hot, still, fetid gloom of the hut. Two pitchforks, some large plastic buckets, a shovel and lengths of rope and chain were strewn about the floor in disorder. A coiled whip and a pump-action shotgun hung from nails hammered into the roof supports.

'What was that?' Zen called.

The man got to his feet.

'The air force. They come here to practise flying low over the mountains. When Signor Burolo was . . .'

He broke off.

'Yes?' Zen prompted.

'They didn't bother us then.'

I bet they didn't, thought Zen. A few phone calls and a hefty contribution to the officers' mess fund would have seen to that.

The low melancholy growl was repeated once more, a feeble echo of the jet's brief uproar, like a child feebly imitating a word it does not understand.

'It does not sound happy, the lion,' Zen observed.

'It is dying.'

'Of what?'

'Of old age.'

'The planes disturb it?'

'Strangers too.'

The man's tone was uncompromising. Zen pointed to the scar on his forearm.

'But it is still dangerous, I see.'

The man brushed past him towards the door.

'A very neat job, though,' Zen commented, following him out. 'More like a knife or a bullet than claws.'

'You know a lot about lions?' the keeper demanded sarcastically, as they emerged into the brilliant sunlight and pure air.

'Only what I read in the papers.'

The man walked over to the smaller hut and brought out a plastic bucket filled with a bloody mixture of hearts, lungs and intestines.

'I notice that you keep a shotgun in there,' Zen pursued, 'so I assume there is reason for fear.'

The man regarded him with blank eyes.

'There is always reason for fear when you are dealing with creatures to whom killing comes naturally.'

Seeing him standing there in open defiance, the bucket of guts in his hand, ready to feed the great beasts that he alone could manage, it was easy to see Furio Padedda's attraction for a certain type of woman. It was to these concrete huts that Rita Burolo had come to disport herself with the lion-keeper, unaware that their antics were being recorded by the infra-red video equipment her husband had rigged up under the roof.

How had Oscar felt, viewing those tapes which – according to gloating sources in the investigating magistrate's office – made hard-core porno videos look tame by comparison? Had his motive for making them been simple voyeurism, or was he intending to black-mail his wife? Was she independently wealthy? Had he hoped in this way to stave off bankruptcy until his threats forced l'onorevole to intervene in his favour? Supposing he had mentioned the existence of the tapes to her, and she had passed on the information to her lover. To a proud and fiery Sardinian, the fact that his amorous exploits had been recorded for posterity might well have seemed a sufficient justification for murder. Or rather, Zen realized, as he sat moodily sipping his *vernaccia*, it could easily be made to appear that it had. Which was all that concerned him, after all.

The bar had emptied appreciably as the men drifted home to eat the meals their wives and mothers had shopped for that morning. Zen stared blearily at his watch, eventually deciphering the time as twenty to nine. He pushed his chair back, rose unsteadily and walked over to the counter, where the burly proprietor was rinsing glasses.

'When can I get something to eat?'

Reto Gurtner would have phrased the question more politely, but he had stayed behind at the table.

'Tomorrow,' the proprietor replied without looking up from his work.

'How do you mean, tomorrow?'

'The restaurant's only open for Sunday lunch out of season.'

'You didn't tell me that!'

'You didn't ask.'

Zen turned away with a muttered obscenity.

'There's a pizzeria down the street,' the proprietor added grudgingly.

Zen barged through the glass doors of the hotel. The piazza was deserted and silent. As he passed the Mercedes, Zen patted it like a faithful, friendly pet, a reassuring presence in this alien place. A roll of thunder sounded out, closer yet still quiet, a massively restrained gesture.

In the corner of the piazza stood the village's only public phone box, a high-tech glass booth perched there as if it had just landed from outer space. Zen eyed it wistfully, but the risk was just too great. Tania would have had time to think things over by now. Supposing she was off-hand or indifferent, a cold compensation for her excessive warmth the day before? He would have to deal with that eventually, of course, but not now, not here, with all the other problems he had.

The village was as still and dead as a ghost town. Zen shambled along, looking for the pizzeria. All of a sudden he stopped in his tracks, then whirled around wildly, scanning the empty street behind him. No one. What had it been? A noise? Or just drunken fancy? 'They must have stumbled on something they weren't supposed to see,' the Carabiniere had said of the murdered couple in the camper. 'It can happen to anyone, round here. All you need is to be in the wrong place at the wrong time.'

As the alcoholic mists in Zen's mind cleared for a moment, he had an image of a child scurrying along an alleyway running parallel to the main street, appearing at intervals in the dark passages with steps leading up. A child playing hide-and-seek in the darkness. But had he imagined it, or had he really caught sight of something out of the corner of his eye, on the extreme periphery of vision, something seen but not registered until now?

He shook his head sharply, as though to empty it of all this nonsense. Then set off again, a little more hurriedly now.

The pizzeria was just around the corner where the street curved downhill, among the new blocks on the outskirts of the village. The exterior was grimly basic – reinforced concrete framework, bare brickwork infill, adhesive plastic letters spelling *'Pizza Tavola Calda'* on the window – but inside the place was bright, brash and cheerful, decorated with traditional masks, dolls, straw baskets and woven and embroidered hangings. To Zen's astonishment, the young man in charge even welcomed him warmly. Things were definitely looking up.

After a generous *antipasto* of local air-cured ham and salami, a large pizza and most of a flask of red wine, they looked even better. Zen lit a cigarette and looked around at the group of teenagers huddled conspiratorially in the corner, the tabletop laden with empty soft-drink bottles. If only he had had someone to talk to, it would have been perfect. As it was, his only source of entertainment was the label of the bottled mineral water he had ordered. This consisted of an assurance by a professor at Cagliari University that the contents were free of microbacteriological impurities, together with an encomium on its virtues that seemed to imply that in sufficient quantities it would cure everything but old age. Zen studied the chemical analysis, which listed among other things the *abbassamento crioscopico, concentrazione osmotica* and *conducibilità elettrica specifica a 18°C.* Each litre contained 0.00009 grams of barium. Was this a good thing or a bad thing?

The door of the pizzeria opened to admit the half-witted midget he had seen outside Confalone's office that morning. She was dripping wet, and Zen realized suddenly that the hushing sound he had been hearing for some time now, like static on a radio programme, was caused by a downpour of rain. The next instant a deafening peal of thunder rang out, seemingly right overhead. One of the teenagers shrieked in mock terror, the others giggled nervously. The beggar woman limped theatrically over to Zen's table and demanded money.

'I gave you something this morning,' Reto Gurtner replied in a tone of distaste.

The owner shouted angrily in Sardinian and the woman turned away with a face as blank as the wooden carnival masks hanging on the wall and went to sit on a chair near the door, looking out at the torrential rain. She must know a thing or two, thought Zen, wandering about from place to place, privileged by madness.

When the owner came to clear Zen's table, he apologized for the fact that he'd been bothered.

'I try to keep her out of here, but what can you do? She's got nowhere to go.'

'Homeless?'

The man shrugged.

'She's got a brother, but she won't live with him. Claims he's an impostor. She sleeps rough, in caves and shepherd's huts, even on the street. She's harmless, but quite mad. Not that it's surprising, after what happened to her.'

He made no effort to lower his voice, although the woman was sitting near by, perched on her chair like a large doll. Zen glanced at her, but she was still staring rigidly at the door.

'It's all right,' the owner explained. 'She doesn't understand Italian, only dialect.'

Zen eagerly seized this opportunity to talk.

'What happened to her?'

The young man shook his head and sighed.

'I wasn't around then, but people say she just disappeared one day, years ago. She was about fifteen at the time. The family said she'd gone to stay with relatives who'd emigrated to Tuscany. Then a few years ago her parents died in . . . in an accident. The son was away doing his military service at the time. When the police went to the house they found Elia shut up in the cellar like an animal, almost blind, covered in filth and half crazy.'

Reto Gurtner looked suitably horrified by this example of Mediterranean barbarism.

'But why?'

The young man sighed.

'Now, you understand, this village is just like anywhere else. Televisions, pop music, motorbikes.'

He waved at the teenagers in the corner.

'The young people stay out till all hours, even the girls. They do what they like. Twenty years ago it was different. People say that Elia was seeing a man from a nearby farm. Perhaps she stayed out too late one summer night, and . . .'

He broke off as the door banged open and three men walked in. The beggar woman sprang to her feet, staring at them like a wild animal about to pounce or flee. One of the men spat a few words of dialect at her. She flinched as though he had struck her, then ran out. The rain had stopped as suddenly as it had begun.

The three newcomers were wearing the local heavyweight gear, durable, anonymous and mass-produced, but there was nothing faceless or conventional about their behaviour. They took over the pizzeria as though it were the venue for a party being given in their honour. The leader, who had obviously had quite a lot to drink already, threw his weight around in a way that seemed almost offensively familiar, going behind the counter and sampling the various plates of toppings, talking continuously in a loud raucous voice. Zen could understand nothing of what was being said, but although the owner kept smiling and responded in the required jocular fashion, it seemed an effort, and Zen thought he would have been happier if the men had gone away.

Having done the rounds, chaffed the owner and his wife and grabbed a plate of olives and salami and a litre of wine, the trio seated themselves at the table next to Zen's. Once their initial high spirits had subsided, their mood rapidly turned sombre, as though all three had immense grievances which could never be redressed. The leader in particular not only looked fiercely malcontent, but was scowling at Zen as though he was the origin of all his troubles. His bristly jet-black beard, curly hair and enormous hook nose gave him a Middle Eastern appearance, like a throwback to the island's Phoenician past. He reminded Zen of someone he had seen earlier, although he couldn't think who. From time to time, between gulped half glassfuls of wine, the man muttered in dialect to his companions, bitter interjections which received no reply.

Zen began to feel alarmed. The man was clearly drunk, his mood explosive and unpredictable, and he was staring at him more and more directly, as though beating up this stranger might be just what was needed to make his evening. To defuse the situation before it got out of hand, Zen leaned over to the three men.

'Excuse me,' he said in his best Reto Gurtner manner. 'Could you tell me if there's a garage round here?'

'A garage?' the man replied after a momentary hesitation. 'For what?'

Zen explained that his car was making a strange knocking noise and he was worried that it might break down.

'What kind of car?'

'A Mercedes.'

After a brief discussion in dialect with his companions, the man replied that Vasco did repairs locally, but he wouldn't have the parts for a Mercedes. Otherwise there was a mechanic in Lanusei, but he was closed tomorrow, it being Sunday.

'You're on holiday?' he asked.

As Zen recited his usual explanation of who he was and what he was doing, the man's expression gradually changed from hostility to sympathetic interest. After a few minutes he invited Zen to join them at their table. Zen hesitated, but only for a fraction of a moment. This was an invitation which he felt it would be decidedly unwise to refuse.

Three quarters of an hour and another flask of wine later, he was being treated almost like an old friend. The hook-nosed man, who introduced himself as Turiddu, was clearly delighted to have a fresh audience for his long and rather rambling monologues. His companions said hardly a word. Turiddu talked and Zen listened, occasionally throwing in a polite question with an air of wide-eyed and disinterested fascination with all things Sardinian. Turiddu's grievances, it turned out, were global rather than personal. Everything was wrong, everything was bad and getting worse. The country, by which he appeared to mean that particular part of the Oliastra, was in a total mess. It was a disaster. The government in Rome poured in money, but it was all going to waste, leaking away through the sieve-like conduits of the development agencies, provincial agricultural inspectorates, the irrigation consortia and land-reclamation bodies.

'In the old days the landowner, he arranged everything, decided everything. You couldn't fart without his permission, but at least there was only one of him. Now we've got these new bosses instead, these pen-pushers in the regional government, hundreds and hundreds of them! And what do they do? Just like the landowner, they look after themselves!'

Turiddu broke off briefly to gulp some more wine and accept one of Zen's cigarettes.

'And when they do finally get round to doing something, it's even worse! The old owners, they understood the land. It belonged to them, so they made damn sure it was looked after, even though we had to break our bums doing the work. But these bureaucrats, what do they know? All they do is sit in some office down in Calgliari and look at maps all day!'

Turiddu's companions sat listening to this harangue with indulgent and slightly embarrassed smiles, as though what he was saying was true enough but it was pointless and rather demeaning to mention it, particularly to a stranger.

'There's a lake up there in the mountains,' Turiddu continued, striking a match casually on his thumbnail. 'A river used to flow down towards the valley, where it disappeared underground into the caves. The rock down here is too soft, the water runs through it. So what did those bastards in Cagliari do? They looked at their maps, saw this river that seemed to go nowhere, and they said, "Let's dam the lake, so instead of all that water going to waste we can pipe it down to Oristano to grow crops."'

Turiddu broke off to shout something at the pizzeria owner in Sardinian. The young man came over with an unlabelled bottle and four new glasses.

'Be careful,' he warned Zen with humorous exaggeration, tapping the bottle. 'Dynamite!'

'Dynamite my arse,' Turiddu grumbled when he had gone. 'I've got stuff at home, the *real* stuff, makes this taste like water.'

He filled the four tumblers to the brim, spilling some on the tablecloth, and downed his at one gulp.

'Anyway, what those clever fuckers in Cagliari didn't realize was that all that water from the lake didn't just disappear. It was there, underground, if you knew where to look for it. All the farms round here were built over caves where the river ran underground. With that and a bit of fodder, you could keep cattle alive through the winter, then let them loose up in the mountains when spring came. But once that fucking dam was built, all the water – *our* water – went down the other side to those soft idle bastards on the west coast. As if they didn't have an easy enough life already! Oh, they paid us compensation, of course. A few lousy million lire to build a new house here in the village. And what are we supposed to do here? There's no work. The mountains take what little rain there is, the winter pasture isn't worth a shit. What's the matter? You're not drinking.'

Zen obediently gulped down the liquid in his glass as the Sardinian had done, and almost gagged. It was raw grappa, steely, unfiltered, virtually pure alcohol.

'Good,' he gasped. 'Strong.'

Turiddu shrugged.

'I've got some at home makes this taste like water.'

The door of the pizzeria swung open. Zen looked round and recognized Furio Padedda, who had just walked in with another man. Zen turned back to his new companions, glad of their company, their protection.

'Tell me, why is that bit of forest on the other side of the valley so green? It almost looks as though someone was watering it.'

Turiddu gave an explosive laugh that turned into a coughing fit.

'They are! We are, with our water!'

He refilled all the glasses with grappa.

'The dam they built, it was done on the cheap. Bunch of crooks from Naples. It leaks, not much but all the time. On the surface the soil is dry, but those trees have roots that go down twenty metres or more. Down there it's like a marsh. The trees grow like geese stuffed for market.'

Zen glanced round at Furio Padedda and his companion, who were sitting near the door, drinking beer. Despite his drunkenness, Turiddu had not missed Zen's interest in the newcomers.

'You know them?' he demanded with a contemptuous jerk of his thumb at the other table.

'One of them. We met today at the villa where he works.'

Turiddu regarded him with a stupified expression.

'That place? You're not thinking of buying it?'

Zen looked suitably discreet.

'My client will make the final decision. But it seems an attractive house.'

The three men glanced rapidly at each other, their looks dense with exchanged information, like deaf people communicating in sign language.

'Why, is there something wrong with it?'

Zen's expression remained as smooth as processed cheese. Turiddu struggled visibly with his thoughts for a moment.

'It used to belong to my family,' he announced finally. 'Before they took our water away.'

He stared drunkenly at Zen, daring him to disbelieve his story. Zen nodded thoughtfully. It might be true, but he doubted it. Turiddu was a bit of a fantasist, he guessed, a man with longings and ambitions that were too big for his small-town habitat but not quite big enough to give him the courage to leave.

The Sardinian laughed again. 'You saw the electric fences and the gates and all that? He spent a fortune on that place, to make it safe, the poor fool. And it's all useless!'

Zen frowned. 'Do you mean to say that the security system is defective in some way?'

But Turiddu did not pursue the matter. He was looking around with a vague expression, a cigarette which he had forgotten to light dangling from his lips.

'Just take my advice, my friend,' he said. 'Have nothing to do with that place. Terrible things have happened there, things you can't wash away with water, even if there was any. There are plenty of nice villas up north, on the coast, houses for rich foreigners. Down here is not the place for them. There are too many naughty boys. Like that one over there, for instance.'

He nodded towards Furio Padedda, who was just finishing his beer.

'Is he a friend of yours?' asked Zen.

Turiddu slapped the table so hard that the bottle nearly fell over.

'Him? He's no one's friend, not round here! He's a foreigner. He's got friends all right, up in the mountains.'

He lowered his voice to a sly whisper.

'They don't grow crops up there, you know. They don't grow anything, the lazy bastards. They just take whatever they want. Sheep, cattle. Sometimes people too. Then they get very rich very quick!'

One of his companions said something brief and forceful in Sardinian. Turiddu frowned but was silent.

A shadow fell across the table. Zen looked up to find Furio Padedda standing over him.

'Good evening, *Herr* Gurtner,' he said, stressing the foreign title.

'What the fuck do you want, Padedda?' growled Turiddu.

'I just wanted to greet our friend from Switzerland here. Been having a drink, have you? Several drinks, in fact.'

'None of your fucking business,' Turiddu told him.

'I was thinking of Herr Gurtner,' Padedda continued in an even tone. 'He should be careful. Our Sardinian grappa might be a little strong for him.'

He called his companion over.

'Let me introduce my friend Patrizio. Patrizio, Herr Reto Gurtner of Zurich.'

Patrizio held out his hand and said something incomprehensible. Zen smiled politely.

'I'm sorry, I don't understand dialect.'

Padedda's eyes narrowed.

'Not even your own?'

A silence like thick fog fell over the pizzeria. You could feel it, taste it, smell it, see it.

'Patrizio spent eight years in Switzerland working on the Saint Bernard tunnel,' Padedda explained. 'He speaks Swiss German fluently. Oddly enough, it seems that Herr Reto Gurtner does not.'

*I knew him at once. They think they're so clever, the others, but their clever-
ness is lost on me. It's a poison that doesn't take, a disease I'm immune to.
Their conjuring tricks are meant for them, the children of the light to whom
everything is what it seems, the way it looks. The policeman just provided
himself with false papers and a big car and – presto! – he was magically
transformed in his own eyes and theirs into a foreign businessman come to
buy property. They believe in property, they believe in documents and
papers, names and dates. How could they not believe in him? Living out a lie
themselves, how could they recognize his lies?*

*But I knew who he was the moment I set eyes on him. I knew why he had
come and why he wanted to see the house. I knew what lay behind his sly
questions and insinuating remarks, his prying and peeping.*

*I was very bold, I confronted him openly. He shied away, seeming not to
know me. The darkness showed its hand for an instant, like a brief eclipse of
the sun, and I read death in his eyes. I'd seen it before with the animals
Father killed. I knew what it meant.*

*Perhaps he too sensed that something was going on. Perhaps he even sus-
pected that his life was in danger. But how could he have had the slightest
idea who it was that represented that danger?*

Sunday, 07.00–11.20

Perhaps if the kidnap attempt had not occurred when he had been driving back from it, Oscar Burolo might have shown his appreciation to the local church by donating a set of real bells. It was the kind of showy gesture he was fond of, stage-managed to look like an impulsive act of generosity, although in fact he would have costed the whole thing down to the last lira and got a massive discount from the foundry in return for some building work using materials recycled from another contract. Nevertheless, the village church would have got its bells. As it was, it had to make do with a gramophone record of a carillon played through loudspeakers, and it was this that woke Aurelio Zen shortly before dawn the following morning. The gramophone record was very old, with a loud scratch which Zen's befuddled brain translated as high-velocity shots being fired at him by a marksman perched in the bell-tower. Luckily, by the time they reached his room the bullets had slowed down considerably, and in the end they just hovered in the air about his face, darting this way and that like dragonflies, a harmless nuisance.

As the recorded bells finally fell silent, Zen opened his eyes on a jumble of colours and blurred shapes, impossible to sort by size or distance. He waited patiently for things to start making sense, but when minutes went by and his surroundings still refused to snap into focus, he began to worry that he had done some permanent injury to his brain. He hauled himself upright in bed, slumping back against the wooden headboard.

Things improved somewhat. True, he still had a splitting headache and felt like he might throw up at any moment, but to his relief the objects in the room began – a little reluctantly, it seemed – to assume the shapes and relationships he vaguely remembered from the previous day. There was the large plywood wardrobe with the door that wouldn't close properly and the wire coat-hangers hanging like bats from a branch. There was the small table with its cumbersome ceramic lamp, and the three cheap ugly wooden chairs squatting like refugees awaiting bad news. From a ceiling the colour of spoiled milk

444

a long rusty chain supported a dim light, whose irregular thick glass bowl must have looked very futuristic in about 1963.

There was the washbasin, the rack for glasses below the mirror and the dud bulb above, the metal rubbish bin with its plastic liner, the barred window lying open into the room. He must have forgotten to close it when he went to bed. That was why the air seemed stiff with cold, and why the sound of the bells had wakened him. He didn't feel cold in bed, though, probably because he was still fully dressed apart from his shoes and jacket. He laboriously transferred his gaze to the floor, a chilly expanse of speckled black and white aggregate polished to a hard shine. There they were, the two shoes on their sides and the discarded jacket on its back above them, like the outline drawing of a murder victim.

He lay back, exhausted by this effort, trying to piece together the events of the previous evening. Quite apart from resulting in the worst hangover he had ever experienced, he knew that what had happened hadn't been good news. But what *had* happened?

He remembered arriving back at the hotel. The bar was empty except for the old man called Tommaso and a younger man playing the pinball machine in the corner. The proprietor called Zen over and handed him his identity card and a bill.

'The hotel's closing for repairs.'

'You didn't tell me when I checked in.'

'I'm telling you now.'

The pinball player had turned to watch them, and Zen recognized him. He even knew his name – Patrizio – although he had no recollection of how or where they had met. What had he been doing all evening?

Abandoning this intractable problem, Zen swung his feet down on to the icy floor and stood up. This was a mistake. Previously he had had to deal with the electrical storm in his head, a stomach badly corroded by the toxic waste swilling around inside it, limbs that twitched, joints that ached and a mouth that seemed to have been replaced by a plaster replica. The only good news, in fact, had been that the room wasn't spinning round and round like a fairground ride. That was why it had been a mistake standing up.

Washing, shaving, dressing and packing were so many stations of the cross for Aurelio Zen that morning. But it wasn't until he lit a cigarette in the mistaken belief that it might make him feel better, and found tucked inside the packet of Marlboros a book of matches whose cover read 'Pizzeria Il Nuraghe', that the merciful fog obscuring the events of the previous evening suddenly lifted.

He collapsed on one of the rickety wooden chairs, its feet scraping atrociously on the polished floor slabs. Zen didn't notice. He wasn't in his hotel room any longer. He was sitting at the table in the pizzeria, drunker than he had ever been in his life; horribly, monstrously, terminally drunk. Five men, three seated and two standing, were staring at him with expressions of pure, malignant hostility. The situation was totally out of control. Nothing he could say or do would have any effect whatsoever.

For a moment he thought that they might be going to assault him, but in the end Furio Padedda and his friend Patrizio had just turned away and walked out. Then the man called Turiddu threw some banknotes on the table and he and his companions left too, without a word.

Outside, the air was thick with scents brought out by the rain: creosote, wild thyme, wood smoke, urine, motor oil. To judge by the stillness of the street, it might have been the small hours. Then a motorcycle engine opened up the night like a crude tin-opener, all jagged, torn edges. The bike emerged from the shadows of an alley and moved slowly and menacingly towards Zen. By the volatile moonlight, he recognized the rider as Furio Padedda. The Sardinian bestrode the machine like a horse, urging it on with tightenings of his knees. From a strap around his shoulders hung a double-barrelled shotgun.

Then a figure appeared in the street some distance ahead of Zen. One ahead and one behind, the classic ambush. The correct procedure was to go on the offensive, take out one or the other before they could complete the squeeze. But if Zen had been following correct procedures he would never have been there in the first place without any back-up. Even in his prime, twenty years ago, he couldn't have handled either man, never mind both of them. As Zen approached the blocker, he saw that it was Turiddu. With drunken fatalism, he kept walking. Ten metres. Five. Two. One. He braced himself for the arm across the throat, the foot to the groin.

Then he was past and nothing had happened. He sensed rather than saw Turiddu fall in behind him, his footsteps blending with the raucous murmur of Padedda's motorcycle. Zen forced himself not to hurry or look round. He walked on past rows of darkened windows, closed shutters and locked doors, followed by the two men, until at last he reached the piazza and the hotel.

Now, mulling it over in his room, his thoughts crawling through the wreckage of his brain like the stunned survivors of an earthquake, Zen realized that he owed his escape to the enmity between the two Sardinians. Each had no doubt intended to punish the impostor, but neither was prepared to allow the other that honour, and cooperation was out of the question. Back at the hotel, the proprietor, alerted by Padedda's associate Patrizio, had delivered his ultimatum. There was no other accommodation in the village, and in any case there was no point in Zen remaining, now that Reto Gurtner had been exposed as a fraud. Whatever he said or did, everyone would assume that he was a policeman, a government spy. The farce was over. He would drive to Cagliari that morning and book a ticket on the night ferry to the mainland. When he returned to the village, it would be in his official capacity. At least that way he could compel respect.

His inability to do so at present was amply demonstrated by the length of time it took him to get breakfast in the bar downstairs. At least half-a-dozen of the locals had drifted in and out again, replete with *cappuccinos* and pastries, before Zen was finally served a lukewarm cup of coffee that tasted as though it had been made from second-hand grounds and watered milk.

'Goodbye for now,' he told the proprietor as he stalked out.

The remark elicited a sharp glance that expressed anxious defiance as well as hostility. It gladdened Zen for a moment, until he reflected that his implied threat was the first step on the path which had led to the Gestapo tactics of the past.

The weather had changed. The sky was overcast, grey and featureless, the air still and humid. Zen's hangover felt like an octopus clinging to every cell of his being. Although weakening, the monster had plenty of life in it yet. Every movement involved an exhausting struggle against its tenacious resistance. He found himself looking forward to sinking luxuriously into the Mercedes' leather upholstery and driving away from this damned village, listening to the radio broadcasts from Rome, that lovely, civilized city where Tania was even now rising from her bed, sipping her morning coffee, even thinking of him perhaps. He could allow himself to dream. Given all he'd been through, he'd surely earned the right to a little harmless self-indulgence.

Half-way across the piazza, beside the village war memorial, Zen had to stop, put his suitcase down and catch his breath. The dead of the 1915–18 war covered two sides of the rectangular slab, the same surname often repeated six or eight times, like a litany. The Sardinians had formed the core of the Italian army's mountain divisions and half the young men of the village must have died at Isonzo and on the Piave. The later conflicts had taken a lesser toll. Thirty had died in 1940–45, four in Spain and five in Abyssinia.

As Zen picked up the leaden suitcase again, he noticed a tall thin man in a beige overcoat staring at him curiously. His deception would be common knowledge by now, he realized, and his every action a cause for suspicion. He dumped the suitcase in the boot of the Mercedes, got inside and turned the ignition on. Nothing happened. It was a measure of his befuddlement that it took him several minutes to realize that nothing was going to happen, no matter how many times he twisted the key. At first he thought he might have drained the battery by leaving the lights on, but when he tried the windscreen wipers they worked normally. He had invented problems with the Mercedes as a way of breaking the ice with Turiddu and his friends the night before, and the wretched car was apparently now taking its revenge by playing up just when he needed it most. Then he noticed the envelope tucked under one of the wiper blades, like a parking ticket.

Zen got out of the car and plucked it free. The envelope was blank. Inside was a single sheet of paper. 'FURIO PADEDDA IS A LIAR,' he read. 'HE WAS NOT IN THE BAR THE NIGHT THE FOREIGNERS WERE KILLED BUT THE MELEGA CLAN OF ORGOSOLO KNOW WHERE HE WAS.'

The message had been printed by a hand seemingly used to wielding larger and heavier implements than a pen. The letters were uneven and dissimilar, laboriously crafted, starting big and bold but crowded together at the right-hand margin as though panicked by the prospect of falling off the edge of the page.

Despite his predicament, Zen couldn't help smiling. So the humiliating disaster of the previous night had worked to his advantage, after all. Turiddu had seen an opportunity to even the score with his rival, no doubt easing his conscience with the reflection that Zen had not yet been officially identified as a policeman. If the information was true, it might be just what Zen needed to fabricate a case against Padedda and so keep Palazzo Sisti off his back. Unfortunately Turiddu's hatred for the 'foreigner' from the mountains, whatever its cause, did not make him a very reliable informant. Nevertheless, there was something about the note which made Zen feel that it wasn't pure fiction, although in his present condition he couldn't work out what it was.

He stuffed the letter into his pocket, wondering what to do next. For no reason at all, he decided to ring Tania.

The phone was of the new variety that accepted coins as well as tokens. Zen fed in his entire supply of change and dialled the distant number. Never had modern technology seemed more miraculous to him than it did then, stranded in a hostile, poverty-stricken Sardinian village listening to a telephone ringing in Tania's flat, a universe away in Rome.

'Yes?'

It was a man's voice, abrupt and bad-tempered.

'Signora Biacis, please.'

'Who's speaking?'

'I'm calling from the Ministry of the Interior.'

'For Christ's sake! Don't you know this is Sunday?'

'Certainly I know!' he replied impatiently. The coins were dropping through the machine with alarming frequency. 'Do you think I like having to work today either?'

'What do you want with my wife?'

'I'm afraid that's confidential. Just let me speak to her, please.'

'Eh no, certainly not! And don't bother ringing any more, signore, because she isn't in! She won't be in! Not ever, not for you! Understand? Don't think I don't know what's going on behind my back! You think I'm a fool, don't you? A simpleton! Well, you're wrong about that! I'll teach you to play games with a Bevilacqua! Understand? I know what you've been doing, and I'll make you pay for it! Adulterer! Fornicator!'

At this point Zen's money ran out, sparing him the rest of Mauro Bevilacqua's tirade. He walked despondently back to the Mercedes. By now the octopus had slackened its grip somewhat, but it still took Zen five minutes to work out how to open the bonnet. Once he had done so, however, he realized at once why the car would not start. This was no credit to his mechanical knowledge, which was non-existent. But even he could see that the spray of wires sticking out of the centre of the motor, each cut cleanly through, meant that some essential component had been deliberately removed.

He closed the bonnet and looked around the piazza. The phone box was now occupied by the man in the beige overcoat. With a deep sigh, Zen reluctantly returned to the hotel. Why on earth should anyone want to prevent him from leaving? Did Padedda need time to cover his tracks? Or was this sabotage Turiddu's way of reconciling his anonymous letter with the burdensome demands of *omertà*?

The proprietor greeted Zen's reappearance with a perfectly blank face, as though he had never seen him before.

'My car's broken down,' Zen told him. 'Is there a taxi service, a car hire, anything like that?'

'There's a bus.'

'What time does it leave?'

'Six o'clock.'

'In the evening?'

'In the morning.'

Zen gritted his teeth. Then he remembered the railway down in the valley. It was a long walk, but by now he was prepared to consider anything to get out of this cursed place.

'And the train doesn't run on Sunday,' the proprietor added, as though reading his thoughts.

A phone started ringing in the next room. The proprietor went to answer it. Zen sat down at one of the tables and lit a cigarette. He felt close to despair. Just as he had received information that might well make his mission a success, every door had suddenly slammed shut in his face. At this rate, he would have to phone the Carabinieri at Lanusei and ask them nicely to come and pick him up. It was the last thing he wanted to do. To avoid compromising his undercover operation, he had left behind all his official identification, so involving the rival force would involve lengthy explanations and verifications, in the course of which his highly questionable business here would inevitably be revealed, probably stymieing his chances of bringing the affair to a satisfactory conclusion. But there appeared to be no alternative, unless he wanted to spend the night in the street or a cave, like the beggar woman.

He looked up as the thin man in the beige overcoat walked in.

Instead of going up to the bar, he headed for the table where Zen was sitting.

'Good morning, dottore.'

Zen stared at him.

'You don't recognize me?' the man asked.

He seemed disappointed. Zen inspected him more carefully. He was about forty years old, with the soft, pallid look of those who work indoors. At first sight he had seemed tall, but Zen now realized that this was due to the man's extreme thinness, and to the fact that Zen had by now adjusted to the Sardinian norm. As far as he knew, he had never seen him before in his life.

'Why should I?' he retorted crossly.

The man drew up a chair and sat down.

'Why indeed? It's like at school, isn't it? The pupils all remember their teacher, even years later, but you can't expect the teacher to recall all the thousands of kids who have passed through their hands at one time or other. But I still recognize you, dottore. I knew you right away. You haven't aged very much. Or perhaps you were already old, even then.'

He took out a packet of the domestic *toscani* cigars and broke one in half, replacing one end in the packet and putting the other between his lips.

'Have you got a light?'

Zen automatically handed over his lighter. He felt as though all this was happening to someone else, someone who perhaps understood what was going on. Certainly he didn't.

The man lit the cigar with great care, rotating it constantly, never letting the flame touch the tobacco. When it was glowing satisfactorily, he slipped the lighter into his pocket.

'But that's mine!' Zen protested, like a child whose toy has been taken away.

'You won't be needing it any more. I'll keep it as a souvenir.'

He stood up and took his coat off, draping it over a chair, then walked over to the bar and rapped on the chrome surface with his knuckles.

'Eh, service!'

The proprietor emerged from the back room, scowling furiously.

'Give me a glass of beer. Something decent, not any of your local crap.'

Shorn of his coat, the man's extreme thinness was even more apparent. It gave him a disturbing two-dimensional appearance, as though when he turned sideways he might disappear altogether.

The proprietor banged a bottle and a glass down on the counter.

'3,000 lire.'

The thin man threw a banknote down negligently.

'There's five. Have a drink on me. Maybe it'll cheer you up.'

He carried the bottle and glass back to the table and proceeded to pour the beer as carefully as he had lit the cigar, tilting the glass and the bottle towards each other so that only a slight head formed.

'Miserable fuckers, these Sardinians,' he commented to Zen. 'Forgive me if I don't shake hands. Someone once told me that it's bad luck, and I certainly don't need any more of that. Strange, though, you not remembering my face. Maybe the name means something. Vasco Spadola.'

Time passed, a lot perhaps, or a little. The thin man sat and smoked and sipped his beer until Zen finally found his voice.

'How did you know where I was?'

It was a stupid question. But perhaps all questions were stupid at this point.

Spadola picked up his overcoat, patted the pockets and pulled out the previous day's edition of *La Nazione*, which he tossed on the table.

'I read about it in the paper.'

Zen turned the newspaper round. Half-way down the page was a photograph of himself he barely recognized. It must have been taken years ago, dug out of the newspaper's morgue. He thought he looked callow and cocksure, ridiculously self-important. Beneath the photograph was an article headed 'NEW EVIDENCE IN BUROLO AFFAIR?' Zen skimmed the text.

'According to sources close to the family of Renato Favelloni, accused of plotting the murders at the Villa Burolo, dramatic new evidence has recently come to light in this case resulting in the re-opening of a line of investigation previously regarded as closed. A senior official of the Ministry's élite Criminalpol squad, Vice-Questore Aurelio Zen, is being sent to Sardinia to assess and coordinate developments at the scene. Further announcements are expected shortly.'

Zen put the paper down. Of course. He should have guessed that Palazzo Sisti would take care to publicize his imminent trip to the area in order to ensure that the 'dramatic new evidence' he fabricated got proper attention from the judiciary.

'Shame I missed you in Rome,' Spadola told him. 'Giuliano spent over a week setting the whole thing up, watching your apartment, picking the locks, leaving those little messages to soften you up. By that Friday we were all set to go. I didn't know you'd sussed the car, though. Giuliano was always a bit careless about things like that. Same with that tape he took instead of your wallet. It comes of being an eldest son, I reckon, mamma's favourite. You think you can get away with anything.'

He paused to draw on his cigar.

'When the cops rolled up I had to beat it out the back way. I was lucky to get away, carrying the gun and all. I had to dump it in a rubbish skip and come back for it later. All that effort gone to waste, and what was worse, they'd got Giuliano. I knew he wouldn't have the balls to hold out once they got to work on him. I reckoned I'd have to lie low for months, waiting for you to get fed up being shepherded about by a minder or holed up in some safe-house. I certainly didn't expect to be sitting chatting to you in a café two days later!'

He broke out in gleeful laughter.

'Even when I read the report in the paper, I never expected it to be this easy! I thought you would be staying in some barracks somewhere, guarded day and night, escorted around in bulletproof limousines. Still, I had to come. You never know your luck, I thought. But never in my wildest dreams did I imagine anything like this!'

The door of the bar swung open to admit Tommaso and another elderly man. They greeted the proprietor loudly and shot nervous glances at Zen and Spadola.

Zen ground out his cigarette.

'All right, so you've found me. What now?'

Spadola released a breath of cigar smoke into the air above Zen's head.

'What now? Why, I'm going to kill you, of course!'

He took a gulp of beer.

'That's why I didn't want to shake hands. One of the people I met in prison used to be a soldier for the Pariolo family in Naples. You worked there once, didn't you? Gianni Ferrazzi. Does the name ring a bell? It might have been after your time. Anyway, this lad had twenty or thirty hits to his credit, he couldn't remember himself exactly how many, and everything went fine until he shook hands with the victim before doing the job. He hadn't meant to, he knew it was bad luck, but they were introduced, the man stuck out his paw, what was he supposed to do? It would have looked suspicious if he'd refused. He still went ahead and made the hit, though, even though he knew he'd go down for it. That's what I call real professionalism.

'To be honest, I thought that it would be a bit like that with you. Impersonal, I mean, anonymous, like a paid hit. That's the way it was with Bertolini, unfortunately. I just hadn't thought the thing through, that first time. The bastard never even knew why he died. I had enough to cope with, what with his driver pulling a gun and his wife screaming her head off from the house. I realized afterwards that I wanted a lot more than that, otherwise I might just as well hire it out and save myself the trouble. I mean the victim's got to understand, he's got to know who you are and why you're doing it, otherwise what kind of revenge is it?

'So I swore that you and Parrucci would be different. I certainly got my money's worth out of him, but you were more difficult. Once this terrorist scare started after I shot Bertolini it seemed too risky to try and kidnap someone from the Ministry. They would have cracked down hard. I had no intention of getting caught. I've done twenty years for a murder I didn't commit, so they owe me this one free!'

He leant back in his chair with a blissful smile.

'Ah, but I never imagined anything like this! To sit here like two old friends, chatting at a table, and tell you that I'm going to kill you, and you knowing it's true, that you're going to die! And all the time those two old bastards over there are discussing the price of sheep's milk or some fucking thing, and the barman's cleaning the coffee machine, and the television's blatting away next door, and the ice-cream freezer in the corner is humming. And you're going to die! I'm going to kill you, while all this is going on! And it'll still go on, once you're dead. Because you're not needed, Zen. None of us is. Have you ever thought about that? I have. I spent twenty years thinking about it. Twenty years, locked up for a murder I didn't even do!'

Spadola squeezed the last puff of acrid smoke from his cigar and threw that butt on the floor.

'You want to know who killed Tondelli? His cousin, that's who. It was over a woman, a bar-room scuffle. Once he was dead, the Tondellis saw a way to use it against me, and paid that cunt Parrucci to perjure himself. You bastards did the rest. But even supposing I had killed him, so what? People die all the time, one way or another. It doesn't make a fucking bit of difference to anything.

'*That's* what you can't admit, you others. That's what scares you shitless. And so you make little rules and regulations, like at school, and anyone who breaks them has to stand in the corner with a dunce's cap on. What a load of bullshit! The truth of it is that *you're* the first to break the rules, to cheat and lie and perjure yourselves to get a lousy rise, a better job or a fatter pension! *You're* the ones who ought to be punished! And believe it or not, my friend, that's what's going to happen, just this once. Take it in, Zen! You're going to die. Soon. Today. And I'm telling you this, warning you, and you know it's true, and yet there's absolutely nothing whatsoever that you can do about it! Not a single fucking thing.'

Spadola put his fingers to his lips and blew a kiss up into the air like a connoisseur appreciating a fine wine.

'This is the ultimate! I've never felt anything like it. It makes up for everything. Well, no, let's not exaggerate. Nothing could make up for what I've been through. But if it's any consolation, you've made me a very happy man today. You destroyed my life, it's true, but you have also given me this moment. My mother, may she rest in peace, used to say that I was destined to great sorrows and great joys. And she was right. She was so right.'

He broke off, biting his lip, tears welled up in his eyes.

'I suppose it's no use telling you that I had nothing to do with the evidence against you being faked,' Zen said dully.

Spadola rocked violently back and forth in his chair as though seized by an involuntary spasm.

'I don't believe it! This is too much! It's too good to be true!' He panted for breath. 'Do you remember what you said that morning at the farm near Melzo? I told you I was innocent. I told you I hadn't done it. I knew I'd been betrayed, and that made it all the harder to bear. If I'd really knifed that fucking southerner you'd never have got a word out of me, but knowing it was all a fix I thought I'd go crazy. And do you know what you said, when I screamed my innocence in your face? You said, "Yes, well you would say that, wouldn't you?" And you looked at me in that sly way you educated people have when you're feeling pleased with yourselves. *Of course* you had nothing to do with it, dottore! Just like this what's-his-name, the politician in this murder case you're investigating. *He* didn't have anything to do with it either, did he? People like you never do have anything to do with it!'

'I don't mean that I didn't plant the knife myself. I mean I didn't even know that it had been planted. It was done without my knowledge, behind my back.'

'Then you're an incompetent bastard. It was your case, your responsibility! I've spent twenty years of my life, the only one I'll ever have, shut up in a stinking damp cell with barely room to turn around, locked up for hours in the freezing-cold darkness . . .'

He broke off, shuddering uncontrollably, his cheeks glistening wet.

'Go on, take a good look! I'm not ashamed of my tears! Why should I be? They're pearls of suffering, *my* suffering. I should make you lick them up, one by one, before I blow your evil head off!'

'Cut the crap, Spadola!' Zen exploded. 'Even if you didn't do the Tondelli job, you were guilty as hell of at least four other murders. What about Ugo Trocchio and his brother? You had them killed and you know it. We knew it, everyone knew it. We couldn't prove it because people were too scared to talk. And so it went on, until some of my colleagues decided that it was time you were taken out of circulation. Since they couldn't do it straight, they did it crooked. As I say, I didn't know. If I had known, I would have tried to stop it. But the fact remains that you earned that twenty-year sentence several times over.'

'That's not the point!' Spadola shouted, so loudly that the men at the bar turned to stare at him. 'Christ Almighty, if everyone who broke the law in this country was sent to prison, who'd be left to guard them? We'd need a whole new set of politicians, for a start! But it doesn't work that way, does it? It's a game! And I was good! I was fucking brilliant! You couldn't pin a damn thing on me. I had you beat inside out. So you moved the goal posts!'

'That's part of the game too.'

Spadola drained off his beer and stood up.

'Maybe. But the game stops here, Zen. What happens now is real.' His voice was perfectly calm again. He stood staring down at Zen. 'I know what you're thinking. You think I'm crazy, telling you what I'm going to do, warning you, giving you a chance to escape. There's no way I can get away with it, that's what you're thinking, isn't it? Not in broad daylight, in the middle of this village. Well, we'll see. Maybe you're right. I agree that that's a possibility. Maybe you're cleverer than me. Maybe you'll figure out a way to save your skin, this time around. That doesn't worry me. I'll get you in the end, whatever happens. And meanwhile that slim hope is part of your punishment, Zen, just like I was tormented with talk of appeals and parole that never came to anything.'

He put on his overcoat. 'You've probably noticed that your car's not working. I removed the distributor and cut the leads. Just to save you time, I'll tell you that the phone box is out of order now, too. As for the locals, I doubt if they'd tell you the time by the clock on the wall. I showed them the paper, you see, told them who you are. Oddly enough, they didn't seem terribly surprised. Between the two of us, I think they must have sussed you out already.

'So I'll see you later, dottore. I can't say when exactly. That's part of the punishment too. It could be in a few minutes. I might suddenly get the urge. Or it might not be until late tonight. It all depends on my mood, how I'm feeling. I'll know when the moment has come. I'll sense it. Don't worry about the pain. It'll be quick and clean, I promise. Nothing fancy, like with Parrucci. I really had it in for him in a big way. They used to call him 'the nightingale', didn't they? Because of how beautifully he sang, I suppose. He turned out to be more of a screamer, though, in the end. I had to take a walk, I couldn't handle it myself. He was tougher than he looked, though. When I got back an hour or so later he was still whimpering, what was left of him. I had to finish him off with a pistol. Sickening, really. Well, I'm off for a piss.'

He walked across the restaurant area and disappeared through a door marked 'Toilets'.

'Let me use your phone!' Zen told the proprietor. 'That man is an ex-criminal. He has threatened to kill me. I'm a Vice-Questore at the Ministry of the Interior. If you don't help, you'll be an accessory to murder.'

The proprietor gazed at him stonily.

'But your name is Reto Gurtner. I've seen your papers. You're a Swiss businessman, from Zurich.'

'My name is Aurelio Zen! I'm a high-ranking official!'

'Prove it.'

'Let me use the phone! Quickly, before he comes back!'

'There's no phone here.'

'But I heard it ringing when I came in.'

'That was the television.'

Given a few more minutes, Zen might have been able to change the man's mind with a combination of threats and pleas. But the few seconds before Vasco Spadola reappeared were too precious to gamble on that slim possibility. Besides, it would take the Carabinieri at least fifteen minutes to reach the village, and that would be plenty of time for Spadola to carry out his threat. Zen turned and ran.

Outside in the piazza, people had begun to gather for the promenade before lunch. Zen stood uncertainly by the door. Who could he turn to? Angelo Confalone? But it was Sunday. The lawyer's office would be closed and Zen had no idea where he lived. For a moment he thought of appealing to the crowd, of throwing himself on their mercy. But there was no time to indulge in public oratory, and besides, he had been branded a spy, a proven liar, an agent of the hated government in Rome. Anyone who helped him would risk placing his own position in the community in jeopardy. Spadola was right. He was on his own.

Then he saw the Mercedes, and realized that there was just one faint hope. It hung by the narrowest of threads, but he had nothing to lose. Anything was better than skulking about the village, hiding in corners waiting to be routed out and killed.

As he shoved his way unceremoniously through the knots of bystanders, Zen noticed Turiddu standing in a group of other men. They were all staring at him, talking in low voices and pointing at a yellow Fiat Uno with Rome number plates parked nearby. To one side, all alone, stood Elia, the mad beggar woman. Zen belatedly noted the resemblance between her and Turiddu, and realized that he must be the brother she had rejected. That explained his anger on finding her at the pizzeria the night before. In a community like this, a mentally ill relative would be a perpetual source of shame.

He released the handbrake of the Mercedes and put the gear-leaver into neutral. Then he got out and started to push with all his might, struggling to overcome the vehicle's inertia and the slight incline leading up to the main street. His headache sprang back into active life and his aching limbs protested. After a violent effort the car rolled on to the cracked concrete slabs of the street. Zen turned the wheel so that it was facing downhill, then got it moving and jumped back inside. Soon the car was rolling quite fast down the steeply inclined main street and round the curve leading out of the village. He wasn't in the clear yet, not by a long way, but he was exhilarated by his initial success. By the time he reached the new houses on the outskirts, the car was travelling as fast as he would have wanted to go anyway. He even had to use the horn several times to warn groups of villagers of his silent approach.

When I saw him leaving I thought everything was lost. I'd followed him everywhere, gun in hand, flitting through the shadows like a swift at dusk. All for nothing. There was always someone there, foiling my plans, as though some god protected him! And now he was beyond my reach.

He thought he was safe, I thought I'd failed. What neither of us understood was that his death was already installed in him, lodged in his body like our sins in the Bleeding Heart above the fireplace. I used to think the heart was from one of the pigs father had slaughtered. I kept expecting to find the beast's guts on another wall and its cock and balls nailed to the door. Once the lamp went out in the middle of a thunderstorm and mother made me get down on my knees and pray to be forgiven or God would strike us dead on the spot. So I knelt to the great pig in the sky whose farts terrified mother, praying it wouldn't shit all over us.

Which is just what it did, a little later on. Be careful what you pray for. You might give God ideas.

I wandered off, neither knowing nor caring where I went. All places were equal now. My feet brought me here, like a horse that knows its own way home. He would be far away, I thought, speeding through the corridors of light in his big white car.

But there was only one exit from the maze in which we both were trapped. Even as I despaired, he was on his way there, bringing me the death I needed.

Sunday, 11.20–13.25

It was only as he approached the series of hairpin bends by which the road descended from the village that Zen realized Vasco Spadola might well have sabotaged the Mercedes's brakes as well as its engine. By then the car was doing almost 50 kph and accelerating all the time.

The brakes engaged normally, and a moment later Zen saw that his fears had been groundless. Spadola's exacting sense of what was due to him made it unthinkable that he would choose such an indirect and mechanical means of executing his revenge. His desires were urgent and personal. They had to be satisfied personally, face to face, like a perverted sex act.

The car drifted downhill in a luxurious silence cushioned by the hum of the tyres and the hushing of the wind. The hairpin bends followed one another with barely a pause. The motion reminded Zen of sailing on the Venetian lagoons, continually putting the boat about from one tack to the other as he negotiated the narrow channels between the low, muddy islets. He felt strangely exhilarated by that moment when life and death had seemed balanced on the response of a brake lever, as on the toss of a coin. In Rome, when he first sensed that someone was on his trail, he had felt nothing but cold, clammy terror, a paralysing suffocation. But here in this primitive landscape what was happening seemed perfectly natural and right. This is what men were made for, he thought. The rest we have to work at, but this comes naturally. This is what we are good at.

Even in this euphoric state, however, he realized that some men were better at it than others, and that Vasco Spadola was certainly too good for him. If he was to survive, he had to start thinking. Fortunately his brain seemed to be working with exceptional clarity, despite the hangover. There was as yet no sign of pursuit on the road above, but as soon as Spadola emerged from the hotel he was bound to notice that the Mercedes was gone, and to realize that it could only have moved under the force of gravity. All he needed to do after that was follow the road downhill, and sooner or later – and it was likely to be sooner rather than later – he would catch up.

Below, the road wound down to the junction where Zen had stopped to consult the map on his way to the Villa Burolo twenty-four hours earlier. On the other side of the junction, he remembered, an unsurfaced track led to the station built to serve the village in the days when people were prepared to walk four or five kilometres to take advantage of the new railway. This station was Zen's goal. There was bound to be a telephone, and the station-master, owing his allegiance – and more importantly his job – not to the locals but to the state, was bound to let Zen use it. All Criminalpol officials were provided with a codeword, changed monthly, which acted as turn-key providing the user with powers to dispose of the facilities of the forces of order from one end of the country to the other. One brief phone call, and helicopters and jeeps full of armed police would descend on the area, leaving Spadola the choice of returning to the prison cell he had so recently vacated or dying in a hail of machine-gun fire. All Zen had to do was make sure the police arrived before Spadola.

He had banked on being able to freewheel the Mercedes all the way, but as soon as he got close enough to see the track, he noticed a feature not shown on the map: a low rise of land intervening between the road and the railway. It was difficult to estimate exactly how steep it was from the brief glances he was able to spare as he approached the last of the hairpin bends. For a moment he was tempted to let the car gather speed on the final straight stretch, gambling that the accumulated momentum would be enough to carry it over the ridge. But the risk was too great. If he didn't make it, he would be forced to abandon the Mercedes at the bottom of the slope, in full view of the road, which would be tantamount to leaving a sign explaining his intentions. When Spadola arrived, he would simply drive along the track, easily overtaking Zen before he could reach the station on foot.

By now he was seconds away from the junction. The only alternative was to turn on to the main road, which ran gently downhill to the right. Trying to conserve speed, he took the turn so fast that the tyres lost their grip on a triangular patch of gravel in the centre of the junction and the Mercedes started to drift sideways towards the ditch on the other side. At the last moment the steering abruptly came back, almost wrenching the wheel from Zen's hands. He steered back to the right-hand side, thankful that there was so little traffic on these

Sardinian roads. As the car started to gather speed again, he glanced at the road winding its way up to the village. Several hundred metres above, he spotted a small patch of bright yellow approaching the second hairpin. Then a fold of land rose between like a passing wave and he lost sight of it.

The road stretched invitingly away in a gentle downward slope. Zen felt his anxieties being lulled by the car's smooth, even motion, but he knew that this sense of security was an illusion. Once on the main road, Spadola's Fiat would outstrip the engineless Mercedes in a matter of minutes, while every kilometre Zen travelled away from the station was a kilometre he would have to retrace painfully on foot. The car was not now the asset it had seemed, but a liability. He had to get rid of it, but how? If he left it by the roadside, Spadola would know he was close by. He had to ditch it somewhere out of sight, thus buying time to get back to the station on foot while Spadola continued to scour the roads for the elusive white Mercedes. Unfortunately the barren scrub-covered hills offered scant possibilities for concealing a bicycle, let alone a car.

Up ahead he saw the junction with the side-road leading down to the Villa Burolo, but he did not take it, remembering that it bottomed out in a valley where he would be stranded. What he needed was a smaller, less conspicuous turn-off, something Spadola might overlook. But time was getting desperately short! He kept glancing compulsively in the rear-view mirror, dreading the moment when he saw the yellow Fiat on his tail. Once that happened, his fate would be sealed.

Almost too late, he caught sight of a faint dirt track opening off the other side of the road. There was no time for mature reflection or second thoughts. With a flick of his wrists, he swung the Mercedes squealing across the asphalt on to the twin ruts of bare red earth. Within moments a low hummock had almost brought the car to a halt, but in the end its forward momentum prevailed, and after that it was all Zen could do to keep it on the track, which curved back on itself, becoming progressively rougher and steeper. The steering-wheel writhed and twisted in Zen's hands until the track straightened out and ran down more gently into a hollow sunk between steep, rocky slopes where a small windowless stone hut stood in a grove of mangy trees.

Zen stopped the Mercedes at the very end of the track, out of sight of the main road. He got out and stood listening intently. The land curved up all around, containing the silence like liquid in a pot, its surface faintly troubled by a distant sound that might have been a flying insect. Zen turned his head, tracking the car as it drove past along the road above, the engine noise fading away without any change in pitch or intensity. His shoulders slumped in relief. Spadola had not seen him turn off and had not noticed the tyre marks in the earth.

He walked over to the hut, a crude affair of stones piled one on top of the other, with a corrugated iron roof. He stooped down and peered in through the low, narrow open doorway. A faint draught carrying a strong smell of sheep blew towards him from the darkness within. It must once have been a shepherd's hut, used for storing cheese and curing hides, but was now clearly abandoned. Zen knelt down and wriggled inside, crouching on the floor of bare rock. The sheepy reek was overpowering. As his eyes adjusted to the obscurity, Zen found himself standing at the edge of a large irregular fissure in the rock. Holding his hand over the opening, he discovered that this was the source of the draught that stirred the fetid air in the hut.

Then he remembered Turiddu saying that the whole area was riddled with caves which had once brought water down underground from the lake in the mountains. The idea of water was very attractive. His hangover had left him with the most atrocious thirst. But of course there was no more water in the caves since they had built the dam. That was evidently why the hut had been abandoned, like so many of the local farms, including the one Oscar Burolo had bought for a song. Presumably this was one of the entrances to that system of caves. It was large enough to climb down into, but there was no saying what that impenetrable darkness concealed, a cosy hollow he could hide in or a sheer drop into a cavern the size of a church.

Nevertheless, he was strongly tempted to stay put. He felt safe in the hut, magically concealed and protected. In fact he knew it would be suicidal to stay. Indeed, he had already wasted far too much precious time. Before long, the road Spadola was following would start to go uphill, and he would know that Zen could not have passed that way. The network of side-roads would complicate his search slightly, but in the end a process of elimination was bound to lead him to this gully and the stranded Mercedes. The first thing he would do then would be to search the hut.

But this knowledge didn't make the alternative any more appealing. The idea of setting out on foot across country with only the vaguest idea of where he was going was something Zen found quite horrifying. His preferred view of nature was through the window of a train whisking him from one city to another. Man's contrivances he understood, but in the open he was as vulnerable as a fox in the streets, his survival skills non-existent, his native cunning an irrelevance. Nothing less than the knowledge that his life was at stake could have impelled him to leave the hut and start to climb the boulder-strewn slope opposite.

He laboured up the hillside, using his hands to scramble up the steeper sections, grasping at rocks and shrubs, his clothes and shoes already soiled with the sterile red dirt, the leaden sky weighing down on him. He felt terrible. His limbs ached, thirst plagued him and his headache had swollen to monstrous dimensions. Half-way to the top he stopped to rest. As he stood there, panting for breath, cruelly aware how unfit he was for this kind of thing, his brain blithely presented him with the information it had withheld earlier. The anonymous note left under the windscreen-wiper of the Mercedes had claimed that Padedda's whereabouts on the night of the Burolo murders was known to 'the Melega clan of Orgosolo'. It was that name which had seemed to authenticate the writer's allegations. Antonio Melega, Zen belatedly remembered, was the young shepherd who had been buried a few days after the abortive kidnapping of Oscar Burolo, having been run over by an unidentified vehicle.

The faint hum of a passing car stirred the heavy silence. The main road was still out of sight, and there was no particular reason to suppose that the vehicle had been Spadola's yellow Fiat. But the incident served as a reminder of Zen's exposed position on the hillside, above the hollow where the Mercedes stood out as prominently as a trashed refrigerator in a ravine. Putting every other thought out of his head, Zen attacked the slope as though it were an enemy, kicking and punching, grunting and cursing, until at last he reached the summit and the ground levelled off, conceding defeat.

Before him the landscape stretched monotonously away towards undesirable horizons. Zen trudged on through a wilderness of armour-plated plants that might have been dead for all the signs of life they showed. To take his mind off the brutal realities of his situation, Zen tried to work out how the information he had obtained might be brought to bear on the Burolo case. And the more he thought about it, the more convinced he became that he had stumbled on the key to the whole mystery.

The irony was that having been sent to Sardinia to rig the Burolo case by incriminating Furio Padedda, he now possessed evidence which strongly suggested that the Sardinian was in fact guilty. With the lions Oscar had bought to patrol the grounds of his villa after the kidnap attempt, had come a man calling himself Furio Pizzoni. His real name, Palazzo Sisti had discovered, was Padedda, and he was not from the Abruzzo mountains but from those around Nuoro. And Padedda's friends, according to Turiddu's drunken revelations the night before, in addition to the traditional sheep-rustling, were also engaged in its more lucrative modern variation, kidnapping. Turiddu's companions had shut him up at that point, but the implications were clear.

There had never been any question that the Melega family, with a dead brother to avenge, had an excellent motive for murdering Oscar Burolo, and the ruthless dedication to carry it out. What no one had been able to explain was how a gang of Sardinian shepherds had been able to gain entrance to the villa despite its sophisticated electronic defences, but given an ally within Burolo's gates this obstacle could have been easily overcome. According to their testimony, Alfonso Bini and his wife had been watching television in their quarters at the time of the murder. If Padedda, instead of drinking in the village, had concealed himself at the villa, there would have been nothing to stop him entering the room from which the alarms were controlled and throwing the cut-out switches. For that matter, he could have carried out the killings himself. The wound on his arm, which had looked suspiciously like a bullet mark to Zen, corresponded to the fact that the assassin had been lightly wounded by Vianello. Padedda would no doubt have used his own shotgun, familiar and reliable, to do the killings, removing one of Burolo's weapons to confuse the issue. Zen recalled the ventilation hole in the wall of the underground vault to which the trail of blood-stains led. Had that been searched for the missing weapon? And had ejected cartridges from the shotgun which Padedda kept hanging in the lions' house been compared with those found at the scene of the crime? Such checks should have been routine, but Zen knew only too well how often routine broke down under the pressure of preconceived ideas about guilt and innocence.

A car engine suddenly roared up out of nowhere and Zen threw himself to the ground. He lay holding his breath, his face pressed to the dirt, cowering for cover in the sparse scrub as a yellow car flashed by a few metres in front of him. It seemed impossible that he had escaped notice, but the car kept going. A few moments later it had disappeared.

He stood up cautiously, rubbing the cuts on his face and hands caused by his crash-landing in the prickly shrubbery. Now that he knew it was there, he could see the thin grey line of asphalt cutting through the landscape just ahead of him. There was no time to lose. Spadola had taken the direction leading down into the valley. He would soon see that the Mercedes was not there and couldn't have climbed the other side, and would cross this road off his list, turn back and try again. Zen's only consolation was that Spadola had not yet found the abandoned car, and therefore did not know that Zen was on foot.

He ran across the raised strip of asphalt and on through the scrub on the other side, hurrying forward until the contours of the hill hid him from the road. He could see the railway now, running along a ledge cut into the slope below. Rather than lose height by climbing down to it, he continued across the top on a converging course which he hoped would bring him more or less directly to the station. Meanwhile the bits and pieces of the puzzle continued to put themselves together in his mind without the slightest effort on his part.

As with Favelloni, it was impossible to know whether Padedda had actually carried out the killings or merely provided access to the villa. On balance, Zen thought the latter more likely. The Melegas, like Vasco Spadola, would have wanted the satisfaction of taking vengeance in person. This also explained the bizarre fact that no attempt had been made to destroy the video tape. It was possible that such unsophisticated men, unlike Renato Favelloni, might have ignored the camera as just another bit of the incomprehensible gadgetry the house was full of. Afterwards the Melegas would have had no difficulty in persuading a few of the villagers to come forward and claim that they had seen Padedda in the local bar that evening, while the age-old traditions of *omertà* would stop anyone else from contradicting their testimony. It all made sense, it all fitted together.

Zen hurried on, forcing himself to maintain a punishing pace. To his right, he could see the whole of the valley stretching across to the ridge on the other side where the Villa Burolo was visible as a white blur. Further up towards the mountains, the unnatural green of the forest fed by the leaking dam stained the landscape like a spillage of some pollutant. A distant rumble gave him pause for a moment, until he realized that it was not a car but two aircraft. After some time he made out the speeding black specks of the jet fighters swooping across the mountain slopes on their low-altitude manoeuvres. Then they disappeared up a valley and silence fell again. He pushed on, torn between satisfaction at having finally cracked the Burolo case and frustration at the thought that unless he managed to get to a telephone before Spadola caught up with him, the villagers' silence would remain unbroken for ever, and Renato Favelloni would be sent to prison for a crime he had not committed. Of course, Favelloni no doubt royally deserved any number of prison terms for other crimes which would never be brought home to him, protected as he was by *l'onorevole*. But, as Vasco Spadola had remarked, that was not the point.

The going was not easy. The red earth, baked hard by months of drought, supported nothing but low bushes bristling like porcupines, with wiry branches, abrasive leaves and sharp thorns that snagged his clothing continually. Fortunately, the plants didn't generally grow very close together, and it was always possible to find a way through. But the constant meandering increased the distance he had to cover, and made his progress much more tiring. And he *was* tired. His dissipations the night before had resulted in a shallow, drunken sleep that had only scratched the surface of his immense weariness.

At last he reached the crest of a small ridge which had formed his horizon for some time, and caught sight of the station for the first time, about half a kilometre away to his right, a squat building with a steeply-pitched roof. The railway itself was invisible at that distance, so the buildings looked as if they had been set down at random in the middle of nowhere. Below, the track that he had originally planned to take in the car wound through the scrub. Zen ran down the hill to join it. The track showed no signs of recent use. Low bushes were growing on it, and rocks had sprouted in the wheel ruts. But now he was within sight of his goal, walking was almost a pleasure.

The first hint of what was to come was that one end of the station roof had fallen in. Then he saw that the windows and doors were just gaping holes. By the time he reached the yard, it was evident that the station was a complete ruin. The ground-floor rooms were gutted, strewn with beams and plaster from the fallen ceiling, the walls charred where someone had lit a fire in one corner. Outside, the gable wall still proclaimed the name of the village in faded letters, with the height in metres above sea-level, but it was clearly many years since the station had been manned. The whole line was a pointless anachronism whose one train a day served no purpose except to keep the lucrative subsidies flowing in from Rome.

Zen shook his head. He couldn't believe this was happening. It was like a bad dream Automatically he reached for a cigarette, only to remember that Spadola had taken his lighter. He blasphemed viciously, then tried to force himself to think. It was tempting to think of spending the night at the station and catching the train the next morning, but that would be as short-sighted as staying in the shepherd's hut. It would be equally foolish to try and make off across country. The Barbagia was one of the wildest and least populated areas of the country. Without a map and a compass, the chances of getting lost and eventually dying of starvation or exposure were very high.

That left just two possibilities: he could walk back along the track to the main road and then walk or try and hitch a lift to the nearest town, or he could follow the railway line up into the mountains. The problem with taking the road was the high risk of Spadola coming along it. Walking along the railway would be a long and tiring business, and he might have to spend a night in the open. But if the worst came to the worst he could flag down the train the next morning, or even jump aboard, at the speed it would be going. The decisive advantage, however, was that the railway was out of sight of the road, which Spadola would now be patrolling with increasing frustration.

The unlit cigarette clenched between his lips, Zen stepped across the disused passing-loop where pulpy cacti ran riot, and started to walk along the line of rusty rails which curved off to the left, following the contours of the hillside. He had imagined walking along the railway as being tedious but relatively relaxing, but in fact it was every bit as demanding as negotiating the scrub. The ancient sleepers, rough-hewn, weathered and split, were placed too close together to step on each one and too far to take them two at a time, while the ballast in between was jagged, uneven and choked with plants.

A thunderous rumble sounded in the distance once again. Zen stopped and looked up to spot the jets at their sport in the mountains. It was only moments later that he realized another sound had been concealed in their cavernous booming, a rhythmic purr that was quieter but much closer. For a moment it seemed to be coming from the railway line, and Zen's hopes flared briefly. Then he swung round and saw the yellow Fiat driving along the track to the station.

Instinctively he crouched down, looking for cover, but this time it was too late. Its engine revving furiously, the Fiat had left the track and was smashing its way through the scrub towards him. Zen leapt up and started to run as fast as he could away from the car. Almost immediately he tripped over a rusty signal-wire and went flying, landing on a small boulder and turning his ankle over agonizingly. Behind him, the frantic roaring of the car engine reached a peak, then abruptly died. A car door slammed. Zen forced himself to his knees. Some fifty metres away the yellow Fiat lay trapped in a thicket of scrub. Beside the car, a shotgun in his hand, stood Vasco Spadola.

Zen tried to stand up, but his left ankle gave way and he stumbled. He tried again. This time the ankle held, although it hurt atrociously. But although he now knew that Spadola was going to kill him, he couldn't just stand there and let it happen, even though it meant torturing himself in vain. He started to hobble away as fast as he could, gasping at every step. Repeatedly he tripped, lost his precarious balance and ended up on his hands and knees in the rocky dust. He did not look back. There was no point. At the best pace he could manage, Spadola would catch up with him in a matter of minutes. He wondered how good a shot Spadola was, and whether he would hear the blast that killed him.

When he finally stopped to look round, he found that Spadola was still some fifty metres away, dawdling along, the shotgun balanced loosely in the crook of his arm. With a groan, Zen hobbled off again. So that was how it was going to be. Spadola was in no hurry to finish him off. On the contrary, the longer he could draw out the agony, the more complete his revenge would be. Only the approach of night would force him to close in for the kill, lest his prey escape under cover of darkness. But that was many hours away yet. In the meantime, he was content to dog Zen's footsteps, not trying to overtake him but not letting him rest either, harrying him on relentlessly towards the inevitable bloody conclusion.

Zen plodded blindly on in a nightmare of pain, confusion and despair. He now neither knew nor cared which direction he was going in. All his hopes and calculations had come to nothing. Unless Palazzo Sisti managed to throw a political spanner in the works at the last moment, Renato Favelloni would be convicted of the Burolo murders, while Furio Padedda and the Melega family watched with ironic smiles, never guessing that they owed their freedom to a vendetta very similar to the one which had cost Oscar and the others their lives. To cap it all, Spadola would probably get away with it too. The villagers would say nothing, particularly since it would involve them as accessories to Zen's murder. When his corpse was eventually discovered, it would be assumed he had fallen victim to the long-running guerilla war between the islanders and the state. His colleagues in Rome would shake their heads and agree that it had been crazy to improvise a one-man undercover operation in Sardinia without even telling anyone what he was doing. 'He was *asking* for it!' Vincenzo Fabri would crow triumphantly, just as people had said about Oscar when he chose a villa so close to the kidnappers' heartland. No one would want to tug too hard on any of the loose ends that remained. As Zen well knew, the police were part of the forces of order in more senses than one. They liked things to make sense, they liked files to be closed. If this order happened to correspond to the truth, well and good, but in the last resort they would rather have a false solution than no solution at all. Certainly there was never any encouragement to throw things back into chaos by suggesting that things might not be quite what they appeared.

Without the slightest warning, something impossibly fast for its monstrous size overshadowed the world and the sky fell apart with a hellish roar. At first Zen thought that Spadola had fired at him. Then, swivelling round, he saw the second jet sharking silently through the air towards him. Absurdly, he started to wave, to call for help! Vasco Spadola broke into hoots of derisory laughter that were lost in the din as the fighter screamed past overhead, not deigning to notice the

antics of the petty creatures which crawled about on the bed of this
sea of air it used as a playground.

After that, Zen lost all track of time. Reality was reduced to a patch
of baked red soil always the same, always different. His sole task was
to find a way through the dense, prickly plants that grew there.
Sometimes they were widely spaced. Then he had only the constant
jarring pain from his ankle to contend with, the choking thirst and
the hammering headache. But usually the plants formed patterns
restricting his moves like hostile pieces in a board-game. Then he had
to raise his eyes and try and find a way through the maze. If he got it
wrong, or when the plants ahead of him closed up entirely, then he
had to force his way through. Branches poked him, thorns ripped his
clothes and scratched his skin. Several times he almost got stuck,
only to wrench himself free with a final effort. But stopping or
turning back was not permitted, though by now he could hardly
remember why.

At some point in this timeless torment he found himself confronted by a new obstacle, unforeseen by the rules of the game which
had absorbed him hitherto. It was a wire-mesh fence, about four
metres high, supported on concrete stakes and stretching away in
either direction as far as the eye could see. Some distance behind it
stood a similar fence of barbed wire.

Zen's first thought was that it was some sort of military installation. It wasn't until he saw a sign reading 'Beware of the Lions' that
he realized he had blundered into the perimeter fence of the Villa
Burolo. He started to follow the fence as it marched up the hillside.
But where it cut effortlessly through the undergrowth, dividing the
wilderness in two with surrealistic precision, Zen had to scramble,
wriggle, dodge and feint. Denser thickets in his path constantly
forced him to seek alternative routes, and as he became more
exhausted he began to lose his footing on the steep slope. His hands
were soon scuffed and scratched, his clothing tattered, his legs
bruised and bleeding.

It was some time before it occurred to him that he might try to
attract attention by setting off the villa's alarm systems. If he could
set the sirens off, the caretaker might turn on the closed-circuit television scanners, see the armed figure of Spadola and phone the police.
The problem was that in order to minimize false alarms, the outer
fence was not connected to the system, so Zen had to lob stones at the

inner fence with its attached sensors. This consisted of single strands of razor wire, and was very hard to hit. Zen's aim gradually improved, but before any of the stones connected with the target something that sounded like a swarm of bees whined past his head. An instant later he heard the gunshot.

When he turned round, Spadola had already broken open the shotgun and was reloading the spent barrel. He gestured angrily at Zen, waving him away from the fence. This incident served to remind Zen of the realities of his situation. The noise the shot made passing overhead suggested it had been travelling fast enough to do significant damage to his hands, face and neck. At the very least such injuries would cause serious loss of blood, in turn inducing a shocked condition in which further resistance would become impossible. Spadola could do that any time he wanted to. The fact that he had deliberately aimed high proved that. He was in total command of the situation, and would carry out the killing when it suited him and not before. Meanwhile, Zen could only struggle like an animal being used for scientific research, its agony the subject of dispassionate study, its feeble attempts to escape as predictable as they are vain.

At length the fence, obeying the forgotten whims of a dead man, changed direction to run north across the mountainside. Zen had now to choose between following it into unknown territory or continuing up the face of the mountain towards the lurid green forest massed at the head of the valley now closed by the dam. And he had to choose quickly, because Spadola was suddenly forcing the pace. But as soon as he saw that his quarry was continuing to struggle up into ever higher and wilder regions, he fell back again. What had concerned him, presumably, was that Zen might try to circle round the Burolo property to the main road. If he asked himself why his victim had selected the harder and more hopeless option, he probably put it down to his growing confusion and disorientation.

Zen toiled up the successive ridges of the mountainside towards the forest. By now the contrast between the hysterical green of the conifers and the sombre tones of the parched, abstemious landscape was less evident than it had been from a distance. Close to, it was not the upper surface of the forest that struck the eye but its lower depths, a dull brown stagnancy killed off by the tall victors of the struggle for survival. Their outspread branches formed a roof which closed off all light to the ground, condemning their own lower branches together with the losers of the race, whose spindly skeletons rose from a mulch of pine needles and rotting branches. This was what Zen had been hoping for. Vasco Spadola thought that he could play cat and mouse with his victim for hours yet, spinning out the game until the approach of night. What he hadn't realized was that in that unnatural forest, beneath those trees gorged on water seeping from the flawed dam, it was *always* night.

Zen glanced back to find that Spadola had broken into a run. Teeth gritted against the stabbing pain in his ankle, Zen ran too. He ran with the desperation of a man who knows that his life depends on it, and for the first crucial moments, despite his injury, he ran faster. After that Spadola rapidly started to narrow the gap, but by then it was too late. Zen had reached the cover of the trees. Another shot rang out, and Zen felt stinging pains all over his arms, legs and back. When he clapped a hand to his neck, as though slapping a mosquito, it came away stained with blood. Then he saw the lead pellets in his hand, little black lumps lodged just under the skin like burrowing ticks.

As Zen made his way deeper into the forest, he knew that there would be no further reprieves. The sadistic pleasure of killing his enemy by degrees had been replaced in Spadola's mind by an urgent desire to finish him off before it was too late.

After so many hours in the open, entering the forest was like stepping into a huge building: hushed, mysterious, dim and intimate in detail, vast and complex in design. Zen barged on, forcing aside the brittle tendrils that waved outwards from the trunks, like seaweed under water. Once his eyes had adjusted, the darkness thinned to a dimness that limited visibility to about ten metres, except when a clearing caused by a rocky outcrop punched a hole in the dense fabric of the forest. In one of these, he suddenly caught sight of a great curtain of concrete, towering above the trees. The thought of that hanging lake increased his impression of being under water. Beyond the immediate circle of bare column-like tree trunks, nothing was visible. Despite the moisture that forced its way out through the faults in the dam to keep the undersoil perpetually damp, nothing grew beneath the killing cover of the trees. The forest was a reservoir of silence and darkness. No breezes entered, nothing stirred.

The bare soil, soft with composted droppings, squelched underfoot. It was that sound which could give him away, he realized. In the deathly hush beneath the trees, the least noise would betray his position, and it was impossible to move without making a noise. But by the same token, Spadola could only hear Zen if he himself stopped moving, in which case he would fall ever further behind, the sounds would grow fainter and his bearings on their source less precise. So Zen's strategy was to plough on without once stopping or looking back, and then, once he was deep inside the forest, to stop and stay absolutely still. Then the tables would be turned. Deprived of any clue as to Zen's whereabouts, Spadola could only beat about at random, while the noise he made doing so would give Zen ample warning of his approach. If necessary, Zen could simply repeat the process until darkness fell. The advantage now lay with him.

The floor of the forest sloped gently to the east, following the contours of the invisible mountainside. Zen pushed on, his arms held up to protect his face from the dead twigs sticking out from the tree trunks. Several times he tripped agonizingly. Once he stumbled on a root surfacing like a monstrous worm and fell against a broken branch that cut his forehead open. But he felt nothing until he stopped, satisfied that he had gone far enough. Then all the injuries he had suffered ganged up to air their grievances. Surrendering to his exhaustion, Zen stretched out on the ground and closed his eyes.

The noises woke him, crashing sounds close at hand, their source invisible in the eerie gloom. He looked round wildly, forgetting for a merciful moment where he was. Then he saw the line of scuffed footmarks running back across the undulating surface and the dangling branches he had broken in his reckless flight, and understood. Far from vanishing into the trackless wastes of the forest, he had left a trail a child could have followed. But the creature following him was no child, and it was almost upon him.

He knew this was the end. Physically exhausted by his ordeal, weakened by hunger, thirst and loss of blood, this final blow had crippled his morale as well. Further resistance was futile. Nothing he had done since leaving the village had made the slightest difference to the outcome. He might just as well have ordered a last drink and sat in the bar waiting to die. Yet to his disgust, for it seemed a kind of weakness, a cowardice, he was unable to let things take their course even now. Instead he must stagger on through that sunken landscape, that lumber room of dead growth, without direction or purpose, out of control to the last.

In this frame of mind, he was incapable of surprise, even when he stumbled across the path weaving through the forest like a road across the bed of a flooded valley. The trodden surface showed signs of recent use, no doubt by animals, though there were no signs of any droppings. In one direction the path ran downhill, presumably leading out of the lower flank of the forest. Zen turned the other way. Encroaching branches beside the path had already been broken off, and his own footsteps were invisible in the general disturbance of the forest floor. If Spadola went the wrong way when he reached the path, Zen would have gained ample time to find a secure sanctuary. Hope teased his heart, banishing the deathly calm of his fatalistic resignation.

The path wound uphill in a lazily purposeful way that lulled Zen's attention, until suddenly he found himself standing on the brink of a deep chasm in the forest floor, scanning the trough of darkness in front of him. He could see nothing: no path, no ground, no trees. It was as if the world ended there.

After standing there indecisively for some moments, he realized the ravine offered the hiding-place he had been seeking, if he could manage to scramble down the precipitous slope below him. Nevertheless, he had to overcome a strong reluctance to descend into that black hole, although he knew this revulsion was the height of foolishness. It was not the dark he should be afraid of but Spadola. He lowered himself on to a rocky outcrop and started to clamber down.

At first the descent was easier than he had imagined, with numerous ledges and projections. But the further down he went, the fainter grew the glimmers of light from the surface far above, until at length he could hardly make out his next foothold. The idea of losing his footing and plunging off into nothingness made his palms sweat and his limbs shake in a way that greatly increased the chances of this happening. The only measure of how deep the chasm was came from the falling rocks he dislodged. Gradually the clattering became briefer and less resonant, until he sensed rather than saw that he had reached the bottom.

As his pupils dilated fully, he could just make out the hunched shapes of boulders all around, and realized that he was standing in the channel cut by the river which had flowed down from the lake above before the dam was built. The huge rocks littering its bed would have been washed down in the former torrent's spectacular seasonal surges.

When he heard the scurry of falling stones behind him, Zen's first thought was that the dam had given way and the black tide, unpenned, was surging towards him, sweeping away everything in its path. Then he realized the sound had come from above.

Frantically, he began to pick his way down the riverbed, crawling round and over the shattered lumps of granite, trying to put as much distance as possible between himself and the killer on his trail. As soon as the noises of Spadola's descent ceased, Zen could go to ground in some obscure nook or cranny. It would take an army weeks to search that chaotic maze.

But, to his dismay, the channel ended almost immediately, widening out into a circular gully closed off by a wall of dull white rock, rounded like the end of a bath. The foliage above was thinned out by this space where nothing grew, allowing a trace more light to filter down to the depths. Zen gazed at the freakish rock formation surrounding him. He did not understand what could have caused it, but one thing was clear. The wall of smooth white rock was at least ten metres high and absolutely sheer. Zen couldn't possibly climb it, and with Spadola hard on his heels he couldn't turn back. He had fallen into a perfect natural trap, a killing ground from which there was no escape.

The sound of tumbling rocks announced the approach of the hunter. With a weary slackness of heart, as though performing a duty for the sake of appearances, Zen knelt down and squeezed himself into a narrow crevice underneath a tilting boulder. As soon as Spadola reached the end of the gully, he would become aware that Zen could not have climbed out and must therefore be hiding nearby. He would flush him out almost at once. This time it really was the end. There was nothing to do but wait. He lay absolutely still, as though part of the rock was pressing in on him.

'Well, fuck me!'

Zen felt so lonely and scared that the words, the first he had heard since leaving the village, brought tears to his eyes. He was suddenly desperate to live, terrified of death, of extinction, of the unknown. How precious were the most banal moments of everyday life, precisely because they were banal!

A mighty roar scoured the enclosed confines of the gully. As the shot echoed away, Spadola's peals of manic laughter could be heard.

'Come on out, Zen! The game's over. Time to pay up.'

The voice was close by, although Zen could see nothing but a jumble of rocks.

'Are you going to come out and die like a man, or do you want to play hide-and-seek? It's up to you, but if you piss me about I might just decide to kill you a little more slowly. Maybe a little shot in the balls, for openers. I'm not a vindictive man, but there are limits to my patience.'

Like rats leaving a doomed ship, all Zen's faculties seemed to have fled the body wedged in its rocky tomb. He was incapable of movement, speech or thought, already as good as dead.

Spadola laughed.

'Ah, so there you are! Decided to spare me the trouble, have you? Very wise.'

Zen still couldn't see Spadola, but somehow he had been spotted. The anomaly didn't bother him. It seemed perfectly consistent with everything else that had happened. Footsteps approached. Zen tried to think of something significant in his last moments, and failed.

Something stirred the air close to his face. Less than a metre away, close enough to touch, a boot hit the ground and a trousered leg swished past.

'There's no point in trying to hide,' Spadola shouted, his voice echoing slightly. 'I can still see you. Let's just get it over with, shall we? It's been fun, but . . .'

There was a loud gunshot, followed by a scream of rage and fury. Then two more shots rang out simultaneously, one deafeningly close to Zen, the other a repetition of the first. Pellets bounced and rattled against the rocks, ricocheting like hailstones.

It seemed impossible that the silence could ever recover from such a savage violation, but before long the echoes died away as though nothing had happened. Zen had no idea what *had* happened, so he waited a long time, sampling the silence, before emerging from his hiding-place. He found Spadola almost immediately, his body flung backwards across the rocks, a limp, discarded carapace. Something had scooped a raw crater out of his belly, around which circles of lesser destruction spread out like ripples on a pond. The shotgun lay close by, wedged between two rocks.

Zen searched dispassionately through the dead man's pockets

until he found his lighter, then sat down on a rock and lit a cigarette. From this perch he could see the end of the gully. Beneath the wall of white rock the ground opened up to form a cavernous sluice funnelling downwards, the edges clean and rounded. As he sat there, the cigarette smouldering peacefully between his fingers, Zen recalled what Turiddu had said about the soft rocks and the hard rocks, and realized that the white surface closing off the gully was the limestone that overlaid the granite at this point, rubbed to a smooth curve by the whirling water before it disappeared underground into the pool of darkness at the base of the cliff which was now a main entrance to the cave system underlying the whole area.

Something glinted in the shadows just inside the cavern. Like the immortal he had once seemed to be, playing God with the video of the Burolo killings, Zen made his way towards it as though immune to danger. The grey rock was stained with something sticky that, smelling it, he knew was drying blood. A double-barrel pump-action Remington shotgun lay near by. The metal was still warm. By the flickering flame of his cigarette lighter, Zen read the inscription engraved on the barrel: 'To Oscar, Christmas 1979, from his loving wife Rita.'

How wrong I was! And how right! Yes, a death was needed, and he brought it. But how did I fail to see that the person whose death would set me free was me?

The darkness is closing in, touching me, taking me like a lover. There was blood then, too. He seemed to expect it, but I was shocked. No one had told me anything. I thought I was going to die. I didn't, though, not that time. But now my long labour is finally accomplished, and the death I have been carrying all these years is about to be delivered. A little more pain and everything will be over. There's nothing more to do, nothing to be done.

And then? I've tried to be a good girl, but trying is not enough. Everything depends on his mercy, or his inattention. It's surprising what you can get away with sometimes, then at others he'll beat you viciously for nothing at all. So in the end justice is done. Who can say? Will my sufferings count for anything, my good deeds? Will I be judged worthy of forgiveness, this time? Of love?

ROME

Friday, 11.20–20.45

'He threatened to kill me?'

'Oh, yes! Me too, for that matter. But it's only talk. He has to call his mother if he finds a spider in the bath. Now if *she'd* said it we might have something to worry about.'

The café on Via Veneto accurately reflected the faded glories of the street itself. The mellow tones of marble, leather and wood predominated. Dim lighting discreetly revealed the understated splendours of an establishment so prestigious it had no need to put on a show. Its famous name appeared everywhere, on the cups and saucers, the spoons, the sugar-bowl and ashtray, the peach-coloured napkins and tablecloth and the staff's azure jackets. The waiters conducted themselves like family retainers, studiously polite yet avoiding any hint of familiarity. A sumptuous calm reigned.

The café was too far from the Viminale to be one of the regular haunts of Ministry personnel, who in any case would have balked at paying 4,000 lire for a cup of coffee they could get elsewhere for 800, with a hefty dose of Roman pandemonium thrown in for free. This was one reason why Zen had invited Tania there for their first meeting since his return from Sardinia. The other was a desire he still didn't completely understand, to do things differently, to break free of old habits, to change his life, *himself.*

'How did he find out?'

She smiled, anticipating his reaction.

'He hired a private detective.'

'To follow you?'

'To follow *you!*'

So that was who Leather Jacket had been working for, thought Zen, not Spadola or Fabri, but Mauro Bevilacqua! Ironically, he might have considered that possibility earlier if it hadn't seemed wishful thinking to imagine that Tania's husband could have any reason to feel jealous of *him.*

'He didn't want to admit even to the detective that his wife might be unfaithful,' Tania explained. 'He was afraid people would laugh at him and call him a cuckold.'

'Which he wasn't, of course. Isn't, I mean.'

'Well, it depends on how you look at it. According to the strictest criteria, a husband is a cuckold if his wife has even *thought* of being unfaithful.'

They exchanged a glance.

'In that case we're all cuckolds,' Zen replied lightly.

'That's why Mauro would claim that his vigilance was completely justified.'

This time they both laughed.

Zen lit a Nazionale and studied the young woman sitting opposite him, her legs crossed, her right foot rising and falling gently in time to her pulse. Clad in the currently fashionable outfit of black mid-length coat, short black skirt and black patterned tights, with bright scarlet lipstick and short wet-look hair, she looked very different from the last time he had seen her. Not that he minded. The Tania he loved – he felt able to use the word now, at least to himself – was invulnerable to change, and as for this new image she had chosen to show the world, he found it exciting, sophisticated and sexy. A week ago he would have hated it, but the life which had almost miraculously been returned to him in Sardinia was no longer quite the same as it had been before he had passed through that ordeal.

'But it must be a nightmare for you,' he said seriously. 'It was bad enough having to live there before, but now that his suspicions have been proven, or apparently proven . . .'

'I don't live there any more.'

For a moment they both remained silent, the news lying on the table between them like an unopened letter.

Tania lifted the pack of Nazionali and shook a cigarette loose.

'May I?'

'I didn't know you smoked.'

'I do now.'

He held the lighter for her. She lit up and blew out smoke self-consciously, like a schoolgirl.

'He hit me, you see.'

Zen signalled his shock with a sharp intake of breath.

'So I hit him back. With the frying pan. It had hot fat in it. Not much, but enough to give him a nasty burn. When his mother found out I thought she'd go for me with the carving knife, but in the end she backed off and started babbling to herself in this creepy way, hysterical but very controlled, saying I was a northern witch who had put her son under a spell but she knew how to destroy my power. It scared me to death. I knew then that I had to leave.'

'Where did you go?'

He dropped the question casually, like the experienced interrogator that he was, as though it were a minor detail of no significance.

'To a friend's.'

'A friend's.'

She took a notebook and pen from her handbag, wrote down an address and handed it to him. He read, 'Tania Biacis, c/o Alessandra Bruni, Via dei Gelsi 47. Tel. 788447.'

'It's in Centocelle. I'm staying there temporarily, until I find somewhere for myself. You know how difficult it is.'

He nodded.

'And Mauro?'

'Mauro? Mauro's still living with his mamma.'

Everything about her had a new edge to it, and Zen couldn't be sure that this wasn't an ironical reference to his own situation.

Ignoring this, he said, 'That restaurant in Piazza Navona, it's open tonight.'

She waited for him to spell it out.

'Would you think of . . . I mean, I don't suppose you're free or anything, but . . .'

'I'd love to.'

'Really?'

She laughed, this time without malice.

'Don't look so surprised!'

'But I *am* surprised.'

Her laughter abruptly subsided.

'So am I, to tell you the truth. I can't quite see how we got here. Still, here we are.'

'Here we are,' he agreed, and signalled to the waiter.

On the broad pavement outside, Zen pulled Tania against him and kissed her briefly on both cheeks in a way that might have been purely friendly, if they had been friends. She coloured a little, but said nothing. Then, having agreed to meet at the restaurant that evening, Tania hailed a taxi to take her to Palazzo di Montecitorio, the parliament building, where she had to run an errand for Lorenzo Moscati, while Zen returned to the Ministry on foot.

The winter sunlight, hazy with air pollution, created a soothing warmth that eased the lingering aches in Zen's body. A surgeon in Nuoro had spent three hours picking shotgun pellets out of his limbs and lower back, but apart from those minor subcutaneous injuries and a slightly swollen ankle, his ordeal had left no permanent scars. He strolled along without haste, drinking in the sights and sounds. How precious it all seemed, how rich and various, unique and detailed! He spent five minutes watching an old man at work collecting cardboard boxes from outside a shoe shop, deftly collapsing and flattening each one. An unmarked grey delivery van with reflecting windows on the rear doors drove past with a roar and pulled in to the side of the street, squashing one of the cardboard boxes. The old man waved his fist impotently, then retrieved the box, straightened it out and brushed it clean before adding it to the tall pile already tied to the antique pram he used as a cart.

Zen walked past the open doorway of a butcher's shop, from which came a series of loud bangs and a smell of blood. The delivery van roared by and double-parked at the corner of the street, engine running. Outside a pet shop, a row of plastic bags filled with water were hanging from a rack. In each bag, a solitary goldfish twitched to and fro, trapped in its fragile bubble-world. A mechanical street-cleaner rolled past, leaving a swathe of glistening asphalt in its wake, looping out round the obstruction caused by the grey van. No one got in or out of the van. Nothing was loaded or unloaded. A tough-looking young man, clean-shaven, with cropped hair sat behind the wheel, staring straight ahead. He paid no attention to Zen.

Up in the Criminalpol suite on the third floor of the Ministry, the other officials were in the midst of a heated discussion with Vincenzo Fabri at its centre.

'The British have got the right idea,' Fabri was proclaiming loudly. 'Catch them on the job and gun them down. Forget the legal bullshit.'

'But that's different!' Bernardo Travaglini protested. 'The IRA are terrorists.'

'There's no difference! Sicily, Naples, Sardinia, they're our Northern Ireland! Except we're dumb enough to respect everyone's rights and do things by the book.'

'That's not the point, Vincenzo,' De Angelis interrupted.

'Thatcher's got an absolute majority, she can do what she wants. But here in Italy we've got a democracy. You've got to take account of people's opinions.'

'Screw people's opinions!' Fabri exploded. 'This is war! The only thing that matters is who is going to win, the state or a bunch of gangsters. And the answer is they are, unless we stop pissing about and match them for ruthlessness.'

He caught sight of Zen sidling past and broke off suddenly.

'Now there's somebody who's got the right idea,' he exclaimed. 'While the rest of us are sweating it out down in Naples, trying to protect a bunch of criminals who would be better off dead, Aurelio here pops over to Sardinia and turns up, quote, new evidence in the Burolo case, unquote, which just happens to put a certain politician's chum in the clear. That's the way to do things! Never mind the rights and wrongs of the situation. Results are all that matters.'

Resignedly, Zen turned to face his tormentor. This was a showdown he could not dodge.

'What do you mean by that?'

Fabri faked a smile of complicity.

'Oh, come on! No hard feelings! In your shoes I'd have done the same. But it just goes to prove what I've been saying. Do things by the book like us poor suckers and what do you get? A lot of head-aches, long hours, and a boot up the bum when things go wrong. Whereas if you look after number one, cultivate the right contacts and forget about procedures, you get covered in glory, name in the paper and friends in high places!'

'To be fair, you should take some of the credit,' Zen replied.

'Me? What are you talking about?'

'Well, you recommended me, didn't you?'

Fabri's eyes narrowed dangerously.

'Recommended you to who?'

'To Palazzo Sisti.'

A moment's silence was broken by a rather forced laugh from Vincenzo Fabri.

'Do me a favour, will you? I don't go to bed with politicians, and if I did I certainly wouldn't choose that bunch of losers!'

'It's all right, Vincenzo,' Zen reassured him. 'They told me. I asked who had put them on to me and they said it was their contact at the Ministry.'

Fabri laughed dismissively.

'And what's that got to do with me?'

'Well, they said this person, this contact, had already tried to fiddle the Burolo case for them, except he'd made a complete balls-up of it. As far as I know, you're the only person here who's done any work on that case.'

'You're lying!'

It was Zen's turn to switch on a smile of complicity.

'Look, it's all right, Vincenzo! We're among friends here. No hard feelings, as you said yourself. I for one certainly don't hold it against you. But then I'm hardly in a position to, of course.'

Fabri stared at him furiously.

'I tell you once and for all that I have nothing whatever to do with Palazzo Sisti! Is that clear?'

Zen appeared taken aback by this ringing denial.

'Are you sure?'

'Of course I'm fucking sure!'

Zen shook his head slowly.

'Well, that's very odd. Very odd indeed. All I can say is that's what I was told. But if you say it's not true . . .'

'Of course it's not true! How dare you even suggest such a thing?'

'Admittedly I can't prove anything,' Zen muttered.

'Of course you can't!'

'Can *you*?'

The reply was quick and pointed. Fabri recoiled from it as from a drawn knife.

'What? Can I what?'

'Can you prove that the allegations made by *l'onorevole*'s private secretary are untrue?'

'I don't *need* to prove it!' Fabri shouted.

No one had moved, yet Zen sensed that the arrangement of the group had changed subtly. Before, he had been confronted by a coherent mass of officials, united in their opposition to the outsider. Now a looser gathering of individuals stood between him and Fabri, shuffling their feet and looking uncertainly from one man to the other.

'Don't you?' Zen replied calmly. 'Oh, well in that case, of course, there's nothing more to be said.'

He turned away.

'Exactly!' Fabri called after him. 'There's nothing more to be said!'

When Zen reached the line of screens that closed off his desk he glanced back. The group of officials had broken up into smaller clusters, chatting together in low voices. Vincenzo Fabri was talking at full speed in an undertone, gesticulating dramatically, demanding the undivided attention he felt was his by right. But some of his listeners were gazing down at the floor in a way which suggested that they were not totally convinced by Fabri's protestations. They accepted that Zen was an unscrupulous grafter on the make. The difference was that they now suspected that Fabri was one too, and that the reason for his bitterness was not moral indignation but the fact that his rival was more successful.

Giorgio De Angelis, keeping a foot in both camps as usual, patted Fabri on the shoulder in a slightly patronizing way before walking over to join Zen.

'Congratulations. It was about time something like that happened to Vincenzo.'

A wan smile brightened Zen's face.

'So tell me all about it!' De Angelis continued. 'How on earth did you manage to do it?'

Zen's smile died. Of all his colleagues, De Angelis was the one with whom he had the closest relationship, yet the Calabrian clearly took it for granted that Zen had 'fixed' the Burolo case. Well, if no one was going to believe him anyway, he might as well take the credit for his supposed villainy!

He turned his smile on again.

'The funny thing is, I hadn't been going to use the woman at all originally. The person I had in mind was Furio Padedda. He seemed the perfect candidate from everyone's point of view.'

'But Padedda was involved too, wasn't he?' said De Angelis.

Zen shook his head. No one seemed to be able to get the story straight, no doubt because the only thing that really concerned them was the headline news which the media, carefully orchestrated by Palazzo Sisti, had been trumpeting all week: that the case against Renato Favelloni had collapsed.

'Padedda and the Melega family were planning to kidnap Burolo, successfully this time, and extort a huge sum of money from the family. They might well have killed him too, after they got paid, but that was all in the future. On the night of the murders, Padedda was attending a meeting of the gang up in the mountains. But I certainly could have used him, if all else had failed. He even had a convenient wound on his arm. His blood group is different from that of the stains at the villa, but we could have got round that somehow.'

One by one, the other officials had approached to hear Zen's story. It was a situation new to him, and one he found rather embarrassing. Unlike Fabri, he had never enjoyed being the centre of attention. But things had changed. If Fabri could no longer count on star billing, neither could Zen avoid the fame – or rather notoriety – which had been thrust upon him.

'But in the event I didn't need Padedda. As soon as I'd visited the scene I knew how I was going to work it. As you probably know, Burolo's villa was originally a farm house. The farms in that area were all built over caves giving access to an underground stream where they got their water. When I inspected the cellar of the Villa Burolo I noticed that the air was very fresh. The caretaker explained that it was naturally ventilated, and pointed out an opening at floor level. Since we were underground, I realized right away that the air could only have come from the cave system.'

The assembled officials nodded admiringly.

'No one else had thought of this as a way around the famous problem of access, for the simple reason that the vent was too small to admit a normal adult. But that was precisely what attracted me to the idea. There were already indications suggesting that the killer might have been exceptionally small. The upward angle of fire, for one thing, and the fact that on the video Burolo and even Vianello's wife, who was tiny herself, look *down* at the person confronting them. Then there was the ghost that child claimed to have seen one night, a woman who looked like a little old witch. As soon as this woman Elia hobbled up to me in the village, asking for money, I put two and two together and made five.'

This elicited a ripple of appreciative laughter.

'But mightn't she have done it?' asked Carlo Romizi earnestly. 'I mean I saw this thing on the television which seemed to be suggesting that . . .'

Zen gestured impatiently.

'Of course she might! She wouldn't have been much use to me otherwise, would she?'

'No, I mean *really*.'

Zen frowned. 'Oh, you mean *really*!'

He turned to the others. 'Quick, someone! Get on the phone to Palazzo Sisti. They'll have your mug all over the morning papers, Carlo. "Italian Believes Favelloni Innocent. After months of research, Palazzo Sisti announced last night that they had located someone who believes in the innocence of Renato Favelloni. 'It's true that he's an Umbrian,' admitted a spokesman for *l'onorevole*, 'but we feel this may be the beginning of a significant swing in public opinion'."'

Zen stood back, letting the waves of laughter wash over him. I could grow to like this, he thought, the good-humoured, easy-going chaffing, the mutual admiration of male society. Fatherless from early childhood, with no one to teach him the unwritten rules, he had always found it difficult to play the game with the necessary confidence and naturalness. But perhaps it wasn't too late even now.

'What I still don't understand is how you managed to tie it up so neatly at the end,' Travaglini commented.

'There was nothing to it really,' Zen replied modestly. 'There were various ways I could have worked it, but when Spadola showed up in the village it seemed a good idea to kill two jailbirds with one stone, so to speak. I couldn't predict exactly what would happen if I brought him and Elia together, but there seemed a good chance that one or both might not survive. Which suited me down to the ground, of course. The last thing I wanted was the magistrates getting a chance to interrogate her.'

'Have they found her body yet?' someone asked.

Zen shook his head.

'The cave system is very extensive and has never been mapped. As you can imagine, the locals don't have much time for speleology. They used the cave mouths for storage and shelter but no one apart from Elia had bothered to explore any further. The Carabinieri flew in a special team trained in pot-holing . . .'

'Complete with designer wet-suits by Armani,' De Angelis put in.

Everyone laughed. The glamorous image of their paramilitary rivals was always a sore point with the police.

'By Wednesday, two of the Carabinieri had managed to get lost themselves,' Zen resumed, 'and the others were busy looking for them. All they found of the woman were a few blood stains matching those at the villa, and a collection of odds and ends she'd apparently stolen, things of no value.'

Travaglini offered Zen a cigarette which he felt constrained to accept, even though it wasn't a brand he favoured. Such are the burdens of popularity, he reflected.

'What are you doing about a motive?'

'No problem. One of the villagers, a man called Turiddu, claimed that his family had owned the farm house which Burolo bought. At the time I thought he was bragging, but it turned out to be true. The Carabinieri also confirmed that Elia was Turiddu's sister, and that she'd been found locked in a cellar. The story is that when she was fifteen she fell in love with someone her father disapproved of. The man suggested that he get her pregnant to force her father to consent to their marriage. Simple-minded Elia agreed. Once he'd had her a few times, the young man changed his mind about marriage, of course. Although she wasn't pregnant, Elia told her father what had happened, hoping he would force the man to keep his word. Unfortunately her lover got wind of this and ran off to a branch of the family in Turin.

'Since he was out of reach, Elia's father took revenge on his daughter instead, locking her up in the cellar and telling everyone that she had gone away to stay with relatives on the mainland. She spent the next thirteen years there, in total darkness and solitude, sleeping on the bare floor in her own filth. Twice a day her mother brought her some food, but she never spoke to her or touched her again. Turiddu told us that he was forbidden to mention her existence, even within the family. This naturally made him even more curious about this strange sister of his, who had committed this terrible nameless sin. He started sneaking down to the cellar when his parents were out, to gawp at her. And then one day, to his astonishment, he found she wasn't there.

'There was nowhere she could be hiding, and it was inconceivable that she had escaped through the bolted door leading up to the house. Eventually he realized that she must have managed to get through the hole leading to the underground stream. He put out his lantern and kept watch, and sure enough, a few hours later he heard her coming back. He struck a match and caught her wriggling in through the hole, which she had gradually worn away by continual rubbing until it was just wide enough for her to get through. His father's ban on acknowledging Elia's existence made it impossible for Turiddu to betray her secret even if he had wanted to. Anyway, it didn't seem important. As far as he was concerned, the caves where the stream flowed were just an extension of the cellar. Elia's prison might be a little larger than her father supposed, but it was still a prison.

'All this came out when we interrogated Turiddu on Monday and Tuesday. At first he played the tough guy, but once I made it clear that his sister was dead, that she was going to take the rap for Favelloni, and that unless he cooperated he would get five to ten for aiding and abetting, he changed his mind. Underneath the bluster, he was a coward with a guilty conscience. There was a running feud between his family and a clan in the mountains. The usual story, rustling and encroachment. Turiddu's father "accidentally" shot one of the mountain men while out hunting, and they got their own back by ambushing his van. Both parents were killed. It was Turiddu's responsibility to carry on the vendetta, but he shirked it. That sense of shame fed his hatred for anyone connected with the mountains, like Padedda. Still, he gave us what we wanted. Once he got started he poured out details so fast that the sergeant taking notes could hardly keep up. "Eh, excuse me, would you mind confessing a little more slowly?" he kept saying.'

Once again, laughter spread through the officials grouped around, hanging on Zen's words.

'So the motive is revenge,' said De Angelis. 'As far as this woman was concerned, whoever lived upstairs in that house was the person responsible for punishing her.'

Zen shrugged.

'Something like that. It doesn't matter anyway. She was crazy, capable of anything. And we don't need a confession. The gun she dropped after shooting Spadola was the one used in the Burolo killings, and her fingerprints match the unidentified ones on the gun-rack at the villa.'

'But how do you explain the fact that Burolo's records had been tampered with?' Travaglini objected.

'Easy. They weren't. In our version, the chaos in the cellar was due to the fact that the new shelving Burolo had put up blocked the vent Elia used to get in and out of her old home. On the night of the murders she worked the fittings loose, then pushed the whole unit over, sending the tapes and floppy disks flying, which is what caused the crash audible on the video recording. By the way, lads, how do you think this is going to make our friends of the flickering flame look? The Carabinieri seized all that material right after the killings. If our murderer didn't erase the compromising data on those discs, who did?'

De Angelis shook his head in admiration. 'You're a genius, Aurelio! How the hell did you ever manage to balls up so badly in the Moro business?'

For a moment Zen thought his façade of cool cynicism would crack. This was too near the bone, too painful. But in the end he managed to carry it off.

'We all make mistakes, Giorgio. The best we can hope for is not to go on making the same one over and over again.'

'I still don't see how you arranged for the shotgun used in the Burolo murders to turn up in the cave where this Elia was,' Romizi insisted. 'Or how you fixed the fingerprints.'

Zen smiled condescendingly. 'Now, now. You can't expect me to tell you all my little secrets!'

'So Renato Favelloni walks free,' Travaglini concluded heavily.

'Not to mention *l'onorevole*,' added Romizi.

For a moment it seemed as though the atmosphere might turn sour. Then De Angelis struck a theatrical pose.

'"I have examined my conscience,"' he declared, quoting a celebrated statement by the politician in question, '"and I find that it is perfectly clean."'

'Not surprisingly,' Zen chipped in, 'given that he never uses it.'

The discussion broke up amid hoots of cynical laughter.

Before meeting Tania Biacis for dinner that evening, Zen had a number of chores to perform. The first of these was to return the white Mercedes. Early on Monday morning a Carabinieri jeep had towed the car back to Lanusei, where it had been repaired. On his return to Rome Zen had left a note for Fausto Arcuti at the Rally Bar, and earlier that morning Arcuti had phoned and told Zen to leave the car opposite the main gates of the former abattoir.

'What about locking the doors?' Zen had asked.

'Lock them, dottore, lock them! The Testaccio is a den of thieves.'

'And the keys?'

'Leave them in the car.'

'But how are you going to open it, then?'

'How do you think we opened it in the first place?' Fausto demanded. Now that the informer was no longer in fear of his life, his naturally irreverent manner had reasserted itself.

After lunch with De Angelis and Travaglini, Zen set off in the Mercedes, reflecting on his conflicting feelings about being readmitted to the male freemasonry which ran not only the Criminalpol department but also the Ministry, the Mafia, the Church and the government. It all seemed very relaxing and attractive at first, the mutual back-scratching and ego-boosting, the shared values and unchallenged assumptions. Yet even before the end of lunch a reaction set in, and Zen found the cosy back-chat and the smug sense of innate superiority beginning to pall. It was all a bit cloying, a bit too reminiscent of the self-congratulatory nationalism of the Fascist epoch. Whatever happened between him and Tania, he knew it would never be easy. But that, perhaps, was what made it worthwhile.

As he queued up to enter the maelstrom of traffic around the Colosseum, Zen noticed an unmarked grey delivery van three or four vehicles behind him. He adjusted the wing mirror until he could see the driver. It didn't look like the man he had seen that morning, but of course they might be working shifts.

He continued south, past the flank of the Palatine, then turned right along the Circus Maximus and crossed the river into Trastevere. The grey van followed faithfully. He was being tailed. This in itself was bad enough. What made it infinitely worse was that Zen felt absolutely sure he knew who was responsible.

Despite his bluster, Vasco Spadola must have known that he couldn't be certain of success in his single-handed vendetta. Things can always go wrong; that's why people take out insurance. There seemed very little doubt that the grey van represented Spadola's insurance. The men he had spotted in the van were not slavering psychotics like Spadola himself, getting a hard-on at the idea of killing. Nor were they third-rate cowboys like Leather Jacket. They were professionals, doing what they had been paid to do, carrying out a contract to be put into effect in the event of Spadola's death. The only other explanation was that Mauro Bevilacqua was pursuing revenge at secondhand, but that seemed wildly unlikely. Tania clearly hadn't taken his threats seriously. In any case, professional killers didn't advertise in the Yellow Pages, and a bank clerk wouldn't have known how to contact them.

Zen turned off the Lungotevere and steered at random through the back streets around the factory where his favourite Nazionali cigarettes were made. The incident had plunged him into apathetic despair. These men wouldn't give up, whatever happened. They had their reputation to consider. There was no point in having the team in the van arrested. They would simply be replaced by another crew. His only hope, a very slim one, was to find out who Spadola had placed the contract with and try to renegotiate the deal. But that was for the future. His immediate task was to lose the tail. Unfortunately this called for virtuoso driving skills Zen didn't possess.

In the end, his very incompetence proved to be his salvation. As he turned out of the back streets by Porta Portese he was so deep in thought about his problems that he failed to notice that the traffic lights had just changed to red. The white Mercedes managed to squeeze between the lines of the traffic closing in from either side, but the grey van remained trapped. Zen crossed the river again, veered round into Via Marmorata and then, once he was out of sight of the van, turned right into the Testaccio. He abandoned the car with the keys locked inside, as Arcuti had instructed him, then worked his way back to Via Marmorata on foot, taking refuge in the doorway of the ornate fire station at the corner until he saw a number thirty tram approaching the stop.

He got off the tram near Porta Maggiore and walked round to Gilberto Nieddu's flat, where his mother had been staying for the past week. Zen had promised to collect her that afternoon, but now he was going to have to ask for more time. Gilberto had insisted that everything had gone well, but he was bound to say that. Zen knew that looking after his mother must have been a terrible imposition, and one that would now have to be prolonged. Until he had resolved the problem of the grey van his mother could not return home. He did not look forward to breaking this news to the Nieddus.

Gilberto was at work, so it was Rosella Nieddu who greeted Zen at the door of their pleasant, modern flat in Via Carlo Emanuele. To Zen's amazement, his mother was playing a board-game with the two youngest Nieddu daughters. It was so long since he had seen her do anything except slump in a comatose state in front of the television that this perfectly ordinary scene of domestic life seemed as bizarre and alarming as if the tram he had just been on had suddenly veered off the rails and started careering freely about the streets, menacing the passers-by.

'Hello, Aurelio!' she called gaily, beaming a distracted smile in his direction. 'Everything all right?'

Without waiting for his response, she turned back to the children. 'No, not there! Otherwise I'll gobble you up like this, bang bang bang bang bang!'

The girls tittered nervously. 'But Auntie, you can't go there, it's the wrong way,' the elder pointed out.

'Oh! So it is! Silly old me. Silly old Auntie.'

Zen felt a pang of jealous hurt, all the stronger for being completely absurd. She's not your auntie, he felt like shouting. She's my mamma! Mine! Mine!

Taking Rosella Nieddu aside, he hesitantly broached the subject of his mother staying one more night.

'That's wonderful!' she replied, interrupting his deliberately vague explanations. 'Did you hear that, kids? Auntie Zen's not leaving today after all!'

A look of sheer delight instantly appeared on the children's faces. They rushed about, doing a sort of war-dance around the old lady, screaming at the top of their voices while she looked on happily, a benign totem-pole.

'What a treasure your mother is!' Rosella Nieddu enthused.

'Why, er, yes. Yes, of course.'

'She's been absolutely tireless with those two. I love them dearly, of course, but sometimes I think they're going to drive me round the bend. But your mother has the patience of a saint. And she knows all these wonderful games and tricks and stories! I haven't had to do a thing. It's been a real holiday for me. I've finally been able to catch up with my own life a bit. Gilberto helps as much as he can, of course, but he's so busy at work these days. Anyway, we've arranged that your mother's going to come round every week, once she goes home, I mean. That's all right, I hope.'

Zen stared at her.

'You *want* her to come?'

Rosella Nieddu's serene features contracted in puzzlement.

'Of course I do! And just as important, she wants to. She said she was . . . Well, anyway, she wants to come.'

Zen eyed her.

'What did she say?'

'I don't expect she meant it.'

'Meant what?'

'Well . . .'

'Yes?'

'It was just a manner of speaking, you know, but she said she'd had enough of being locked up at home.'

'Locked up?' Zen shouted angrily. 'What the hell do you mean? She's the one who refuses to set foot outside the flat!'

'Well, she's been out a lot while she's been with us.'

'She never wanted to move here in the first place. She hates Rome!'

'No she doesn't! We all went to the Borghese Gardens on Sunday. She couldn't believe all the joggers and cyclists, and the fathers pushing babies. Afterwards we went to the zoo and then had lunch out. We had a really good time. She said she hadn't enjoyed herself so much for years.'

Zen stood open-mouthed. This is not my mother, he wanted to protest, it's an impostor! My mother is a crabby old woman who spends her time shut up at home in front of the television. I don't want this wonderful, patient, inventive old lady with a zest for life! I want my mamma! I want my mamma!

'I'm glad to hear it, I'm sure,' he said drily. 'So it'll be no trouble if she stays another night, then?'

'It'll be a pleasure.'

Zen rode the lift downstairs feeling irritated, relieved and obscurely guilty. It wasn't his fault, of course. How could it be? He hadn't locked his mother up in the flat. She'd locked herself up. It was true that he had accepted that, because it was convenient, because it had left him free to do what he wanted, particularly when he'd been seeing Ellen. He'd always avoided confronting his mother with that relationship, preferring to shut her out of that area of his life. That was apparently one of the things that had made Ellen leave him in the end. Perhaps it *was* partly his fault, in a way. He hadn't created the situation, but he'd connived at it, used it, acquiesced. He hadn't been cruel, but he'd been lazy. He'd been thoughtless and selfish.

He stopped in the first café he came to and phoned the caretaker at home. Then he walked back to Porta Maggiore and took a number nineteen tram all the way round the city to its terminus a short walk from where he lived. As he had expected, there was no sign of the grey van, but the chances were that the house was under surveillance. Zen walked casually down the street and into the shop next door to his house, an outmoded emporium selling everything from corkscrews and hot-water bottles to dried beans and herbal remedies. It had the air of a museum rather than a shop, and the elderly woman who ran it had the haughty, disinterested manner of a curator.

'You're from the Electricity?' she demanded as Zen threaded his way through the shelves and cupboards to the counter.

'That's right.'

She jerked her thumb at a door at the rear of the shop. The array of mops and brooms which normally concealed it had been cleared to one side.

'Don't you dare touch anything!' she admonished. 'I know where everything is! If anything's missing, there'll be trouble, I promise you.'

Zen opened the door. Inside was a dark passageway almost completely filled with boxes of various sizes. At the end was a second door, opening into the courtyard of his own house. In the hall he found Giuseppe and thanked him for getting the shopkeeper to unlock the doors.

'So what's the problem, dottore?' the caretaker asked anxiously.

'Just a jealous husband.'

Giuseppe cackled and waggled a finger on either side of his forehead.

'He has good reason, I'll bet!'

Zen shrugged modestly. Giuseppe redoubled his cackles.

'Like we say in Lucania, there may be snow on the roof but there's still fire in the furnace! Eh, dottore!'

Once he had showered and shaved, Zen put on a suit of evening dress exhumed from the oak chest in which it had laid entombed since the last time he had had occasion to attend a formal gathering. He wandered dispiritedly through to the living room, struggling with a recalcitrant collar-stud. In the absence of his mother and Maria Grazia, the lares and penates of the place, the flat felt hollow and unreal, like a stage set which despite its scrupulous accuracy does not quite convince.

Catching sight of himself in the mirror above the sideboard, Zen was surprised to find that he did not look flustered and absurd, as he felt, but elegant and distinguished. What a shame that Tania would not see him in his finery! But it was clearly out of the question to keep their appointment as long as hired assassins were pursuing Spadola's vendetta from beyond the grave. He had already put her life at risk once too often.

He picked up the smooth pasteboard card propped against the mirror and scanned the lines of engraved italic copperplate requesting the pleasure of his company at a reception at Palazzo Sisti that evening at seven o'clock. Even *l'onorevole* and his cronies didn't have the gall to celebrate openly the collapse of the case against Renato Favelloni, so the reception was nominally in honour of one of the party's rising stars, who had recently been appointed to a crucial portfolio in the government's newly reshuffled cabinet. Zen had been very much in two minds about attending, particularly after Vincenzo Fabri's attack on him that morning, but the appearance of the grey van had removed his lingering doubts.

There was no point in him trying to buy off the people Spadola had hired. Even if he'd had the money to do so, the underworld had a strict code of consumer protection in such matters. Spadola would have made a substantial payment up front, with the balance in the hands of a trusted third party. The deposit was unreturnable now that Spadola was dead, so any failure to carry out the hit would amount to breach of contract. These rules of conduct were extremely rigid. Zen's only recourse was to try and persuade the organization involved that it was in its own interests to make an exception in this case. He himself didn't have the necessary clout to do this, but *l'onorevole* should, or would know who did. And *l'onorevole* owed him.

He reached for the phone and dialled the number Tania had given him that morning, to cancel their date, but there was no reply. By now it was ten to seven, and there was no sign of the taxi he had ordered, so he rang to complain. To his dismay, the dispatcher not only disclaimed all knowledge of his previous call but even hinted that Zen had invented it in order to jump the forty-five minute waiting period that now existed. After a brief acrimonious exchange Zen slammed down the receiver and headed for the door. The evening was fine and it was not too far to walk. Even if he didn't manage to pick up a taxi on the way he would arrive no more than fashionably late.

He raced down the stairs two at a time and out on to the street, trying to work out how best to phrase his petition without making it look as though he took Palazzo Sisti's underworld connections for granted. So preoccupied was he that he didn't notice the unmarked grey delivery van that was now double-parked further down the street, nor the dark figure that slipped out of a doorway near by and began to follow him.

His route was the same as he and Tania had taken a week earlier: past the law courts, across the river and south through Piazza Navona. He strode rapidly along, oblivious to the stares he was attracting from passers-by curious about this image of sartorial rectitude hoofing it through their vulgar streets like Cinderella going home from the ball.

When he reached the small piazza facing the grimy baroque church of Sant'Andrea della Valle, he was halted for some time by the traffic on Corso Vittorio Emanuele. A woman getting out of a car parked by the fountain shouted something and pointed. Zen turned to find a slight, swarthy man brandishing a pistol at him.

'You have disgraced my marriage bed and . . .'

He paused, breathless with the effort of running to keep up with Zen.

'. . . and brought dishonour on my house! For this you shall pay, as my name is Mauro Bevilacqua!'

So this is the way it's going to end, thought Zen. He almost laughed to think he had survived the worst a Vasco Spadola could do, only to fall victim to the ravings of a jealous bank clerk.

'You thought you had it all worked out, you two, didn't you?' Bevilacqua sneered. 'You thought you could have fun and games at my expense and get away scot-free. Well let me tell you . . .'

Tyres squealed as the grey van slewed to a halt by the neat Fascist office block at the other side of the piazza. Men in grey overalls bearing the word POLIZIA in fluorescent yellow leapt out, clutching submachine guns.

'Don't move!' boomed a harshly amplified voice. 'Drop your weapon!'

Mauro Bevilacqua looked about him in utter bewilderment. He turned to face the van, the pistol still in his hand. A volley of shots rang out. There was a sound of breaking glass and a woman's scream.

'For Christ's sake drop the fucking thing before they kill us all!' Zen hissed.

The pistol clattered to the cobblestones.

'It's only a replica,' Bevilacqua muttered.

The woman who had shouted to Zen stood looking with a shocked expression at her car, whose windscreen was now crazed and punctured by bullet holes. Two of the men in grey overalls threw Bevilacqua against the side of the car, arms on the roof, and searched him roughly. Another walked up to Zen and saluted.

'Ispettore Ligato, NOCS Unit 42! I trust you're unharmed, dottore? Sorry about losing contact this afternoon. You were a bit too quick for us at the lights. Still, no harm done. We were here when it counted.'

He walked over to Bevilacqua, who was now lying face down on the cobblestones, his arms tightly handcuffed behind his back. Ligato gave him an exploratory kick in the ribs.

'As for you, you bastard, you can count yourself lucky you're still alive!'

Zen laid a restraining hand on the official's shoulder.

'Don't be too hard on him,' he said. 'His wife's just left him.'

Palazzo Sisti was lit up and humming like the power-station it was. Zen walked buoyantly across the courtyard, passing a queue of limousines waiting to discharge their illustrious passengers. Things were looking up, he thought. At this rate, he might be able to keep his date with Tania after all. But first there was the reception to be got through.

The minuscule porter, beside himself with the importance of the occasion, was haranguing a chauffeur who was trying to park in a space reserved for some party dignitary. Zen slipped past him and climbed the stairs. At the top, he encountered a familiar ape-like figure unconvincingly got up in a footman's apparel.

'Good evening, Lino.'

The bodyguard scowled at Zen. 'That way,' he said, jerking his thumb.

'This way?' Zen inquired brightly.

Lino's scowl intensified. 'Don't push me too far!' he warned.

'Sorry, too late. Someone has already threatened to kill me this evening. In fact there's a waiting list, I'm afraid. I could pencil you in for some time next month.'

'You're crazy,' muttered Lino.

Zen walked past a mutilated classical torso which revived memo-

ries of a particularly nasty murder case he had once been involved
in. A pair of rosewood doors opened into a series of salons whose
modest dimensions and exquisite decoration reflected the tone of the
palace as a whole. The rooms were packed with people. Those nearest the door scanned Zen's features briefly, then turned away. But
though they did not recognize him, he saw many faces familiar from
the television and newspapers. As he hovered on the fringes of the
gathering, unable to find an opening, Zen found himself reminded
oddly of the village bar in Sardinia. If the contrasts were obvious, so
were the similarities. He couldn't get a drink here either, for one
thing, the white-jacketed waiters always passing by just out of his
reach, ignoring his signals. But more important, here too he was an
intruder, a gate-crasher at a private club. These people were constant
presences in each other's lives, meeting regularly at functions such as
this, not to mention other more significant reunions. Nothing any of
them did or said could be indifferent to the others. They were a family,
a tribe to which Zen did not belong. They had felt obliged to invite
the man who did their dirty work for them, but in fact his presence
was an unwelcome embarrassment, to himself and everyone else.

To Zen's dismay, the first familiar face he saw was that of Vincenzo
Fabri, resplendent in an aerodynamically styled outfit that made
Zen's look as though it had been rented from a fancy-dress agency.
Fabri approached with a smile that boded no good.

'I didn't know you'd be here, Zen.'

'Life's full of surprises.'

'Isn't it just?'

Fabri beckoned him closer with a crooked finger. 'Guess what?'

Zen gazed at him bleakly.

'I've made Questore!' Fabri crowed in a triumphant whisper.

He extended the forefinger of his right hand and poked Zen in the
chest.

'To be fair, I suppose you should take some of the credit, as you
said this morning. But it's results that count in the end, isn't it? Bari
or Ferrara seem the most likely prospects at the moment, unless I
decide to take a few months' leave and wait for something better to
come up. They say Pacini won't last much longer in Venice. Now
there's a thought, eh? Well, I must circulate. See you at the Ministry.
I'll be in to clear my desk.'

Zen knew he had to leave quickly, before he said or did something unforgivable. As he pushed through the crowd, he felt a grip on his arm.

'Wherever are you going in such a hurry, dottore? I was just about to, ah, . . . that's to say, I was on the point of, ah, bringing your presence to the attention of someone who has taken a very close, very personal interest in the events of the past few days.'

The young secretary steered Zen towards a distinguished-looking figure in his mid-sixties who was holding court in the centre of the room, where the throng was thickest. Zen recognized him immediately. Unlike the other celebrities, whose fleshly reality often jarred uncomfortably with their etherealized media image, this man's appearance coincided perfectly with the photographs Zen had seen of him. Elderly without frailty, experienced but not resigned, he gave the impression of just having reached the prime of life.

'We were talking about you earlier,' the young man resumed, effortlessly inserting himself and Zen into the inner circle of initiates. 'Indeed, I trust you will not think me indiscreet if I mention that *l'onorevole* was pleased to remark how deeply indebted we are to you for your, ah, effective and timely intervention.'

The distinguished figure, deep in conversation with two younger men whose enthusiastic servility was embarrassing to behold, paid not the slightest attention.

'It would be no exaggeration to say that the Party has been spared a most trying experience as the result of your, ah, initiative,' the young man went on. 'It's true that we were at first somewhat surprised by the choice of . . . that's to say, by the fact that this woman, ah, proved to be the guilty party. However, on mature consideration we unreservedly approve of this solution, more especially since it allows us to retain the Padedda option as a fall-back position should any further problems arise. We are really most grateful, most grateful indeed. Isn't that so, *onorevole*?'

For a second, the elder man's eyes swept over Zen's face like the revolving beam of a lighthouse.

'If there's ever anything you need . . .' he murmured.

Zen made the appropriate noises, then gracefully withdrew. As he headed towards the door, towards his evening with Tania, the words were still ringing in his ears. 'If there's ever anything you need . . .' Better than money in the bank, he thought. Better than money in the bank!

Cabal

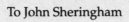
To John Sheringham

I, on the other hand, believe that the whole affair, today as yesterday, was bound up with games of make-believe in which every role was itself playing a double role, of false information taken to be true and true information taken to be false: in short, with the sort of atrocious nonsense of which we Italians have had so many examples in these past few years.

Leonardo Sciascia

1

'... *quia peccavi nimis cogitatione, verbo, opere et omissione: mea culpa, mea culpa, mea maxima culpa.'*

Amplified both by the loudspeaker system and the sonorous acoustics of the great basilica, the celebrant's voice reverberated with suprahuman authority, seemingly unrelated to the diminutive figure beating his breast like a hammy tenor in some provincial opera house. The fifty or so worshippers who had turned out on this bleak late-November evening were all elderly, and predominantly female. The apse and the chapel of the *cattedra*, itself a space larger than many churches, had been cordoned off for the service by uniformed attendants, but in other regions of St Peter's basilica tourists and pilgrims continued to promenade, singly or in groups, dazed by the sheer scale of the sacred and secular claims being made on every side, numbly savouring the bitter taste of their individual insignificance.

For some, the tinkling of the bell, the strains of the organ and the procession of red-clad priest and ministers had come as a welcome relief from these oppressive grandeurs, rather as though afternoon Mass were a dramatic spectacle laid on by the authorities in an attempt to bring this chilly monstrosity to life, a *son et lumière* event evoking the religious function it had originally had. Curious as children, they crowded behind the ropes dividing off the apse, gawking at Bernini's shamelessly showy sunburst and the great papal tombs to either side. For a time the rhythmic cadences of the Latin liturgy held their attention, but during the reading from the Apocalypse of St John many drifted away. Those who remained were fidgety and restless, whispering to each other or rustling through their guide-books.

One man, standing slightly apart on one side of the crowd, was ostentatiously paying no attention at all to the service. He was wearing a suede jacket and a flowery print shirt opened at the neck to display the thick gold chain which nestled in the lush hairs on his chest. His big arms were crossed, the sleeve of the jacket riding up to reveal the gold Rolex Oyster watch on his left wrist, and his large,

round, slightly concave face was tilted upwards like a satellite dish
tracking some celestial object invisible to the naked eye, high above,
in the vast dark recess of the unlighted cupola. Not far away, at the
base of one of the massive whorled columns supporting the fantastic
canopy of the bronze baldacchino over the papal altar, a woman was
also absorbed by the spectacle above. With her grey tweed coat, black
tailored wool jacket, calf-length velvet skirt and the white silk scarf
over her head, she looked like a designer version of the aged crones
who constituted the majority of the congregation. But her lipstick, a
blare of brilliant red only partially qualified by her cold blue eyes,
sent a very different message.

The homily which followed the reading sounded less like a learned
discourse than a spontaneous outburst of sour grapes on the part of
the priest, nettled by the poor turn-out. Once upon a time, he complained, the church had been the centre of the community, a privileged place where the people gathered to experience the presence of
God. Now what did we see? The shops, discotheques, night clubs,
beer bars and fast food outlets were all turning people away, while
the churches had never been so empty. The touristic passing trade
had by this time largely dispersed, but this line of argument
appeared to risk alienating even the core of the congregation,
reminding them painfully of their status as a marginalized and ana-
chronistic minority, representatives of an outmoded way of thinking.
Coughing, shuffling and inattention became endemic.

A brief diversion was provided by the arrival of a buck-toothed,
bespectacled nun, breathless and flurried, clutching a large bouquet
of flowers. She apologized to the attendants, who shrugged and
waved her through the ropes. Depositing the bouquet on the balus-
trade surrounding the colossal statue of St Veronica, the nun took her
place on a bench near the back of the congregation as the priest began
reciting the Credo. A plainclothes security man who had been looking on from the fringes of the crowd walked over, picked up the
flowers and inspected them suspiciously, as though they might
explode.

'*Et iterum venturus est cum gloria, judicare vivos et mortuos . . .*'

At first the noise sounded like electronic feedback transmitted via
the loudspeakers, then the screech of a low-flying aircraft. One or two
departing tourists glanced up towards the looming obscurity of the
dome, as the man with the suede jacket and gold chain and the

woman in the tweed coat and white scarf had been doing all along. That certainly seemed to be the source of the eerie sound, somewhere between a whine and a growl, which billowed down to fill the basilica like coloured dye in a tank of water. Then someone caught sight of the apparition high above, and screamed. The priest faltered, and even the congregation twisted round to see what was happening. In utter silence all watched the black shape tumbling through the dim expanses towards them.

The sight was an ink-blot test for everyone's secret fears and fantasies. An arthritic seamstress who lived above an automobile body shop in the Borgo Pio saw the long-desired angel swooping down to release her from the torments of the flesh. A retired chemist from Potenza, on the other hand, visiting the capital for only the second time in his life, recalled the earthquake which had recently devastated his own city and saw a chunk of the dome plummeting down, first token of a general collapse. Others thought confusedly of spiders or bats, super-hero stunts or circus turns. Only one observer knew precisely what was happening, having seen it all before. Giovanni Grimaldi let go of the nun's bouquet of flowers, which scattered on the marble floor, and reached for his two-way radio.

Subsequent calculations demonstrated that the period of time elapsing between the initial sighting and terminal impact cannot have exceeded four seconds, but to those watching in disbelief and growing horror it was a period without duration, time-free. The figure might have been falling through a medium infinitely more viscous than air, so slowly did it appear to descend, revolving languidly about its own axis, the long sustained keening wrapped around it like winding robes, the limbs and trunk executing a leisurely sarabande that ended as the body smashed head first into the marble paving at something approaching seventy miles per hour.

No one moved. The glistening heap of blood and tissue subsided gently into itself with a soft farting sound. Priest and congregation, tourists and attendants, stood as silent and still as figures in a plaster Nativity. In distant nooks and crannies of the vast enclosure, the final echoes of that long scream died away. Then, as strident as trumpets, first one, then many voices took up the strain, shrieking hysterically, howling, sobbing and gasping.

Giovanni Grimaldi started towards the body. It seemed to take for ever, as in a bad dream, the crowd perpetually closing up right in front of him, denying him passage. Then he was through the inner circle, beyond which no one was prepared to go, and promptly slipped and fell, his radio dropping with a loud clatter. Instinctively the crowd drew back, terrified by this renewed proof of the malignant power possessed by this killing floor. The screaming redoubled in volume as those at the back were toppled and trodden underfoot. As the attendants ran to try and contain the crowd, Grimaldi stood up, his blue suit stained with the blood on which he had slipped. It was almost invisible on the marble slabs, a light spattering that blended perfectly with the scarlet veins beneath the highly polished surface of the stone.

He retrieved his radio and pressed the call-up button. While Control took their sweet time about answering, as usual, Grimaldi looked round to try and find the man in the suede jacket and the woman in the tweed coat, but they were no longer there.

'Well?' a crackly voice demanded crossly in his ear.

'This is Grimaldi. We have a jumper in the basilica.'

'In progress or complete?'

'Complete.'

He switched off the radio. There was no need to say more. Suicides were a regular occurrence in St Peter's, partly due to the vertiginous attraction of high places in general, but still more to a popular belief that those who died on the Apostle's tomb went straight to heaven, by-passing the normal red tape and entry quotas. The Church had preached repeatedly and at length against this primitive superstition, but in vain. The part of the inner gallery beneath the dome that was open to the public had been fitted with a two-metre-high wire-mesh security fence, but if folk want to kill themselves badly enough it's impossible to prevent them doing so.

Nevertheless, this particular jump was unique, at least in Grimaldi's experience. As far as he knew, no one had ever managed to commit suicide while Mass was being said, for at such times there was no access to the dome.

Grimaldi's message set in motion a well-established routine. The first step was to clear the basilica. Those witnesses suffering from shock were led across the piazza to the Vatican's first-aid post, pausing briefly to allow the passage of an ambulance from the nearby Santo Spirito hospital. When there was life to be saved, as when Papa Wojtyla had been shot, the Church preferred the high standards of its own Policlinico Gemelli, but when it came to carting away corpses the institutions of the Italian state were good enough.

The ambulance slowed at the gate beneath the Arch of the Bells where the Swiss Guards, who had been advised of the situation, waved it through into the succession of small, dark courtyards flanking the east side of St Peter's. Just beyond the enormous bulge of the transept a uniformed member of the Vigilanza, the Vatican Security Force, waved the vehicle to a halt. The ambulance men got out, opened the rear doors and lifted out a stretcher. Then they followed the security guard through a door into a bare sloping passage tunnelled into the massive lower walls of the basilica. They passed through two small antechambers, then through a doorway concealed beneath the beckoning skeletons of Bernini's funeral monument to Alexander VII, and thence into the basilica itself.

In the open space between the apse and the papal altar, a team of cleaners in blue overalls waited with their mops and buckets, ready to expunge every physical trace of the outrage once the body had been removed. A bishop would then be summoned to perform the spiritual equivalent, a rite of reconsecration. The ambulance men put down their stretcher and set about unwrapping the green plastic sheeting used to wrap the remains. At this point Giovanni Grimaldi turned aside, his stomach thrashing like live fish in a net. It was precisely to avoid having to witness things like this that he had come to work for the Vatican in the first place.

The son of a fisherman from Otranto, Grimaldi had started his career in the Carabinieri, and as a brighter-than-average recruit was rapidly promoted to investigative work. He had stuck it for four years, struggling heroically with a squeamishness which he knew would master him in the end. Every time he had to go to the scene of a violent crime his guts tightened up, his breath choked like an asthmatic's, his skin became filmy with perspiration and his heart went wild. For days afterwards he couldn't sleep properly, and when he did, the dreams were so horrible that he wished he hadn't.

His colleagues seemed to think nothing of spending the morning poking around a burnt-out car containing the remains of four local mobsters and then tucking into a nice charred roast at lunch, but Grimaldi lacked this ability to detach his professional and private lives. The experience had marked him even physically. His body was hunched, his head lowered, face averted, and his eyes peered up with the guarded, wary look of abused children. His hair had started falling out at an alarming rate, while deep wrinkles corrugated his face until by now he looked older than his own father – who still put to sea each night with his crew of illegal Algerian immigrants, and didn't give a fuck about anything.

The usual fate of ex-Carabinieri is to join one of the many armies of private bank guards, but thanks to a local politician who had a word with a bishop who mentioned the matter to a monsignore in the Curia who had the ear of a certain archbishop in the Palazzo del Governatorato, Giovanni Grimaldi moved to Rome and became a member of the Vigilanza. Because of his experience and abilities, he was soon transferred to a select detective unit responsible directly to the Cardinal Secretary of State. In addition to investigating such minor crime as occurred within the Vatican – mostly petty theft – this group allegedly carried out a variety of covert operations which were the subject of considerable gossip among employees of the Curia. His children only visited him in the holidays now, and his wife in his dreams, for she had contracted cancer the year after he settled in the capital. The children now lived in Bari with Grimaldi's sister, while he himself eked out a solitary life in a church property near the Vatican, trying to make ends meet for his absentee family, and to put a little aside for the future.

Despite himself, Grimaldi glanced over as the ambulance men transferred the corpse to the plastic sheeting. He noted with impersonal curiosity, as though watching a film, that the blue lounge suit in which the shattered body was clad was of the highest quality, and that one of the black brogues was missing. He looked again at the material of the suit. It looked oddly familiar. His breath started to come in heaves and gasps. No, he thought, not that. Please not that.

The ambulance men had already started to parcel up the body.

'Just a minute,' Grimaldi told them. 'We need to know who he was.'

'That's all done at the hospital,' one of the men replied dismissively, not even looking up.

'The victim must be identified before the body is released to the representatives of the Italian authorities,' Grimaldi recited pedantically.

The ambulance man looked up wearily, as though dealing with a halfwit.

'All the paperwork's done back at the morgue. We've got a strict turn-around time.'

Grimaldi planted his foot on the plastic sheeting just inches from the man's hand.

'Listen, this may be just another bit of Trastevere to you, but when you drove through the archway out there, past our Swiss friends in their fancy dress, you left Italy and went abroad. Just like any other foreign country, this one has its own rules and regulations, and in the present case they stipulate that before this cadaver can be released to the representatives of the Italian state – that's you – it must be identified to the satisfaction of an official of the Vatican City State – which in this case means me. So let's get busy. Pass me the contents of his pockets.'

The ambulance man heaved a profound sigh, indicating helpless acquiescence in the face of might rather than right, and started to go through the dead man's clothing. The trouser pockets and the outer ones of the jacket were empty, but a zipped pocket inside the left breast of the jacket yielded a large metal key, seemingly new, and a worn leather wallet containing an identity card and driving licence. The security man scanned these documents, then brusquely turned his back on everyone and switched on his radio again.

'This is Grimaldi,' he said, his voice hoarse with excitement. 'Tell the chief to get over here immediately! And you'd better notify His Excellency.'

Aurelio Zen, on the other hand, was to remember that particular Friday as the night the lights went out.

His first thought was that it was a personal darkness, like the one which had descended without warning a few months earlier on poor Romizi. 'Come on, Carlo, at least try and *look* like you're working!' one of the other officials had jeered at the sight of the Umbrian frozen at his desk, a grey, sweating statue of flesh. Romizi had always been a laughing-stock in the Criminalpol squad. Only that very morning Giorgio De Angelis had retailed yet another apocryphal story about their hapless colleague. 'Romizi is detailed off to attend a conference in Paris. He rings the travel agent. "Excuse me, could you tell me how long it takes to get to Paris?" "Just one moment," says the travel agent, reaching for his timetable. "Thanks very much," says Carlo, and hangs up.'

But Romizi's fate hadn't been funny at all. 'A clot on the brain,' the doctor had explained when Zen looked in at the San Giovanni hospital. When asked what the prognosis was, he simply shook his head and sighed. Anna, Romizi's wife, and his sister Francesca were looking after him. Zen recognized Anna Romizi from the photograph of her as a young mother which Carlo had kept on his desk, their twin baby boys on her lap. Now those fresh, plumpish features had been rendered down to reveal the bedrock Mediterranean female beneath, grim, dauntless, enduring. Zen said his piece and left as soon as he could, fearful and depressed at this reminder of the primitive, messy plumbing on which all their lives ultimately depended. It didn't seem remotely surprising that it should break down without warning. On the contrary, the miracle was that it ever functioned in the first place. In growing panic he listened to the thudding of his heart, felt the blood coursing about the system, imagined the organs going about their mysterious, secretive business. It was like being trapped aboard an airplane piloted by an on-board computer. All you could do was sit there until the fuel ran out, or one of the incomprehensibly complex and delicate systems on which your life depended suddenly failed.

Which is what he thought had happened when the darkness abruptly enveloped him. He was on foot at the time, heading for an address in the heart of the old city. The same raw November evening which had culled the congregation in St Peter's kept people indoors. The streets were lined with small Fiats parked nose to tail like giant cockroaches, but there was no one about except a few youths on scooters. Zen made his way through the maze of the historic centre by following a succession of personalized landmarks, a painted window here, a patch of damaged plasterwork there, that rusty iron rib to stop men peeing in the corner. He had just caught sight of the great bulk of the Chiesa Nuova when it, and everything else, abruptly disappeared.

In different circumstances the wails, groans and curses that erupted from the darkness on every side might have been distinctly unnerving, but in the present case they were a welcome token that whatever had happened, Zen was not the only one affected. It was not a stroke, then, but a more general power failure, the umpteenth to strike the city this year. And the voices he could hear were not those of the restless dead, seeping like moisture out of the ancient structures all around to claim the stricken Zen as their own, but simply the indignant residents of the neighbourhood who had been cooking or watching television or reading when the lights went out.

By the time he realized this, the darkness was already punctuated by glints and glimmers. In a basement workshop, a furniture restorer appeared, crouched over the candle he had just lit, one hand cupped around the infant flame. The vaulted portico of a renaissance palace was illumined by a bow-legged figure clutching an oil-lamp which cast grotesque shadow images across the whitewashed walls and ceiling. From a window above Zen's head a torch beam shone down, slicing through the darkness like a blade.

'Mario?' queried a woman's voice.

'I'm not Mario,' Zen called back.

'So much the better for you!'

Like a vessel navigating an unfamiliar coast by night, Zen made his way from one light to another, trying to reconstruct his mental chart of the district. Reaching the corner, he got out his cigarette lighter. Its feeble flame revealed the presence of a stone tablet mounted on the wall high above, but not the name of the street incised in it. Zen made his way along the houses, pausing every so often to hold his lighter up to the numbers. The flame eventually wilted, its fuel used up, but by its dying flickers he read a name off the list printed next to the button of an entry-phone. He pushed one of the buttons, but there was no response, the power being dead. The next moment his lighter went out, and his attempts to relight it produced only a display of sparks.

He got out his key-holder and felt the differing shapes and position of the keys. When he had identified the one he was looking for, he reached out both hands and palpated the surface of the door like a blind man until he discovered the keyhole. He fitted the key into it and turned, opening the invisible door into a new kind of darkness, still and dense with a dank, mildewy odour. He started groping his way up the stairs, hanging on to the handrail and feeling with his foot for each step. In the darkness the house seemed larger than he remembered, like the family home in Venice in his childhood memories. As he made his way up the steep flight of steps to the top floor, he heard a male voice droning on, just below the threshold of comprehension. Zen cautiously traversed the open spaces of the landing, located the door by touch, knocked. The voice inside did not falter. He knocked again, more loudly.

'Yes?' a woman called.

'It's me.'

After a moment, the door opened to reveal a tall slim figure silhouetted against a panel of candle-gleam.

'Hello, sweetheart!'

They fell into each other's arms.

'How did you get in? I didn't hear the buzzer.'

'It's not working. But luckily someone had left the door open.'

He didn't want her to know that he had keys to the house and the flat.

'. . . *from the gallery inside the dome. According to the Vatican Press Office, the tragedy occurred shortly after 5.15 this evening, while Holy Mass was being celebrated in the . . .*'

Tania covered Zen's face with light, rapid, bird-like kisses, then drew him inside. The living room looked and smelt like a chapel. Fat marbly candles flooded the lower regions of the room with their unctuous luminosity and churchy aroma while the pent-roof ceiling retreated into a virtual obscurity loftier than its real height.

'*. . . where he had been a virtual prisoner since a magistrate in Milan issued a warrant for his arrest in connection with . . .*'

Tania broke free of his embrace long enough to switch off her small battery-operated radio. Zen sniffed deeply.

'Beeswax.'

'There's an ecclesiastical wholesaler in the next street.'

She slipped her hands inside his overcoat and hugged him. Her kisses were firmer now, and moister. He broke away to stroke her temples and cheeks, gently follow the delicate moulding of her ear and gaze into the depths of her warm brown eyes. Disengaging himself slightly, he ran his fingers over the extraordinary garment she was wearing, a tightly clinging sheath of what felt like velvet or suede and looked like an explosion in a paint factory.

'I haven't seen this before.'

'It's new,' she said lightly. 'A Falco.'

'A what?'

'Falco, the hot young designer. Haven't you heard of him?'

Zen shrugged.

'What I know about fashion you could fit on a postcard.'

'And still have room for "Wish you were here" and the address,' laughed Tania.

Zen joined in her laughter. Nevertheless, there's one thing I do know, he thought – any jacket sporting the lapel of a 'hot young designer' is going to cost. Where did she get the money for such things? Or *was* it her money? Perhaps the garment was a present. Pushing aside the implications of this thought, he produced a small plastic bag from his pocket, removed the neatly wrapped package inside and handed it to her.

'Oh, Aurelio!'

'It's only perfume.'

While she unwrapped the little flask, he added with a trace of maliciousness, '*I* wouldn't dare buy you clothes.'

She did not react.

'I'd better not wear it tonight,' she said.

'Why not?'

'It'll come off on your clothes and *she*'ll know you've been unfaithful.'

They smiled at each other. 'She' was Zen's mother.

'I could always take them off,' he said.

'Mmm, that's an idea.'

They had been together for almost a year now, and Zen still hadn't quite taken the measure of the situation. Certainly it was something very different from what he had imagined, back in his early days at the Ministry of the Interior, when Tania Biacis had been the safely inaccessible object of his fantasies, reminding him of the great Madonna in the apse of the cathedral on the island of Torcello, but transformed from a figure of sorrow to one of gleeful rebellion, a nun on the run.

His fancy had been more accurate than he could have known, for the breakup of her marriage to Mauro Bevilacqua, a moody bank clerk from the deep south, had transformed Tania Biacis into someone quite different from the chatty, conventional, rather superficial woman with whom Zen, very much against his better judgement, had fallen in love. Having married in haste and repented at leisure, Tania was now, at thirty-something, having the youthful fling she had missed the first time around. She had taken to smoking and even drinking, habits which Zen deplored in women. She never cooked him a meal, still less sewed on a button or ironed a shirt, as though consciously rejecting the ploys by which proto-mammas lure their prey. They went out to restaurants and bars, took in films and concerts, walked the streets and piazzas at all hours, and then went home to bed.

Things notoriously turned out differently from what one had expected, of course, but Zen was so used to them turning out worse, or at any rate *less*, that he found himself continually disconcerted by what had actually happened. Tania loved him, for a start. That was something he had certainly never expected. He had grown accustomed to thinking of himself as essentially unlovable, and he was finding it difficult – almost painful – to abandon the idea. He was comfortable with it, as with a well-worn pair of shoes. It would no longer do, though. Tania loved him, and that was all there was to it.

She loved him, but she didn't want to live with him. This fact was equally as real as the first, yet to Zen they were incompatible. How could you love someone with that passionate intensity, yet still insist on keeping your distance? It didn't make any sense, particularly for a woman. But there it was. He had invited Tania to move in with him and she had refused. 'I've spent the last eight years of my life living with a man, Aurelio. I married young. I've never known anything else. Now I'm finally free, I don't just want to lock myself up again, even with you.' And that was that, a fact as unexpected and irreducible as her love, handed him to take or leave.

He'd taken it, of course. More than that, he'd schemed and grafted to grant her the independence she wanted, and then conceal from her that it was all a sham, subsidized by him. If Italian divorce rates were still relatively low, this was due less to the waning influence of the Church than to the harsh facts of the property market. Accommodation was just too expensive for most single people to afford. When Zen and his wife had broken up, they had been forced to go on living together for almost a year until one of Luisella's cousins found room to take her in. Tania's clerical job at the Ministry of the Interior had been a nice little perk for the Bevilacqua household, but it was quite inadequate to support Tania in the independent single state to which she aspired.

So Zen had stepped into the breach. The first place he'd come up with had been a room in a hotel near the station which had been retained by the police for use in a drug surveillance operation. In fact the subject of the investigation had been killed in a shoot-out with a rival gang several months earlier, but the officer in charge had neglected to report this and had been subletting the room to Brazilian transvestite prostitutes. As illegal immigrants, the *viados* were in no position to complain. Neither was Zen's informant, a former colleague from the Questura, since the officer in question was one of his superiors, but Zen was under no such constraints. He sought the man out, and by a mixture of veiled threats and an appeal to masculine complicity had got him to agree to let Zen's 'friend' have the use of the room for a few months.

It was only when they met at the hotel to exchange keys that Zen quite realized what he'd got himself into. Quite apart from the transvestites and the pushers, the room was filthy, noisy, and stank. It was unthinkable that he could ever suggest that Tania move in there, still less visit her, surrounded by the sounds and smells of commercial sex. Unfortunately they had already celebrated the good news, so he had had to find an alternative, and quickly.

The solution came through an expatriate acquaintance of Ellen, Zen's former lover, who had been renting a flat right in the old centre of the city. The property had been let as an office, to get around the *equa canone* fair rent laws, and the landlord took advantage of this to impose a twenty per cent increase after the first year. The American quickly found an apartment he liked even better, but in order to cause his ex-landlord as much grief as possible, he suggested that Tania come and live in the original flat as his 'guest', thus forcing the owner to go through a lengthy and costly procedure to obtain a court order for his eviction. The rent still had to be paid, however, and since Zen had boasted of his cleverness in getting Tania a place for nothing – he told her that the American was away for some months and wanted someone to keep an eye on the flat – he had to foot the bill.

In the bedroom, Tania removed her clothes with an unself-conscious ease which always astonished Zen. Most women he'd known preferred to undress in private, or in the intimacy of an embrace. But Tania pulled off her jeans, tights and panties like a child going swimming, revealing her long leggy beauty, and then pulled back the covers of the bed and lay down half-covered while Zen was still taking off his jacket. Her straightforwardness made it easy for him, too. His doubts and anxieties dropped away with his clothes. As he slipped between the cool sheets and grasped Tania's warm, silky-smooth flesh, he reflected that there was a lot to be said for the human body, despite everything.

'What's that?' Tania asked some time later, raising her head above the covers.

Zen raised his head and listened. The silent dimness of the bed-room had been infiltrated by an electronic tone, muffled but just audible, coming in regular, incessant bursts.

'Sounds like an alarm.'

Tania raised herself up on one elbow.

'Mine's one of the old ones, with a bell.'

They lay side by side, the hairs on their forearms just touching. The noise continued relentlessly. Eventually Tania sat up like a cat, flex-ing her back, and crawled to the end of the bed.

'It seems to be coming from your jacket, Aurelio.'

Zen pulled the covers over his head and gave vent to a loud series of blasphemies in Venetian dialect.

'Your position here is essentially – indeed, necessarily – anomalous. You are required to serve two masters, an undertaking not only fraught with perils and contradictions of all kinds but one which, as you may perhaps recall, is explicitly condemned by the Scriptures.'

Juan Ramón Sánchez-Valdés, archbishop *in partibus infidelium* and deputy to the Cardinal Secretary of State, favoured Aurelio Zen with an arch smile.

'One might equally well argue, however,' he continued, 'that the case is exactly the opposite, and that so far from serving two masters, you are in fact serving neither. As a functionary of the Italian Republic, you have no *locus standi* beyond the frontiers of that state. Neither, clearly, are you formally empowered to act as an agent of either the Vatican City State or the Holy See.'

Zen raised his hand to his mouth, resting his chin on the curved thumb. He sniffed his fingers, still redolent of Tania's vagina.

'Yet here I am.'

'Here you are,' the archbishop agreed. 'Despite all indications to the contrary.'

And just my luck too, thought Zen sourly. Like every other Criminalpol official, he had to take his turn on the night duty roster, on call if the need should arise. In Zen's case it never had, which is why he hadn't at first recognized the electronic pager which had sounded while he and Tania were in bed. He shifted in his elegant but uncomfortable seat. Unachieved coition made his testicles ache, a common enough sensation in his adolescence but latterly only a memory. Tania had said she'd wait up for him, but it remained to be seen when – or even whether – he would be able to return to the flat.

On phoning in, he'd been told to report to the Polizia dello Stato command post in St Peter's Square. The telephonist he spoke to was reading a dictated message and could not elaborate. The taxi had dropped him at the edge of the square, and he walked round the curve of Bernini's great colonnade. As part of the Vatican City State, St Peter's Square is theoretically off-bounds to the Italian police, but in practice their help in patrolling it is appreciated by the over-stretched Vigilanza. But this is strictly the small change of police work, concerned above all with the pickpockets and the 'scourers', men who infiltrate themselves into the crowds attending papal appearances with the aim of touching up as many distracted females as possible. The high-level contacts between the Vatican security force and the police's anti-terrorist DIGOS squad, set up in the wake of the shooting of Pope John Paul II, were conducted at a quite different level.

The patrolman on duty called a number in the Vatican and announced Zen's arrival. He then waited a few minutes for a return call, before escorting Zen to an enormous pair of bronze doors near by, where two Swiss Guards in ceremonial uniforms stood clutching halberds. Between them stood a thin man with a face like a hatchet, wearing a black cassock and steel-rimmed glasses, who introduced himself as Monsignor Enrico Lamboglia. He inspected Zen's identification, dismissed the patrolman, and led his visitor along a seemingly interminable corridor, up a set of stairs leading off to the right, and through a sequence of galleried corridors to a conference room on the third floor of the Apostolic Palace, where he was ushered into the presence of Archbishop Juan Ramón Sánchez-Valdés.

The Deputy Cardinal Secretary of State was short and stout, with a face which seemed too large to fit his skull, and had thus spilled over at the edges in an abundance of domed forehead, drooping jowls and double chins. His dull green eyes, exposed by the flight of flesh towards the periphery of the face, were large and prominent, giving him an air of slightly scandalized astonishment. He was wearing cheap grey slacks, a dark-green pullover with leather patches on the elbows, and an open-necked shirt. This casual dress, however, did not detract from the formidable air of authority and competence he radiated as he reclined in a red velvet armchair, his right arm resting on an antique table whose highly polished surface was bare except for a white telephone. The hatchet-faced cleric who had escorted Zen stood slightly behind and to one side of the archbishop's chair, his head lowered and his hands interlocked on his chest as though in prayer. On the other side of the oriental rug which covered the centre of the lustrous marble floor, Zen sat on a long sofa flanking one wall. Three dark canvases depicting miracles and martyrdoms hung opposite. At the end of the room was a floor-length window, covered by lace curtaining and framed by heavy red velvet drapes.

'However, let us leave the vexed issue of your precise status, and move on to the matter in hand.'

Several decades in the Curia had erased almost all traces of Sánchez-Valdés's Latin-American Spanish. He fixed Zen with his glaucous, hypnotic gaze.

'As you may have gathered, there was a suicide in St Peter's this afternoon. Someone threw himself off the gallery inside the dome. Such incidents are quite common, and do not normally require the attention of this department. In the present instance, however, the victim was not some jilted maidservant or ruined shopkeeper, but Prince Ludovico Ruspanti.'

The archbishop looked significantly at Zen, who raised one eyebrow.

'Of course, the Ruspantis are no longer the power they were a few hundred years ago,' Sánchez-Valdés continued, 'or for that matter when the old Prince, Filippo, was alive. Nevertheless, the name still counts for something, and no family, much less an eminent one, likes having a *felo de se* among its number. The remaining members of the clan can therefore be expected to throw their not-inconsiderable weight into a concerted effort to discredit the suicide verdict. They have already issued a statement claiming that Ruspanti suffered from vertigo, and that even if he had decided to end his life, it is therefore inconceivable that he should have chosen to do so in such a way.'

The middle finger of Sánchez-Valdés's right hand, adorned by a heavy silver ring, tapped the tabletop emphatically.

'To make matters worse, Ruspanti's name has of course been in the news recently as a result of these allegations of currency fraud. To be perfectly honest, I never really managed to master the ins and outs of the affair, but I know enough about the way the press operates to anticipate the kind of malicious allegations which this is certain to give rise to. We may confidently expect suggestions, more or less explicit, to the effect that from the point of view of certain people, who must of course remain nameless, Ruspanti's death could hardly have been more convenient or better-timed, etcetera, etcetera. Do you see?'

Zen nodded. Sánchez-Valdés shook his head and sighed.

'The fact is, dottore, that for a variety of reasons which we have no time to analyse now, this little city state, whose sole object is to facilitate the spiritual work of the Holy Father, is the object of an inordinate degree of morbid fascination on the part of the general public. People seem to believe that we are a mediaeval relic which has survived intact into the twentieth century, rife with secrecy, skulduggery and intrigue, at once sinister and colourful. Since such a Vatican doesn't in fact exist, they invent it. You saw the results when poor Luciani died after only thirty days as pope. Admittedly, the announcement was badly handled. Everyone was shocked by what had happened, and there were inevitably delays and conflicting stories. As a result, we are still plagued by the most appalling and offensive rumours, to the effect that John Paul I was poisoned or suffocated by members of his household, and the crime covered up.

'Now a prince is not a pope, and Ludovico Ruspanti no Albino Luciani. Nevertheless, we have learned our lesson the hard way. This time we're determined to leave nothing to chance. That is why you've been invited to give us the benefit of your expert opinion, dottore. Since Ruspanti died on Vatican soil, we are under no *legal* obligation to consult anyone whatsoever. In the circumstances, however, and so as to leave no room for doubt in anyone's mind, we have voluntarily decided to ask an independent investigator to review the facts and confirm that there were no suspicious circumstances surrounding this tragic event.'

Zen glanced at his watch.

'There's no need for that, Your Excellency.'

Sánchez-Valdés frowned.

'I beg your pardon?'

Zen leaned forward confidentially.

'I'm from Venice, just like Papa Luciani. If the Church says that this man committed suicide, that's good enough for me.'

The archbishop glanced up at Monsignor Lamboglia. He laughed uneasily.

'Well!'

Zen beamed a reassuring smile.

'Tell the press anything you like. I'll back you up.'

The archbishop laughed again.

'This is good to hear, my son. Very good indeed. If only there were more like you! But these days, alas, the Church is surrounded by enemies. We cannot be too careful. So although I applaud your attitude of unquestioning obedience, I fear that we need more than just a rubber-stamped *nihil obstat*.'

Sánchez-Valdés rose to his feet and walked over to stand in front of Zen.

'I shall introduce you to one of our security officers,' he continued quietly. 'He was at the scene and will be able to tell you anything you wish to know. After that you are on your own. Inspect, investigate, interrogate, take whatever action you may consider necessary. There is no need for you to consult me or my colleagues.'

He stared intently at Zen.

'In fact it is imperative that you do not do so.'

Zen looked him in the eye.

'So as to preserve my independent status, you mean?'

The archbishop smiled and nodded.

'Precisely. Any suspicion of collusion between us would vitiate the very effect we are trying to produce. Do whatever you need to do, whatever must be done to achieve the desired result. I have been assured by your superiors that you are an extremely capable and experienced operative.'

He turned to Monsignor Lamboglia.

'Fetch Grimaldi in.'

On the wall of the antechamber in which Giovanni Grimaldi had been kept waiting for the best part of two hours hung a large, murky canvas. It depicted a number of armed figures doing something extremely unpleasant to a nude male in the foreground, while a group of senior citizens with haloes looked on with expressions of complacent detachment from the safety of a passing cloud. Closer inspection revealed that the prospective martyr was being torn apart by teams of yoked buffaloes. Grimaldi winced sympathetically. He knew exactly how the poor bastard felt.

His initial reaction to what had happened was one of straight-forward panic. He had been entrusted with a job whose delicacy and importance had been repeatedly stressed. It was a chance to prove himself once and for all, to make his mark as a responsible and trustworthy employee. And he had blown it. If only he hadn't allowed himself to be distracted by that man with the gold chain, the flashy watch and the nasal accent who had apparently become detached from the *Comunione e Liberazione* sightseeing group which had passed through a few minutes earlier. The man had approached Grimaldi as he stood at the rail of the external balcony at the very top of St Peter's, apparently absorbed in the stupendous view, and fired off an endless series of questions about where the Spanish Steps were and which hill was the Aventine and whether you could see the Coliseum from there. Grimaldi had known he had better things to do than play the tourist guide, but his pride in knowing Rome so well, being able to identify each of its significant monuments, had been too great. It was such a thrill to point out the principal attractions of the Eternal City with languid, confident gestures, as though he were the hereditary landlord.

Besides, his quarry was in plain view, standing by the railing a little further round the balcony, chatting up that classy number with the white silk headscarf who had been all alone on the balcony when they arrived. Grimaldi didn't blame him! He might have had a go himself if he hadn't been on duty. Not that he'd have stood a chance.

It looked like she might well go for the Prince, though. They were standing very close together, and their conversation looked unusually animated for two people who had only just met. Meanwhile he was stuck with this northerner and his dumb questions. 'And is that the Quirinale Palace?' he whined, pointing out the Castel Sant'Angelo.

The next time Grimaldi had looked across to the other side of the balcony, the Prince and his pick-up had disappeared. Abandoning the inquisitive tourist in mid-sentence, he clattered down the steel ladder leading to the precipitous stairway, crazily slanted and curved like a passage in a nightmare, which led down to the roof of the basilica. The cupola was riddled with such corridors and stairs, but most had been sealed off, and those open to the public were clearly signposted so as to send visitors on their way with the minimum of delay or confusion. There was nowhere to get lost, nowhere to hide. Minutes after leaving the lantern, Grimaldi was down in the nave of St Peter's, and knew that he had lost the man he had been given strict orders to keep in view at all costs.

It was clear what had happened. The whole thing had been carefully set up. While the Vigilanza man's attention was distracted by the supposed *Comunione e Liberazione* truant, Ruspanti had been whisked away by his female companion. They could be anywhere by now. Grimaldi wandered disconsolately around the basilica, where preparations for the evening Mass were in progress. He was merely postponing the moment when he would have to report back to headquarters and reveal his failure. Then he caught sight of the woman in the grey tweed coat and white silk headscarf, and began to feel that everything might turn out all right after all. When the man in the suede jacket turned up a few minutes later, he felt sure of it. The two did not look at each other, but they were aware of each other's presence. They were a unit, a team. Only Ruspanti was still missing, but Grimaldi now had no doubt that the Prince would also reappear in due course.

And indeed he *had*, although not in quite the manner the Vigilanza man had imagined. It certainly wasn't the perfect outcome, from his point of view, but on the other hand it could have been worse. Rather than going on bended knees to Luigi Scarpione, his boss, and admitting that he had fallen for a trick which shouldn't have fooled an untrained rookie, he had found himself summoned to the Secretariat of State, no less, in the Apostolic Palace itself, next door to the pope's private quarters, a *sanctum sanctorum* guarded by a hand-picked élite of the Swiss Guards, where the riff-raff of the Vigilanza were not normally permitted to set foot. Not only had he set foot there, he'd actually met the legendary Sánchez-Valdés face to face.

Normally, the special security unit to which Grimaldi belonged liaised with the Curia through the archbishop's secretary, Lamboglia, a cold and charmless man who received minions in his anonymous office in an obscure building off Via del Belvedere, in the Sant'Anna district. The clergy might need the likes of Grimaldi to do their dirty business, but that didn't give him entry to a society which had almost as little time for laymen as for women. However, the implications of Ruspanti's death were so dramatic that this caste system had been temporarily suspended, and on this occasion Grimaldi was received not just by Lamboglia but by Juan Ramón Sánchez-Valdés himself. By all accounts, it was this Latin American who more or less ran the domestic side of the Holy See's affairs, leaving His Eminence the Cardinal Secretary of State at liberty to devote himself to the complexities of foreign policy.

Unfortunately Grimaldi was unable to savour this exceptional honour as fully as it deserved, since he was preoccupied with the delicate question of deciding exactly how much of the truth to reveal. The aim was no longer simply to disguise his own incompetence. There was more at stake than that. Once the initial shock of the horror he had witnessed had worn off, Grimaldi had dimly begun to perceive possibilities of personal advantage which took precedence even over his innate desire to impress his superiors. He wasn't quite sure whether he was going to exploit them, never mind how, but in the meantime he wanted to keep all his options open, and that meant not giving too much away.

In the event, his performance seemed to have gone down quite well. Sánchez-Valdés had accepted that Grimaldi's inability to keep track of Ruspanti's movements had been due to circumstances beyond his control, namely the press of tourists in the dome of St Peter's that day. No attempt had been made to reprimand or punish him. Grimaldi was just congratulating himself on his success, when he was called back from the antechamber where he had been sent to kick his heels and introduced to a newcomer, a man he had never seen before. Slightly taller even than Lamboglia, he had fine, slightly wavy hair and a face stretched as tautly over its bones as a drum. His angular nose and square, protuberant chin might have looked strong, but the mouth was weak and indecisive, as were the opaque grey eyes. Or so Grimaldi thought, until they turned towards him. It only lasted a moment, but he felt as though he had never been looked at before.

'This is Dottor Aurelio Zen, a specialist investigator dispatched by the Italian authorities in response to an urgent request conveyed by the apostolic nuncio,' Sánchez-Valdés announced. 'He is lending us the benefit of his experience and expertise to ensure that no possible doubt remains concerning this tragic event. You are to accompany him wherever he wishes to go and to see that he is accorded total cooperation in carrying out his duties.'

Zen shook hands with Sánchez-Valdés, and was accompanied to the door by Monsignor Lamboglia. Grimaldi was about to follow when the archbishop called him back.

'You need say nothing about the other business,' he murmured *sotto voce*.

'The surveillance?'

Sánchez-Valdés nodded.

'Or the whereabouts of the deceased prior to today's events. As far as our guest is concerned, Ruspanti appeared from nowhere to obliterate himself on the floor of St Peter's. *Descendit de caelis*, as you might say.'

Grimaldi blushed, shocked by the levity of the reference. The archbishop flapped his right hand rapidly, urging him to join the others.

Lamboglia led Zen and Grimaldi out of the Apostolic Palace by a circuitous route which brought them out directly in St Peter's. In the nave, workmen were shifting benches into position in readiness for Saturday's papal Mass, but the area beyond the crossing was still sealed off by plastic tape and patrolled by two uniformed Vigilanza officials.

'I look forward to hearing from you,' Lamboglia told Zen, and strode off. After a brief word with the uniformed guards, Grimaldi led Zen over the tape and round the baldacchino. The body had been covered in a tarpaulin borrowed from the *sampietrini*, the workers responsible for maintaining the fabric of St Peter's. Once the identity of the illustrious corpse had been established, the ambulance men from Santo Spirito hospital and the cleaning crew had been hurriedly dismissed until further notice. No one was to approach the body and nothing was to be removed or otherwise disturbed without an explicit order to that effect from the office of the Cardinal Secretary of State.

Grimaldi looked away as Zen lifted the tarpaulin to view the tangle of broken bone, unsupported flesh and extruded innards that constituted the remains of Prince Ludovico Ruspanti. *He* certainly didn't appear bothered by such things, Grimaldi noted, risking a quick glimpse. Indeed, he seemed almost indecently unimpressed, this hot-shot from the Interior Ministry, squatting over the corpse like a child over a box of hand-me-down toys, lifting the odd item which looked as though it might be of interest, bending down to sniff the blood-drenched clothing and inspect the victim's shoes.

'Looks like he thought about slashing his wrists first,' Zen murmured, indicating the thin red weals on the victim's wrists. Deliberately unfocusing his eyes, Grimaldi turned his head towards the horror.

'Preliminary cuts,' Zen explained. 'But he didn't have the nerve to go through with it, so he decided to jump instead.'

Grimaldi nodded, though he could see nothing but a merciful blur.

'We're going to have do something about these shoes,' added Zen.

The offending items, cheap brown suede slip-ons with an elastic vent, stood side by side on the marble flooring. Both were spotlessly clean, as was the stocking covering the victim's left foot. The other sock was covered in rust-red bloodstains.

Grimaldi was on the point of saying something, but then he remembered that the shoes had been Scarpione's idea. The Vigilanza boss had appeared at the scene before any of the clerics could get there. 'Save trouble all round,' he'd said, giving the necessary orders. Apparently he'd been wrong, but Grimaldi knew better than to get involved.

'What about them?' he asked.

Zen looked at him sharply, then shrugged.

'Very well, I'll raise it with Monsignor Lamboglia.'

The lift had been shut down for the night, so they had to walk all the way up to the roof of the basilica. They climbed the shallow steps of the spiral staircase in silence. Zen had no small-talk, and Grimaldi had decided to volunteer no information. This official from the Interior Ministry, despite his lethargic manner, might not be as easy to fool as Archbishop Sánchez-Valdés.

They found Antonio Cecchi, chief of the *sampietrini* maintenance men, in one of a cluster of sheds and workshops perched on the undulating roof of the basilica like a lost corner of old Rome. Cecchi was a compact, muscular man of about fifty with the face of a gargoyle: thin, splayed ears protruding prominently from a bulbous skull topped by a shock of short wavy hair like white flames. Grimaldi explained the situation. With a sigh, Cecchi picked up a torch and led them up a short flight of steps on the outside of the dome. As they waited for Cecchi to find the right key on the huge bunch he produced from the pouch of his blue overalls, Zen studied a large crack in the wall. A number of marble strips had been bridged across it to keep track of its progress, the earliest being dated August 1835. He was not reassured to note that all the tell-tales were broken.

Inside the door, a ramp led up to a door opening on to the internal gallery at the base of the drum. The roof outside gave such a strong illusion of being at ground level, with its alleys and piazzas, its washing lines and open casements, that it was a shock to realize just how high they were. Zen peered through the safety fence at the patterned marble floor over a hundred and fifty feet below. The fence ran inside the original railings, all the way from the floor to a point higher than Zen's head, closing off the half of the gallery which was open to the public.

'This is supposed to stop jumpers,' Cecchi explained, shaking the mesh with his powerful fingers.

'This one went off the other side,' put in Grimaldi.

He pointed across the circular abyss to a door set in the wall of the drum opposite, giving on to a section of the gallery that was not open to the public, and hence was protected only by the original railings.

'The stairs leading down from the top of the dome pass by that door,' Grimaldi explained. 'The door's kept locked, but he somehow got hold of a key.'

Zen frowned.

'But he would have been seen by anyone standing over here.'

'The dome was closed by then. This part of the gallery would have been shut and locked. Only the exit was still open.'

Zen nodded.

'Sounds all right. Let's have a look round the other side.'

Cecchi led the way along a corridor which ran around the circumference of the dome in a series of curved ramps. When they reached the doorway corresponding to the one by which they had left the gallery on the other side, the building superintendent produced his keys again and unlocked the door. Zen pushed past him and stepped out on to the open section of the gallery. The finger he wiped along the top of the railing came away covered in dust.

'They don't bother cleaning here,' Cecchi remarked. 'No call for it.'

Halfway between the gallery and the floor, the roof of the baldacchino rose up towards them, surmounted by a massive gold cross. Bernini had not envisaged his showpiece being seen from this angle, and it had an awkward, clumsy look, like an actress glimpsed backstage without her costume or make-up. Immediately underneath the gallery ran a wide strip of gold, like an enormous hatband, with a Latin inscription in blue capitals: TV ES PETRVS ET SVPER HANC PETRAM EDIFICABO ECCLESIAM MEAM. The air was filled with a sonorous squealing as the staff, far below in the body of the nave, manoeuvred the heavy wooden benches into place for the papal Mass. It reminded Zen of the sirens of fog-bound shipping in the Venetian lagoons.

Telling Cecchi and Grimaldi to wait there, he walked round this semi-circular section of the gallery, inspecting the railing and floor carefully. He sighed heavily and consulted his watch. Then he leant over the railing, looking up at the sixteen frescoed segments into which the interior of the dome was divided. Beneath each segment was a huge rectangular window consisting of thirty enormous panes, like a monstrous enlargement of an ordinary casement. The glass was dark and glossy, reflecting back the glare of the floodlights which Cecchi had turned on as they entered the dome. Each pair of windows was separated by a double pilaster whose cornices supported a ledge topped with what looked like railings.

Zen walked back to the waiting Vatican employees.

'Is there another gallery up there?' he asked.

Cecchi nodded.

'It's locked, though.'

'So was this one.'

'He had a *key* to this one,' said Grimaldi, as though explaining the obvious to a child.

Zen nodded.

'I'd like to have a look at the upper gallery, if that's possible.'

Cecchi sighed heavily.

'It's possible, but what's the point? There's nothing to see.'

'That's what I want to make sure of,' Zen replied.

On the landing outside, two doorways faced one another. The one on the right was the lighted public way leading down from the lantern. Cecchi turned to the other, a locked wooden door. After searching through his keys for some time, he opened it, revealing yet another ramp curving upwards into darkness. The ramp ended at a narrow spiral staircase bored through the stonework between the gargantuan windows. At the top, another door gave access to a second gallery in the floodlit interior of the dome, sixty feet above the lower one.

Zen looked over the railing at the vertiginous prospect below. From here, the tarpaulin was a mere scrap of blue. Again he told Grimaldi and Cecchi to wait while he walked slowly round the ledge, running his finger along the top of the railing and examining the floor. He had gone about a quarter of the way round when he stopped abruptly and glanced back at the other two men. They were standing near the door, chatting quietly together. Zen bent down beside the object which had caught his attention. It was a black brogue shoe, resting on its side between two of the metal stanchions supporting the railing. The toe, its polish badly scuffed, protruded several inches over the void.

A moment later he noticed the twine. Thin, colourless, almost invisible, it was tied to one of the stanchions against which the shoe rested. The other end dangled over the edge of the gallery. Zen pulled it in. There were several yards of it. He got out his lighter and burned through the twine near the knot securing it to the metal post. Straightening up again, he stuffed the twine into his pocket with the plastic bag in which the perfume had been wrapped.

Looking over the railing, he studied the scene below. The workmen were still shifting benches further down the nave, but the area below was deserted. With a gentle kick, Zen eased the black shoe off the edge of the gallery and watched it tumble end over end until he could make it out no longer. Whatever sound it made as it hit the floor of the basilica was lost in the squealing and honking of the benches. Rubbing his hands briskly together, Zen completed his circuit of the gallery, returning to the spot by the door where Grimaldi and Cecchi were in conversation.

'Quite right,' he told the building superintendent. 'There's nothing to see.'

Cecchi sniffed a told-you-so. Zen tapped Grimaldi's two-way radio.

'Does this thing work up here?'

'Of course.'

'Then get hold of Lamboglia and tell him to meet me by the body in ten minutes.'

He glanced at his watch again.

'And then call a taxi to the Porta Sant'Anna,' he added.

When Zen and Grimaldi emerged into the amplitude of the basilica, like woodlice creeping out of the skirting of a ballroom, Monsignor Lamboglia was waiting for them. Zen regretted not having paid much attention to Sánchez-Valdés's secretary earlier, since it meant dealing with an unknown quantity at this crucial juncture. If he played it smart, he could be back in bed with Tania in half an hour. He therefore studied the cleric as he approached, trying to gather clues as to how best to handle him. Lamboglia's gaunt, craggy face, a mask of gloomy disapproval which looked as though it had been rough-hewn from granite, gave nothing away. But the rapid tapping of his fingers and the darting, censorious eyes betrayed the testy perfectionist who loved catching inferiors out and taxing them with inconsequential faults. It was this that gave Zen his opening.

'Well?' demanded Lamboglia brusquely, having dismissed Grimaldi with a curt wave of the hand.

Zen shrugged.

'More or less, yes. Apart the business of the shoes, of course.'

Lamboglia's lips twisted in disapproval and his eyes narrowed.

'Shoes? What do you mean?'

Zen pulled the edge of the tarpaulin back, exposing the victim's feet and the brown suede slip-ons.

'The archbishop said you people had learned a thing or two from the way Papa Luciani's death was handled,' he remarked contemptuously. 'You wouldn't know, judging by this sort of thing.'

By now Lamboglia looked apoplectic. For an instant, Zen caught a glimpse of the little boy, desperate to please, yet finding himself unjustly accused, fighting to restrain the tears, the panicky sense that the universe made no sense. The boy was long gone, but the strategies he had worked out in his misery still determined the behaviour of the man.

'If you have noticed anything amiss,' the cleric snapped, 'then kindly inform me what it is without further prevarication.'

Zen handed him one of the shoes.

'For a start, these shoes have only ever been worn by a corpse. Moreover they are mass-produced items totally out of keeping with the quality of the victim's other garments. On top of that, they're *brown*. A man like this wouldn't be seen dead – to coin a phrase – wearing brown shoes with a blue suit. And finally, the stocking on the right foot is stained with blood all the way down to the toe, and must therefore have been uncovered when the body struck the ground.'

After inspecting the shoe carefully, Monsignor Lamboglia nodded. His panic was subsiding, converting itself into a cold anger which would eventually be discharged on the appropriate target.

'And what conclusion do you draw from these observations?' he demanded challengingly.

Zen shrugged.

'You'd need to interrogate your staff to find out exactly what happened. My guess is that when the body was discovered, one of the shoes was missing. Some bright spark realized that this might look suspicious, and since they couldn't find the missing shoe, a different pair was substituted. But people are superstitious about letting their shoes be worn by a dead man, so they used a new pair. Result, an amateurish botch-job calculated to arouse exactly the sort of suspicions it was meant to allay.'

Lamboglia measured Zen with a cold glare. It was one thing for *him* to criticize his underlings – and whoever was responsible for this was going to wish he had never been conceived – but that did not mean he was prepared to condone gratuitous insults from outsiders.

'Nevertheless,' he pointed out, 'the problem remains. No one's going to be prepared to believe that Ruspanti walked up to the dome with one shoe off and one shoe on.'

Zen nodded slowly, as if recalling something.

'Ah yes, the shoe.'

Strolling over to the benches of pews lined up in the north transept, he walked along them until he saw the missing black brogue. He picked it up and walked back to Lamboglia.

'Here you are.'

Lamboglia turned the shoe over as though it were a property in a magic trick.

'What was it doing there?' he demanded.

'It must have got pulled off as Ruspanti clambered over the railings. Perhaps he changed his mind at the last minute and tried to climb back.'

Lamboglia thought about this for a moment.

'I suppose so,' he said.

'There are no further problems as far as I can see,' Zen told him briskly. 'But you can of course contact me through the Ministry, should the need arise.'

Lamboglia glared at him. Although the man's behaviour couldn't be faulted professionally, his breezy, off-hand manner left a lot to be desired. Lamboglia would dearly have loved to take him down a peg or two, to make him sweat. But as things stood there was nothing he could do except give him the sour look which his subordinates so dreaded.

'Are you in a hurry, dottore?' he snapped.

'I have a taxi waiting.'

Lamboglia's glare intensified.

'Another appointment? You're a busy man.'

Zen looked at the cleric, and smiled.

'No, I just want to get to bed.'

2

On the face of it, the scene at the Ministry of the Interior the following Tuesday morning was calculated to gladden the hearts of all those who despaired of the grotesque overmanning and underachievement of the government bureaucracy, a number roughly equal to those who had failed to secure a cushy *statale* post of their own. Not only were a significant minority of the staff at their desks, but the atmosphere was one of intense and animated activity. The only snag was that little or none of this activity had anything to do with the duties of the Ministry.

In the Ministerial suite on the top floor, where the present incumbent and his coterie of under-secretaries presided, the imminent collapse of the present government coalition had prompted a frantic round of consultations, negotiations, threats and promises as potential contenders jockeyed for position. On the lower floors, unruffled by this *aria di crisi*, it was business as usual. The range of services on offer included a fax bureau, an agency for Filippino maids, two competing protection rackets, a Kawasaki motorcycle franchise, a video rental club, a travel agent and a city-wide courier service, to say nothing of Madam Beta, medium, astrologer, sorcerer, cards and palms read, the evil eye averted, talismans and amulets prepared. One of the most flourishing of these enterprises was situated in the Administration section on the ground floor, where Tania Biacis ran an agency which supplied speciality food items from her native Friuli region.

Tania had got the idea from one of her cousins, who had returned from a honeymoon trip to London with the news that Italian food was now as much in demand in the English capital as Italian fashion, 'only nothing from our poor Friuli, as usual!' At the time this had struck Tania as little more than the usual provincial whingeing, all too characteristic of a border region acutely aware of its distance from the twin centres of power in Rome and Milan. It had been the energies released by the break-up of her marriage which had finally driven her to do something about it. Claiming some of the leave due to her, she had travelled to London with a suitcase full of samples rounded up by Aldo, the husband of her cousin Bettina, whose job with the post office at Cividale gave him ample opportunity for getting out and about and meeting local farmers.

Posing as a representative, Tania had visited the major British wholesalers and tried to convince them of the virtues of Friuli ham, wine, honey, jam and grappa. Rather to her surprise, several had placed orders, in one case so large that Aldo had the greatest difficulty in meeting it. Since then, the business had grown by leaps and bounds. Aldo and Bettina looked after the supply side, while Tania handled the orders and paperwork, using the Ministry's telephones and fax facilities to keep in contact with the major European cities, as well as New York and Tokyo. One of Agrofrul's greatest successes was a range of jams originally made by Bettina's aunt; this had now been expanded into a cottage industry involving several hundred women. Genuine Friuli grappa, made in small copper stills, had also done well, while the company's air-cured hams were rapidly displacing their too-famous rivals from Parma as the ultimate designer charcuterie.

Tania had told Aurelio nothing of all this. Her nominal reason for reticence was that he was a senior Ministry official, and although everyone knew perfectly well what went on in the way of moonlighting, scams and general private enterprise, she didn't want to compromise her lover by making him a party to activities which were theoretically punishable by instant dismissal, loss of pension rights and even a prison sentence. Tania was pretty sure that no one would throw the book at *her*. The rules were never enforced on principle, only as a result of someone's personal schemes for advancement or revenge, and she simply wasn't important enough to attract that kind of negative compliment. Moreover, as a result of her six years service in the Administration section she was now privy to most of her colleagues' dirty little secrets, which in itself would make any potential whistle-blower think twice.

Aurelio's situation was quite different. By nature a loner, his reputation damaged by a mistaken fit of zealousness at the time of the Moro affair, he was promoted to the Ministry's élite Criminalpol squad as a result of an unsavoury deal during his comeback case in Perugia, and had subsequently been connected with a heavily compromised political party at the time of the Burolo affair. As a result,

Zen was surrounded by enemies who would like nothing better than to implicate him in a case involving misuse of bureaucratic resources and conspiracy to defraud the state, not to mention a little matter of undeclared taxes amounting to several million lire.

The fact that they were lovers would just make the whole scandal even more juicy, but it also explained Tania's unadmitted reason for not telling Aurelio about the success of Agrofrul. She was well aware that the story he had told her about the flat was not true. It supposedly belonged to an American who was out of the country on business for a few months and was happy to have someone looking after the place, but this was clearly nonsense. Where were this American's belongings? Why did he never get any post? Above all, why had he handed it over free of charge to the friend of a friend, a person he'd never even met, when he could have sub-let it for a small fortune? Flats as gorgeous as that, in such a sought-after district, didn't just fall into your lap free of charge. Someone was paying for it, and in the present case that someone could only be Aurelio Zen.

This put Tania in an awkward position. Eight years of marriage to Mauro Bevilacqua had left her with no illusions about the fragility of the male ego, or the destructive passions that can be unleashed without the slightest warning when it feels slighted. She knew that Zen had already been hurt by her refusal to move in with him, and she guessed that his belief that he was supporting her financially might well be the necessary salve for this wound. He could accept Tania's independence as long as he was secretly subsidizing it, as long as he believed that she was only *playing* at being free. But how would he react if he learned that his mistress was in fact the senior partner in a business with a turnover which already exceeded his salary by a considerable amount? She had no wish to lose him, this strange, moody individual who could be so passionately there one moment, so transparently distant the next, who seemed to float through life as though he had nothing to hope or fear from it. She wanted to know him, if anyone could, and to be known in return. But not possessed. No one would ever own her again, on that she was quite adamant.

She pulled the phone over, got an outside line and then dialled a restaurant in Stockholm's business district where a brambly *refosco* made by a relative of Aldo's sister had become a cult wine. The distributor who had been importing Agrofrul's produce had recently gone bankrupt and the restaurant now wanted to know if they could obtain supplies direct. Using her limited but serviceable English, Tania ascertained that the proprietor had not yet arrived but would call back. She lit a cigarette and turned her attention to the newspaper open on the desk in front of her, which was making great play with allegations of a cover-up in the death of a Roman nobleman in the Vatican.

Tania turned the page impatiently. She had no appetite for such things any more, the grand scandals which ran and ran for years, as though manipulated by a master storyteller who was always ready with some fresh 'revelation' whenever the public interest started to wane. The one thing you could be sure of, the only absolute certainty on offer, was that you would never, ever, know the truth. Whatever you did know was therefore by definition not the truth. Like children playing 'pass the parcel', the commentators and analysts tried to guess the nature of the mystery by examining the size, shape and weight of the package in which it had been concealed. But the adult game was even more futile, for once the wrappings had all been removed the parcel always proved to be empty.

The shrilling of the phone interrupted her thoughts. Pulling over the rough jotting of proposals she had prepared for the Swedish restaurateur, Tania lifted the receiver.

'*Good morning,*' she said in English.

'Who the hell is this?'

The speaker was male, Italian, and very angry. Tania immediately depressed the rest with her finger, breaking the connection. A moment later the phone rang again. She let it go on for some time before lifting her finger and snarling 'Yes?' in her best bureaucratic manner, bored and truculent.

'Is that Biacis?' demanded the same male voice.

'Who do you think, the Virgin Mary?'

There was a furious spluttering.

'Don't you dare talk like that to me!'

'And how am I supposed to know how I should talk when you haven't told me who you are?' Tania snapped back.

In fact she knew perfectly well who it was, even before the caller angrily identified himself as Lorenzo Moscati, head of the Criminalpol division. Within the caste system of the Ministry, Moscati was a person of considerable stature, whose relation to a mere Grade II administrative assistant such as Tania was roughly that of one of the figures in the higher reaches of a baroque ceiling-piece, almost invisible in the refulgence of his glory, to one of the extras supporting clouds or propping up sunbeams in the bottom left-hand corner. But Tania didn't give a damn. As a successful independent business-woman, she had no reason to be impressed by some shit-for-brains with the right party card and an influential clique behind him. Even the Russians were finally having second thoughts about the virtues of such a system. Only the Italian state apparatus remained utterly immune to the effects of *glasnost*.

'Zen, Aurelio!' Moscati shouted.

'What about him?'

'Where is he?'

'How should I know? This isn't Personnel.'

Moscati's voice modulated to a tone of unctuous viciousness.

'I am aware of that, my dear, but all Ciliani can tell me is that he's off sick. So I called his home number and asked if I could speak to the invalid, only to find that his mother hasn't seen him since yesterday and seems to think he's gone to Florence for work.'

'So? What have I to do with it?'

Moscati gave a nasty chuckle.

'To be perfectly honest, I thought he might be holed up at your little love-nest.'

Tania gasped involuntarily. Moscati chuckled again, more confidently now.

'No wonder he needs a day off to recover, poor fellow,' he continued in the tone of silken brutality he used with female underlings. 'All that night service, and at his age, too. Anyway, that's another matter. The fact is that our Aurelio is deep in the shit, wherever he may be. Have you seen the papers? These allegations are extremely serious, even alarming, but as his colleague I naturally feel a certain solidarity. That's why I'm giving him one last chance to put things right. Have him call me, now.'

He hung up. Tania stubbed out her cigarette, which had burned down to the filter, and dialled a Rome number. It rang for some time before a sleepy voice answered.

'Yes?'

'Did I wake you, sweetheart?' she asked gently.

A pleased grunt.

'Not exactly. I've been lying here beside you. The pillow is still shaped by your head, and the sheets smell of you. There's really quite a lot of you still here.'

'More than there is here, believe me. Look, I'm sorry to have to be the one to break this to you, but Moscati has been on to me. He's after your blood for some reason.'

There was a brief silence.

'Why did he call you?' Zen asked.

He sounded wide awake now.

'He knows, Aurelio.'

'He can't!'

The exclamation was as involuntary as a cry of pain.

'I'm afraid he does,' said Tania. 'And about the flat, too.'

A silence. Zen sighed.

'I'm sorry,' he muttered almost inaudibly.

'It doesn't make any difference. Not to me, at any rate. You'd better phone him, Aurelio. It sounded urgent.'

Another sigh.

'Any other messages?'

Tania leafed through the mail for the Criminalpol department, which she planned to deliver when the pressures of business permitted.

'Just a telegram.'

'Let's have it.'

Tania tore open the envelope and read the brief typed message.

'It sounds like some loony,' she told him.

'What does it say?'

'"If you wish to get these deaths in the proper perspective, apply at the green gates in the piazza at the end of Via Santa Sabina."'

He grunted.

'No name?'

'Nothing. Don't go, Aurelio. It could be a nutter.'

She sounded nervous, memories of Vasco Spadola's deadly vendetta still fresh in her mind.

'When was it sent?'

'Just after five yesterday afternoon, from Piazza San Silvestro.'

He yawned.

'All right. I'd better ring Moscati now.'

'What's it all about, Aurelio? He said it was in the papers.'

'Well, well. Fame at last.'

Tania said nothing.

'I'll ring you later about tonight,' he told her. 'And don't worry. It's just work, not life and death.'

The letters had been faxed from the Vatican City State to the Rome offices of five national newspapers about ten o'clock on Monday evening. The time had been well chosen. The following day's editions were about to go to bed, while most people in the Vatican had already done so. There was thus no time to follow up the startling allegations which the letter contained, still less to get an official reaction from the Vatican Press Office, notoriously reticent and dilatory at the best of times.

The anonymous writer had thoughtfully included a list of the publications to whom he had sent copies of the document. The editors phoned each other. Yes, they'd seen the thing. Well, they were undecided, really. They weren't in the habit of printing unsubstantiated accusations, although these did seem to have a certain ring of authenticity, and if by chance they were true then of course ... Nevertheless, in the end all five agreed that it would be wiser to hold back until the whole thing could be properly investigated. Chuckling with glee at their craftiness in securing this exclusive scoop, each then phoned the newsroom to hold the front page. Here was a story which had everything: a colourful and notorious central character, a background rife with financial and political skulduggery, and – best of all – the Vatican connection.

Aurelio Zen read the reports as his taxi crawled through the dense traffic, making so little progress that at times he had the impression that they were being carried backwards, like a boat with the tide against it. He had bought *La Stampa*, his usual paper, as well as *La Repubblica*, *Il Corriere della Sera*, and, for a no-holds-barred view, the radical *Il Manifesto*. Each served up the rich and spicy raw materials with varying degrees of emphasis and presentation, but all began with a résumé of the affair so far which inevitably centred on the enigmatic figure of Prince Ludovico Ruspanti, an inveterate gambler and playboy but also a pillar of the establishment and a prominent member of the Knights of Malta. Unlike the vast majority of the Italian aristocracy – most notoriously the so-called 'Counts of

Ciampino' created by Vittorio Emanuele III before his departure into exile from that airport in 1944 – the Ruspantis were no parvenus. The family dated back to the fifteenth century, and had at one time or another counted among its members a score of cardinals, a long succession of Papal Knights, a siege hero flayed alive by the Turks, the victim of a street affray with the Orsini clan and a particularly gory uxoricide.

After unification and the collapse of the Papal States, one junior member of the Ruspantis had sensed which way the wind was blowing, moved to the newly emergent power centre in Milan and married into the Falcone family of textile magnates. The others remained in Rome, slowly stagnating. Ludovico's father, Filippo, had succumbed to the febrile intoxications of Fascism, which had seemed for a time to restore some of the energy and purpose which had been drained from their lives. But this drunken spree was the Ruspantis' final fling. Filippo survived the war and its immediate aftermath, despite his alleged participation in war crimes during the Ethiopian campaign, but the peace slowly destroyed him. The abolition of papal pomp and ritual in the wake of the Second Vatican Council was the last straw. Prince Filippo took to his bed in the family palazzo on Lungotevere opposite the Villa Farnesina, where he died anathemizing the 'antipope' John XXIII who had delivered the Church into the hands of the socialists and freemasons. Lorenzo, the elder of Filippo's two sons, had been groomed since birth for the day when he would become Prince, but in the event he survived his father by less than a year before his Alfa Romeo was crushed between an overtaking truck and the wall of a motorway tunnel. And thus it was that Ludovico, to whose education and character no one had given a second thought, found himself head of the family at the age of twenty-three.

The young Prince appeared at first a reassuring clone of his late brother, doing and saying all the right things. As well as joining such exclusive secular associations as the Chess Club and the Hunting Club, he also put himself forward for admission to the Sovereign Military Order of Malta, like every senior Ruspanti for the previous four hundred years. He hunted hard, gambled often, and busied himself with running the family's agricultural *tenuta* near Palestrina. His political and social opinions were reassuringly predictable, and he expressed no views on the controversial reforms instituted by John XXIII, or indeed on anything else apart from hunting, gambling and running the aforementioned country estate. The only thing which caused a raised eyebrow among certain ultras was the reconciliation with the family's mercantile relatives in Milan. This event, which most people considered long overdue, unfortunately came too late for the Falcone parents, who had paid the price of their high industrial and financial profile by falling victim to the Red Brigades, but Ludovico went out of his way to cultivate his cousins Raimondo and Ariana – to such an extent, indeed, that malicious tongues accused him of having conceived an unhealthy passion for the latter, a striking girl who had never fully recovered from her parents' death. Such improprieties, however, even if such they were, occurred a world away, in the desolate, misty plains of Lombardy. Where it mattered, in the salons of aristocratic Rome, Ludovico's behaviour seemed absolutely unexceptionable.

Nevertheless, as the years went by the family's financial situation gradually began to slide out of control. First sections of the country estate were sold off, then the whole thing. Palazzo Ruspanti was next to go, although Ludovico managed to retain the *piano nobile* for the use of himself and his mother until she died, when he sold up and moved to rented rooms in the unfashionable Prenestino district. Friends and relations were heard to suggest that marriage to some suitably endowed young lady might prove the answer to these problems. Such things were a good deal rarer than they had been a hundred years earlier, when a noble title counted for more and people were less bashful about buying into one, but they were by no means unheard of.

Ludovico, though, showed no interest in any of the potential partners who were more or less overtly paraded before him. This indifference naturally added fuel to the rumours concerning his love for Ariana Falcone, whose brother Raimondo had recently and quite unexpectedly achieved fame as a fashion designer. Other versions had it that Ruspanti was gay, or impotent, or had joined that inner circle of the Order of Malta, the thirty 'professed' Knights who are sworn to chastity, obedience and poverty – cynics joked that Ludovico would have no difficulty with the final item, at any rate. Then there was the question of where all the money had gone. Some people said it had been swallowed by the Prince's cocaine habit, some that he had paid kidnappers a huge ransom for the return of his and Ariana's love-child, while others held that the family fortune had gone to finance an abortive monarchist *coup d'état*. Even those who repeated the most likely story – that Ludovico's inveterate love of gambling had extended itself to share dealing, and that his portfolio had been wiped out when the Wall Street market collapsed on 'Black Monday' – were careful to avoid the charge of credulous banality by suggesting that this was merely a cover for the *real* drama, which involved a doomsday scenario of global dimensions, involving the CIA, Opus Dei and Gelli's P2, and using the Knights of Malta as a cover.

Thus when word spread that Ruspanti had taken refuge with the latter organization following his disappearance from circulation about a month earlier, the story was widely credited. The official line was that Ruspanti was wanted for questioning by a magistrate investigating a currency fraud involving businessmen in Milan, but few people were prepared to believe that. Far larger issues were clearly at stake, involving the future of prominent members of the government. This explained why the Prince had chosen a hiding place which was beyond the jurisdiction of the Italian authorities. The Sovereign Military Order of Malta has long lost the extensive territories which once made it, together with the Knights Templar, the richest and most powerful mediaeval order of chivalry, but it is still recognized as an independent state by over forty nations, including Italy. Thus Palazzo Malta, opposite Gucci's in elegant Via Condotti, and the Palace of Rhodes on the Aventine hill, headquarters of the local Grand Priory and chancery of the Order's diplomatic mission to the Holy See, enjoy exactly the same extraterritorial status as any foreign embassy. If the fugitive had taken refuge within the walls of either property, he was as safe from the power of the Italian state as he would have been in Switzerland or Paraguay. Whatever the truth about this, Ruspanti had not been seen again until his dramatic reappearance the previous Friday in the basilica of St Peter's.

This event initially appeared to render the question of the Prince's whereabouts in the interim somewhat academic, but the letter to the newspapers changed all that with its dramatic suggestion that his death might not be quite what it seemed – or rather, what the Vatican authorities had allegedly been at considerable pains to *make* it seem. According to the anonymous correspondent, in short, Ludovico Ruspanti – like Roberto Calvi, Michele Sindona and so many other illustrious corpses – had been the subject of 'an assisted suicide'.

The letter made three principal charges. The first confirmed the rumours about Ruspanti having been harboured by the Order of Malta, but added that following his expulsion, which took place after a personal intervention by the Grand Master, the Prince had been leading a clandestine existence in the Vatican City State with the full connivance of the Holy See. Moreover, the writer claimed, Ruspanti's movements and contacts during this period had been the subject of a surveillance operation, and the Vatican authorities were thus aware that on the afternoon of his death the Prince had met the representatives of an organization referred to as 'the Cabal'. But the item of most interest to Zen was the last, which stated categorically that the senior Italian police official called in by the Holy See, a certain 'Dottor Aurelio Zeno', had deliberately falsified the results of his investigation in line with the preconceived verdict of suicide.

Almost the most significant feature of the letter was that no more was said. The implication was that it was addressed not to the general public but to those in the know, the select few who were aware of the existence and nature of 'the Cabal'. They would grasp not only how and why Ruspanti had met his death, but also the reasons why this information was now being leaked to the press. 'In short,' *Il Manifesto* concluded, 'we once again find ourselves enveloped by sinister and suggestive mysteries, face to face with one of those convenient deaths signed by a designer whose name remains unknown but whose craftsmanship everyone recognizes as bearing the label "Made in Italy".'

'This one?'

The taxi had drawn up opposite an unpainted wooden door set in an otherwise blank wall. There was no number, and for a moment Zen hesitated. Then he saw the black Fiat saloon with SCV number plates parked on the other side of the street, right under a sign reading PARKING STRICTLY FORBIDDEN. It could sit there for the rest of the year without getting a ticket, Zen reflected as he paid off the taxi. Any vehicle bearing *Sacra Città del Vaticano* plates was invisible to the traffic cops.

A metal handle dangled from a chain in a small niche beside the door. Zen gave it a yank. A dull bell clattered briefly, somewhere remote. Nothing happened. He pulled the chain again, then got out a cigarette and put it in his mouth without lighting it. A small metal grille set in the door slid back.

'Yes?' demanded a female voice.

'Signor Bianchi.'

Keys jingled, locks turned, bolts were drawn, and the door opened a crack.

'Come in!'

Zen stepped into the soft, musty dimness inside. He just had time to glimpse the speaker, a dumpy nun 'of canonical age', to use the Church's euphemism, before the door was slammed shut and locked behind him.

'Follow me.'

The nun waddled off along a bare tiled corridor which unexpectedly emerged in a well-tended garden surrounded on three sides by a cloister whose tiled, sloping roof was supported by an arcade of beautifully proportioned arches. Zen's guide opened one of the doors facing the garden.

'Please wait here.'

She scuttled off. Zen stepped over the well-scrubbed threshold. The room was long and narrow, with a freakishly high ceiling and a floor of smooth scrubbed stone slabs. It smelt like a disused larder. The one window, small and barred, set in the upper expanses of a bare whitewashed wall, emphasized the sense of enclosure. The furnishings consisted of a trestle table flanked by wooden benches, and an acrylic painting showing a young woman reclining in a supine posture while a bleeding heart hovered in the air above her, emitting rays of light which pierced her outstretched palms.

Zen sat heavily on one of the benches. The tabletop was a thick oak board burnished to a sullen gleam. He took the cigarette from his lips and twiddled it between two fingers. It seemed inconceivable that only half an hour earlier he had been lying in a position not dissimilar from that of the female stigmatic in the painting, wondering if it was worth bothering to get out of bed at all given that Tania would be back shortly after two. For no particular reason, he had decided to treat himself to a couple of days' sick-leave. Like all state employees, Zen regularly availed himself of this perk. A doctor's certificate was only required for more than three days' absence, and as long as you didn't abuse the system too exaggeratedly, everyone turned a blind eye. That was how Zen had known that something was seriously wrong when Tania told him about Moscati checking up on him.

When he phoned in, Lorenzo Moscati had left him in no doubt whatever that the shit had hit the fan.

'I don't know how you do it, Zen, I really don't. You take a simple courtesy call, a bit of window-dressing, and manage to turn it into a diplomatic incident.'

'But I . . .'

'The apostolic nuncio has intervened in the very strongest terms, demanding an explanation, and to make matters worse half the blue bloods at the Farnesina were fucking *related* to Ruspanti. Result, the Minister finds himself in the hot seat just as the entire government is about to go into the blender and he had his eye on some nice fat portfolio like Finance.'

'But I . . .'

'The media are screaming for you to be put on parade, which is all we need. We're saying you're in bed, not with la Biacis but a fever, something nasty and infectious. We've sent Marcelli along to handle the press conference. All you need to do is fiddle a doctor's certificate and then keep out of sight for a day or two. But first get along to Via dell'Annunciata in Trastevere, number 14, and make your peace with the priests. You'd better turn on the charm, Zen – or Bianchi, as they want you to call yourself. Remember how the Inquisition worked? The Church graciously pardoned the erring sinners, and then turned them over to the secular authorities to be burnt alive. And that's what's going to happen to you, Zen, unless you can talk your way out of this one.'

The implications of this threat could hardly have been more serious. If the Vatican lodged a formal complaint, the Ministry would have no option but to institute a full internal inquiry. The verdict was almost irrelevant, since the severity of the eventual disciplinary proceedings was as nothing compared to the long, slow torment of the inquiry itself, dragging on for month after month, while the subject was ostracized by colleagues wary of being contaminated by contact with a potential pariah.

So gloomy were these speculations that even the arrival of Monsignor Lamboglia was a distinct relief. The cleric was wearing a plain dark overcoat, grey scarf and homburg hat and carrying a black leather briefcase, and his sharp-featured face looked even grimmer than usual.

'Will that be all?' murmured the elderly nun from the doorway.

Lamboglia scanned the room slowly through his steel-rimmed glasses. He might have been alone for all the sign he gave of having noted Zen's existence. Without turning round, he nodded once. The nun backed out, closing the door behind her.

The cleric took off his overcoat, folded it carefully and laid it beside his hat and briefcase on the table. He opened his briefcase and removed a portable tape-recorder, then looked at Zen for the first time since entering the room.

'You may smoke.'

Zen twirled the unlit cigarette between his lips.

'Do I get a blindfold as well?'

Lamboglia regarded him like an entomologist confronted by an unfamiliar insect whose characteristics had nothing much to recommend them from a personal point of view, but which would have to be catalogued just the same. He sat down opposite Zen, set the tape-recorder on the table mid-way between them and pressed the red RECORD button.

'Did you send that letter to the papers?' he asked.

Zen gazed at him in shock, then growing anger. He nodded.

'There hasn't been enough aggravation in my life recently. I'd been wondering what to do about it.'

It was Lamboglia's turn to get angry.

'So you find this funny, do you?'

'Not at all. I find it *stupid*.'

He fixed Lamboglia with a steady glare.

'Look, if I were crazy enough to risk my career by pointing out irregularities in the conduct of an investigation for which I was responsible, I'd at least have done it properly!'

He tapped the pile of newspapers lying at his elbow.

'This letter is all bluff, a farrago of vague, unsubstantiated generalities. Now I don't know anything about this secret society which Ruspanti was apparently involved with, but as far as the manner of his death is concerned there is absolutely no doubt in my mind. I know what happened, and when, and how.'

Impressed despite himself by Zen's confident, decisive manner, Lamboglia nodded.

'So there's no truth in these allegations?'

'What allegations?'

Lamboglia tapped the table impatiently.

MICHAEL DIBDIN

'That Ruspanti was murdered!'
Zen frowned.
'But of *course* he was murdered!'
The two men gazed at each other in silence for some time.
'You mean you didn't know?' Zen asked incredulously.
Behind the twin discs of glass, Lamboglia's eyes narrowed dangerously.
'What made you think we did?'
'Well, according to the letter, Ruspanti was living in the Vatican and you were keeping him under surveillance.'
'But you didn't know that on Friday!'
'It's true, then?' Zen asked quickly.
Lamboglia turned off the tape-recorder, rewound the cassette briefly, and pressed PLAY.
'. . . *keeping him under surveillance.*'
The cleric looked at Zen.
'You were quite right, dottore – your career *is* at risk. Don't try and catch me out again. Just answer my questions.'
He pressed the RECORD button.
'It is your professional conduct on Friday which is the subject of this inquiry, dottore. At that time, you had no reason to assume – rightly or wrongly – that we had any idea that Ruspanti might have been murdered. The word was never even mentioned in the course of your interview with Archbishop Sánchez-Valdés.'
At last, Zen lit his cigarette, then looked round in vain for an ashtray. Irritated by this delay, Lamboglia waved dismissively.
'Use the floor. The nuns will clean it up. That's what nuns are for.'
Zen released a breath of fragrant smoke.
'It was precisely the fact that no one mentioned the possibility of murder which I found so significant,' he said.
Lamboglia gave a sneering laugh.
'That's absurd.'
'On the contrary. I wasn't asked to investigate Ruspanti's death but to confirm that he had committed suicide. When I offered to do so without more ado, as a good Catholic, the archbishop made it quite clear that he wanted more than that. "Do whatever you need to do," he told me, "whatever must be done to achieve the desired result."'
'Exactly!' cried Lamboglia. 'To determine the truth!'
Zen shrugged.

'No one mentioned that word either.'

'Because it was taken for *granted*!'

Zen tapped his cigarette, dislodging a packet of ash which tumbled through the air to disintegrate on the smooth flag-stones.

'Then the members of the Curia are a great deal less subtle than they have been given credit for,' he replied.

Lamboglia rapped the table authoritatively.

'Don't be impertinent! You had no right to conceal anything from us.'

'Excuse me, monsignore, but Archbishop Sánchez-Valdés explicitly instructed me to take whatever action I considered necessary without consulting him or his colleagues.'

'Yes, but only to avoid compromising your status as an independent observer. No one asked you to cover up a murder!'

Zen tossed the butt of his cigarette under the table and crushed it out.

'Of course not. It would have been impossible for me to do so if I'd been asked openly. That's why murder was never once mentioned, despite the fact that there was no sense in calling me in unless there was a real possibility that Ruspanti had been murdered. By the same token, I couldn't reveal the evidence I subsequently discovered without making it impossible for you to sustain the suicide verdict.'

And for me to get home to Tania, he thought, for the decisive factor that evening had been his eagerness to return as soon as possible to the bed from which he'd been ejected by the electronic pager. Any hint of what he had discovered would have put paid to that for good.

'Let's be honest, monsignore,' he told Lamboglia. 'You didn't want me coming to you and saying, "Actually Ruspanti didn't fall from the gallery he had the key to but the one sixty feet above it." You didn't want to know about it, did you? You just wanted the matter taken care of, neatly and discreetly. That's what I did, and if someone hadn't decided to give the game away, no one would be any the wiser.'

Lamboglia stared at him across the table in silence. Several times he seemed about to speak, then changed his mind.

'That's impossible,' he said at last. 'The dome was closed when Ruspanti fell. The killer would have been trapped inside.'

'The killers – there must have been at least two – left fifteen or twenty minutes earlier.'

Lamboglia laughed again, a harsh, brittle sound.

'And what did Ruspanti do during that time, may I ask? Hover there in mid-air like an angel?'

'More or less.'

'You forget that we have extensive professional experience of false miracles.'

'This wasn't a miracle. They trussed the poor bastard up with a length of nylon fishing line and left him dangling over the edge of the gallery.'

'*Fishing* line?'

Zen nodded.

'Thin, transparent, virtually invisible, but with a breaking strain of over a hundred kilos. I found several metres of the stuff tied to one of the railing supports on the upper gallery. I removed it, of course.'

Lamboglia suddenly held out a hand for silence. He got up and walked quickly to the door, which he flung open dramatically. The elderly nun almost fell into the room, clutching a mop.

'Jesus, Mary and Joseph! Forgive me, monsignore, I didn't mean to startle you. I was just scrubbing the floor . . .'

'Cleanliness is indeed a great virtue,' Lamboglia replied in a tone of icy irony, 'and the fact that you have seen fit to undertake this menial labour yourself, rather than delegate it to one of your younger colleagues, indicates a commendable humility. If your discretion matches your other qualities – as is fervently to be hoped – then your eventual beatification can be only a question of time.'

He glowered at the nun, who gazed back at her tormentor with an expression which to Zen's eyes at least appeared frankly erotic.

'Such a degree of sanctity no doubt makes any contact with the secular world both painful and problematic,' Lamboglia continued remorselessly. 'Nevertheless, I'm sure that someone as resourceful as yourself will find a way to procure us two coffees, easy on the milk but heavy on the foam, and a couple of pastries from a good bakery, none of that mass-produced rubbish.'

Abandoning her mop, the nun scampered off. Lamboglia slammed the door shut and returned to the table. He rewound the tape to the beginning of the interruption and replaced the recorder in front of Zen.

'You say you found this twine attached to the upper gallery. But what made you look there in the first place?'

'I examined the lower gallery, the part that is closed to the public, overlooking the spot where Ruspanti fell. It was at once obvious that no one had thrown himself from there. There was an undisturbed layer of dust all along the top of the guardrail, and even on the floor. Besides, there was no sign of the missing shoe there. The upper gallery was the only other possibility.'

Lamboglia frowned with the effort of keeping up with all this new information.

'But we found the shoe in the basilica, under one of the benches. You said it had fallen there separately from the body.'

Zen nodded.

'Separately in space *and* time. Several hours later, in fact, while I was searching the gallery.'

There was a timid knock at the door and the elderly nun appeared, carrying a tray covered with a spotless white cloth. She set it down on the table and removed the cloth like a conjuror to reveal two steaming bowls of coffee, an appetizing assortment of pastries and a glass ashtray. The cleric gave a curt nod and the nun slunk out.

'So none of this can now be proved?' Lamboglia asked.

Zen selected a pastry.

'Well, there were some marks on Ruspanti's wrists. I thought at first that they were preliminary cuts showing where he'd tried to slash his wrists, but in fact they must have been weals made by the pressure of the twine. A post-mortem might reveal traces of the chloroform or whatever they used to keep him unconscious, but I don't suppose there's the faintest possibility of the family agreeing to allow one.'

'But if the killers left before Ruspanti fell, how did they release the bonds that were holding him to the gallery?'

Zen washed down the pastry with a long gulp of the creamy coffee and got out his cigarettes.

'They didn't. *He* did.'

Lamboglia merely stared.

'This is just a guess,' Zen admitted as he lit up, 'but they probably tied him up with a slippery hitch and looped the free end around his wrists. The family said that Ruspanti suffered from vertigo, so when he came round from the chloroform to find himself suspended two hundred feet above a sheer drop to the floor of the basilica he would have panicked totally. The witnesses all talked about the terrible screams which seemed to start several seconds before the body appeared. During those seconds Ruspanti would have been desperately struggling to free his hands so that he could reach the railings and pull himself to safety. What he didn't realize was that by doing so, he was clearing the hitch securing him to the gallery.'

Lamboglia stuck one finger between his teeth for a single moment which revealed him to be a reformed nail-biter.

'You should have informed us.'

Zen shrugged.

'The way I read it, you either knew or you didn't want to. Either way, it was none of my business to tell you.'

Lamboglia stood up. He switched off the tape-recorder and replaced it in his briefcase.

'Look, there's no problem,' Zen told him, getting up too. 'Just deny everything. I'll back you up. Without hard evidence, the media will soon drop the case.'

Lamboglia buttoned up his coat and took his hat.

'There is also the question of the mole.'

'You want me to tackle that?' offered Zen, eager to show willing. 'Someone must have supplied Ruspanti's killers with keys to the galleries. I could make a start there.'

Lamboglia stared at the wall as though it were an autocue from which he was reading a prepared text.

'The matter of the keys can be left to our own personnel. As far as the mole is concerned, we already have a suspect. The anonymous letter was faxed to the newspapers from a machine in the offices of Vatican Radio. At ten in the evening, there is only a skeleton staff on duty, and it was a fairly simple matter to eliminate them from suspicion. The only other person who had access to the building that evening was the duty security officer, Giovanni Grimaldi.'

Zen let his cigarette fall to the floor and stepped on it carefully.

'The man who showed me round on Friday?'

Lamboglia inclined his head.

'He was at the scene when Ruspanti fell, wasn't he?' Zen demanded. 'Was he already involved in the case in some way?'

The cleric looked at him blankly.

'That is neither here nor there. We are concerned to determine whether or not he sent that letter to the press, and if so to prevent it happening again. The problem is that Grimaldi is himself a member of the force which normally undertakes operations of this kind.'

'*Quia custodet ipsis custodies,*' murmured Zen.

'*Quis custodiet ipsos custodes,* actually. But you've got the right idea. Who is to investigate the investigators? We normally have every confidence in our staff, but in this case it is simply too much of a risk to expect Grimaldi's colleagues to act against him. It is essential that the mole shouldn't be tipped off before we can act.'

He looked at Zen.

'Which is where you come in.'

Zen returned his stare.

'You want me to . . . "act"?'

Lamboglia placed his hands on the table, fingers splayed as though on the keyboard of an organ.

'A positive and decisive intervention on your part would contribute greatly towards bringing this unfortunate episode to a mutually satisfactory conclusion,' he said.

Zen nodded.

'But this time, perhaps you'd better tell me exactly what you want done,' he said. 'Just to avoid the possibility of any further confusion.'

'The first thing is to search Grimaldi's room. With any luck, you might find some incriminating material which we can use. He's on duty this afternoon, so you won't be disturbed.'

He handed Zen a brown envelope.

'This contains his address and a telephone number on which you can call us this evening to relay your findings. Any further instructions will be conveyed to you at that stage.'

He turned to go.

'Oh, there's just one more thing,' Zen said.

The cleric turned, his glasses gleaming with reflected light like the enlarged pupils of a nocturnal predator.

'Yes?'

'Can you recommend a good doctor?'

He closed the door with great care, lifting it slightly on its hinges to prevent the tell-tale squeak, and stood listening. The sounds he could hear would have meant little to anyone else, but to Zen they provided an invaluable guide to the hazards he was going to have to negotiate.

At the end of the hallway, beyond the glass-panelled door to the living room, his mother was talking loudly in short bursts separated by long intervals of silence. Zen couldn't make out what she was saying, but the singsong intonations and the buzzing of the Venetian 'x' revealed that she was speaking in dialect rather than Italian. So unless she was talking to herself – always a distinct possibility – then she must be on the phone, almost certainly to Rosalba Morosini, their former neighbour in Venice, whom she called regularly to keep in touch with the news and gossip in the only city that would ever be quite real for her.

Further away, a mere background drone, came the sound of a vacuum cleaner, indicating that Maria Grazia, the housekeeper, was at work in one of the bedrooms at the far end of the apartment. Zen moved cautiously forward along the darkened hallway. The room to his left, overlooking the gloomy internal courtyard, was crammed with boxes of papers and photographs, trunks full of his father's clothes and miscellaneous furniture which had been transferred wholesale to Rome when his mother had finally been persuaded to abandon the family home just off the Cannaregio canal. The thought of that emptied space pervaded by the limpid, shifting Venetian light made Zen feel as weightlessly replete as a child for a moment.

With extreme caution, he opened the door opposite. The elaborate plaster moulding, picture rail and ceiling rose revealed that this had been intended to serve as the dining room, but following his mother's arrival Zen had commandeered it as his bedroom. As far as he was concerned, whatever it lacked in charm and intimacy was more than compensated for by its proximity to the front door. High on the list of problems caused by his mother's presence in the house

566

was the fact that every time she saw him putting on his coat Signora Zen wanted to know where he was going and when he'd be back, while on his return she expected a detailed account of where he'd been and what he'd been doing. Exactly as though he were still ten years old, in short. It was, Zen had concluded, the only way in which mothers could relate to their sons, and therefore not something for which they were to be blamed, still less which there was any point in trying to change. Nevertheless, it got on his nerves, particularly since his relationship with Tania Biacis had begun to make ever greater demands on his time.

Zen had been separated from his wife Luisella for over a decade, but in the eyes of the Church and Zen's mother they were still married. In his previous affair, with an American expatriate, Zen had used this as a way of maintaining his distance. Ellen had ultimately returned to New York, disappointed by Zen's unwillingness to commit himself to her more fully. Now the tables had been turned with a vengeance. Zen would have been more than happy to present Tania to his mother as his *fidanzata*, that usefully vague category somewhere between steady girlfriend and future wife. It was she who had refused, with a light laugh which, had he been less in love, might have seemed almost insulting.

'I'm sorry, Aurelio, but after eight years of Signora Bevilacqua I can't face having to deal with another *mamma* just yet.'

So it was back to the lies and deceptions which had characterized his affair with Ellen. If he felt less guilty about them, it was not only because his feelings for Tania had a self-justifying intensity, but because his mother was no longer the pathetic figure she had been at that time. The change dated from the previous year, when the Zens' apartment had been broken into by Vasco Spadola, an ex-mobster bent on revenge. Signora Zen had been forced to go and stay with Gilberto and Rosella Nieddu, where she had proved to be such a hit with the Nieddu children that she now spent two afternoons a week looking after them.

The effect of this surrogate auntyhood – greatly appreciated by the Nieddus, whose relatives were all in their native Sardinia – had been to transform Signora Zen from a semi-comatose recluse, parasitic on the imported soap operas doled out by Channel 5, into a sprightly, inquisitive old person with opinions and interests, still sharply critical of the city in which she lived like a foreigner, but also aware of its attractions and possibilities. Zen had had mixed feelings about this at first, since it meant revising a number of his own attitudes and habits, but he soon came to appreciate the fact that Signora Zen was out of the house more. It was easier in every sense to sneak off and spend time with Tania when he knew that his mother was happily occupied elsewhere.

He still needed to keep his stories straight, though, and in the present case that meant not being seen at home. He had been away from both home and work for the past two days, but as far as his mother was concerned his absence was not caused by illness but by an urgent mission to Florence. Alarmed by the effects of Moscati's call to the house, Zen had phoned her that morning from Tania's bed and repeated the story, so it would be difficult for him to explain his abrupt return just a few hours later. Hence the extreme caution with which he closed himself into his bedroom and walked across to the chest of drawers, making sure to avoid the creaky floorboard near the foot of the bed.

He eased the middle drawer open as gingerly as though it were filled with unstable high explosive, although at first sight it seemed to contain nothing but socks and underwear. Zen moved a pile of vests at the back of the drawer and pulled out a small scarlet plastic bag marked *Profumeria Nardi*. He opened the mouth of the bag and peered at the tangled plastic twine inside, the end melted to a blob by the flame of his lighter. The remaining portion would still be there, tied to the foot of the railing on the upper gallery of the dome of St Peter's. It too would have a terminal blob of transparent plastic, slightly darkened by the flame.

He stuffed the bag into his coat pocket and went over to the wardrobe in the corner. Pulling up a rickety wooden chair which stood near the wash-basin in the corner, Zen lifted down the small leather suitcase on top of the wardrobe. He snapped the catches quietly and opened the lid. The suitcase was almost full with packets, boxes and papers. Zen removed a small flat wooden box, which must have been upside down, for the hinged lid opened and the contents clattered all over the floor.

His mother either didn't hear the noise or must have assumed that it came from outside, for she didn't stop talking. Zen knelt down and collected the tools and instruments. One had rolled right under the bed, and when Zen crawled in there to retrieve it he caught sight of some writing on the wooden bedstead. With an effort, he could just make out the irregular lettering: *Zen, Anzolo Zuane, 28 March 1947.* The inscription blurred and he felt a terrible panic grip him. Seizing the metal instrument he had come in search of, he thrust himself out from under the dream-soaked structure of the bed, back into the light and the air of the room. The name written on the bedstead was his father's – Angelo Giovanni in Italian – but the writing was his own, and by 1947 the man named must have been long dead in some frozen swamp or Soviet prison camp. Only his son had continued to insist, secretly, magically, on his father's continuing presence in the house.

He stood up and dusted himself down, then tiptoed over to the door leading to the hallway. Pressing against the door to prevent the catch snapping against the edge of the mortise, he gripped the handle and turned. He put his ear to the crack and listened. To his dismay, the aural radar on which he depended had gone dead. The only sound was the continual murmur of traffic in the street outside. With a glance at his watch, he opened the door quickly. The hinges shrieked.

'Is that you?' called his mother.

'Eh?' shouted Maria Grazia from the bedroom.

'Was that you?'

There was a pause as the housekeeper interrupted her work and appeared in the doorway of the living room.

'What, signora?'

'Was that you?'

'Was what me?'

'That noise.'

'What noise?'

'It sounded like . . . like the front door opening.'

His mother sounded anxious. Homes never feel the same after they've been violated by a break-in. Maria Grazia's bulky form suddenly appeared in outline on the glass-panelled door to the living room. Zen stepped back hastily.

'It's shut,' the housekeeper reported, having presumably taken a look down the hall.

'Go and check!' Zen's mother insisted.

Zen tried to close the door, but it was too late.

'Mother of God!' cried Maria Grazia as she caught sight of him.

'What is it?' Signora Zen called from the living room. 'What's happened?'

'I'm not here!' Zen whispered urgently to the housekeeper.

Maria Grazia put her hand on her abundant bosom and mimed relief.

'It's all right, signora,' she yelled. 'I just banged my elbow.'

She opened the front door and made energetic shooing gestures to Zen, who left his hiding place and slipped out on to the landing and down the stairs to freedom with a smile of gratitude.

His local café had seen much less of him now that he regularly slept at Tania's, and when he asked the cashier for *gettoni* he received a qualified welcome hinting at both the promise of rehabilitation if he ceased to patronize rival establishments and the threat of being reduced to the status of a casual customer if he didn't. Zen went to the pay-phone and called the doctor whose name he had extracted from Lamboglia. At a pinch he could probably have got a certificate from his own doctor, but the last thing he wanted was to drag someone he knew and respected into this murky affair. If the press got suspicious about his 'illness', let them hound someone else.

The Vatican contact, a Doctor Carmagnola, said that he had heard from Monsignor Lamboglia, and would influenza or infectious gastro-enteritis do or did he want to be quarantined? Zen said that there was no need to exaggerate, and Carmagnola told him he could collect the certificate from the reception of the Ospedale del Bambino Gesù. Zen picked up a taxi in Piazza Cavour and went first to the hospital on the Gianicolo, and then on to one of the more illustrous of Rome's hills. They drove along the Tiber as far as the Palatino bridge, then across the river and up a narrow, curving lane. Following Zen's directions, the driver turned right and continued along a wealthy residential street past a public garden planted with orange trees. They passed two churches on the right, then a consulate on the left. A police jeep was parked opposite, and the two bored patrolmen watched the taxi drive past and park in the small piazza enclosed by a high wall.

A stiff breeze hissed in the trees all round, and from a nursery school near by came the sound of children at play. There was no other sound. Zen walked over to the pair of large green gates set in the wall at one side of the piazza. The letters SMOM were etched on a small brass plate above the bell. Zen pressed the button.

'Yes?' replied a crackly voice from the entry-phone.

'This is Dottor Aurelio Zen. I understand there is a message for me.'

'One moment.'

There was a brief pause before the voice resumed.

'I regret that we have no knowledge of any such message.'

Zen wasn't surprised. In his bones he'd known all along that the errand was a hoax set up by some prankster who had read his name in the newspaper reports of Ruspanti's death. He might even be here, watching the success of his stratagem. Zen glanced around, but there was no one to be seen except an elderly couple sitting on a bench at the other side of the piazza. He made one more attempt.

'Listen, I'm a police official! I received a message telling me to come to this address.'

'We have no knowledge of this matter,' the voice insisted with finality.

'Who's "we"?' snapped Zen, but the entry-phone had clicked off. He stood staring up at the tall green gates. The stone lintel above them was decorated with a cross whose arms grew broader towards their forked tips. A Maltese cross, thought Zen. SMOM: the Sovereign Military Order of Malta. These were the gates of the Palace of Rhodes, the Order's extraterritorial property where, according to rumour, Ludovico Ruspanti had taken refuge from the rigours of Italian justice.

Perhaps the message hadn't been a hoax, after all. But in that case what did it mean? 'If you wish to get these deaths in the proper perspective, apply at the green gates in the piazza at the end of Via Santa Sabina.' Zen focused his eyes with an effort. The gates were high and tightly closed. The only opening of any kind was an ornamental metal plate set close to the edge of the left-hand gate. The plate was of bronze, worked by hand in a complex elliptic pattern, with a plain circular keyhole in the centre. Zen bent down and squinted through the keyhole.

He expected the hole to be covered at the other end, so it was a shock to find, on the contrary, a view arranged specifically to be seen from that point. It was still more of a shock to realize that what he was looking at – framed by an alley of tall evergreen shrubs and centred in the keyhole like the target in a gun-sight – was the dome of St Peter's. Despite the distance, he could count each of the ribs protruding through the leading of the roof, and the tiny windows lighting the internal gallery from which Prince Ludovico Ruspanti had plunged to his death.

An hour later Zen was in a take-out pizzeria just outside the walls of the Vatican City. The other side of the street was lined with the boutiques which had recently sprung up in this area, once notorious as a haunt of thieves and prostitutes. One window was bisected by a huge poster reading FALCO, which Zen remembered as the name of the 'hot young designer' whose creation Tania had been wearing the previous Friday. This must have been a mistake, however, for the window was that of a bookshop. Next door stood a doorway giving access to the residential floors where Giovanni Grimaldi lived.

Zen finished his square slab of sausage-meat and mushroom *boscaiolo* pizza and wiped his hands on the paper napkin in which it had been wrapped. Time to go. He had not actually seen Grimaldi leave the building, but he must be at work by now. The only person who had gone either in or out, in fact, had been a young woman in a long tweed coat with a white scarf over her head who had appeared about ten minutes earlier. As for Grimaldi, he had probably opted for a lunch in the heavily subsidized Vatican canteen. Zen tossed the soiled napkin into a rubbish bin and walked out into the hazy sunshine.

Like a quarter of all the real estate in Rome, including the house in which Zen himself lived, the building opposite was owned by the Church, in this case an order of Carmelite nuns. This was not an investment property, however, but one of those set aside to provide cheap accommodation as part of the package which the Vatican offered in an effort to attract and retain its low-paid employees, the other principal incentives being access to duty-free goods and exemption from Italian income tax. From Zen's point of view there were both pros and cons to the building's low-rent status. On the plus side, there was no caretaker to worry about. The problem was that there was no lift either, and Grimaldi lived on the top floor.

The stairwell was dark, and the timer controlling the lights had been adjusted for the agility of a buck chamois in rut rather than a middle-aged policeman going about his dubious business. Lamboglia had told Zen that 'with any luck' he might 'find some

incriminating material which we can use'. There were various ways
you could read that, quite apart from the literal meaning, which was
in fact the only one Zen was prepared to discount entirely. The question was not whether Lamboglia had expected him to plant evidence
in Grimaldi's room – that was taken for granted – but what that
evidence was to prove. After due consideration Zen had decided to
go for broke and frame Grimaldi for the murder. The way things
were looking, the Vatican was going to need a scapegoat. Grimaldi
would do nicely, particularly if, as Zen suspected, he had been part
of the team carrying out surveillance on Ruspanti.

The top floor of the building differed from the others only in that
the rectangular circuit of bleak barracks-like corridors was lit by a
succession of grimy skylights. The stench of carbolic cleanser was
fighting a losing battle against a guerilla force of odours associated
with stale food, dirty clothes, clogged drains and night sweats. The
only sounds were the murmur of a distant radio and a steady hushing as of rain. Zen made his way along the corridor to a brown-
painted door marked 4W, a loosened screw having allowed the 3 to
flop over on its face.

There was no sound inside, but as a precaution Zen knocked
gently before getting out the wooden box he had removed from the
suitcase in his bedroom at home. The door was fitted with a Yale-type
lock above the handle and a deadlock with a keyhole below. Zen bent
down and squinted into the opening of the lower lock, but the key
was in position. He frowned briefly, then shrugged. Presumably
Grimaldi only used the Yale lock when he went out.

He opened the tool kit and selected a device like a pair of callipers,
which he inserted into the upper lock. Zen had acquired the tools
during the years he had spent in Naples. He had been directing a
plan to bug the beachside villa of a prominent *camorra* boss when a
burglar had broken into the property. He couldn't arrest the intruder
without compromising the original operation, but the burglar didn't
know that, and was delighted when Zen offered to drop all charges
in return for the tool kit and a series of masterclasses in its use. It was
some time since he had needed to put these skills to the test, but he
was nevertheless surprised to find that the lock totally resisted all his
efforts.

The lack of play in the lock was so marked that if the lower lock
hadn't had the key in it, he might have thought that the catch was

snibbed back. But it had, and an unoccupied room couldn't very well be locked from the inside. He stood listening to the hushing of the rain and staring at the stubborn door. Wrapping a handkerchief around the door handle, he shoved his shoulder hard against the edge, to see which lock gave. The next thing he knew, the door had swung effortlessly open, depositing him on his knees in the middle of the floor.

A dull prickle of apprehension ran over his scalp as he got up again. Surely Giovanni Grimaldi's work could not have left him with such a rosy view of human nature that he went off to work leaving his belongings in an unlocked room in an unguarded building? The only possible answer seemed to be that he didn't *have* any belongings, or at least none worth stealing. Apart from a few magazines, a small radio, a cheap alarm clock, some empty soft-drink bottles and the clothes hanging in the closet and laid out on the bed, the place looked as impersonal as a hotel room. The furniture must have been an eyesore even when new, which it hadn't been for a very long time.

Zen looked around for somewhere to hide the plastic twine. The obvious candidate was the chest of drawers, a hideous monstrosity with bandy metal legs and a synthetic woodgrain top. The drawers were slightly open and the contents in disarray. Of course, men who live alone tend to be either obsessionally tidy or total slobs, and it might simply be that Grimaldi was one of the latter. Nevertheless, Zen once again felt the warning prickle.

On top of the chest of drawers lay a leather wallet, a bunch of keys, a red plastic diary, some loose change, an open letter and a framed photograph of a young woman holding two small children by the hand. A faded chrysanthemum lay on its side in front of the picture. Zen picked up the letter, from some relative in Bari, and skimmed through it. It was mostly about Grimaldi's children, who were apparently well and 'as happy as can be expected', although they sometimes confused their mother's absence with their father's, thinking that he was in heaven and she in Rome. Zen put the letter down beside the flower of death. He stepped over to the window and looked down at the street below, sighing deeply as though gasping for breath. By the entrance to the pizzeria opposite a group of men were standing in the mild sunshine, arguing good-naturedly.

Zen whirled round as though someone had touched him. There was no one there. *There was no one there*. The unlocked door, the clothes laid out on the bed, the wallet and money and keys all ready, the drawers in disorder, the sound of rain while the sun shone . . . As if sleepwalking, Zen crossed the room and opened the door. Along the floor of the corridor, a long mobile tongue of dark liquid was making its slow way, curling this way and that across the red tiles. Zen set off towards the direction from which it was coming. At the end of the corridor was a door painted glossy white, with no number and no lock, just a semi-circular metal handle. The sound of falling water grew louder as Zen splashed his way towards it. Light streamed out of the cracks around the door on three sides, water on the fourth.

He rapped loudly on the white panelling. When there was no reply, he pulled and then pushed the door handle. The door rattled, but it was bolted on the inside. Zen stepped back, measuring his distance carefully. He bent his right leg and raised his foot to about the level of the internal bolt, then kicked out hard. The door burst inwards, but held.

'Hey!'

A man had poked his head out of a doorway further along the corridor. Zen ignored him. He brought his leg up again and smashed his foot viciously at the door. This time the bolt gave way and the door sagged in. A wave of water poured down the steps into the corridor, creating a series of miniature waterfalls.

'What the hell do you think you're doing?' the man demanded.

Zen didn't even look round. He was staring at the water running down the white porcelain tiles of the floor, at the drenched dressing-gown which had for some time stemmed the flood under the door, at the eight-pointed cross roughly chalked on the wall, at the naked body slumped in the shower, blocking the drain, and at the face of Giovanni Grimaldi staring back at him, seemingly with an astonishment to match his own.

If the man had done as Zen had told him – phoned the police, and then waited outside for them to arrive – there would have been no problem. There was no phone in the building, so he had to go across the road to the pizzeria. That should have left plenty of time for Zen to subject Grimaldi's room to a thorough search. As it was, he had barely started when he heard voices on the stairs. He hastily stuffed the red plastic diary into his pocket and regained the corridor just before the neighbour returned with a Carabinieri patrolman whose 850cc Moto-Guzzi had been parked outside the pizzeria while its driver demolished a piece of ham-and-mushroom within.

Apart from forcing him to curtail his search, this coincidence meant that Zen was cast in the role of Material Witness in the ensuing investigation, which went on for the rest of the afternoon. Faced with a couple of subordinates from his own force, he could have made a brief statement and then buggered off, but the paramilitary Carabinieri saw no reason to stretch the rules to accommodate some big shot from their despised civilian rivals. On the contrary! The inquiry into Giovanni Grimaldi's death was handled strictly according to the letter of the law, with every t crossed, every i dotted, and every statement, submission and report written up in triplicate and then signed by the witnesses and counter-signed by the officials.

Not that there was the slightest doubt as to the cause of the tragedy. 'I always said it was just a matter of time before something like this happened,' the dead man's neighbour told the patrolman as they gazed in through the open doorway of the shower. Marco Duranti was one of those florid, irascible men who have the answer to all the world's problems. It's all so very simple! The solution is right here, at their fingertips! Only – and this is what drives them *mad* – no one thinks to ask them. Not only that, but when they offer the information, as a disinterested gesture of goodwill, people take no notice! They even turn away, muttering 'Give it a rest, Marco, for Christ's sake!' That's what Grimaldi had done, the last time he'd warned him – purely out of the kindness of his own heart – about that damned shower. It was thus understandable that Duranti's grief was tempered by a certain satisfaction that his oft-repeated warnings of disaster had been proved right.

He drew the attention of the Carabinieri patrolman to the electric water heater supplying the shower. Sellotaped to the wall near by was a piece of paper in a plastic cover punched for use in a folder. A faded message in red felt-pen indicated that the heater should always be turned off before using the shower. Now, however, the switch was clearly set to ON.

'It should have been replaced years ago,' Duranti went on indignantly, 'but you can imagine the chances of that happening. The Church has always got enough money to keep Wojtyla jetting about the world, but when it comes to looking after its own properties and the poor devils who live in them – eh, eh, that's another matter! This whole place is falling to pieces. Why there was someone in only yesterday morning poking about in the drains. The next thing we know the floor will be running with shit, never mind water!'

By this time a small group of residents, neighbours and hangers-on had gathered in the corridor. No one wanted to go into the bathroom while the water was still potentially lethal, so Duranti fetched a hook with a long handle which was used for opening the skylight windows, and after several abortive attempts the patrolman managed to flip the heater switch to the OFF position. Protected by the solid leather soles of his magnificent boots, he then ventured into the flooded cubicle and turned off the water just as the *maresciallo* arrived with three more patrolmen and a doctor. No one paid any attention to the design chalked on the wall, and by the time they all adjourned to the local Carabinieri station it had been rubbed by so many sleeves and shoulders that it was no longer recognizable.

For the next few hours, Zen, Duranti and a selection of the other residents were questioned severally and together. Zen told them that he had gone to the house while following up a lead in a drugs case he was engaged on, details of which he could not disclose without authorization from his superiors. The lead had in fact been false – an address on the fifth floor of a building which only had four – but when he reached the top of the stairs he had noticed the water seeping along the corridor. Having traced the source to the shower, he attempted to communicate with the occupant, and when that failed he had kicked the door down.

It was this homely gesture which had finally won the Carabinieri over. They glanced at each other, nodding sympathetically. Confronted by an obstinately locked door and a stubborn silence on the other side of it, that was what you did, wasn't it? You kicked the fucking thing down. It might not do the door any good, but it would sure as hell make the next one think twice about messing you around. The *maresciallo* thanked Zen for his cooperation and told him he could go. Marco Duranti, on the other hand, was detained for a further forty minutes. Zen spent the time in a café across the road, making a number of phone calls. The first was to the contact number he had been given in the Vatican. This was engaged, so he phoned Tania.

'Hello?'

It was a man's voice, with a reedy timbre and clipped intonation.

'Sorry, I must have a wrong number.'

He dialled again, but now this number was engaged as well, so he fed the two-hundred lire piece back into the slot and called Paragon Security Consultants. A secretary made him hold the line for some time before putting him through to the managing director.

'Gilberto Nieddu.'

'This is the Ministry of Finance, dottore. Following a raid by our officers on a leading firm of accountants, we have uncovered evidence which suggests that for the last five years your company has consistently failed to declare twenty-five per cent of its profits.'

There was silence at the other end.

'However, we have no time to concern ourselves with such small-time offenders,' Zen continued, 'so we'd be prepared to overlook the matter in return for the services of a discreet, qualified electrician.'

This was greeted by a sharp intake of breath.

'Is that you, Aurelio?'

Zen chuckled.

'You sounded worried, Gilberto.'

'You bastard! You really had me going there!'

'Oh come on, Gilberto! You don't expect me to believe that you're fiddling a quarter of your taxes, do you?'

'Of course not, but . . .'

'It must be a hell of a lot more than that.'

Nieddu made a spluttering sound.

'Now about this electrician,' Zen went on.

'Look, Aurelio, it may have escaped your attention, but I'm not running a community information service. You need an electrician, look in the *pagine gialle*.'

'I'm not talking about changing a plug, Gilberto.'

'So what *are* you talking about?'

Zen told him. Nieddu gave a long sigh.

'Why do I let you drag me into these things, Aurelio? What's it got to do with me? What's it got to do with *you*, for that matter?'

He sighed again.

'Give me the address.'

When they'd agreed a rendezvous, Zen called Tania again. The same male voice answered.

'Who's that?' demanded Zen.

There was a brief interval of silence, then the receiver was replaced. Zen immediately redialled, but the phone rang and rang without any answer. He hung up, went to the bar and ordered a double espresso which he gulped down, searing his throat. He got out the red plastic-bound diary which he had removed from Giovanni Grimaldi's room. It turned out to be dated the following year, a freebie given away with a recent issue of *L'Espresso*. He riffled through it, but the pages were blank except for a few numbers and letters scribbled in the Personal Data section. Replacing the diary in his pocket, Zen touched his packet of Nazionali cigarettes. He took one out and lit it, then returned to the phone. There was still no reply from Tania's number, so he tried the Vatican again. This time the number answered almost immediately.

'Yes?'

'This is Signor Bianchi.'

'Yes?'

It was a voice Zen didn't recognize.

'I've just seen Signor Giallo.'

He felt ridiculous, but Lamboglia's instructions had been quite clear: even on this supposedly secure line, Zen was to refer to Grimaldi only by this code name.

'He's dead.'

There was a brief silence.

'Is there anything else?' asked the voice.

'You mean any other deaths?' Zen shouted. 'Why, how many are you expecting?'

He slammed the phone down. When he turned, the barman and all five customers were staring at him. He was about to say something when he saw Marco Duranti emerge from the Carabinieri station and set off along the street at a surprisingly brisk trot. Zen tossed a five-thousand-lire note in the general direction of the barman and ran after him.

'Excuse me!'

Duranti swung round with a wary, hostile expression. When he saw Zen he relaxed, but only slightly.

'It's about this maintenance man you saw in the building yesterday,' Zen told him.

'Yes?'

Zen pointed across the street.

'Are you going home? We could walk together.'

Duranti shrugged gracelessly.

'I was wondering if there might be a connection with this case I'm working on, you see,' Zen told him as they set off together. 'They could be using the sewers as a place to hide their drug cache. Where was he actually working?'

'I didn't look. All I know is he had the electric drill going for about half an hour just when I'm trying to have my siesta. Of course they *would* have to pick the week I'm on night shift.'

They were just passing the Porta Sant'Anna, the tradesman's entrance of the Vatican City State. A Swiss Guard in the working uniform of blue tunic, sleeveless cloak and beret set at a jaunty angle was gesturing with white-gloved hands to a driver who had just approached the security barrier. Meanwhile his colleague chatted to a girl on the pavement. A little further up the street was a second checkpoint, manned by the Vigilanza. Their uniform, dark blue with red piping, badly cut and with too much gold braid, made a sad contrast with the efficient elegance of the Swiss. Revolver on his hip, radio on his shoulder, the Guard held up his hand to stop the car, which had now been permitted through the first barrier, and swaggered over to give the driver a hard time.

'What did this man look like?' Zen asked.

Duranti shrugged.

'Stocky, muscular, average height, with a big round face. He wasn't Roman, I'll tell you that.'

'How do you know?'

'The accent! All up here in the nose, like a real northerner.'
Zen nodded as though this confirmed his suspicions.

'That's very helpful. You make an excellent witness, signore. If only everyone was as observant.'

They had reached the corner of the street where Duranti lived. Zen thanked him and then waited until he had disappeared before following him down the street to the pizzeria where he had had lunch.

Normality had already returned to the neighbourhood. In an area where safety standards were rarely or never observed, domestic accidents were even more frequent than suicide attempts in St Peter's. In the pizzeria, the owner and three cronies were discussing the recent and spectacular explosion of a butane gas cylinder which had blown a five-year-old girl clean through the window of the family's third-floor apartment. The child landed on the roof of a car below, unhurt but orphaned, her father having been disembowelled by a jagged chunk of the cylinder while the mother succumbed to brain injury after part of the wall collapsed on her.

Zen elbowed his way through to the counter and ordered another slab of pizza to keep him going until, God willing, he finally got to eat a proper meal. The baker had just pushed a large baking tray filled with bubbling pizza through the serving hatch from the kitchen next door, and the *pizzaiolo* hacked out a large slice which he folded in two and presented to Zen with a paper wrapper. He moved to the back of the shop and leant against a stack of plastic crates filled with soft-drink bottles, munching the piping-hot pizza and awaiting the arrival of Paragon Security's electrician.

A blowsy near-blonde of rather more than a certain age walked in and greeted the four men with the familiar manner of one who has seen the best and worst they could do and not been at all impressed. She ordered one of the ham and mozzarella pasties called *calzoni*, 'trousers'. The men guffawed, and one remarked that that was all Bettina ever thought about. She replied that on the contrary, *calzoni* these days were usually a disappointment, 'delicious looking from the outside, but with no filling worth a damn'. The owner of the pizzeria protested that his 'trousers', on the other hand, were crammed with all the good things God sends. Bettina remained unimpressed, claiming that while his father had known a thing or two about stuffing, the best the present proprietor could manage was a pathetic scrap of meat and a dribble of cheese.

Zen's left elbow turned to a burning knob of pain.

'Hi there.'

The pain vanished as suddenly as it had begun. Zen looked round to find Gilberto Nieddu grinning puckishly at him.

'I didn't expect you to come personally,' said Zen.

He still found it odd to see Nieddu's rotund, compact body dressed in a smart suit and tie. Gilberto had been running an independent security firm for years now, and very successfully too, but Zen still thought of him as the colleague he had once been, and was always vaguely taken aback to see him disguised as a businessman. Nieddu set down the small metal case he was carrying.

'You don't think I'd risk one of my lads getting involved with your crazy schemes?'

Zen waved at the counter.

'Want something?'

Nieddu shook his head.

'I've got a meal waiting for me at home, Aurelio. If I ever *get* home.'

Zen finished his pizza and lit a Nazionale.

'Okay, this is the situation. Like I said on the phone, someone was killed in an accident this afternoon, only I don't think it was an accident. The victim lived in a run-down tenement where the wiring was installed around the time Caesar got mugged in the Forum. The water heater in particular is very dodgy, and tenants have been warned to switch it off before using the shower. It seems to me that all someone needed to do was fix the heater so that it became seriously dangerous, and then wait for the victim to trot along and electrocute himself. In short, the perfect murder.'

'Give me a smoke, polenta-head,' said Nieddu.

'I thought you'd given up.'

'I've given up *buying* them. Don't laugh. My doctor says it's a first step.'

He lit up and exhaled mightily, then shook his head.

'It wouldn't work,' he said. 'They'd need to get out the element, for a start. That's a major job even with a new heater. If this one's as old as you say, the nuts will have rusted up. Anyway, the thing's bound to be checked, and it'll be clear that it's been tampered with. There's no chance of it being mistaken for an accident.'

'So it can't be done?'

'Of course it can be done, but not like that. What you want to do is by-pass the heater altogether. Where exactly is this rundown tenement?'

'Right across the road.'

Gilberto glanced at his watch.

'Let's have a quick look. Then I really must go, or Rosella will think I'm having an affair.'

The hallway was dark and dank, the only sound the brushing of Zen's sleeve on the plaster as he groped for the switch.

'No!' whispered Nieddu.

He opened the metal case and removed a small torch. A beam of light split the darkness, precise as a pointing finger, indicating walls and ceiling, doorways, steps, painting brief slashes and squiggles in the stairwell as they walked upstairs. On each floor they could hear the murmur of radios and televisions, but they saw no one. When they reached the top, Zen led the way along the corridor. Light showed under the door of Marco Duranti's room, but there was no sound inside. Zen tried the door to Giovanni Grimaldi's room, but it was now locked. The shower sported a brand-new hasp and a large padlock, as well as a sign reading 'OUT OF ORDER'.

Zen opened his burglary kit and got to work on the padlock. Despite its impressive appearance, it was a cheapie. He had barely started work before it snapped open. Nieddu gave a low whistle.

'When you finally get the boot, Aurelio, you give me a call. We can always use people with skills like yours.'

He pushed the door open. The broken hinges protested loudly and the base scraped across the tiles like fingernails down a blackboard. Zen shoved him inside quickly and pushed the door closed as someone came out of a room further along the corridor. Nieddu doused the torch and he and Zen stood side by side in the darkness. Footsteps approached, then retreated again. A door closed and feet receded down the stairs.

Nieddu switched on the torch. The beam bounced and skittered around the glazed white tiles, picking out the water heater resting on its wooden trestle near an oblong window high up in the whitewashed wall.

'Give me a leg up.'

Zen locked his hands together to make a step. With the adroitness of an acrobat, the Sardinian hoisted himself up, gripping the trestle with one hand and resting his foot on the wall screening off the shower cubicle.

'Just as I thought,' he said, his voice reverberating off the bare walls. 'The threads are all corroded to hell. No one's touched this for years.'

He dropped back to the floor and padded around the bathroom, shining the torch over the glossy tiles and matt-white plaster. When he reached the partition wall beside the door, he grunted significantly.

'Ah.'

'Found something?' queried Zen.

Nieddu eased the door open and stepped outside. He shone the torch into the angle of the wall. Inside, a thin pencil of light appeared in the darkness. Zen bent down and inspected the wall. A small hole had been drilled right through it. He went out to join Nieddu in the corridor. The torch beam was now pointing along the wall at an electric junction box a few yards away.

Outside in the street, a police car approached at high speed, siren howling. The walls and ceiling of the corridor pulsed with a revolving blue light. Down below, in the entrance hall of the building, an excitable voice which Zen recognized as that of Marco Duranti yelled 'This way!' The stairwell resounded to the sound of voices and clattering boots.

'Time to go?' asked Nieddu calmly.

Zen nodded. The Sardinian opened the metal case and removed something which looked like a large firework. He ran along the corridor to the head of the stairs, tossed it down and came running back.

'Smoke bomb,' he explained. 'Should hold them for a while.'

There was an acrid smell in the air, and the sounds below turned to coughing and spluttering. They ran back to the bathroom, where Nieddu held his hands cupped while Zen hoisted himself clumsily up to the wooden trestle. Nieddu then passed up his dispatch case. Going into the shower, he gripped the metal piping and pulled himself up on the wall around the cubicle. From there he leapt across to join Zen on the trestle, which creaked ominously under their combined weight. Nieddu clambered on top of the water heater.

'Fuck!'

'What's the matter?'

'I've snagged my jacket on a nail.'

'Christ, is that all?'

'*All*? It's brand-new, from Ferre.'

He leant across to the window and pulled it open. Taking the metal case from Zen, he pushed it through the opening, then sprang after it and held his hands out to Zen, who had clambered up on top of the tank. He tried not to look down. The trestle was still groaning and the window looked a long way away.

'It's no good,' he said suddenly. 'I can't do it.'

The Sardinian sat down facing the window, his feet braced on either side.

'Give me your hands.'

Zen leaned forward across the gap and Nieddu gripped his wrists. In the corridor outside he could hear a stampede of approaching boots. He kicked off from the heater, scraping his shoes desperately on the wall, and somehow Nieddu dragged him through the opening and out on to the sloping tiled roof.

'Come on!' the Sardinian said urgently. 'I've got some stun grenades, but you wouldn't want me to have to use those. They cost a fortune, and you already owe me for the suit.'

They ran off together across the roofs towards the lights of the next street.

3

If Zen had spent the night at home instead of at Tania's, he could have walked to his first appointment next morning. As it was he ended up on foot anyway, the taxi he summoned having ground to a halt outside the Liceo Terenzio Mamiani, just round the corner from Zen's apartment. Wednesday mornings were always bad, as the usual rush-hour jam was supplemented by the influx of pilgrims heading for the weekly papal audience. Zen paid the driver and strode off past lines of honking, bleating vehicles, including coaches whose utilitarian styling and robust construction exuded a graceless charm which awakened nostalgic memories of the far-off, innocent 1950s. From portholes wiped in their misted-up windows, the Polish pope's compatriots peered out at the Eternal City, perhaps wondering if the last kilometre of their pilgrimage was going to take as long as the previous two thousand.

Zen crossed Piazza del Risorgimento and followed the towering ramparts of the Vatican City State up the hill, passing women carrying wicker baskets and plastic bags of fruit and vegetables home from the Trionfale market. The bells of the local churches were in some disagreement about the exact moment when nine o'clock arrived, but the Vatican itself opened its doors dead on time, as though to emphasize that although *in* Rome, it was by no means *of* Rome. The handful of tourists waiting for the museums to open began to file inside. Zen followed them up the curving ramp to the cash desk, where he plonked down his ten-thousand-lire note with the rest. Then, like someone doing Rome in two days, he hurried through the collections of classical antiquities, following the arrows marked 'Raphael Stanze and Sistine Chapel Only'.

A marble staircase brought him to a gallery receding as far as the eye could see. The walls were hung with tapestries and painted maps alternating with windows overlooking a large courtyard. Dust swarmed like a school of fish in the sunlight streaming in through the windows. Zen had already left the other early visitors far behind, and this part of the museums was deserted. At the end of the gallery, he turned left into a chamber hung with enormous battle scenes, then down a staircase to a suite of rooms on the lower floor overlooking a courtyard patrolled by a Swiss Guard. Zen smiled wryly, thinking of the night before. Following their hasty exit from the house where Giovanni Grimaldi had been murdered, he and Gilberto Nieddu had climbed down a fire escape into the internal courtyard of a building in the next street and then sneaked past the lodge where the *portiere* was watching television.

'Never again, Aurelio!' Gilberto told him as they parted in the street. 'Don't even bother phoning.'

Back at Tania's, Zen had called his mother to tell her that his duties in Florence unfortunately required him to stay another night but he would be back for sure the following day.

'That's all right,' his mother replied. 'At least you ring up and let me know what's happening, not like some.'

'What do you mean, mamma?'

'Oh, that Gilberto! It makes me furious, it really does! Rosella phoned here only half an hour ago, to ask if I knew where you were. Apparently Gilberto called her this afternoon and said he might be a bit late home this evening because he was meeting *you*, if you please! Can you believe the cheek of it? Poor Rosella! Come nine o'clock there's no sign of him and the dinner's ruined, so she phones me to try and find out what's going on. Of course I didn't know any of this at first, so I just told her the truth, that you were in Florence. It's the old story. I told her. Just look the other way. There's no point in making a fuss. You're not the first and you won't be the . . .'

'Listen, mamma, I'm running out of tokens. I'll see you tomorrow.'

'Wait, Aurelio! There's a message for you. This gentleman called, he wouldn't leave his name, but he said it was about a Signor Giallo. He asked you to phone him immediately.'

Zen dialled the number he had been given by Lamboglia. It was answered by a different voice, this time with a foreign intonation. But why not? The Vatican was the headquarters of an international organization.

'Your presence is required tomorrow morning,' the man told him. 'Come to the main entrance to the Vatican Museums, pay in the normal way, then follow these directions.'

Zen noted them down.

'Now there's something I want *you* to do,' he told the anonymous voice. 'Contact whoever is responsible for the maintenance of the building where Signor Giallo lived and find out whether a workman was sent there yesterday to investigate the sewers.'

He had hung up just as Tania walked in naked from the shower, looking rather like the gracefully etiolated females in the frescos which covered the chamber where he now found himself. The subjects were nominally biblical, but the action had been transferred from the harsh realities of historical Palestine to a lush Italian landscape peopled by figures of an ideal renaissance beauty. On one wall, ships navigated under full sail and armies manoeuvred for battle. Another showed a large chamber where men were disputing and orators pronouncing. The painted room was about the same size and shape as the one on whose wall it was depicted, and the artist had cleverly included a painted door at floor level, creating the illusion that one could simply turn the handle and step into that alternative reality. Zen was just admiring this amusing detail when the handle in fact turned and the door opened to reveal the stooping figure of Monsignor Lamboglia.

'Come!' he said, beckoning.

Inside, a spiral stone staircase burrowed upwards through the masonry of the ancient palace. They climbed in silence. After some time, Lamboglia opened another door which led into a magnificent enclosed loggia. The lofty ceiling was sumptuously carved and gilded, the rear wall adorned with antique painted maps representing a world in which North America figured only as a blank space marked *Terra Incognita*. The large windows opposite offered an extensive view over St Peter's Square, now reduced to serving as a parking lot for those pilgrim coaches which had managed to fight their way through the traffic.

Zen followed his guide through a door at the end of the loggia, beneath a stained-glass light marked 'Secretariat of State' and into a vaulted antechamber. The walls and ceiling were covered in fantastic tracery, fake marble reliefs and painted niches containing *trompe l'oeil* classical statues. Lamboglia pointed to one of the armless chairs upholstered in grey velvet which stood against the painted dado, alternating with carved wooden chests and semi-circular tables supporting bronze angels.

'Wait here.'

He disappeared through a door at the end of the corridor. Zen sat down in the designated chair, which proved to be as uncomfortable as it was no doubt intended to make the occupant feel. The windows on the opposite wall were covered in lace curtaining which strained the sunlight like honey through muslin. Zen closed his eyes and tried to concentrate on what he was going to say. Try as he would, though, his thoughts kept drifting away to the night before. Tania had lied to him, there was no doubt about that. Not just filtered the truth, as he would shortly do for the benefit of the Vatican authorities. No, Tania had lied.

'Were you out this afternoon?' he had asked casually as they lay in bed together.

'Out?'

He ran his fingertips lightly over her ribs and belly.

'Mmm. About six o'clock.'

She pretended to think.

'Oh yes, that's right. I stepped out for a moment to do some shopping. Why?'

'I tried to phone. To tell you I'd be late.'

He rolled up on his side, gazing down at her.

'A man answered.'

A distant look entered her eyes, and he knew she was going to lie. The rest was routine, a matter of how hard he wanted to press, how much he could bully her into revealing.

'You must have got a wrong number,' she said.

He looked away, embarrassed for her, regretting that he'd brought it up. Nevertheless, he couldn't help adding. 'It happened twice. I dialled again.'

She laughed lightly.

'Probably a crossed wire at the exchange. It's a pity the Vatican doesn't run a phone system as well as a postal service. They fly their mail out to Switzerland to be sorted, you know, yet it still arrives in half the time it takes the post office.'

He accepted the diversion gratefully.

'That's because the post office sends it to *Palermo* for sorting. By boat.'

She laughed again, with amusement and relief. Thinks she's got away with it, Zen thought to himself. Already he was getting used to the idea of her treachery. To be honest, once he'd recovered from the initial shock it was almost a relief to find that she was indeed deceiving him. The immense and unconditional gift which Tania had made of her love still amazed him. Being worthy of it had been a bit of a responsibility. This discovery evened things up considerably. All in all, he told himself, it was probably the best thing that could have happened.

The door at the end of the corridor opened and Lamboglia reappeared. He extended his right hand, palm down, and waggled the fingers beckoningly. Zen rose and followed him into the office where he had been received by the Cardinal Secretary of State's deputy the previous Friday. On this occasion, Juan Ramón Sánchez-Valdés was in his full episcopal regalia, an ankle-length soutane with a magenta sash, piping and buttons. The crown of his head was covered by a skullcap of the same colour. The rim of an ecclesiastical collar was just visible beneath the soutane, while a plain silver cross hung from its chain at the base of the archbishop's chest.

As before, Zen was placed on the long red sofa while the archbishop sat in the high-backed armchair by the table. At his elbow, beside the white telephone, lay a single sheet of paper with some lines of typing. Lamboglia took up his earlier position, just behind the archbishop's shoulder, but Sánchez-Valdés waved him away.

'Sit down, Enrico! You make me nervous, hovering there like a waiter.'

Flinching as though he'd been struck, poor Lamboglia trotted off across the elaborately patterned rug with the quick fluttering gait of a woman, all stiff knees and loose ankles, and subsided into a chair on the end wall.

'Enrico is from Genoa,' Sánchez-Valdés remarked to Zen. 'On the other hand I seem to recall that you, dottore, are from Venice. The two cities were of course fierce trading rivals, and vied with each other to supply us with transportation for the Crusades. I came across rather a good comment on the subject just the other day, in a dispatch from our nuncio in Venice at the turn of the century – the thirteenth century, that is. He advises the Holy Father to treat with the Doge, exorbitant though his terms might seem, explaining that while both the Genoese and the Venetians will gladly offer to sell you their mothers, the crucial difference is that the Venetians will *deliver*.'

Although he was aware of being manipulated by a skilled operator, Zen could not help smiling.

'I gather it was you who found poor Grimaldi's body,' the archbishop went on without a pause.

Zen's smile faded.

'What a terrible tragedy!' sighed Sánchez-Valdés. 'Those poor children! First they lose their mother to illness, and now . . .'

He broke off, seemingly overcome by emotion. Lamboglia was rubbing his hands together furiously, as though to warm or wash them.

'I believe Enrico informed you that we had strong reason to suppose that Grimaldi was the author of that anonymous letter to the press,' Sánchez-Valdés continued. 'Needless to say that fact has now become one more of the many embarrassments which this case threatens to cause us. If it became known, one can easily imagine the sort of vicious insinuations and calumnies which would inevitably follow. No sooner is the identity of the "Vatican mole" discovered than he is found dead in the shower. How very convenient for those who wish to conceal the truth about the Ruspanti affair, etcetera, etcetera.

'That's why we've summoned you here this morning, dottore. Enrico has explained to me your unfortunate misunderstanding of our intentions with regard to the death of Ludovico Ruspanti. On this occasion I want to leave you in no doubt as to our position. Fortunately it is very simple. With Grimaldi's death, this tragic sequence of events has reached its conclusion. Any mistakes or miscalculations which may have occurred are now a matter for future historians of Vatican affairs. As far as the present is concerned, we shall instruct the Apostolic Nuncio to convey our thanks to the Italian government for your, quote, discreet and invaluable intervention, unquote.'

The archbishop lifted the sheet of paper from the table and scanned it briefly.

'Enrico!' he called.

Lamboglia sashayed back across the carpet to his master's side. Sánchez-Valdés handed him the paper.

'There is just one remaining formality,' he told Zen, 'which is for you to sign an undertaking not to disclose any of the information which you may have come by in the course of your work for us.'

Lamboglia carried the paper over to Zen, who read through the six lines of typing.

'I'm sorry,' he said. 'I can't sign this.'

'What do you mean?' snapped Lamboglia, who was waiting to convey the signed document back to Sánchez-Valdés.

'To do so would risk placing me in an untenable position with regard to my official duties.'

Sánchez-Valdés hitched up the hem of his soutane to reveal a pair of magenta socks.

'You didn't display such exaggerated scruples the last time we spoke,' he said dryly.

'That was altogether different, Your Excellency. Ruspanti's death occurred in the Vatican City State, and was therefore not subject to investigation by the Italian authorities. When I acted for you in that affair, I did so as a free agent. If Grimaldi had also died within the walls of the Vatican, I would have been happy to sign this undertaking. But he didn't, he died in Rome. If I sign this, and Grimaldi's death is subsequently made the subject of a judicial investigation, I would be unable to avoid perjuring myself whether I spoke or remained silent.'

Archbishop Sánchez-Valdés laughed urbanely.

'But there's no possibility of that happening! Grimaldi's death was an accident.'

Zen nodded.

'Of course. Just like Ruspanti's was suicide.'

The two clerics stared at him intently. The archbishop was the first to break the silence.

'Are you suggesting that Grimaldi did *not* die accidentally?' he asked quietly.

'That's absurd!' cried Lamboglia. 'We've seen the Carabinieri report! There's no question that Grimaldi was electrocuted by a faulty shower.'

Zen shook his head.

'He was electrocuted *in* the shower, not *by* the shower.'

Sánchez-Valdés looked up at the ceiling, as though invoking divine assistance.

'There's no doubt about that?' he murmured.

'None at all.'

The archbishop nodded.

'A pity.'

'Indeed,' agreed Zen. 'Nevertheless, although I am unable to sign this undertaking, I can assure you that I will honour it in practice. Your secrets will go no further.'

He smiled shyly.

'As I mentioned the first time Your Excellency honoured me with an audience, whatever the Church decides is good enough for me.'

Sánchez-Valdés looked at Zen with amusement.

'You're a great loss to the Curia, dottore,' he remarked, shaking his head. 'A very great loss indeed! But then of course they already accuse us of creaming off the best administrators in the country.'

He got to his feet, sighing.

'Thank you, Enrico, that will be all.'

After a momentary hesitation, Lamboglia left sullenly. When the door had closed behind him, Sánchez-Valdés walked over to the window. He pulled aside the screen of the net curtaining, allowing a beam of raw sunlight to enter.

'What a lovely morning.'

He turned to Zen.

'I think we should take a walk, dottore.'

Zen stared at him blankly.

'A walk?'

'That's right. A walk in the woods.'

'Have you heard the one about the whore and the Swiss Guard?' asked the archbishop.

Zen, who was lighting a cigarette, promptly choked on the smoke. When the fit of coughing had subsided somewhat, he shook his head.

'I don't think I have.'

Sánchez-Valdés face beamed with expectation.

'This new recruit has just arrived in Rome, fresh from the mountains. On his first evening off duty he decides to explore the city a little. He wanders out through the Sant'Anna gate and down into the Borgo, where he is accosted by a lady of the night.'

He paused to inspect a flowering shrub in the rockery they were passing.

'"It's just like my friends told me," thinks Hans. "These Roman women can't resist a blond hunk of manhood like me." When they reach Asphasia's business premises, she says, "Before we go any further, let's settle the little matter of the fee." The Swiss smiles complacently. "Out of the question! I wouldn't dream of accepting money from a woman."'

Zen laughed politely.

'I heard that one from Scarpia, the head of the Vigilanza. His real name is Scarpione, but Paul VI always called him Scarpia, like the police chief in *Tosca*. No one was sure whether it was a mistake or a joke, and Montini wasn't the kind of person you could ask, but somehow the name stuck, perhaps precisely because anyone further removed from Puccini's villain would be hard to imagine. Poor Luigi is all home and family, mild and jovial to a fault. But you'll be able to judge for yourself.'

They passed an elaborate fountain in the form of an artificial grotto from which a stream issued to pour over a series of miniature falls while two stone cherubs watched admiringly from the pool below. The path they were following led straight uphill through a coppice of beech trees. Except for a faint background murmur of traffic, they might have been deep in the country.

'Anyway,' Sánchez-Valdés went on, 'that joke sums up the way the Vigilanza regard their colleagues in the Cohors Helvetica, as Nordic yokels with a superiority complex, so stupid they think they're smart. The Swiss, for their part, look down on the security men as jumped-up traffic wardens. This conceit is perhaps understandable in a corps which not only enjoys an unbroken tradition of service stretching back almost five hundred years, but is charged with responsibility for guarding the person of the Holy Father. As for the Vigilanza, their duties are indeed fairly mundane for the most part, but there is a small élite unit within the force which undertakes more specialized and sensitive tasks. The existence of this unit is officially denied, and we never discuss its operations. If I've decided to make an exception in your case, it's because you already know too much. The Ruspanti affair has got completely out of control, and we must proceed as they do with forest fires, separating off the affected area and letting the flames burn themselves out.'

Perhaps affected by this metaphor, Zen ground his spent cigarette out with exaggerated caution, creating an unsightly smudge of soiled paper and tobacco shreds.

'There's no filter,' he explained awkwardly. 'It'll wash away as soon as it rains.'

He felt constrained to apologize by the extreme tidiness of the gardens. There was something not quite real about the Vatican, he was beginning to feel. It was like Rome devoid of Romans, peopled instead by a quiet, orderly, industrious race. There was no litter, no graffiti, no traffic. Cars were parked strictly within the painted boxes allotted for the purpose, and the few people about walked briskly along, intent on their business. The grass was not only neatly trimmed and innocent of used condoms, spent syringes and the sheets of loose newspaper used as curtains by courting couples in their cars, it was also a richer, more vibrant shade of green, as though it were part of the divine dispensation that the Holy City received more rain than the secular one without the walls. Trees and shrubs, hedges and flowerbeds, all appeared vibrant and vigorous like illustrations from a theological textbook exemplifying the argument from design. In principle, this was all extremely pleasant. In practice it gave Zen the creeps, like a replica which everyone was conspiring to pass off as the real thing.

'Among the responsibilities of this special Vigilanza department,'

Sánchez-Valdés was saying, 'is the covert surveillance of individuals living or working within the Vatican City State whose activities have for one reason or another attracted the attention of my department. Until last Friday, one of these was Prince Ludovico Ruspanti.'

The archbishop broke off as they approached a team of gardeners at work resetting a rockery. He nodded at the men, who inclined their heads respectfully. Once they were out of earshot again, Sánchez-Valdés resumed.

'As you are no doubt aware, Ruspanti was under investigation by the Italian judiciary for his part in the illegal export of currency. What you probably do not know, since the matter was *sub judice*, is that his part in this alleged fraud consisted of recycling large sums through his account at the Institute for the Works of Religion. In short, the Prince was accused of using the Vatican bank to break Italian law. After the scandals surrounding the collapse of the Banco Ambrosiano, we clearly could not be seen to be sheltering him from justice. But although we had our own reasons for allowing Ruspanti the temporary use of a grace-and-favour apartment while he sorted out his affairs, we weren't naïve enough simply to leave him to his own devices.'

Zen looked up at the crest of the hill above them, where the mighty bastion of the original fortifications was now crowned with the transmitting aerials of Vatican Radio.

'In that case . . .' he began, then broke off.

Sánchez-Valdés finished it for him.

'In that case, we should know who killed him, just as the anonymous letter to the papers claimed. Yes, we should. The problem is that the official assigned to Ruspanti on the day he died was . . .'

'Giovanni Grimaldi.'

The archbishop gestured as though to say 'There you are!' The alley they were following had reached a roundabout from which five others led off in various directions, each with its name inscribed on a travertine slab mounted in a metal stand. Sánchez-Valdés turned left along a straight gravel path running along the foot of a section of the original Vatican walls, towering up thirty metres or more to their machicolated battlements.

'Grimaldi was presumably debriefed before I arrived that Friday,' Zen commented.

Sánchez-Valdés nodded.

'He said he had lost Ruspanti among the throng of tourists up on the dome of St Peter's and was trying to find him again in the basilica when the body fell. At the time there seemed no reason not to believe this. The first thing which alerted our suspicions was the disappearance of the transcript which had been made of Ruspanti's telephone conversations. Ah, there's Luigi!'

A plump man with carefully permed silvery hair and a benign expression stood by a pine tree beside the path, watching them approach. Zen felt a surge of revulsion. He suddenly couldn't wait to get out of this place where even the chief of police looked like a parody of a kindly, absent-minded village priest.

'We made the inquiries you requested,' Scarpione told Sánchez-Valdés once the introductions had been performed. 'The supervisor responsible for the Carmelites' holdings says that no repair work had been ordered in the house where Grimaldi lived.'

The archbishop looked at Zen.

'Well, there's the answer to the question you put to us last night. What is its significance?'

'Grimaldi's neighbour, Marco Duranti, said that someone was working there on Monday afternoon with an electric drill, supposedly repairing the drains.'

'And someone was there again last night,' Scarpione broke in, proud of his scoop. 'I've just had a call about it from the Carabinieri. They were called out by this Duranti, but unfortunately the intruders managed to escape by using some sort of smoke bomb.'

Zen coughed loudly.

'They probably came back to search Grimaldi's room again.'

The archbishop frowned.

'Again?'

'They tried once before, after they killed him.'

Luigi Scarpione took a moment to react. Sánchez-Valdés turned to Zen, indicating the Vigilanza chief's stunned and horrified expression as proof that the Vatican's hands were clean of Grimaldi's death. Zen held up his palms in token of the fact that he had never for a moment believed otherwise.

'But the Carabinieri . . .' Scarpione began.

'The Carabinieri don't know about Grimaldi's involvement in the Ruspanti case,' Zen broke in. 'In fact they don't even know that there *is* a Ruspanti case. If they did, they might have concluded that two such deaths in five days was a bit too much of a coincidence, and taken the trouble to investigate the circumstances of Grimaldi's "accident" a little more thoroughly, as I did. In which case, they would no doubt have discovered that the workman who came to the house on Monday afternoon had drilled a hole through the wall between the bathroom and the passage outside, enabling him to connect an electric cable to the water pipes feeding the shower. A woman was round at the house on Monday morning, talking to Grimaldi, and I saw her leave on Tuesday, just after he died. She would have waited for him to go into the shower, as he did every day before starting work, and then thrown the switch. The moment Grimaldi stepped under the water he was effectively plugged into the mains. Afterwards the woman pulled the cable free and removed it, leaving an electrocuted body inside a bathroom bolted from the inside. Of *course* the Carabinieri thought it was an accident. What else were they supposed to think?'

Scarpione shuddered. Sánchez-Valdés patted him reassuringly on the shoulder and led the way past the helicopter landing pad from which the pope set off to his villa and swimming pool in the Alban hills, or on one of his frequent foreign trips.

'And what about you, dottore?' he asked Zen. 'What do *you* think?' Zen shrugged.

'What had Grimaldi been working on this week, since Ruspanti's death?'

'A case involving the theft of documents from the Archives,' said Scarpione. 'Giovanni was patrolling the building, posing as a researcher.'

'Not the sort of thing people would kill for?'

'Good heavens, no! A minor trade in illegal antiquities, that's all.'

'In that case, my guess is that he tried to put the squeeze on the men who murdered Ruspanti. That transcript that's gone missing probably contained some reference implicating them. Grimaldi put two and two together, stole the transcript, and offered to sell it for the right price. That would also explain why he sent the anonymous letter to the papers. He couldn't blackmail the killers without casting enough doubt on the suicide verdict to get the case reopened.'

The three men passed through a gap in the battlemented walls, the truncated portion covered with a rich coat of ivy, and started downhill, through the formally landscaped gardens, the dome of St Peter's rising before them in all its splendour.

'Have you located the source of the keys which Ruspanti's killers used?' Zen asked casually.

Sánchez-Valdés nodded.

'Yes indeed! Tell Dottor Zen about the progress we've been making this end, Luigi.'

Scarpione glanced at the archbishop.

'All of it?'

'All, all!'

The Vigilanza chief cleared his throat and began.

'We thought at first it might be one of the *sampietrini*.'

He lowered his voice discreetly.

'There have been complaints on several occasions from some of the younger workers about the behaviour of Antonio Cecchi, their boss.'

'A little matter of attempted buggery, to be precise,' Sánchez-Valdés explained cheerfully.

Scarpione coughed again.

'Yes, well . . .'

'Like many people,' the archbishop went on, speaking to Zen, 'Luigi makes the mistake of supposing that we priests are either ignorant of or embarrassed by the facts of life. If he had spent half as much time in a confessional as we have, he would realize that there is nothing likely to shock us very much. Carry on, Luigi!'

'Well, anyway, in the end one of the uniformed custodians who patrol the dome during the hours of public access admitted that he had been responsible. He said he was approached by a man who represented himself as a monsignore attached to the Curia. This person claimed that a party of notables from his native town were visiting the Vatican, and said he wanted to give them a private tour of the basilica. He would be so obliged if it would be possible for him to borrow the keys for an hour or two.'

'All such requests are supposed to be submitted in writing,' Sánchez-Valdés explained, 'but no lay worker in the Vatican is going to refuse a favour to a member of the Curia.'

Zen grunted.

'Only in this case, he wasn't.'

'We have a description of the impostor,' Scarpione assured him. 'He was of average stature, quite young, with fair hair and fine features.'

'Well, that rules out la Cicciolina.'

'I'm sorry?'

'Dottor Zen is being ironic,' Sánchez-Valdés explained heavily. 'His implication is that while the description you have given may effectively exclude the ex-porn queen and present Radical Party deputy from suspicion, it is imprecise enough to cover almost everyone else.'

'I'm sure you did the best you could,' Zen murmured, glancing at his watch.

They had reached a terrace overlooking a formal garden in the French style. In a cutting below, a diesel locomotive hooted and started to reverse around a freight train on the branch line linking the Vatican to the Italian state railway system.

'We mustn't detain you any longer, dottore,' Sánchez-Valdés told Zen. He turned to Scarpione. 'How can we get him out of here without attracting attention, Luigi? The last thing we want is a front-page photograph of the man from the Ministry of the Interior leaving the Vatican after high-level consultations at the Secretariat of State when he's supposedly too ill to answer questions from the press.'

'How did he get in?' asked Scarpione.

'Through the museum. But that'll be too risky at this time of day.'

The Vigilanza man pondered for a moment.

'I suppose I could get one of my men to smuggle him out in a delivery van or something . . .'

Sánchez-Valdés shook his head.

'I don't want to subject their loyalty to any further tests just at present,' he remarked acidly.

He snapped his fingers.

'I know! That train looks like it's about to leave. Go and have a word with the crew, Luigi, and ask them to drop our visitor off at the main-line station. It's only a short ride, and that way he's sure to be unobserved.'

Scarpione hurried off, eager to prove that *his* loyalty, at any rate, was unimpeachable. As soon as he was out of earshot, Sánchez-Valdés turned to Zen.

'Despite what our detractors say, dottore, I urge you to accept that the Vatican has no vested interest in obscurity or mystification, still less in such wickedness as these killings. Our only wish is to see the perpetrators brought to justice, and I can assure you that we will bend all our efforts to that end. On the basis of the information you have provided today, I shall make representations to the Carabinieri to reopen their investigation into Grimaldi's death . . .'

'Without mentioning my name,' Zen insisted.

Sánchez-Valdés waved his beringed hand to indicate that this might be taken for granted. Outside the huge unused station building below, the diesel locomotive blew its horn. Luigi Scarpione stood on the platform near by, beckoning frantically.

'It's about to leave,' said Sánchez-Valdés.

Zen turned to him suddenly.

'What about the Cabal?'

A distant look entered the archbishop's eyes.

'What?'

'Grimaldi's letter to the newspapers claimed that on the day he died, Ruspanti had been going to meet the representatives of an organization called the Cabal. His other allegations have turned out to be true. What about that one?'

Sánchez-Valdés laughed lightly.

'Oh, *that*! No, no, that was just some nonsense Ruspanti dreamed up.'

'Ruspanti?'

'Yes, he used it as bait, to tempt us into giving him sanctuary. It's rather embarrassing, to tell you the truth! He took us in completely with this cock-and-bull tale about some secret inner group within the Knights of Malta which supposedly . . .'

Zen stared.

'The Knights of Malta?'

'Absurd, isn't it? That bunch of old fogies and social climbers! Mind you, Ruspanti was one of them himself, which lent his claims a certain *prima facie* credibility. In return for our assistance, he promised to spill the beans on the various political conspiracies which this group was supposedly planning. As soon as we examined his claims, of course, it was evident that there was nothing in them.'

The diesel hooted again, longer this time.

'Hurry, dottore, or they'll leave without you!' Sánchez-Valdés urged. 'We don't want to create an international incident by preventing the departure of an Italian train, do we? Incidentally, you're probably the first person to leave the Vatican by train since Papa Roncalli went on a pilgrimage to Assisi back in the sixties. What about that, eh? Something to tell your grandchildren!'

'Deuce!'

'Thirty–forty, isn't it?'

'No, no, my friend. It was thirty–forty after you fluffed my last service return.'

'All right, all right.'

Rackets were raised once more, the fluffy yellow ball sped to and fro, the players pranced about the pink asphalt. The server sported a racy Sergio Tacchini outfit whose top, shorts, socks, trainers and sweatbands were all elements in the same bold abstract pattern. His opponent had opted for a classic all-white image by Ellesse, but it was falling flat. Having just blown the opportunity to save the set, he looked plain rather than restrained, not timeless but out of date.

'Advantage!' called Sergio Tacchini confidently.

'It was out!' whined Ellesse.

'Says who?'

'I saw it cross the line! It was nowhere near!'

'Oh! Oh! Gino, don't try this stuff on with me!'

'I tell you . . .'

'All right, let's get a neutral opinion.'

The server turned to the man who was looking on from the other side of the tall mesh netting which surrounded the court.

'Hey, you! You saw that shot? It was in, wasn't it?'

'Come off it, Rodolfo!' his opponent objected. 'If they let the guy up here, he must work for you. Do you think he's going to tell his own Minister that his shot was too long?'

'On the contrary, everyone knows I'll be on my way once this reshuffle finally hits. I can't even get a cup of coffee sent up any more. In fact, he's going to give it *your* way, Gino, if he's got any sense. For all anyone knows, you could be his boss next week!'

He turned again to the onlooker, a gaunt, imposing figure with sharp, angular features and a gaze that hovered ambiguously between menace and mockery.

'Listen, er – what's your name?'

'Zen, Minister. Vice-Questore, Criminalpol. I'm afraid I didn't see the ball land.'

Rodolfo returned to the base-line shaking his head.

'Fine, we'll play a let. I don't need flukes to beat you, Gino. I've got in-depth superiority.'

He skied the ball and whacked it across the net with a grunt suggestive of a reluctant bowel motion. Zen clasped his hands behind his back and pretended to take an interest in the progress of the game. Fortunately there were other distractions. Despite being located on the least illustrious of Rome's seven hills, the roof of the Ministry of the Interior still afforded extensive views. To the right, Zen could admire the neighbouring Quirinal and its palace, once the seat of popes and kings, now the official residence of the President of the Italian Republic. To the left, the ruined hulks of ancient Rome's most desirable residential quarter gave a rural appearance to the Palatine. In between, the densely populated sprawl of the city centre, covered by a veil of smog, resembled the treacherous marshland it had once been. In the hazy distance below the hills of the far bank of the Tiber, the dome of St Peter's hovered, seemingly weightless, like a baroque hot-air balloon.

The sun was hidden behind a skin of cloud which diffused its light evenly across the flat roof. The Ministry's complex system of transmitting and receiving aerials, towering above like ship's rigging, increased Zen's sense of detachment from the mundane realities of life in the invisible streets far below. The train which had carried him back to Italy that morning consisted of four empty wagons which had discharged their duty-free imports and one flat-bed laden with the mosaics which were the Vatican's only material export. Zen had looked back from the cab of the superannuated green-and-brown diesel locomotive at the massive iron gates closing behind the train, just as all the Vatican gates still did at midnight, sealing off the one-hundred-acre City State from its encircling secular neighbour. The complexities of the relationship between the two were something that Zen was only beginning to appreciate now that he found himself trapped between them like a speck of grit caught in the bearings of power.

Despite his promise to Sánchez-Valdés, he had every intention of filing a full report on the Ruspanti affair. The first rule of survival in any organization is 'Cover thyself.' No matter that Moscati had told

Zen that he was on his own, that it was between him and the Vatican, that the Ministry didn't want to know. None of that would save Zen if – or, as now seemed almost inevitable, when – the tortuous and murky ramifications of the Ruspanti affair turned into a major political scandal. If Zen failed to keep the Ministry fully briefed, this would either be ascribed to devious personal motives or to twitchings on the strings by which one of the interested parties controlled him. Either way, his position would be untenable. A man as sophisticated as Sánchez-Valdés must have known this, so Zen assumed that the real purpose of that 'walk in the woods' had been to pass on information which the Curia could not release officially, to smuggle a message out of the Vatican in much the same way as Zen himself. It was now up to Zen to make sure that the message got through.

Under normal circumstances, his section chief would have been the person to go to, but after hearing Tania recount Moscati's gloating remarks about their relationship Zen didn't trust himself to handle the conversation with the necessary professional reserve. Then he recalled something that Moscati had said when they had spoken on the phone the previous morning. 'Result, the Minister finds himself in the hot seat just as the entire government is about to go into the blender and he had his eye on some nice fat portfolio like Finance.' So the Minister was not only aware of Zen's gaffe, but had been politically embarrassed by criticism from the 'blue-bloods at the Farnesina', the Ministry of Foreign Affairs, who would have sustained the full wrath of the Apostolic Nuncio. By the time the Vatican goods train drew into the station of San Pietro F.S., Zen had decided that this was a case for going straight to the top. That way, when the lies and obfuscations started, he would at least know their source. He would speak to the Minister personally, tell him what had happened and what Archbishop Sánchez-Valdés had said. Then, later, he would write up a full report of the incident (with an editorial slant favourable to him, naturally) to be filed in the Ministerial database as permanent proof, dated and signed, that he had fulfilled his duties.

Until recently, San Pietro had been a little-used suburban halt on an antediluvian branch line to Viterbo. All that had changed with the decision to upgrade part of the route as a link between Stazione Termini and the new high speed *direttissima* line to Florence. As a result, the tunnel under the Gianicolo hill had been reconstructed and the station remodelled in the latest colour-coordinated

Eurostyle. The local services hadn't improved, however, so Zen walked out of the station and took the 62 bus across town, slipping into the Ministry through a side entrance to elude any reporters who might be around. Now, watching the tennis players swooping and reaching in the mild sunlight, that interlude seemed to him like a brief dip into the polluted and treacherous waters separating the verdant isle of the Vatican City State from this stately cruise liner where the Minister and his opponent were disporting themselves. Gino was an under-secretary in the Ministry of Health, which occupied the other half of the huge building on the Viminal hill. To satisfy the elaborate formulas of the *manuale Cencelli*, by which positions of power are distributed amongst the various political parties, this post had been allocated to a member of the moribund Liberal Party, while Rodolfo was a well-known figure on the Andreotti wing of the Christian Democrats. But although they were nominally political rivals, the contest that the two men were currently engaged in was infinitely more keenly fought than any which was ever allowed to disrupt the stifling calm in which the country's *nomenclatura* basked and grew fat.

'Game, set and match!' called the Minister as the ball scudded off the asphalt out of reach of Gino's racket.

'Lucky bounce, Rodolfo.'

'*Balle*, my friend. You have just been outplayed physically and intellectually. My own surprise is that you still haven't learned to lose with grace. After all, it's all your party has been able to do for the last thirty years.'

He strode over to Zen, his skin gleaming with perspiration and flushed with victory. The Minister's even, rounded features expressed an image of sensitivity and culture that was fatally undermined by the mouth, a cramped slot which might have been the result of plastic surgery.

'You wanted to see me?'

Zen assumed his most respectful demeanour.

'Yes, sir. I have a message for you.'

The Minister laughed shortly.

'The problem of overmanning must be even more dire than I'd imagined if we're using senior Criminalpol officials as messengers.'

He turned back to his opponent.

'Consolation prize, Gino! You get to have first go in the shower while I see what this fellow wants.'

Rubbing his head vigorously with a towel, the Minister led the way down a short flight of stairs into his suite on the top floor of the building and threw himself down on a black leather sofa. Zen remained standing.

'It's about the Ruspanti case,' he said hesitantly.

He expected some furious response, threats or insults, demands for apologies and explanations. The Minister merely stared up at him slightly more intently.

'I'm sorry if . . . I mean, I understand that there were some . . . That's to say . . .'

Zen broke off, disconcerted. He belatedly realized that he had allowed himself to be tricked into the elementary blunder of implying that what underlings like him did or failed to do could seriously affect anyone other than themselves. Moscati's phrase about the Minister finding himself 'in the hot seat' as a result of Zen's mishandling of the Ruspanti affair was pure hyperbole. Politicians could no more be brought down by such things than a ship could be capsized by the actions of fish on the ocean bed. It was the weather on the surface, in the political world itself, that would determine the Minister's career prospects. Judging by his manner, the forecast was good.

'I don't want to rush you, er . . . what did you say your name was?' he grunted, getting to his feet, 'but if you have a message for me, perhaps you could deliver it without too much further delay. I have to see the Prefect of Bari in twenty minutes to discuss the Albanian refugee problem.'

He stretched out full length on the floor and started doing push-ups. Zen took a deep breath.

'Yes, sir. The fact is, I've just returned from the Vatican, where I had an audience of His Excellency Juan Ramón Sánchez-Valdés, First Deputy to the Cardinal Secretary of State. His Excellency gave me to understand that he was entirely satisfied with my, quote, discreet and invaluable intervention, unquote. An official communiqué to this effect will be forwarded by the Papal Nuncio in due course.'

The Minister rolled over on to his back, hooked his toes under the base of the sofa and started doing sit-ups.

'And you just wanted me to know that you're happy as a pig in shit?'

'No, sir. There's more.'

'And better, I hope.'

'Yes, sir. His Excellency Sánchez-Valdés confirmed that Prince Ludovico Ruspanti had been living in the Vatican City State for some weeks prior to his death. Not only that, but a special undercover unit of the Vigilanza Security Service was tapping Ruspanti's phone and maintaining surveillance on his movements. The implication is that some people at least knew from the beginning that Ruspanti had not committed suicide, and perhaps even knew the identity of his killers.'

That made the Minister sit up, and not just for exercise.

'Go on,' he said.

'One of those people was Giovanni Grimaldi, the Vigilanza official who was assigned to Ruspanti on Friday afternoon. He also had access to the transcript of the Prince's phone calls, which subsequently disappeared. The Curia also have evidence that Grimaldi was the source of the anonymous letter sent to the newspapers on Monday evening.'

'Bet you're glad you're not in his shoes, eh, Zeppo?'

'Zen, sir. Yes, sir. He's dead. It was disguised as an accident, but he was murdered, presumably by the people who killed Ruspanti. His Excellency Sánchez-Valdés mentioned that the Vatican was induced to give Ruspanti sanctuary by the promise of information about a secret political conspiracy within the Order of Malta, a group called the Cabal. Nothing more seems to be known about this organization, but the implication must be that it was their agents who faked Ruspanti's suicide and arranged for Grimaldi to have his fatal accident.'

The door opened and Gino strode in, spick and span in a Valentino suit, reeking of scent, his hair implant cockily bouffant.

'All yours, Rodolfo.'

The Minister got up heavily. He looked older and moved stiffly.

'Just a moment, Gino. I won't be long.'

Gino shrugged casually and left. It was he who looked the winner now. The Minister mechanically towelled away the sweat on his brow and face.

'Is that all?' he muttered.

'Almost,' nodded Zen. 'There's just one more thing. Yesterday I received an anonymous telegram saying that if I wanted to "get these deaths in perspective", I should go to a certain address on the Aventine. It turned out to be the Palace of Rhodes, the extraterritorial property of the Order of Malta.'

The Minister grimaced contemptuously.

'So what? Someone saw your name in the paper and decided to have a bit of fun at your expense. Happens all the time.'

'That's what I thought at first. But the message referred to "deaths", *plural*. At the time it was sent, only one person had died – Ludovico Ruspanti. But the people who sent the telegram already knew that Giovanni Grimaldi would be killed the following day. They'd spent the Monday afternoon making the necessary arrangements. And on the wall of the room where Grimaldi was killed, they'd chalked an eight-pointed Maltese cross.'

The Minister regarded Zen steadily for what seemed like a very long time. All his earlier facetiousness had deserted him.

'Thank you, dottore,' he said finally. 'You did right to keep me informed, and I look forward to receiving your written report in due course.'

He flung his towel over his shoulder and padded off to the bathroom.

'Can you find your own way out?'

The lift was through the Minister's office, where Gino was studying a framed portrait photograph of the Minister with Giulio Andreotti. He smiled cynically at Zen.

'Behold the secret of Rodolfo's success,' he said in a stage whisper.

Zen paused and looked up at the large photograph, which hung in pride of place above the Minister's desk. Both politicians were in formal morning dress. Both looked smug, solid, utterly sure of themselves. Beneath their white bow-ties, both wore embroidered bands from which hung a prominent gilt pendant incorporating the eight-pointed cross of the Sovereign Military Order of Malta.

'With Big Ears by his side,' Gino explained, 'he'll go all the way.'

'And how far is that?' asked Zen.

Gino stabbed the outer fingers of his right hand at the photograph in the gesture used to ward off evil.

'All the way to hell!'

The lift seemed to have a mind of its own that day. Zen was sure that he had pushed the right button, but when the doors slid apart the scene which greeted him was very different from what he had expected. Instead of the polished marble and elegant appointments of the Criminalpol offices on the third floor, he found himself in a cavernous hangar, ill-lit and foul-smelling. The oppressively low ceiling, like the squat rectangular pillars that supported it, was of bare concrete. The air was filled with a haze of black fumes and a continuous dull rumbling.

'What can I do for you, *dottó*?'

A dwarf-like figure materialized at Zen's elbow. The empty right sleeve of his jacket, flattened and neatly folded, was pinned back to the shoulder. The face, shrivelled and deeply lined, expressed a readiness to perform minor miracles and cut-price magic of all kinds.

'Oh, Salvató!' Zen replied.

'Don't tell me. You couldn't get through on the phone.'

Salvatore ejected an impressive gob of spittle which landed on the concrete with a loud splat.

'I had your boss Moscati down here the other day. Salvató, he says, I've been on the phone half an hour trying to get through, finally I decided it was quicker to come down in person.'

He waved his hand expressively.

'But what can I do? All I've got is one phone. One phone for the whole Ministry to book rides, *dottó*! You need a switchboard down here, Moscati says to me. Don't even think about it, I tell him. Look at the switchboard upstairs. The girls are so busy selling cosmetics and junk jewellery on the side that you can't get through at all!'

They both laughed.

'Where to, *dottó*?' asked Salvatore, resuming his air of professional harassment.

Zen was about to confess his mistake, or rather the lift's, when an idea sprang fully-formed into his mind.

'Any chance of a one-way to Fiumicino in about half an hour?'

Salvatore frowned, as he always did. Then an almost incredulous smile spread slowly across his face.

'You're in luck, *dottó*!'

He pointed across the garage towards the source of the rumbling noise. Now that his eyes had adjusted to the dimness, Zen could just make out a blue saloon with its bonnet open. A man in overalls was bent over the engine while another sat behind the wheel with his foot on the accelerator.

'We've been having a spot of trouble with that one,' Salvatore explained, 'but it's almost sorted out now. It's the grace of God, *dottó*. Normally I'd have been a bit pushed to come up with a vehicle at such short notice.'

This was an understatement. The real point of the joke at which Salvatore and Zen had laughed a moment before was that the garage phone was largely tied up by the demands of the private limousine service which Salvatore and his drivers had organized. Their rates were not the lowest in Rome, but they had the edge over the competition in being able to penetrate to any part of the city, including those officially closed to motor vehicles. For a special rate, they could even lay on a police motorcycle escort to clear a lane through the Roman traffic. This was a boon to the wealthy and self-important, and was frequently used by businessmen wishing to impress clients from out of town, but it did have the effect of drastically restricting use of the pool by Ministry staff.

'The airport in half an hour?' beamed Salvatore. 'No problem!'

'Not the airport,' Zen corrected as he stepped back into the lift. 'The *town* of Fiumicino.'

In the Criminalpol suite on the third floor, Zen flipped through the items in his in-tray. It was the first time he had been into work since Friday, so there was quite a pile. Holding the stack of papers, envelopes and folders in his left hand, he dealt them swiftly into three piles: those to throw away now; those to throw away later, after noting the single relevant fact, date or time; and those to place in his out-tray, having ticked the box indicating that he had read the contents from cover to cover.

'*Dominus vobiscum*,' a voice intoned fruitily.

Zen looked up from an internal memorandum reading 'Please call 645 9866 at lunchtime and ask for Simonelli.' Giorgio De Angelis was looking round the edge of the hessian-covered screen which divided off their respective working areas.

'According to the media, you're dangerously ill with a rare infectious virus,' the Calabrian went on, 'so I won't come any closer. This miraculous recovery is just one of the perks of working for the pope, I suppose. Pick up thy bed and walk and so on. How did you swing it, anyway? They say you can't even get a cleaning job in the Vatican these days unless you have Polish blood.'

For some time after his transfer to Criminalpol, Zen had been slightly suspicious of De Angelis, fearing that his apparent bonhomie might be a strategy designed to elicit compromising admissions or disclosures. The promotion of Zen's enemy Vincenzo Fabri to the post of Questore of Ferrara, combined with Zen's coup in solving the Burolo affair to the satisfaction of the various political interests involved, had changed all that. With his position in the department no longer under direct threat, Zen was at last able to appreciate Giorgio De Angelis's jovial good-humour without scanning everything he said for hidden meanings.

The Calabrian produced a newspaper article which quoted Zen as 'reaffirming that there were no suspicious circumstances surrounding the death of Ludovico Ruspanti' and dismissing the allegations in the anonymous letter as 'mischievous and ill-informed'.

'Impressive prose for a man with a high fever,' he commented, running his fingers through the babyish fuzz which was all that now grew on the impressive expanses of his skull. 'I particularly liked the homage to our own dear Marcelli.'

Zen smiled wryly. The phrase 'mischievous and ill-informed rumours' was a favourite of the Ministerial under-secretary in question, who had almost certainly penned the statement.

'But seriously, Aurelio, what really happened? Is there any truth in these allegations that Ruspanti was murdered?'

Catching the eager glint in De Angelis's eyes, Zen realized he was going to have to come up with a story to peddle round the department. At least half the fun of working there was the conversational advantage it gave you with your relatives and friends. Whether you spoke or kept silent, it was assumed that you were in the know. As soon as his colleagues discovered that Zen was no longer 'ill', they were all going to want him to fill them in on the Ruspanti affair.

'Who's to say it *was* Ruspanti?' he replied.

De Angelis goggled at him.

'You mean . . .'

Zen shrugged.

'I saw the body, Giorgio. It looked like it had been through a food processor. I'd be prepared to testify that it was human, and probably male, but I wouldn't go any further under oath.'

'Can't they tell from the dental records?'

Zen nodded.

'Which may be why the body was handed over to the family before anyone had a chance. The funeral's being held this afternoon.'

De Angelis gave a low whistle.

'But why?'

'Ruspanti was broke and had this currency fraud hanging over him. He needed time to organize his affairs and play his political cards. So he decided to fake his own death.'

De Angelis nodded, wide-eyed at the sheer ingenuity of the thing.

'So who died in St Peter's?' he asked.

'We'll never know. You'd need a personal intervention by Wojtyla to get an exhumation order now. It was probably someone you've never heard of.'

De Angelis shook his head with knowing superiority.

'More likely a person of the very highest importance, someone they needed to get out of the way.'

Zen gestured loosely, conceding that this too was possible.

'Let's talk about it over lunch,' the Calabrian suggested eagerly.

'Sorry, Giorgio, not today. I've already got an appointment. Now if you'll excuse me, I have to make a phone call.'

As his colleague left to circulate the true story behind the Ruspanti affair through the department, Zen pulled the phone over and dialled the number written on the message form.

'Hotel Torlonia Palace.'

The calm, deep voice was in marked contrast to the usual Roman squawk which hovered as though by an effort of will on the brink of screaming hysteria. Zen had never heard of the Hotel Torlonia Palace, but he already knew that you wouldn't be able to get a room there for less than a quarter of a million lire a night.

'May I speak to Dottor Simonelli, please.'

'One moment.'

After a brief silence, a male voice with a distinct reedy timbre came on the line.

'Yes?'

'This is Vice-Questore Aurelio Zen, at the Interior Ministry. I received a message . . .'

'That is correct. I am Antonio Simonelli, investigating magistrate with the Procura of Milan. Am I right in thinking that we've been in contact before?'

'Not as far as I know.'

'Ah,' the voice replied. 'I must have confused you with someone else. Anyway, I was hoping it would be possible for us to meet. I have some questions I wish to ask you relative to my investigations. Could you call on me this afternoon?'

Although his heart sank, Zen knew that this was one more hurdle he was going to have to go through. They made an appointment to meet at four o'clock in the lobby of the hotel. Zen hung up with a massive sigh and hastened downstairs to find Tania. This damned case was a hydra! No sooner had he seen off the Vatican, the Minister and an inquisitive colleague than up popped some judge from Milan.

Of all the offices in the building, those occupied by the Administration department most clearly betrayed the Ministry's Fascist birthright: a warren of identical hutches, each containing six identical desks disposed in the same symmetrical order. Tania shared her cubicle with three other women and two men, both of whom had unwittingly been auditioned by Zen for the part of her mysterious lover. But their voices didn't match the one he had heard on the phone, and besides, he doubted whether Tania would have gone for either the fat, balding father-of-three or his neighbour, the neurotic obsessive with bad breath. He doubted, but he couldn't be sure. You could never tell with women. She had gone for *him* after all. With taste like that, who could tell what she might stoop to next?

Tania was talking on the phone when he walked in. As soon as she caught sight of Zen, a furtive air came over her. Shielding her mouth with one hand, she spoke urgently into the phone as he strode towards her. All he could make out before she hung up was 'I'll speak to you later,' but it was enough. The form of the verb was familiar, her tone conspiratorial.

'Who was that?' he demanded

'Oh, just a relative.'

She actually blushed. Zen let it go, out of self-interest rather than magnanimity. What with the stresses and strains of the morning, and those that loomed later in the afternoon, he needed an interval of serenity. In a way it didn't even seem to matter that her love was all a fake. If she was making use of him, then he would make use of her. That way they were quits.

He stared at the computer screen on the desk, which displayed a list of names and addresses, many of them in foreign countries. Surely they couldn't *all* be her lovers? Tania depressed a key and the screen reverted to the READY display.

'Shall we go?' she asked.

But Zen continued to gaze at the screen. After a moment he pressed one of the function keys, selecting the SEARCH option. SUBJECT? queried the screen. Zen typed 'Malta/Knights'. The screen went into a brief coma before producing two lines of print: SOVEREIGN MILITARY ORDER OF MALTA/KNIGHTS OF MALTA/KNIGHTS OF ST JOHN OF JERUSALEM/KNIGHTS HOSPITALLERS: 1 FILE(S) 583 INSTANCE(S).

'What does that mean?' he asked Tania.

She surveyed the screen with the impatience of a professional aware of the value of her time.

'It means, first of all, that these people evidently can't make up their minds what to call themselves, so they are referred to under four different titles. The database holds one report specifically dedicated to this organization. There are also five hundred plus references in other files.'

'What sort of references?'

Tania's swift, competent fingers rattled the keyboard with panache. AUTHORIZATION? appeared. ZEN, she typed. Again the screen faltered briefly, then filled with text which proved to be an extract from the Ministry's file on a Turin businessman who had been convicted of involvement in a local government corruption scandal in the early eighties. The reference Zen had requested was picked out by the cursor: 'Member of the Sovereign Military Order of Malta since 1964 with rank of Knight of Magisterial Grace.'

That sort of thing was apparently all there was, at least in the open files. He got Tania to run him off a copy of the report on the Knights of Malta, even though he knew that anything really worth knowing would be held in the 'closed' section of the database, accessible only with special authorization restricted to a handful of senior staff. The files stored there supposedly detailed the financial status, professional and political allegiances, family situation and sexual predilections of almost fourteen million Italian citizens. Like everyone else, Zen had often wondered what his own entry contained. Was his connection with Tania included by now? Presumably, judging by Moscati's mocking remarks. How much more did they know? Reading such an entry would be like seeing a copy of your own obituary, and just as difficult.

4

They strolled along the quay, hand in hand, fingers entwined. It had rained while they were in the restaurant, briefly but hard. Now the sky had cleared again, every surface glistened, and the air was flooded with elusive, evocative scents.

The little town of Fiumicino, at the mouth of the narrower of the two channels into which the Tiber divided just before it met the sea, was somewhere Zen always returned to with pleasure. The scale of the place, the narrow waterway and the low buildings flanking it, the sea tang, the bustle of a working port, all combined to remind him of the fishing villages of the Venetian lagoon. In addition, Fiumicino contained several restaurants capable of doing justice to the quality and freshness of the catches which its boats brought in.

Replete with *crema di riso gratinato ai frutti di mare* and grilled sea bass with artichokes, he and Tania wandered along the stone quays like a pair of young lovers without a care in the world.

'. . . the best artichokes in the world,' she was saying. 'My aunt prepares the hearts, then they bottle them in oil, ten kilos at a time.'

'You're making me hungry again.'

'You must try them, Aurelio! I'll get Aldo to send an extra jar with the next batch of samples . . .'

She broke off.

'Batch of what?' Zen asked mechanically, so as not to reveal that he hadn't been listening, absorbed in the spectacle of a skinny cat stalking a butterfly across a pile of empty fish crates.

'The next time one of the family comes to Rome, I mean,' said Tania.

'Look!'

Balanced on its hind legs like a performing monkey, the cat was frantically pawing at the air, trying in vain to seize the elusive, substanceless quiver of colour.

'You'll never catch it, silly!' laughed Tania in a slightly tipsy voice. 'And even if you do, there's nothing there to eat!'

Still intent on its prey, the cat stepped off the edge of the boxes. It twisted round in mid-air and landed on its feet, shooting a hostile glance at the couple who had witnessed its humiliation.

'Actually I may go myself, this weekend,' Tania announced as they continued on their way.

'Go? Where?'

'Home to Udine, to see my cousins.'

Zen freed his hand.

'Suppose I came too?'

Tania shot him a panicky glance.

'You? Well . . .'

She gave an embarrassed laugh.

'You see, Bettina and Aldo don't actually know about you.'

A few minutes earlier, as they walked together along the quay, Zen had found himself thinking, 'This, or something very like it, is happiness.' That exaltation now looked like nothing more special than a side effect of the *verdicchio* they had drunk at lunch. Now the hangover had arrived.

'So who *do* they know about?' he demanded truculently.

Tania looked at him, a new hardness in his eyes.

'They know I'm no longer with Mauro, if that's what you mean.'

He didn't say whether it was or not.

'So they think you're living alone.'

'Well, aren't I?'

They faced each other for a moment over that. Then Tania broke into a smile and took his arm.

'Look, Bettina's my cousin, the second daughter of my father's younger brother. It's not an intimate relationship, but since my parents died and Nino emigrated to Australia it's the best I've got. Bettina doesn't burden me with her problems and I don't burden her with mine.'

'I didn't realize I was a problem,' he replied, snapping up the cheap shot on offer.

'I didn't mean that, Aurelio. I mean that we don't share our inner-most preoccupations, good or bad. We keep our distance. That's the best way sometimes, particularly with relatives. Otherwise the whole thing can get out of control.'

'And control is important to you, is it?'

He hated the snide way he said it. So did Tania, it soon became clear.

'And why not?' she snapped. 'Damn it, I spent the first thirty years of my life asleep at the wheel. You saw the result. Now I've decided to try taking charge for a while and see how that goes. I mean is that all right?'

Aware of the weakness of his position, Zen backed down.

'Of course. Go where you like. It looks like I might have to work, anyway.'

The fishing boats which had landed their catches early that morning were now tied up two abreast on either side of the channel, stem to stern. Two crewmen were mending nets spread out over the quay, and Tania and Zen chose to go opposite ways around them. As they joined up again, she said, 'What *is* this work you're doing, anyway?'

Partly out of fatigue with the truth, partly to get his own back for her own evasions, Zen decided to lie.

'The Vatican have got a problem with documents disappearing from the Secret Archives,' he said, recalling the case which Grimaldi had been working on at the time of his death. 'They can't use their own security people because they think some of them may be involved.'

'And you hang around like a store detective waiting for someone to lift a pair of tights?'

'More or less. It's a hell of a way to make a living, but if I crack the case I get a full plenary indulgence.'

Tania laughed.

'Not that I really need one,' he went on, eager to please. 'I'm already owed over a hundred thousand years' remission from purgatory. In fact I'm a bit worried that I might soon reach the stage where my spiritual credit exceeds any practical possibilities I have of sinning. Just think what a ruinous effect that would have on my moral fibre.'

'How did you get to be so holy?'

'Oh, I used to be quite devout in my way. I loved the idea of collecting indulgences, like saving up coupons for a free gift. If I said three *Pater nosters* after confession, I got three hundred years' remission from purgatory. That seemed an incredible bargain! I couldn't believe my luck. It takes maybe a minute or so, if you gabble, and for that you got off three hundred years of unspeakable torture! I couldn't understand why everyone wasn't taking advantage. I and Tommaso, my best friend, used to vie with each other. I had well over a hundred thousand years' worth stored up before I finally fell in love with Tommaso's sister. After that, the next world no longer seemed quite so important.'

His words were drowned by the roar of a plane taking off from the international airport just a few kilometres to the north.

'Anyway,' he concluded, 'having attended Mass on the first Friday of each month for the nine months after my First Communion, I'm assured of dying in a state of grace whatever happens.'

To his surprise, Tania immediately reached out and touched the nearest metal – a mooring bollard – for good luck.

'Don't mention such things, Aurelio.'

He took her in his arms, and she kissed him in that way she had, making him wish they were in bed.

'Sweetheart,' she said.

He laughed, moved despite himself, despite his knowledge that she was cheating him.

'I didn't know you were superstitious,' he said as they walked on. 'You've spent too long living with southerners.'

'Now, now! Don't start coming on like some regionalist red-neck who thinks that the Third World starts at the Apennines.'

'Of course it doesn't! It starts at Mestre.'

'Mauro may have been a creep, but . . .'

'*May*? Tania, you once described Mauro Bevilacqua as someone for whom strangling at birth would have been too good.'

Perhaps that was who she was seeing on the side, he thought. Perhaps Mauro would have the last laugh after all, and Zen suffer the ignominy of being cuckolded by his lover's husband.

'. . . but not *all* southerners are like that,' Tania continued. 'Mauro's elder brother, for example, is a charming man, scholarly and cultured, with a nice dry wit.'

'Oh yes?' demanded Zen, his jealousy immediately locking on to this new target.

'In fact you might see him while you're snooping around the Vatican Archives. He works for the region's cultural affairs department, and he spends a lot of time there researching material for exhibitions and so on.'

'Maybe he's the one who's been stealing the stuff,' Zen muttered moodily.

'From what Tullio says, I'm surprised the thefts were ever noticed.

According to him the Vatican collections are so vast and so badly organized that you can spend days tracking down a single item. It's more like a place for hiding documents than for finding them, he says.'

She broke off, frightened by the intensity with which he was staring at her.

'What's the matter, Aurelio? Did I say something wrong? You seem so strange today, so moody and unpredictable. Is there something you haven't told me?'

There was a deafening siren blast as a large orange ocean-going tug slipped her moorings on the other side of the river. Zen transferred his obsessively fixated gaze to the vessel as it proceeded slowly downstream towards the open sea.

'Do you ever see this . . . what's his name?'

Now it was Tania's turn to stare.

'Just exactly what is that supposed to mean?'

He looked at her and shrugged, ignoring her indignant tone.

'What it says.'

They faced each other like enemies.

'Do I ever see Tullio Bevilacqua?' Tania recited with sarcastic emphasis. 'No, I haven't seen him since Mauro and I broke up. Does that satisfy you?'

'But are you on good terms? Would he do you a favour?'

'What sort of favour?' Tania shouted, scaring away the seagulls. 'What the hell are you talking about, Aurelio?'

So he told her.

They returned by train. Tania got off at Trastevere and got a bus back to her flat, while Zen continued to the suburban Tiburtina station. The determined effort they both made to part on good terms was itself the clearest indication yet of the growing crisis in their relationship, and of their mutual sense that things were no longer quite what they seemed.

From the station, Zen caught a taxi to the Hotel Torlonia Palace. On the way he looked through the Ministry's file on the Knights of Malta. As he had expected, the document was entirely non-controversial, amounting to little more than an outline of the organization's history, structure and overt aims. Founded in 1070, the Sovereign Military Hospitaller Order of St John of Jerusalem, of Rhodes, and of Malta was the third oldest religious Order after the Benedictines and Augustans, and the first to consist entirely of laymen. The Order was originally formed to staff and run infirmaries during the Crusades, but soon took on a military role as well. At the end of the twelfth century the Knights retreated to Rhodes, from where they conducted covert operations all over the Middle East until their expulsion by the Turks in 1522. Thereafter they led a token existence in Malta until Napoleon's conquest of the island once again forced them into exile, this time in Rome.

The Knights had thus lost their original religious and political relevance by 1522, and the last fragment of their territorial power three centuries after that. Nevertheless, like an archaic law which has never been repealed, the Order still enjoyed the status and privileges of an independent nation state, with the power to mint coins, print stamps, license cars, operate a merchant fleet and issue passports to its diplomats and other favoured individuals. 'Like Opus Dei [q.v.],' Zen read, 'the Order is exempt from the jurisdiction of local bishops, being under the direct authority of the pope, exercised through the Sacred Congregation for Religious and Secular Institutes. The contradiction between the obedience required by this relationship and the independence inherent in the Order's sovereign temporal status has on occasion led to acrimonious conflicts.'

Zen scanned the rest of the report, which sketched the structure of this very exclusive organization. At least sixteen quarterings of noble blood were required for membership, except in a special category – Knights of Magisterial Grace – created to accommodate prominent but plebian Catholics. At the core of the Order were the thirty 'professed' knights, or Knights of Justice, who had taken a triple vow of poverty, chastity and obedience. 'Governed by His Most Eminent Highness the Prince and Grand Master with the help of a "general chapter" which convenes regularly, the Order donates medicine and medical equipment to needy countries and performs humanitarian work throughout the Third World . . .'

The text began to blur in front of Zen's eyes. It was clear what was involved: a snobbish club designed to give the impoverished remnants of the Catholic aristocracy access to serious money, while bestowing a flattering glow of religious and historical legitimacy over the ruthlessly acquired wealth of the *nouveaux riches*. Under cover of the Order's meritorious charitable work, its members could dress up in fancy red tunics, flowing capes and plumed hats and indulge themselves to their heart's content in the spurious rituals and meaningless honours of a Ruritanian mini-state. All very silly, no doubt, but no more so than most pastimes of the very rich. What was really silly was the idea that such an organization might be capable of plotting – never mind executing – the cold-blooded murders of Ludovico Ruspanti and Giovanni Grimaldi.

The taxi drew up in the courtyard of an *umbertino* monstrosity on a quiet street overlooking the gardens of the Villa Borghese. The uniformed doorman surveyed Zen without notable enthusiasm, but eventually let him pass. Zen identified himself at Reception, walked across the spacious lobby and flopped down in a large armchair, wondering what he was going to say. He knew it wasn't going to be easy. Antonio Simonelli had a vested interest in establishing that Ruspanti's death was connected with the currency fraud which he had been investigating. If it wasn't, then his entire dossier on the affair, painstakingly compiled over many months of arduous work, would become so much wastepaper. Since Ruspanti had died in St Peter's, which was technically foreign soil, Simonelli could not pursue his suspicions officially without the cooperation of the Vatican, which was not forthcoming. Zen was therefore the magistrate's only hope.

What Simonelli wanted from him was some inside information, some awkward fact or compromising discrepancy, which he could use to bring pressure to bear on the Vatican authorities to permit a full official investigation of Ruspanti's death to be carried out by him in collaboration with one of the Vatican's own magistrates. The affair would then drag on inconclusively for years, until it petered out, smothered beneath the sheer volume of contradictory and confusing evidence. That would be of no concern to Simonelli, who would meanwhile have established himself as one of the rising stars of the judiciary, a man to watch. As for Zen, he would be used and abused without respite by all sides in the affair, and would be lucky to keep his job. Unless he scotched this thing now, he would never hear the end of it.

There was a buzz of voices behind him.

'I have nothing further to say!'

'According to Giorgio Bocca, your philosophy encapsulates the shallow, a-historical consumerism of the nineties. Do you accept that?'

Zen turned to find a strikingly attractive man in his mid-twenties standing at bay before a pack of reporters brandishing notebooks and microphones. His sleek, feral look jibed intriguingly with his boyish fair hair and the candour of his pale blue eyes. His movements were almost feminine in their suppleness, yet the look of breathtaking insolence with which he confronted the journalists could hardly have been more macho.

'Bocca can say what he likes. No one's listening anyway. As for me, my clothes speak for me!'

They certainly did, a layered montage of overlapping textures and colours so cunningly contrived that one hardly noticed where one garment ended and another began. Especially in motion, the resulting flurry of activity was so distracting that you hardly noticed the man himself.

Another reporter waved a microphone in the man's face.

'Camilla Cederna has said, "The one thing that is clear from this book is that it was composed by a ghost-writer. Since the invented personality the author describes is equally substanceless, the whole exercise amounts to one ghost writing about another." Any comment?'

'If la Cederna is so out of touch with the rhythms of contemporary reality, perhaps she should restrict herself to a topic more suited to her talents, for example needlework.'

This caused some laughter.

'Fortunately the thousands of people who read my book and wear my clothes have no such difficulties,' the man continued. 'They understand that what I am is what I have made myself, using nothing but my own genius. I owe nothing to anyone or to anything! I am entirely my own creation! I am Falco!'

'Dottor Zen?'

A corpulent man had approached the chair where Zen was sitting and stood looking down at him with a complacent expression.

'I am Antonio Simonelli.'

They're letting all sorts in these days, thought Zen as they shook hands. With his crumpled blue suit and hearty manner, Simonelli seemed more like a provincial tradesman than a magistrate. But this might well be a deliberate ploy designed to lull Zen into a false sense of security. And indeed Simonelli at once struck a confidential note.

'You know who that was, of course?'

The media star had swept out by now, surrounded by his entourage, and the lobby was quiet again.

'Some designer, isn't he? I don't really keep up with such things.'

Simonelli subsided into a leather chair opposite, which resembled an overdone soufflé.

'Falco, he calls himself,' Simonelli explained in his Bergamo whine, like an ill-tuned oboe d'amore. 'He's based in Milan, but he's down here promoting some book he's published, explaining his "design philosophy" if you please. Of course he *would* have to choose the very hotel where I always stay. It's terrible. You can't move for reporters.'

He signalled a waiter. Zen ordered an espresso, Simonelli a *caffè Hag*.

'It's my heart,' he explained, unwrapping a panatella cigar with his big, blunt fingers. 'One of my colleagues dropped dead just last month. He was fifteen years younger than me. Gave me a bit of a jolt, so I had a check-up, and it turns out I'm at risk myself.'

Zen smiled politely.

'Anyway, I mustn't bore you with my problems,' the magistrate went on. 'Except for the Ruspanti case, that is. I don't know how much you know about the investigation I have been involved in . . .'

'Only what I've read in the newspapers.'

'It's all water under the bridge now, of course,' Simonelli sighed mournfully. 'With my key witness dead, there's no case to be made. This is really only a private chat, just to satisfy my curiosity. Naturally whatever is said between us two will remain strictly off the record.'

He broke off as the waiter brought their coffees. Simonelli emptied two sachets of sugar into his cup and looked across the table at Zen as he stirred.

'So tell me, what really happened? Did he fall, or was he pushed?'

It had been perfectly done, thought Zen. The illusion of a personal rapport, the implied assumption that they were associates and equals, the casual request for information 'just to satisfy my curiosity', the assurance that Zen could speak freely in the knowledge that what was said would go no further, even the facetious touch of the final question. If Zen hadn't been expecting something of the kind, he might well have fallen for it hook, line and sinker – and then spent the next few years wriggling and thrashing as Simonelli reeled him in. As it was, the magistrate's adroitness merely reinforced Zen's determination to give nothing away. Reticence would be a mistaken tactic, however, merely confirming that there were significant secrets to be learned. The true art of concealment, Zen knew, lay not in silence but garrulity, in rumour and innuendo. Best of all was to let the victim spin the web of deceit himself. That way, it was bound to conform perfectly to his fears and prejudices, forming a snug, cosy trap from which he had no desire to escape.

'I found no evidence to suggest that Ruspanti's death was anything other than it appeared to be,' he declared firmly.

Simonelli gazed at him levelly.

'So you accept that he committed suicide.'

'I see no reason not to.'

The magistrate lit his cigar carefully, rotating the end above the flame of his lighter.

'Even in the light of this second fatality?'

Zen looked blank.

'I'm sorry?'

'The Vatican security man, Giovanni Grimaldi. You don't think his death was connected in any way to Ruspanti's?'

Zen downed his coffee in three swift gulps.

'How do you know about that?' he asked casually.

Simonelli sipped his coffee and puffed at his cigar, making Zen wait.

'Grimaldi was what the espionage profession calls a double agent,' he explained at last. 'In addition to his duties for the Vigilanza, he was also working for me as a paid informant.'

Zen knew that this revelation was intended to encourage him to make one in return, but he was too intrigued not to follow it up.

'So you knew that Ruspanti had taken refuge in the Vatican?'

Simonelli nodded.

'After the Maltese kicked him out. Yes, I knew. But I couldn't prove it, and if I'd spoken out they'd have spirited him away before anyone could do anything. So I bided my time and used Grimaldi to keep track of what was happening. Until last week, he was providing me with regular, detailed reports of Ruspanti's movements, the people he met, the calls he made, and so on. Most of it was irrelevant, all about some organization which Ruspanti was threatening to expose if they didn't help him. But the first thing I did when I heard of Ruspanti's death was to try and contact Grimaldi. He didn't return my calls, so I flew down here to look him up, only to find that he was dead.'

Zen sat perfectly still, eyeing Simonelli. His racing pulse might have been due to the coffee he had just drunk.

'What was the name of this organization Ruspanti was threatening?' he asked.

Simonelli looked annoyed at this reference to something he had made clear was a side-issue.

'I really don't remember.'

'The anonymous letter to the papers spoke of a group calling itself the Cabal,' said Zen.

'Yes, that's right. The Cabal. Why? Do you know any more about it?'

Zen shrugged.

'To be honest, I assumed it referred to this group of businessmen you've been investigating.'

To his surprise, Simonelli reacted with a look of total panic. Then it was gone, and he laughed.

'Really?'

Zen said nothing. Simonelli broke a baton of ash off his cigar into the glass ashtray on the table.

'According to Grimaldi's reports, I'd rather gathered that it had some connection with the Knights of Malta,' he said.

Zen raised his eyebrows.

'It's the first I've heard of it.'

Simonelli gasped two deep breaths.

'Anyway, we've rather got away from my original question, which was whether you think that Grimaldi's death could have been connected in any way to Ruspanti's.'

Zen frowned like a dim schoolboy confronted by a concept too difficult for him to grasp.

'But Ruspanti committed suicide by jumping off the gallery in St Peter's and Grimaldi was electrocuted in his shower by a faulty water heater. What connection could there be?'

'The two deaths occurring so close together was just a coincidence, then?'

'I can't see what else it could be.'

In his heart he apologized to Ruspanti and Grimaldi for adding such insults to the fatal injuries they had sustained. But it was all very well for the dead, he thought to himself. They were well out of it.

'That anonymous letter to the press certainly was neither an accident nor a coincidence,' Simonelli remarked with some asperity. 'Someone wrote it, and for a reason. Do you have any ideas about that?'

Zen looked shiftily around the lobby, as though checking whether they could be overheard.

'One thing I did find out is that certain people in the Vatican are not satisfied with the official line on Ruspanti's death,' he confided in an undertone. 'The Vatican isn't a monolith, any more than the Communist Party – or whatever it's calling itself these days. There are different currents, varying tendencies, opposed pressure groups. One of them might well have wished to try and throw doubt on the suicide verdict.'

Simonelli plunged his cigar into the dregs of his coffee, where it expired with a hiss.

'An official leak, then.'

Zen tipped his hand back and forth.

'Semi-official disinformation.'

'It must have been embarrassing for you,' Simonelli suggested, 'to have your professional integrity publicly attacked like that.'

Zen shrugged.

'One has to live with these things.'

Simonelli hitched up the sleeve of his jacket, revealing a chunky gold watch.

'Well, thank you for taking the trouble to come and satisfy my interest in this business,' he said.

'Not at all. If that's all, I'd better be getting back to the Ministry.'

Simonelli raised his eyebrows.

'Working?' he demanded coarsely. 'At this time?'

The magistrate's manner was so familiar that Zen almost winked at him.

'Thanks to this Vatican business, I've got a backlog of other work to catch up on,' he confided. 'I thought I might as well get paid overtime for doing it.'

Simonelli laughed.

'Quite right, quite right!'

Just inside the hotel's revolving door, they shook hands again.

'Perhaps we'll meet again some time,' Zen found himself saying.

Simonelli's eyes were enlivened by some expression which he couldn't read at all.

'I shouldn't be surprised, dottore. I shouldn't be at all surprised.'

AUTHORIZATION?

Zen gazed at the band of green script which stared back at him, as unwavering as a reptile's eye. Something had gone wrong, but he had no idea what. True, he was no longer as utterly innocent of computers as he had once been. He had no map to the computer's alien landscape, and wouldn't have been able to read it if he had, but he had laboriously learned to follow a number of paths which led to the places he wanted or needed to reach. As long as he stayed on them, he could usually reach his goal, given time. But if by accident he pushed the wrong key, producing some unforeseen effect, there was nothing for it but to return to the beginning.

That was what must have happened now, it seemed. He had intended to open a file in which to enter the outline details of the Ruspanti case which he had passed on orally to the Minister earlier in the day. He wanted to do this now, while they were still fresh in his mind. Then, later in the week, he would call up the file and rewrite it as a proper report, which he would then save to the database as a 'Read Only' item, imperishably enshrined in electronic form for any interested party to consult. Something had gone wrong, however. When he tried to open a file to jot down his notes, the computer had responded as though he had asked to read an already-existing file, and demanded an authorization reference. With a sigh, Zen pressed the red 'Break' button and began all over again.

The window beside the desk where the terminal was installed was steadily turning opaque as the winter dusk gathered outside. Down below in Piazza del Viminale the evening rush hour was at its height, the gridlocked vehicles bellowing like cattle in rut, but no sound penetrated the Ministry's heavy-duty reflective triple glazing, proof against everything from bullets to electronic surveillance. Zen gazed at that darkened expanse of glass where he had once caught sight of Tania, seemingly floating towards him in mid-air across the piazza outside. Searching his own personal database, he identified a day shortly before he went to Sardinia for the Burolo case, the day when

Tania had come to lunch at his apartment. Although little more than a year earlier, that period already seemed to him like a state of pre-lapsarian innocence. What was Tania doing now, he wondered, and with whom? Concentrating his mind with an effort, he once again ran through the procedure for opening a file and pressed 'Enter'. As before, the screen responded with a demand for his security clearance. Infuriated, Zen typed 'Go stuff your sister.' AUTHORIZATION INVALID the computer returned priggishly.

It was not until the third time that he finally caught on. He had been scrupulously careful on this occasion, moving the cursor through the menus line by line and double-checking every option before selecting it. When SUBJECT? appeared, he carefully typed 'Cabal', the working title he was using for his notes. He was certain that he had observed all the correct procedures, yet when he pressed the 'Enter' key, the computer once again flashed its demand for authorization like some obsessive psychotic with a one-track mind. To dispel the urge to stick his fist through the screen, he swivelled round in his chair and stood up – and suddenly the solution came to him, huge and blindingly obvious. The computer was not stupid or malicious, just infinitely literal-minded. If it was treating his attempt to open a file named 'Cabal' as a 'read' option, it could only be because *such a file already existed*.

He turned away from the screen as though it were a window from which he was being watched. His skin was prickling, his scalp taut. Grabbing the keyboard, he called up the directory. No such file was listed. That meant it must be stored in the 'closed' section of the database, whose contents were not displayed in the directory.

Somewhere in the office behind him a phone was ringing. He reached out blindly, picked up the extension by the computer terminal and switched the call through.

'Criminalpol, Zen speaking.'

He was sure it must be Tania. No one else would ring him at work at that time. But to his disappointment, the voice was male.

'Good evening, dottore. I'm calling from the Vatican.'

Zen knew he had heard the voice already that day, although it didn't sound like either Sánchez-Valdés or Lamboglia.

'How did you know I was here?' he asked inconsequentially.

'We tried your home number first and they said you were at work.

Listen, we need to see you this evening. It's a matter of great urgency.'

'Who is this?'

'My identity is not important.'

Zen reduced his voice to a charged whisper.

'I'm afraid that's not good enough. I have been assured on the highest authority that my involvement with the Ruspanti affair is over. I'm currently preparing a report on the incident for my superiors. I can't just drop everything and come running on the strength of an anonymous phone call.'

There was a momentary silence.

'This report you're writing,' said the voice, 'is it going to mention the Cabal?'

Zen raised his eyes to the glowing screen.

'What do you know about the Cabal?'

'Everything.'

Zen was silent.

'Come to St Peter's at seven o'clock exactly,' the voice told him. 'In the north transept, where the light shows.'

The phone went dead. Zen blindly replaced the receiver, still staring at the word AUTHORIZATION? and the box where the name of the official seeking access to the file would appear. As though of their own volition, his fingers tapped six times on the keyboard, and the box filled with the name ROMIZI. This was a perfectly harmless deception. If anybody bothered to check who had tried to read the closed file on the Cabal, it would at once be obvious that a false name had been used. Poor Carlo Romizi, helplessly comatose in the Ospedale di San Giovanni, clearly couldn't be responsible.

As he expected, though, the only response was AUTHORIZATION INVALID. Zen sat gazing at the screen until the words blurred into mere squiggles of light, but the message itself was so firmly imprinted on his eyeballs that it appeared on walls, floors, windows and doors long after he had turned off the computer and left the building, imbuing every surrounding surface with a portentous, threatening shimmer.

When he got home, a familiar voice was holding forth in his living room about the philosophy of fashion. Glancing at the television, Zen recognized the young man he had last seen delivering an impromptu press conference in the lobby of the Hotel Torlonia Palace. He was now perched on a leather and chrome stool, being interviewed by Raffaella Carrá about his book *You Are What You Wear*.

'. . . not a question of dressing up, like draping clothes over a dummy, but of recreating yourself. When you put on a Falco creation, you are reborn! The old self dies and a new one takes its place, instantly, in the twinkling of an eye . . .'

Zen crossed to the inner hallway.

'Hello? Anyone there?'

'. . . if you're so insecure you need a label to hide behind, then by all means buy something by Giorgio or Gianni. I've got nothing against their stuff. It's very pretty. But I'm not interested in merely embellishing a preconceived entity but effecting a radical transformation of . . .'

He looked into the kitchen, the dining room, the bathroom and his mother's bedroom. The flat was empty.

'. . . clothes for people who don't want to look like someone else but to make themselves apparent, to create themselves freely and from zero, every instant of every day. People like me, who have nothing to hide, who are neither more nor less than what they seem to be . . .'

'And who *are* you?' Raffaella Carrá demanded. 'Who *is* Falco?'

'What can I say? There's no mystery about me! What you see is what you get. I am nothing but this perpetual potential to become what I am, this constant celebration of our freedom to exorcize the demons of time and place, or who and what, where and why, and escape towards a goal which is defined by our approach to it . . .'

As he reached to switch off the television, Zen saw the note in his mother's spidery handwriting on top of the set.

Welcome back Aurelio – Lucrezia from downstairs asked if I could keep an eye on her two boys while she collects her brother and his wife from Belgium – they were supposed to arrive yesterday evening but the plane was delayed – I'll be back in time for dinner – don't turn TV off as I am recording the last episode of *Twin Peaks* – Rosella and I have a bet on who did it but I think she has been told by Gilberto's brother in America where it was on last year

Your loving mother

Zen put the note down with a sigh. They had had a video recorder for two years now, but his mother still refused to believe that it was possible to tape a television programme successfully without the set being switched on and the volume turned up.

'. . . refuse to recognize deterministic limitations on my freedom to be whoever I choose. No one has the right to tell me who I am, to chain me to the Procrustean bed of so-called "objective reality". *All* that counts is my fantasy, my genius, my flair, eternally fashioning and refashioning myself and the world around me . . .'

The voice vanished abruptly as Zen twisted the volume control. He took out his pen and scrawled a message at the bottom of his mother's note to the effect that he had got back safely from Florence and would see her for dinner. For some reason he found his mother's absence disturbing. It was good that she was out and about, of course, keeping herself busy. Nevertheless, there was something about the whole arrangement which jarred. He set the note down on top of the television, walked back down the hallway and opened the last door on the right.

The pent-up odours of the past broke over him like a wave: camphor and mildew, patent medicines and obsolete toiletries, stiffened leather, smoky fur, ghostly perfumes, the whiff of sea fog. He pushed his way through the piles of overflowing trunks, chests and boxes. Spiders and woodlice froze, then broke ranks and scattered in panic as the colossus approached. There it was, in the far corner, perched on a plinth of large cardboard boxes containing back-numbers of *Famiglia Cristiana* from the early fifties. The gaily painted wooden box had originally been stamped with the insignia of the State Railways and a warning about the detonators it had contained. Zen still lucidly recalled his wonder at the transformation wrought by his father's paintbrush, which had magically turned this discarded relic into a toy box for little Aurelio.

Reaching over so far his stomach muscles protested, he pulled the box down and removed the lid. Then he sifted through the contents – clockwork train set, tin drum, lead soldiers and battleships – until he found the revolver which had been made specially for him by a machinist in the locomotive works at Mestre. The man had been an ardent Blackshirt, and although unfireable, the gun was an accurate replica of the 9mm Beretta he carried when he went out to raise hell with his fellow *squadristi*. Zen weighed it in his hand, tracing the words MUSSOLINI DUX incised in the solid barrel, remembering epic battles and cowboy show-downs in the back alleys of the Cannaregio. The pistol had been the envy of all his friends, but its connections with the leader whose adventurism had caused his father's death perhaps explained Zen's lifelong reluctance to carry a firearm, or even learn to use one.

He squeezed his way back out of the storeroom with a sigh of relief, as though emerging from a prison cell. The past was always present in the Zen family. Nothing was ever thrown away, and even the dead remained unburied. That man Falco talked a load of pretentious rubbish, of course, but it was easy to see the attractions of his shallow, consumerist credo. Fascism had perhaps offered similar raptures and consolations to the people of his father's generation.

It was ten to seven when he left the house, the replica pistol concealed in his overcoat pocket. The streets were crowded with shoppers and people going home from work or out on the town, and when he emerged into the vacant expanses of St Peter's Square it was like stepping into another city. The throng of pilgrims and their coaches had long since departed, and the only people to be seen were two Carabinieri on patrol. Zen climbed the shallow steps leading up to the façade of St Peter's and passed in under the portico.

Apart from a party of tourists who were just leaving, the basilica seemed as deserted as the piazza outside. Zen walked down the nave to the baldacchino, then turned right into the north transept. Between each of the three chapels stood a curvacious confessional of dully gleaming mahogany which reminded Zen of his mother's wardrobe. There were six in all, but only one showed a light indicating the presence of a confessor. The gold inscription above the entrance read EX ORDINE FRATRVM MINORVM. For a moment Zen hesitated, feeling both ridiculous and slightly irreverent. Then, with a shrug, he approached the recess and knelt down.

It was at least three decades since he had been to confession, but as he felt the wooden step beneath his knees and looked at the grilled opening before his face, the years slipped away and he once again felt that anxious sense of generalized guilt, assuaged by the confidence of possessing a system for dealing with it. So strong were these sensations that he was on the point of intoning 'Forgive me, Father, for I have sinned' when a voice from the other side of the grille recalled him to the realities of his present situation.

'Can you hear me, dottore?'

Zen cleared his throat.

'Only just.'

'I prefer not to speak too loudly. Our enemies are everywhere.'

It was the man who had phoned him earlier at the Ministry.

'You are probably wondering why you have been summoned at such short notice, and in this unusual fashion. I shall be frank. Many people think of the Curia as a monolith expressing a single, unified point of view. This is not surprising, since we spend a considerable amount of time and trouble cultivating just such an impression. Nevertheless, it is a fallacy. To take the present instance, considerable differences exist over the handling of the Ruspanti affair. There have been some heated exchanges. I represent a group who believe that the issues at stake here are too serious to be swept under the carpet. If our arguments had been rejected by the Holy Father, we should of course have submitted. We have in fact repeatedly urged that the matter be placed before him, but on each occasion we have been overruled. The decision to cover up the truth about the Ruspanti case has been taken by a small number of senior officials acting on their own initiative.'

Zen glanced at the grille, but the interior of the confessional was so dark that he could not make out anything of the speaker.

'What have you been told about the Cabal?' the man asked abruptly.

Zen cleared his throat.

'That according to Ruspanti there was an inner group within the Order . . .'

'Speak up, please! I'm rather hard of hearing.'

Zen raised his mouth to the grille.

'I was told that Ruspanti claimed that there was an inner group within the Order of Malta known as the Cabal. These claims were investigated and found to be false.'

'Nothing more?'

'*Is* there more?'

The response was a low chuckle which sent a shiver up Zen's spine.

'Both more and less. Some of what you've been told is true, but the manner of its telling has been deliberately designed to mislead you into discounting it and concentrating your efforts elsewhere. Certainly Ludovico Ruspanti approached us with allegations about a secret society within the Order of Malta, of whom he was himself of course a distinguished member, and with whom he had taken refuge before we gave him sanctuary. We had received similar information before, but this was the first emanating from an authoritative source and which offered the possibility of verification. Ruspanti claimed to be able to provide names, dates and full documentation. Relations between the Holy See and the Order of Malta have been strained for some time . . .'

The man's voice faded under a ululating howl which seemed to come from inside the confessional. It grew quickly louder until it was deafening, then gradually faded to nothing.

'What was *that*?' asked Zen.

'What?'

'That noise.'

'I heard nothing. As I was saying, relations between the Holy See and the Order of Malta have been strained for some time, but our first reaction was indeed one of suspicion. To our dismay, however, our preliminary investigations substantiated every single claim which Ruspanti had made. Far from finding his allegations baseless or false, we uncovered evidence of the most alarming kind. I hasten to add that these findings did not in any way implicate the Order of Malta as a whole, which is and has always been an admirable body, tireless in its charitable exertions and unwavering in its loyalty to the papacy. The Cabal is something quite different, a parasitic clique, a sinister inner coterie hidden within the ranks of a respectable organization, like Gelli's P2 within the Masonic Order.'

The voice fell silent. For a moment, Zen thought he heard the rustling of paper.

'You may remember the Oliver North scandal in the United States,' the man continued. 'A small group of influential people in the Reagan administration decided that there were actions which needed to be taken, actions which the President would certainly approve, inasmuch as they were logical developments of his avowed policies, but whose existence and implementation he could not afford to know about. These men therefore decided to take matters into their own hands, since Reagan's were tied by his constitutional and legal obligations.'

Hearing footsteps behind him, Zen looked round. One of the blue-jacketed attendants wearing the red leather badge of the basilica staff was passing on his rounds. He glanced briefly at the kneeling peni-tent, but with no more than the usual impersonal curiosity which anyone might feel, wondering what secrets were being divulged in muttered undertones. Zen shifted his position slightly. His knees were beginning to ache.

'The idea behind the Cabal is very similar,' the man went on. 'In short, they believe they know what the Holy Father wants better than he does himself – or at any rate, better than he can afford to express openly. Like many of us, they are disturbed by the decline in church attendance and in the numbers presenting themselves for the priest-hood, and by the rampant hedonism and materialism of society today. Wojtyla's early life was dominated by the struggle against a godless ideology, but he has come to feel that we now face an even more implacable foe than Communism. The sufferings of the Church in Poland and elsewhere ultimately served to strengthen the faith of believers. But what the Communists failed to destroy with force and terror is now in danger of decaying through sheer apathy and neglect.'

Zen emitted a grunt, of pain rather than agreement. Had some malicious cleric selected this rendezvous as a way of making him appreciate his place in the Vatican's scheme of things?

'In this situation, it is inevitable that some people should cast envi-ous glances at the very different situation in the Muslim world. While our young people seem to think of nothing but the instant gratifica-tions of a materialist society, theirs are gripped with a religious fer-vour of undeniable intensity, for which they are prepared both to die and to kill. While our cities are flooded with drugs and pornography, theirs are rigorously patrolled by religious police with summary powers of arrest and punishment. And while the authority of our leaders, including the Holy Father himself, is challenged on all sides, a single pronouncement by one of theirs is sufficient to force a celebrated writer to go to ground like a Mafia supergrass. Can you doubt that there are those of us who are nostalgic for the days when our Church was also capable of compelling respect, by force if necessary? Of *course* there are!'

Once again the brief pause, the slight rustle of paper. Was the man reading a prepared text?

'But while some may idly regret an era which has passed for ever, others are scheming to bring it back. These people have noted Wojtyla's effect on the cheering crowds who come to greet him in their hundreds of thousands during his tours of Africa and Latin America. Here is a man who has both the potential and the will to bring about a radical desecularization of society. Naturally the Holy Father cannot be seen to harbour any such ambitions, still less endorse the tactics of destabilization necessary to bring them to fruition. But by his sponsorship of such organizations as Opus Dei and *Comunione e Liberazione*, Wojtyla has made it quite clear in which direction he wishes the Church to move.'

Zen tapped impatiently on the wall of the confessional. It resounded hollowly, like a stage property.

'This is all very interesting,' he remarked in a tone which suggested just the opposite, 'but I'm not a theologian.'

'Neither are the members of the Cabal! Like the original Knights of Malta, from whom they draw their inspiration, they are men of action, men of violence, organized, capable and ruthless. What happened to Ruspanti is proof of that.'

'And what *did* happen?'

'Ruspanti made the mistake of trying to play a double game. On the one hand he was trading information for protection here in the Vatican, doling it out scrap by scrap, feeding us just enough to whet our appetite for what was still to come. He described the structure and aims of the Cabal in general terms, named a few of the minor players and hinted that under the right circumstances he would be prepared to identify the leaders, including well-known figures in the political, industrial, financial and military worlds. At the same time, he was also trying to put pressure on the Cabal itself, threatening to expose them if they didn't meet his terms. That was a mistake which proved to be fatal. Last Friday he was summoned to a meeting with two senior representatives of the Cabal, here in St Peter's, and . . .'

Zen wasn't listening. He had just realized why his mother's absence from home had seemed so oddly disturbing. When this man had phoned him at the Ministry, he claimed to have tried Zen's home number and been told he was at work. That was a lie. There had been no one at home to answer the phone. The deception was trivial, but it altered Zen's whole attitude towards this faceless informant. No longer did he feel constrained or deferential. He felt rude and sassy. His knees were killing him, and he was going to get even.

'. . . that the Cabal is everywhere, even within the Curia,' the man was saying. 'Any opposition to their aims, any threat to their secrecy, is punished by instant death.'

'If they're so clever, why haven't they found the transcript of Ruspanti's phone calls?' demanded Zen.

There was silence in the confessional.

'Grimaldi had it, so they killed him,' Zen went on. 'But they didn't find it.'

'How do you know?'

'Because I did.'

It was a shot in the dark, but he had nothing to lose. The urgent tremor in the speaker's voice revealed that it had gone home.

'You have the transcript?'

There was a sudden eruption of sound, as though a bomb had gone off.

'Hello?' cried the voice. 'Are you still there?'

Now the source of the noise was visible: a rack of spotlamps being lowered from their position high above the south transept.

'Yes, I'm here,' said Zen.

Why couldn't the man see him?

'Where is the transcript?'

'Where Grimaldi hid it. It was I who discovered his body, and I had time to search his room before the Carabinieri got there. Someone else had been there too, but they didn't know what to look for.'

Beyond the grille, the confessional was as silent as the grave.

'Among Grimaldi's belongings was a red plastic diary,' Zen continued. 'It was for the new year, so it was mostly empty, but he had noted down a series of letters and numbers that leads straight to the transcript, assuming you know where to look.'

'And where's that?'

Zen laughed teasingly.

'Have you told anyone else where it is?' the man demanded.

'Not yet. It's hard to know who to tell, with so many conflicting interests involved.'

There was a considerable silence.

'Naturally you want to do the right thing,' the voice suggested more calmly.

'Naturally.'

Again the man fell silent.

'This revelation changes everything,' he said at last. 'This is not the time or place to discuss it further, but I do urge you most strongly to take no further action of any kind until we contact you again.'

'Wait a minute,' Zen replied. 'I don't even know who you are. Suppose you step out of there and let me see your face.'

The sinister chuckle sounded again.

'I'm afraid that's not possible, dottore.'

Zen took the fake pistol from his pocket. He had been right to bring it after all.

'You're taking a big chance,' he warned the man. 'Supposing I decide to let someone else have the transcript instead?'

'But how would you know it *was* someone else? You know nothing about us.'

One hand gripping the wooden railing, Zen raised himself pain-fully to a crouching position. Then he straightened up, gritting his teeth against the fierce aching of his knees. The revolver in one hand, he swept aside the heavy curtain covering the entrance to the confessional.

'I do now!' he cried.

He gazed wildly around. There was no one there. Then he heard the low chuckling once again. It was coming from a small two-way radio suspended from a nail which had been driven into the wall of the confessional, just below the grille.

'You know nothing about us,' the voice repeated. 'Nothing at all.'

5

Ever since his transfer to the capital from Naples, Aurelio Zen had travelled to and from work by bus. His removal from active duty at the Questura at the time of the Aldo Moro kidnapping had had no effect on this, since the Ministry of the Interior – where he had been allocated a menial desk job – was only a few blocks from police headquarters. Even the opening of the new underground railway line had not induced him to change his habits, despite the fact that the terminus at Ottaviano was only a few blocks from his house, and the Termini stop a short walk from the Ministry. But experience showed that twenty minutes in the tunnels of the Metropolitana A left Zen's day spavined before it had even begun. The bus journey was by no means an unrelieved joy, but at least it took place in a real city rather than that phantasmagoric subterranean realm of dismal leaky caverns which might equally well be in London, or New York – or indeed the next century.

Tania Biacis had changed Zen's habits in this respect, as in so many others. They spent about three nights a week together, absences which Zen explained to his mother in terms of overtime or trips away from Rome. But whether Zen had slept at the flat or not, he and Tania travelled to work together by taxi every morning. It was yet another aspect of the new arrangement which was costing a small fortune, but it seemed worth it just to have that precious interval of time with Tania before they separated to go about their different jobs at the Ministry. He was perfectly willing to pay, Zen reflected as his taxi crossed Ponte Cavour on the way to Tania's that Thursday morning. The problem was his ability.

The simple fact was that he could no longer go on supporting two households in this kind of style, and what was the point in doing it if not in style? Mistresses were not something you could get on the cheap, any more than champagne or caviar. They were a luxury, a self-indulgence for the rich. If you couldn't afford them, you had to do without. Zen couldn't do without Tania, but it was becoming clear that he couldn't really afford her either – unless he found some way of making a large sum of money overnight. As the taxi turned right along the embankment of the Tiber, he found himself wondering idly how much the transcript of Ruspanti's phone calls would fetch, assuming that his intuition about the hiding-place proved correct.

The idea was absurd, of course! He couldn't contemplate making a personal profit from a piece of evidence which would presumably make it possible to bring the murderers of Ludovico Ruspanti and Grimaldi to justice. Of course, a cynic might argue that there was no chance of the murderers being brought to justice anyway, if the issues involved in the case were anywhere near as extensive as they appeared to be. Such a cynic – or a realist, as he would no doubt prefer to be called – might claim that in this particular case, as in so many others, justice was simply *not an option*, and to pretend otherwise was mere wishful thinking masquerading as idealism. In reality, there were only two possible outcomes. Zen could sell the transcript, thereby solving all his problems, or he could create a host of new problems for himself by setting in motion a major scandal with repercussions at every level of society. A rational man, the realist might well conclude, should be in no doubt which course to choose.

The taxi drew up in the narrow street, scarcely wider than an alley, where Tania lived. Almost at once the door opened and she appeared. It was a measure of what was happening to them that while Zen would once have been glad of a promptitude which allowed them a few extra minutes together, he now wondered whether she was anxious to prevent him seeing who was in the flat.

'I phoned Tullio,' she said, slipping in beside him with a seemingly guileless kiss. 'He sounded very keen. He'll see you this morning at his office in EUR.'

'What time?'

'About ten,' he said.

'Did you tell him who I was?'

'Of course not! As far as he knows, you're just a high-ranking colleague of mine at the Ministry who needs a favour done. Not that Tullio would care. He's made a pass or two at me himself, if it comes to that.'

Zen inspected her.

'And did it?'

She sighed.

'Give me a break, Aurelio!'

It was a windless grey morning, humid and close. The taxi was now wedged into the flank of the phalanx of traffic on Corso Vittorio Emanuele. Zen patted her knee.

'Sorry.'

She flashed him a smile.

'Shall we eat out tonight?'

He nodded.

'I'll be out till about eight,' she said. 'Perhaps we could try that Chinese place behind Piazza Navona.'

Zen grunted unenthusiastically. Oriental cuisine, the latest Roman craze, left him cold. The food was excellent, but it seemed to him an exoticism as irrelevant to his life as Buddhism. The way he looked at it, you were either a Catholic or an atheist. There was no point in shopping around for odd doctrines, however original, nor eating odd food, however delicious.

The taxi dropped Tania first, at the corner of Via Venezia and Via Palermo, then drove round to the other side of the Ministry, where Zen paid it off. Lorenzo Moscati's jibes had made it clear that their efforts to keep the affair secret had been a failure, but there was still a difference between accepting that people knew what was going on and flaunting it in their faces. The porter ticked Zen's name off in the ON TIME column of his massive ledger.

'Oh, dottore! They want to see you up in Personnel.'

Zen rode the lift up to the office on the fourth floor where Franco Ciliani, a tiny balding tyrant given to Etna-like eruptions of temper, presided over the thankless task of trying to complete the jigsaw of staff allocation when over half the pieces were missing at any one time.

'What are you doing here?' he demanded as Zen appeared.

'Ciccillo said you wanted to see me.'

'That's not what I mean! As far as I'm concerned, you're in Milan.'

Zen gestured a comically excessive apology.

'Sorry, but I'm not, as you see.'

Ciliani gave a brutal shrug.

'I don't give a damn where you are in reality. That's entirely your affair. I'm talking about what's down on the roster, and that tells me you're in Milan. So when I get a call yesterday asking why you haven't turned up, I naturally wonder what the hell.'

'Who did you speak to?'

651

Ciliani made a half-hearted attempt to locate something in the chaos of papers on his desk.

'Shit. Sermonelli? Something like that.'

'Simonelli?'

'That's it. Antonia Simonelli.'

'Yesterday?' queried Zen, ignoring the little matter of Simonelli's gender.

'That's right. Real ball-breaker. You know what the Milanese are like.'

'There must be some mistake. Simonelli's here in Rome. We met yesterday.'

'I said you'd be there by tomorrow at the latest.'

'But I just told you . . .'

'Told me?' demanded Ciliani. 'You told me nothing. We aren't even having this conversation.'

'What do you mean?'

Ciliani sighed deeply.

'Look, you're in Milan, right? I'm in Rome. So how can I be talking to you? It must be a hallucination. Probably the after-effects of that fever you had.'

Zen stared up at the fault-line of a huge crack running from one end of the ceiling to the other.

'When did the original notification come through?'

Ciliani consulted his schedule.

'Monday.'

'I was off sick on Monday.'

He suddenly saw what must have happened. Simonelli had summoned Zen to Milan on Monday, then decided to come to Rome himself to investigate Grimaldi's continuing silence. He had then got in touch with Zen direct, but presumably his secretary in Milan – the officious woman Ciliani had spoken to – had not been informed of this, and was still trying to complete the earlier arrangement.

'Fine!' said Ciliani. 'I'll give Milan a call and explain that your departure was unavoidably delayed due to medical complications, but you have since made a swift and complete recovery and will be with them tomorrow. Speaking of which, it's tough about Carlo, eh?'

'What?'

'Romizi, Carlo Romizi.'

'Oh, you mean his stroke? Yes, it's . . .'

'Haven't you heard the news?'

'What news?'

Ciliani stuck his finger in his ear and extracted a gob of wax which he scrutinized as though deciding whether to eat it.

'He went last night.'

'Went? Went where?'

Ciliani looked at him queerly

'Died.'

'No!'

Such was the emotion in Zen's voice that Ciliani lowered his voice and said apologetically, 'Excuse me, dottore, I didn't know you were close.'

We are now, thought Zen. Trembling with shock, he left Ciliani and joined the human tide which was beginning to flow in the opposite direction, as those dedicated members of staff who had reported for duty on time rewarded their efficiency by popping out for a coffee and a bite to eat at one of the numerous bars which spring up in the vicinity of any government building like brothels near a port. Zen scandalized the barman by ordering a *caffè corretto*, espresso laced with grappa, a perfectly acceptable early-morning drink in the Veneto but unheard of in Rome.

He stood sipping the heady mixture and gazing sightlessly at the season's fixture list for the Lazio football club. From time to time he took a stealthy peek at the idea which had leapt like a ghoul from the grave when Ciliani gave him the news of Carlo Romizi's death. It didn't go away. On the contrary, every time he glanced at it – surreptitiously, like a child in bed at the menacing shadows on the ceiling – it looked more substantial, more certain.

The pay-phone in the bar was one of the old models that only accepted tokens. Zen bought two thousand lire's worth from the cashier and ensconced himself in the narrow passage between the toilet and a broken ice-cream freezer. A selection of coverless, broken-spined telephone directories sprawled on top of the freezer. Zen looked up the number of the San Giovanni hospital. The first four times he dialled, it was engaged, and when he finally did get through the number rang for almost five minutes and was then answered by a receptionist who had taken charm lessons from a pit bull terrier. But she was no match for a man with twenty-five years' experience as a professional bully, and Zen was speedily put through to the doctor he had spoken to the week before.

All went well until Zen mentioned Romizi's name, when the doctor suddenly lost his tone of polite detachment.

'Listen, I've had enough of this! Understand? Enough!'

'But I . . .'

'She's put you up to this, hasn't she?'

'I'm simply . . .'

'I refuse to be harried and persecuted in this fashion! If it continues, I shall take legal advice. The woman is mad!'

'Please understand that . . .'

'In a case of this kind prognosis is always speculative, for the very good reason that a complete analysis is only possible post-mortem. I naturally sympathize with the widow's grief, but to imply that the negligence of I or my staff in any way contributed to her husband's death is slanderous nonsense. There were no unusual developments in the case, the outcome was perfectly consistent with the previous case-history. If Signora Romizi proceeds with this campaign of harassment, she will find herself facing charges of criminal libel. Good day!'

There were two columns of Romizis in the phone book, so Zen got the number from the Ministry switchboard. Carlo's sister Francesca answered. Having conveyed his condolences, Zen asked if it would be possible to speak to Signora Romizi.

'Anna's just gone to sleep.'

'It must have been a terrible shock for her.'

'We've both found it very hard. They'd warned us that Carlo might not recover, but you never really think it will happen. He had seemed better in the last few . . .'

Her voice broke.

'I'm sorry to distress you further,' Zen said. 'It's just that I heard from someone at work that Signora Romizi felt that the hospital hadn't done everything they might to save Carlo.'

There was no reply.

'I was wondering if I could do anything to help.'

'It's kind of you.' Francesca's voice was bleak. 'The problem is that Anna is finding it hard to accept what has happened, so she's taking it out on the people there. And of course there's plenty to complain about. Carlo had a bed in a corridor, along with about thirty other patients, some of them gravely ill. There are vermin, cockroaches and ants everywhere. The kitchen staff walked out last week after some junkie's relatives held them up at gun point, and the patients might have starved if the relatives hadn't got together and provided sandwiches and rolls. That's on top of taking all the sheets home to wash, of course. Meanwhile when the politicians get ill, they go to the Villa Stuart clinic and get looked after by German nuns!'

'If it's not too painful, could you tell me what actually happened?'

Francesca sighed.

'We had been taking it in turns to sit up with Carlo round the clock, so that there would always be a familiar face there at his bedside if he regained consciousness. Last night it was Anna's turn to stay up. She says she dozed off in her chair and some time in the middle of the night a noise woke her. She sat up to find a doctor standing by the bed, someone she had never seen before. He seemed to be adjusting the controls of the life-support apparatus. When Anna asked him what he was doing, he left without . . .'

Francesca Romizi's quiet voice vanished as though the barman pointing his remote control unit at Zen had changed the channel of his life. From the huge television set mounted on a shelf at the entrance to the passage, the commentary and crowd noises of a football match which had taken place in Milan the previous evening boomed out to engulf the bar.

'Can you speak up?' Zen urged the receiver.

'. . . grew light . . . cold and pale . . . nurse was . . . told her . . .'

High on the wall above the telephone was a black fuse-box. Standing on tiptoe, Zen reached for the mains cut-out. As abruptly as it had started, the clamour of the television ceased again, to be replaced by the groans of the staff and clientele.

'Not again!'

'This is the tenth time this month!'

'I'm not paying my electricity bill! They can do what they like, send me to prison, anything! I'm not paying!'

'The government should step in!'

'Rubbish! The abuse of political patronage is the reason we don't have a viable infrastructure in the first place.'

Zen covered one ear with his hand and pressed the other to the receiver.

'I'm sorry, I missed that.'

'I said, Anna thinks that the doctor who tampered with the electronic equipment was some intern, not properly trained. She's threatening to sue the hospital for negligence.'

Zen struggled to keep his voice steady.

'Have you any evidence?'

'Well, they haven't been able to identify the doctor concerned so far. But Anna could have dreamed the whole thing, or even invented it to relieve her guilt at the fact that she had been sleeping while Carlo died. Such strong emotions are unleashed at these moments that really anything is possible.'

Zen asked Francesca to convey his profoundest sympathy to Signora Romizi and offered to help in any way he could. As he replaced the receiver with one hand, he reached for the mains switch with the other, and the bar sprang to rowdy life again.

Back at the counter, Zen consumed a second coffee, this time without additives. Like Francesca Romizi, but for very different reasons, he was sceptical about the idea of negligence on the part of the hospital staff. Carlo's death had no more been an accident than Giovanni Grimaldi's. From the moment Zen used his name in an unsuccessful attempt to access the Ministry's 'closed' file on the Cabal, Carlo Romizi had been doomed. No wonder the hospital had been unable to trace the mysterious doctor who had visited his bedside in the small hours of the night. There was no doctor, only a killer in a white coat.

The demonstrable absurdity of this response merely guaranteed its authenticity. The comatose Romizi, utterly dependent on a life-support system, could not conceivably have been responsible for the electronic prying carried out in his name at the Ministry the night before. His death had been intended to serve as a message to Aurelio Zen. The Cabal had of course seen through Zen's feeble attempt at disguise, but they had gone ahead and killed Romizi anyway, knowing that he had nothing whatever to do with it. It was a masterstroke of cynical cruelty, calculated not only to strike terror into Zen's heart but also to cripple him with remorse. For it was he who had condemned Carlo Romizi to death. If Zen had chosen another name, or used his own, the Umbrian would still be alive.

These reflections were much in Zen's mind as he arrived at the ponderous block in Piazza dell'Indipendenza which housed the consulate of a minor South American republic, three *pensioni* patronized largely by American backpackers, a cut-price dental surgery, a beauty salon, and the headquarters of Paragon Security Consultants. Zen was still too shocked by the reality of what had happened to work out the long-term implications, but of one thing he was absolutely determined. The file which had cost Carlo Romizi his life was going to give up its secrets. If that part of the database was 'closed', then he would break in. Zen had no idea how to do this, but he felt sure that Gilberto Nieddu would know someone who did.

Gilberto at first seemed something less than enchanted to see his friend.

'No!' he cried as Zen walked in. 'No, no, no, no, no, no, no, no!'

'I haven't said anything yet.'

'I don't care! Jesus, last time I agree to look at a faulty water heater for you, and what happens? Not only do I end up having to tear-gas the Carabinieri and then risk my neck escaping across the rooftops, but when I get home my wife assaults me with the pasta rolling-pin, accusing me of having another woman on the side! Well that *was* the last time, Aurelio, the very last! From now on . . .'

Zen got out his cigarettes and offered them to Nieddu, who ignored the gesture.

'I'm really sorry about that, Gilberto. You see, I'd told my mother I was in Florence so that I could spend a few nights with a friend. We should all get together some time. You'd like her. She's called Tania and . . .'

'Oh I see! You sin and I pay the price.'

'I'll explain to Rosella . . .'

'If she thinks that I've buddy-buddied you into covering up for me, she'll kill us both.'

'All right then, I'll get *Tania* to call her.'

'She'd assume that she was my mistress, pretending to be yours. Can you imagine what Rosella would do if she thought I'd tried to con her like that? Sardinian girls learn how to castrate pigs when they're five years old. And they don't forget.'

Zen blew a cloud of smoke at the rows of box-files and tape containers stacked on the shelves.

'She'll get over it, Gilberto. It might even be a good thing in the end. There's nothing like jealousy to liven up a marriage.'

'Spare me the pearls of wisdom, Aurelio. I'm up to my eyes in work.'

He bent ostentatiously over a blueprint of an office building which was spread out across his desk.

'I need to see some classified information held in a computer database,' said Zen.

Nieddu unstoppered an orange highlight pen and marked a feature on the plan.

'I was wondering how you'd go about that,' Zen went on.

'Who runs the computer?' asked Nieddu without looking up.

'The Ministry.'

The Sardinian shot him a quick glance.

'But you have clearance to that.'

'Not this part.'

Nieddu shook his head and pored over the blueprint again.

'I know someone who can do it. It'll cost you, though.'

'That's no problem. But it's urgent. I have to go up to Milan on the early train tomorrow, and I need to set it up before leaving. What's the address?'

'I'll run you out there before lunch.'

'I don't want to put you to any more trouble, Gilberto.'

Nieddu gave him a peculiar smile.

'You'd never find the place,' he said. 'And anyway, you don't just turn up. You have to be *presented*.'

The new metro was going to be wonderful when it was finished, but then Romans had been saying that about one grandiose and disruptive construction project or another ever since Nero set about rebuilding the city after the disastrous fire of July 64. The national pastime of *dietrologia*, 'the facts behind the facts', was also well established by that time, and many people held that the blaze had been started deliberately so as to facilitate the Emperor's redevelopment scheme. Nero's response to these scurrilous rumours of state terrorism had an equally familiar ring. The whole affair was blamed on an obscure and unpopular sect of religious fanatics influenced by foreign ideologies such as monotheism and millennialism. One of the victims of the resulting campaign of persecution was a Jewish fisherman named Simon Peter, who was crucified in the Imperial Circus and buried near by, in a tomb hollowed out of the flank of the Vatican hill.

This stirring historical perspective, far from inspiring Aurelio Zen to a sense of wonder and pride, merely intensified his oppressive conviction that nothing ever changed. Being stuck for twenty minutes at Garbatella station because of a signalling fault hadn't exactly helped his mood. The work in progress to integrate the grubby old Ostia railway into the revamped Metropolitana B line to EUR had resulted in the partial paralysis of services on both. Nevertheless, it would be wonderful when it was finished – until it started to fall apart like the A line, which had been open for less than a decade and already looked and smelt like a blocked sewer.

The short walk to the office where Tullio Bevilacqua worked helped restore Zen's spirits, although he wouldn't have dreamed of admitting this to anyone. For both political and aesthetic reasons, it was wholly unacceptable to admire the monumental EUR complex, conceived in the late thirties for a world fair designed to show off the achievements of Fascist Italy. The war put an end to the project for an *Esposizione Universale di Roma*, but the architectural investment survived and, as usual in Rome, was recycled for purposes quite different from that intended by its creator.

The resulting complex – the only example of twentieth-century urban planning attempted in the capital since the First World War – had a freakish, hallucinogenic appearance at once monumental and two-dimensional, like a film set designed by Giorgio de Chirico for a production by Dino de Laurentiis. The vast rectangular blocks of white masonry evenly distributed along either side of the broad straight thoroughfares locked together at right angles created a succession of perspectives which seemed designed to demonstrate and also subvert the laws of perspective. Despite the crushing scale and geometric regularity, the effect was curiously insubstantial, abstract and ethereal, diametrically opposed both to the poky confines of the old city centre and to the sprawling jumble of the unplanned *borgate* on the outskirts.

Tullio Bevilacqua looked like a caricature of his brother, the same features exaggerated into an extravagance larger than life. Tullio was not just overweight but grossly fat. His balding scalp was beaded with sweat, his nose glistened with grease, his moustache bristled and curled in anarchic abandon. Seeing him, Zen felt his first twinge of sympathy for fastidious, pedantic Mauro.

Zen introduced himself as Luigi Borsellino and outlined the cover story which he had prepared.

'The case is still *sub judice*, but without going into details I can tell you that it concerns a drug-smuggling ring which has been bringing in heroin in consignments of tinned tuna from Thailand destined for the Vatican supermarket. Such goods are exempt from inspection by our customs officials, of course. The box containing the hot tuna is then moved across the unguarded frontier into Italy for distribution.'

Bevilacqua raised his eyebrows and whistled. Zen nodded.

'The problem is that the resulting scandal would be so damaging for the Vatican that unless we go to them with a watertight case they might try and hush it up. What we're doing at the moment is assembling a jigsaw of apparently unrelated pieces, one of which consists of some papers which we believe may be concealed in the Archives. But since we're not liaising officially with the Vatican, we have no way of getting at them. That's why your assistance would be invaluable – if you would be prepared to collaborate.'

He needn't have worried. Tullio Bevilacqua was one of those men who are fascinated by police work. He clearly felt thrilled and privileged at the idea of becoming a part of this investigation, even on the basis of such a flimsy briefing. Zen had been prepared for awkward questions and hard bargaining, but Tullio had no more intention of quibbling about the details than a small boy who has been invited on to the footplate by the engine driver will stop to ask where the train is going.

'We believe that the papers have been concealed in or near the document filed under this reference,' Zen explained.

He passed Bevilacqua a card on which he had written the sequence of numbers and letters which Giovanni Grimaldi had noted in his diary.

'Do we know what it looks like?' asked the new recruit.

What a thrill that 'we' gave him!

'It's probably a number of typed pages, possibly with a printed heading of some sort to make it look official. In any case, it should stand out like a sore thumb in the middle of all those mediaeval manuscripts. Don't worry about the contents. The information we need will be coded. Just get us the document and we'll take care of the rest.'

Zen hoped that Grimaldi would have had the sense to remove any reference to Ruspanti on the cover of the transcript, and that the document itself would conform to the standard practice, identifying the telephone numbers involved rather than the speakers' names. At any rate, Tullio Bevilacqua gave every impression of having been convinced by the story Zen had told him, and promised to do what he could to help. He gave Zen his home phone number and told him to ring between seven and eight that evening.

At the intersection just beyond offices of the *assessorato alla cultura*, four sets of converging façades combined to produce a perspective of vertiginous symmetry. Zen stood motionless at the kerb, gazing at the seemingly endless vistas on every side. In the even pearly light, the outlines of the buildings appeared to blur and merge into the expanse of the sky. It was impossible to say how much time passed before the metallic grey Lancia Thema screeched to a halt beside him.

'Hop in,' said Gilberto Nieddu.

The Sardinian had changed out of the jeans and polo-neck he had been wearing earlier that morning into a sleek suit with matching tie and display handkerchief.

'You look like a pimp at a wedding,' Zen told him sourly as they

swept off along the broad central boulevard running the length of
EUR.

'I've got an important lunch coming up,' explained Nieddu. 'It's all
very well for you, Aurelio. You can wear any old tat. In business, if you
want to be rich and successful you have to look like you already are.'

Zen flushed indignantly. His suits came from an elderly tailor in
Venice who had once supplied his father. They might not be in the
latest style, but they were sober, durable, well-cut and of excellent
cloth. To hear them denigrated was like hearing someone speak ill of
a friend.

'You sound like that jerk I saw on television yesterday,' he retorted.
'He claims that you are what you wear.'

'Falco?' exclaimed Nieddu. 'He's a genius.'

'What!'

'Well he's done all right for himself, hasn't he? Which reminds me,
have you got the cash?'

'Of course I've got it.'

The envelope containing the five fifty-thousand-lire notes was safely
lodged in his jacket pocket. At this rate he was going to be broke by the
New Year. They left the confines of EUR and drove along a road whose
original vocation as a winding country lane was still perceptible
despite the encroaching sprawl of concrete towers and jerry-built
shacks which continually spilt across it. Nieddu punched the buttons
of the radio without finding anything which satisfied him.

'Want to hear a joke?' he said. 'This priest is playing bowls with the
village drunk. Every time the drunk misses his shot, he yells, "Jesus
wept!" "Don't take Our Lord's name in vain," the priest tells him.
Next shot, the drunk is wide again. "Jesus wept!" "If you blaspheme
like that, God will strike you dead," warns the priest. They
play again, again the drunk misses. "Jesus wept!" Sure enough, a
black thundercloud covers the sky, a bolt of lightning sizzles down
and strikes dead . . . the priest. And from the heavens comes a
tremendous cry, "*Jesus wept!*"'

Nieddu turned off on to a dirt track running through an enclave of
shacks and shanties to the right of the tarred road. The Lancia
bumped over dried mud ruts and a collapsed culvert. Three toddlers
standing on a rusty pick-up perched on concrete blocks watched
solemnly as they passed by. Just before the track turned left to rejoin
the road, Nieddu stopped the car.

Like its neighbours, the house at the corner had apparently been cobbled together out of materials scavenged from other jobs. The walls were formed from breeze-blocks, roof tiles, bricks of varying shape and shade, and sections of concrete and tile piping, all stuck together with plenty of rough thick cement. The property seemed to have grown organically, like a souk, further sections being added as and when required. Some of these were roofed with tiles, others with corrugated iron or asbestos sheeting, one with a sagging tarpaulin. There were few windows, and one of these, its wooden frame painted a lurid shade of puce, was nailed to the outside of the wall, presumably for decorative effect. The house was surrounded by a large expanse of bare earth, every growing thing having been consumed by the pigs and goats which roamed the property freely except for a small fenced-off area of kitchen garden. The entire lot was surrounded by a mesh fence against which two savage-looking mongrels were hurling themselves, their fangs bared at the intruders.

Nieddu locked the car, having first set and tested an alarm which briefly silenced the dogs. As he and Zen walked up to the gate they renewed their aggressive clamour, only to be stilled again, this time by a voice from inside the house. The front door opened and a shapeless, ageless creature appeared on the step. It was wearing a long robe of bright yellow silk, a crimson sash and a tiara set with green, blue and red stones.

Gilberto Nieddu raised his right hand in a gesture of salutation.

'Peace be with you, signora!'

'And with you.'

The voice was loud, coarse, hopelessly at odds with the archaic formulas of greeting.

'We would fain speak with him that abideth here, yea, even with Mago,' intoned Gilberto in a fruity tone, before adding prosaically, 'I phoned earlier this morning.'

The figure screamed incomprehensible abuse at the dogs, who looked as though they might burst into tears at any moment, and slunk off to the rear of the property. Gilberto opened the gate and led the way across the yard to the door where the robed figure stood to one side, gesturing to them to enter.

The interior of the house was cool and dark and smelt strongly of animal odours. They walked along a passage which twisted and turned past a succession of open doorways. In one room a young man stripped to his underpants lay asleep on an unmade bed, in another an elderly man pored over a newspaper with a magnifying glass, in a third two teenagers wearing crinkly black acrylic shell suits with bold coloured panels sat watching a television set on top of which a cockerel perched, watching them in turn.

The next doorway was covered by a heavy velvet curtain.

'Make ready your offering,' hissed their guide.

Nieddu nudged Zen, who produced the envelope containing a quarter of a million lire. A plump hand appeared, its slug-like fingers bedecked with an assortment of jewelled rings, and the envelope vanished into the folds of the yellow robe.

'Wait here while I intercede with Mago, that he may suffer you to enter in unto him.'

The creature drew back one edge of the curtain a little, releasing an overpowering whiff of fetor, and slipped inside. The curtain dropped into place again.

'My grandfather used to move his bowels first thing every morning,' Nieddu remarked conversationally. 'Afterwards, he'd inspect the result carefully, then go outside and eat the appropriate herb or vegetable, raw, with the dirt still on it. He lived to be a hundred and four. He saw Garibaldi once.'

There were muffled voices from behind the curtain, which twitched aside to reveal the robed figure.

'Mago is graciously pleased to grant your request for an audience.'

As the two men stepped inside, the curtain fell shut behind them, leaving them in a darkness which was total except for a glow emanating from the far side of the room. Nauseating odours of unwashed flesh, stale sweat and spilt urine made the air almost unbreathable. As Zen's eyes gradually adjusted, he made out the reclining figure bathed in the toneless radiance.

'Hi, Gilberto!'

'Nicolo! How's it going?'

Nieddu put his arm around Zen, forcing him forwards.

'Let me introduce a friend of mine. This is Aurelio. Aurelio, meet Nicolo.'

Propped up in bed lay a teenage boy with delicate features, flawless pale skin and fine dark hair. His big expressive eyes rested briefly on Zen, and his slender hand stirred in welcome from the keyboard where it had been resting. A length of coiled wire connected the keyboard to a stack of electronic equipment on a table beside the bed. On an old chest of drawers at the foot of the bed stood a video screen.

'Aurelio's got rather an amusing little puzzle for you,' said Nieddu.

'Oh goody!' the boy cried gleefully. 'It's been a bit boring lately. Is it like that one I did for you last month, Gilberto, the one where you wanted to find out how much money . . . ?'

'No, no,' Nieddu interrupted, 'it's nothing to do with that at all. Aurelio wants to break into a database at the Ministry of the Interior.'

The boy's face fell.

'Government systems are easy peasy.'

Nieddu nudged Zen.

'Tell Nicolo what you want to know, Aurelio.'

Zen was busy trying to block his nasal passages against the pervading stench.

'I want a copy of a confidential file on an organization called the Cabal.'

The supine figure fluttered his fingers over the keyboard like a blind man reading braille.

'Like that?' asked Nicolo.

Zen followed his gaze to the glowing screen, which now read CABAL. He nodded.

'It's in a part of the database which you need special security clearance to get into,' Zen explained. 'The problem is that it's quite urgent. Have you any idea how long it might take?'

Nicolo gave a contemptuous sniff.

'I could get the system on-line while you wait, but if this is restricted-access data that isn't going to help.'

He stared at the screen in silence for a while.

'There are various ways we could do it,' he mused. 'There are probably a few guest passwords left lying around in the system. We might be able to use one of those.'

Zen shook his head.

'How do you mean?'

'Well, let's say some VIP like Craxi comes to visit the place, they'll set up a password customized just for him, for example . . .'

'*Duce*,' suggested Nieddu.

Zen laughed. Bettino Craxi, the leader of the Socialist Party, was notoriously sensitive about comments likening his appearance and style to that of Benito Mussolini. Nicolo paid no attention to the joke.

'Yes, that would do. After the visit, the guest password is supposed to be erased, but half the time people forget and it's left sitting in the control system, waiting to be used. And it's easier to guess a password than you might think. They have to be relatively straightforward, otherwise the designated users can't remember them. Anyway, that's one possibility. Another would be to run a keystroke-capture programme, but if this level is classified then it may be accessed relatively infrequently, so that would take time.'

'I need to know in the next day or two,' Zen told him.

Nicolo nodded.

'In that case, we'd better go in via Brussels. I cracked the EEC system last month. This mate of mine in Glasgow and I had a bet with the Chaos crowd in Hamburg to see which of us could get in there first and leave a rude message for the others to find. We won. From Brussels we can log on to the anti-terrorist data pool, and then access the Ministry from say London or Madrid. That way we circumvent the whole password procedure. If you're on-line from a high-level international source like that, you come in with automatic authorization.'

Zen nodded as if all this made perfect sense.

'Oh, and just one other thing,' he said. 'If you do manage to access this area of the computer, I'd like to see the file on an official named Zen. Aurelio Zen.'

Nieddu looked at him sharply but said nothing.

'Zen,' said Nicolo, spelling the name on the screen. 'I'll get to work on it right away. Give me a ring tomorrow. With any luck I should have something by then.'

Gilberto bent over the bed and handed something to the boy, who slipped it hastily under the covers with a guilty grin as the curtain drew aside again and the robed figure reappeared to usher the visitors out.

Back in the car, Zen burst into the hysterical laughter he had been suppressing. Nieddu grinned as he slalomed the Lancia through the twists and turns of the narrow country road.

'I know, I know! But believe me, Nicolo's the best hacker in Italy, and one of the best in Europe. He's done things for me I didn't believe were possible. And when he says he'll get to work right away, he means exactly that. The boy lives and breathes computers. He's capable of going for forty-eight hours without sleep when he's on the job.'

'But that . . . *thing* in the fancy dress!'

'That's his grandmother. Nicolo was born with a spinal deformity so severe he wasn't expected to live. The family's from a village near Isernia. Nicolo's parents had their hands full working the land and looking after their other seven children, so they handed him over to Adelaide, who'd moved up here to Rome with her other daughter. One of the grandsons was given a computer for Christmas, but he couldn't figure out how to work it properly, so they passed it on to Nicolo. The rest is history.'

'But what's all this Mago business?' demanded Zen.

Nieddu laughed.

'Adelaide thinks the whole thing is a con. Well, what's she supposed to think? Here's this crippled adolescent invalid, never leaves his bed, can't control his bladder, kicks and screams when she tries to change the sheets, yet is supposedly capable of roaming the world at the speed of light, dodging in and out of buildings in Amsterdam, Paris or New York and bringing back accounts, sales figures, medical records or personnel files. I mean *come on*! I'm in the electronics business and even I find it barely credible. What's a sixty-year-old peasant woman from the Molise to make of it all? Yet the punters keep rolling up to the door and pressing bundles of banknotes into her hand! It's a scam, she thinks, but it's a bloody good one. So she's doing her bit to help it along by dressing up like a sorcerer's assistant.'

Zen lit cigarettes for them both.

'What did you give the boy at the end?'

'Butterscotch. It's some sort of speciality from Scotland. This friend of his in Glasgow – they've never met, needless to say – sent him a packet, and now Nicolo can't get enough. I've bought a supply from a specialist shop in Via Veneto and I take him some every time I go.'

They had reached the Via Appia Nuova, and Gilberto turned left, heading back into the city. Zen felt totally disoriented at the sight of the shiny cars and modern shopping centres, as though he'd awakened from a dream more real than the reality which surrounded him.

'So what is this Cabal?' Nieddu said suddenly. 'It was mentioned in that anonymous letter to the papers about the Ruspanti affair, wasn't it? Are you still investigating that?'

'No, this is private enterprise.'

Nieddu glanced at him.

'So what is it?'

'Oh, something to do with the Knights of Malta,' Zen replied vaguely.

Nieddu shook his head.

'Bad news, Aurelio. Bad news.'

'Why do you say that?'

'Well for a start-off, the Knights of Malta work hand in glove with the American Central Intelligence Agency and with our own Secret Services.'

'How do you know that?'

'I get around, Aurelio. I keep my ears open. Now I don't know what you mean by private enterprise, but if you're thinking of trying anything at all risky, I would think again. From what I've heard, some of the stuff the Order of Malta have been involved in, especially in South America, makes Gelli and the P2 look small-time.'

They drove in silence for a while. Zen felt his spirits sink as the city tightened its stranglehold around them once more.

'Like what?' he asked.

'Like funding the Nicaraguan Contras and mixing with Colombian drug barons,' Nieddu replied promptly. 'You remember the bomb which brought down that plane last year, killing a leading member of the Brazilian Indian Rights movement? Every item of luggage had been through a strict security check, except for a diplomatic pouch supposedly carrying documents to one of the Order's consulates.'

Zen forced a laugh.

'Come on, Gilberto! This is like claiming that Leonardo Sciascia was a right-wing stooge because his name is an anagram of CIA, CIA and SS! The Order of Malta is a respectable charity organization.'

Nieddu shrugged.

'It's your life, Aurelio. Just don't blame me if you end up under that train to Milan instead of on it.'

Tania Biacis had said that she wouldn't be home until eight o'clock, so Zen got there at six thirty. This time there were no problems with the electricity, but as he pushed the button of the entry-phone to make sure that the flat was in fact unoccupied, Zen couldn't help recalling the night when Ludovico Ruspanti had died and all the lights went out. As the darkness pressed in on him, Zen had thought of his colleague Carlo Romizi. That association of ideas now seemed sinister and emblematic.

There was no answer from the entry-phone, and the unshuttered windows of the top-floor flat were dark. Zen let himself in and trudged upstairs. On each landing, the front doors of the other apartments emitted tantalizing glints of light and snatches of conversation. Zen ignored them like the covers of books he knew he would never read, his mind on other intrigues, other mysteries. A series of loud raps at the front door of Tania's flat brought no response, so Zen got out the other key and unlocked the door.

Once inside, he turned on the hall light and checked his watch. He had plenty of time to search the flat and then retire to the local bar-cum-pizzeria, run by a friendly Neapolitan couple, before returning at about ten past eight for his dinner date with the unsuspecting Tania. First of all, though, he phoned his mother to make sure that Maria Grazia had packed his suitcase. His train left at seven the next morning, and he didn't want to have to do it when he got home.

'There's a problem!' his mother told him. 'I told Maria Grazia to pack the dark-blue suit but she said she couldn't find it! She wanted to pack the black one or the dark-grey, but I said no, the black is for funerals, God forbid, and the grey one for marriages and First Communions. Only the blue will do, but we can't find it anywhere, I don't know where it's got to . . .'

'I'm wearing it, mamma.'

'. . . unless we find it you won't be able to go. We can't have you appearing at an official function looking less than your best . . .'

'Mamma, I'm wearing the blue suit today!'

669

'. . . so important to make a good impression if you want to get ahead, I always say. People judge you by your clothes, Aurelio, and if you're inappropriately dressed it doesn't matter what you do . . .'

'Mamma!!!'

'. . . watching on television while I was at Lucrezia's yesterday, ever so nice, and talented too! He's written this book called *You Are What You Wear*, which is precisely what I've been trying to say all along, not that anyone ever has me on TV or even listens to me for that . . .'

Zen depressed the rest of the telephone, cutting the connection. He counted slowly to ten, then dialled again.

'Sorry, mamma, we must have got cut off somehow. Listen, apart from the blue suit, is my case packed?'

'All except your suit, yes. We looked everywhere, Maria Grazia and I, but we just couldn't find it. Perhaps it's at the cleaners, I said, but she . . .'

'I've got to go now, mamma. I'll be back late. Don't wait up for me.'

'Oh listen, Aurelio, I almost forgot, someone phoned for you. They were going to ring again tomorrow but I told them you were going to Milan on the early train and they said they needed to speak to you urgently and so they gave me a number you're to ring at seven thirty tonight.'

'Who was it, mamma?'

'I don't remember if he gave a name, but he said it was about something you had for sale. It's not any of the family belongings, I hope?'

Zen felt his heart beating quickly.

'No, no. No, it's just something to do with work. Give me the number.'

He noted down the seven digits and stared at them for some time before setting to work. Like a burglar, he made his way steadily through the flat, turning out drawers and searching cupboards, wardrobes and shelves. He became much better acquainted with Tania's taste in clothes and jewellery, including a number of unfamiliar items bearing designer labels which even Zen had heard of. He had been allowed to see the Falco sweater, but the others had been concealed from him. None, he reckoned, could have cost much less than half a million lire.

As he passed by the extension phone in the hallway, he had an idea. He dialled the Ministry, quoted the Rome number which his mother had passed on, and asked them to find out the subscriber's name and address. Then he went into the kitchen. Spreading an old newspaper over the floor, he lifted the plastic rubbish sack out of its bin and emptied out the contents. When the phone rang, he was on his hands and knees, separating long white worms of cold spaghetti from the whiffy mess in which they were breeding, poring over fish bones, separating scraps of orange peel from the gutted hulks of burst tomatoes. Wiping his hands quickly on a towel, he took the call in the hallway. It was the Ministry with the information he had requested.

'The number is a public call-box, dottore, in the lobby of the Hotel Torlonia Palace. The address is . . .'

'It's all right, I know the address.'

'Very good, dottore. Will that be all?'

Zen closed his eyes.

'No. Contact the Questura and have a man sent round there to watch the phone. He's to take a full description of anyone using it around seven thirty. If the person is a guest, he's to identify him. If not, follow him.'

Back in the kitchen, he resumed his analysis of the mess on the floor. Deep in the ripest purée of all, which had been fermenting for days at the bottom of the sack, he found the first scrap of paper. Gradually he recovered the others, one by one, from a glutinous paste of coffee grounds moistened with the snot of bad egg white. In the end he traced all but two of the sixteen irregular patches into which the sheet had been torn, and carefully pieced it together again on the kitchen counter.

Dear Tania,

It's great news that you can make it on the 27th. Let me know which flight you'll be on and I'll meet you. I have to take my wife to the opera that evening, but we can have lunch and then spend the afternoon together. I'm really looking forward to it.

All the best,
Primo

Zen crunched the fragments into a clammy wodge which he tossed back on to the pile of smelly rubbish. Then he rolled up the sheets of newspaper and stuffed the bundles back into the plastic sack. The 27th was the following Saturday, when Tania claimed she was going back to Udine to spend the weekend with her cousin. When the rubbish was bagged, he opened the window to air out the kitchen. It was just after a quarter past seven, time to find out if his hunch about Giovanni Grimaldi's hiding place for the transcript had been correct. Going back to the living room, he phoned the number Tullio had given him. A girlish voice answered before being silenced by a rather older boy. A brief struggle for the phone ended with a slap and crying.

'Who is it?' asked the victor.

'Luigi Borsellino,' said Zen. 'Let me speak to your dad.'

Cutlery and crockery pinged and jangled distantly above the chatter of a family mealtime, and then a gleeful voice in Zen's ear exclaimed 'I've got it!'

'It was there?'

'Exactly where you said, interleaved between the pages of a fourteenth-century treatise on some obscure Syrian heresy.'

'And you brought it out with you?'

'No problem. The security at that place is a joke. Anyway, if they'd tried to stop me I'd have pointed out that fourteenth-century Syrians didn't use typewriters.'

'What does it look like?'

'There's about twenty pages. It starts with a list of what looks like telephone numbers.'

'No, those will be the numbers of the bank accounts the gang uses to launder the money from the drug sales,' Zen replied glibly. 'Just read them out to me, will you? I'll pick up the document itself later on this evening, but we need to take action to freeze those accounts as soon as possible.'

There were about twenty numbers altogether. Zen wrote them down in his notebook on the same page as the number his mother had passed on. To his surprise, one of the numbers Bevilacqua read out was the same, the pay-phone in the lobby of the Hotel Torlonia Palace. But the Torlonia Palace was of course one of the leading luxury hotels in Rome. It was perfectly natural that the intimates and associates of Prince Ruspanti should choose to stay there, just like other eminent visitors to the city such as Antonio Simonelli.

'... before nine o'clock all right?' Tullio Bevilacqua was saying.

Zen glanced at his watch. Christ! Seven thirty-one!

'Yes, yes! I'll see you then! Bye!'

'But I haven't given you the address!' squawked Bevilacqua.

'I'll get it from . . .'

Zen broke off in confusion. 'From Tania', he had been going to say.

'. . . from the Ministry computer.'

Bevilacqua gasped.

'You mean . . . you've got a file on me?'

'We've got a file on *everyone*.'

He hit the receiver rest repeatedly until he got a dialling tone, then punched the number which now figured twice on the notebook page open on his knee. It was answered immediately.

'You're late.'

It was the voice which had spoken to Zen the night before from the confessional in St Peter's. The man's arrogant tone triggered an instinctive response for which Zen was quite unprepared

'I've cornered the market in the commodity you're interested in. I'll be as late as I fucking well choose.'

'Can you prove you have possession?'

The voice was the same as the night before, but the background was now thoroughly worldly: a babble of voices competing for attention against the synthetic battery of a pop band.

'Well, I could read you a list of phone numbers, but that would be giving away information which I could sell elsewhere. Just as a taster, though, one of the numbers which Ruspanti phoned just before he died is the same as the one on which you are now speaking. But I expect you already knew that.'

There was a brief pause.

'But now we know that *you* know. That makes all the difference.'

Zen said nothing.

'Hello? Are you still there?' the man queried peevishly.

'I'm here. I'm waiting for you to say something worth listening to. I got an earful of your waffle last night.'

'How much do you want?'

This was the crunch. If Zen had been bluffing, his bluff had been called. And what else could he have been doing? The idea of selling evidence to the highest bidder, never more than an idle speculation in the first place, was out of the question after what had happened to Carlo Romizi. It was unthinkable to imagine disposing of the transcript for his personal advantage, merely to restore his flagging finances and win back Tania from the rich young shit beside whom he looked drably impoverished, timidly conventional.

'How much?' prompted the voice impatiently.

'Rather more than Grimaldi asked, and rather less than he got.'

The man laughed. He could relax, the deal was in the bag. Money would never be a problem for these people.

'We offered Grimaldi thirty million, but he tried to hold out for more. I think we would be prepared to improve the price this time, to let us say fifty. But I would very strongly urge you to accept.'

Zen kept silent. What was the man talking about? The transcript wasn't for sale, not at any price. It was sacred, stained with the innocent blood of his colleague, Carlo Romizi.

'That figure of course applies only to the *original*,' the voice stressed. 'As you rightly surmised, the contents are already known to us.'

'Grimaldi showed you a photocopy, I suppose, to whet your appetite for the real thing?'

'We'll contact you in the next day or two, dottore. I understand you're going to Milan tomorrow?'

'Yes, but . . .'

'We shall know how to contact you. *Buon viaggio.*'

Zen replaced the phone slowly. Then he shrugged, as though shaking off a bad dream. Nothing would come of it. Tomorrow he would take the transcript to Milan and hand it over to Antonio Simonelli or his secretary. Then it would be out of his hands, and just as well too. He didn't trust himself to do the right thing any longer.

The thought of Milan made him get out his notebook and look again at the list of phone numbers which Ruspanti had called from his hideaway in the Vatican. As he thought, in addition to those in Rome, there had been several calls prefixed 02, the code for Milan. Zen picked up the phone and dialled one of them, just out of curiosity. There was no answer. He tried another and got an answering machine.

'*This is 879 4632. There is no one able to answer the phone at present. If you wish to leave a message . . .*'

The voice sounded rather like the man he had just been speaking to a moment ago in the Hotel Torlonia Palace. Which all went to show that one person can sound much like another, particularly on the telephone. There was one other Milan number on the list, and Zen was just about to dial it when the phone suddenly started to ring.

'Yes?'

'This is the Questore, dottore. The Ministry asked us to contact you about the phone you wanted watched. I'm afraid the situation was a bit confusing. Apparently there was some sort of publicity event being held at the hotel, a launch party for some book, so the place was thick with media people and the phones were in use all the time.'

'I see. Thank you.'

He had expected something of the kind. The men he was dealing with were too clever to allow themselves to be trapped in that way. Zen picked up the phone again and dialled the last of the Milan numbers which Ludovico Ruspanti had called in the final week of his life.

'Yes?'

The voice was that of a young woman. She spoke hesitantly, as though expecting a reprimand. Zen realized that he had no idea what to say.

'It's me,' he murmured finally.

There was a brief pause.

'Ludo?'

The woman sounded tentative, incredulous. Not half as incredulous as Zen, though.

'Who else?'

There was a stifled gasp.

'But they told me you'd had to go away. They told me I'd never see you again . . .'

Her voice trailed away. Perhaps she too had become aware of the altered acoustic on the line. Someone, somewhere, was listening in.

'Listen, can I see you tomorrow?' Zen went on quickly.

'You're coming here? To see *me*?'

'Yes! I'll ring when I arrive.'

'But remember to let it ring and then call back, so that I have time to get rid of Carmela. You forgot this time, silly! Luckily her sister is visiting this week and they're out every evening. Well, she couldn't very well bring her here, could she?'

Zen caught sight of the clock on the sideboard opposite. It showed five to eight, long past time for him to be gone.

'Till tomorrow, then!'

'Oh, I can't wait, I can't wait!' the woman cried girlishly. 'You promise?'

'I promise.'

'Cross your heart and hope to die?'

A superstitious revulsion rose like nausea in Zen's throat.

'I'll ring you tomorrow,' he said, and hung up.

He couldn't believe what had just happened. Seemingly the number in Milan belonged to one of 'Ludo' Ruspanti's mistresses, and – incredible as this seemed – she was apparently unaware that her lover was dead. His elation was briefly dimmed by the knowledge that someone had been eavesdropping on their conversation. Nevertheless, here was a golden opportunity which, if he could only find the right way to handle it, might lead him to the heart of the . . .

'All right, Aurelio, who is she?'

Zen looked up to find Tania Biacis glowering at him from the doorway.

'Come on!' she shouted, advancing into the room. 'Don't try palming me off with clever lies. I've seen you taking in too many other people to fall for it myself. Just tell me the truth, then get to hell out of here!'

He had never seen her like this, furious, overbearing, utterly sure of herself. He got up, gesturing weakly.

'You don't think . . .'

'I don't *think* anything!' she broke in brutally. 'I just heard you speaking to her on the phone, fixing a rendezvous for tomorrow. "Oh, I can't wait, I can't wait!" Sounds like hot stuff, this lady of yours!'

'So it was *you* listening in, on the extension in the hallway!'

'I wasn't *listening in*. I was trying to use my phone. I had no idea you were here. How the hell did you get in, anyway? You've had a key all along, I suppose. I might have known!'

'The American gave me a spare key. I thought I'd hang on to it, just in case . . .'

'So I get home and pick up the phone, only to hear this woman practically sticking her tongue into your ear. So you're going away tomorrow, right? A sudden urgent mission of the highest importance to – where did you say she lives?'

'And what about you, my dear?' Zen retorted. 'Who were you

trying to phone so urgently the moment you got in? Was it that man who answered the phone when I called here on Tuesday?'

Tania held up her hands.

'All right, I admit it. It wasn't a wrong number. It was Aldo, my cousin Bettina's husband. He was here on business.'

'Business? You told me he worked for the post office.'

She flapped her hands in evident confusion.

'Well, there was some . . . conference or something.'

The evident lie stung him to push things to the limit.

'All right, then, let's forget Aldo. But you still haven't told me who you were trying to phone. Was it Primo, by any chance?'

The pink flush around her high cheek bones revealed that the name had had its effect.

'It's too bad he's got to take his wife to the opera in the evening, isn't it?' Zen carried on. 'Still, he's going to pick you up from the airport and take you out to lunch, and after that, who knows?'

'Is that why you broke in here? So that you could snoop around reading my mail? You . . . you . . . you COP!'

'I can think of an even more insulting epithet to apply to you, if I chose to use it!'

'Fuck off! Just fuck off out of my house!'

Zen measured her with a look.

'What do you mean, *your* house?'

Tania tossed her head contemptuously.

'Oh, you mean because you've been secretly paying someone to rent this place to me? Well I'd guessed that, as it happens. I'm not *stupid.* The only reason I hadn't told you I knew was that I didn't want to hurt your feelings. Oh, it's so fucking pathetic, the whole thing . . .'

To Zen's utter consternation, she turned away and burst into tears. Not as a ploy; that he could have withstood. But she had moved beyond him, into uncharted areas of real grief. Yet how could it be real when she was false, and believed him to be? It didn't make sense. None of it made sense. So he fled, leaving her to her intolerable mysteries. The real world awaited him: his distraction, his toy.

6

The piazza in front of Rome's Stazione Termini, normally thronged with buses, cars, traders' vans and lorries, with crowds of commuters, tourists, beggars, transients and the forlorn Senegalese and Filipino immigrants who used the place as an informal clubhouse, information centre and canteen, was now a bleak, empty, rainswept wasteland. As Zen stared out of the window of the taxi at the porticoed arcade to one side and the blank wall closing off the vista, he slipped back into the dream from which the alarm clock had saved him less than half an hour earlier.

He'd been walking across just such a piazza, but in broad daylight, beneath a brutal summer sun. The light flattened the ground at his feet, reducing it to a featureless expanse bordered by a row of broken columns, the last of which cast a perfect shadow of itself on the hot paving, like the hands of a clock showing one minute to twelve. That was indeed the time, and he would never manage to catch the train, which left on the hour from the station whose enormous façade sealed off the perspective. Already he could see the plume of smoke as the locomotive pulled away from the invisible platform, inaccessible behind a high wall . . .

The taxi hit one of the kerbs delineating the bus lanes, jolting him awake again. The dream was still horribly vivid, though: the stillness, the stifling heat, the paralysis of his limbs, the sickening perspectives of the piazza, at once vertiginous and claustrophobic. He sat up straight, willing himself back to the here and now. It was only a dream, after all.

Having paid off the taxi, he carried his bag through the booking hall into the main concourse of the station. It was twenty past six. He'd spent a quarter of an hour blundering around the apartment, worrying that he'd remembered to pack everything except the one essential item, whatever it was, without which his journey would be in vain, and was just wondering whether to take the replica revolver when the taxi arrived, ten minutes early. In the end he'd thrown the thing into his suitcase along with a couple of spare shirts, grabbed his briefcase with the precious transcript, and rushed downstairs. As a result of that unnecessary haste, he now had forty minutes to hang around the draughty public spaces of the station.

The cafeteria was still closed, but a small kiosk was dispensing coffee to a huddle of early arrivals. Zen joined the queue, eventually obtaining a double espresso which he knocked back like a shot of spirits. The warning glow of caffeine hit his bloodstream, adding the depth of memory to his two-dimensional consciousness. He winced, recalling his parting from Tania the night before, the unforgivable things said on either side, the way he had walked out without any attempt at reconciliation. Well, what was the point? It was over, that was clear enough. Tania might be ludicrously mistaken about his supposed amours, but he certainly wasn't about hers. There was too much evidence, both material and circumstantial, and he was too experienced an investigator to be led astray. Besides, Tania had made it plain that after the years of confinement in a joyless marriage to Mauro Bevilacqua she wasn't prepared to submit to the straitjacket of another exclusive relationship. Why insist on freedom and then leave it untasted?

Zen tossed the disposable plastic cup into the rubbish bag provided and turned to survey his fellow passengers. They looked bizarrely out of place, an elegant, wealthy throng clustered around the mini-bar like factory workers on the early shift. Power dressing was the order of the day, both men and the few women present discreetly flaunting an understated sartorial muscle based on cut, finish and quality fabrics. The only exception was a tense-looking man wearing the undress uniform of the Church the world over, a plain clerical suit and white collar clutching a locked attaché case under his arm. Zen instinctively glanced at his own battered leather briefcase, leaning against the overnight bag at his feet.

After storming out of Tania's apartment the night before, he had gone to the bar round the corner and shared some of his problems, suitably depersonalized, with the Neapolitans over a hot chocolate. Since he couldn't very well ask Tania for her brother-in-law's address, Zen looked it up in the phone book and then took a cab round there to pick up the transcript. Unfortunately, Tullio Bevilacqua was so proud of the part he had played in the relentless struggle against organized crime that he had invited his brother to witness this historic event.

The last time Zen had seen Tania's husband, Mauro Bevilacqua was waving a gun in his face and threatening to exact revenge for the insult done to his family honour, so his unexpected appearance at this juncture seemed likely to result in all manner of problems, both professional and personal. In the event, the encounter was less fraught than it might have been. After a brief but violent internal tussle, Mauro opted for a pose of contemptuous indifference, as though to emphasize that the doings of his estranged wife were of no concern to him. Only at the end, when Zen was about to leave, did his mask slip for a moment.

'We mustn't detain our guest any longer, brother. He has important work to do keeping prostitution off the streets.'

Tullio frowned.

'Dottor Borsellino isn't in the Vice Squad.'

Mauro gave a smile of exquisite irony.

'Borsellino?' he enquired archly. 'Ah, excuse me! I was confusing him with an official who used to work with all the sluts of the city. A slimy, venal little *faccia di culo* by the name of Aurelio Zen.'

He turned to face Zen.

'Do you know him by any chance, dottore?'

Zen nodded.

'I'll tell him what you said.'

'Yes, do that. Not that I've got anything personal against him, you understand. In fact he did me a favour once. Took this *whore* off my hands.'

Mauro Bevilacqua smiled reminiscently.

'I wonder who's she with now!'

Since Zen was wondering almost exactly the same thing, he was unable to come up with a suitably crushing reply. Back home, his mother had kept him up late with a long and involved story about some childhood friend of hers who had moved to Milan with her husband and been killed during the war when an Allied bomb struck the laundry where she worked. By the time he extricated himself, Zen had felt too tired to do more than go straight to bed and hope that he would feel better in the morning.

He walked over to the news-stall, which had just opened, and looked through the serried ranks of magazines. The cover of the new issue of *Moda* showed an extraordinary peacock of a man, a shimmering apparition in heavy grey and gold silks, his guileless blue eyes turned levelly towards the camera. The caption read 'Falco: A Philosopher in the Wardrobe'. Just then a subliminal frisson spread through the group of men standing at the news-stall, leaping from one to another like an electric charge. Zen turned his head along with all the others, but it was too late. The woman who had generated all this excitement had already passed by, and all he could see of her was her shoulder-length blonde hair and the back of her dark-cream trenchcoat, the hem oscillating back and forth above her suede bootees. With a sigh he picked up his luggage and followed her and the other passengers towards the platform where *il pendolino*, as the pride of the Ferrovie dello Stato was popularly known, was now boarding.

The eight carriages which made up the ETR 450 high-speed unit, with a bullet-shaped cab at each end, were mounted high above the bogies on which they tilted to maintain stability at speeds of up to 150 mph – hence its nickname, 'the pendulum'. All seats were reserved and first class only. Zen's carriage was towards the middle of the train. In the vestibule, a uniformed attendant checked his ticket and directed him to his place. Two rows of reclining seats ran the length of the coach, just as in an airplane. Indeed, the *pendolino* was the next best thing to a plane, covering the four hundred miles between Rome and Milan in under four hours.

Having stowed the suitcase in the luggage rack, Zen lowered the table attached to the back of the chair in front, opened his briefcase and extracted the sheaf of papers which it contained. Apart from the initial reference list of phone numbers, the transcript consisted of twenty-two pages headed UFFICIO CENTRALE DI VIGILANZA and covered in single-spaced typing, divided into blocks headed with a date, time and telephone number. Each represented one phone call which Ruspanti had made. Incoming calls did not figure. Ruspanti presumably hadn't given his phone number to anyone, either because the 698 prefix would have revealed his presence in the Vatican City State, or because he knew or suspected that the line was being tapped.

There was a whistle blast from the platform outside, a whine as the automatic doors closed, then a slight jolt of movement. Zen glanced at his watch. Seven o'clock on the dot. A moment later the window was covered in a speckle of rain as the train emerged into the grey dawn. Inside, the broad strip of fluorescent panelling on the ceiling of the coach bathed everything in a coolly efficient radiance. Zen lowered his head over the papers again and started to read.

Some time later he sensed someone standing behind him, craning over him. He hastily covered the typewritten page, but it was only one of the stewards, offering him an airplane-style breakfast tray, an assortment of sad pastries and unloved rolls in plastic shrouds. Zen waved it away, then reclaimed the cup and asked for coffee. Beyond the window, the flat expanses of the Tiber flood-plain slipped past like a video being fast-forwarded. They were on the new *direttissima* line by now, the train humming purposefully along at its top speed on the custom-built high-speed track.

Zen read quickly through the rest of the transcript, then laid it on the table, face down, and sighed. Giovanni Grimaldi had been felled in his shower like a beast at the abattoir because he had threatened to reveal the contents of this document, yet Zen had just read it from cover to cover and it meant almost nothing to him.

He turned back to the beginning and read it through once more. Whether Ruspanti had been aware of the tap on his own line, or was concerned about possible eavesdroppers the other end, he had gone to great pains to say nothing of any consequence. About half the calls amounted to little more than requests to be contacted 'at the usual number' or 'in the normal way'. In others, Ruspanti referred to 'the sum agreed' or 'under discussion', or urged that 'the measures previously outlined be put into immediate effect'. Only twice did he mention anything more specific. The first instance occurred in the course of the call to the pay-phone in the lobby of the Hotel Torlonia Palace the previous Thursday. His patience had finally run out, Ruspanti said. If 'Zeppegno' couldn't be persuaded to 'do the decent thing' by the weekend at the latest, then he would 'have no alternative but to make public the matter which you know about'.

This might well have some bearing on the circumstances of Ruspanti's death, given the timing. But as the nature of the secret he threatened to make public was not even hinted at, and the name mentioned was presumably false, it did not amount to very significant evidence. The other call was to the last of the Milan numbers which Zen had tried the night before, but although it sounded an intimate note perceptible even in the unrelievedly literal transcription, its significance remained equally cryptic.

'Hello?'

'Ludo! Where are you? Are you coming here?'

'I'm not in Milan, my love.'

'Where, then?'

'I'm . . . moving around a bit. Here today, gone tomorrow.'

'Sounds like fun.'

'In fact I was talking to someone about you just the other day, Ariana. Someone who works for a magazine.'

'About *me*?'

'That's right. I told him all about your dolls. He sounded very interested. In fact he wants to write an article about them.'

'Don't make fun of me, Ludo. It isn't fair.'

'I'm not! This is quite serious.'

'But why would anyone be interested in my dolls?'

'You'd be amazed, Ariana. So would your brother!'

'You haven't told him, have you?'

'No, I can't seem to get hold of him. Why don't *you* tell him? Tell him to get in touch and let me know what he thinks about the idea. He knows how to contact me, if he wants to.'

'But when will I see you?'

'As soon as all this is over.'

'All what? There's some problem, isn't there? I can feel it. What is it, Ludo? Tell me!'

'Oh nothing. Just the silly games we boys play. Girls are more sensible, aren't they?'

Zen looked at the window, but the train was running through a tunnel, and all he could see was the reflection of his own features, baffled and haggard. Perhaps a reader more familiar with the details of the case against Ruspanti might glean something more substantial from the transcript. Since someone had been prepared to kill Grimaldi and bribe Zen to obtain the damn thing, there must be some clue hidden there. The reference to 'dolls' might be a code of some kind. What would Ruspanti's mistress be doing playing with dolls? Perhaps Antonio Simonelli would know what it meant.

The roar of the tunnel faded as the train emerged into bright sunshine. A moment later they had crossed the Arno and rejoined the old line running through the outskirts of Florence. Zen replaced the transcript in his briefcase, which he locked and placed on his knee as the train drew into the suburban station of Rinfredi, which it used to avoid the timewasting turnround at the Florentine terminus of Santa

Maria Novella. The stop was a brief one, and by the time he had had
a chance to skim *La Stampa* they were once again under way, along
the fast straight stretch to Prato.

'Good morning, dottore.'

Zen looked up from his newspaper. The voice was both distinctive
and familiar, but it still took him a moment to recognize the man
standing beside his seat, an umbrella in one hand and a briefcase in
the other, gazing down at Zen with a smile of complicity. It was the
man who had been in his thoughts just a few minutes earlier, the man
he was going to Milan to see, Antonio Simonelli.

'Have you brought the transcript?'

They had barely settled down in the seats to which Simonelli had led the way. When the magistrate suggested that Zen join him in the next carriage, he had at once agreed. Policemen are accustomed to obeying the instructions of the judiciary, and besides, seeing Simonelli was the reason for Zen's trip to Milan. This chance meeting – the magistrate had apparently just joined the train at Florence, where he had been attending a meeting – was simply a happy coincidence. Or so it had seemed, until Simonelli mentioned the transcript.

Zen instinctively tightened his grip on the briefcase, which was lying on his knees. The train rounded a curve, and sunlight suddenly streamed in through the window. In the lapel of Simonelli's jacket, something glimmered. Zen looked more closely. It was a small silver eight-pointed cross.

'You're a member?'

The magistrate glanced down as though noticing the insignia for the first time.

'I am, actually.'

'Like Ruspanti.'

Simonelli's laugh had an edge to it.

'Hardly! Ruspanti was a Knight of Honour and Devotion. You need at least three hundred years of nobility behind you to achieve that. I'm just a simple Donat, the lowest of the low.'

It was only when Zen felt the magistrate's restraining hand on his wrist that he realized that he had reached for his cigarettes. Simonelli indicated the sign on the window with a nicotine-stained finger.

'No smoking.'

Zen let the muscles of his eyes unclasp, projecting his point of focus out of the train, beyond the dirt-flecked window with its prohibitory sign and into the landscape beyond. The slanting winter light streaked the narrow gorge of the Bisenzio where road and railway run side by side until the river peters out in the southern flanks of the Apennines. Then the road, largely disused since the motorway was opened, begins the long climb to the pass thousands of feet above, while the railway plunges into the eleven-mile tunnel under the mountains.

Why had Simonelli reserved a seat in a non-smoking section when he was himself a smoker? There were plenty of single seats available in the smoking coach where Zen was sitting, but not two together. If Simonelli had already known that the seat beside his was unoccupied, this could only be because he had booked them both in advance. The implications of this were so dizzying that he hardly heard Simonelli's next words.

'After all, it wouldn't do for a judge and a policeman to break the law, would it?'

Zen glanced round at him witlessly.

'Or at least,' corrected Simonelli, 'to be *seen* to do so.'

'Seen to . . . How?'

'By smoking in a non-smoking carriage.'

Zen nodded. Antonio Simonelli joined in until both their heads were wagging in the same tempo. They understood each other perfectly.

'It *is* the original, I trust.'

Once again the magistrate's nicotine-stained finger was extended, this time towards the briefcase Zen was hugging defensively to his body.

'As my colleague explained to you on the phone, we're not interested in purchasing a copy.'

Zen's mouth opened. He laughed awkwardly.

'No, no. Of course not.'

Simonelli glanced out of the window at the landscape, which was growing ever more rugged as they approached the mountain chain which divides Italy in two. With its many curves and steep gradients, this difficult section of line was the slowest, and even the *pendolino* was reduced to the speed of a normal train. Simonelli consulted his watch.

'Do you think we're going to be late?' Zen asked.

'Late for what?'

The Maltese cross in the magistrate's lapel, its bifurcated points representing the eight beatitudes, glinted fascinatingly as the contours of the valley brought the line into the sunlight.

'For whatever's going to happen.'

Simonelli eyed him steadily.

'All that's going to happen is that you give me the transcript, and I take it to an associate who is seated in the next carriage. Once he has confirmed that it is the original, I return with the money.'

Zen stared back at the magistrate. Marco Duranti had described the supposed maintenance man who hot-wired the shower to kill Giovanni Grimaldi as stocky, muscular, of average height, with a big round face and a pronounced nasal accent, 'a real northerner'. The description fitted Simonelli perfectly. And would not such a humble task befit 'a simple Donat, the lowest of the low'? Despite the almost oppressive warmth of the air-conditioned carriage, Zen found himself shivering uncontrollably.

Simonelli tugged at the briefcase again, more insistently this time. Zen held on tight.

'How do I know I'll get paid?'

'Of course you'll get paid! No one can get off the train until we reach Bologna anyway.'

As the train glided through the station of Vernio and entered the southern end of the long tunnel under the Apennines, Zen's attention was momentarily distracted by the woman who had caused such a stir at the terminus in Rome. She was making her way to the front of the carriage, and once again he only saw her clothes, a cowl-neck ribbed sweater and tightly cut skirt. She left a subtle trail of perfume behind her, as though shaken from shoulder-length blonde hair like incense from a censer.

'If the transcript is safe with you, the money is safe with me,' Zen found himself saying above the roaring of the tunnel. 'So give it to me now, before you take the transcript.'

He had hoped to disconcert Simonelli with this demand, to force him to consult his associate and thus give Zen more time to consider his next move. But as usual, he was a step behind. With a brief sigh of deprecation at this regrettable lack of trust on Zen's part, Simonelli opened his briefcase. It was full of serried bundles of ten-thousand-lire notes.

'Fifty million,' the magistrate said. 'As we agreed.'

He closed the lid and snapped the catches, locking the case, then stood up and laid it on his seat.

'Now give me the transcript, please.'

Zen stared up at him. Why struggle? What difference did it make?

He had been going to hand the transcript over to Simonelli anyway, in Milan. This way the result was the same, except that he came out of it fifty million lire better off. Even if he wanted to resist, there was nothing he could do, no effective action he could take. The only weapon he had was the fake revolver buried inside his suitcase in the luggage rack at the end of the next carriage. But even if he had been armed to the teeth, it wouldn't have made any difference in the long run. The Cabal would get their way in the end. They always did.

He lifted his arm off his briefcase. Simonelli reached across, opened the briefcase and removed the transcript.

'I shall be no more than five minutes,' he said. 'We have several men on the train. If you attempt to move from this seat during that time, I cannot be responsible for your safety.'

He strode off along the carriage towards the vestibule where the blonde woman was now smoking a cigarette. The train seemed to be full of masochistic smokers, Zen reflected with a forlorn attempt at humour. He stared out of the window, trying to think of something other than the humiliation he had just suffered. Although he had been travelling this line for years, the ten-and-a-half-minute transit of the Apennines was still something which awed him. His father had impressed the young Aurelio with the history of the epic project which had gripped the imagination of the nation throughout the twenties. Although marginally shorter than the Simplon, the Apennine tunnel had been infinitely more difficult and costly to construct, running as it did a nightmarish schist riddled with pockets of explosive gas and unmapped underground lakes which burst forth without warning, flooding the workings for months on end. Zen was lost in these memories and speculations when, just like the previous Friday, all the lights went out.

A moment later the secure warmth of the carriage was gutted by a roaring torrent of ice-cold air. The train shuddered violently as the brakes locked on. Cries of alarm and dismay filled the carriage, turning to screams of pain as the train jerked to a complete stop, throwing the passengers against each other and the seats in front.

Once Zen's eyes had adjusted to the darkness, he discovered that it was not quite total after all. Although the lights in this carriage had failed, those in the adjoining coaches reflected off the walls of the tunnel, creating a faint glimmer by which he could just make out the aisle, the seats and the vague blurs of the other passengers moving about. Then two figures wielding torches like swords appeared at the end of the carriage. A moment later, the fluorescent strip on the ceiling of the carriage came on again.

It was a perfect moment for a murder, Zen reflected afterwards. The killers would be wearing sunglasses, and while everyone else was blinded by the sudden excess of light, they could carry out their assignment as though in total darkness. Fortunately, though, the men who had entered the carriage were not assassins but members of the train crew. Zen followed them to the vestibule at the front of the carriage, where he made himself known to the guard, a grey-haired man with the grooming and gravity of a senior executive.

The gale-force wind which had stripped all the warmth out of the carriage had diminished now the train had come to a halt, but there was still a vicious draught streaming in through the opened door. Zen asked what had happened. The *capotreno* indicated a red lever set in a recess in the wall near by. Shouting to make himself heard over the banshee whining in the tunnel outside, he explained that the external doors on the train were opened and closed by the driver, but that this mechanism could be overridden manually to prevent people being trapped inside in the event of an emergency. The lever was normally secured in the up position with a loop of string sealed like a mediaeval parchment with a circle of lead embossed with the emblem of the State Railways. This now dangled, broken, from its support.

'As soon as this lever is thrown, a warning light comes on in the driver's cab, and he stops the train. Unfortunately some people like to kill themselves this way. I don't know why, but we get quite a few.'

Just like St Peter's, thought Zen.

'But why did the lights go off?' he asked.

The guard indicated a double row of fuses and switches on the wall opposite, protected by a plastic cover which now swung loose on its hinges.

'The fuse for the main lighting circuit was missing. We've swapped over the one for the air-conditioning thermostat, just to get the lights back on before the passengers started to panic. He must have done it himself, so he couldn't see what was going to happen to him.'

The toilet door opened with a click and the blonde woman stepped out. She looked slightly flustered by so much male attention.

'Has something happened?' she asked.

Close to, her skin showed a slight roughness that made her seem older. Her pale blue eyes looked at Zen, who sniffed. Apart from her perfume, there seemed to be another new odour present – the smell of burning.

'Did you hear anything?' he said.

The flaxen hair trembled as she shook her head.

'Just the roaring noise when the lights went out. Has some-one . . . ?'

The *capotreno* dismissed the woman with a wave and told two of his assistants to keep the passengers off the vestibule.

'We'd better have a look on the track,' he said.

The *pendolino* had never seemed more like an airplane to Aurelio Zen than when he stepped out of its lighted sanctuary into the howling storm outside. The Apennines form a continuous barrier running almost the entire length of the Italian peninsula, and the prevailing climatic conditions are often very different on either side. This man-made vent piercing the range thus forms a conduit for violent air currents flowing in one direction or the other as the contrasting weather systems try to find their level.

The high pressure was in Tuscany that day, so the wind was flowing north, battering the faces of the men as they walked back along the track. While they were still alongside the train, the lights streaming from the windows high overhead, Zen found the experience just about tolerable. But when they passed the final coach and struck out into the midst of that turbulent darkness which corroded the fragile beams of their torches, wearing them away, using them up, until they could hardly see the track in front of them, he was gripped by a terror so real it made anything else appear a flimsy dream of security, a collective delusion provoked by a reality too awful to be contemplated.

The noise was already deafening, but as they moved forward, breasting that black tide that threatened at every moment to sweep them away with it, it became clear that its source lay somewhere in front of them. The five men trudged slowly on, leaning forward as though pushing a laden sledge, their feeble torch beams scanning the ballast, sleepers and rails. The occasional patch of toilet paper, a soft-drink can or two, an ancient packet of cigarettes and a newspaper was all they found at first. Then something brighter, a fresher patch of white, showed up. One of the train crew picked it up and passed it to the *capotreno*, who held up his torch, scanning the line of heavy type at the top: UFFICIO CENTRALE DI VIGILANZA.

As the clamour up ahead grew ever more distinct and concentrated, the movement of the air became stronger and more devious, no longer a single blast but a maelstrom of whirling currents and eddies fighting for supremacy. Without the slightest warning a giant beacon appeared in the darkness behind them and swept past, forging south into the gale. As the locomotive passed, the darkness was briefly swept aside like a curtain, revealing the vast extent of the cavity where they cowered, deafened by the howl of its siren. Then the darkness fell back, and all other sounds were ground out by the wheels of a seemingly endless succession of unlighted freight wagons.

At length two red lights appeared, marking the last wagon. As it receded into the distance, the men started to move forward again and the original, primitive uproar reasserted itself, an infinitely powerful presence that was seemingly located somewhere in the heart of the solid rock above their heads. The train crew shone their torches upwards, revealing a huge circular opening in the roof of the tunnel. It was almost impossible to stand here, in the vortex of the vicious currents spiralling straight up the mountaintop thousands of feet above.

The *capotreno* beckoned to Zen, who lowered his ear to the man's mouth.

'Ventilation shaft!'

They found the body a little further on, lying beside the track like another bit of rubbish dropped from a passing train in defiance of the prohibition in several languages. One leg had been amputated at the thigh and most of the left arm and shoulder was mangled beyond recognition, but by some freak the face had survived without so much as a scratch. The Maltese cross glinted proudly in the lapel of the plain blue suit, and the fingers of the right hand were still clutching several pages of the transcript which now appeared to have claimed its second victim.

The power and influence of Milan – Italy's rightful capital, as it liked to call itself – had never appeared more impressive to Aurelio Zen than they did as he strode along the corridors of the Palazzo di Giustizia late that afternoon. The office to which he had been directed was in an annexe built on at the rear of the main building, and its clean lines and uncluttered spaces, and still more the purposeful air of bustle and business, was as different as possible from other sites sacred to the judiciary. If Milan was capable of influencing, even superficially, an organization in which the bacillus of the 'Bourbonic plague' was preserved in its purest and most virulent form, then what couldn't it do?

He rounded a corner to find a woman looking towards him from an open doorway. A helmet of lustreless black hair cropped at the nape framed her flat, open face, the bold cheeks and strong features blurred by menopausal turmoil like a damp-damaged fresco. She wore a slate-grey wool jacket with a matching skirt cut tight just below the knee.

'Antonia Simonelli,' she said. 'Come in.'

He followed her into an office containing two teak desks. One, pushed into a corner, was almost invisible beneath a solid wall of stacked folders reaching up to within a metre of the ceiling. The other was completely bare except for a laptop computer. At the other side of the room, a large window afforded an excellent view of the gothic fantastications of the cathedral and the glazed roofs and dome of the Galleria Vittoria Emanuele.

The woman sat at the bare desk and crossed her long legs. Zen took the only other seat, a hard wooden stool.

'I must apologize for the spartan furnishings,' the woman said. 'My office is in the part of the main building which is being renovated, and meanwhile I'm sharing with a colleague whose tastes and habits are very different from mine. Gianfranco likes the blinds drawn and the lights on, even in high summer. That's his desk. I sometimes feel I'm going to go crazy just looking at it.'

Zen looked at the rounded peak of her knee and the tip of her grey suede court shoe, which rose above the sheeny expanse of the desktop like a tropical island in a calm sea.

'He didn't have any ID,' he murmured.

The woman bent forward, frowning slightly.

'I beg your pardon?'

Zen looked up at her.

'The man on the train. He didn't have any identification. But I suppose *you* do.'

He produced his own pass certifying him as a functionary of the Ministry of the Interior and laid it on the desk.

'Anyone could walk in here,' he remarked earnestly. 'We've never met before. How would you know it wasn't me?'

The woman regarded him fixedly.

'Are you feeling all right?' she asked guardedly.

Zen tapped the desk where his identification lay. The woman opened her black grained-leather bucket bag and passed over a laminated card with her photograph and an inscription to the effect that the holder was Simonelli, Antonia Natalia, investigating magistrate at the Procura of Milan. Zen nodded and handed it back.

'I'm sorry,' he said. 'I suppose I must have sounded a bit crazy.'

The woman said nothing, but her expression did not contradict the idea.

'I've had a slight shock,' Zen explained. 'On the way here a man fell fr~·¬ the train. I had to help retrieve the body from the tunnel.'

'Tha╵ can't have been very pleasant,' the magistrate murmured sympathetically.

'I had been talking to him just a few moments earlier.'

'It was someone you know, then?'

He looked at her.

'I thought it was you.'

The woman's guarded manner intensified sharply.

'If that was intended as a joke . . .' she began.

'I don't think the people involved intended it as a joke.'

She eyed him impatiently.

'You're speaking in riddles.'

Zen nodded.

'Let me try and explain. On Wednesday I received a message at the Ministry asking me to call a certain Antonio Simonelli at a hotel in

Rome. When I did so, he identified himself as an investigating magistrate from Milan working on a case of fraud involving Ludovico Ruspanti, and asked me to meet him to discuss the circumstances of the latter's death.'

The woman seemed about to say something, but after a moment she just waved her hand.

'Go on.'

Zen sat silent a moment, considering how best to do so.

'At the time I thought he was trying to obtain information off the record which might help him prosecute the case against Ruspanti's associates. That risked placing me in a rather awkward position. When the Vatican called me in, I was asked to sign an undertaking not to disclose any information which I came by as a result of my investigations. I therefore answered his questions as briefly as possible.'

The woman opened a drawer of her desk and removed a slim file which she opened.

'Go on,' she repeated without looking up.

Zen pretended to look at the view for a moment. He decided to make no mention of the transcript of Ruspanti's phone calls. That was lost for ever, scattered beyond any hope of retrieval by the gale which had sucked it away and strewn it the length of the eleven-mile tunnel. The only thing to do now was to pretend that it had never existed.

'On the train up here this morning,' he continued, 'I was approached by the same man. He asked why I was travelling to Milan. I said I had an appointment with one of his colleagues at the Procura. He must have realized then that the game was up, I suppose. He went off towards the toilets, fused the lights and threw himself out.'

The woman looked steadily at Zen.

'Describe him.'

'Burly, muscular. Big moon face, slightly dished. Strong nasal accent, from the Bergamo area, I should say. Smoked panatellas.'

Antonia Simonelli selected a photograph from the file lying open on the desk and passed it to Zen. A paper sticker at the bottom read ZEPPEGNO, MARCO. Zen suppressed a gasp of surprise. There had been so many fakes and hoaxes in the case so far – including the fifty million lire, which had turned out to consist of a thin layer of real notes covering bundles of blank paper – that he had assumed that the names which appeared in the transcript were also pseudonyms. But perhaps Ruspanti had deliberately raised the stakes by mentioning the real name of one of the men he was threatening on a phone he knew to be tapped, making it clear that he was ready to start playing dirty. That would certainly explain why the individual concerned had been desperate to suppress the transcript by any means, including the murder of Giovanni Grimaldi.

Zen handed the photograph back.

'You know about him, then?'

Antonia Simonelli nodded.

'I know *all* about him!'

'Including whether he is – was – a member of the Order of Malta?'

She looked at him with surprise.

'What's that got to do with it?'

Zen said nothing. After a moment, the magistrate tapped the keyboard of the laptop computer.

'Since 1975,' she said.

'It wasn't an aspect of his activities that concerned you?'

She gave a frown of what looked like genuine puzzlement.

'Only in that it was perfectly typical of him. Joining the Order is something that businessmen like Zeppegno like to do at a certain point. It provides social cachet and range of useful contacts, and demonstrates that your heart is in the right place and your bank account healthy. But I repeat, why do you ask?'

Zen shrugged.

'He was wearing the badge, on the train. I asked him if he was a member, and he said he was. I just wondered if that was a lie too, like everything else he had told me.'

Antonia Simonelli wagged her finger at him.

'On the contrary, dottore! Apart from the little matter of his identity, everything he told you was true.'

A smile unexpectedly appeared on the woman's face, softening her features and providing a brief glimpse of the private person.

'Antonio Simonelli, indeed!' she exclaimed. 'You have to hand it to the old bastard. What a nerve! Supposing we had been in touch before, and you were aware of my gender?'

'He checked that by suggesting that we had. It was only when I said I didn't know him – you – that he asked to meet me.'

She sighed.

'So he's dead?'

'Well, the identification still has to be confirmed, of course, but . . .'

'Who's handling the case?'

'Bologna. That took another half hour to work out. He jumped out right on the border between Tuscany and Emilia-Romagna. In the end we had to get a length of rope and measure the distance from the body to the nearest kilometre marker.'

'And there's no doubt that it was suicide?'

Zen looked away. This was the question he had been asking himself ever since the torch beams picked out the corpse sprawled by the trackside. The circumstances had conspired to prevent anything but the most cursory investigation at the scene. Short of closing the Apennine tunnel, and thus paralysing rail travel throughout Italy, the corpse could not be left *in situ* while the Carabinieri in Bologna dispatched their scene-of-crime experts. Fortunately there happened to be a doctor travelling on the train who was able to pronounce the victim dead. Zen then carried out a nominal inspection before authorizing the removal of the body. By the time the train reached Bologna, no one had the slightest interest in questioning that they were dealing with a case of suicide. The only remaining mystery was the victim's identity, since there were no papers or documents on the body.

Zen shook his head.

'The only person who was anywhere near him when he fell from the train was a woman who had gone to the toilet, and she wouldn't have had the strength. Anyway, she was a German tourist with no connection with the dead man. No, he must have done it himself. There's simply no other possibility.'

Antonia Simonelli got up from her desk.

'I'm sure you're right, dottore,' she said. 'It's just that I'd come to know Zeppegno quite well, and if you'd asked me, I'd have said that he just wasn't someone who would ever commit suicide. He thought too highly of himself for that.'

She waved at the file, the photographs, the computer.

'For the past five years I have been painstakingly assembling a case against a cartel of Milanese businessmen. Zeppegno was typical. His family were provincial bourgeois with aspirations. His father ran an electrical business in a town near Bergamo. By a combination of graft and hard work, Marco gradually built up a chain of household appliance suppliers in small towns across Lombardy. As an individual unit, each of his outlets was modest enough, but taken together they represented a profitable slice of the market.

'Like other entrepreneurs, Zeppegno hated paying taxes and wanted to be able to invest his money freely. The answer was to cream off a percentage of his pre-tax profits and invest them abroad. The problem was how to do it. Big businesses have their own ways around the currency control laws, of course. You order a consignment of raw material from a foreign supplier who is prepared to play along. This is duly invoiced and paid for, but the goods in question are never shipped, and the money ends up in the off-shore bank account of your choice. There's an element of risk involved, but in a big outfit with a complex structure and a high volume of foreign trade the danger is minimal. The bogus orders can be hidden amongst a mass of legitimate transactions, and if all else fails *i finanzieri* have on occasion been known to look the other way.'

Zen acknowledged the gibe with a blink. The venality of the Finance Ministry's enforcement officials was legendary.

'The turnover of a company like Zeppegno's was far too small to conceal that sort of scam successfully. Which is where the late Ludovico Ruspanti came in. It didn't hurt that he was an aristocrat, of course. Self-made provincials like Zeppegno tend to retain the prejudices of their class. A title like "Prince" not only helped convince them that their money was safe in Ruspanti's hands, but reassured them that what they were doing was nothing much to be ashamed of, since a man like him was involved. The procedure itself couldn't have been simpler or more convenient. You simply wrote Ruspanti a cheque for whatever amount you wished to dispose of. If you preferred, of course, you could hand it over in cash. He deposited the money in his account at the Vatican bank, and it was then transferred – less his fee – to your foreign bank account.

'The fascinating thing about this arrangement is that while the ensemble constitutes a flagrant breach of the law, each of the individual operations is in itself perfectly legal. There is no law against one Italian citizen donating a large sum of money to another. If the recipient happens to be one of the privileged few who enjoy the right to an account at the Institute for the Works of Religion, it is perfectly in order for him to deposit the money there. And since that institution is extraterritorial, what subsequently happens to the money is of no concern to the Italian authorities.'

She gave a bitter laugh.

'They talk about the rival claims of London and Frankfurt as the future financial capitals of Europe, but what about Rome? What other capital city can boast the convenience of an offshore bank, completely unaccountable to the elected government, subject to no verifiable constraints or controls whatsoever and located just a brief taxi-ride from the centre, with no customs controls or security checks to pass through? Ludovico Ruspanti could walk in there with a billion lire, and when he came out again that billion had effectively vanished! Poof!

'The only weak point in all this was Ruspanti himself. The cut he took counted as unearned income, and of course he couldn't declare it – even supposing he wanted to – without giving the game away. That was the lever I planned to use to squeeze Ruspanti for information on the whole operation, and I must say I was very hopeful of success. But without him, there is literally no case. I naturally couldn't help wondering whether this might not have occurred to some of the other interested parties. That's what I really want to know, dottore. Forget Zeppegno for a moment. You investigated Ruspanti's death. Tell me, did he fall or was he pushed?'

Zen smiled.

'Funnily enough, those were exactly the words that Simonelli used when I spoke to him in Rome.'

The magistrate stared at him coldly.

'*I* am Simonelli.'

'Of course! Please excuse me. I meant Zeppegno, of course.'

He tried to think clearly, but his experiences on the train and in the tunnel seemed to have left him incapable of much more than reacting to immediate events. The only thing he was sure of was the single thread, flimsy but as yet unbroken, which he still held in his hand. It might yet lead him to the heart of this affair, but it would not bear the weight of a judicial process. So although he found himself warming to Antonia Simonelli, he was going to have to stall her for the moment.

'Ruspanti was murdered,' he replied. 'So was the minder the Vatican had assigned to him.'

The magistrate stared at him fixedly.

'But you were quoted in the papers the other day as saying that the allegations that there were suspicious circumstances surrounding Ruspanti's death were mischievous and ill-informed.'

'I wasn't consulted about the wording of that statement.'

He had Simonelli hanging on his every word. The dirtier and more devious it got, the better she liked it. The case she thought was dead had miraculously sprung to life before her eyes!

'The familiar tale,' she said, nodding grimly.

Zen stood up and leaned across the desk towards her.

'Familiar, yes, but in this case also long and complex. You will naturally want to get in touch with the authorities in Bologna, and possibly even go there in person. I therefore suggest that we postpone further discussion on the matter until then.'

She glanced at her watch.

'Very well,' she said. 'But please don't imagine that this is any more than a postponement, dottore. I am determined to get to the bottom of this business, whatever the vested interests involved. I hope I shall have your entire cooperation, but if I have any reason to suspect that it is not forthcoming, I shall have no hesitation in using my powers to compel you to testify.'

Zen held up his hands in a protestation of innocence.

'There'll be no need for that. I've been put in an impossible position in this case, but basically I'm on the side of the angels.'

Antonia Simonelli looked at him with a finely judged mixture of wariness and confidence.

'I'm not concerned with angels, dottore. What I need is someone who's on the side of the law.'

The house was not immediately recognizable as such. The address, in a back street just north of the Teatro alla Scala and west of the fashion alleys of Via Monte Napoleone and Via della Spiga, appeared at first to be nothing more than a slab of blind walling, slightly less high than the modern apartment buildings on either side. It was only as his taxi pulled away that Zen noticed the doors, windows and balconies painted on the plaster, complete with painted shadows to give an illusion of depth. The façade of a severe late-eighteenth-century Austro-French *palazzo* had been recreated in considerable detail, and the fact that the third dimension was missing would doubtless have been less apparent by daylight than it was under the intense glare of the streetlamps, diffused by the pall of fog which had descended on the city with the coming of dusk.

It took Zen some time to locate the real entrance, a plain wooden door inset in the huge *trompe l'oeil* gate framed by pillars at the centre of the frontage. There was no name-plate, and the grille of the entry-phone was disguised in the plumage of the hawk which rose in fake bas-relief above an illusory niche where the actual button figured as the nippled peak of a massive painted metal bell-pull. Zen had barely touched the button when, without a challenge or a query, the door release buzzed to admit him. Only after he stepped inside did he realize, from the shock he felt, what it was he had been expecting: some aggressively contemporary space defined by the complex interaction of concrete, steel and glass. The punch-line of the joke façade, he had tacitly assumed, must lie in the contrast with something as different as possible from historical gentility.

It was the smell which initially alerted him to his error. The musty odours which assailed him the moment he stepped over the thresh-old were quite incompatible with the processes of late-twentieth-century life. Nor could they be reproduced or mocked up. Dense and mysterious, with overlapping strata of rot and mould and fume and smoke, they spoke of years of habitation, generations of neglect. He looked around the cavernous hallway, a huge vaulted space feebly lit by a lamp dangling from a chain so thickly encased in dust and spider-webs that it seemed to be this rather than the rusted metal which was supporting the yellowing bulb. He had a sudden urge to laugh. This was a much better joke than the predictable contrast he had imagined. It was a brilliant coup to have the fake and the reality *correspond*. Evidently the house really was what it had been made to resemble, an aristocratic residence dating from the period when Milan was a city of the Austro-Hungarian Empire.

At one end of the hallway, an imposing stone staircase led upwards into regions of murky obscurity. There was no sound, no one in sight. 'You remember how to get here?' the voice on the phone had asked when he rang that afternoon from his hotel. The same girlish tones as before. For her part, though, she had remarked this time that he 'sounded different, somehow'. He had got the address from SIP, the telephone company, via the Ministry in Rome. They had also supplied the names of the other two subscribers whom Ruspanti had called in Milan. One, predictably enough, was his cousin, Raimondo Falcone. The other was Marco Zeppegno. The woman had told him to arrive at eight o'clock. Apparently Carmela was taking her sister to the opera that night, and would have left by then.

The stairs led to a gallery running the length of the building on the first floor, which was conceived on a scale such as Zen had seen only in museums and government offices. Stripped of the trappings and booty which it had been designed to show off, the gallery looked as pointless and slightly macabre as a drained swimming pool. Such furnishings as there were related neither to use nor comfort. There were no chairs, but a wealth of wooden chests. A fireplace the size of a normal room took up much of one wall, but there was no heating. Acres of bare plaster were relieved only by a series of portraits of men with almost identical beards, whiskers, cravats and expressions of earnest insolence.

'You're not Ludo!'

He whirled round. The voice had come from the other side of the gallery, but there seemed to be no one there. Then he noticed what looked at first like a full-length oil portrait of the woman he had seen on the train, her light blue eyes turned towards him, her head surrounded by a nimbus of fine flaxen hair. He squinted at her. The air seemed thick and syrupy, as though the fog outside were seeping into the house, distorting distances and blurring detail.

'He couldn't come,' Zen ventured.

'But he *promised*!'

He saw now that the supposed canvas was in fact a lighted doorway from which the woman was observing his advance, without any alarm but with an expression of intense disappointment which she made no effort to disguise.

'I spoke to him just this afternoon, and he promised he would come!'

She was wearing a shapeless dress of heavy black material which accentuated the pallor of her skin. Her manner was unnervingly direct, and she held Zen's gaze without any apparent embarrassment.

'He *promised*!' she repeated.

'That's quite right. But he's not feeling very well.'

'Is it his tummy?' the woman asked serenely.

Zen blinked.

'Yes. Yes, his tummy, yes. So he asked me to come instead.'

She moved towards him, her candid blue gaze locked to his face.

'It was you,' she said.

Had she recognized him from the train?

'Me?' he replied vaguely.

She nodded, certain now.

'It wasn't Ludo who rang. It was you.'

He smiled sheepishly.

'Ludo couldn't come himself, so he sent me.'

'And who are *you*?' she asked, like a princess in a fairy story addressing the odd little man who has materialized in her bedchamber.

Zen could smell her now. The odour was almost overpowering, a heady blend of bodily secretions that was far from unpleasant. Combined with the woman's full figure and air of childish candour, it produced an overall effect which was extremely erotic. Zen began to understand the Prince's attraction to his cousin in Milan.

'Do you remember Ludo mentioning that he'd spoken to someone who worked for a magazine?' he said.

The woman's face creased into a scowl, as if recalling the events of the previous week was a mental feat equivalent to playing chess without a board. Then her frowns suddenly cleared and she beamed a smile of pure joy.

'About my dolls!'

Zen smiled and nodded.

'Exactly.'

'It was you? You want to write about them?'

She bit her lower lip and wrung her thin hands in agitation.

'Will there be photographs? I'll need time to get them all looking their best. To tell you the truth, I thought Ludo was only joking.'

She smiled a little wistfully.

'He has such a queer sense of humour sometimes.'

Zen explained that although they would of course want to take photographs at some later stage, this was just an introductory visit to get acquainted. But Ariana Falcone didn't seem to be listening. She turned and led the way through the doorway as though lost in the intensity of her excitement.

'Just think! In the magazines!'

By contrast with the cold, formal, antiquated expanses of the gallery, the room beyond – although about the size of a football pitch – was reassuringly normal in appearance. The architectural imperatives of the great house had been attenuated by the skilful use of paint and light, and the furnishings were comfortable, bright and contemporary. But to Zen's dismay, the place was filled with a crowd numbering perhaps fifty or sixty people, standing and sitting in complete silence, singly or in groups.

Their presence struck Zen with panic. Ariana might have accepted his story at face value, but it was unlikely to bear scrutiny by this sophisticated host. Zen had never been so conscious of himself as the dowdy government functionary, encased in his anonymous suit, as when he ran the gauntlet of that fashionable throng, each flaunting an outfit so stylish and exotic that you hardly noticed the person wearing it. And in fact it was not until Ariana swung round with a grand gesture and announced, 'Well, here they are!', that Zen realized they were all mannequins.

'Some of them are upstairs, being fitted,' she went on. 'Raimondo gave me a copy of *Woman's Wear Daily* recently. I got lots of ideas from that. Which magazine do you work for, by the way?'

'Er . . . *Gente*.'

'Never heard of it.'

You must be the only person in Italy who hasn't, thought Zen. She didn't know what had happened to Ludovico Ruspanti, either. Was there a connection?

'It's about famous people,' he explained. 'Stars.'

'All Raimondo brings me are fashion magazines. And I can't go out, of course, because of my illness. Anyway, what do you think?'

She pointed around the room, watching anxiously for Zen's reaction.

'It's magnificent,' he replied simply.

He meant it! Whatever the implications of this peculiar ensemble, the scale of the conception and the quality of the execution were quite astonishing. Each of the 'dolls' – a full-size figure of articulated wood – was fitted out with a costume like nothing Zen had ever seen. Sometimes the fabrics and colours were boldly contrasted, sometimes artfully complementary. The construction often involved a witty miracle in which heavy velvets apparently depended from gossamer-fine voile, or tweed braces supported a skirt which might have been made of beaten egg whites. Even to someone as deeply ignorant of fashion as Zen was, it was clear that these garments were very special indeed.

'Raimondo is your brother?' he asked.

Ariana's face, which had been beaming with pleasure at his compliment, crumpled up. She nodded mutely.

'And what does he do?' Zen inquired.

'Do? He doesn't do anything. Neither of us *do* anything.'

Zen laughed lightly and pointed to the dolls.

'What about all this?'

She made a moue.

'Oh, that's play, not work.'

He walked about through the throng of figures inclined in a variety of life-like poses. One costume in particular caught his eyes, a clinging cardigan of stretch panne velvet textured to resemble suede and dyed in clashing patches of brilliant primary colours. He had seen it before, and not on a mannequin.

'Do you really make them all yourself?' he asked.

'Of course! I used to have little dolls, but that was too fiddly, so Raimondo got me these.'

She pointed to a male figure on Zen's right.

'I made that outfit last year. It's based on something I saw in a men's fashion magazine Raimondo left lying around, a leather blouson and jeans. I thought that was a bit boring, so I let those panels into the suede to reveal a false lining made of blue shot silk, which looks like bleached denim. The slacks are in brushed silk, mimicking the suede.'

Zen looked at it admiringly.

'It's wonderful.'

Her pixie face collapsed into a scowl.

'*He* doesn't think so.'

'Your brother?'

She nodded.

'I'm surprised he agreed to let you come, actually. I think he's a bit ashamed of my dolls. When I told him what Ludo had said about the magazine when he phoned last week, Raimondo got terribly angry.'

Zen gazed at the stretch panne-velvet cardigan, his mind racing. Was it possible?

'And where is he now?' he asked.

'Raimondo? Oh, he's away in Africa, hunting lions.'

Zen nodded sagely.

'That must be dangerous.'

'That's just what *I* said when he told me. And do you know what he replied? "Only for the lion!" '

He looked at her, and then at the mannequins. The contrast between their astonishing garments and the woman's shapeless black apparel, imbued with the heady reek of the living body within, could not have been more marked.

'Do you ever wear any of the clothes yourself?' Zen asked.

She frowned, as though he'd said something that made no sense.

'They're *dolls'* clothes!'

'They look quite real to me.'

She shrugged jerkily.

'It's just something to keep me amused while I'm ill. When I get better again, and Mummy and Daddy come back, we'll put them all away.'

He gestured around the room.

'What a huge house!'

She looked at him blankly.

'Is it?'

He was about to say something else when she went on, 'Daddy used to say it was like a doll's-house, with the windows and doors painted on the front.'

'Why is it like that?'

She made an effort to remember.

'It happened in the war,' she said at last. 'A bomb.'

'Ah. And do you and Raimondo live here all alone?'

'No, he's got a place of his own somewhere. He doesn't want to catch my illness, you see.'

Zen nodded as though this made perfect sense.

'Is it infectious, then?'

'So he says. He told me that if he stayed here any longer he'd end up as crazy as I am. That's why Mummy and Daddy left, too. I drive people away. I can't help it. It's my illness . . .'

Her voice trailed away.

'What is it?' asked Zen.

She stood listening, her head tilted to one side. He peered at her.

'Is something . . . ?'

'Ssshhh!'

She started trembling all over.

'Someone's coming!'

Zen strained his ears, but couldn't detect the slightest sound.

'It must be Carmela! I don't know what's happened! The opera can't be over yet.'

She clapped her hands together in sheer panic.

'Oh, what are we going to do? What are we going to do?'

Zen stood looking round uncertainly. Suddenly Ariana looked at him intently, sizing him up.

'Take off your coat and jacket!' she hissed.

She darted to the mannequin near by, removed the blouson he was wearing and tossed it to Zen. Then she bundled up his overcoat and jacket and stuffed them hurriedly under a chair. Feeling absolutely ridiculous, Zen struggled into the blouson. Ariana snatched a sort of fisherman's cap off another dummy and put it on him.

'Now stand there and *don't move!*'

There was a sound of footsteps.

'Ariana? Ah, there you are!'

Zen recognized the voice at once. Indeed, it seemed as if he'd been hearing nothing else for the past week. The speaker was out of sight from the position in which Zen was frozen, but he could clearly hear the tremor in Ariana's voice.

'Raimondo!'

'Who were you expecting?'

'Expecting? No one! No one ever comes here.'

You're overdoing it, thought Zen. But the man's brusque tone revealed no trace of suspicion.

'Can you blame them?'

The woman moved away from Zen.

'I thought you were in Africa,' she said. 'Hunting lions.'

He laughed shortly

'I killed them all.'

Zen's posture already felt painfully cramped and rigid. To distract himself, he stared at the costume of the mannequin opposite him, an extraordinary collage of fur, leather, velvet and silk apparently torn into ribbons and then reassembled in layers to form a waterfall of jagged, clashing fabrics.

'Did you see Ludo?' the woman demanded suddenly.

The eagerness in her voice was unmistakable.

'Cousin Ludovico?' the man drawled negligently. 'Yes, I saw him.'

'When? Where? How is he? When is he coming back?'

'Oh, not for some time, I'm afraid. Not for a long, long time.'

His voice was deliberately hard and hurtful.

'Did a lion hurt him?'

She sounded utterly desolate. The man laughed.

'What nonsense you talk! It wasn't a lion, it was *you*. He can't stand being around you, Ariana. It's your own fault! You drive everyone away with your mad babbling. Everyone except your dolls. They're the only ones who can put up with you any longer.'

There was a sound of crying.

'I hope you've kept yourself busy while I've been away,' the man continued.

'Yes.'

'Then stop blubbering and show me. Where are they? Upstairs in the workroom?'

'Yes.'

'Come on then.'

Suddenly the man was there, close enough for Zen to touch. The woman followed, her head lowered, sobbing. She gave no sign of being aware of Zen's presence.

'I'll have to keep an eye on you, Ariana,' the man remarked coldly. 'It looks to me as if you might be going to have one of your bad patches again.'

'That's not true! I've felt ever so well for ages now.'

'Rubbish! You have no idea whether you're well or not, Ariana. You never did and you never will.'

They went out of a door at the far side of the room, closing it behind them. Zen hastily removed the blouson and cap, retrieved his coat and jacket and put them on again. The gallery was as cold and silent as a crypt. Zen tiptoed across it and pattered downstairs to the hallway, where he opened the wooden door set in the painted gate and let himself out. The fog was thicker and denser by now, an intangible barrier which emerged vampire-like every night, draining substance and solidity from the surroundings to feed its own illusory reality. Zen vanished into it like a figment of the city's imagination.

7

Zen's hotel was next to the station, a thirty-storey tower topped with an impressive array of aerials and satellite dishes. The next morning, shaved and showered, his body pleasantly massaged by the whirl-pool bath, clad in a gown of heavy white towelling with the name of the hotel picked out in red, he sat looking out of the window at the streets far below, where the Milanese were industriously going about their business beneath a sky of flawless grey.

Opposite Zen's window, a gang of workers were welding and bolt-ing steel beams into place to form the framework of what, according to the sign on the hoarding around the site, was to be another hotel. Judging by the violence of their gestures, there must have been a good deal of noise involved, but within the double layer of tough-ened glass the only sounds were the hiss of the air conditioning, the murmur of a newscaster on the American cable network to which the television was tuned, and a ringing tone in the receiver of the telephone which Zen was holding to his ear.

'Peace be with you, signora,' he said solemnly, as the phone was answered with an incomprehensible yelp.

'And with you.'

'This is the friend of Signor Nieddo. I would fain speak with Mago.'

'Hold on.'

The receiver was banged hollowly against something. Zen turned to the television. He picked up the remote control and shuffled ran-domly through a variety of game shows, old films, panel discussions, direct selling pitches and all-day sportscasts. Spotting a familiar face in the welter of images, he vectored up the sound.

'. . . whatsoever. Would you agree with that?'

'I agree with no one but myself.'

'What's your position on the hemline debate?'

'It's an irrelevance. My clothes are based on the simple complexi-ties at the heart of all natural processes. Nature doesn't ask whether hemlines are long or short this season. I seek to echo in fabric the

regular irregularity of windblown sand, the orderly chaos of breaking waves . . .'

Zen pressed the MUTE button as the receiver was picked up again.

'Mago is graciously pleased to grant your request. Lo, hearken
unto the words of Mago.'

There was a click as the extension was picked up.

'Hello?' said the boyish voice.

'Nicolo, this is Aurelio, the friend of Gilberto. Have you had any
luck with the little puzzle I set you?'

'Just a moment.'

Zen closed his eyes and saw again the casbah-like shack amid the
sprawling suburbs of Rome's Third World archipelago and the fetid
stall at its heart, dark but for the glowing VDU screen from which the
bedridden boy with the etiolated grace of an angel played fast and
loose with the secrets of the material world.

'It's dated Wednesday, the day before you came to see me,' said
Nicolo, picking up the receiver again. 'The text reads as follows.
"Anonymous sources in the Vatican allegedly assert that there is a
secret group within the Order of Malta, called the Cabal. The exis-
tence of this group was allegedly revealed to the Curia by Ludovico
Ruspanti in exchange for asylum in the weeks preceding his death.
Reported verbally to RL by Zen, Aurelio."'

There was a long silence. Then Zen began to laugh, slowly and
quietly, a series of rhythmic whoops which might almost have been
sobbing. So this was the information which he had supposed so
sensitive that Carlo Romizi had been killed to preserve its confi-
dentiality! The Ministry had no 'parallel' file on the Cabal. All
they knew about it was what they had been told by Zen, who knew
only what he had been told by the Vatican, who knew only what
they had been told by Ludovico Ruspanti, who had made it up.

'I did a series of searches for the classified file on this Aurelio Zen,'
Nicolo continued, 'but I didn't come up with anything.'

'You mean it's inaccessible?'

'No, it doesn't exist. There's an *open* file, in the main body of the
database. I made a copy of that which I can let you have if you're
interested, although frankly it sounds like he's had a pretty boring
life . . .'

Zen spluttered into the mouthpiece.

'Thank you for your help, Nicolo.'

'It's all been a bit of a waste of time, I'm afraid.'

'Not at all. On the contrary. Everything's clear now.'

He put the phone down with an obscure sense of depression. Everything was clear, and hateful. Perhaps that was why everything normally remained obscure, because people secretly preferred it that way. It was certainly a very mixed pleasure to discover that he was considered so unimportant that the powers that be hadn't even bothered to keep tabs on him. Any relief he felt was overwhelmed by shame, anger and hurt. Was he worth no more than that? Evidently not. Well, it served him right for wanting to read his own obituary. He had just done so: *a pretty boring life.*

On the table lay a message which had been brought up with his breakfast, telling him that Antonia Simonelli expected to see him in her office at eleven o'clock that morning. Zen looked at it, and then at the television, where 'the philosopher in the wardrobe' was still holding forth. He identified the name of the station – a private channel, based in the city – and got the number from directory inquiries. It was answered by a young woman who sounded quite overwhelmed by the excitement of working in television.

'Yes!'

'This talk show you've got on now, is it going out live?'

'Live! Live!'

'I need to speak to your guest.'

'Our guest!'

'Get him to leave a number where I can contact him later this morning.'

'Later! Later!'

'Tell him it's urgent. A matter of life and death.'

'Life! Death!'

'Yes. The name is Marco Zeppegno.'

Before getting dressed, Zen made one more call, this time to Rome. Gilberto Nieddu was initially extremely unenthusiastic about doing what Zen wanted, particularly on a Saturday, but Zen said he'd pay for everything, even a courier to the airport.

After leaving the hotel, Zen strolled down the broad boulevard leading from the fantastic mausoleum of the Central Station to the traffic-ridden expanses of Piazza della Repubblica. This was in fact one of the least propitious parts of the city for a pleasant walk. Because of the proximity of the railway yards, Allied bombers had given it their full attention during the closing stages of the war, and the subsequent reconstruction had taken place at a time when Italian architecture was still heavily influenced by the brutal triumphalism of the Fascist era. Zen wasn't concerned about his surroundings, however. He just needed to kill a little time.

He idled along, staring in the shop windows, studying the passers-by, lingering in front of an establishment which sold or hired Carnival costumes. Eventually he reached Piazza della Repubblica, whose oval and rectangular panels of greenery still showed signs of the damage they had incurred during the building of the new Metropolitana C line. At a discreet distance from the piazza, beyond a buffer zone of meticulously trimmed and tended lawns, stood one of the city's oldest and most luxurious hotels. As Zen turned back, his attention was attracted by a young couple walking down the strip of carpet beneath the long green awning towards the waiting line of taxis. The woman looked radiant in a cream two-piece suit which effortlessly combined eroticism and efficiency, while the man, his cherubic face set off by a mass of curls, was a lively and attentive escort. Zen stopped, quite shamelessly gawking. The woman looked mysteriously familiar, like a half-forgotten memory. So bewitching was the vision that it was only at the very last moment, as the taxi swept past, bearing the woman and her young admirer from the scene of past pleasures to that of future delights, that Zen recognized her as Tania Biacis.

He promptly sprinted up the drive towards the next taxi in line, which was coming alongside the awning to pick up a pair of Japanese men who had just emerged from the hotel. Ignoring the shouts of the doorman, an imposing figure clad in something resembling the dress uniform of a Latin American general, Zen opened the passenger door and got in.

'Follow that taxi!' he cried.

The driver turned to him with a weary expression.

'You've been watching too many movies, *dottó.*'

'This rank is for the use of our guests only!' thundered the doorman, opening the door again.

The two Japanese looked on with an air of polite bewilderment. It was too late now anyway. The other vehicle was already lost to view amid the yellow cabs swarming in every direction across the piazza. Zen got out of the taxi and walked slowly back down the drive, shaking his head. At the corner of the block opposite, beneath the high portico, a red neon sign advertised the Bar Capri. Whether intentionally or not, the interior, a bare concrete shell, vividly evoked the horrors of the speculative building which has all but crushed the magic of that fabled isle. Zen went to the pay-phone and dialled the number which had been left for him at the television studio. There was no ringing tone, but almost at once the acoustic background changed to a loud hum and a familiar voice barked, 'Yes?'

Until that moment, Zen had had no clear idea of what he was going to say, but the encounter outside the hotel seemed to have made up his mind for him. The sight of Tania and her young admirer had inspired him with a fierce determination to win her back at any cost. And cost – money – was the key. If Primo could afford to take her to a hotel like that, he must be *loaded*! He had probably paid for her flight, too. Of course, Primo had personal attractions as well, but then so had Zen. What he didn't have was cash, and that was going to change. He had been a sucker for long enough, beavering away at a meaningless job without either thanks or reward. It was success people respected, not diligence or rectitude. Gilberto patronized him, his colleagues patronized him, and now it turned out that Tania was having a fling with some married man with enough money to offer her a good time. And quite right too, he thought. He didn't blame her. What was the point in playing safe when you could end up like Carlo Romizi at any moment? Would it be any consolation, in that final instant of consciousness, to reflect on how *correctly* one had behaved?

'Good morning, dottore,' he said, putting on the singsong accent of an Istrian schoolmaster whom he and his schoolfriends had once used to delight in imitating. 'I saw you on television this morning. A very fine performance, if I may say so.'

'Who is this?'

'The name I gave earlier was Marco Zeppegno, but as you know, dottore, Marco's phone has been disconnected.'

In the background there was the constant hum of what sounded like a car's engine.

'I wonder why,' Zen continued. 'Didn't he pay his bills? Or had he started to make nuisance calls, like Ludovico Ruspanti?'

'Who are you? What do you want?'

Zen chuckled.

'Bearing recent experiences in mind, I'm sure you'll understand if I decline to answer just now. Tapping a phone in the Vatican is a matter for professionals like Grimaldi, but any radio ham can listen in to a mobile phone.'

The connection went dead. For a moment Zen thought that the man had hung up, but he came back at once, calling 'Hello? Hello?'

'It was only interference,' Zen assured him. 'Don't worry, you won't get rid of me that easily!'

'What is it you want?'

'I'll tell you when we meet this afternoon.'

'Impossible! I have a . . .'

Once again the connection was broken for several moments.

'. . . until six thirty or seven. I could see you then.'

'Very well.'

'Come to my office,' the man said after a long pause. 'It's just off Piazza del Duomo. The main entrance is closed at that time, but you can come in the emergency exit at the back. The place was burgled last week and the lock hasn't been repaired yet. It's in Via Foscolo, next to the chemist's, the green door without a number. My offices are on the top floor.'

In Piazza della Repubblica, Zen boarded a two-coach orange tram marked 'Porta Vittoria'. A notice above the large wooden-framed windows set out in considerable detail the conditions governing the transport of live fish and fowl. Goldfish and chicks, Zen learned, would be conveyed (up to a maximum of two per passenger) providing that the containers, which might under no circumstances be larger than a 'normal parcel or shoe box', were neither rough nor splintery, dirty nor foul-smelling, nor yet of such a form as to cause injury to other passengers. The remainder of the text, which laid down the penalties for flaunting these regulations, was too small to read with the naked eye, but the implication was that any anarchistic hotheads who took it upon themselves to carry goldfish or chicks on trams without due regard for the provisions heretofore mentioned would be prosecuted with the full rigour of the law.

Zen recalled the bewilderment of the Japanese businessmen as he barged in like a truculent drunk and attempted to commandeer their taxi. 'Is it always like this?' they were clearly asking themselves. 'Is this the rule, or just an exception?' If they really wanted to understand Italy, they could do worse than give up taxis, take to public transport and ponder the mysteries of a system which legislated for circumstances verging on the surreal yet was unable to ensure that the majority of its users even bought a ticket.

He got off at the stop opposite the Palazzo di Giustizia and ran the gauntlet of the traffic speeding across the herringbone pattern of smooth stone slabs. As he reached the safety of the kerb, a taxi drew up and Antonia Simonelli got out. She looked severe and tense.

'It was Zeppegno all right,' she nodded. 'There doesn't seem any question that it was suicide.'

There was a squeal of tyres at the kerb and someone called his name. Turning round, he found himself face to face with Tania Biacis. Another taxi had pulled up behind the first. The young man who had left the hotel with Tania sat watching from the rear seat of the taxi with an expression of alarm.

'Okay, Aurelio,' shouted Tania, thrusting a finger aggressively towards Antonia Simonelli. 'I've asked you before and I ask you again. Who is she?'

Arm in arm, visibly reconciled, Tania and Zen walked across the pedestrianized expanses of Piazza del Duomo. At the far end, the upper storeys of several buildings were completely hidden behind a huge hoarding displaying three faces represented on the gargantuan scale which Zen associated with the images of Marx, Lenin and Stalin that had once looked down on May Day parades in Moscow's Red Square. But like Catholicism, its old rival, Communism was no longer a serious contender in the ideological battle for hearts and minds. The icon which dominated Milan's Cathedral Square was that of the United Colors of Benetton: the vast, unsmiling features of a Nordic woman, a Black woman and an Asian baby. These avatars of the new order, representatives of a world united by the ascendant creed of consumerism, gazed down on the masses whose aspirations they embodied with a look that was at once intense and vapid.

'They're suing the hospital,' said Tania.

'Good for them.'

'This is all between us, but apparently Romizi's wife was having an affair with Bernardo Travaglini.'

'You're joking!'

'Once she'd got over the shock of Carlo's death, she got in touch with Bernardo and told him her suspicions about what happened. He and De Angelis went round to the hospital with a couple of uniformed men in a squad car and put the fear of God into the director.'

Zen could easily picture the scene, the two plainclothes officials wandering menacingly about the director's office, their words a mixture of bureaucratic minutiae and paranoia-inducing innuendo, while their uniformed cohorts guarded the door. Yes, Giorgio and Bernardo would have had the director eating out of their hands in no time at all. The irony was that Zen might have done something of the sort himself if he hadn't been so convinced that Carlo had been the victim of the Cabal. But it now appeared that Romizi's death had been caused by a different sort of plot.

'Under pressure from Travaglini and De Angelis, the director came up with the name of the intern who visited Romizi that night,' Tania continued. 'When they called on him, the intern claimed that he had been acting on orders. He'd never been trained to use life-support equipment, and had no idea what the effect would be. He was told to reset such-and-such a knob to such-and-such a setting, and that's what he did.'

'They needed the bed?'

Tania shrugged.

'That's what it looks like. The hospital is denying the whole thing, of course. Signora Romizi's suing the hospital, the intern and the doctor in charge have been suspended, and the Procura has opened a file on the affair.'

They crossed the square and entered the glazed main aisle of the Galleria Vittorio Emanuele. The elegant mall was almost empty, the offices on the upper floors and the exclusive shops at ground level both shut. Tania lingered for some time in front of a window displaying the latest creations from the teeming imagination of the legendary Falco. With a shove half-playful, half-serious, Zen propelled her towards the one establishment still open for business, the Café Biffi. They sat outside, under the awnings whose function here was purely decorative, in an area cordoned off from the aisle by a row of potted plants on stands. Tania opted for a breaded veal cutlet and salad. Zen said he'd have the same.

'But if you specialize in products from the Friuli,' Zen asked, picking up a conversation they had had earlier, 'what are you doing here?'

'We want to diversify, keeping the original concept of traditionally-made items from small producers whom a big exporter company won't handle because they can't deliver in quantity. Primo is based here in Milan, so . . .'

'Don't tell me he's a farmer!'

'God, you don't let up, do you?'

Her look wavered on the edge of the brink of a real challenge. Don't push me too hard, it said. Zen grinned in a way he knew she found irresistible.

'You know what the police are like.'

'Yes,' she said. 'They're bastards.'

Their food arrived, and for a while everything else was forgotten. It was almost two o'clock by now, and they were starving. Once the embarrassment and confusion of the initial confrontation in front of the lawcourts had been cleared up, there had been no time to do anything but arrange to meet later. Then Zen had accompanied Antonia Simonelli to her office, where he provided her with a detailed and largely accurate account of the circumstances in which Ludovico Ruspanti had died, while Tania had gone off to 'talk business' with Primo.

Now they were together again, other commitments suspended for an hour. But although both seemed eager to dispel the suspicions which had arisen as a result of past evasions, the explanations and revelations came unevenly, in fits and starts, a narrative line deflected by questions and digressions, forging ahead towards the truth but leaving pockets of ambiguity and equivocation to be mopped up afterwards. Amongst these was the one Zen had just tackled, and to which he returned once they had satisfied their immediate hunger.

'So, about Primo . . .'

Tania wiped her lips with a napkin which looked as though it had been carved from marble.

'Primo is a middleman representing a network of small producers stretching from Naples to Catanzaro.'

Zen nodded slowly.

'Oh, you mean he works for the mob! No wonder he can afford to stay at that fancy hotel. They probably own it.'

Tania twitched the hem of her cream skirt.

'Aurelio, I'm going to get really angry in a moment. Quite apart from anything else, it so happens that *I'm* the one who's staying there.'

Zen raised his eyebrows, genuinely disconcerted.

'Well, well.'

'It's my little indulgence.'

'Not *that* little. You must be doing well.'

She nodded.

'We are. Very well. But I'm increasingly realizing that the future is in the south. Up here, agriculture is getting more and more com-mercialized, more industrialized and centralized. You're no longer dealing with individual producers but with large agribusinesses or cooperatives whose managers think in terms of consistency and volume. The south has been spared all that. It's just too poor, too fragmented, too disorganized, too far from the centre of Europe. Those factors are all drawbacks for bulk produce, but once you're talking designer food then the negatives become positives . . .'

She broke off, catching sight of his abstracted look.

'I'm boring you.'

He quickly feigned vivacity.

'No, no.'

'It's all right, Aurelio. There's no reason why you should be interested in the wholesale food business.'

He pushed the last piece of veal cutlet around his plate for a moment, then laid down his knife and fork.

'It's just a shock to find that you're so . . . so successful and high-powered. It makes me feel a bit dowdy by comparison.'

If his words sounded slightly self-pitying, the look he gave her immediately afterwards was full of determination.

'But that's going to change.'

'Of course. You'll soon get used to it.'

'I don't mean that.'

'Then what do you mean?'

'You'll see.'

A pair of Carabinieri officers in full dress uniform strode by, murmuring to each other in a discreet undertone. With their tricorn hats and black capes trimmed with red piping, they might have passed for clergy promenading down the apse of this secular basilica, oriented not eastward, like the crumbling gothic pile in the square outside, but towards the north, source of industry, finance and progress.

'So he works for you?' asked Zen, lighting a cigarette.

Tania pushed her plate aside.

'Primo? No, no, we don't pay salaries. Piece-rates and low overheads, that's the secret of success. Look at Benetton. That's how they started out. Run by a woman, too.'

She took one of her own cigarettes, a low-tar mentholized brand. Zen had tried one once. It was like smoking paper tissues smeared with toothpaste.

'No, Primo works for the EC,' she said. 'He goes round farms assessing their claims for grants. We pay him on a commission basis to put us in touch with possible suppliers.'

He nodded vaguely. She was right, of course. He wasn't interested in the details of the business she was running. He *was* interested in the results, though. Tania had rejected the idea of moving in with Zen, on the grounds that his flat was too small. But if he could bring off the little coup he had planned for that evening, he would have the cash for a down-payment on somewhere much larger, perhaps with a separate flat for his mother across the landing. And as a double-income couple, they could pay off the loan with no difficulty.

He looked around the Galleria, smoking contentedly and running over the idea in his mind. This was a new venture for him. He had cut corners before, of course. He had bent the rules, turned a blind eye, and connived at various mild degrees of fraud and felony. But never before had he cold-bloodedly contemplated extorting a large sum of money for his personal gain. Still, better late than never. Who the hell did he think he was, anyway, Mother Theresa? Not that there was any great moral issue involved. Antonia Simonelli might succeed in embarrassing the Vatican, but she had no real chance of making a case against those responsible for killing Ludovico Ruspanti. One of them, Marco Zeppegno, was already dead, and with his death the other man had put himself beyond the reach of justice. But not beyond the reach of the Cabal, thought Zen.

He leant back, looking up at the magnificent glass cupola, a masterpiece of nineteenth-century engineering consisting of thousands of rectangular panes supported by a framework of wrought-iron ribs soaring up a hundred and fifty feet above the junction of the two arcaded aisles. The resemblance to a church was clearly deliberate: the four aisles arranged like an apse, choir and transepts, the upper walls decorated with frescoed lunettes, the richly inlaid marble flooring, the vaulted ceilings, the central cupola. Here is *our* temple, said the prophets of the Risorgimento, a place of light and air, dedicated to commerce, liberty and civic pride. Compare it with the oppressive, dilapidated pile outside, reeking of ignorance and superstition, and then make your choice.

'What now?' asked Tania.

He gave a deep frown, which cleared as he realized that she meant the question literally.

'I've got to go to the airport.'

'You're not leaving already?'

'No, no. I have to pick up something which is being air-freighted up here. Something I need for my work.'

'What are you doing here, anyway?'

He shrugged.

'Just following up some ramifications of the Ruspanti affair. Nothing very interesting.'

She signalled the waiter and asked for two coffees and the bill. Zen raised his eyebrows slightly.

'I'll put it on expenses,' she said.

'Fiddling already?'

'Actually I'm saving money. If I hadn't bumped into you, I'd be lunching Primo instead, the full five courses somewhere they really know how to charge.'

'Whereas I get a snack in a café, eh?' he retorted in a mock-surly tone.

Tania smiled broadly and stroked his hand.

'I'll make it up to you tonight, sweetheart.'

His face clouded over.

'Is there a problem?' she asked.

'Well, I may not be free until nineish.'

She patted his hand reassuringly.

'That's all right. I shall just have to go and buy some very expensive clothes to while away the time. There's a wonderful new outfit by Falco I just *crave*. Jagged strips of suede and silk and fur arranged in layers like a pile of scraps, just odds and ends, but somehow holding together, though you can't see how. Did you see it in that shop, towards the back?'

He smiled mysteriously.

'I've seen it, but not in a shop.'

She looked at him with interest.

'You've seen someone wearing it?'

'Not exactly.'

The waiter arrived with the coffee, and Zen took advantage of the interruption to change tack slightly.

'Are his clothes very expensive?'

'Hideously!' she cried. 'But each one is an original creation. It's an investment as well as a luxury, like buying a work of art.'

Zen's mysterious smile intensified.

'All the same, if I were you I'd put my money into something else. I have a feeling that the market in Falco creations might be about to take a tumble.'

Tania patted his hand indulgently.

'Aurelio, you're a dear, sweet man, but you haven't a clue about fashion.'

The man stepped off the exercise bicycle and surveyed himself in the mirror. His lithe, slender body was covered with a pleasing sheen of sweat, creating highlights and chiaroscuro and emphasizing the contours of the evenly tanned flesh, hardened and sculpted by workouts such as the one he had just completed. So satisfied was he by what the mirror showed him that he lingered there a moment longer under the spell of that unattainable object of desire.

'Without my clothes, I feel naked,' he had once remarked to an interviewer, who had laughed uproariously at this witticism. It was in fact the literal truth. Even his own nudity was only tolerable when reflected back to him from the mirror. The idea of other people's was quite repugnant to him. His secret fantasy was to *become* that glistening image, to break through the glass and merge with that substanceless child of light, for whom being and seeming were one and the same. As for the others, as imperfect as himself, and a good deal less fastidious in most cases, he did not particularly care to share a room with most of them, never mind anything more intimate. With a final, flirtatious glance at the mirror, he turned away and flounced off to the bathroom.

Ten minutes later, dressed in jeans and a leather jacket, he walked through to the adjoining pair of offices. The clock on the wall showed twenty to seven. The suite was located on the top floor of a block backing on to the Galleria Vittorio Emanuele, and commanded a striking view of the great glazed cupola, swelling up into the night sky like a luminous balloon. He had switched off all the lights, and this background glimmer, softened by the thickening fog, was the only source of illumination. Feeling a prickle of sweat break out on his stomach and back, he opened the window slightly. Coolness was the key to everything. The secret of his success lay in the ability to remain perfectly calm whatever happened, to manipulate events and perceptions so that people saw only what he wished them to see.

He picked up a canvas bag lying on the desk and went into the workroom next door. The walls were covered with sketches and photographs, the floor littered with irregular off-cuts of the fine paper used for sizing garments. Only a tiny fraction of the light from the Galleria penetrated to this internal room, but he moved through it with total confidence, skirting the pin-studded mannequins and sidestepping the benches draped with silk and velvet, cashmere and wool, leather and tweed. As he passed each one, he let his fingers run over the material, and shivered sensuously.

The one way in which he revealed himself to be his father's son was his passion for materials: their look, their feel, their smell. Umberto used to bring samples home from the mills at Como and stroke the boy's infant cheeks with them. The idea was to train Raimondo from the earliest possible age for his future role as heir to the family textile business. But the child had misunderstood, as children are prone to do. He thought his father was caressing him, expressing a love that so rarely manifested itself on other occasions.

At the door leading to the hallway, he paused briefly and listened. All was quiet. He unlocked the door, went out and closed it behind him, pulling until the lock engaged with a precise click. He removed a pair of disposable rubber gloves from the bag and put them on, then took out the cold chisel and hammer. Working the chisel into the crack between the lock and the jamb, he struck it repeatedly until the lock shattered. Then he replaced the chisel and hammer in the bag, peeled off the rubber gloves with a shudder of disgust – they reminded him of condoms – and went back inside, leaving the door slightly ajar.

As he passed one of the worktables, his fingers touched a garment which he could not for a moment identify. He paused to stroke it delicately, grazing the surface of the fabric like a lover exploring the contours of his partner's body. A languid smile of recognition softened the normally rigid contours of his lips. Of course! It was the model for the new line of jeans which he was going to unleash on the world next year, a move calculated to reaffirm the atelier's revolutionary reputation. Not that demand for the existing lines had in any way slackened. On the contrary, business was booming. But he knew that the time to abandon a successful formula was before it began to pall. That way, you retained the initiative. You weren't running for cover, you were 'making a statement'.

In the present instance, this meant abandoning the complex, multi-layered pyrotechnics for which he'd become famous in favour of something plain and popular, something strong and simple, something *ecological*. Jeans were all these things, of course, but their appeal was fatally diminished by the fact that they were also durable, and cheap. The response of the leading designers had been to price them up, to sell the price rather than the garment.

Such a solution was worthy of the shallow, conventional minds who ran the major fashion houses. Anyone could license a line of designer denims and sell them at a five hundred per cent mark-up – at least, anyone with a name like Armani or Valentino could. It had been left to him, the newcomer, to achieve a truly creative breakthrough. His fingertips caressed the soft brushed silk which he'd had tinted to resemble worn and faded denim. Naturally no one in their right minds would be prepared to pay Falco prices for real denim, which would last for years. These, on the other hand, although virtually indistinguishable from the real thing to the naked eye, would tolerate only the most limited wear before falling apart. People were going to *kill* for them.

Back in his private sanctum, he sat down at his desk and held his watch up to the glimmer from the window. Five to seven. He opened the middle drawer of the desk and took out the pistol he had brought from home. The gun had belonged to his father, a service-issue revolver which he had retained illegally at the end of the war as a souvenir. As far as he knew, Umberto had never used the weapon in anger, not that it would have done him much good against the Red Brigades' Kalashnikovs. But that would just make the authorities more sympathetic when his son acted a trifle hastily in a similar situation. Not that anyone was likely to think twice about the matter anyway. Break-ins and muggings were everyday events in the junkie-ridden centre of Milan. What was more natural than that he should keep his father's old service pistol at the office where he often worked late and alone? Or indeed that he should use it when the need arose?

'I was walking towards my desk, officer, when I heard a sound in the outer office. I'd just had a shower. I suppose that's why I hadn't heard the noise of the door being forced. I ran to the desk and got out the pistol I've kept there since the building was broken into last week . . .' After that, it would depend on whether his visitor proved to have been armed, something which he could easily verify after shooting him dead. If he wasn't, then it might be marginally more difficult, although accidents did notoriously happen in these circumstances. But this was unlikely. The overwhelming probability was that the intruder would have a gun too. He sounded like Zeppegno, a wannabee thug full of tough talk and cheap threats. To scum like that, a gun was like an American Express card. It said something about you. People treated you with respect and said, 'That'll do nicely, sir.' You didn't leave home without it. All he needed to do was put on the rubber gloves and fire a few rounds from the victim's gun into the walls and furniture, then transfer the sheaths to the dead man's hands, thus explaining the lack of fingerprints, and call the police. If he got anything more than a fine for possessing an unregistered firearm, there would be a universal outcry among the good burghers of Milan. What, an eminent designer could be threatened by some doped-up hoodlum in his own office without even being permitted to defend himself? What was the world coming to?

He placed the gun on the desk within easy reach and lay back in his swivel chair, thinking about his father. His parents were not often in his thoughts. Indeed, people had called him cold and unnatural at the time of the tragedy, but it would be truer to say that he felt little or nothing, and refused – this was the scandal, of course – to pretend that he did. He had never tried to get anyone else to understand his views on the subject, which all came down to the fact that he did not consider Umberto and Chiara to be his parents at all, except in the most reductive genetic sense. Their children were Raimondo and his sister Ariana. He, Falco, owed them nothing.

His cousin Ludovico Ruspanti had been an early inspiration. He had made everyone else in Raimondo's circle seem wan and insipid. When Umberto and Chiara became martyrs of the class struggle, his father dying in a hail of machine-gun fire sprayed through the windscreen of their Mercedes, his mother succumbing to her injuries a few days later, he had remembered Ludovico's deportment on the occasion of his own bereavements. He must have handled it badly, though. No one had criticized Ludovico's play-acting, even though he had turned to wink broadly at his cousin after making some fulsome comments about his late brother, as though to say 'We know better, don't we?' Raimondo, on the other hand, had made the mistake of being frank about his feelings, or lack of them, and for this he had never been forgiven.

What no one could ever deny was that he had coped extremely

well with orphanhood, while Ariana had been broken. She had worshipped her parents, particularly her mother, to whom she had always been close. Raimondo had made no secret of the fact that he disapproved of her childlike dependency, of that physical intimacy prolonged well into adolescence. He found it cloying and excessive, and he had been proved right. When the walls of her emotional hothouse were so brutally shattered by the terrorists' bullets, Ariana had collapsed into something very close to madness.

This fact had been hushed up by the services of exclusive and discreet private 'nursing homes' which existed for just this very purpose, and by the use of such euphemisms as 'prostrated by grief' and 'emotionally overwrought'. The plain truth was that Ariana Falcone had gone crazy, as her brother had not scrupled to tell her to her face shortly after the funeral. Enough was enough! He had always resented the exaggerated fuss which had been made of Ariana, the way her every wish and whim was pandered to. This excessive display of temperament was just another blatant example of attention-seeking, and in extremely poor taste too, trading on their parents' violent deaths for her own selfish ends, and trying – with a certain amount of success, moreover – to make him look cold and heartless by comparison. The sooner she faced up to the realities of the new situation the better. Their parents were dead and he was in charge. What Ariana needed was a series of short, sharp shocks to bring this home to her, and it was this which he had set out to provide.

Although he had applied his treatment rigorously, Ariana stubbornly refused to respond. On the first anniversary of the killings, he had given her one last chance, ordering her to appear at a memorial service which was being held at their local church. Not only had she refused, but the only reason she deigned to give was that she wanted to play with her collection of dolls which were kept in the beautiful wooden toy-house which her parents had given her for her eighth birthday. Her brother's response had been swift and decisive. Tying her to a chair, he had doused the doll's-house in paraffin and set fire to it before her eyes, with the dolls inside.

But Ariana's petulance seemingly knew no bounds. Far from accepting that it was time to stop these embarrassing and self-indulgent games, she had sunk into a condition verging on catatonia. Eventually Raimondo found a doctor who was prepared to prescribe an indefinite course of tranquillizers which kept Ariana more or less amenable, and their Aunt Carmela was brought in to act as minder. Raimondo moved out to a small modern flat near the university, where he had been re-enrolling for years without ever taking his exams. The huge palazzo which Umberto's father had bought in the twenties was turned over to Carmela and Ariana. A new play-house was obtained and stocked with dolls. It was not quite the same, but Ariana showed no sign of noticing the difference, or of remembering what had happened to the original. She spent her days happily sewing clothes for her dolls based on ideas culled from Carmela's discarded magazines.

What happened next was completely unpredictable. Appropriately enough, the whole thing had been intended as a joke. Paolo, one of Raimondo's student acquaintances, had always dreamt of becoming a fashion designer, much against his parents' wishes. It was he who told Raimondo about the competition being run by a leading fashion magazine to find the 'designers of tomorrow'. He was submitting a portfolio of drawings and sketches, which he described to his friends at every opportunity. If he won, he explained, then his parents would be obliged to let him follow his genius instead of taking a job in a bank. Paolo went on at such length about it that Raimondo finally decided to play a trick on him. One evening when Ariana had gone to bed, he borrowed a dozen of her dolls, complete with the miniature costumes she had made for them, removed the heads to make them resemble dressmaker's mannequins, and then photographed them carefully with a close-up lens. Next he took the prints to a commercial art studio and had them reproduced as fashion sketches, which he triumphantly showed to Paolo as *his* entry.

If Paolo had taken the thing in the spirit in which it had been intended, Raimondo would have admitted the truth, had a good laugh, and that would have been that. To his amazement, however, Paolo reacted with a torrent of vituperative abuse. Raimondo's designs were impractical nonsense, he claimed. No one could ever make such things, let alone wear them. In short, it would be an insult to submit them for the competition. Until that moment, Raimondo had not had the slightest intention of doing so, but Paolo had been so unpleasant that he sent the drawings in to spite him. When the results were announced three months later, he was awarded the first prize.

His first reaction was one of incredulity. The joke had gone far enough – much too far, in fact. He must put a stop to it at once. But that wasn't so easy, not with all Milan beating a path to the door. Paolo couldn't have been more wrong, it seemed. The designs Raimondo had submitted were judged to be daring but accessible, refreshingly different, striking just the right balance between novelty and practicality. He was offered contracts, more or less on his own terms, with several of the city's top fashion houses.

If Ariana had been in her right mind, he would have let her take the prize and the fame and fortune that went with it. As it was, this was out of the question. His sister was quite incapable of sustaining the ordeal of public exposure. Apart from Aunt Carmela and Raimondo himself, the only person she ever saw was her cousin Ludovico, on whom she seemed to have developed a schoolgirlish crush. She always brightened up before, during and after his visits, which had grown quite frequent. Apparently Ludo had some business interests in Milan, although it was never very clear what they were. When he was around, Ariana could almost pass for normal, but this was an illusion. Ariana lived in a self-contained world, talking to no one but her dolls. She had never watched television or read the papers since the day a report about some terrorist atrocity had caused a lengthy relapse. Her world had a lot to recommend it, from her point of view. It was warm, stable and quiet. There were no nasty surprises. Love might safely be invested, secure in the knowledge that no harm could befall.

For Raimondo to admit the truth would only have served to kill a goose whose eggs, it seemed, were of solid gold. But it wasn't really a question of money. The Falcone family fortunes, although no longer quite what they had been when Umberto was running the business, were still in an altogether different league from those of their Roman cousins. No, it was the original element – that of the practical joke, the elaborate prank – which swayed him in the end. If fooling Paolo had seemed a worthwhile thing to do, the idea of fooling *everybody* was completely irresistible.

It took him a while to find his feet. The freelance contract didn't work out in the end. When the house involved requested small changes in various details, he'd had to refuse, for the simple reason that he was unable to draw. His arrogance and intransigence attracted criticism at the time, but in the long run the episode merely strengthened his hand, increasing his reputation as a wayward, uncompromising genius who worked alone by night and then appeared with a sheaf of sketches and said, 'Take it or leave it!'

When he launched his own ready-to-wear line the following March, it was only a modest success. The fashion world in Italy is dominated by a handful of big names whose control is exercised through exclusive contracts with textile producers, insider deals in which the fashion press allocate editorial space in direct proportion to the amount of advertising bought, and licensing arrangements for perfumes, watches, lighters, glasses, scarves and luggage which make such 'concession tycoons' multi-millionaires without their having to lift a finger. What was being sold was an image created by the designers' *haute couture* range, shown three times a year in Rome and abroad. Such garments, selling for tens of billions of lire, were out of reach to anyone but the super-rich, most of them in America and the Gulf oil states, but the image of luxury and exclusivity were available to anyone prepared to pay a modest sum for a 'designer-labelled' product which might in fact have been produced in a Korean sweat shop. The sweat didn't stick, the chic did. That was the trick of it.

As sole owner of a large textile mill, Raimondo Falcone was in a unique position to break the cartel on raw materials. The problem lay in generating the desirable image. He clearly couldn't go into *couture*. As the word implies, this means being able to cut, to go into a fitting room with the client, pick up a length of cloth and a pair of scissors and produce something which looks like it has grown there. This was clearly not a possibility for Raimondo, who couldn't cut a slice of *panettone* without wrecking the entire cake. Then he had his inspiration, one day when he was being interviewed on television. His sudden emergence on to the fashion scene, as though from nowhere, was already the stuff of legend. People were naturally curious about him, his background, his working methods, his philosophy. While he was telling the interviewer a pack of lies – 'I always thought of it as a hobby really, I used to scribble ideas on the back of an envelope and then lose it somewhere . . .' – it occurred to him that what people really wanted from their clothes was the kind of miraculous transformation like the one which so fascinated them about him. They wanted to be able to put on a new personality like putting on a shirt. Fashion wasn't just about attracting sexual partners or showing off your wealth. It was a search for metamorphosis, for transcendence.

And who better to offer it than a man who appeared unfettered by the constraints within which ordinary mortals were forced to operate?

From that moment, he had never looked back. It took no more than an occasional grudging, condescending word of praise from him to keep Ariana busy. Censored extracts from fashion magazines, from which all reference to Falco designs had of course been removed, kept her fantasy world in touch with the colours, lines and fabrics which were currently in vogue. Once he had succeeded in convincing her that she needed big dolls to play with now, being a big girl herself, the trick-photography and out-of-house sketches could be dispensed with. From time to time he removed a selection of the garments she made and handed them over to his subordinates, a tight, highly-paid and very loyal team who relieved the maestro of the tiresome day-to-day business of putting his creations into production from the original models. All he had to do was tour the country, appearing at shops and on television, telling people that they were what they wore, and that in the late twentieth century it was ideologically gauche to suggest otherwise.

He sat upright suddenly, listening intently. Then he heard it again, a distant metallic sound somewhere far below. Once again, a smile bent his lips. He knew what it was: the discarded filing-cabinet shell which had been sitting on the landing of the first floor for as long as anyone could remember. When he arrived, having smashed off the padlock used to secure the emergency exit since the break-in, he had pulled the metal cabinet out from the wall so that it all but blocked the way upstairs. Its faint tintinnabulation was as good as a burglar alarm to him.

He picked up the pistol and walked with rapid, light steps into the workroom, where he knelt down behind one of the tables with a clear view of the door. The moment it opened, the intruder would be framed in a rectangle of light, peering into a dark, unfamiliar territory where the only recognizable targets were the mannequins. But *he* would be ready, his eyes perfectly adjusted to the fog-muted glimmer from the Galleria outside, the pistol steadied against the edge of the table and trained on its target. It would be like shooting rabbits leaving the burrow.

Then a miracle occurred. That, at least, is how he explained it to himself in that initial instant of wordless awe. After that it was pure sensation, pure experience. Later he realized that the whole thing could have taken no more than a few seconds, but while it lasted there was nothing else, only the noise and the light. The light was the kind you might see if they skinned your eyeballs, pickled them in acid and trained lasers on them. As for the *noise* . . .

When he was a boy, he had once been allowed up the campanile of the family church. After endless windings, the spiral staircase broadened into a chamber where the bells hung, great lumps of dull metal, seeming no more resonant than so many rocks. Yet when the clapper struck, they could be heard over half the city. He had wondered ever after what it would have sounded like if they'd started pealing while he was standing there. Now he knew. His whole body thrilled and jangled, every cell and fibre quivering in exquisite agony as the overtones and reverberations of that blow died away. Another such would kill him, he thought as he lay in a heap on the floor, clutching his head. But there wasn't another. This puzzled him at first. Once the clapper was set swinging with that kind of violence, it was bound to come back to strike the other side, just when you were least expecting it.

Hands moved lightly and rapidly all over his body, like a couturier fitting a client. He opened his eyes. A tall figure wearing a black clerical suit stood looking down at him, a revolver in each hand. Above the trim white collar rose a garish latex Carnival mask representing the bluff, benign features of John Paul II.

From the other side of the latex mask, Aurelio Zen surveyed the situation with a sense of satisfaction and relief. He had been extremely dubious about the outcome of this venture ever since picking up the package that afternoon at Linate. He had no idea what stun grenades looked like, but given what Gilberto had told him they were going to cost, he was expecting something pretty impressive. Gleaming stainless-steel canisters with spring-action triggers and time-delay settings, slightly greasy to the touch – that sort of thing. Above all, he was expecting them to *weigh*. 'We are the goods,' he expected them to tell him as he staggered away from the airline counter with a metal case marked DANGER – HIGH EXPLOSIVE.

Instead of which the clerk had casually tossed him a padded envelope which felt almost empty. Zen left feeling like the victim of a confidence trick. Matters did not improve when he opened the envelope in the taxi on the way back to the city. Inside, he found two grey plastic tubes, each about the size of a toothpaste dispenser, lashed together by a rubber band looped over on itself. At one end, a red plastic peg with a ridged grip protruded a few centimetres from the body of the tube, the junction being sealed with a pull-tab. There was also a note in Gilberto's jauntily precise writing.

To avoid accidents, remove seal at last moment. After pulling out the red pin, you have 3 seconds to deliver the grenade and get out. The effects last 5 seconds or more, depending on the physical condition of the opposition, their degree of preparation and training, etc. One pack is enough for an average-sized room; larger areas may require two.

Just like air freshener, thought Zen disgustedly. Four hundred thousand lire each, Gilberto was charging him for these! 'And that's cost price, Aurelio. In fact *below* cost, because it's what I paid three months ago. God knows what the replacement cost will be.' As an added irony, the source was one of Zen's colleagues. The reason the grenades were so expensive was that very few came on to the market. Any equipment on general military or police issue could be had at massive discounts, for that was very much a buyer's market. But stun grenades were supplied only to a few specialist units in the police and Carabinieri. Nieddu's supplier was connected to the Interior Ministry's DIGOS anti-terrorist squad, whose morale was at an all-time low these days – which no doubt explained why they were resorting to private enterprise, like everyone else.

In the event, though, Zen had to admit that his doubts had been decisively confounded. The grenades might not look much, but they packed one hell of a punch. Even from the other side of the door, the effect had been that of the firework to end all fireworks. He hadn't been sure how large the room was, but at almost half a million lire a go, Zen decided that one was going to have to be enough. Which it certainly had been. When he charged in, Falcone was lying on the floor, his hands to his head and his knees drawn up, like one of the victims overwhelmed by lava at Pompeii. Setting down his replica revolver, Zen grabbed the pistol which the man had been holding and frisked him swiftly for other weapons. Then he picked up his toy gun and stepped back.

After a few seconds, Falcone moaned and rubbed his eyes as though stirring from sleep. He stared incredulously at Zen, who smiled in the privacy afforded by the latex mask. The fancy dress had been another aspect of the affair which he had been unsure about. Some disguise was certainly necessary. He didn't want to give the game away too soon, not without finding out as much as he could. This was his first deliberate attempt at criminal extortion, and he didn't want to bungle it. The single card he had to play should certainly be enough to extract a cash settlement, but if his victim could be kept in suspense about who he was and what he wanted, then other potentially profitable facts might well emerge. At the very least, the aura of psychological domination thus established would work strongly to Zen's advantage when it came to agreeing terms.

The moment he thought of disguises, he recalled the fancy-dress shop he had seen that morning in Via Pisani. At that time of year, they had an extensive selection available for hire, but in the end Zen had opted for a clerical outfit. The mask, a pudgy parody of Wojtyla's Slavic features, had then been an obvious accessory. Nevertheless, it remained to be seen how it went down on the night. As it turned out, there were no worries on that score. Falcone couldn't keep his eyes off it.

'You're a bit early for Carnival,' he eventually remarked with a brave attempt at reasserting himself.

'It's for your protection,' Zen replied in the singsong accent he had used on the phone.

'For *yours*, you mean.'

The plastic pope's face moved from side to side in a gesture of negation that made a macabre contrast with its expression of benevolent paternalism.

'If I were not masked, you might recognize me,' Zen explained. 'Then we would have to kill you.'

He waited a moment for this to sink in.

'We may decide to do so anyway in the end, of course. That depends on whether you are able to furnish a satisfactory explanation of your conduct with regard to the Ruspanti affair.'

Falcone tried a laugh.

'What have *I* to do with that? There's absolutely no evidence linking me to the Ruspanti affair.'

'Evidence is for judges. I am not a judge, I am an executioner. Sentence has already been passed. Unless you can persuade me otherwise in the next few minutes, it will be carried out.'

In the pools of shadow on the floor, Falcone squirmed like a stranded fish.

'But what have I done, for God's sake? What have I done?'

'You have taken our name in vain! You have slandered our organization and circulated lies about our aims and activities. You have stirred up a hornet's nest of speculation and rumour that is causing us considerable embarrassment. In short, you have attempted to make use of us.'

The black holes of the mask's eyes bored into Falcone.

'The Cabal does not allow itself to be made use of.'

Once again Falcone tried to laugh, but it broke from him like a belch, uncontrolled and shameful.

'Listen, there's been a terrible mistake! I had no idea that any such organization as the Cabal even existed! Ruspanti told me he had dreamed it up as a way of getting the Vatican to give him refuge. He was very proud of how clever he'd been, of how the priests were swallowing it all and coming back for more. I thought that's all it was, just something he'd made up!'

'That's not what you told the police.'

At this, Falcone visibly shrank.

'What?'

'The police official from the Ministry of the Interior who was called in by the Vatican to investigate the Ruspanti affair. You didn't tell *him* that you thought the whole thing was a hoax. On the contrary, you went to great lengths to ensure that he thought that the Cabal was behind the whole affair.'

Falcone gasped.

'You know about that?'

'It will save a lot of time if you just assume that we know *everything*. Now answer my question! Why did you go to such extraordinary lengths – breaking into a confessional in St Peter's, setting up a shortwave radio link – just so as to smear an organization whose existence you now say you didn't believe in?'

'I never intended to smear anyone . . .'

'Well you certainly succeeded! The Ministry of the Interior even opened a file on us. Fortunately one of our men was able to have it suppressed, but the effects could have been incalculable. For the last time, *why*?'

Falcone looked up at the pistol in the man's right hand. It was now pointing directly towards him. With absolute clarity, he realized that he was going to die – and by his own gun, or rather his father's.

'It was just a bluff!' he cried. 'We suspected that the police knew more than they were officially admitting. The idea was to convince the officer in charge that Ruspanti's death was not a criminal matter but a political one, and that the guilty party might include anyone and everyone from his own boss to the President of the Republic.'

The papal mask nodded like an obscene parody of a priest hearing confession.

'But who is this "we"? And why should you care what line the police were taking?'

'I meant the Falcone family. Ruspanti was a distant cousin of ours, and we were worried that . . .'

A harsh cackle from the lips of the plastic pope cut him off.

'Oh come, now! You had rather more reason to worry about than the family connection, didn't you?'

'I don't know what you mean.'

'Then let me fill you in. Friday last week, you and Marco Zeppegno murdered Ludovico Ruspanti by throwing him from the upper gallery in St Peter's . . .'

'We didn't *throw* him!'

Too late, he realized the trap he had fallen into.

'Quite right,' the intruder continued gloatingly. 'You lashed him to the railings with a length of fishing twine fastened in such a way that once he regained consciousness, his own struggles precipitated him to his death. Four days later, you electrocuted Giovanni Grimaldi in his shower . . .'

'I had nothing to do with that!'

The cry was spontaneous, an affirmation of an innocence he really felt. Although it had been he who had connected the electric cable to the mains and listened to the dying man's screams, the elimination of Grimaldi had served only Zeppegno's interests. The photocopy of the transcript he had been shown on the Monday afternoon confirmed that there was nothing to compromise him, particularly since Grimaldi had obviously been totally taken in by his female clothing – even to the extent of doing a half-hearted number on him!

To be honest, it might have been that which sealed the Vigilanza man's fate. He'd been shocked to find himself the object of that kind of attention, just because he'd put on a skirt and blouse. Of course this merely confirmed what he'd claimed all along – fixed categories were an illusion, you were what you appeared to be – but it was one thing to theorize about such things, quite another to see a man eye you up and down in that smug, knowing way. There was nothing remotely sexual about his cross-dressing. It was just an extension of the possibilities open to him, that was all, a blurring of distinctions he had already proclaimed meaningless. He would even more happily have dressed as a child, if that had been possible.

But Giovanni Grimaldi had made the mistake of making sexual advances to him, so when Marco had said they were going to have to move, he had agreed, even though he himself was not at risk. The telephone call from Ludovico to Ariana which had originally forced him to intervene was recorded in the transcript, but Ludo was still being careful at that point, and he had said nothing that would make any sense to an outsider. But by the eve of his death, Ruspanti had thrown caution to the winds, and Zeppegno's name appeared in black and white. If the police got hold of it, they'd beat the truth out of Marco in no time at all. That was another reason why he'd decided to play along at the time, and later too, negotiating by phone from the lobby of the hotel in the middle of a party to celebrate the publication of his new book. It was only then that he realized that his own interests would be better served by killing Zeppegno himself.

'I had nothing to do with that!' he repeated.

The intruder seemed at first to understand.

'"You are what you wear."' I didn't realize you took your own slogan so seriously! Very well then, Zeppegno's accomplice wasn't you but a woman of similar build and bone structure. Oddly enough, yesterday yet another young woman – clearly no relation, because she was wearing brown instead of black – pushed Marco Zeppegno out of a train in the middle of the Apennine tunnel. Quite an eventful week they've had, these girls, whoever they may be.'

Raimondo Falcone had once watched a pig gutted, out at the villa where Carmela used to live. The beast was suspended by its hind trotters from a hook. The knife was plunged in below the pink puckered anus and tugged down like the tag of a zipper, opening the animal's belly, releasing its heavy load of innards. The plastic pope's words had a similar effect on him now. The man had not exaggerated. He *did* know everything.

Well, not *every*thing. He knew about Ruspanti and Grimaldi. He even knew about Zeppegno. But that was only the wrapping on the real secret, the key to all the others and the reason why he had originally suggested to Zeppegno that they pool forces and pay a visit to the Prince in Rome. Ironically enough, it was Ruspanti himself who had brought Falcone and Zeppegno together in the first place, when he learned that his cousin had abandoned the derelict family mansion to mad Ariana and moved into a smart new apartment block which also happened to house one of the former clients of his currency export business. At first the Prince merely asked Falcone to pass on his demands and menaces to Marco Zeppegno, who could in turn relay them to the other men under investigation by Antonia Simonelli. When Raimondo balked, his cousin reminded him that it was in his own interests to see the affair settled quietly. A major scandal would reflect badly on everyone in the family, especially a young designer at such a delicate stage of his career, just starting to rise in the world, but still within reach of jealous rivals who would seize on any excuse to burst the bubble of his success.

At the time Falcone had understood this as an observation, not a threat, and had agreed to act as go-between. Zeppegno, for his part, refused to be drawn on the specific commitments Ruspanti wanted, claiming that he needed more time, and that dramatic interventions by influential people were just around the corner. To Falcone he was less diplomatic, perhaps hoping that some echo of this might get back to the Prince. 'It was a business arrangement. He did the job, we paid him well. If the bastard's in the shit now, let him look after himself. I've got problems of my own without adding conspiracy to pervert the course of justice.' Raimondo took little interest in the matter one way or the other until the day Ruspanti dropped an oblique reference to Ariana's dolls. A few days later he mentioned the dolls again, this time referring to their 'extraordinarily inventive' costumes. In a panic, Falcone hung up. When the phone rang again, he did not answer it. He did not answer it for the next week, but when he dropped in to pick up a consignment of costumes from Ariana, she told him about Ludovico's story about meeting a reporter who was interested in writing an article about her and her dolls. The implication was clear. If his demands were not met, Ruspanti would reveal to the world that Falco was a fake, a pretentious posturer who had deceived everyone by cynically exploiting the talents of the traumatized sibling he kept locked up at home.

It was then he decided that his cousin must die. Ruspanti had in fact seriously miscalculated. Not for a moment did Falcone think of agreeing to the Prince's demands, which now ran to private planes to smuggle him out of the country and secret hideouts in Switzerland or Austria where he could lie low until the affair blew over. It was not just his commercial success that was at stake, but his very self! He was no longer Falcone, but Falco. If Falco were to be revealed as a void, an illusion, then what would become of *him*? As long as Ludovico Ruspanti remained alive, Falco's existence had hung in the balance.

As it did now, he thought. The intruder stood quite still, the pistols aimed at his queasily yawing head.

'Until this moment, I had no idea that any such organization as the Cabal existed,' Falcone said wearily. 'If I have inadvertently offended or inconvenienced you, I apologize. If there is any way in which I can make reparations, I am more than willing to do so.'

The man in cleric costume raised his hands slowly.

'No!' shrieked Falcone in sheer terror. 'For the love of God forgive me, I beg of you!'

The empty eyes of the mask stared at him.

'I? I have nothing to do with it.'

Falcone grovelled on the floor, abasing himself utterly.

'I meant the Cabal.'

The intruder laughed.

'The Cabal doesn't exist.' And he raised his mask like a visor.

The effect was as stunning as the detonation of the grenade. Slack-jawed, pale, seemingly paralysed, Falcone just stared and stared. He, who had fooled everyone around him for so long, had now himself been made a fool of – and by a dowdy creep whose suits looked as though they were made by his mother! How was it possible? Why had it been permitted? The world had stopped making sense.

'Don't worry, dottore, you're in good company,' said Zen, tossing the latex mask aside. 'The best minds in the Vatican fell for it when Ruspanti spun them the tale. The press and the public fell for it when Grimaldi wrote his anonymous letter. I fell for it myself when the Vatican seemed to be covering the matter up, and the top man at the Ministry did when I passed the story on.'

Falcone studied him watchfully from the floor.

'The shock's wearing off now, isn't it?' Zen continued. 'You're starting to ask yourself why I bothered going to all this trouble. After all, everyone else has had a reason. Ruspanti used the Cabal to get into the Vatican. Grimaldi used it to stir up speculation about Ruspanti's death, so that he could put the squeeze on you and Zeppegno. You two used it to try and lead me up a blind alley. But what's in it for me? That's what you're asking yourself, isn't it dottore?'

He took out his packet of Nazionali and lit up.

'Of course, I could say that I'm just getting even for that session in the confessional. My knees just about seized up solid! Where were you, anyway?'

Falcone gave a pallid grin. He didn't know what this man wanted, but he sensed that his life was no longer in danger

'In a car on the Gianicolo hill. It was Marco's idea. He provided the gadgetry and set it all up. Mind you, we had a few tricky moments, like when that police car passed by with its siren going.'

'What you told me about the Vatican – the schisms and feuds, all the various groups jockeying for position – sounded very authentic.'

'I got all that from Ludovico. He knew all the right-wing weirdos and religious eccentrics in Rome, of course. These people are actually quite harmless, like the ones who want to restore the monarchy. All I did was make them sound a significant threat.'

Zen nodded.

'It sounds like you were on quite good terms with your cousin. And Ariana is still in love with him, isn't she?'

A chill ripple passed over Falcone's skin.

'What?' he croaked.

Zen waved a pistol casually.

'Look, let's get one thing clear. I'm not here in my professional capacity.'

Falcone stared at him.

'You mean . . .'

'I mean I'm on the make,' Zen replied. 'I'm a corrupt cop. You've read about them in the papers, you've seen them on television. Now, for a limited period only, you can have one in your own home or office.'

Raimondo Falcone stood up, facing Zen.

'How much?'

Zen let his cigarette fall to the floor and stubbed it out with the toe of his right shoe. Falcone watched anxiously to make sure it was properly extinguished. Fire in the atelier was the great terror of every designer.

'How much do you think it's worth?'

Falcone's eyes narrowed.

'How much *what*'s worth?'

Zen looked past him at the window of the inner office, where the lighted dome of the Galleria rose into the gathering fog.

'You killed your cousin to keep it secret,' he said as though to himself. 'That would seem to make it quite valuable.'

Again the chill spread over Falcone, eating into his complacency like acid. With an effort, he pulled himself together. There was no need to panic. He was in no danger. All this crooked, taunting bastard wanted was money. Give it to him, promise him whatever he wanted, and get him the hell out of here.

'We agreed fifty million for the transcript,' he said decisively, the businessman in him taking charge.

'I no longer have the transcript.'

Falcone couldn't help smiling. He knew that, having wrested most of it from Zeppegno before pushing him out of the train. Instead of hanging on to the door, poor obtuse Zeppegno had clutched the transcript, still believing that it was the real object of the exercise. The idea had been that Zeppegno would join the *pendolino* at Florence, engage Zen in conversation and get hold of the document. Falcone, in drag again, would go to the vestibule as they approached the Apennine tunnel and turn off the lights. While Zeppegno walked through to the next carriage, Falcone was to go back to the seat where Zen was sitting and shoot him dead.

At least, that's what Zeppegno thought was going to happen. Falcone had quite different ideas, and in the event they prevailed. Once he'd opened the door and pushed his startled accomplice out, he'd taken the part of the transcript he'd managed to seize back to the lavatory. Luckily it included the page where Ruspanti phoned Ariana. He'd burnt that and flushed the ashes down the toilet. This was no doubt an unnecessary precaution, but he preferred to err on the safe side. Then he'd pushed the other pages out of the window, checked his appearance in the mirror and gone out to face Zen and the train crew. As he'd expected, all they'd looked at was his bum.

'I'm not interested in the transcript,' he said.

'There's no reason why you should be,' agreed Zen. 'You weren't even mentioned.'

'I was simply using that figure as a benchmark.'

'Your sister was, though.'

For a moment Falcone hoped he'd misheard, even though he knew perfectly well he hadn't.

'And her dolls,' added Zen. 'And the journalist who supposedly wanted to write about them. That's who she thought I was when I went there yesterday. What really shook me was that she seems to think that Ruspanti is still alive.'

Falcone stood perfectly still, his hands clasped and his eyes raised to the ceiling, like a plaster statue of one of the lesser saints.

'Of course, given the isolation in which she lives, there's no reason why she should ever find out. Unless someone told her.'

There was no reaction apart from a fractional heightening of Falcone's expression of transcendental sublimity.

'I'm no psychologist,' Zen admitted, 'but I'd be prepared to bet that if Ariana was told that her beloved cousin Ludo was dead, and exactly how he died, then the consequences would be extremely grave.'

He waved casually around the workshop.

'At the very least, the supply of new Falco designs would be likely to dry up for some considerable . . .'

Then the other man was on him, grabbing the pistol in his right hand. Zen tried to shake him off, but Falcone hung on like a terrier. In the end he had to crack him across the head with the other pistol before he would let go.

'There's no need for this,' Zen told him. 'All I want is a reasonable settlement. We can come to terms. I'm not greedy.'

But Falcone was beyond reach. Shaking his woozy head like a boxer, he came forward again. Zen cocked the replica revolver and pointed it at him.

'Keep your distance!'

There was a deafening bang. This time both men looked stunned, but Zen recovered first. He wasn't still groggy from the first time, for one thing. But the main point was that he had felt the revolver rear up in his hand, and realized what had happened. Falcone didn't seem to have been hit, thank God, but his face was that of a man in hell.

'It was a mistake!' Zen assured him. 'I got the pistols mixed up. I fired yours by mistake. Mine's just a replica.'

But Falcone was gone, turning on his heel and sprinting through to the next room.

'Come back!' yelled Zen, chasing him. 'You're in no danger! All I want is money!'

When he reached the door of the office, it was empty. He searched the gymnasium and bathroom beyond, but there was no sign of Falcone. Only then did he notice the open window. The offices formed part of the south end of the Galleria's main aisle, the lower floors having windows which opened directly on to it, beneath the glazed-barrel vault roof. This floor was at roof level, and it was only a short drop from the window to one of the iron girders which supported the large panes of glass. Catwalks ran the length of the main supporting struts, giving access to the roof for cleaning and maintenance. Along one of these, Raimondo Falcone was now running for his life.

'*Merda!*' shouted Zen.

He was disgusted with his clumsiness, his unbelievable gaucheness, his limitless ineptitude. Couldn't he do *any*thing right? What would Tania think of him, after all his proud boasts about things changing? Nothing had changed. Nothing would ever change. In sheer frustration he fired the pistol again and again, blasting away as though to punch new stars in the night sky.

The renewed firing made Falcone run even faster. He had reached the cupola now, and started to climb the metal ladder which led from the catwalk up the curving glass slope of the dome to the ventilation lantern at the top. Through the shifting panels of fog, Zen could just see Falcone moving rapidly across the panes of lighted glass like a nimble skater on a luminous mountain of ice. It thus seemed no great surprise when, in total silence and with no fuss whatsoever, he abruptly disappeared from view.

Down in the Galleria itself, Christmas was in the air. The shops, cafés and travel agencies were all doing a thriving business. Giving and receiving, eating and drinking, skiing and sunning and all the other rituals and observances of the festive season ensured that money was changing hands in a manner calculated to gladden the hearts of the traders. Any modern Christ who had attempted to intervene would himself have been expelled in short order by the security guards employed to keep this temple of commerce free of beggars, junkies, buskers, religious fanatics and other riff-raff.

Nevertheless, it was some such gesture of protest that sprang to most people's minds when they heard the sound of breaking glass. The shop windows were a powerful symbol of the socio-economic barriers against which the poor were constantly being brought up short. They could gawk at the goodies as much as they liked, but they couldn't get at them. Sometimes, especially around Christmas, the disparity between the way of life on display and the one they actually lived became too much to bear, and some crazed soul would pick up a hammer and have a go.

Even the screaming seemed at first to fit this scenario, until some people, more acute of hearing, realized that it was not coming from on-lookers in the immediate vicinity of the presumed outrage, but from somewhere else altogether – in fact from *above*. When they raised their eyes to the roof to see what it could be, the expression of amazement on their faces made their neighbours do the same, until in no time at all everyone in the Galleria was gazing upwards. It must have looked extraordinary, seen from above, this crowd of faces all tilted up like a crop of sunflowers.

Until then, the distribution of people in the aisles of the Galleria had been fairly even, but they now began to scatter and press back, forming clusters near the walls and rapidly evacuating the space at the centre of the building, where the arms of the House of Savoy were displayed in inlaid marble. The clearing thus formed might have been destined for an impromptu performance of some kind, a

751

display of acrobatics or some similar feat of skill or daring. But the crowd's attention was high above, where the vast, dark opacity of the cupola weighed down on the lighted space below. Now the shock was over, they were reassured to realize that the body plummeting to earth amid a debris of broken glass must be a spectacle of some kind got up to divert the shoppers, an optical illusion, a fake. Clearly no one could have *fallen* through the enclosure overhead, as solid and heavy as vaulted masonry. It was all a trick. A moment before impact the plunging body would pull up short, restrained by hidden wires, while the accompanying shoal of jagged icicles tinkled prettily to pieces on the marble floor before melting harmlessly away.

In the event, though, it turned out to be real.

flaunting! p.720